MW01007948

"*Exciting hunting scenes and a tender love story with two well-developed characters.*"

-*Kirkus Reviews*

"*Benjamin Barnette's novel is a fascinating journey into the Paleolithic which chronicles the daily life of the Mammoth Hunters... The novel reflects in-depth environmental research and presents an enthralling description of the Paelo-environment of the ancient Bering Sea land bridge and its prehistoric inhabitants.*"

-*Douglas B. Sims, Ph.D.*
Professor of Environmental Science
College of Southern Nevada

"*The Ice Age world comes to life under Barnette's hand, while the emotional connections between characters keep readers engaged... The story line and history are impeccable, making Winds Across Beringia a superior read that is especially highly recommended for fans of prehistoric fictional adventure stories.*"

-*Midwest Book Review*

"*Fifteen thousand years ago, the world was very different. Mammoths and other great mammals that are now extinct roamed the northern reaches of North America and Asia, and the people who hunted them lived different lives than any of us can know... Most often their findings and theories are presented in documentaries or scientific papers, but Dr. Barnette chose to breathe life into his mammoth hunters and present bits of what could have been their lives in a novel... Dr. Barnette's expertise shows in every page, bringing the world to* life with rich detail; this is a perfect example of why historians should write more fiction."

-San Francisco Book Review, Star Rating: 4/5

"Barnette's language offers lyrical and smooth descriptions of the Ice Age world sparsely populated by early humans and ancient mammals... Fiction readers with an interest in anthropology and Earth science will relish this highly researched and visceral offering."

-The BookLife Prize

WINDS ACROSS BERINGIA

WINDS ACROSS BERINGIA

BENJAMIN H. BARNETTE

MILL CITY PRESS

Mill City Press, Inc.
2301 Lucien Way #415
Maitland, FL 32751
407.339.4217
www.millcitypress.net

© 2012 by Benjamin H. Barnette

Map of Beringia:
Design by Benjamin H. Barnette
Cartography Artwork by Christopher Martin,
Hilo, Hawaii

Cover Photographs:
NASA image by Antartis. ID 42054455
"Mammoth (Skelton)" by Beatrissa

All rights reserved solely by the author. The author
guarantees all contents are original and do not
infringe upon the legal rights of any other person or
work. No part of this book may be reproduced in any
form without the permission of the author. The views
expressed in this book are not necessarily those of
the publisher.

This is a work of fiction. Names, characters, business,
events and incidents are the products of the author's
imagination. Any resemblance to actual persons, living
or dead, or actual events is purely coincidental.

Printed in the United States of America.

Library of Congress # 2019917434

ISBN-13: 978-1-5456-8140-4

ACKNOWLEDGMENTS

I owe deep thanks and gratitude too many people who helped me take this work from an unfinished manuscript to a complete self-published novel. Retired educator Jo-Anna Broadhurst; fellow author Fred 'Kett' Fischer (*Marilyn Monroe Versus the Nazi Colonel*); archeologist and artist, S. Neal Crozier; Doug Sims, Ph.D., College of Southern Nevada; and lifelong friend Steve Ball all read and edited the manuscript and offered excellent advice and words of encouragement.

Winds Across Beringia is dedicated to the late Dr. Gilbert V. Oliver, D.M.D. who made his home in Walnut Creek, California but also sojourned winters on the Big Island of Hawaii. We enjoyed many pleasurable discussions on the beach at Kailua-Kona, Hawaii as I was writing the book. He advised me on several medical aspects and was the first to read a very rough draft and offered continued encouragement. I miss him and those enjoyable conversations.

CONTENTS

INTRODUCTION

The world appeared dramatically different 15,000 years ago than it does today. It was a wondrous world bursting with breathtaking sights and sounds, teeming with exotic, astonishing animals. A world overflowing with surprising daily adventure but equally filled with painful hardships, unending struggle, and constant death.

Near the top of the world, enormous mountainous glaciers and vast, thick ice sheets covered much of the northern hemisphere including most of North America, Europe, and Asia. During this tumultuous geological epoch, commonly called the Ice Age, massive glaciation covered the mountainous regions of southern Alaska and huge areas in the north within the Brooks Range, including large sections of the Seward Peninsula. Likewise, in Siberia, vast walls of ice were formed in the mountainous regions of the Chukchi Peninsula and areas to the south and west.

So much of the world's seawater was "locked up" in the form of ice that sea levels around the world dropped hundreds of feet, exposing land surfaces now submerged by ocean depths. The most famous inundated land mass once connected Asia and North America across the Bering Sea, linking modern day Alaska and Siberia. Named "Beringia" by contemporary scholars, this "lost continent" extended some 1,000 miles wide when fully exposed, supporting an environment of a cold, dry, grass-covered plain known as a steppe. The great rivers such as the Yukon and the Kuskokwim in Alaska and the Anadyr in Siberia continued to flow hundreds of miles across Beringia to the Bering Sea to the southwest. These grand rivers and their tributaries formed narrow wooded zones which meandered across the grassy steppe in much the same manner as forested rivers wander across the Great Plains of North America today.

This vast grass land sustained an abundant array of wildlife including now extinct animals such as the woolly rhinoceros, Chersky horse, steppe bison, short faced bear, and lion but also several species whose progeny survived into modern times such as the muskox and caribou. The most celebrated species however, extinct or not, and without question remains the woolly mammoth. So renowned is this species that the extensive grass lands which spanned the northern regions from Alaska, across Siberia, Beringia, and into Europe were named the Mammoth Steppe.

In turn, abundant wildlife supported human populations. Prehistoric hunters in Europe, Asia, and the lost continent of Beringia followed and hunted the game animals, especially the plentiful mammoth. So large in size was the mammoth that even a single kill would have provided a treasure trove of meat, oil, hide, and bone; but it was also a life-threatening risk pursuing such a dangerous, powerful animal. As the prehistoric hunters of Beringia followed the great mammoth herds, they stepped foot into what is now Alaska, becoming the ancient ancestors to all Native American peoples of North and South America.

Modern DNA studies of living Native American people of North America reveal that when the first American people ventured into our northern continent, they did not come alone. They brought with them the Caucasian genes of Europeans, albeit a very small percentage. It seems feasible to me that if we could watch a migrating band of Paleo people entering North America from Beringia who carried European genes, we would not recognize any difference from the Native American features of black hair and dark skin in any of the group's features. Conversely, it remains just as likely that a few members might actually be European individuals with fair skin and light-colored hair who, for whatever reason, married into the Asian bands of Beringia. It would require only three or four generations for those fair- colored features to dissipate and not be noticeable in the people's physical attributes; the DNA, however, would remain forever.

As "historical fiction" this book follows the fascinating prehistoric people who lived on the lost Beringia Continent and centers on a tribal group named the Wind Band who depended on the majestic mammoth for their livelihood. Obviously, the characters are fictional and various aspects of their culture are in some instances presumed or extracted from historically known native groups of North America. Nonetheless, the manner in which they survived and their environment was very real and thus is described from many years of research.

The Wind Band follows the mammoth as they migrate along their river valley homeland with the change of each season. But they are not alone. Likewise, other groups, both friend and foe, make the lost mammoth continent of Beringia their home.

The lives of the Wind Band reflect a double-edged blade-both a wondrous adventure and a desperate struggle. Pitted against an unforgiving environment and huge dangerous animal adversaries, they stay alive with only the tools of bone, wood, and stone at their disposal, yet they possess the extraordinary human mind and an enduring will to survive.

A FINAL NOTATION

There are two appendices and a bibliography noted in the back of this novel. I developed each one to help the reader gain a better understanding of North America's and thus Beringia's prehistoric past. Appendix I lists the animals, plants, and birds that are mentioned and discussed in the novel and would have, I believe along with many noted scholars, lived on Beringia. Each species would have been a common inhabitant of the environment and interacted to some measure with the human populations.

Some species the reader will recognize as common throughout North America, while others are specific to the northern regions and a steppe environment. A few species, such as the mammoth, are members of a long list of animals, especially large mammals that became extinct at the end of the Ice Age.

Appendix II is a discussion and description of the cultural material common to Paleo-people in the novel and to prehistoric people in general. It provides a small insight into the terms, artifacts, and material used in prehistory and understood by archeologists. For instance, most of the stone arrowheads people find along creek banks or in plowed fields, actually aren't arrowheads.

Finally, the bibliography, although far from complete, includes most of the reference material I referred to while writing the novel. The reader may find these sections interesting and is encouraged to refer to both appendices and any source listed in the bibliography while reading the novel.

A MUSCOGEE (CREEK) LEGEND

Long before it was politically correct and popular to use the term Native American, the Muscogee (Creek) Indian Tribe struggled and survived in the State of Oklahoma, which was once called "Indian Territory." The small town of Okmulgee, located in the central portion of the state, was and remains their capitol. Numbering some 44,000, the Creeks are the 9th largest Indian Tribe in United States. They call themselves the "Muscogee" which also identifies their language. They have not always lived in Oklahoma.

In the 1830s, along with other tribes in the Southeast, the Muscogee were forcibly moved from their homeland in the Southeastern Region, the current states of Georgia and Alabama, by the American government lead by President Andrew Jackson. Driven like cattle to Oklahoma on a long, hard, dreadful and forced march, many died of hunger, exposure, and exhaustion along the way. That appalling event is etched into Indian memory as the "Trail of Tears." How or when the Muscogee came to the Southeast is not known. But they do have a legend.

In the beginning, the Muscogee people lived in a far Western land beside mountains that reached to the sky that they called the "backbone of the earth." Then, a thick fog descended upon the earth and the Muscogee drifted apart, became lost and were divided into smaller groups although the groups stayed close to each other. Finally, the Master of Breath, "Father Creator" Esaugeta Emissee had mercy on them and the wind began to blow away the fog. The Muscogee followed the wind toward the sunrise. They crossed a great river and went to the Southeastern corner of the United States. Each group gave themselves names. The group that went first, that was the farthest east and the first to see the sunrise, praised the wind that blew away the fog and called themselves the Wind Band and were always considered the first band and the aristocracy of all the bands. Each group then named themselves for the first animal they saw. And the Master of Breath spoke and said you are the beginning of each of your families. Live up to your names and the Muscogee will always be a powerful force.

Siberia

Kolymskoye Glacier

Apalche Mountain Range

Gokonhe Mountain

Onna's Land
Zaliv. Plain

Koryak Glacier

Kolavinarak River

Kamchatka Mountains

Up'nerkillermiut

Bering
"Great Sea"

Beringia Map

= GLACIERS   60 MILES

Part One
RITE OF PASSAGE

*"Utilize your Rite-of-Passage journey as a trading
adventure as well and visit the Canineqmiut Eskimo
village on the coast of the Great Sea," challenged
Cheparney. "Broaden your endeavor."*

Chapter 1:

SUMMER KILL

T he thunderous clamor of the mammoth ruptured first from one direction, then another. Echoing off a nearby cliff face, it swirled around like a great whirl of wind, finally roiling upward into the sky. The noise was deafening. The boisterous blast of trumpeting calls, the sudden crash of broken tree limbs, and the stomps of heavy feet crashing through the underbrush caused the earth to quake. The great majestic beasts had arrived.

While mammoth can trudge across the open grassy steppe or through patches of thick forest in a silent march resembling lumbering giant shadows, they seldom do. They maintain constant communication with each other through earsplitting trumpeting calls. Throughout their migration they seldom walk around anything, other than huge trees, smashing through and over small trees and underbrush as their heavy footsteps shake the earth. This herd was no exception.

Harjo was all too familiar with this raucous herd as he had hunted, followed, and studied them nearly all his life. He stood with his back against a huge malformed cottonwood tree that in one volatile moment in the distant past had been struck by lightning. The bolt had split and burned the lower portion of the trunk creating a mysterious man-sized enclave. Harjo wedged himself tightly into this curved tree trunk niche.

The huge distorted tree grew on the terrace of a narrow spring-fed wooded drainage called Wekiwa by his people. It meandered by a small group of low, steep, rocky hills. The terrace was not high in elevation yet was abrupt as it tapered off down toward the stream's edge. A sheer cliff lay adjacent on the other side of the stream. This wooded stream and the rocky outcrop island lay within the vast steppe grasslands that stretched in all directions as far as the eye could see and beyond-much farther still-for Harjo believed the great Mammoth Steppe extended to the ends of the earth. This mammoth herd followed the small Wekiwa drainage as it flowed southeast to empty into the larger Echota River that formed a wide, shallow, valley; home to Harjo's band, his tribe, and this mammoth drove.

This collected movement of the woolly mammoth was not an actual migration, not as the massive fall and spring migrations are, but rather, a relocation. As the herds consumed the tall steppe grass in one region-a small valley, drainage, or meadow-they relocated to another area. And now, in early summer, the herds dispersed from their open spring calving grounds back into the lush meadows of the Echota Valley.

Although they trekked with earsplitting noise, the mammoth moved in a slow steady gait. Their long flowing hair, longer than a man's arm, was blown by the wind like the tall summer grass and falling past their flanks, it nearly reached

2

the ground. But their most striking feature was their large, curved, white ivory tusks. The tusks of the female cows were smaller with less curvature and so preferred as construction supports for winter mammoth lodges but were still so large, it required two men to carry one. Overdeveloped, the bull's tusks extended from the upper jaw, side-by-side, and then spread apart, outward and downward, forming inward into huge spectacular circles reaching 10 to 12 paces in length. Their tusks continued to grow throughout their life, the tips actually crossed on the oldest aging bulls.

While a mammoth herd appeared as one continuous mass of individual animals, many seasons of close observation had taught Harjo a mammoth herd was really a combination of many smaller herds. Mammoth lived in extended family groups consisting of a bull, his female harem, and their offspring. The immense herd was thus composed of enumerable family clusters numbering eight to 12 in each group. During migrations and herd movements, the family formed a strict configuration designed to protect the calves. An older dominant female went first out ahead of the family group. Next the mature females formed two lines on either side of the youngsters and babies who were clustered in the center. Finally, the patriarchal bull, nearly twice the size of the females, followed just behind. All adults were prepared to defend the family, but the bulls were especially aggressive, fearless, and dangerous attacking any animal that might wander in too near to the family group and its calves.

Meanwhile, the bachelor males, mostly young adults and adolescents, traveled alone or in small groups on the outside edge of the herd at large. Akin to humans, the young bachelors were unafraid at their own peril, risk takers with an unquenchable thirst of curiosity. These were the ones Harjo waited for, tucked into the enclave of the mystical tree.

Harjo had carefully chosen this tree adjacent to the stream. Mammoth loosely follow the drainage but go around the low steep hills avoiding the cliff area so that they paraded by only on one side of the tree avoiding the side with the enclave hiding spot that concealed Harjo. But more importantly, he selected this tree because mammoth had rubbed and scratched on the tree shaving of the tree's bark leaving their scent and hair behind. In fact, he had used this 'Spirit Tree' off and on nearly all his adult life, last utilizing it several summers ago. Accordingly, he knew that eventually one of the young bulls would be attracted to the tree and the lingering mammoth scent. In preparation, he had scattered mammoth dung around the base of the tree. The whole Mammoth Steppe was dotted with mammoth dung. He had similarly piled tall clumps of grass stained with mammoth urine around the tree along with branches of fragrant sage limbs, which he stacked next to him in the enclave. He also rubbed the sage leaves and branches in the palms of his hands and on his fur parka and pants to release the heady but appealing odor of the pungent plant. The mammoth dung, urine, and the sage plants would all help to mask his human scent.

Mammoth have poor eyesight yet an exceptional sense of smell. They can detect water from the next valley over and danger in the form of men or lions from a great distance. A man's scent, his dung, and his urine can be discerned by the mammoth as far as the horizon. Thus, failure awaits the hunter who fails to take the necessary measures to eliminate these odors. Harjo bathed last afternoon in preparation for today's hunt. He also took the necessary steps to insure residues of animal blood, dung, urine, and even saliva did not stain his clothing. Remarkably, the scent from campfire smoke did not alert the mammoth or other game animals.

Smoke from wildfires remained common events and part of the natural environment across the Mammoth Steppe.

Relying on all of these precautions to mask his scent, Harjo now stood poised in the shelter of the giant tree with mammoth nearly surrounding him. The earth shook as a nearby bull stomped the ground trumpeting a call so loud that it momentarily blocked out all other sound. Then, as the trumpet call faded, he could hear the collapse and breakage of nearby trees and bushes as the mammoth smashed through the underbrush. To be detected now would almost certainly mean death. Harjo's emergency plan, if he were discovered, would be to run down the terrace embankment, across the stream, and hope to climb up the rock cliffs. Mammoth are swift afoot and can easily run down a man, but steep slopes and embankments slow them down, and he hoped this delay would give him a path to escape. The possibility he could make this escape was unlikely, still better than no chance at all.

Suddenly, just to Harjo's left, a large bull came to the stream to drink. Slow and somewhat cumbersome, the beast stepped down off the terrace into the edge of the water. He called out in a high-pitched trumpet as another nearby mammoth answered. Harjo watched undetected as the bulky bull gracefully sucked up a trunk full of water then curved it into his mouth. Filling his trunk again, he sprayed himself with a light shower, then with another ear-shattering trumpet turned to continue his march.

Harjo remained motionless, wedged into the secret enclave grasping his spear in front of him. Well made, his spear was a composite manufacture tipped with a fine thin point. A poorly knapped projectile point that might break on impact or fail to penetrate deeply would spell doom for an ill-equipped hunter.

Mammoth are a lethal adversary. Without reserve or any remorse, they will crush and trample a man, woman, or child, if given the opportunity to do so. Harjo remained calm and dauntless. Fear can be the killer. He stared straight ahead without emotion, waiting for his opportunity. And then it came.

One of the great beasts stopped and rubbed against the lightning scared tree. Harjo could feel the whole tree shake with the weight of the beast and he could hear the rubbing sound as both rough bark and long hair was being scrapped off. He could also hear the low bellowing noise of the mammoth that told him his quarry was in fact a young bull as he anticipated. As the beast rubbed, Harjo raised his spear straight up, moving only his hands and arms so that the spear point was now arm's lengths above his head as he grasped the shaft near the end. The mammoth stopped rubbing and began to move on. Now was his opportunity-now!

Harjo first stepped out forward just enough to clear the enclave, then he sidestepped with his left foot followed by his right, which he planted firmly on the ground. Suddenly, all the tumultuously clambering noise around him became still and he seemed to move in slow, silent motion. As he cleared past the huge tree and turned to his left, he now stood less than an arm's length from the giant beast. He could smell the powerful aroma of the magnificent creature. The mammoth stepped, moving its right leg. Harjo could see the muscles of the mammoth's shoulder and its ribs flex through the beast's long flowing hair. Standing only slightly higher than the animal's knee, he must now make a quick decision-to aim for the heart or the lungs.

The heart was preferred but added an element of increased risk. Higher up the chest cavity the ribs of the mammoth were rounded, consequently easier for the point to slip between, thus piercing the lungs. The lower chest cavity, however, housed the heart. But here the wider, flat rib bones made this area more difficult to puncture. He picked a spot on the animal, aimed at his heart, and concentrated completely on that one, small imaginary location. In fact, the only part of the animal he saw was his shoulder, ribcage, and the upper leg. And now, still concentrating with all his strength, he thrust his spear into that single spot.

He thrust not with just the strength of his arms but with the power of his shoulders, his stomach, and most importantly with his legs. His strike was true.

He watched the spear point slip by the ribs, the foreshaft plunge into the mammoth, and the spear shaft itself sank into the mammoth's chest. He could feel the spear point touch the mammoth's heart.

The huge wounded animal exploded with a deafening trumpeting call of terror that seemed to be both a high pitched and a low guttural sound at the same instant. Harjo glanced up and was afforded his first view of the animal's head which was raised up—his trunk likewise raised and curled. The beast slung his head, first to the left and then to the right. Harjo let go of his spear shaft and at the same moment ducked low to the ground, then leaped to the side, and back behind the tree just as the mammoth slung his head to the right. His curved ivory right tusk crashed against the tree just above Harjo's head. Had he hesitated even briefly; Harjo would have been crushed by the bull's great tusk against the tree. But now, with that same yowl of horror and panic, the injured mammoth launched off into a dead run, but he was not alone.

Alerted by the distress calls, other mammoth trumpeted loudly and joined their wounded herd-mate in stampede. All up and down and around this edge of the great herd, panicked mammoth called out running away from the giant cottonwood tree and the rocky hills. The wounded mammoth, however, did not run far, fewer than 100 paces. He collapsed to the ground first on his front knees, then to his chest, and then on his back knees. Finally, his great head and massive tusks hit the tall steppe grass. Then, in one last final gasp for life, the mortally struck mammoth raised its stately head and bellowed out one last trumpet call, then fell over on its left side and lay silent.

For a temporary, brief monument the whole Mammoth Steppe, now lush with tall green early summer grass, lay silent. But only for a monument-perhaps the hush lasted but the blink of an eye. Then, a gentle summer breeze broke the silence, prompting Harjo to take a deep long breath. The air was filled with the scent of grasses mixed with flowers and the strong but pleasant aroma of sagebrush, mammoth dung, and the warm sweet summer sun.

Now, all the many common sounds of the steppe returned. Overhead, a black soaring raven, upon seeing the newly slain mammoth, called out to alert his comrades of an impending feast. Then, a shrill whistle, a human sound, caught Harjo's ear. He answered with his own whistle, looking up to see three approaching figures, three of his four sons, who had been waiting concealed downstream ready to launch lethal darts into the wounded fleeing mammoth if necessary. They followed the stream toward the slain beast.

Harjo had temporarily stowed his own quiver of darts, foreshaft quiver, and atlatl throwing board in the giant tree's enclave. He tied his belt with the attached foreshaft quiver around his waist, then grasped the quiver of darts and slipped the quiver strap over his head, adjusting it on his back. Then, he tucked the atlatl into his belt. He had removed those weapons to allow complete freedom of movement while he attacked the mammoth. Glancing up, he reached out and touched the giant cottonwood tree. He briefly paid homage to the spirit of the tree. It did possess a spirit. Certainly, it was not the same as the spirit of a man or even that of an animal, but a spirit, nonetheless. Harjo had known this Spirit Tree all his life. He, as his father before him, and his father before him, had slain many mammoth here on this very spot with the help of this noble tree. With respect duly given, he walked toward the still giant animal. During the wounded mammoth's run, Harjo's spear shaft worked its way free from the animal, leaving the foreshaft and point embedded into the beast-the shaft lay on the ground. He picked it up on the way and reaching into the smaller foreshaft quiver attached at his side, he drew a spear foreshaft and point and attached it to the spear shaft thus rearming his spear with a lethal point.

He approached the mammoth with caution watching closely for any signs of life and stopped several paces from him to continue his meticulous observations. He glanced up only for a moment to see his sons still approaching. Then, holding his spear out to full length by grasping the butt end, he cautiously approached the mammoth and touched the point of his spear to the animal's eye. If any life at all remained within the mammoth, he would respond, so sensitive is the eye. If so, Harjo would ram his spear into the eye, through the skull, and into the brain of the animal causing instant paralysis and death. There was no reaction or response; the young large bull had journeyed to the other side.

As the three young figures approached, they were laughing and jubilant because they realized what this kill would mean. There would be enough food to quell the hunger of the entire band for at least 60 days, nearly the entire summer. The carcass location was perfect, as the bull had fallen in an open and flat area, void of obstructing trees or rocks and near the Wekiwa Stream. Owing to its great size, unless a slain mammoth can be completely surrounded, a complete skinning and butchering could not be realized thus precious meat and hide would be abandoned to scavengers. Skinning and boning a mammoth required an enormous amount of hard, filthy labor. Band members could expect to be covered with slippery oil, guts, and brown blood for several days and under constant threat from savage scavengers and the boys realized much of the workload would fall to them.

Even then, the labor remained incomplete. The meat needed to be cured, dried, roasted, smoked, and jerked, and the huge heavy hide had to be scraped of fat, meat and then treated. Finally, the fat would be rendered into oil and stored in skin pouches. Yes, the Wind Band would certainly enjoy nearly 60 days of meat but during the next several days, during processing, they were going to earn everyday of it.

The three boys greeted their father with laughter, handshakes, and embraces. Chate was the oldest. He completed his Rite-of Passage journey several cycles ago and bought a girl from the Wolf Band. Her name was Hokte and she proved to be an excellent choice as wife, fitting neatly into the family. Hokte was now ripe with pregnancy, expecting to deliver this summer. Echo, the second in line, returned from his Rite-of-Passage last fall. Although now legally an adult male, he would also be recognized at the impending First Kill Ceremony. The accompanying feast provided by his father with this slain mammoth promised to be an occasion to remember. Fus was the third oldest and would probably seek his Rite-of-Passage in the next two perhaps three summers.

Harjo addressed his third in line. "Fus go and inform the band the location of the kill and remind Micco Yarda that we need to begin dressing the mammoth as soon as possible. He'll say something but just say you are only delivering my message. Then, escort your mother here to the kill and don't let her take you both across the meadow, follow the stream. Don't run, but don't stroll.

"Alright Erke," replied a jubilant Fus. He used the Muscogee term for father "Erke" rather than the usual term from their mother's language. Good, thought Harjo to himself. It was not a far distance but youngsters of Fus's age welcomed the opportunity to travel alone especially on any mission, minor or otherwise. To be selected to carry a message from the Micco of one band to the Micco of another remained a relished duty.

Harjo offered some last-moment advice. "The mammoth have only temporarily vacated this area and they will soon return, so pay attention."

Anxious to leave, Fus fidgeted with excitement. "I won't let a mammoth come up behind me, Erke and I'll keep all paths to escape in sight and mind," he said with a big smile.

The other boys laughed, as did Harjo, as they had heard this same advice nearly all their lives and at some point, they will need to remember it. Harjo acknowledged he was probably over cautious. "Alright," he said, "Go on."

Fus did some kind of silly hand gesture with his brothers and they exchanged words in their mother's language which they all three spoke more fluently than their native Muscogee, then he headed off toward the Wind Band encampment. He was handsome thought Harjo; he favored his mother, Onna. The other boys weren't ugly but were of a dark complexion resembling him more. Onna's two natural born youngest, however, Fus and his younger sister, Loni, bore Onna's likeness, their beautiful fair-skinned mother.

Harjo and his two sons walked around inspecting the imposing creature. The boys were jubilant. Chate and Echo remained in admiration and awe of their father, for they knew the combined hunting skills and courage required for a single hunter to bring down a mammoth. No other predator across the whole Mammoth Steppe can kill a mammoth, only a man. And among the entire Muscogee Tribe, few men could accomplish such a feat alone. But in that way, a single hunter risked only one life, his own.

They examined the entry wound and Harjo offered some up close and hands-on advice and instruction in making that one, all important, thrust with the spear. That one single plunge of a spear meant life and or death for both the hunter and the prey.

With the inspection of the slain mammoth complete, Harjo asked, "Who has the ax?" Chate held it up. "Good, Chate you cut some drying rack poles and Echo you start dragging some wood over here for fires. We will want several fires around the kill and processing area tonight."

"Alright Erke," replied both youngsters about the same moment. All three boys must have made some agreement to now use the Muscogee word for father-Erke. "Good," Harjo again said to himself. They turned and left together toward the stream, still laughing and talking in their mother's language. Harjo understood portions of their conversation. It had nothing to do with the best way to approach their assigned tasks but related to the impending celebrations and girls-one girl in particular.

Suddenly, a single young bull announced his arrival with a loud trumpeting call some 50 paces away. Harjo answered with a shrill whistle directed at the mammoth but also to alert his two boys who immediately whistled a response. He now yelled a call to insure the bull recognized his presence. If he charged, Harjo could use the body of the slain mammoth as protection. The young bull made several attack lunges and other aggressive gestures, then he moved off at a quick pace. Harjo looked back toward the stream. Chate and Echo stood ready with darts nocked in their atlatls. On seeing the mammoth exit, they waved and returned to their chores. Harjo then noticed a single black wolf at a safe distance, standing and watching. He often remarked to himself how the color black could serve as sufficient camouflage in both a snow-covered landscape and also in brown and green woodlands. It seemed contrary and yet a black-colored animal remained difficult to see. "A scout," said Harjo to himself. "He will take the knowledge of this mammoth kill to his pack and they most certainly will return, probably tonight."

A calling raven circled low overhead and then surprisingly landed on the mammoth with little fear of Harjo. He laughed to himself. Onna's pet raven announces her arrival.

Harjo looked up to see a distant lone figure approach, following the wooded edge of the Wekiwa Stream. He could tell by the shape of the parka it was a woman and by the corresponding gait that it was Onna. She should not be crossing the meadow alone. He presumed Fus would accompany her back, but apparently not. As he explained to the boys, in spite of this kill, mammoth will continue to migrate through this area. He considered whistling for one of the boys, sending him to escort their independent mother, but decided that was futile. She would soon arrive.

As Onna grew near, he saw she carried her woman's bag on her shoulder and a spear. Smiling, he thought to himself, "at least she carries her harpoon. How long had she had that spear and her woman's bag now?" His mother had sewn the bag and given it to him as he departed on his "Rite of Passage." Later, on that same momentous journey, he had given it to Onna. Likewise, he had crafted her spear from a sapling willow on that same journey well over 20 seasons ago. Certainly, the point and foreshaft had been replaced but the shaft was the original. He would not expect willow to last this long but Onna took good care of her harpoon and her bag.

As Onna approached, she smiled and waved by holding her hand up overhead, palm forward, and moving it side to side. Harjo likewise responded with a cheerful wave. Only a few paces away, she held her harpoon up and stuck the butt end into the ground and approached. She obliviously saw the great slain beast but walked straight up to Harjo, took his hands, and stood up on the toes of her skin boots and kissed him.

"Are you alright?" she asked.

Harjo nodded yes. Nonetheless, she stepped back still holding his hands and looked him over. Then, she looked into his eyes. Many seasons of experience had taught her he might conceal an injury, subsequent to a hunt, because in his words he would not want to create a fuss.

"I am alright," replied Harjo in a no-need-to-worry tone. "He did not hurt me." Onna could tell by his eyes and the manner of his response he was truthful. Satisfied he was not injured and becoming emotional, she embraced Harjo and put her head against his parka chest.

"Thank you, Harjo," she whispered as tears begin to swell in her eyes, "Thank you for taking care of me and risking so much for all of us."

"You're very welcome," Harjo replied as he lifted up her head, gazed into her face and smiled. He reached out with his rough calloused thumb and gently wiped the tears from under each of Onna's eyes.

Onna looked up to his face with a teary-eyed smile. "Look at me," she said as she sniffed, "I am crying like a baby."

"You can cry when you want," Harjo replied, "You are free." Still gently holding her chin, he kissed each of her eyes then tenderly kissed her mouth.

Still sniffling, Onna turned to the great silent mammoth and clapped her hands together, her voice now expressing joy. "Oh, Harjo, he is beautiful, so large and healthy. This will be a wonderful summer, Harjo and we can spend most of it at Wetumka, and Echo can have a wonderful feast to celebrate the return from his Rite-of Passage." She stopped and looked around. "Where are my boys?"

"Supposedly, your two oldest are collecting wood from the stream for fires and to construct drying racks and Fus is with you. Apparently, he is not, so I don't know where he is."

She looked around and again stood up on her toes and gave Harjo a kiss on the side of this mouth. "Fus is bringing one of our sleds and coming with Micco Yarda. Harjo, it is so difficult moving all the sleds tied on top of the travails now that the snow is melted."

She took Harjo's hand walking toward the mammoth, then began a pace around the great beast, continuing, "Micco Yarda is sending about one-half of the band to skin and prepare the meat. He knows I want the whole hide for the new winter lodge. Mmm, fresh roasted mammoth, Harjo, oh, it makes me hungry. The others will stay and set up the Wetumka camp."

They stopped and she touched the mammoth's tusks. "He has such beautiful tusks, doesn't he, Harjo?" Harjo nodded his head in agreement, and they continued on.

"We have two more boys to send on their Rite-of-Passage journey, Harjo, and one girl to marry off."

"You're forgetting Summer's three children," reminded Harjo.

"I'm not forgetting them; I'm just not going to consider them now. We will both likely die before those two baby boys and that sweet infant girl reach maturity."

They paused for a moment as Onna reached out, touching the mammoth's small ears, then she continued. "Ayuko, Hokte, and Loni will stay at camp caring for all the band children including Summer's so that she can come and help process the mammoth. Oh, yes, and our handsome

Caribou hunter son will stay guarding the camp and help set it up as you directed."

As they continued their inspection of the great slain animal, the remaining members of the mammoth herd carried on with their migration. Most would avoid this area of the kill, keeping a reasonable distance. A loud, close trumpeting call caused Onna and Harjo to glance toward the sound, then back to each other. "An old bull orders his young females to stay in line," smiled Onna, "Bossy old bulls!" They stopped again as Onna touched and examined the back of the giant beast.

"I wish I could go with the family when they leave for Coweta this summer to construct the new mammoth lodge and I am still apprehensive of the idea of you exploring the upper Big River all alone this summer. Harjo! Better still I wish we could take a trip together, just you and I, in the same way when we traveled during your Rite-of-Passage-remember?"

"Of course, I remember," answered Harjo, as he gently squeezed her hand. "Your oldest son's young wife is due to have her first baby this summer and you can't leave."

"I know," answered Onna, "I just wish we could take a trip before I get too old."

"Besides, you need to stay and find a wife for Echo," joked a smiling Harjo.

"No-no, that's up to you men. Women have no say, especially mothers." Then, Onna thought for a moment.

"Harjo, have you heard something?"

"Chate and Echo were discussing a girl earlier."

"Oh," said Onna, "Which one?"

"I'm not sure," answered Harjo, "but I don't think she is from the Wind Band."

"Another band," mused Onna, as she looked skyward touching her chin-mostly thinking out loud.

16

"Oh Harjo, I just remembered. I finally asked the Lion Shaman if any other Muscogee woman has ever accompanied her husband on his Rite-of-Passage journey."

"I thought you were afraid to talk to him."

"I was afraid, but I asked him anyway. Echo's return from his Rite-of Passage journey renewed my curiosity so, I approached him by his fire at the edge of our camp. He said no. Just that, no other words or explanation."

Ravens and magpies were gathering in the tops of nearby trees calling to spread the news of the mammoth kill. They both looked up at the scavenger birds, smiling at each other, recalling past events of the birds calling to them from the tops of trees. Onna held out her hand and made a strange sound so that her pet raven flew over landing on it. She laughed as she struggled to hold up the weight of the large black bird. She petted it saying something in her language as the bird talked back to her in raven language. She laughed, tossing her hand so that the bird flew up and landed on the mammoth, then it strutted around looking for a likely place to begin a meal.

Chate emerged from the stream with a stack of cut posts and carried the heap up near the mammoth, dropping the load. He then went to greet his mother who grasped both his elbows and stood up on her toes to kiss him.

"Father, I can make some racks on the stream using the trees as post.

"Alright," replied Harjo.

"Make sure they are in the sun," added Onna.

Chate returned to the stream as Echo emerged dragging a large dead log loaded with smaller limbs of dead wood. He dropped off the pile and likewise went to his mother for a similar kiss, and then he too returned to the stream.

Onna and Harjo looked up to see some 20 or so people coming across the meadow, some pulling sleds and other's

travails-the Wind Band's mammoth meat and hide processors would soon arrive. Onna again took Harjo's hand,
leading him to the log that Echo had just delivered. She
reached up and took off his dart quiver. "Sit and relax," she
ordered, "You have done enough for today."

Harjo complied. Onna looked around to see if anyone
was watching that could see her and after taking off her
woman's bag, she pulled her fur parka over her head, dropping it on the log. She was now naked except for her fur
boots as she reached inside her bag pulling out a long furless caribou buckskin frock. Harjo smiled, then reached up,
kissed his fingers, and laid his hand on her soft yellow colored patch of pubic fur.

"Harjo," she whispered loudly, then touched his hand
and quickly looked around to see if there were any close
prying eyes, especially those of the boys toward the stream.
She quickly pulled the caribou buckskin over her head. She
would wear this garment with all the fur removed, while
she joined the butchering work. She then set down on the
ground and began to remove her boots, smiling up at Harjo.
She would also work barefoot as she usually did.

Watching Onna on the ground as she removed her
boots brought back Harjo's memories. Reminiscences travel
the paths of their own choice across the terrain of the past
but watching Onna and that certain smile she always wore
took him back to his Rite-of-Passage journey so many, many
seasons ago.

Chapter 2:

THE JOURNEY OF YOUTH

Should fortune smile upon a Mammoth Hunter baby and the child lived to reach the age of five or six summers, the journey from childhood to adult began. It was a long, hard journey fraught with difficult, often cruel lessons, learned each day with the rising and setting of the sun. Women followed the path of a seamstress and mother but for a man, hunting remained a rewarding although equally dangerous and difficult occupation. Few men lived to become grey headed as most were killed by mammoth or other dangerous animals during a hunt or slaughtered by ever present Enemy Warriors. Nonetheless, hunting sustained all people across the unforgiving yet abundant Mammoth Steppe.

Harjo like all Muscogee boys began training with spears and darts at the age of five or six summers learning from their fathers and other men in their family. Expectantly, after ten seasonal cycles and reaching 15 or 16 summers, Muscogee boys had mastered the weapons to at least be a capable hunter and hopefully, an accomplished master. But utilizing the weapons was only part of their learned skills. Crafting the weapons likewise required daily effort by the Muscogee boys and ten summers of training to finally grasp the necessary skills to manufacture adequate weapons.

All youth, in every Muscogee band and throughout the entire Muscogee Tribe, must successfully complete a Rite-of-Passage to become a full-fledged adult member of the Tribe, their band, and become eligible for marriage. For a young boy who has reached the tender age of 15 or 16 summers, the Rite-of-Passage demands that he undertake and complete a journey to some distant place lasting an extended period and then return with items of proof that he arrived at that destination. This journey demonstrated he had attained the skills necessary to survive the harsh Mammoth Steppe and to support a family. Also, during this epic journey, he will realize a vision quest.

Harjo's mother told him he was born during the summer, the best season for birth. So, it was during his 16th summer, Harjo knew the journey and the test he would face on what many considered the most important and certainly the first epic undertaking a Muscogee mammoth hunting boy would take-the Rite-of-Passage. He decided he would travel to the west and northwest with the Great Sea as his destination. His mother said her people, the Canineqmiut who live on the coast, call the Great Sea "Imarpik." He actually made the decision the previous summer and approached his father, Cheparney, with the revelation that he believed he was ready for his Rite-of Passage. After a little consideration, his father provided an even more challenging undertaking.

"Utilize your Rite-of-Passage journey as a trading adventure as well and visit the Canineqmiut Eskimo village on the coast of the Great Sea," challenged Cheparney. "Broaden your endeavor. You could pull a sled packed with mammoth resources and trade with the Canineqmiut for seacoast resources, in particular, the sea mammal pelts. I am confident you will be successful and experience a wonderous adventure. You might also find yourself in an envious and prestigious position within the band or with the whole tribe for that matter."

Harjo listened intently as his father laid out an attractive plan. "Allow yourself at least one whole cycle and more beginning from this summer to include the next two winters to prepare. I have taught you for ten summers and will help you kill your first mammoth. I helped your brothers kill their first mammoth when they were your age and you are ready for that hunt. Now, assuming the mammoth doesn't kill us," he laughed with a joking smile, "You will then have a store of mammoth resources-pelts, dried and smoked cured meat, valuable mammoth oil, and mammoth ivory. The Canineqmiut men are avid carvers and appreciate mammoth ivory. You will also have plenty of opportunity to process some of our red chert tool stone. Heated treated bifaces always trade well. Those Canineqmiut men will trade their daughters for that tool stone. Chert is all but absent in the Coastal Zone, consequently, they generally use ground slate for their points and knives. They also admire other inland animal pelts to trim their parkas. Build a sturdy dependable sled. Then, during the middle or end of the second winter, you will be ready. Plan to arrive at the Canineqmiut village in early spring just as they are arriving from their winter villages and the beginning of their sea mammal hunting season. Everyone in the family will help. Your mother would love a meal of that nasty tasting sea mammal meat. I am certain she will ask you to return with a healthy portion." Cheparney chuckled to himself, "I could only eat that animal when faced with starvation; nonetheless, it is something to experience."

Cheparney proposed a difficult and ambitious under-taking for such a young Mammoth Hunter although it was tailored made it for Harjo. After all, his mother was a Yupik woman, a Canineqmiut, born and raised in the coastal village they call "Up'nerkillermiut." Harjo heard this story of how this situation came to pass on many nights at the band campfire in front of the Chokofa Tent related by his uncle, Micco Yarda. He always began the tale the same way.

"Many cycles and seasons ago Cheparney, distraught by the death of his first wife during childbirth, left his two young sons with me and set out alone on a journey. He did not know, nor did he care of neither his destination nor how long he would be gone. He made his way to the coast of the Great Sea and sojourned with the Canineqmiut. How he overcame the language barrier no one knows. Several seasons passed, more than a whole cycle. We had all given him up for lost."

Taking a deep breath, he continued. "Then one spring day, to all's surprise, he returned pulling a sled laden with sea mammal pelts and a beautiful young Canineqmiut girl named Ayuko. Cheparney spoke very little Yupik, still does, and she spoke no Muscogee. Nonetheless, they set up a mammoth lodge. Ayuko adopted Cheparney's first two boys who reciprocated and adopted her as mother. Ayuko bore more children, Harjo and his sister, Chucuse."

Consequently, and by Canineqmiut reckoning, which recognizes kinship through both parents, Harjo had relatives at the village in the persons of his uncle, his mother's brother, and his cousin, his uncle's son. Harjo and his sister spoke Yupik fluently and over the years listening to his mother's stories, he learned much about the Canineqmiut culture.

And so, it was that Harjo spent the whole cycle and more, beginning from that summer and the next two winters, he prepared for his great adventure with help and guidance from his family especially his father. And late during the cold, dark winter season, as all the Muscogee bands were camped at the winter village of Coweta, Harjo was ready to leave.

The wondrous Echota River rose from tall glacier-capped mountains located far to the north and was fed by many smaller headwater streams and springs. This vital watercourse formed the beautiful, wide Echota Valley as it meandered southward to ultimately empty into the even grander Big River. The mammoth and other steppe animals spent the spring and summer in the open headwater regions of the Echota and each winter they migrated along the length of the Echota Valley to the wooded low valley of the Big River, including the mouth of the Echota Valley.

As the Echota River widened to intersect with the Big River, it meandered past an impressive, strange, some say mystical, lofty rocky mountain formation. Laid out in a northwest/southeast orientation, it took a single hunter a long summer day to walk from end to end along the long narrow formation, and it took the Wind Band nearly three days to pass the extent of this rugged creation on a migration march. From a distance, this impressive brown rock formation appeared as the skeletal backbone of a large animal, perhaps a mammoth.

Following the mammoth, the Wind Band, as did the other bands of the Muscogee Tribe, spent the winter at the confluences of the two great rivers and built their winter villages they called Coweta along the base of this rocky formation of towering peaks, tall narrow pentacles, deep caves, and wide steep cliffs. The tall pentacles and steep cliffs could not be climbed but the formation offered many locations of high altitude where one could view the horizon in a complete circle.

Before a young boy leaves for his Rite-of Passage journey, he first secures the blessings from various male Elders of his band. This is not permission, but a blessing. The consulting Elders include the Band Micco or Headman and often the Band Shaman and perhaps the boy's grandfather or older uncles. It presumes the boy's father agrees and has prepared the boy for this event all of his young life. The journey also proposes the opportunity to benefit the band at large in that the youngster will likely return with information concerning resources, landscapes, or other human groups of another area which maybe hereto little or unknown. Occasionally, the boy may know he is ready for the journey but does not have a particular destination in mind; if this is so, the "Council of Elders" will suggest an appropriate voyage.

During the course of this journey, the boy will realize a "Vision Quest." It may come to him in a dream while asleep or in a vision while awake. It may be induced by sleep or food deprivation, through meditation, or on rare occasions by pain. He does not necessarily need to know the meaning of his vision or dream, but it is something he will keep all his life.

The boy will return with something to show he reached the journey's destination. It is not prescribed but something identifiable for that area. For instance, if he is destined for the sea coast, he might return with something from the sea or coast such as various sea shells, which are highly prized by Muscogee women as necklaces and decorations for their parkas.

On return the boy again meets with the Council of Elders. This occasion would include the band's Shaman. The boy thus relates the story of his journey presenting the items of his success. He also relates the circumstances of and the story of his vision. The Elders will then judge the successful completion of the Journey or not. They will also offer words of wisdom and advice upon becoming a man and most often attempt an interpretation of his vision. This is generally in the area of the Shaman's wisdom. An interpretation of the vision, however, is not necessary. The vision's meaning will be revealed to the young man during the course of his life as deemed appropriate by the spirit world and the Father Creator.

With the successful completion of the journey and acknowledgment by the Elders, a gathering of the band at large is called. The Micco declares to all present that the youngster has made "the Journey" from boy to adulthood and that he is now afforded all the rights, privileges, and responsibilities of an adult male member of the band, including the right to marry if he so chooses. His family and or the village Elders will present him with some token to symbolize his passage and sponsor a feast in his honor.

Seeking council with Micco Yarda left Harjo with an uneasy feeling even though Yarda was his uncle. And now it seems the band Shaman, the powerful, mysterious Lion Shaman, had likewise been requested to attend the council, which only added to Harjo's anxiety. To his way of thinking, asking for a blessing and to some degree permission to go out on the journey for the Rite of Passage seemed unnecessary and a troublesome formality. He maintained the deepest respect for these two elders, admiration for their wisdom and gratitude for their long service to the Wind Band, but he knew he was ready as did his father. He also knew he would begin his journey with or without the Micco's blessing. But still, it was what his parents, in fact his whole family, expected, so he would, although somewhat begrudgingly, comply so he could please his family.

As he approached Micco Yarda's mammoth lodge, Harjo noticed Micco Yarda's wife, Us'se, and other women and children leaving the lodge. He took a deep breath and frowned. Micco Yarda or the Lion Shaman must have asked Us'se and her guest to leave the lodge so as to conduct a private council. He did not appreciate this attention drawn to him.

Micco Yarda's mammoth lodge was not only his family's residence but also served the band and the Muscogee Tribe at large, as a meeting and council house. Here band leaders met to discuss the course of action the band should take and equally important the miccos, leaders, and elders of the other bands met to discuss Tribal affairs. The winter Tribal Council meeting was conducted in this very lodge which also housed visiting guest from other bands, traders from other Tribes, or anyone from the Wind Band who required shelter.

As he continued, Harjo approached the rock wall that held down the mammoth hide covering of the lodge, securing it to the ground. He walked around the wall to the mammoth tusk arched opening of the entry room and stood by one of the support posts. He noticed a strange marking on the post, the mark of a bird track deeply carved into the wood. Harjo smiled. The peculiar mark was his; left there by his own hand some three summers ago and he fondly recalled the incident.

That summer he, his father and brothers, Yahola and Chilocco, and other selected men and boys journeyed to the Coweta winter village to reconstruct the entry room of Micco Yarda's mammoth lodge. Any entry room was constructed in the same manner as the main lodge room only smaller and without an excavated pit floor. Four support posts were selected and cut, each just less that the height of two men, perhaps three long paces in length and each forked at the top. The posts were debarked, dried, and treated with mammoth oil. Ideally, the whole post was treated but at least the bottom portion that was set into the ground. The posts were then buried into postholes at equal height. Next, four cross beams were secured to the top of the post using the forks of the post then secured with lashing. Six mammoth tusks were then selected, each the same size and with the same curvature as much as possible.

Below Coweta, along the banks and higher terraces of Big River, an extensive mammoth bone bed littered the area. The origin of the bone bed afforded many long debates with a wide range of explanations, particularly among the old men, including those who held the phenomena as a vengeful act of the Father Creator. Cheparney believed and explained to his boys the bone bed represented a natural calamity not necessarily vengefulness of the Father Creator.

"Imagine," he lectured, "a large mammoth herd on migration traveling along the banks of Big River somewhere upriver. There was a great landslide perhaps during the rare occasions when the great river forges a new channel. A great number of the mammoth were lost into the river and their carcasses deposited here by the natural flow of the currents. Possibly, several mammoth were lost in each migration if they followed the great river upstream and thus were deposited in this eddy."

Cheparney's theory seemed to be verified because a recently deposited rotting mammoth carcass lay on the shore as the work crew collected the six mammoth tusks as support structures. Tusks of cows and young bulls were selected because those of old bulls were too spiraled to be practical as lodge supports.

The tips of the tusks were attached to the cross pieces, three on each side and lashed into place. The bases of the tusk were likewise lashed to a large length of pole to secure them at the ground level. Occasionally, the ends of the tusks were buried to hold them in place. Thus, the completed super structure formed a curved or half circle appearance.

In new construction, an entry tunnel was excavated about a pace wide, extending from the ground and slanted toward and below the excavated pit floor of the main room. This creates a "cold trap" and catches the cold air below the lodge floor so that it does not penetrate the lodge. Steps are cut from the sidewall to allow easy access from the entry tunnel in to the lodge. The step sidewalls are braced with mammoth long bones and the sidewalls of the tunnel are likewise lined with poles to keep the walls from collapsing. As Harjo's work party reconstructed the entry room, they simply used the existing entry tunnel, widened it, and repaired the retaining walls.

Finally, the super structure was covered with prepared and fitted mammoth hides. The entry room is not heated so the wool side of the hide remains on the outside. In the heated lodge room, the wool and hair are on the inside of the lodge. The edges of the hide cover are secured and held down with a rock wall. Rocks are abundant along the Backbone Mountains. Occasionally, mammoth bones are used to hold down the cover, especially jaw bones. Those heavy bones were stacked on top of each other forming a heavy wall especially if filled with dirt, although it remained a rugged chore to collect the number of mandibles necessary to secure the cover. Railing is constructed around the open tunnel of the more elaborate lodges including Micco Yarda's lodge to insure visiting Elders would not fall into the tunnel and to provide easy storage for weapons before entry into the lodge.

That summer had been one of Harjo's most enjoyable adventures especially for a boy of only 13 or 14 summers to be selected to accompany a party of renowned warriors, including his father. It was such an honor and he remained grateful. Perhaps having a renowned warrior father and an uncle as band Micco had its advantages.

To see the Coweta winter village and the Big River during the summer was a wondrous experience. Harjo could not have imagined how deep and lush the forest was along the Big River as compared to the same thin open forest in winter. The river was so wide from the snow and glacier melt and the number and variety of birds was simply astonishing. Harjo vowed to himself that one day he would explore the upper regions of the Big River.

Harjo was tasked to select, cut, and manufacture the four main structural posts. When completed, all the men commented on such a fine job he had done leaving young Harjo with a sense of pride. He carved the track of the bird in each post so as to represent his family name of Fus Chate or Red Bird. The carvings also corresponded to his magnificent atlatl, which was carved by his grandfather in the form of a strange bird. His grandfather had described the bird as a very brilliant red. Harjo reached up to touch the carvings and smiled. He then recalled he was on his way to an important meeting.

Harjo left his spear in the entry room and proceeded into the entry tunnel and up the steps. He passed the first arc of mammoth tusks and the center support posts of the lodge and stood by the hearth. A large fire burned in the hearth and the skylight was opened. Micco Yarda sat on a rare bearskin robe. He killed the bear as a young hunter. He was the only man Harjo knew who had ever slain one of the huge great bears. Next to him, the Lion Shaman sat on a bison rope-both Elders leaned against backrests.

The Lion Shaman was dressed for ceremony making Harjo all the more uneasy. He wore the white pelt of a lion, which included the skin from the animal's head and legs.

The head, upper jaw, and fangs were attached to a hood that sat on top of the shaman's head. The front legs of the pelt with the claws attached were folded over his shoulders and then tied in a knot on his chest. The rest flowed down his back like a cape. The cape pelt, placed on top of the Shaman's head, gave him the strange mystical appearance as a lion form. He did not wear a shirt and Harjo could see the scars of a wound made by a lion's claws on his shoulders. Harjo had always wondered if a lion tore the flesh from the Shaman's shoulders or if he accomplished the wounds himself. He also wondered if the Shaman had killed the lion. A hunter who is able to kill a lion and lives to tell the tale is a brave one indeed.

"Oh yes, Harjo my boy, come in, come in and sit by the fire," said Micco Yarda. His uncle had a calming voice and a way of easing possible tension. Harjo complied. "We understand you are ready for your Rite of Passage. Would you mind telling us what you had in mind for your journey?"

Of course, they already knew where he was going and what he planned to do, but Harjo related the story, following this custom. When he finished, both Elders agreed it was a remarkable journey, but one ready made for him. They wished him good fortune and advised him on several precautions. They also advised him on various responsibilities of adulthood and marriage. Micco Yarda did most of the talking while the Lion Shaman listened, occasionally moving his head in agreement. Harjo also nodded his head yes in agreement although he did not really hear what his uncle said, and he was sure he had heard this same advice on other occasions in the past. Micco Yarda thanked him for coming and as he rose to leave, the Lion Shaman raised his hand as to motion Harjo, he had something to say. Harjo sat back down.

The old Shaman kept his hand up and looked into Harjo's face. Harjo also looked back into the Shaman's face, ancient with age and wrinkles, but also filled with wisdom and a strange sense of power. The Shaman's voice was clear, direct, and commanding.

"Your vision will not be realized by pain or by depriving yourself food or sleep. Do not waste your efforts and strength to employ these methods. Your vision will be realized by meditation and will be sent to you on the wind-the strong, powerful, mystic steppe wind. Do you understand?"

Young Harjo was stunned. He had never been so directly addressed by the Shaman, the powerful Lion Shaman. He nodded his head and managed to say a subdued, "Yes."

"Good," the Shaman replied. "You will fare well." Then he lowered his hand as if giving Harjo permission to leave. Thus, Harjo complied and got up, leaving through the lodge tunnel entryway. As he picked up his spear in the entry room, Harjo now felt eerie about his impending journey and vision quest because of the Shaman's words. But on the other hand, he also felt good about it because in the same peculiar fashion, the Shaman guaranteed he would have a vision. He was now more anxious than before to begin his journey.

Shortly before he left on his Rite-of-Passage, Cheparney took Harjo up the Backbone Mountains to a vista in the early morning light and together they watched the breath-taking view of the great Mammoth Steppe now blanketed with winter snow. In such places where the horizon could be seen in all directions in a "Great Circle" many Muscogee warriors and hunters meditated, seeking inspiration from the "Master of Breath," Father Creator, Esaugeta Emissee.

On this day, Cheparney enlightened Harjo with a piece of great wisdom. "The world appears," explained Cheparney pointing to the horizon, "as a great flat circle that we can see in all directions to the horizon. But it is not. The world is not flat nor is the horizon the end of the earth or the Mammoth Steppe. It only appears to be. The great grassland steppe also appears to be flat as we look to the horizon. But as we traverse it, we know it is not. There are deep gullies and streams, rolling hills, high and low areas. The landscape is anything but flat. The horizon is just the distance that we can see. We know it is not the end of the steppe. If we are higher up as now, we can see farther, but we can still only see to the horizon. Why? Because the world curves. It curves in all directions. It does so because it is round. That is why when you see something on the horizon such as a rock formation, a cluster of tall trees, or a small hill, you can mark it. It is on the horizon so you cannot see past it. But as you walk toward it and reach it, you can still see beyond to the next horizon. And you can see back to the horizon that you came from."

Cheparney looked around and found a patch of wet snow sheltered in the shade of a large rock and packed it together to make a round ball. "The world," he explained, "is a huge ball, larger than we will ever know-larger than we can comprehend." He held the snowball down at arm lengths. "See, it appears to be a flat circle and everywhere you will go, it will appear so." Harjo looked down at the snowball to see what he meant. Again, Cheparney looked around and found a small pebble then stuck it to the ball. He held it up for Harjo to see. "We see the image as the pebble on the horizon, but we cannot see past the horizon. That is until we walk to it. Then we see a new horizon. "Or," he continued, turning the snowball in explanation, "We do not see the formation as we walk toward the horizon, but then it slowly begins to appear." Cheparney handed the snowball to Harjo who took it, rotated it, watching the pebble appear and disappear on rotation.

Cheparney continued. "I believe a man could walk to the west and return to his place of origin from the east going completely around the world; only it would take several life spans to do so. I am not sure what all this means, except that the world, the land, and the sea is much greater than we can imagine. And there are distant lands yet unknown, but they are reachable." In silence, Harjo nodded that he understood.

Cheparney put his arm around his son, giving him a one-arm hug. "Ready to leave?" he asked. Harjo only smiled, nodding his head yes, then dropped the snowball to the ground. "It is an exciting moment for us as well as for you. Remember, stay ever vigilant, don't take any unnecessary risks, and if things seem too quiet and peaceful, become more alert. Too quiet is often the Father Creator's way of sending you a warning. When you feel something in the wind, respond to it."

"Yes, I will," answered Harjo in a shy way.

"Well, we should head back down," Cheparney said with a smile. "There must be at least one little 'bunny of a girl' that wants to say her goodbyes to you." Harjo likewise only smiled shyly as the two made their way down the rocky peaks back to Coweta.

Chapter 3:

CHUFE

Muscogee women adore the pelts of the hare, especially the thick white winter coat. The thinner brown summer pelt was less desirable, so much that summer hares were seldom killed. Ptarmigan and hare were the preferred quarry of Muscogee boys growing up and learning to hunt. Ptarmigan meat was delicious, while hare, although nutritious enough, produced a bland, less desirable flavor. A young hunter often kept the meat of a hare but offered its fur to a woman, his mother, sister, favored aunt, or if possible, a young woman or better yet, a girl he hoped to impress. Young boys hunted them in the fall and winter, keeping women supplied with pelts. Often, young boys would exchange a pelt to young attractive women for a kiss.

Some women owned a hare pelt rug created by sewing together as many as ten hare pelts, but every woman possessed a least one hare pelt that she kept in her woman's bag as an all-purpose washing pelt while many kept a furless pelt for washing as well. Every woman decorated their parkas, some more, some less, and hare was regarded as the prized pelt for adornment. Women sewed strips of fur on the sleeves, skirts, and shoulders of their parkas. Those who were more daring added circular patches on the front to suggest breast or triangular patches in the groin and vulva area, and occasionally a woman may sew a hare tail on her tail end. More commonly, the white hare tail was attached to a feather and worn in a women's hair.

The Muscogee language expressed this relationship between women and hare with the term "bunny." Children used the term bunny expressed in "child's talk" to mean hare. It actually refers to a baby hare. Making a comparison between a bunny and a woman however could be either a complement or an insult. In turn then, an attractive young woman might be called a pretty young bunny. On one side, a young woman might be called a "bunny" to mean she was attractive which represents the most common usage.

On the other side, a woman might be identified as a "little bunny" to suggest she was of low morals and would probably engage in sex with any man. This association also referred to a woman's changing emotions as the hare changes color each season, from brown in the summer to white in the winter.

Young, beautiful Chufe was a pretty bunny. Her parka was elaborately decorated with hair pelts to emphasis her breast and vulva area, including a hair tail sewn on the small of her back to focus on her bottom. When she walked by, and she had a lovely walk, men would watch her "bunny tail" as the pretty young woman strolled past.

A young hunter from a prominent family of the Lion Band had purchased Chufe from her father following Muscogee marriage customs. It seemed to be a good match. Unfortunately, the adventurous Chufe enjoyed sexual relationships with a wide variety of Muscogee men young and old.

For a married woman, adultery was a very serious offence that could lead to death. The offended husband might kill his adulterous wife although that was very rare. He might also drag her into the center of the village and administer a public beating by severely whipping her legs with a switch, then returning her to her father, but likewise, that too occurred only on rare occasions. More commonly, the offended husband dragged the wife back to her father. This divorce was a public embarrassment and a manner of honor for the family and the father. All property, including any children remained with the husband and the divorced woman took only the clothes on her back and her personal women's bag back to her father's lodge. This had been Chufe's fate, returned to her father's lodge by the young man from the Lion Band.

Chufe lost a baby. Undeniably tragic, but yet was a common and expected hardship. All women lose nearly one-half of their babies during the first season subsequent the birth. Many babies die at birth. It was a predictable hardship of life that a woman would lose at least one baby but generally three or five during her childbearing age. Perhaps losing her first baby, in some way provoked Chufe to be unfaithful.

Harjo carried his spear leaving his atlatl and darts at his family's lodge as he walked by Chufe's father's lodge. She stood outside in the entryway room.

"Harjo," she called out. Harjo stopped and looked in her direction as if to say "yes."

"Harjo, come here please, I want to ask you something."

Harjo walked over, stopping close to her. They had known each other all of their young lives. Chufe had always been sexually adventurous as a girl and there were few secrets at Coweta.

"Yes, Chufe?" he asked.

She reached out and took his hand and moved closer to him. "It's been so long since I've seen you or talked with you, Harjo. How have you been?"

"Frantic. It's been very frantic lately. A lot of work."

"Yes, I heard you were going to the coast on your Rite-of-Passage journey." She still held Harjo's hand. Slowly, she reached her free right hand up and pushed her parka hood back revealing her hair. Then, she rubbed and stretched her neck using slow, seductive motions.

"Harjo, will you buy me from my father and marry me when you return?" she asked with a beautiful, tempting smile.

"I don't know," replied a startled Harjo with a stutter.

"If you're not ready for marriage Harjo, will you ask your father to buy me as a second wife?"

"I suppose I could ask him after I return." He answered in a mumbled way.

"I was just teasing you, Harjo," she said laughing. "But I do want to ask you. Will you bring me some shells from the coast?"

"She is so beautiful," thought Harjo, "such a beautiful smile. It is difficult to say no to her. Uh-maybe," he replied.

"Oh yes, a whole handful," she said, holding out her cupped hand. "Will you, please?" she pleaded, still smiling.

"I suppose I could bring some shells back for you."

Cautiously, Chufe looked around to see is anyone was watching, then, still holding his hand, she looked up smiling into his face.

"Come with me," she whispered as she tenderly led him into her father's lodge. In the entry room she took his spear and leaned it against the wall. She picked up a "snow beater" stick, handed it to Harjo, then turned around and slightly bent over in a slow seductive manner with her hands on her knees.

"Will you knock the snow off my bottom please?"

Harjo looked to see she had sat down in the snow, so he gently swatted her butt to clean the snow off her parka and her bunny tail.

"Thank you," she said, looking back over her shoulder still smiling. "My father is out hunting, and my mother is staying with my brother's wife. They asked me to spend the nights with them while the men were gone but I would rather stay alone."

Again, she took his hand and while rubbing it, she smiled into his face. "You have such strong, large, powerful hands, Harjo, and your palms are so hard." She then led him down the entry tunnel into the lodge.

The skylight was opened while the hearth in the center of the lodge glowed with coals. The corners of most lodges were quartered off as sleeping areas by hanging animal skin curtains from the support beams. Not only did this provide a small measure of privacy but helped warm the lodge. Chufe led Harjo to a corner and drew back the curtain to reveal a knee-high platform bed layered with furs. A woven grass mat lay on the hard-packed dirt floor in front of the bed. She set down, untied her boots, and pulled them off along with her socks. She patted the bed next to her to invite Harjo to sit down. He complied.

Slowly, she got up, then moved down on her knees to the grass mat and untied Harjo's boots then slowly pulled them off along with his mammoth wool socks. During the removal, she occasionally glanced up at Harjo smiling but did not say anything. She then stood up.

Grasping her parka sleeve, she pulled her arm out of her parka followed by the other, then pulled the knee length garment over her head. She tossed the parka onto the bed then shook her long beautiful black hair combing it with her hands. She was not wearing any pants even though it was winter. Now naked from head to toe Harjo could see

38

how beautiful she was with her stunning face and fine fea-
tures-large firm breasts, curved narrow waist, and ample
hips. Chufe motioned for Harjo to stand up and then with
a near silent but stimulating laughter, helped him remove
his parka.

Then she put her arms around his waist pulling him
close. He put his arms around her shoulders. She looked
up, smiled into his face, and kissed him full on the mouth.
The warmth of her kiss and the warm softness of her breast
against his chest began to move Harjo, stirring his burning
young blood.

Harjo had not enjoyed sex before. Oh, there had been
quick childlike encounters of kissing and handling with
girls from his band and other bands, including Chufe,
but not the complete sexual act. The inexperienced Harjo
did not want Chufe to know this would be his first sexual
adventure, although she probably did. The well-experienced
Chufe did not care; although the prospect of being his first
excited her, hence she remained more than willing to guide
him on this new arousing journey.

"I have wanted you since we were children, Harjo. Do
you remember?"

"I remember you were the prettiest girl in the band.
You still are."

Flattery will get you anything. She now untied the
drawstrings to his pants pulling them down.

Warmly-softly-she kissed him again gently but seduc-
tively rubbed her vulva against his now swollen manhood.
His pants were at his ankles and she put her foot on top of
them between his legs. "Pull your feet out," she whispered.
Her warm wet mouth kissed and sucked on his nipple, then
sliding her wet tongue across his chest she so stimulated
the other.

"When a woman does something to a man, Harjo, often it is a signal she wants him to do the same to her."

Following her not so subtle suggestion, Harjo took her soft brown nipple in his mouth sucking, kissing, and stimulated it until it became hard and tumid. At the same moment, he massaged her other large gorgeous breast with his hands and fingers.

"Oh yes, Harjo," she whispered and gently kissed his neck and ears. She reached down to tenderly fondle his testicles.

"I'll be your bunny Harjo, if you will be my warrior?" she asked with panting breath. Harjo thought before he answered.

These two terms, bunny and warrior, carried subtle but important meanings in a Mammoth Hunter male/female relationship. A mated pair, husband and wife, often referred to each other with private nicknames. Very often the husband called his wife "his bunny" and the wife called her husband "her warrior." As a result, a woman who would call a man "her warrior" means a man who fights for her and protects her; he is probably her husband but not necessarily. That is, a young girl may refer to her father or even an older brother as "her warrior." Consequently, to become a woman's warrior would constitute a meaningful relationship.

At this point, and so aroused, Harjo did not consider the complete consequences of becoming "Chufe's warrior," but he saw no harm.

"Yes," he answered, "I'll be your warrior."

Chufe was pleased with his answer thus continued to fondle and caress him. Thinking to herself, she pondered, "He is so handsome, muscular, and strong like his father. I have always wanted to entice Cheparney into my bed, but the son will make a wonderful choice as well. He is tall and built like his father, but he favors the face of his mother-Ayuko. Perhaps that is why he is so handsome. His mother, although Canineqmiut and from the coast, is the prettiest woman in the whole Muscogee Tribe. It must be true what I have heard the old women say-a pretty mother has pretty babies."

Chufe turned around, then rubbed her buttocks against his pelvis and reached her arms back behind his neck inviting him to kiss her neck and massage her breast. She then put her arms down to reach back and gripped his buttocks still moving hers in a slow circular motion. She then crawled into the platform bed on her hands and knees looking back over her shoulder.

"Come take me, Harjo," she gasped in a low seductive voice.

Harjo followed her on his knees onto the bed moving behind her. He gazed at her exquisite buttocks and the beautiful dark vulva between her thighs. He could just make out her black pubic hair and the sight of her hair and vulva lips heightened his passion and desire for her. But he also noticed several small, red welt marks laid across her stunning thighs. Chufe realized he must see the welts and looking back over her shoulder whispered, "We can't let my father catch us Harjo or he will give me another switching. If he catches me again, he said he would switch my legs and my bottom.

"He won't catch us," he replied, rubbing her gorgeous behind with both of his hands. Of course, he could not prevent her father from suddenly returning from his hunt and walking into his own mammoth lodge to discover the now naked lovers. But his words seem to offer her some comfort.

He moved forward on his knees as his ridged manhood probed for her female entrance. She reached between her legs to helped guide him and he followed her path. As he entered her warm, wet womanhood, he felt a whole new feeling of unmatched wonder. Slowly, but with determination, he pushed-completely filling her.

Again, Chufe looked back over her shoulder. "Oh, Harjo," she whispered in a panting voice, "You're so big. Go slow at first and then faster."

Harjo complied and withdrew his manhood to its head then slowly penetrated her again-then again-and another.

"Oh yes, oh yes" she called out in a desperate whisper. He grasped her ample hips, withdrew, and sank into her over and over then began to increase his speed. Chufe arched her back, moaning and panting as she squirmed pushing back against him. Harjo remained silent offering only a few moans but Chufe continued with her verbal, although quiet stimulation.

"That's it! That's it! Oh faster! Oh faster," she panted." Harjo continued to follow her directions but then her passion surprised him.

"Spank me, Harjo, spank me! Spank your naughty bunny!"

Following directions, Harjo raised his hand and gave her a playful swat on each bottom cheek.

"Harder," she cried out!"

He raised his hand again and delivered a hard slap.

But again, she cried out, "Harder, Harjo, harder with the rough palm of your tough hand! Spank me hard-hard!"

Now, as more of a challenge, he brought his powerful hand down on one stunning buttocks cheek and then the other as hard as he could. He continued spanking her until she was satisfied.

"Oh stop, oh stop!" She called out in a screaming whisper as she buckled and convulsed with orgasm. Her head went down to the bed on the side of her face as her hands clenched the soft fur bed cover. Then, following several gasping moans, she raised her head and arched her back moving back to him.

"Kiss me, Harjo, kiss me!"

Harjo leaned forward with his chest on top of her back and put his left hand down on the hare blanket. He was surprised to discover that he could kiss her in this position. He reached out his right hand with his fingers pointing up to the side of her face with his palm under her chin then gently pulled her head to the side. At the same moment, he leaned over her back and kissed her warm open mouth. She passionately returned his kisses.

He leaned back, returning his hands to her hips but decided he wanted to see more. He caressed the red skin and finger marks his spanks left on her cheeks, which were hot to his touch. He then spread her cheeks, then leaned back and looked at himself moving in and out of her womanhood and at her anus. He then slid his thumb down between her checks touching that tiny brown mystery.

Looking back over her shoulder, she spoke while panting. "I'll let you have that little hot spot one of these days, Harjo. Would you like that, hmm? Faster, Harjo, faster, pound me, pound me!"

She dropped down to her elbows and pushed against him meeting his thrust with hers. She felt herself reaching orgasm again. "Faster Harjo, faster, pound me just as a bunny-a bunny-pound against my bottom-harder!" She then lifted her feet sliding them over his ankles and pinned him down.

Harjo placed his hands on her hips and discovered with her feet holding down his ankles, he could thrust with more speed and power and he did-as hard and as fast as he could. Chufe convulsed and contracted again with orgasm.

"Fill me Harjo-fill me!"

He did not hold out much longer as he gasped and groaned with ejaculation and following Chufe, Harjo drifted over into the spirit world of mating. From the natural world of male and female, from the beginnings before life, they both entered the spirit world of the Creator Father. All the animals of the steppe, especially the mammoth, enter the spirit world during mating. The aggressive males fight for access to the females-the coy female's desire for the strongest males. All move with the rhythm of life, if only for one brief but glorious moment, drifting from the natural world to taste the wonderful, mystical, the unseen and unexplained spirit world.

Chufe collapsed on her hare skin blanket and slowly stretched out. Harjo, with his palms on the blanket, eased down with her. They lay exhausted, panting, and delighted.

After they had recovered, Chufe whispered. "Your bunny still needs attention Harjo. Don't neglect her."

Harjo rose up on his hands, kissing her neck, ears, and then gently sucked on her ear lobes and that fold of skin just below the lopes. He rolled over as she turned into his arms snuggling against his chest. He kissed and caressed her. He then whispered into her ear what a wonderful lover she was, how beautiful she was, and that she was the prettiest girl in the Tribe. Soon, she drifted off to sleep.

Harjo lay with her for a while, then got up and dressed. He looked down at a beautiful sleeping Chufe curled up on her side somehow more striking while asleep. At the end of her bed lay a mammoth pelt blanket. He unrolled the blanket, covering her. Then, he drew her skin curtains and headed out through the entry tunnel into the entry room of the mammoth lodge. He found it hard to believe he had just had sex with such a beautiful girl. It clouded his mind like the frozen ice fog that settles on the hides of the mammoth lodges during deep, cold winters. He was not sure he understood, but he did realize the experience was more enjoyable than he had ever imagined. He picked up his spear and walked with a smile and a bounce toward his own family's mammoth lodge. He was too young to realize it then, at that moment; too young and overwhelmed with his first sexual escapade to appreciate the fact that he would never be the same again.

Chapter 4:

LEAVING

The Muscogee Mammoth Hunters reckoned traveling distance by the distance individuals or groups could achieve in a day considering the long daylight hours of the summer and short days of winter. The first distance was one that a young warrior could accomplish in one day taking only his weapons and thus engaged in a desperate flight, such as pursuing or being pursued by a warrior band. This, of course, would represent unusual circumstances. Nonetheless, if one hunter would ask another how far from this location to another and the answer was "the distance a desperate warrior could travel in a day" then each would have a mental construct of that distance.

More common would be the distance a hunter could travel by walking and again taking only his weapons but also such supplies as a backpack, shoulder bags, or other pouches. This would relate to the circumstance of a long-distance explorer. This was likewise a less common event.

The most frequent and the one generally referred to was the distance a hunter could traverse while pulling a sled loaded with supplies, trading goods, or the products of a large game kill. Muscogee Mammoth Hunters epitomized adventure. Distant trading forays to exchange mammoth products with the caribou hunters to the north were common. Occasionally, a daring trader may also take the dangerous journey to the southwest to the land of the Sea Mammal Hunters. Also, a single hunter may venture out on a hunting trip with a near empty sled and return with a load of meat and hides. Bison were commonly taken in this manner.

Finally, the expanse a whole band could cover in a day loomed as the most important travel distances. Composed of many sleds and the added travel limitations of children and the elderly, this distance loomed the most important consideration for the leaders of a Muscogee band. In planning a band migration, a micco must know how many days it would take his band to travel from one location to the next without exhausting the more fragile members of his band. Also, he must consider that his band could only travel so many consecutive days before stress and fatigue would jeopardize migration success.

Harjo discussed the best path to the coast with Cheparney on several occasions and listened to his father's counsel. "I believe your best route," Cheparney advised, "is to follow the Echota River northwest on the same route the band takes on spring migration. You've traveled this segment of the journey on many occasions. It takes three days to pass the Backbone Mountains. Then, as the river turn northward, you should continue northwest across the steppe."

"Once on the open steppe," continued Cheparney, "navigation will be more difficult. Use the sun, the North Star at night, and at first the Backbone Mountains until those jagged peaks slip below the horizon. All combined, these will help you keep your bearing."

"Father, how may days pulling sled to reach the coast?"

Cheparney pondered the question for a moment then answered. "It requires approximately nine days to cross the steppe and to reach the Coastal Zone. The flat treeless terrain of the Coastal Zone will offer a greater challenge of navigation and require about four days to traverse. I count 16 days total, give or take three days, until you reach the coast. If you're lucky, you will come upon the Canineqmiut village of Up'nerkillermiut situated at the north end of Tununeq Bay. If less lucky, you will reach the coast at the bay at large and then you would follow the coast north to the village."

As they often did, the Fus Chate men gathered around the burning hearth of their mammoth lodge inspecting and repairing weapons. It remained a critical, never-ending task. The fire provided a low light as did other burning mammoth oil lamps but because of the poor light, the men would inspect and repair but wait until daylight before crafting any new weapons. This would be Harjo's last opportunity to repair any flaws in his weapons. The mood remained quiet and somber for all of the family members.

The next morning at daylight, the Fus Chate family met outside their mammoth lodge to bid farewell to their adventurous son. All knew the risks of a Rite-of-Passage journey but understood it must be taken. And more so with Harjo's journey as his would be froth with danger. If tragedy befell Harjo, his family may never see him again and if so, would most likely never learn what became of him.

He embraced his older brothers Yahola and Chilocco who wished him luck. His uncle, Micco Yarda, shook his hands and told him he would do well. Yarda's wife, Us'se, took his arms and kissed her nephew. Having lost her two sons to mammoth, she now put the trust of her old age into the hands of her nephews. Yahola's young wife, Kak-ke, likewise kissed Harjo although she did not know him very well; nonetheless women always kissed the men in their family. Beautiful little weeping sister Chucuse jumped to put her arms around her tall brother's neck, then smothered his face with kisses.

"Harjo, please be careful, please."

"I will," he promised as he took her by the waist to set her down.

Cheparney embraced Harjo and smiled. He was proud that his son was so well prepared for this journey and up to the task—he could think of nothing else to say.

Harjo's sturdy sled was tightly packed and tied down with strong rawhide ropes. His well-made spruce shaft spear was pushed behind the sled's rawhide tie-downs, but his dart quiver lay across his back, his foreshaft quiver and knife were attached to his belt. His magnificent heirloom atlatl was also pushed into his belt.

Also, in tears, Ayuko went to her son, grasping his arms and stood on her toes to kiss him. It is a bittersweet moment for all mothers as their sons leave on their Rite-of-Passage Journey.

"He looks so handsome," thought Ayuko, "Where did that little boy who played the fox chase game go? I can't believe he is nearly a man." She wanted her son to complete his right and journey but being alone on the Mammoth Steppe was a very dangerous undertaking. She knew by firsthand experience as she had made the journey from the coast with Cheparney when just a budding girl. She had also endured the journeys of her first two sons and would similarly endure Harjo's.

Ayuko handed her son a well-made women's bag full of extra camping supplies as a gift. It contained extra items that a mother would pack for a boy such as soap, food bowls, and extra socks. Items that he would not necessarily think to pack himself.

"I don't expect you to wear the bag," she said in Yupik, smiling with tears silently running down her face. "But I expect you will give it to a pretty young girl when you return."

He thanked her and kissed her again. There was nothing more to say. Cheparney put his arm around Ayuko and they watched their youngest son make his way toward his sled.

Harjo leaned against the sled harness. It required more pull than he thought it would to budge the fully loaded sled, but it finally creaked as the dry snow's hold on the bone runners gave way and at long last, the journey of a life span began. He turned for one final smile to his parents and family. The excitement sparked through him like lightning striking a tree and although he tried to hide his enthusiasm, he could not camouflage his smile. He would always recall this particular moment in his life as one of the defining events that would otherwise epitomize youth.

Other members of the Wind Band, who were out early this morning, offered Harjo a wave, a shout, or a whistle of encouragement and good luck. Especially the older men, upon seeing Harjo off on his Rite-of-Passage, were sparked into pleasant memories of their journey and the adventurous days of their youth. Even pretty, naughty, little Chufe was out to see Harjo off. Standing out of view to all but him, she raised her parka, bent over, and offered Harjo a view of her bare bottom. Then, looking back over her shoulder, gave him a kiss on her hand. Harjo was fond of Chufe and wanted the best for her. He was sorry about her divorce even though she brought it on herself. As she was pretty, Harjo believed it would not be long before another man bought her from her father, perhaps as a second wife. Then, it occurred to him. What if his father purchased Chufe as a second wife? "Would that not be strange," he said smiling to himself. Well, he had more serious concerns but still beautiful Chufe will certainly be recalled on many forthcoming, cold, lonely nights.

The thought and the idea of being alone-really alone-on the great wide Mammoth Steppe was both thrilling and somewhat unsettling. He welcomed the challenge, the adventure, even the hardship of pitting himself against all the danger the steppe could provide. But, on the other side, there would be no one to turn too-save himself.

He was also anxious to see for himself what the landscape was like to the west. He had heard so much about the Coastal Zone. How would it really appear? Cheparney said it takes four days to cross the zone. Harjo suddenly recalled hearing his father, Micco Yarda and other Elders discussing the changing landscape-trees growing into the grasslands where none had grown before. Harjo wondered, that being true, would trees then grow into the Coastal Zone? He did not know. And was the Great Sea as large as he had heard? He found it hard to visualize a water body that stretched to the horizon and the Canineqmiut, hunting animals in the sea from floating watercraft. All was hard to visualize.

What would the Canineqmiut and their massive village look like? According to his mother, they would accept him as one of their own. How very strange, men he had not seen who were related only to his mother, according him kinship. The thrill urged him to push hard and fast, but he knew a steady, even pace was the best strategy.

Harjo followed the flat wooded area that formed between the Echota River and the higher elevations and hilly terrain along the foothills of the Backbone Mountains. Twice each cycle, late fall and early spring, the Wind Band journeyed with their sleds along this natural wide path during spring and fall migrations. Harjo pulled sleds up and down the Echota River as far back as he could remember, first as a Ptarmigan Boy, and then later in support of his family. The rocky formations, rugged terrain of the Backbone Mountains, and the trees of the woodland provided plenty of safe cover in case of an encounter or attack from mammoth as he followed the west side of the Echota River.

Each winter, the bulk of the mammoth herd congregated on the east side of the Echota and the north side of Big River. There at the confluence of the two rivers, impenetrable, vast, thickets of willow and alder and the spacious open meadows provided winter forage and the dense woods along Big River provided cover from winter winds and cold. Consequently, a mammoth encounter on this side of the Echota would be rare.

Although the Echota flowed nearly due south, this section along the Backbone Mountains the river meandered southeast thus Harjo would follow the mountains in a northwest direction. Generally, pulling a loaded sled through the forest was a difficult task even in winter. The reduced amount of snow cover and plenty of obstacles such as fallen trees, trunks, and other debris often blocked the way, but this natural path generally remained clear. Once Harjo cleared the mountains and headed northwest across the open steppe, the sled would glide more easily.

Toward the end of the day, Harjo came upon one of the many Wind Band camping locations where, along with his family, he had camped here on several previous migrations. The area narrowed between the Echota Riverbank and the Backbone Mountain base promoting a thick grove of white cottonwood trees. These small white barked relatives of the large cottonwood flourished in clusters along the river. Their small round leaves created an unusual but familiar sound when blown by the wind, especially in fall. The steep hill cliff face along the mountain side, the grove of white cottonwoods, and several large trees all combined to form a protected area with shallow snow accumulation which created excellent camping conditions. Harjo noticed several rock-lined hearths formed in linear spacing along the path and several cut horizontal poles set into notched trees.

He could easily cover considerably more ground this day and in fact, he could probably clear the mountains with a two days hard march. But this was not an endurance journey or a desperation flight.

As advised by his father, "Set yourself an easy pace, don't travel the whole daylight, and most importantly enjoy yourself. Not to mention you would need the opportunities to meditate in order to realize your vision. I doubt a vision can be achieved while pulling the sled."

Thus, Harjo stopped here, setting up his first camp. He selected a likely spot by one of the hearths surrounded by rocks with a large "sitting log" near the hearth. It was mostly cleared of snow with a good location for his mammoth bed. He noticed there was old water boiling rocks set on top of the hearthstones left by the last campers. In fact, he thought this location may have been where his family camped late last fall.

A low rock formation was located some 15 paces west. A large ancient cottonwood tree grew on top of the small flat area with its aged roots protruding through the surrounding rocks. Long exposure of the large tree roots gave them a tree limb form rather than a buried root appearance. That strange combination of rocks, soil, and roots created a primordial amalgamation.

A pair of eagles built and maintained a large nest high in the center of this ancient tree. The eagles nested here as far back as Harjo could remember. The huge nest appeared to measure some two paces across. The pair also roosted in this tree during the winter and thus it formed the center of their lives as they returned to it nearly every night. Numerous eagle pairs nested in the high-protected cliffs of the Backbone Mountain, but they seldom roosted there in winter, preferring the large river trees. The icy rocks of the mountain were too cold for winter comfort. Harjo remembered playing around the base of the giant tree with its mystical formation of rocks and roots as a young boy. He also recalled that the occasions of finding an eagle feather were always a welcomed delight.

The first thing Harjo did was to count this day. He kept a length of rawhide rope attached to the top rail of the sled and every evening he planned to tie a knot to keep track of the number of days in his journey. He laughed at himself as this was the same technique women used to keep count of their menstruation days. Women employed "counting chords" to count the number of days within their menstrual cycle simply by tying a loose knot in the chord to represent one day thus helping signal their day of pregnant ripeness. Usually a length of small rawhide strips they kept in their women's bag served the purpose or often by tying knots in the draw chords of their pants. Frequently, the end of the chord was attached to a bone or ivory figurine to identify it as the "menstrual chord" because other chords were likewise kept counting other important days, cycles, or events. Carved female figurines with enlarged breasts and buttocks were popular as menstrual chord carvings.

He gathered a stack of firewood, which lay in abundance around the camp and formed a small stack of dry sticks and tender in the hearth. Then, he took his utility bag from the sled, pulling out his fire-starting kit. Such kits were common to all and nearly everyone throughout all the Bands of the Muscogee owned one.

A man usually started the first fire at camp or the Coweta Village while the whole band of women waited around and then used a burning stick to start their own fire once he had a flame burning. During the summer celebrations of the "First Kill" the Lion Shaman started the fire during the "First Fire" ceremony and the rest of the band ignited their family hearths from this one fire. Boys were also motivated to start the fires especially during spring and summer migrations. Harjo recalled he often started the family fire. For some reason, boys find it fun.

A drilling procedure started the fire by friction heat. He laid out the four components of the kit, a mouthpiece, a drill stick, a bow piece, and a fire stick. Dry tender was needed, usually fur pulled from a pelt or various small "fur like" grasses. Harjo kept a wad of dry tender with his kit.

As the fire burned, Harjo set up the rest of his camp. He untied his mammoth bed from the sled and laid it out near the fire and the log. His mother made the bed for him. She sewed it from one long piece of winter mammoth pelt folded together with the thick, warm, mammoth wool inside, the color of yellow ocher. He could sit on top of the bed pelts as a ground blanket and tend the fire, then sleep between them at night.

Harjo was anxious to brew some mammoth tea. People used the strongly aromatic leaves of the plant across the Mammoth Steppe from the coast to the caribou hunters far to the north. The yellow brew was the favored drink of the Muscogee people and was consumed at nearly every meal and throughout the day as well. Both men and women often sat around a campfire at night consuming a ladle or bowl of the aromatic tea before heading off to bed. He could readily use his current supply because the plant was more plentiful as he approached the Coastal Zone. He set a boiling pouch near the fire to brew the tea.

His fur clothing required a considerable amount of maintenance work to keep them in useable condition, especially boots. Wet clothing was a lethal enemy and during all seasons, except summer, would most likely cause frostbite which in turn caused pain, discomfort, and lameness. And for a lone hunter on the frigid Mammoth Steppe those conditions eventually led him down a path to death.

Harjo brought an extra set of boots, parka, pants, mittens, wool and grass socks, and boot pads. He also brought a caribou skin shirt. With all the hair removed from the hide, it made a fine warm weather shirt. He often wore it in the afternoon around camp.

He strung a rawhide rope line between two trees and pulled the boot pads and socks from his boots and hung them up to dry overnight. He also hung up his parka and pants likewise to dry and put on his extra boots, pants, and caribou shirt.

He took his boots, inspected them, and hung them up as well. In the morning, after the boots were dry, he would soften the soles with a flat bone tool or stone. Then, he would use his boot sole creaser to get into the toes and heals to soften those hard to reach areas and to keep the tine pleats in order. A boot sole creaser was a flat bone tool resembling a knife and about the same size.

After a meal of mammoth jerky and tea and some moments in meditation by the fire, Harjo was ready for bed. The distant hoot of a horned owl reminded him to be sure all was ready before retiring. Harjo slept in various amounts of clothing from completely dressed to completely naked depending on the circumstances, real or predicted. More commonly, he slept in his caribou shirt and grass sock, which he chose for his first night. With all chores complete, he slept with his weapons nearby, leaning against the sitting log. Because of the tall trees, he could only see a portion of the sky and stars straight up from his bed. He lay on his back watching the stars. His thoughts turned to Chufe. Her warm soft body would be a welcome pleasure right now. He smiled thinking of her. He called out a few horned owl hoots, tricking the owl into answering which brought another smile to his face. Although generally uneventful, his first day concluded with a sense of pleasure; in fact, it had been fun.

Chapter 5:

CROSSING THE STEPPE

The all too familiar trumpeting call, resembling a nearby clash of thunder, jolted Harjo, jerking him from what had been a peaceful sleep and an otherwise calm night. As he sprang from bed, he grabbed his spear, belt, and fore shaft quiver and ran for the large tree atop the rock and tree root formation. What was once his childhood playing area now became a lifesaving strong hold. He ducked behind the tree, turning back toward his camp. It remained dark as the morning sun just began its short spring journey from the east, but Harjo could make out the dark figure of a large bull mammoth. It raised its head and trunk to let out another loud trumpeting call. The bull had followed the riverbank downstream and stopped some 20 paces from camp. It assumed a combatant stance, drug his great tusks across the ground, and then charged toward the camp but stopped adjacent to Harjo's bed and the now smoldering fire.

Harjo expected the mammoth to stomp on his bed and perhaps even damage his darts and atlatl left leaning against the log. But the bull watched Harjo making several aggres-sive gestures toward him. Even with its poor eyesight, the mammoth could see that Harjo was relatively safe on top the rock/tree root formation and behind the large tree. The mammoth could also realize that Harjo was armed with a deadly spear. And so, the great beast, having decided that he had made his own personal statement, turned and ran back toward the river and then turned down the trail toward Coweta. It stopped at a safe distance and continued in a walking gait on his way without looking back.

"Well, there is nothing like a mammoth charge to get your early morning blood stirring and boost your morning hunger," laughed Harjo out loud, realizing good fortune was with him. The mammoth could have charged through the camp trampling him as he slept in his mammoth bed. Perhaps, because it was still too dark, the mammoth stopped to deliver a warning call instead of charging. Sleeping late can be a fatal mistake on the Mammoth Steppe but it is usu-ally safe on this side of the river during the spring season. Harjo was reminded to take more care in camp selection and to remember that the behavior of young bull mammoth always remains unpredictable.

Harjo urinated on the large tree then returned to his camp. He rekindled the fire using the smoldering coals. After inspecting and preparing his boots for today's march, he dressed and put away his sleeping clothes. He took a drink of water and a slab of mammoth jerky and decided to practice with darts and a spear while the fire heated his water boiling rocks. The trail itself provided a good prac-tice range and a small bush and grass clump a good target.

Once satisfied with his practice, which included many handheld spear throws, he brewed some mammoth tea drinking, two ladles full and ate some more mammoth jerky. Then he took his warm water pouch, spear, and bison robe and headed for the rock formation. He stripped, squatted, left dung, and then washed himself. Harjo had always been amazed at how quickly wet things dried even when there was still snow on the ground and he wondered why warm water quickly disappeared and snow did not. Harjo laughed at himself, "a question for the Lion Shaman."

All packed and loaded, Harjo started his second day's journey that began with a discourteous mammoth awaking. Ravens and magpies were abundant along the wooded rivers especially in winter. They also followed the mammoth herds, benefiting from the cold nights that took the weak, sick, and old. The feathered scavengers could not open a mammoth carcass but would wait patiently taking second place after wolves or lions. During the summer, the thick wooded streams were also rich with passerine birds, especially the Big River and to a lesser number the Echota. The farther north on the Echota, as it narrowed, splitting into tributaries and smaller streams, the woodlands likewise dissipated. The narrow upland streams supported few trees if at all, perhaps only small patches of willow. The birds were attracted to thick forest and the insects found in abundance on the Big River and the lower region of the Echota. The insects hibernated in the winter and thus the birds flew south and southeast.

But, as the birds left the steppe migrating south and southeast, they must fly over the huge glacier that formed the southern boundary of Muscogee Tribe's world. The birds could not live on the frozen glacier; consequently, there must be land on the other side. How far? No one knew. How far can the birds fly? Perhaps that was another question for the Lion Shaman.

Harjo watched another beautiful sunny day unfold on the Mammoth Steppe. He was covering more distance than he anticipated and now on his fifth day, traversed the more open flat terrain that allowed the heavy sled to pull easily across the shallow snow. He cleared the wooded zone of the Echota River two days ago. Most late winter and early spring days were sunny, reasonably warm, accompanied by clear starlit nights. But the nights were very cold, and Harjo was grateful for his mother's mammoth bed. Last night in the stars he first found the Big Dipper then the North Star. He marked its location on the ground in the snow with a line pointed at the top. Now, as he stood facing north with the new morning sun, he could get his bearings and noted the northwest direction he wanted to travel. Watching the sun on the flat open terrain nearly every day all his life taught a young traveler how to keep his bearings and destination. On the horizon, he saw another tree clump. It was not in the exact line he wished to travel but close enough and he would adjust with his next alignment. Today he would begin his march heading for that clump. As he moved ahead, he could use this tree clump, his current camp, as a back bearing. He also looked to see how his shadow matched up with the north direction and at least for a short while, before the sun moved too far into the sky, he would have another reference for north and thus his northwest destination. All these elements combined to keep Harjo traveling in the right, linear direction.

Later in the morning, Harjo crossed over a bison trail and watched a small herd in the distance. Suddenly, he stopped. Slow and easy, he reached back over his shoulder with his right hand and lifted the sled harness off, over his head. He let it fall past his arms but needed to quickly trade his spear from his left to his right hand allowing the harness to drop to the ground. Slowly, deliberately, he reached over his shoulder pulling out a dart-off in the distances-a lion. It was a mature female following the bison trail stalking one of its favored quarries. The wind was blowing in the right direction taking his scent away from the lioness. Positioned behind the lioness, which focused her attention toward the wondering bison, Harjo remained unnoticed. He armed his dart with a fore shaft and then fixed the bone-notched end into his atlatl-he was ready. He watched as the lion continue to stalk the bison remaining focused on its prey. Lions are beautiful, magnificent creatures and fearfully deadly.

During the winter, lions carry a thick white fur adorned with subtle black spots. The tufted fur on the male's neck and under its chin immediately identifies him. In the summer, their fur changes to a brownish-white color. A large male stands about chest high to a man and is nearly four paces long.

Lions are usually not hunted but generally killed in self-defense, usually by a group of hunters. Every hunter knows he will someday face a lion, alone or in a group, and more than likely, be attacked by a lion. Thus, the common reasoning follows, why hunt the lion, as sooner or later he will hunt me and provide the hunter a close opportunity to kill the magnificent beast or be killed by it. The powerful lion can easily crush and rip a man apart, killing him in the blink of an eye. Its neck and shoulder muscles are of such strength, the lion can drag a caribou carcass a great distance. A male lion can carry off a child in its ruthless jaws with little effort.

Young hunters will occasionally pursue a lion because of the notoriety gained in killing such a magnificent lethal animal. The meat, however, provides poor quality food. The lion's pelt, on the other hand, is highly desirable, particularly by women. It was common knowledge among Muscogee men that the pelts of two animals stimulate a woman, sexually—the lion and the hare. It was often a topic of discussion by young men and boys. The Lion Shaman says, Harjo stopped and corrected himself. He had not actually heard the Lion Shaman say this—but according to "boy stories" the Shaman said, "A hunter who can kill a lion proves he could protect a woman thus the lion's pelt simulates her. The hare is sexually promiscuous producing many babies; consequently, the hare pelt similarly stimulates the female." Whatever the reasons, women were fond of lion pelts.

Lions take their number of humans, generally unlucky hunters or women or children who unwisely stray from camp. They generally do not approach habitation areas, however, and band members are generally safe in camps, villages or around fires.

Children are taught from a very early age not to stray from camp and require a constant eye to ensure their safety. Similarly, women know the mortal risk of wandering away from village protection. Lions are intelligent hunters and stalkers. They pick and choose their prey and know the difference between an armed warrior who might injure the lion and an unarmed, smaller woman or better yet, a child. With bison, they will likewise avoid a bull with large horns and strong necks and seek out a female or more often a calf.

Harjo watched as the lioness reached a safe distance and continued to stalk the bison. He took the dart from his atlatl then slipped his renowned thrower back into his belt. He decided he would carry the dart with his spear for a while. Harjo surveyed the horizon in all directions especially behind him. He decided he would make stops to look behind him more frequently than he normally would as he now approached an unfamiliar landscape. He heard the cry of a red-tailed hawk and looked up to admire the great bird. He saw a pair as they soared around in great slow circles. They were reaching the extent of their range. They seldom flew this far out of the Echota Valley, preferring the safety of the large trees. Harjo leaned against his heavy sled and moved on.

On his tenth day, Harjo stopped at the bottom of a low hill near a rocky ravine. The small chasm formed a head-water catchment, which in turn supported a small wooded patch just a short distance down the hill. It was much too early in the day to camp. Besides, he calculated there would be plenty of comfortable wooded camping spots ahead, although he noticed these oases seemed to be fewer as he neared the coast.

Medium-sized cottonwood trees along with large willows grew in this small rocky ravine with thick brush surrounding the base of the trees. The loud chattering and over activity of a group of magpies around the trees caught his attention. He could see the remnants of last year's nests scattered in the trees that this was a favored brooding location of the noisy, long tailed, black and white birds that paid little attention to him. The rocky ravine, water, and thick brush would discourage predators from climbing the trees, providing protection to the nests and sleeping magpies. Perhaps it was not a good camping spot after all as the loud birds would certainly prove to be a nuisance.

Harjo first thought to go around the hill, but he reconsidered. "No, I'll pull to the top of the hill and have a good look around," he said out loud. He pulled the sled around the brush thicket, however, and then slowly up the hill. About midway up, he realized the incline was steeper than he thought, but the snow was soft thus he maintained good footholds. After a mild struggle, he pulled the sled across the top. "Yes," he said out loud and panting, "This is a good view and I can re-establish my bearings." With his hand, he guarded his face as he glanced up to the sun and then at his shadow on the ground. He looked back toward the horizon and he could see the clump of trees that marked last night's camp. "Good," said Harjo, "perfect." With good back bearings he now had true bearings and looked ahead to the northwest. He could make out another clump of tall trees on the horizon, which would provide him another guide and target destination to the next horizon.

He dropped the sled harness, took off his belt and dart quiver, laying them on the sled. He decided to take a rest, drink some water, and enjoy the view. He took his water pouch and jumped on the sled and sat. The cry of an eagle caught his ear and he looked up to see a single soaring bird. He noticed the eagle shared the sky with the pair of red-tailed hawks that likewise soared across the mid-morning sky. So clear was the sky and so blue, not a cloud for as far as he could see. The dark body and white head and tail of the eagle stood out in contrast, painting a magnificent display of color against the clear blue sky. He also watched the red-tail hawks and smiled when he caught a flash of red from their tails as they turned in slow, lazy arcs.

In all directions, he could see the horizon. He sat in the center of the great circle and in the center of the great sphere of the Mammoth Steppe. He held up his hand. Not a hint of wind or breeze. Again, he looked up at the birds. How could they soar so long with no flapping, without the aid of the wind? He did not know. Perhaps the Father Creator formed some sort of wind high in the air that he could not detect on the ground.

He looked down the hill in another direction to another clump of woods. He noticed a disturbance. The tops of the trees swayed back and forth, then seemed to move in a circular fashion. The exposed dry grass and snow in front of the trees also swayed in a wind disturbance. It was an approaching strong breeze. He could see the grass, dirt, and snow debris swirl around in the whirlwind breeze as it approached him. He watched the impressions the wind formed on the ground, like tracks in the snow. The wind reached the bottom of the hill and he began to feel the breeze. He put one hand on his belt and dart quiver to hold them in place then held up his other hand to protect his face as the wind slammed against him along with the swirling debris.

Suddenly, an intense glow of light brighter than the sun encompassed him. It surrounded and enclosed him. It blocked out all sound, all feeling, all thought, and all sight. There was only the overwhelming light. "The Master of Breath"-Father Creator-Esaugeta Emissee sent Harjo a vision and his breath fell upon Harjo like a great wind that was born in the spirit world.

From above, the Father Creator showed Harjo his homeland, the great Mammoth Steppe, and the whole world. He could see the world as though he was high above standing on the clouds. The Big River flowed far from the east from a land that no man has ever seen or touched. It meandered west between two enormous mountains of ice, one on the north and one on the south. Then it continued to flow west to finally empty into the Great Sea. It divided the whole world in half.

To the east, grasslands formed on each side of the Big River as it flowed between the two mountains of ice. This great grassland was abundant in game—great herds of mammoth—but untouched by any man. The land then headed south, still wedged between two huge mountains of ice. It extended on until it reached the ends of the world.

And far to the north, lay a great frozen ocean, which has been frozen for all seasons. This massive frozen ocean reached northward to the ends of the world.

And to the west, there were great mountains of ice but between the mountains were grassland valleys full of life.

And still farther west was a great Mammoth Steppe similar to his homeland teaming with mammoth and other animals, many he did not recognize. But the steppe continued west to the end of the world.

And the Great Sea lay to the south, but the sea continued on farther than anyone can comprehend. And it reached the shores of the great land to the east, and the great steppe to the west, and to the great frozen ocean to the north. How this could happen he could not understand.

And suddenly, the grasslands of the steppe began to grow bushes. The bushes grew becoming trees. The mountains of ice and the frozen ocean to the north began to melt but the weather grew colder and colder. The water from the Great Sea began to rise, as did the water in the Big River that divided the world in half. And the mammoth on the north side of the Big River began to migrate north and then west and the mammoth on the south side of the river began to migrate east then south. All of the animals of the steppe followed the mammoth.

And the water from the Great Sea flowed north; the water from the Great Frozen Ocean in the north flowed south; and the water from the Big River rose. All the waters came together and all the land between the waters was lost-flooded.

And as suddenly as it had appeared, the light vanished, and all his senses returned. Harjo could see, feel, and hear again. He quickly looked behind him as the whirlwind continued on its way. It was like a dream-a dream during the day. A dream that seems to last the entire night but after you awake, you realize it lasted only an instant. How long did the vision last? The whirl was just past him. It lasted only a brief moment.

"A vision," yelled Harjo out loud in excitement! "It happened as the Lion Shaman foretold. It came with the wind!" The Father Creator sent Harjo a vision on the spirit of the wind. So, his spirit must also be part of the Wind Spirit.

Again, Harjo yelled out loud-he laughed out loud. He jumped from the sled and jumped up and down laughing and clenching his fists then slapping his hands on the stack of mammoth pelts piled on his sled. Looking up, he yelled up to the sky.

"Thank you, Master of Breath-Father Creator! Thank you for your vision! I will use it wisely! Thank you!" He then thought to himself he must rethink the vision, out loud and to himself least he forgets. Repeat it as often as necessary until it was remembered-remembered for all his life.

It did not take long, and Harjo knew he had the vision cut into his memory, never to be lost. He did drink some water, adorned his weapons, then took up the harness and continued on his trek. He looked up to see the eagle and the red-tails still soaring; they seemed to be following him.

"They must want to know my vision," he said jokingly, "That is why they follow me. Alright, great scavenger and great predator, although the scavenger does prey and predator does scavenge, a vision is not secret. I will recite my vision to you, even though I do not know what it means, and you are free to tell all you meet." Harjo pulled his heavy-laden sled down and off the low small hill heading toward the distant clump of trees reciting his vision out loud to the eagle and the red-tails. Slowly, but with sure certainty, life flows with the rhythm of the seasons. And the boy grows into a youth, and the youth becomes a man, and he would never be the same again.

Harjo camped in a small wooded oasis that consisted of one medium-sized cottonwood tree and several smaller arboreal offspring including a scattering of willow and alder all clustered on a low hillock. Springs or low water catchments provided the water source for these dwindling small islands of trees and brush. This particular oasis might represent the last wooded patch or a single tree he would encounter before reaching the Coastal Zone. Standing on the low rise at early dawn, looking west and northwest he saw nothing but flat, seemingly treeless terrain as far as he could see. He checked his counting chord. This was his 12th day of travel and he should reach the Coastal Zone today or tomorrow. He decided he would take some firewood with him stacked on the sled. Not much, only enough for a small fire. He leaned into this sled—another day began.

Harjo's father often discussed the Coastal Zone as Harjo was growing up, but he mostly recalled his mother's description of this far away land. He could tell she missed the seacoast environment of her youth as she depicted it with warm memories. Brought from the Canineqmiut village by his father as a nascent girl, she never returned to the coast nor as far as Harjo knew ever expressed any desire to do so. She often mentioned that in late summer how wonderful, sweet, and abundant the berries were in the Coastal Zone. Harjo now pulled his sled across a foreign landscape, leaving no doubt he was in the great Coastal Zone.

Generally, the landscape was described as a narrow band that runs the length along the coast of the Great Sea that is very different than that of the interior Mammoth Steppe. The most obvious difference was the coastal zone's flat, treeless terrain. It supported a "tundra vegetation community" composed of a continuous mat cover of moss, lichens, grasses, and sedges, which in turn was densely rooted with low-growing shrubs. The most abundant woody shrubs were dwarf birch and of course, several edible berry bushes. This moss, lichen, grass, and sedges mat cover stretches endless across the flat, tundra terrain. Someone from the interior with an untrained eye could easily overlook the low woody shrubs that seldom reached more than a little finger in height.

Interior Mammoth Hunters are accustomed to the thick wooded zones that flourished along rivers in the interior, especially the Big River; however, as these streams meandered toward the coast and into the coastal zone, they become void of trees. Although treeless, the coastal area is not woodless. The interior rivers that flow to the coast, in particular the Big River, bring with them huge amounts of wood fragments and trees. Each spring as the winter ice melts, floods, breaks up, and flows to the coast, it carries with it the uprooted trees and wood debris, which are deposited on the coast as driftwood. Over the course of hundreds of seasons, all sizes and shapes of drifted wood lie in huge piles along the coast providing an easy resource for the Canineqmiut. Wood is so abundant along the coastal shores and up the river systems, that the Canineqmiut line the interior of their underground sod winter houses with wood. All they need do is search the driftwood piles on the coast to find any size or any shape of wood they need to fit their desire. This condition is much easier than cutting wood from a standing tree.

As described to Harjo, there are occasional uplifts and rock outcrops such as the low mountains on the northern end of Tununeq Bay where the Canineqmiut built their spring coastal village. Many small drainages and an occasional spring flow from these low mountains to feed and thus form the Tununeq River, which in turns flows to the sea. High bush thickets of willow and alder cluster around the narrow ephemeral drainages in the high altitudes. The brushy trees can grow up to a man's height and perhaps reach wrist size in diameter at the base. Occasionally, the thickets appear as a towering forest on an otherwise treeless landscape. Small wandering herds of musk oxen often browse around and through the willow and alder thickets and in the summer leave large clumps of fur scattered throughout the groves.

Harjo began to see an abundance of Mammoth Hunter tea. The plant was easy to detect as it appears as a low, slow-growing shrub with evergreen leaves. In Yupik, the plant is called *ayuk* and the term in caribou hunter's language, for some reason, now escaped him. The leaves appear smooth on top with wrinkled edges and are fussy underneath. The small white fragrant flowers grow in hemispherical clusters. The leaves are picked by both men and women through all seasons but always done so with care. Because the plants are scarce in Harjo's homeland and grow at such a languid rate, the harvesters systematically pick the leaves enabling the plants to continue their growth. Every so often they pull the plants growing adjacent to the mammoth tea to leave more water and soil for the favored vegetation. The aromatic plant is also brought into the winter mammoth lodges to help mask some of the pungent lodge odor that persists during periods of intense winter cold. Prudent hunters likewise utilize the plant to hide their human scent when hunting. It was surprising and so unique to see so much of this plant growing. It would also be a welcome change to find wood to build a fire and be able to brew a pouch of the wondrous tea.

Chapter 6:

THE GREAT SEA

O n his 16th day, Harjo stood near the top of a low oblong shaped mountain. From his father's description, he knew the Canineqmiut call this mountain *Nulluuk* and that it was located less than one-half a day's journey west of the Canineqmiut village of Up'nerkillermiut. He could not see the village as it was still too far, but before him laid the beautiful Tununeq Bay and renowned Great Sea. He had heard about the Great Sea all his life and now there it was, a flat solid sheet of ice stretching to the horizon and beyond. Suddenly, it occurred to Harjo it would be equally inspiring to see the great body of water during the summer after the ice melts. "Another journey worth consideration," he said out loud.

This was the first topographic relief he had seen in days. As foretold by his father, it required four days to cross the Coastal Zone and through the whole stretch it remained flat as flat could be, nearly as flat as the Great Sea itself now appeared. To the north end of Tununeq Bay, Harjo could make out another single mountain formation. "That must be *Ugcirnaq,*" he said. His eyes followed the mountain and he could see it extended from the shore inland for perhaps one-half day's journey. And, likewise on the southern end of Tununeq Bay, was another mountain range, which must be *Kitniq*. It followed a similar pattern. Thus, Tununeq Bay and the smaller Nulluuk Mountain on which he stood were features of this small but very impressive coastal valley.

Numerous small drainages cut down from all three mountains and carried enough water to form the Tununeq River that meandered through the valley and emptied into the bay. The littoral village of Up'nerkillermiut would be strung out along both the seacoast and the river's bank. Up'nerkillermiut was a spring village and the Yupik term for spring is *up'nerkilleq*. The Canineqmiut also maintained winter villages they call *uksuilleq* and the summer villages termed *neqlilleq,* both located in the interior. The bounty of the spring and summer in the form of stored food supplied the bulk of their winter needs. According to Harjo's mother, the Canineqmiut celebrated, danced and feasted during the winter.

He could determine by the "lay of the land and sea" he should approach the village from the south; otherwise he would be obliged to cross the river. It would certainly be frozen, the same as the sea, but he did not know if it would hold him without breaking. There was no need to take extra risks.

Up in the higher elevations where Harjo now stood, he could see the drainages supported thick waist-high brush of willow and alder, with an occasional tree reaching head high but then dissipated long before the drainages emptied in to the Tununeq River. "Such a unique landscape," he said to himself, "where the brush and small trees live only in the higher elevations and the flat tundra moss and grass ground cover thrives in the lower terrain-strangely unique."

He decided he would camp here tonight. He could at last build a fire with plenty of dead brush for wood and finally brew some tea and descend to the shoreline and the village in the early morning. Harjo felt good-satisfied that one part of his journey was complete. He was anxious to actually stand by the Great Sea, see the village, and to meet the Canineqmiut. His mother's people, according to their beliefs, would include him as one of them.

With a good fire burning, camp chores complete, clothes drying and all ready to go in the morning, Harjo sat on the mammoth bed leaning against the sled. The snow was deeper here but soft so that it kicked away easily. Drinking a ladle of hot tea, he watched the sun set below the expanse of the Great Sea. It was spectacular. He anticipated the sunrise to be of equal splendor.

As he planned, Harjo approached Up'nerkillermiut from the south and followed the shore. And now, up close, the Great Sea presented a view more spectacular than what had been described to him. The size and magnitude alone overpowered Harjo and yet this vast body of water remained incredibly simple. It now lay dormant. A smooth frozen surface as far as he could see, extending to the horizon. A flat sheet of surface ice covering a sea of unknown depth that expanded to an unknown distance. This prospect was too overwhelming for young Harjo to completely comprehend. He could only gaze in awe.

He took a deep breath. The smell of the Great Sea was strange, and he could detect a hint of salt water. What was more noticeable to Harjo were the missing elements. The smell of grass, even when covered with snow, was always odorous in the interior steppe. Missing was the smell of vegetation, soil, and of course, the smell of mammoth dung. He had not smelled mammoth dung since coming into the Coastal Zone.

Becoming adventurous, Harjo temporarily abandoned his sled walking out on the sea's surface, but only a few paces. Such an eerie feeling arose inside of him—walking on the surface of the Great Sea. He knew the Canineqmiut hunters pulled their sleek sea-crafts, loaded on small sleds, out from the shore to where the sea was opened and thawed. And there they hunted the sea mammals on the open sea-water and floating ice flows. Harjo thought to himself, "To maneuver such a craft, which they call kayaks, across the Great Sea, what an adventure!" But that adventure awaited another day and another journey as he must see to the undertaking at hand. He returned to his sled and continued down the coast.

The snow was deeper here on the coast than on the low mountain and as described, large piles of driftwood lined the whole length of the shore. "How easy to find construction timbers," he thought. "Simply search through the debris piles until the desired timbers are found, then pull them out and carry them off." To the inland Mammoth Hunters, seasoned driftwood was a welcomed luxury and here it lay in huge great piles. As the wind blew across the great expanse of the frozen Great Sea, it was much colder. Harjo retrieved his mittens, which he carried on the sled stuck behind the rawhide ropes that secured the load and put them on.

Suddenly, in the distance he saw a lone figure, which appeared to be a man pulling a sled and a kayak. Harjo whistled and waved his arms over his head. He wanted to be sure the man saw him because he did not want him to think that he approached in stealth.

As he drew near to the man, he saw he was middle aged and held the straps to this sled loaded with his kayak in one hand and a lethal looking harpoon in the other. "I come in peace," Harjo said with the most friendly and clearest voice he could gather. The man watched Harjo with caution. "My name is Harjo. I am a Mammoth Hunter of the Muscogee Wind Band." He pointed to his sled. "I have come to trade."

Instinctively, the man looked to Harjo's sled then spoke. "I am Kailukiak. How is it you speak Yupik, Harjo?"

"I am a Mammoth Hunter, but I am also a Canineqmiut. My mother's name is Ayuko. She is Canineqmiut but lives in the land of the mammoth. My uncle's name is Akagtak and my cousin is Angaiak."

"Oh yes," replied Kailukiak slowly. "I have heard the story of Ayuko. The young woman who married a Mammoth Hunter and lives with them. I believe I traded with your father many seasons ago. I know your uncle and your cousin." Kailukiak walked to Harjo extending his hand and Harjo followed. "Mammoth Hunters are welcomed here, and we welcome the opportunity to trade. The only thing my wife talks about anymore is her endless desire to have a mammoth pelt for a bed. She complains about it from dawn to dusk."

"Well," answered Harjo with a grin, "your opportunity to shut her up and provide her with one or more pelts now stands before you."

Kailukiak laughed. "The sealing season promises to be good this year and the hunters have been going out and have returned with many kills. So far, I have not been fortunate to take one."

"I will save you at least one mammoth pelt Kailukiak. Certainly, your luck will change."

"I appreciate that Har...jo. Did I pronounce your name correctly?"

"Yes," replied Harjo.

"Come along, Harjo. I am headed back to the village. I think I know where your uncle might be."

"I would be pleased with that," said Harjo. He turned and looked at Kailukiak's kayak. "I have heard so much about those ocean craft. May I take a look at it?"

"Of course," Kailukaik answered. They both dropped their sled lines and walked to stand beside the sleek seal skin watercraft.

Harjo looked up and down the vessel and then bent down and looked under it. "May I touch it?" asked Harjo.

"Of course," answered Kailukiak.

Harjo laid his mittens on the craft and then looked inside the cockpit opening. "Nearly all of what I know about the Canineqmiut I learned from my mother. And of course, she knows nothing about hunting or about kayaks."

"Married women will help their husbands treat their kayaks with seal oil but otherwise they don't handle them," said Kailukiak. "I have never seen a woman ride in a kayak. I understand your mother was very young when she left with your father. It is quite likely that she has never touched one."

As Harjo looked the craft over, he smiled. It was uniquely magnificent. "Can all men build a kayak?"

Kailukiak thought for a moment. "Probably all older men could if necessary. My grandfather built this one. Kayaks are handed down, father to son, over many generations. Components are replaced as the need arises but the craft as a whole may endure many seasons. I could probably build one from raw material, but I wouldn't attempt the task without the help of a skilled Elder."

Satisfied, Harjo returned to his sled and Kailukiak to his. Then, he and his new acquaintance headed toward the village, which was teaming with activity. Harjo saw hunters coming and going to the sea, pulling sleds loaded with kayaks and occasionally dragging a seal from the shore back to the village. Excitement penetrated the air and Kailukiak sensed it affected Harjo.

"The hunt stirs a man's blood even if the prey is unknown."

Harjo readily agreed. "Oh, yes, and I am anxious to see a sea mammal up close."

Kailukiak grinned, "There are many types of sea mammals. The type we hunt is called the seal and there are several kinds of seals."

Ahead of them, Harjo saw two men dragging a large seal across the snow by lines affixed to its small head. The strange creature left a trail of blood. Kailukiak called out to them. They stopped and waited until Kailukiak and Harjo approached. Harjo could see that one man was young but the other was a veteran hunter. "This is Harjo," said Kailukiak, "a young Mammoth Hunter who comes to trade. You'll be surprised."

Suddenly, the older man greeted Harjo in Muscogee. Taken aback, Harjo returned the greeting. "May I examine the seal?" asked Harjo.

The two men looked at each other astonished. "You speak Yupik, young Mammoth Hunter," replied the older man.

"He is the son of Ayuko, wife of a Mammoth Hunter," explained Kailukiak.

"Oh yes," said the older man. "I hunted with Ayuko's father." He stepped forward and presented his hand in friendship and the younger man followed. Harjo took both of their hands. The older man motioned his hand to the seal and all the men gathered around the animal. "It is a large one," said the older man "and takes us both to drag it."

Harjo studied the seal in amazement. It was nearly four paces in length and hip high. Its oblong-shaped body was a plain grey/brown color. Its small head reminded Harjo of a lion. But, the most amazing characteristic—it had no legs or feet. It propelled itself through the water with what the

Yupik called "flippers." There was no comparable term in Muscogee. "May I touch it?" asked Harjo.

"By all means," answered the older man.

Harjo looked at him with a little smile. The older man squatted down and laid his hands on the seal and rubbed it. Harjo followed. "You are wise to be cautious, Mammoth Hunter," said the older man. "Their heads are small, but they can deliver a terrible and infectious bite."

Harjo rubbed the seal's fur. He now saw why it was prized as boots. Such fur could easily shed the snow, wet, and cold and he could tell by its feel it would be amazingly lite in weight and easy to walk in. "Is this seal called a mukluk?" asked Harjo, "the same word as boot?"

"That's a slang term," replied the elder man. "The correct name is bearded seal. I suppose because it has thick whiskers."

"Can it walk on land?" asked Harjo.

"Not well. It moves in a slow sliding hop. It is a creature of the sea," answered the older man.

Harjo gave the seal a final rub and stood up and the others followed. "Thank you for your wisdom," said Harjo. The men all nodded their heads in agreement and took up their loads and continued on into the village.

As the four men came into the village area, the older and younger men went on their way and Kailukiak and Harjo continued on side by side. Up'nerkillermiut Village was complex and cluttered much in the same manner as his own winter village of Coweta. Harjo recognized nearly all of the village components such as the earth pit houses, post-racks, and cache pits. Drying seal meat hung from some post-racks while others supported kayaks and sleds. Harjo also noticed several unfamiliar log structures built on top of posts. He knew such structures were above ground storage caches, but the Mammoth Hunters did not use such features.

Harjo had only seen the male hunters outside the village on the coast, but once within the village, the whole population of women and children bustled with calm commotion, all related to processing seal. His mother had told him the Canineqmiut follow a strict division of labor by gender. The men hunt and help skin a large animal but then the women take possession of the hides and carcass, processing all the food and tanning the hides. The meat was cut from the bone with the majority left to dry on the racks, although, smaller portions were also boiled in sea water, roasted, and smoked. In the Mammoth Hunter's world, a whole band was involved in some way in processing a taken mammoth, including older children.

Harjo saw seal hides everywhere. Many were staked out on the ground and others were stretched perpendicular on a square rack-post while the women worked vigorously dressing the hides. Seal blubber was another important product of the seal. It was rendered into clear, fine oil then stored in sturdy rawhide containers.

The village men they passed offered joyous greetings to Kailukiak and Harjo as the two likewise responded with acknowledgement. They passed one woman hanging seal meat on a rack, so Harjo offered a pleasant "Good morning." The woman looked up, frowned and said nothing. He looked over to Kailukiak.

"My mother told me the women would not say hello when I went through the village, so I wanted to see if she was correct."

"Your mother was right, Harjo. But don't give it a second thought, they won't say hello to me either and I am related to most of them. That is the way women are. No one knows why." Both men laughed.

As they continued on through the village, an eager Harjo looked around, taking in all the excitement. Then they pulled their sleds past a woman dressing a hide staked out on the ground. As Harjo looked over to the woman, only a few paces away, she raised her head looking back at him with her parka hood pushed back, and the bright sun shining on her. Harjo saw the face of a young girl. Suddenly, without warning, her image instantly stunned him. It was the same feeling as when he experienced his vision. Everything was somehow blocked out except for her figure and her bright shining face. He thought he could hear Kailukiak speaking but as though from a far distance so that he could not make out what he was saying. But then, he did not care to as he was focused with enchantment on the face of the girl. It was the most beautiful face he had ever seen. And more, much more, for something flowed from her that somehow touched him inside-deep in his heart. Something he could not explain, only feel. When her eyes met his, she only partially smiled but her expression was so pleasant and at the same moment, it cried out to him. She mesmerized him and he stood gazing at her in awe-and such wonderful extraordinary colors.

To his complete amazement, her hair shined a beautiful strange yellow color, matted and dirty, but yellow. It was similar in color to winter grass. Harjo knew only people with black hair. Everyone across the whole Mammoth Steppe must have black straight hair, so he had believed all his short life. And yet, there she was with striking yellow hair and it was twisted. There was no term for its condition except that it was not straight.

He was further mystified by the light color of her facial skin. The first word that came to his mind was white, but it was not white, not like snow but it was so much lighter in color than his. Everyone, every human, until now, he had ever seen or knew of had dark brown skin about the same color as his. And there she sat on the ground only a few paces from him with light-colored skin. Then suddenly, he saw an instant flash of him taking off her parka and pants for some serious reason. As a result, he would learn if all her body was the same surprising color as her face.

Harjo was close enough to see her eyes, which startled him even more because everyone Harjo knew, or knew of, had narrow black eyes. But hers-hers were an extraordinary blue, the color of the sky and they were wide and round. And there was still more, as her lips were also a strange, reddish color that he did not know a matching term or representative color. Her face and hands were dirty and oily as was her worn out clothes but still-she was the most enchanting creature he had ever seen.

As she looked at him, she glanced at his sled then back to his face. He thought he recognized a slight hint of a smile. Then she looked around as though she might be caught doing something wrong and returned to fleshing the hide with a scrapping tool.

"Did you hear?" asked Kailukiak as he pulled his sled on. "I think your uncle is this direction."

Instinctively, Harjo followed. "Who is that girl?" he asked.

"What girl?"

"The girl on the ground just behind us—scrapping the hide."

Kailukiak looked behind. "Oh her, strange, isn't she? I don't know her name; she is a slave girl belonging to Ilalke. She comes from somewhere far to the west, on the other side of the Koryak Glaciers. Your uncle can tell you the story. I think she is ugly, don't you? Well, ugly might be unfair, but I don't think she is attractive. Although, she certainly is very young and appears to be strong and healthy."

Harjo looked back over his shoulder. "A servant girl," he said to himself. She glanced up again at him then back to her work. He must learn more about her.

They came upon one of the larger sod houses with a large rack-post constructed in front of the entryway and an above ground storage feature nearby. Also, near the sod house was a kayak set upside down on two "cross piece" posts. An older man and a woman were busy rubbing and treating the kayak with seal oil. As they approached, Kailukiak called out.

"Akagtak, this young Mammoth Hunter here says he is your nephew!" Akagtak, the older man, and the woman stopped and looked up at them in amazement and silence.

Harjo spoke up. "Yes, my name is Harjo of the Wind Band of the Muscogee Mammoth Hunters. I am the son of Ayuko."

The eyes of Akagtak and the woman grew wide as they gazed at each other in astonishment then looked back to Harjo. The older man repeated, "Ayuko?"

"Yes," repeated Harjo. "I am the son of your sister Ayuko who was purchased by a Mammoth Hunter many seasons ago and is married to him still. I have come to trade."

Uncle Akagtak stepped forward to Harjo with both arms out. "Well, young Harjo, I hear my sister taught you to speak Yupik."

"That she did," replied Harjo as he dropped his sled harness to the ground, and they grasped hands. Harjo noticed that Uncle Akagtak's hands were covered with seal oil from the kayak treatment. It by no means bothered him; he only thought it interesting. His mother taught him that seal oil was interwoven into the daily lives of the Canineqmiut; so much so, it often went unnoticed to them. "You will need to become accustom to seal oil and urine," she warned him.

Uncle Akagtak turned and said, "This woman is Ciriiq, wife of your cousin Angaiak."

The woman stepped forward with a beautiful smile. She took Harjo's hands but also leaned up and rubbed noses with him. Harjo was aware of this unusual greeting custom and had often rubbed noses with his mother as a boy, but it still caught him by surprise, forcing him to grin.

"Welcome, Harjo," she said smiling. As she spoke, Harjo caught a whiff of her breath, which was not unpleasant, although the smell of seal and seal oil was more powerful than he had imagined.

As Harjo's mother had taught him, many Muscogee words are difficult for the Canineqmiut to pronounce in Yupik, but "Harjo" would not be one of them. In fact, that was why she had implored Cheparney to give Harjo his name because it was easily pronounced by a Yupik speaker. One of course was her.

"Well, I am off," said Kailukiak as he pulled his sled harness and began to walk away. "Good luck, Harjo." He raised his hand in a parting wave. The remaining three likewise waved a farewell.

"Well, is that a sled piled with mammoth pelts I see?" Asked Uncle Akagtak.

"It is," replied Harjo, "and I intend to trade it for a sled piled with seal pelts."

All three walked to Harjo's sled to briefly examine the prized mammoth pelt sections. "You will find plenty who will want to exchange with you, Harjo," stated Akagtak. "It has been a while since a Mammoth Hunter has come to trade."

"I'll take you around the village," suggested Akagtak, "to introduce you to some men, then perhaps we will journey to the beach and see if your cousin Angaiak has returned from his hunt. If so, we can help him pull his seal."

"Alright," agreed Harjo.

"You can leave your sled and weapons under that storage cache," suggested Akagtak. He sensed Harjo's apprehension. "Theft is not practiced or known among the Canineqmiut," said Akagtak using a tone of reassurance. "I realize you live in a world where attack from enemy raiders remains a constant threat. No such threat is found here. Besides, Ciriiq will keep a watch for you."

Harjo agreed and pulled his sled to the above ground cache then removed his weapons and tucked them under the rawhide tie downs. "My mother taught me many Canineqmiut ways," said an apologetic Harjo, "but I've not experienced them."

As the two men walked on through the village, Harjo noticed the earth pit houses appeared as snow covered mounds and generally aligned side by side with the entry ways pointing to the sea. The houses also appeared to be bunched in linear alignment likely representing family units thought Harjo. Akagtak concurred that families tend to construct their houses together.

They periodically stopped and Uncle Akagtak introduced Harjo, especially if they met an older man. Then they circled away from the village and visited the Canineqmiut burial grounds located inland of the village complex. They did not explore the cemetery grounds but observed from the edge. The manner of burial was another strange Canineqmiut custom that Harjo thought odd. Akagtak explained the procedure.

"Graves were placed above the ground in some type of wooden coffin constructed of logs or split logs," he remarked. "Posts and crosspieces marked the graves. On these were placed various grave goods associated in some way with the buried person. Weapons for men and household or cooking utensils for women are the common grave goods," explained Akagtak.

Harjo also noticed kayaks and sleds as grave goods. As the graves aged, the deteriorated coffins exposed the human bones, which seemed strange to Harjo.

They circled back to the village and then down to the coast, meeting cousin Angaiak returning with a seal. As they approached, Uncle Akagtak spoke right up.

"Son, I want you to meet your mammoth hunting cousin. His name is Harjo."

Angaiak froze and stared at his father, then at Harjo, obviously surprised. "Is he Ayuko's son?"

"Absolutely," laughed Uncle Akagtak, "all the way from the land of the mammoth and he brings a sled load of mammoth pelts to trade."

"I seem to catch everyone off guard," said Harjo as he walked forward with his hand extended.

Angaiak appeared speechless but took Harjo's hand and managed an astonished, "Welcome, Harjo."

"You two get acquainted and I'll retrieve Angaiak's kayak," said a still jubilant Uncle Akagtak who did not wait for any response from the other two but turned and left.

Following an awkward pause, Harjo pointed to cousin Angaiak's catch. "I've not seen this type of seal,"

"It's called a spotted seal," said cousin Angaiak as they both advanced toward the animal. Harjo saw it looked the same as the other seal in body shape but was smaller, about two paces in length and about knee high. The fur, however, was a beautiful light brown color with dark brown spots. Harjo had noticed that most boot tops were made from this seal. They both rubbed the animal's fur as cousin Angaiak explained various characteristics of the seal. Harjo still thought it odd that seals had no ears.

Uncle Akagtak returned, pulling a kayak on a small sled and the three returned to the above ground cache and the large sod house. Harjo learned that this large sod house was a men's house where Uncle Akagtak and cousin Angaiak lived. Angaiak's wife, Ciriiq, lived in her own house next door. Harjo would stay in the men's house. Angaiak and Ciriiq took the seal to begin processing it and Uncle Akagtak escorted Harjo to the men's house. They first went through a rack post porch lined with benches constructed outside the entry tunnel. Harjo followed Akagtak through the entry into the men's house.

He saw the Canineqmiut men's house was similar to a mammoth lodge with some differences. Whereas the Canineqmiut used earth and logs as building material, the Muscogee utilized mammoth hides and tusks. Both houses however were semi-subterranean and once inside, the light from the skylight revealed the interior.

An excavated pit in the center of the house held the hearth, lined with rocks and surrounded by many boiling pouches. The men do not cook but they brew and consume huge quantities of tea. Wooden sleeping benches lined the walls.

"Cousin Angaiak and I sleep here on these two benches," said Akagtak, pointing to the beds covered with grass mats and furs. "You can take this one as it is reserved for guests."

Harjo walked over to the bench, laying his hands and weight on it as if to test its strength. It was constructed of boards fashioned from split logs and looked comfortable enough. Harjo looked up, "This will be good."

He then followed Akagtak through the entryway back out to the porch. Akagtak talked as they walked. "These spring houses are simple constructions, but you should see the winter sod houses, now those are admirable constructions, something a man can be proud of. These are more akin to sod tents."

As they reached the outside porch, Akagtak set down on one of the benches and Harjo followed. He noticed his sled and materials appeared to be in place and Angaiak and Ciriiq seemed to have vanished with the seal. "Uncle Akagtak, my mother told me that Canineqmiut men and women live apart. I was not sure I believed her."

Akagtak laughed. "I suppose it seems strange to a Mammoth Hunter, but it is a simple practice. The men and boys of our village reside in these sod lodge structures we call *gasgiqs* or men's house, which serve as our communal residence. And, as I just said, the spring and the summer house as well, are poor examples of what a sod house should be."

"Nonetheless, here we sleep, eat, repair and prepare tools, tell stories, and take sweat baths. You must enjoy at least one sweat bath, nephew. As you just saw, a gasgiqs measure five to seven paces wide and also doubles as the community lodge where village dances and celebrations take place, hence the largest structures in the village complex. There are three or four men's houses here at Up'nerkillermiut. We enjoy most of our celebrations and dancing in the winter. You should see those."

Scratching his head, Akagtak continued. "Let's see, when a boy turns five or six summers, he is sent from the women's house to the men's house and begins his rigorous training of hunting and survival under the watchful instruction of his father and uncles. The boys are also assigned the domesticated chores around the men's lodge."

"Women, girls and young boys on the other hand reside in the second house type called a "*nepiaq*" the women's lodge. Certainly, more numerous than the men's house and noticeably smaller, about three or four paces wide."

"I see a large number of children running around the village," remarked Harjo with a smile. The separation of husbands and wives does not seem to interrupt romantic relations."

Uncle Akagtak held his head back, laughing out loud. "Well, young nephew, I would wager that Mammoth Hunting men are away from their lodges so much, that the women and girls of a particular family remain alone together through those extended periods. There probably isn't that much difference." Harjo smiled in agreement.

Harjo recognized the similarities but also the differences between the two cultures and still considered it odd that a whole family would not be found sitting around the fire eating and telling stories. As he took his mammoth bed and weapons from the sled into the gasgiq and laid them on his assigned bed platform, he recalled one of his mother's lessons.

All adult Canineqmiut men hunt for at least one woman. Generally, she is his wife but could also be his mother or some other relative. As the men live in the gasgiq, the women will bring them their meals, serving the man or men who hunt for her. The most important meal occurs late in the afternoon.

Cousin Angaiak returned and said he had gone down to another men's house for a sweat bath and to help spread the word of a Mammoth Hunter trader. "I think you could have a good trade tomorrow afternoon after the morning hunt and before we have a sweat bath here in our gasgiq," predicted Angaiak.

At the appropriate moment, Ciriiq brought food for her three men. Ciriiq was a mature married woman holding a position of some respect among the village women. Yet, it still excited her to be serving a Mammoth Hunter, as if he also hunted for her even though he was still a boy, a large and very handsome boy, but old enough. She had never seen a mammoth but had heard stories of their size and danger. Being in this close association with a Mammoth Hunter was exciting although she was mature enough not to let it show.

Harjo experienced his first taste of seal meat, roasted on this occasion. The taste was nastier than he imagined. His two kinsmen consumed the dark oily meat with smiles and laughter as though feasting. Although nutritious, Harjo considered any land mammal or bird to be of superior flavor. He also took this opportunity to ask Uncle Akagtak about the strange servant girl who belonged to Ilalke. He also lived in their gasgiq but apparently utilized another men's house with some regularity. After questions of "Where did she come from? How did she get here?" Uncle Akagtak decided he would answer with a story. Ilalke's brother brought her here from some distant land far to the west. He died but had been a lifelong friend of Uncle Akagtak. The Canineqmiut avoid speaking the name of someone who is dead.

"I say his name once with respect," began Uncle Akagtak. "Tangkak was husband to Usugan, brother to Ilalke, and owner of the servant girl. He was a good hunter. He was brave, but more than anything else, he was an adventurer. Following the end of the seal-hunting season, my friend did well and killed many seals that season. He filled his kayak with hides, oil, and meat and left the remainder of the seal season's catches and departed. His kayak was sleek, durable, and very well made. Perhaps the best kayak I have ever seen. Imarpik, or the Great Sea as you call it Harjo, was now completely open and he followed the shore northwest then west."

"The great Northwest Glacier does not end at the sea. It continues on a great distance to the southwest and helps to form a huge peninsula. He called the peninsula

Kamchatka. It formed a massive mountain glacier called Kamchatka Peninsula, which extended southwest a distance three or four lengths greater than the distance between the Northwest and the Southeast Glaciers. The Great Sea encloses the Kamchatka on the east and west sides. The massive Northwest Glacier only represents the northern "top" portion of the peninsula landmass. The world and the Mammoth Steppe extends much greater than we have considered."

Harjo listened intensely. The Muscogee Mammoth Hunters call the Northwest Glacier Koryak and the Muscogee believed that it blocked the Great Sea and thus ended there. His people believed the northwest glacier was formed by the same situation and condition as the even larger glacier to the southeast. Uncle Akagtak continued.

"My friend did not tell me how many days he followed the coast. But he did say the coast was difficult to follow because of the numerous enormous bays and equally dangerous due to the huge chunks of ice that dislodged from the glacier. He went farther than any Canineqmiut had ever gone. And to his surprise, he came to a large village. The village was located in a large protected bay and the people there lived similar to the Canineqmiut, but they spoke a strange language. They hunted seals although the seals were a strange type he had never before seen. They called their village Ostrov. He said they traded with an even stranger and more distant people who lived on the other side of Imarpik, the Great Sea, which forms the western boundary of the Kamchatka Peninsula. Accordingly, there is another landmass on the far western extent of Imarpik. They told him this land consisted of tall glacier mountains and wide low valleys. Some of the glacier mountains were cut with rivers that could be followed during the summer. The valleys between the glaciers are grasslands rich with mammoth.

The servant girl comes from that distant land. The warriors from Ostrov were somehow able to approach the servant girl's village and by raid, abduct her and others. My friend seemed to feel the Ostrov warriors were partners with other warriors in the girl's land. He did not say how he communicated with them."

"He bought the servant girl there at that village Ostrov. His good kayak became part of the barter. As part of the deal, he returned with the girl in an umiak and a group of those men. Perhaps they intended to open up some type of trade with us or maybe they were just as curious and adventurous as he was. They stayed two days then returned to the sea heading back the way they came. Journeys across the open sea or along the shore of the great walls of ice are exceedingly dangerous. I would wager that the umiak and all the men aboard were lost. My friend died and his brother, Ilalke, took over the responsibilities of his wife and ownership of the servant girl. That is all I know."

Although all the men in the gasgiq had heard this story before they all listened, and a quiet hush fell. But Harjo was not one to hold back. "What if they intend to return as warriors to attack?" asked Harjo.

"We don't know," responded Uncle Akagtak. "But they must first wait for Imarpik to completely thaw. By then we have left Up'nerkillermiut and the bay having gone up the Kolavinarak River to our summer camps and eventually to our winter villages. Besides, as I just stated, a journey that follows alongside the great glacier or over the open sea would be a perilous one indeed. The risks seemingly far outreach the gain." Another hush fell over the men's house.

"Well," said Uncle Akagtak, Elder of the gasgiq. "A long day of hunting awaits us tomorrow and trading with our young Mammoth Hunter nephew in the afternoon. A good night's sleep will be appreciated." The others agreed and made their way to their platform beds.

Ilalke walked through the village in a gritty step. He had waited long enough and was determined to take his rightful pleasure. He entered Usugan's house. She was kneeling by the central hearth—he stood over her. "Get out woman," he ordered. "I am taking my servant girl on her 'First Rites' journey. I wager the dirty little brat has never been penetrated!"

"We have had this discussion before, Ilalke," answered Usugan in anger. "I will not let you rape that girl."

"You will not let me," he mocked and scoffed in sarcasm. "She is my servant and I will rape her if it pleases me."

"She is your servant and property by custom and law. I am your wife because you are brother to my dead husband. You can beat me—you can take me—but not her!"

Ilalke slapped Usugan across her face. "I am taking that girl!" he yelled.

The poor frightened servant girl did not know what to do. She stood with her hands clasped under her chin nearly in tears. She could not understand all the Yupik words but enough to know what was happening.

"You can beat me, Ilalke," growled Usugan, "but stay away from her. I'll scream, Ilalke, and I'll keep screaming as loud as I can. I'll go to the Elders in their gasgiqs and stand in front of them screaming into their faces. I'll scream at Akagtak in his face at your gasgiq until they make you stop!"

"Take your clothes off brat and get into that bed," ordered Ilalke.

"No, Ilalke," then Usugan let out a loud scream.

All the helpless servant girl could do was to clasp her hands and whisper "no-no-no" to herself.

Usugan screamed again. Ilalke picked up a wooden bowl and threw it on the floor. He growled something unintelligible, turned, and stormed out through the entryway. Usugan went to the girl and put her arms around her, comforting her. "It will be alright girl," whispered Usugan in a soothing voice. The servant girl cried as she hugged and rocked with Usugan. Embracing the girl comforted Usugan as well.

Chapter 7:

TRADING

The next morning, the three kinsmen took the recently seal oil-treated kayak down to the coast. Harjo and Uncle Akagtak accompanied cousin Angaiak out on the Great Sea but only for a safe distance. If the sea ice gave away to thaw, there would only be one kayak for the three men and certain death for two. They waved as Angaiak continued on alone and returned to the shoreline. Harjo helped Akagtak treat their other kayak with seal oil as Ciriiq worked hard processing the seal meat and hides. She was boiling some meat in sea water for their next meal hoping to encourage Harjo to eat more. Cousin Angaiak returned empty handed this day but had earlier brought in several large bearded seals leaving no shortage of hides or meat. Ciriiq actually looked forward to a small break in processing as she had more work than one woman could handle. Early in the afternoon after the morning hunt, the Canineqmiut men began to gather at the trading site with their seal pelts in hand ready to trade.

The rack-post porch located in front of the entryway of the gasgiq which housed Harjo provided a perfect site for the trade. Low sitting benches and long sections of logs lined the sides of the porch. Cross-posts were affixed to the upright post about waist high and along with the top post supplied ample space for Harjo to display his cut sections of mammoth pelts. Harjo also noticed wooden pegs were driven into the post seemingly at any location that would accommodate them. Later he would discover why. He unloaded his sled and draped the pelts over the cross-posts. Then he laid his bison robe on the ground, which along with his sled, he used to display his other wares, mammoth ivory, oil, meat, and the red chert bifaces.

Harjo decided he would just accept all reasonable offers and not barter. The first man offered two bearded seal skins for one of Harjo's mammoth pelt sections and he agreed. Harjo probably could have traded one mammoth pelt section for three seal pelts had he bartered. But Harjo was not there to become wealthy in seal skins. He was there to establish relationships and, more importantly, for the thrill of adventure. Also, honestly and realistically, he could carry back only so many hides on his sled and he intended to leave any extra hides with his new Canineqmiut family as gifts.

The next man offered one bearded seal skin for one mammoth pelt section and Harjo agreed, setting the standard for the rest of the trade. Another man offered two smaller spotted seal hides for one mammoth hide section and Harjo agreed which likewise set up a norm.

Later during the trade, an older man approached Harjo with a large bag of sea shells and proposed a trade for one mammoth pelt section. Harjo looked the bag over. All the men gathered there knew Harjo could easily gather his own shells from the coast. But, because the man was elderly, Harjo traded, besides he would rather spend his days in more adventurous pursuits than shell gathering. Harjo laughed to himself as he examined the shells. "Would Chufe share her exotic pleasures with him for each handful of shells?" Harjo noted there were many handfuls in the bag.

Suddenly, a man stepped up to Harjo with an article of clothing. He held it up for Harjo to see, then laid it down for him to examine. "How many mammoth furs for this?" he asked.

Harjo took the article and examined it. The Canineqmiut people called it an *atkuk qaraliq* or "fancy parka" and its attractive appearance left little doubt it was manufactured by a woman of considerable sewing talent. The skilled seamstress had chosen fall caribou as the primary fur, the preferred pelt for all parkas, but also utilized other furs to add artistic and aesthetic value. It was the type of clothing that women adored.

Men remain content with plain, practical clothing and see value in skilled sewing that keeps out wet and cold and traps in warm body heat. The body of a man's parka is commonly sown from two animal pelts with side seams. Women, on the other hand, hold clothing comprised with many stitched parts, several patterns, various furs, and intricate fringing in high esteem. This parka appeared to have both.

The overall shape of the parka identified it as a woman's, tailored to fit a thin woman of average to small size. It was narrow at the shoulders then curved out over the hips and finally curved inward at the skirt end. Harjo saw that the parka body was shaped somewhat like a boot sole with the shoulder placed at the heel of the sole and the bottom skirt at the toes. By contrast, the body of a man's parka was broader at the shoulders then dropped straight down to the end and then straight across.

The parka also supported a hood, a back pouch to accommodate a baby, and of course arms attached at the shoulders. The arms and upper one-half of the garment were sewn from the dark brown back fur of the caribou while the bottom one-half was made from the white colored under belly of the animal and then seamed together creating a unique, artistic contrast. Additionally, the top and skirt were attached with the top cut in a curved, overlapping frontal piece keeping with the curved flow of the skirt. The hood and sleeves were fringed with black wolf's fur because water and breath condensation will not freeze on wolf's fur adding warmth and protection to the wearer.

The shoulders, arms, skirt, and seams were fringed with strips of marmot fur. The fur of the marmot is a light grey color with black feet and tail. The animal has two black strips across its head and one on each shoulder. As another trick of beauty, the front of the parka was overlaid with marmot fur so that the black stripes outlined the location of a woman's breast. Finally, mittens were attached to the sleeves of the arms. Many women preferred to have mittens so attached. The parka was an article of beauty and it would bring any woman to tears.

Harjo was reminded that both the Canineqmiut and Muscogee wore caribou "buckskin" clothing during the summer. All the fur was removed from buckskin. Men wore buckskin pants and shirts while women wore long buckskin dresses, they called frocks. Men's clothing remained plain while women found numerous ways to decorate their frocks.

Following his examination, Harjo commented on the beauty and skilled craftsmanship of the parka. The man and the other traders standing around nodded in agreement. Thinking to himself Harjo did not want to barter but the man did ask. He thought the parka was certainly worth two perhaps three mammoth pelts but probably not four. "Two mammoth pelts," was his reply.

The man thought for a monument then answered, "Maybe it is worth three mammoth pelts?"

Harjo thought for a moment then replied. "It is a trade."

The trading went well, and Harjo traded nearly all of his goods for Canineqmiut products and would return to the Echota River Valley with a sled load of prized seal furs, meat, oil, sea shells, and a few other coastal products. All traded well except for the mammoth meat. It seems the Canineqmiut do not favor the grass-fed flavor of mammoth and those that tasted it did so more for the experience which often ended with facial expressions of disgust. It was just as well with Harjo as he preferred to travel back supplied with mammoth pemmican and jerky rather than that nasty seal meat. He would return with just enough seal meat for his mother and not be forced to eat it himself.

Kailukiak finally showed up with a bearded seal skin. As he promised, Harjo set aside one mammoth section for him. "Something for you to consider young Harjo." advised Kailukiak. "You and two other trading partners could arrive here with one full sled of mammoth resources and two or three empty sleds in tow. After a fair-trading session, you could return home with three full sleds of seal hides. Something else, I believe the ivory and red stone, a less heavy burden, may trade just as well as the heavier mammoth pelts."

"I will keep that in my memory," replied Harjo. He shook hands with Kailukiak, and they gripped each other's shoulder. Harjo had won a friend in Kailukiak.

As the sun began to set, word spread throughout the village that the trading had gone well, and it was the topic of discussion in each gasgiq. Usugan prepared the late after-noon meal at the hearth in the center of her house. The ser-vant girl assisted, kneeling next to her holding the wooden bowls. She pulled something out of her woman's bag, a small pair of new woven grass socks and handed them to the servant girl. "A gift for you," she said with a motherly smile.

"For me," replied the girl with her unusual child-like voice.

Usugan shook her head yes.

The girl folded her hands around the socks and held them to her breast. "Thank you-thank you much." Instantly, she began to take off her worn boots to put on the new socks.

"The women's gossip around the village says the trading went well," said Usugan. "I hear the Mammoth Hunter is a generous young man. He will return to his homeland tomorrow or the next day. Also, the moon will be bright and nearly full the next day or so." She reached her hand up then petted the side of the girls face and spoke in a whisper. "I can do little to help you, poor girl. Take advantage of this young Mammoth Hunter. Do you understand?"

The servant girl did not say anything but shook her head yes. She understood. Usugan put some food in the bowls as the girl held them out. "Here, take some food to Ilalke in the men's house. I don't feel up to seeing or talking with him." The servant girl took the bowl and left.

Harjo, cousin Angaiak, and Uncle Akagtak were seated in their respected gasgiq along with other village men including Ilalke. The trading had gone well but now they discussed the possibilities of cousin Angaiak pursuing a trading mission.

"How many days did it take you to travel from your valley to the coast?" inquired Angaiak.

Harjo replied, "Sixteen."

"And the red stone?" he asked.

"I would need to show you where the stone is located," replied Harjo.

"Would you?" asked Angaiak.

"Most certainly," answered Harjo.

"What about other Mammoth Hunters? Do they claim ownership of the stone and would they think me a thief if I took some?"

"No," replied Harjo. "The red stone is a gift from the Father Creator, a gift for all. Besides the Mammoth Hunters believe the stone by itself has no value except at a distant location. It requires the skill and the knowledge of the knapper to turn the raw stone into a useful tool. The same concept applies to the hide of a mammoth. That is, the hide has no value as long as the mammoth wears it."

"I think I could make such a trip," replied an enthusiastic Angaiak.

"Of course, you could," agreed Harjo.

"But you should not go alone," interrupted Uncle Akagtak. "I wish I was young enough to go with you," he said as he put his hand on his son's shoulder giving it a good grip. "Take at least one partner may be two, and as Kailukiak advised Harjo, take empty sleds, then return with them loaded with mammoth skins and red stone. And maybe a mammoth girl or two," laughed the old uncle.

All three men looked at each other and laughed. "I know one mammoth girl you could buy from her father for less than a seal skin," joked Harjo.

"Would she make a good wife?" asked Angaiak.

"Probably not," replied Harjo, "but she is pretty, soft, and warm." Again, the trio looked at each other then laughed.

"But you must know," cautioned Harjo. "The lion and the mammoth are dangerous animals and will kill a man if given the slightest opportunity to do so."

"Are other inland animals dangerous?" asked Angaiak.

"The wooly rhinoceros should be afforded due respect," offered Harjo, "but most other animals of the steppe are dangerous only if you hunt them. But the lion and the mammoth are treacherous whether you hunt them or not."

"Will you tell me more about the lion and mammoth?" asked Angaiak.

"I certainly will," Harjo replied.

Suddenly, to all the men's surprise, the servant girl appeared through the entryway of the gasgiq sod house carrying a wooden bowl of food and stood near the entryway. The trio of men now realized they were getting hungry. Ilalke got up and walked over to the girl, taking the bowl from her.

Unexpectedly, he slapped the girl hard across the face, knocking her down to the ground. She lay crying of the floor. "You're late!" he grunted out loudly and seemed particularly pleased with himself as though he had just demonstrated some brave act of superiority. A silent hush fell over the whole lodge-only the girl's sobs could be heard.

Harjo could take no more. Forgetting he was a guest in a strange land, he got up and stepped between the girl and her abuser standing only a pace distance from him. He looked straight into the older man's face. "Leave her alone!" he ordered in a stern combative voice. All the men in the gasgiq heard and watched. Still, the only noise was the slight crying from the girl. The older man looked into the youngster's face expecting to see fear or uncertainty; he saw neither. But he did see anger and determination which sent a ripple of fear into him and he eagerly sought a way out. Harjo hoped Ilalke would attack him as he would enjoy repaying the coward for his cruelty. But the older man stepped back, blurted out a single note laugh, and turned his back with both hands on the bowl, then walked back to the benches on the other side of the men's house.

Harjo turned to the girl still on the floor but now sitting up. He did not say anything but held out his hand to her. She looked up at him then slowly reached up taking it. He helped her up and holding her hand, escorted here to the entryway then through the entry passage, the porch, and outside and to the back of the large sod house. Harjo looked back as he led her, and she gently smiled at him. Harjo felt he could take her all the way to the Echota Valley and she would gladly follow.

Still holding her hand and now in the brighter outside light, Harjo looked into her face. He saw the burning red finger marks left by the cowardly slap, a charcoal smeared forehead, and a dirty, grease-smudged face. But still to his wonderment, as when he first noticed, her skin was such a light color-so fair-so much lighter than his. Her hair, although also dirty and matted, appeared a strange but wonderful color, like the color of winter grass. Her lips and mouth were beautiful and also a strange color. A color he could not define. But more intriguing were her magnificent eyes that were so clear, bright, the color of the sky on a sunny day. He found it hard to imagine someone with blue-colored eyes and yet there she stood before him. She likewise looked into his face. Her tears left a muddy trail running down her dirty cheeks. As Harjo looked into her young face, he became spellbound. Not in his wildest dreams could he have imagined such a girl could be. He was over whelmed at how beautiful she was.

He had certainly seen beautiful women before. There were many beautiful women in the Wind Band, Chufe for one, and in the Canineqmiut village as well. His mother was beautiful as was his sister. But she was somehow different, more than beautiful. She was enchanting.

He was still holding her hand but not tightly and then she gently pulled her hand free, turned, and ran in such a way that only girls can run. She then stopped, turned around, and ran back to stop in front of him. She reached out, taking hold of his sleeve and looked into his face. "Thank you," she said almost in a whisper.

She spoke Yupik but in a strange accent he had not heard. Her voice, even in those two simple words, was so pleasant he wanted to hear more. She smiled a beautiful smile then turned and ran away. She was the prettiest girl Harjo had ever seen and she had touched his heart in a way it had not been touched before.

Harjo returned to the gasgiq and sat again with his kinsmen. He noticed that Ilalke had left. "Few Canineqmiut men are cruel," remarked Akagtak in an angry tone. "Survival dictates," he glanced at Harjo, "in the same vein of the mammoth hunting Muscogee men, that we are lethal. We kill game and enemy warriors without hesitation or any remorse. But Ilalke's treatment of his servant girl was cruel. We hunters and warriors would understand and to some degree condone punishment for a servant or slave girl or any woman for misdeeds such as laziness, disobedience, or back talk, but his unprovoked slapping and severe spankings of the girl survives silently unapproved. His cruelty has yet to draw any reprisal, but such malice was gathering attention."

Akagtaq looked down on the ground and spit. "As an Elder, I should have said something by now but have not. I suppose out of some respect for his dead brother."

Uncle Akagtak's tone then changed to a happier mood. "Well, nephew, have you ever taken a sweat bath?" asked Akagtak.

"No, but I have listened to plenty of stories," replied Harjo.

"Your father enjoyed them immensely as I recall and when one of the men's houses 'fired up,' he was one of the first one's present."

"Yes," Harjo replied. "He spoke fondly of the experience."

Generally, only one gasgiq fired up each evening in a loose rotation and all the village men who wished to sweat would visit that lodge. It seems the gasgiq that housed Harjo and his Canineqmiut family was a village favorite and was fired up more often than the others.

First, in preparation, anything the men did not want cooked or steamed was removed from within the structure. Conversely, any item they may want steamed or heated was brought in. Harjo removed all his property from the men's house and put them with his sled, stored under the adjacent above ground storage.

Then, a large fire was started in the hearth pit while the men from the gasgiq waited outside in the porch. Cousin Angaiak did the honors of starting the fire and later poured the steam water. He was afforded these simple honors as his father was a gasgiq Elder. Harjo had not noticed before, but the hearth was stacked wide with rocks, peculiar for a hearth unused for cooking. A youngster climbed on top of the men's house and closed the skylight with a seal gut cover. Older boys usually joined the men while younger ones waited outside and played.

Soon, men began to arrive from around the village and greeted each other warmly. Canineqmiut are very gregarious people, and although the men refrain from open emotions, they truly enjoy each other's company. Harjo noticed one man wearing only a seal skin cape and hood, grass socks, and nothing else. He prompted laughter from the others as he walked through the village in his "sweat clothes". He would dress after he returned to his own men's house.

Several boys entered the gasgiq loaded with buckets of water and urine, and ample buckets were left throughout the men's house. Canineqmiut men carve wooden food bowls and bent wood buckets for their women that display unique designs, decoration, and unequaled craftsmanship. Bent wood used to hold water and urine in both the men's and women's houses caught Harjo's attention. The bottom of a bucket, similar to a wooden bowl, was carved from a single piece of wood and the top edges were carved to a flare to fit into the beveled bucket sides. Those sides are fashioned from thin slabs of wood and beveled at the bottom to match the carved bottom piece then steamed and bent into the desired shape. Finally, the ends were stitched together with willow root after being fitted around the bottom piece. The wares are often decorated with charcoal pigment mixed with seal blood. Somehow, the pigment is fixed by the blood and does not come off from contact with water or hot food.

The men's house, turned sweat lodge, was ready as Harjo and the other men gathered in the porch. They undressed and hung up their clothing, then entered with voices in good cheer. The lodge was already warm.

"Older men and boys usually set near the entryway," advised Akagtak, "and the more adventurous men near the fire hearth. Sit with me some distance from the fire. The trick is to relax, don't move fast or breathe hard. It can become very hot depending on who is doing the pouring. I am not worried about you, young nephew, as I see no fear in you at all. Stay calm, no deep breaths, move slow with care and caution, and enjoy yourself."

As all the men were seated, Harjo watched while cousin Angaiak took a ladle of water and poured it slowly on glowing hot rocks. The lodge filled with steam and heat. Harjo began to sweat. The heat was soothing, relaxing and it rose in intensity. He had never imagined a house structure could become that extremely hot. He could feel the immense heat all around. Like so many worthy experiences, the steam bath was exciting, enjoyable, and equally fearful. As Uncle Angaiak had predicted, the heat became so hot that to take a deep breath would have scalded Harjo's lungs and killed him instantly. If he were to panic and stand up quickly, the heat would have roasted the skin from his bones. He slowly moved his hand to test the air and could feel the heat against it. If he were to move it in any rapid motion, it would sear the skin.

Harjo later learned that because cousin Angaiak was pouring the water, and thus controlling the heat, the lodge did not become as hot as it could. All the men understood a beginner was present. Nonetheless, Harjo thoroughly enjoyed the experience and welcomed future sweats of even hotter intensity. Eventually the heat dissipated, and the men began to wash.

Angaiak joined them and Akagtak offered Harjo a full bucket of water and one of urine. Harjo watched as the men throughout the lodge dipped their hands in the urine buckets and splashed double hands-full on their chest and rubbed vigorously and mixed the urine with body oil and formed lather. As acidic urine will take oil, fat, and flesh from a fresh seal hide the Canineqmiut were certainly clean, but the smell of urine was strong. Human scent, especially urine and dung, was a liability to a Muscogee hunter in pursuit of any animal, in particular the mammoth. Harjo was not quite ready for this particular custom.

Harjo held up his pouch of soap. "I noticed that pouch," said cousin Angaiak. "I thought it strange to have a pouch in a steam bath. What is it?"

"It is soap," smiled Harjo.

"Soap," answered Angaiak. "What is soap?" he asked as uncle Akagtak likewise looked on with curiosity.

"It's used for bathing in place of urine," answered Harjo. "Mammoth can smell urine on a man from as far as the horizon. I realize that seal hides are treated with urine, but they will be aired out."

Uncle Akagtak and cousin Angaiak looked at each other in agreement. Harjo handed cousin Angaiak the pouch and he opened it, smelled, and passed it over to Uncle Akagtak who likewise smelled. Returning the pouch to Harjo, Uncle Akagtak said, "I believe we will stay with urine, creatures of habit."

"How is it made?" asked Uncle Akagtak. As the three men washed, Harjo explained the process.

"Mammoth hunting women, including Ayuko, make soap from wood ash and mammoth oil. I recall as a small boy watching with mild curiosity my mother and other band women as they made soap. The process remained simple but involved a rigorous effort, at least to a small boy. The normal method utilized a heavy skin pouch; perhaps an old drinking bag so that the bag could be filled from the top, closed up, and then drained from the bottom by a stopper. Then a layer of small rocks and grass were pushed in the bottom of the bag. Handfuls of wood ash were scooped into the bag and then it was filled with water. The pouch was allowed to set for two or three days. Then an appropriate amount of the "leached" water was drained off and mixed with mammoth oil. The mixture was shaken up until it turned into froth and thus used in bathing. Many women also added fragrant plants such as sage. Ayuko added sage and some other fragrant plant to this pouch of soap."

Once the men were lathered from head to foot, they poured buckets of water over themselves. The water was comfortably warm. The steam quickly dissipated and now the air within the gasgiq lingered warm and dry. The ritual silence, observed during the ultra-hot steaming, now turned to conversation as the men enjoyed each other's company.

Eventually, and now clean and dry, the men began to file out to the entry porch to dress. Harjo now saw the fur clothes hanging from all the wooden pegs in the porch post.

The men chuckled at the boys who ran out, grabbed their clothes, and ran back in to dress in the warmth of the gasgiq. Slowly the visitors returned to their own men's house. As Harjo, Uncle Akagtak, and cousin Angaiak awaited Ciriiq to bring their evening meal, they sat and talked.

"Let us talk about a topic that some might consider a delicate subject," said Uncle Akagtak.

"Alright," agreed Harjo.

"I understand a married woman who commits adultery among the Mammoth Hunters has committed a serious offense, even a crime. Such behavior may dissolve the marriage."

"Yes," answered Harjo. "Under such conditions, an offended husband may return the wife to her father and dissolve the marriage and there usually remains animosity between the offended husband and his former wife's lover. It may also end in the death of one or the other."

"I understand," acknowledged Uncle Akagtak. "Among the Canineqmiut, it is different, nearly opposite. If a man dies, his brother takes over all his responsibilities including his wife, his children, and his property. A man may be another's brother in friendship, especially those who do not have a brother as kin. Consequently, they may forge an agreement that if one dies, the other will take care of his wife and children. To help insure that each will assume those responsibilities, they have usually slept and had sex with the other's wife. It is possible that the children are actually the brothers. A woman welcomes this custom because it insures that if her husband dies, his brother and or dear friend will provide for her and her children, which otherwise, she would not have. To the Canineqmiut, it is a matter of survival."

"Cousin Angaiak and myself want you to sleep with and to have sexual relations with Ciriiq. She also wants you, too."

"I can guarantee," added cousin Angaiak, "it will be a night you will never forget."

Harjo considered the proposition. "What if I refuse?" he asked.

"Well then, we will feel that we have failed in our hospitality and Ciriiq will feel bad as though you think there is something wrong with her. But more importantly, she will believe that if some tragedy befell Angaiak, you would not help her or come to her aid."

"Well," answered Harjo. "I certainly do not want to offend you or Ciriiq and I don't want her to think I would not help her. And she indeed is very attractive."

"Excellent," said Uncle Akagtak as cousin Angaiak reached out taking his hand.

"What do I do?" inquired Harjo.

"Simply go to her house and bed this evening and spend the evening," answered cousin Angaiak.

"I will," said Harjo, as the other two looked at each other and nodded in agreement.

Chapter 8:

RETURNING

Harjo sat up in the bed blanketed with seal pelts leaning back on his arms braced behind him—the palms of his hands on the bed. Ciriiq stood beside the bed. Her hood was pushed back to reveal her braided hair and face. Harjo had not really taken a good close look at her but did so now. "She is older," he thought, "maybe 35 summers." Ciriiq was certainly not a nubile girl but she was nonetheless very attractive, and her manner was both soothing and somehow seductive.

"So young Mammoth Hunter named Harjo, you are a very handsome young man," she stated with a calm pleasant voice reflecting an attitude of confidence. "I have a question for you."

"Yes," Harjo replied.

"Can you kill a mammoth?"

"Not alone," he answered. "But I have killed one with my father. You have seen the animal's meat and hide."

She paused for a moment to consider his answer then calmly stepped over to one of the four earth lodge support posts. She picked up her woman's bag, which hung by a peg on the post. She then returned to the platform bed. As she rummaged through her bag, Harjo heard the clinking of her bone and ivory sewing tools. Then she produced an oblong-shaped stone about two fingers wide and a hand's length. The stone was obviously used to soften hides. To Harjo's surprise, she ran the stone over the nail of her middle finger of her right hand. Then she 'checked' the fingernail by rubbing it with her thumb. "How strangely curious," thought Harjo to himself. She then returned the stone to her bag and then looked at Harjo with a pleasant but serious expression.

"If my husband Angaiak comes to the land of the mammoth, to your river valley to trade, will you help him?"

Harjo replied with an enthusiastic answer. "Yes, I will. He can stay with me in my father's mammoth lodge. I will speak for him and help negotiate the trade."

She paused, smiled, and raised her eyebrows as if to say that was the answer she hoped to hear. "Are the lions in the land of the mammoth dangerous?"

"Yes, very dangerous. They take mammoth hunter lives. The mammoth are equally lethal, both require many precautions. A wise traveler should gain knowledge of certain habits and behaviors concerning lions and mammoth before crossing the Mammoth Steppe and descending into the valleys of the mammoth."

She leaned down, putting her palms on the bed, moving close, gazing into Harjo's face. "Will you advise Angaiak on such a journey, its dangers, and the directions?"

Harjo now had a better look into her face. Her expression remained calm-somehow seductive-reflecting both experience and beauty. "Most certainly I will."

Ciriiq stood back up with an air of contentment, took her woman's bag back to the post, and returned to the platform bed. Then, without further questions, she smiled and pulled her parka over her head and undressed. She then stood naked before Harjo confirming to him that she was very attractive. Slowly, she got into bed. Then on her knees she reached out gently taking Harjo's shoulders. She was very seductive. She slowly moved close to him, and then gently kissed his neck and ears, caressing him with her warm breath from her mouth and nose.

Ciriiq was strong with odor. Not necessarily unpleasant, just strong. Her scent of woman was aromatic and sexually appealing in an animal way. She also smelled like sea mammal and sea mammal oil. Those aromas were equally neither pleasing nor unpleasant but were simply foreign. Slowly, meticulous, she caressed, fondled, and kissed Harjo. She was an experienced seductress easily overcoming her young victim.

"Do you have a pretty young mammoth girl in your village?" she asked whispering into his ear.

"Yes," he answered beginning to breathe heavily.

"I will show you bed things she does not know." Then she kissed him passionately sucking on his tongue in a way he had not experienced. She placed her warm hands on his chest rubbing his nipples.

"Lay back, relax, young Mammoth Hunter," she said in a low, seductive whisper. "Let me take you to a spirit world you have yet to visit. You will enjoy it-remembering it always."

Gently, Ciriiq pushed Harjo onto his back then pulled the seal pelt cover from him. "That's it my little puppy, just relax.

"Puppy?" asked Harjo.

"A puppy is a baby seal," she replied as she slowly straddled him and languidly rubbed her pubis against him in a circular motion. He looked to her seductive smile and the movement of her full plump breast then to her vulva. He could feel her black pubic hair on his stomach. She then came down on to her elbows cupping the side of his face with her hands then kissed him again full on the mouth-a hot, passionate, fervent kiss.

The pleasure she could render with her mouth lay beyond explanation. Harjo did not know such pleasure could be felt or experienced. Of course, he had only kissed one girl in his short life, pretty Chufe, thinking she kissed well. It was certainly most pleasurable. Ah, but this woman. The way she ran her warm tongue along the edges of his lips, the manner she sucked on his lips, and the skills she employed kissing him was beyond his comprehension.

"Open your mouth," she ordered in a low pleasant whisper. She was confident, direct, and Harjo eagerly obeyed. "Wider-that's it." Then she kissed him in such manner he had not been kissed before. He began to fell his spirit slipping away-beginning its journey to the spirit world of pleasure.

Then, she kissed and licked him from his neck down to his groin. Slowly, meticulously, Ciriiq eased her way down. She slid her wet hot tongue along his chest, stopped to toy with his nipples, and then kissed her way slowly to his stomach. Simultaneously, she massaged him with her warm breast until finally each brown nipple was caressing his knees.

Then, every so tenderly, she massaged his testicles then bending her head down, she took his swollen manhood into her mouth. "Hmm," she groaned and thought to herself. "His balls are large, full of fluid and his manhood is equally hefty." She went up and down his ridged male bone but did not want him to orgasm just yet. "Don't give me your male fluid just yet handsome puppy." She reached out and took his erection between her thumb and forefinger giving him a vigorous squeeze. Then, she slowly got up and straddled him once more and holding his erection in one hand, she gently eased down on him sliding his erection slowly into the moist warmth internal of her womanhood.

She moved slowly in a circular motion then up and down. Harjo felt himself slipping farther and deeper into the spirit world. But he could still see her as she looked at him with a beautiful, seductive face. "You feel so good in me," she panted in her low whisper of a voice. Such a large puppy, does it feel good, hmm?" Her warm, wet vagina felt better than anything he had felt before. He answered, "yes" softly-he wanted it to last longer.

"Are you ready to give me your male fluid?"

A panting "yes" was all Harjo could manage as he neared the spirit world.

"Not just yet puppy," she said as she slid down to lay out flat on top of him. She put her hands behind his neck. "Roll with me-that's it-roll."

Harjo followed and rolled with her so that he was on top of her resting on his elbows. Ciriiq locked her heals behind his knees then grabbed his buttocks with both of her hands. She held him tight-she had him trapped. He felt her reach her hand between them thinking she was massaging herself, but she was moistening her fingers with her own wetness. Then, she ran her fingers between the cheeks of his buttocks finding that small anal opening, then to his wonderment and surprise, she slowly inserted her wet finger.

She then whispered loudly into his ear, "Now-puppy-now, give me your male fluid. Fill me now-fill me now!"

He was able to thrust into her only once, then twice, in and out, and at that moment, she pulled all of him into her sinking her small wet finger deep into his anus touching his gland, his male gland, deep inside of him. Suddenly, Harjo released his male fluid in a passion of light and power that was nearly the same fervor as a vision. He cried out in a loud agonizing groan. Every muscle in his body contracted. Ciriiq held and gripped him so tight he could not have escaped from her had he wanted. It was as though she pulled all of him into her. He convulsed, shaking with such intensity that he flew through the spirit world of pleasure like a bolting dart hurled from a magical atlatl that flexed up and down as it soared, or a bolt of lightning thrown from the mystic sky. He shook as though taken by powerful thunder. He could not determine if life was being taken or forced into him. He collapsed on top of Ciriiq, exhausted and unable to move.

Ciriiq had guided him into the spirit world and entered herself but not as far. As she now returned from that numinous place, she realized just how large and heavy he was. She heard Harjo moaning as he slowly returned from the mystical side of that joyous yet unexplained world. She would tolerate his weight a while longer as she rubbed his back and patted his buttocks helping him to return.

Finally, Harjo got up on his hands then began to rise.

"Don't get up," she said, "just lay with me on your side."

Harjo did as she asked.

As they lay together, Ciriiq's fingers gently caressed his face. "The infinite 'Hunter Spirit' is with this one," she thought to herself. "He is destined for something great and now a small part of him belongs to me."

After a quiet moment had passed, she asked, "Are you satisfied?"

"Yes," was too easy of an answer. Harjo got up and put his hands on the side of her face and kissed her as passionately as he knew how. Then looking into her face, he replied, "I have not had such pleasure or been on such a journey. I did not know it was possible." She smiled likewise touching his face.

Then curiosity reached up and whispered into Harjo's ear. He must ask. "Did you find pleasure as well?"

"Why yes," she smiled and touched his face again, "such a sweet thoughtful puppy. Not quite the same as yours but still pleasure. I derived gratification from giving you satisfaction. If you were my hunter, strong and brave enough to kill a mammoth, I would take your male fluid every day, if you desired, and make sure your balls were never full of white male liquid. But certainly, if you were my hunter, I would teach you how to give me sexual pleasure as well." She paused for a moment. "Let me show you something."

Ciriiq reached her hand down to her glistening black pubic hair and the mounds of her vulva. She spread her lips apart with her fingers to reveal her clitoris. "Lick your fingers," she instructed, "then touch this little female organ- very gently as it is tender and sensitive." Harjo did as she asked but he also noticed his male fluid was beginning to seep out of her vagina.

Ciriiq sighed and gently moved her hips. "This little female organ," she continued, "is the heart of a woman's pleasure. It is similar to a male organ, only obviously, much smaller. Learn to gently and tenderly stimulate this little female organ with your fingers, better yet your tongue, and still better with both and you will send your girl on a spirit journey of immense pleasure. Learn to stimulate her little female organ with your large erect organ as you thrust in and out of her. Arouse the female organ of that pretty mammoth girl of yours and she will never forget you. And, if she has a cold, naughty, closed little vagina she will open up like a wet warm flower as when an icicle is dropped by a flaming hearth-she will melt, spreading wide for you."

Harjo gently massaged her clitoris as she smiled and moaned then she patted his hand. "That's enough," she whispered. He lay back down and she rose up, then kissed him and caressed his face. She smiled at him speaking softly close to his face.

"You are both a strong mammoth hunter and a baby seal puppy. I wish I had you when you were a little boy just beginning to grow pubic hair," she said laughing. "I would hold you down, grip your little penis, and spank your little butt until you gave me your male fluid. I would be the first woman to take your fluid and I would spank every drop out of you." As she spoke, she reached down and lightly spanked his thigh emphasizing her words. Harjo chuckled.

She then looked into his face with a more serious expression. "When I become old, young Harjo, and if I have no man to hunt for me, will you be my hunter?"

Harjo answered without thought. "If I was in your village or camp, I would be your hunter, Ciriiq. I would not allow you to live with hunger or without skins for clothes or sleep outside. I would make sure you had food, clothing, and a warm lodge to live in."

Ciriiq smiled then kissed him again. "I must go to work; I have food to prepare. You may remain here if you like or not. I'll soon take this evening's meal to Angaiak and our uncle. You may eat here or in the men's house."

She rose from the bed, dressed, and was headed out through the entry tunnel as Harjo lay in the bed. She turned back looking at him. "Remember, brave young Mammoth Hunter of the Muscogee Tribe. My bed is always open to you." She offered one last smile then vanished through the tunnel.

Harjo lay back in her bed with his arms behind his head. Then curiously, he thought, "What if cousin Angaiak journeys to the Echota Valley to stay with the Wind Band? Will he expect me to reciprocate sharing my wife with him?" Then he laughed. He did not have a wife, so it does not matter. He thought again of beautiful, mature Ciriiq. He may take her offer of another encounter. He felt good-content-hungry but content.

Sealskins should not be that much different to load than sections of mammoth pelts thought Harjo, but it seems he loaded and unloaded his sled numerous occasions before the load was near to what he wanted. It was later in the morning than he had planned to leave but he was satisfied with his load and ready to go. His new Canineqmiut family was there to see him off and he was returning with warm greetings for both his father and mother. He thanked his new family for their hospitality.

"Meeting you will remain an experience to recall for many seasons to come, young nephew," said Uncle Akagtak. "I hope you return to visit us some day-take care on your return trip." They embraced in farewell.

He likewise embraced cousin Angaiak. "Thank you, cousin, for your wisdom and knowledge on crossing the Mammoth Steppe," said Angaiak. "Look for us to arrive at your village two or three winters from now."

"I will," replied Harjo. "Don't take any unnecessary risks, and you will fare well."

Ciriiq stepped up to Harjo. "You know I am going to kiss you, Harjo," she smiled, "so don't shy away. Only family members are watching." She grasped his elbows then stood up on her toes and kissed him full on the mouth. He returned her kiss. "Promise me you will return to your village unharmed."

"I promise," said Harjo. Ciriiq reached up again giving him another quick kiss. The Canineqmiut family members stood together watching their young relative pull his sled harness over his head, then with a final wave, headed off back to the land of the mammoth. As he moved through the village, many men waved and called out a farewell. At the southern end of the village, Kailukiak also came out to say his farewell.

"I am glad I met you mammoth hunter," said Kailukiak. "I hope we meet again."

"I believe we will, Kailukiak," answered a joyful Harjo. "I want you to teach me how to paddle a kayak."

"I will," Kailukiak said with a vigorous wave, "I will!"

Harjo came to realize the Canineqmiut were a generous and sharing people. Until now, the Muscogee Mammoth Hunters were the only people he had ever lived with and even then, only with the Wind Band. As his mother was Canineqmiut, he learned of their customs growing up but still it was not the same experience as actually living with another people. On one side, the Canineqmiut and the Muscogee lifestyles were completely different, a mammoth hunting people versus a sea mammal hunting people. But on the other side, deep human values such as sharing, and generosity were uniquely the same. And what of the exotic servant girl thought Harjo? All things were not as they seem.

On his trek to the Canineqmiut village, Harjo made a mental note to remember this location as it was an excellent temporary camp and he planned to return to it. It was situated at the head of a small brushy drainage that first trickled down west then southwest and ultimately it emptied into the Tununeq River, the seacoast, and the Canineqmiut village. The stream seeped from a small rock outcrop with patches of willow and alder thickets thriving along its banks. Several large stones were scattered around the area surrounded by tall dead grass. Adjacent the stream and situated on a small circular rise grew several large willow trees. Large for the coastal area, their trunks were nearly wrist size, and they reached about the height of two men. Two large rocks also lined the small knoll along with several large dead branches for firewood. Protected by the large willow trees and brush patches, little snow accumulated on the circular rise. Throughout the general area dried grass and leaves cluttered the ground surface. If necessary, he could tie his bison skin to the tree trunks or limbs to create a roof in case of snow, but the sky was clear, and he anticipated a starlight night.

In fact, the moon will be nearly full tonight and complete its 30-day cycle tomorrow. So tonight, as it was last night, a bright mystical world filled with strange shadows will tease the imagination. The clear endless sky, unnumbered brilliant stars, a mystic vivid moon, and the snow-covered landscape all combined to create a dazzling, nearly day-like night where one could envision mystical creatures sneaking along the bright tundra plain. On such nights, a traveler could make his way across the landscape, with reasonable caution. Harjo pushed his sled into the shelter of the trees then uncovered it to pull out the necessary camping tools. He started a fire near one of the large stones that would make a good backrest then surrounded it with rocks. He spread the bison robe near the fire. He unpacked the sled, stacking his pelts and other material adjacent to one of the large rocks. He would sleep in the sled tonight. Lined with a few sea mammal skins and the mammoth bed, the sled promised to be a comfortable bed.

After the fire burned awhile, he set up his water boiling pouch, added water, and then selected some hot water boiling rocks. Some warm drinking water or perhaps some bitter Canineqmiut tea would be palatable. The Canineqmiut call this plant *yuurqaq*, which generally means tea. It is an upright plant with finger-sized, serrated leaves grouped in threes. The red flower tops of the plant are gathered in great quantity, dried, and used to brew tea that is consumed daily. It is often called redtop plant and although it grows in abundance on the coast, it remains rare in the interior steppe. Harjo was bringing back a large bag of the plant flowers for his mother.

The Muscogee Mammoth Hunters brew tea from a similar plant called marsh locks, which grows in marshy wet areas although not as abundantly. The plant is easily recognized by its attractive purple flowers. The leaves are collected and dried when it is encountered especially during spring and summer migrations. Marsh locks also thrive on the coast where the Canineqmiut collect and the dry the leaves for tea. They call the plant *pingayunelgen*. Harjo did not particularly like this tea and similar to the majority of Mammoth Hunters, he preferred mammoth tea.

It would be dark soon. After feasting on the dwindling supply of dried mammoth meat, Harjo sat on the bison robe leaning with his back against the tall end of the sled. He looked out over the fire toward the direction of Up'nerkillermiut village, now a short distance of two days away. His spear, darts and quiver, and atlatl leaned against one of the adjacent large stones.

Harjo had devised a plan to return in secret to Up'nerkillermiut and steal or as he preferred the term 'rescue,' the beautiful servant girl from Ilalke, her Canineqmiut master. He had traveled two days but was only one long day from Up'nerkillermiut. He first traveled one very short day and camped. He arrived here the next day at this current pre-selected camp. If by some outside chance Ilalke thought Harjo was up to something, he might follow Harjo to ensure that he did leave the coast. Upon reaching Harjo's first abandoned camp, Ilalke would then presume he had headed off back to mammoth land. The passing of two days would reinforce the belief to all the Canineqmiut that he was in fact gone. Now he would return with the sled loaded only with the mammoth bed, food and water, the bison robe, two or three seal pelts, his utility bag, and weapons. In one long day's journey, he would reach Up'nerkillermiut. Then, as night fell and the Canineqmiut slept, he would sneak down into the village and take the girl. He had learned enough about the village layout that he could slip through unseen. He knew what sod house she stayed in and she would be alone with Usugan who would not say anything. In fact, she would probably help. Harjo and the girl would then sneak out of the village to the awaiting sled. Uncle Akagtak had said it himself—theft was not known to the Canineqmiut and they remain unprepared for an attack. Harjo was certain he could sneak in and out with the girl undetected.

They would then make the long trek and return to this camp. If she grew weary-he already knew her clothes were not fit for travel-she could ride in the comfort of the sled, covered in the mammoth bed. Once they arrived back at this camp, they could prepare for the long journey back to his homeland. If by some chance he lost all his pelts and supplies that he left cached at this camp to scavengers or for some reason they could not return to this camp, they retained enough resources with the sled to make the trip.

Harjo was proud of his plan, remaining confident it would be successful. On the narrow chance it failed, he had other options. He still had ample resources including some mammoth meat, many sea mammal pelts, and good tool stone. Perhaps he could buy the girl. Or better yet, he could just kill the bastard and take her. Few people in the village would care, he thought. He laughed to himself thinking, if he returned to the Wind Band with the head of a worthless Canineqmiut man, would that stand as proof he had reached the coast?

Harjo chuckled to himself then checked the horizon to see if the moon had risen when suddenly he caught a glimpse of a distant dark figure. Instinctively, he reached over grasping his nearby spear. He knew lions rarely journeyed to the coast, as did the huge bear, still he watched intently on full alert. To his surprise, he saw it was a human figure that had fallen forward in the shallow snow. The figure rose, stumbled for several steps then fell again forward, but now it fell with arms spread and appeared lifeless.

Harjo climbed out of the sled with his spear in hand and hurried down the gentle slope to the fallen figure. He stuck the butt end of his spear into the ground and got down on one knee next to the face down body. He was nearly certain who it was before he rolled the body over but after he did, he clearly saw the face. His suspicions were confirmed. "The servant girl," he said out loud. She appeared near death from cold and exposure, and he knew he must move as fast as possible to save life and limb.

Still on one knee, Harjo reached out, grabbing her parka by the front. "Now if this worn out piece of carrion she wears as a parka won't rip," he said to himself out loud as he pulled her upright to a sitting position. She had a woman's bag across her shoulder. He slipped it off, dropping it to the ground. He then took her right wrist lifting it up and at the same movement ducked his head under her armpit and thus pulled her arm over the back of his neck. Then he slid his left hand under her buttocks and thigh, grabbed a fist full of her baggy pants, and lifted her up and over his left shoulder, rising up to both feet all in one single motion. He clamped his left forearm on the back of her knees, grasped his spear, bent down by bending his knees and grabbed her bag, and hurried back to camp as fast as he could. She was light but dead weight is still dead weight.

When he reached camp, he planted his spear upright in the ground, dropped her bag, and took her to the bison robe laid out on the ground next to the fire. He kneeled on one knee next to the robe. As she was over his left shoulder, he quickly changed hands and put his right arm across the back of her knees bringing his left hand to the back of her neck. He bent over slightly and let her slide off his shoulder then onto the robe as he caught her.

Quickly, he untied the draw straps on her worn *mukluk* boots then pulled one off. He breathed a small sigh of relieve as she was wearing a new, well-made grass sock woven from the tough "salt grass" that grows only on the coast. He pulled off the soaking wet sock then quickly examined her feet and did likewise with her other foot. He breathed a complete sigh of relieve. Her feet were red and cold but not frozen. She had been spared frostbite. Her *mukluk* boots were worn and not fit to wear but the new grass socks had saved her feet, but he still needed to move quickly.

Her parka sleeves were long, and her hands were inside the sleeves. He pushed them up to quickly look at her hands, which like her feet were red and cold but not frozen. She was not wearing mittens; however, the long parka sleeves protected her hands. He pushed the bottom of her parka up then pulled her up to a sitting position, struggling to pull her soaked parka off. "This must be something a mother learns by undressing a sleeping child," he said to himself out loud. He momentarily considered cutting the parka off but then discovered that if he pulled her arms out first, he could manage to pull the parka off. He continued to hurriedly undress her but could not help but notice, as she was naked from the waist up, the remarkable light color of her skin. He had only seen her face at the Canineqmiut village and now to see her light complexion from the waist up was even more of a wonderment. He also could not but help to notice her breasts were small but very firm, attractive, and incredibly appealing.

He found the drawstring for her pants, untied it, rolled her over on her stomach and then pulled her pants off. It was fortunate she was wearing pants; many women don't, relying on extra-long parkas for protection. Unlike her parka, he also noticed that her pants were in fair condition. Now that she was naked, he could not help but to look at all of her. Akin to her face, she had a lovely body. She was well formed, slender and muscular. He also now recalled his "flash vision" of undressing her that had now come to pass. She was dirty and smelled with pungent body odor. Her worn out clothes also carried an unfavorable aroma. But it was probably not her fault or desire. Harjo was sure a servant girl would not be allowed to bath very often, if at all, and undoubtedly would not possess clean clothes sewn from new pelts. He then noticed several, ugly, red switch mark welts across her buttocks. She had been recently punished with a switch. He gently touched the welts, painful but her skin was not broken, and he saw no evidence of blood. He rolled her over on her back, picked her up, and hurriedly carried her to the sled and the mammoth bed. He thought to himself, "Is that all her idiot master could think of to do with a beautiful behind like hers, beat it with a stick? What a fool!" As he slid her into the mammoth bed, her arms fell above her head. He noticed her vulva area and armpits, marveling at the color of her hair. That small patch of beautiful pubic fur and smaller patches of underarm fur reflected the same wondrous yellow color of her hair.

He pulled her arms to her side then quickly got up and went to the fire, selecting two clean rocks he used for boiling which were warm but not hot as he could hold them in his hands. Hurriedly, he went to the stack of pelts and grabbed his caribou shirt and returned to the sled. He wrapped the warm rocks and her feet together with the shirt then pulled the top cover over her. The mammoth bed was wider than the sled and if the edges of the bed were pushed down into the sled, it formed a perfect body size nest. He then took several sea mammal pelts then pushed them around her body and her head, thus tucking her in. Only her unconscious face was exposed.

Harjo considered taking off his clothes and getting in bed with her to warm her up. It remains a lifesaving technique. If she woke up, however, she would be frightened and she might go into a hysteria fit, which may be more harmful to the girl than the cold. So, he decided the thick mammoth bed was enough and she would warm up quickly. Luck certainly followed her this day.

Had she fallen a mere 100 paces farther down the slope, Harjo would not have seen her, and she would have died long before morning. She was cold and exhausted with death stalking her, but now tucked into the mammoth bed, she would warm up quickly, sleep all night, and recover by dawn. She would wake in the morning, thirsty, hungry, probably in mild shock, but otherwise all right.

Kneeling by the sled, he looked into her sleeping face. So beautifully strange, he said to himself. His curiosity reached its peak and compelled him to reach over then tenderly caress her hair. Then, with his fingertips, he gently traced the feathery arch of her eyebrows and again marveled because her brows were the same strange color as her hair. He could not help himself and slowly eased his face down close to hers smelling her hair. He pulled his head back with a frown. Although a beautiful wondrous color, it was dirty and smelled bad like her dirty body. "Dirt and body odor wash off easily," he said to himself. Then, with his nose next to her slightly parted lips, he smelled her breath. It was warm and sweet. He gave her a slight kiss on her lips and then smiling at himself, he sat back. He would stay awake tending the fire all night in case she woke. Then he could calm her, although, as he already told himself, she would probably sleep all night and wake in the morning. He had some camp chores to complete.

He took her smelly clothes and washed them off in the stream although the parka, pants, and boots were already wet. He stretched a rawhide line between the trees and hung her clothes up to dry including her grass socks, the only decent article of clothing she wore. Then thinking further, he reached inside her boots to discover a pair of grass pads, so he hung those up as well. He also took off his mammoth boots along with his mammoth wool socks and hung them to dry utilizing the line and nearby tree limbs. Normally, he might just wear his buckskin shirt at night instead of a parka, but currently it was wrapped up in dirty little feet. Harjo gathered a pile of wood and tended the fire, ate some more mammoth meat, drank more tea, and waited out the gorgeous bright night.

Part Two

THE JOINING

Onna quickly looked up at Harjo. Her expression showed such intensity. "You no take I back." "I no take you back," repeated Harjo. "You will not go back. You are free."

Chapter 9:

I AM ONNA

Early dawn, the nearly full moon was still aglow. Harjo sat by the fire enjoying the antics of a pair of snow buntings. The little birds were only the size of a man's two fingers. The Father Creator provided many animals and birds of the Mammoth Steppe with the perfect camouflage of white in the winter and brown in the summer. The snow bunting's disguise matched their name. The male was nearly all white with the tips of his wings and tail coated in black, while the female supported a black and brown back and elsewhere was white. The pair were investigating the low rock outcrop for a likely nesting location. Snow buntings build their nest deep in rock crevices, out of reach from preying paws and teeth. He recalled the little white birds were abundant all along the Backbone Mountain formation at the winter village during the summer but migrated out across the steppe in the winter.

Grasping another small dry log, Harjo tossed it on the fire. Anticipating a thirsty and equally famished refugee, he brewed some fresh tea but was also preparing a stew. Utilizing his other boiling pouch, he cut up some generous pieces of the dwindling dried mammoth meat and was stewing the chunks in hot water. The warm soft meat and broth would hasten her recovery.

Suddenly, he heard a quiescent moan from his slumbering guest. She was waking earlier than he predicted. She stirred and moved with several little high-pitched girl's moaning sounds and then opened her eyes. Seeing Harjo, she jumped-startled with an "oh!"-Harjo could see the worried but frightened look on her face. He did not move, waiting a brief moment before speaking. He did not want to alarm her.

"Don't be afraid," he said calmly. "You're alright." After a moment of silence, he continued, relaxed and confident. "You remember me from the Canineqmiut village?"

She nodded her head yes, looking into his face, not frightened but still apprehensive.

Then suddenly, she quickly sat up in the mammoth bed. Somehow, without exposing her breasts, she pulled her knees up and reached down to her feet to anxiously grasp at them through the mammoth bed cover.

"Your feet are good. You did not freeze anywhere, only cold and red." Harjo picked up the ladle and filled it full of warm tea. He sipped the tea with his lips to ensure it was not too hot.

"Are you thirsty?"

Holding the mammoth cover up under her chin she nodded her head in a silent yes. Harjo stood up with the full ladle, then went over and knelt down by the side of the sled. He held the ladle up to her lips and she drank-first with a sip-then she slurped the rest down so that she formed a partial smile.

"Do you remember who I am?"

"Yes," she replied in a quiet, soft voice. "You name Harjo. You Mammoth Hunter."

She was obviously limited speech wise in Yupik, but her manner of verbalization enticed Harjo. She spoke with such a wonderful accent. He had never heard anyone talk in such a manner. He wanted to hear more.

"Don't be afraid," he repeated calmly. "I will not harm you." She looked into his face then shook her head yes and again made a half-hearted attempt to smile.

"What is your name?"

She looked surprised as if she was taken aback that someone cared about her name and answered, "I name?"

"Yes," he responded, "What is your name?"

"Onna," she said now with a near full smile. "I am Onna." Then she reached her hand out from under the mammoth cover and touched the ladle with her finger. "Have more?" she asked in a quiet pleasant whisper.

"Most certainly," Harjo replied with a smile and then he got up and went to the pouch to return with a full ladle. Now she had both hands out from under the mammoth cover and somehow it still kept her breasts covered. Harjo considered a bit of modesty as admirable. She examined and rubbed her hands checking for frostbite. Harjo handed her the ladle of tea and she quickly consumed it. He went back to the fire then returned with the whole pouch of tea, setting it up next to her and the sled so that she could refill the ladle herself.

"You must be very thirsty." The Muscogee people know the Mammoth Steppe, although covered with shallow snow in the winter, remains very dry and nearly void of moisture. Thirst can be dangerous and eating snow can be more dangerous. "Drink all you want. I have plenty. Are you hungry?"

Onna's eyes lit up and she responded by nodding her head yes and also whispering, "Yes."

Harjo went to the pile of supplies then took a wooden bowl from the woman's bag his mother packed for him. At the fire, he filled the bowl with the mammoth stew then he returned to the sled, handing the bowl to Onna.

Onna held the bowl in both hands smelling the steaming stew. She looked up at Harjo with a joyful look of surprise and exclaimed, "Mammoth!"

"Yes," Harjo replied. He remained fascinated by the wonderful sky-blue color of her eyes now red and swollen. She was still exhausted.

"Oh-long I have mammoth." Onna drank from the bowl and then took a piece of meat with her fingers. She looked up smiling at Harjo while she was chewing. Seeing her happy and eating gave Harjo a warm feeling.

"I think you will be fine now, but you nearly died. I was lucky to find you."

Onna thought for moment then responded after a swallow. "I run-go. Walk day-night. Moon bright. I follow you. Feet, sled, snow."

Now Harjo was surprised. "Your clothes and your boots are old and worn. You will freeze. You have no food, no bed, no robe-you could not go very far."

"Yes," she said. "I have sock, Usugan make I grass. I hope find you, follow you, take try do."

There was another long pause. Then she looked up at Harjo with such a serious and desperate expression. She was telling him by the determination in her face that she will risk all she has, including her life. He had not experienced such resolve from a girl before.

"I no stay Canineqmiut. I no servant girl. Canineqmiut men, Ilalke, master, he can kill I. Cold can kill I. Mammoth Steppe can kill I." She paused for a moment. "You-understand?"

The intensity and sincerity of her voice moved Harjo's emotions. It was not loud or harsh or in anger, more of a whisper. Yet her determination was inspiring. Harjo remained silent. Following a short pause, she spoke again.

"I know I no talk Yupik good. You can take I back. I can no stop. I no-I hope you no do. You help I Up'nerkillermiut. I hope you help I." Onna looked back at the bowl of stew then took another bite of meat and continued to look down at the bowl.

She had risked her life on the unlikely chance she could follow and overtake Harjo. She risked all for a chance of freedom. Harjo was deeply moved. He took a silent but deep breath and then spoke.

"Yes, I understand. I will not take you back to Up'nerkillermiut," he stated as a matter of fact.

Onna quickly looked up at Harjo. Her expression showed such intensity. "You no take I back."

"I no take you back," repeated Harjo. "You will not go back. You are free. You can come with me, if you want, to the land of the mammoth."

Onna made a little whimpering sound. Her face began to take on a "crying expression." Harjo saw her bowl was empty. He gently reached down, taking the bowl. She easily gave it up. "We talk," he said. Onna lightly shook her head yes then folded her hands together under her chin. The gesture seemed unusual to Harjo.

Harjo went to the fire and filled the bowl with more stew, but he also grabbed the bison robe then dragged it back to the sled. He handed her the bowl, pulled the robe up by the sled, and made himself comfortable on the robe and began. Onna drank some broth, took a bite of meat, and listened with her head bowed.

"I was coming back to the village for you today."

Onna was sniffling but did not seem ready to cry and looked up. "You come for I?"

" Yes," Harjo said sternly. "I was going to sneak into the village at night, slip into your sod house, and take you out of the village, stealing you from Ilalke."

"You-take-I Ilalke, village, night? He no, know?" asked a whispering Onna.

"That is right," replied Harjo who gently smiled at her double no. After a slight pause, Harjo asked. "Do you want to come with me to the land of the mammoth?"

Onna had somehow finished the bowl placing it in her lap. Again, her hands were folded in that strange manner. "Oh yes Harjo. I can go-you I-land of mammoth?" Onna began to cry. She could not help herself. She rocked forward and back still with her hands folded on her breasts touching her chin. Harjo was not sure what to do. Instinctively, he gently reached his hand out to her. Onna took his hand and kissed the back, the palm, and then cupped it with her hands holding it to her breasts, gently rocking and crying. Onna's hands were small with rough palms. Harjo could sense she was much stronger than her small size indicated. Her silent tears rolled down her face gently falling onto both of their hands.

Her tears also fell into Harjo's heart. Only on one other occasion in his young life had he been so moved by anyone. Ill equipped with poor clothing, no weapons, no food, not even a bison robe, she strikes out alone challenging the Mammoth Steppe. She risked her life for a small, unlikely chance to be free. This strange, beautiful, exotic girl had touched him in a way he could not understand.

Suddenly a sharp wind blew through the camp. Onna raised her head and the wind picked up her hair blowing it back to reveal her beautiful tear stained face. The wind sends him a sign. Harjo looked into her face, Onna smiled, and her smile touched him as well. What seemed to be opposites, tears and smiles, both captured his feelings. And yet the opposite ends of a spear are both sharp. This spear lay on his heart and would not be removed.

Onna gently laid Harjo's hand down on the mammoth bed. She was still in tears but able to talk. "Harjo, I afraid."

"Afraid," repeated Harjo. "Why?"

"Ilalke-more Canineqmiut men-come take I. Oh Harjo, I afraid men come take I."

Harjo changed positions on the bison robe then suddenly realized how close he had shifted toward her, but he did not move back. He looked sincerely into her face. "I do not think he will come after you," he stated in an honest tone. "I do not think any Canineqmiut man in Up'nerkillermiut will attempt to follow you." He now wondered if his speech was too detailed and she failed to understand.

"But I," she paused in the middle of her sentence. Then, with her mouth slightly opened, her big tearful eyes looked upward as she concentrated on the right words and to mentally translate words and her meaning from her language to Yupik.

"When she looks up like that," Harjo thought to himself, "she is so serious and in such serious thought, but she also poses such a pleasing, beautiful, 'enchanting' expression." It inspired him to smile but he did not.

Turning back to him, Onna quickly and with only a hint of tears softly exclaimed, "Property-I property. He can trade I, away."

"Yes," Harjo agreed. "You are property, valuable property." He paused, putting his thoughts together, then continued.

"First," he began, holding up his index finger on his right hand. He now had all his reasoning mentally laid out in sequential order one-two-three believing that approach would improve communication.

But then she delicately reached up with both hands. Her left hand tenderly grasped his index finger and with two fingers of her right hand she gently touched his lips so that he paused. "What first?" she asked in a whisper.

What a polite way to interrupt, he thought, but then not wanting to become too complicated, he changed his word. "One", he replied.

"One?" she answered. Thinking for a moment, she withdrew her hands and then said, "Oh, yes, one!"

"One." he continued again and again holding up his right index finger. "I don't think Ilalke will come after you. He is lazy and a coward." Onna looked seriously into his face with anticipation of what he had to say next. This was a new experience for young Harjo. Someone, especially a girl, anticipating what he had to say as though it carried some level of importance. He enjoyed that concept, but it likewise seemed to place a responsibility on him to deeply consider what he was saying-that he was accurate-and most importantly that he meant what he was saying. Raising two fingers he continued.

"Two: I don't think any man in Up'nerkillermiut will come after you. I think they are glad you have gotten away with a chance for freedom." Onna continued to listen intently as Harjo lifted up three fingers.

"Three: I will not allow Ilalke to take you back. I will fight him and if necessary, I will kill him."

With that response, her still moist eyes suddenly grew wide. Her face, although still pleasant to look upon, changed to an expression of surprise or disbelief. She reached out and again touched his hand looking into his face, deep into his eyes, she asked in what seemed to be a hopeful astonished whisper.

"You fight for I?"

"Yes!" he answered.

She paused and thought seriously for a moment. "You kill Ilalke, he no take I?"

"Yes!" he answered seriously, "if need be and he is foolish enough to try."

Harjo saw her facial expression change. Her lips tighten and tears began to swell in her sky-blue eyes once more as she began to cry again. She reached out with her small but strong calloused hands to gently grasp his right hand. Tears ran down her beautiful light-colored face and in a tearful voice she asked, "You take I, your land, land of mammoth?"

"Yes," he answered, "I will take you to the land of the mammoth and to my village."

"We hurry-go now?" she asked still crying.

"No," he answered with a smile. "We don't need to hurry or to run. We can go at our own pace-go slow!"

"Go slow?" she asked.

"Yes," he replied still smiling. "We go slow."

"I can go sleep?" she asked still in a tearful voice and gently crying.

"Yes, you can go back to sleep-sleep more."

She gently pulled his hand to her lips and giving them a third kiss, but then alertly looked up.

"Men, Ilalke, come yes, maybe!" she asked with a hint of excitement.

"I will watch," he answered. "You can go back sleep."

Her crying eased but still sniffling, she asked, "You stay?"

At first Harjo wasn't quite sure what she meant. He briefly pondered her question and then replied, "yes."

Onna wiped the tears from her face then slipped down into the soft mammoth wool bed pulling the top pelt up over her shoulder. She then turned over on her right side and pulled her knees up. Harjo also got up off his knees and repositioned himself so that he sat on the bison robe leaning against the sled and could watch back toward the direction of the Canineqmiut village. Onna, somehow, reached out then grasped the little finger on his left hand and pulled it down near to her face. Harjo relaxed to allow her to manipulate his hand so that now she lay holding his left hand next to her nose and lips. Harjo sat, somewhat uncomfortable, with the palm of this right hand flat on the bison robe. It did not take long, and she relaxed her grip on his finger. He could tell by her breathing she was sound asleep. She was still exhausted from her desperate flight.

He gently pulled his hand free then turned and got up on his knees with both hands on the top sled rail. He reached down brushing her hair back toward her ear and still again marveled at its color-the color of the fall grass or the yellow ocher paint he thought. He adjusted the mammoth bed top pelt over her shoulder. Then, the same as last night, he was unable to help himself, he bent down and kissed her tear-smudged face receiving a salty taste. Deep in sleep, Onna breathed quietly then with a childlike sigh moved her lips and slightly opened her mouth. Bending down toward her again, he put his nose to her lips and smelled her breath. It was intoxicating and stirred his young, warm blood. With a little more daring, he tenderly kissed the side of her mouth then discovered his manhood had grown to a ridged erection.

Moving his head back, he admired her beautiful sleeping face with such a dirty, smelly, little body. He quietly laughed to himself then softly spoke out to her in a whisper. "Now my beautiful little Onna, we need a plan and preparation. We do not need to hurry but we need to take advantage of the snow-covered frozen ground. Once the snow melts and the frozen ground thaws, it will be much more difficult to pull the sled across the dried grass steppe.

And when we reach the Echota River Valley just where will my family and the Wind Band be and how far will they have migrated from the winter village up the river valley to the first spring camp?"

He thought again, feeling a strange since of responsibility. Everyone he knew could take care of themselves or otherwise be taken care of should some tragedy befall him—until now. Every child in the Wind Band, including his younger sister Chucuse would be provided for if he did not return to the Echota Valley. Now it was different. He must teach Onna the knowledge she would need to travel to the Echota River on her own should something happen to him. It was a new, somewhat strange feeling. It did not cause him anxiety; it just could not be put off.

Chapter 10:

PREPARING

Harjo leaned against the large backrest rock near the fire. He had just retied his bird dart and examined it. He considered making another bird dart then decided one would suffice. He inspected each of his darts, looking down the length then straightening each as needed. If necessary, a shaft could be heated by the fire and straightened. He checked each bone notch at the notching end, the feather fletching, and most certainly, the points and bindings.

He heard a soft voice say his name. He looked over to see Onna was awake, sitting up, and smiling. He smiled too and repeated her name, "Onna." She had not slept very long as it was mid-day, the weather sunny, warm, and beautiful.

"Harjo," Onna said smiling. "I can wet?"

"Yes," he replied then pointing around. "There is plenty of tall grass."

"Harjo," she giggled. "I no can have clothes."

Harjo followed her path then began laughing. "Oh," he said laying the darts aside. He got up, shook the bison robe out, and took it to her laying it on the sled. When he turned to walk back to the fire, she got up, wrapped herself in the robe, and gently made her way back to the tall grass. Harjo put away his dart making material. When Onna finished urinating, she returned and set down on the end of the sled. Harjo brought her a ladle of tea and she took it with a big smile and a thank you.

"I'll leave for a while so you can have some privacy," stated Harjo. "After I return, we'll talk and devise a plan. Do you understand?"

Onna looked up from taking a drink and shook her head. "No understand."

Harjo thought for a moment then tried a different language path. "I'll go hunt. You clothes and eat. Understand?"

Onna nodded her head. "Yes, understand clothes, eat. No understand plan?"

"Plan," Harjo thought. "We need clothes, food, and weapons to travel to the land of the mammoth. A plan is how we prepare-get ready."

Onna replied, "Yes, plan, get ready, go mammoth land." She finished with the ladle and put it in her lap.

Harjo thought again. "Can you whistle?"

Onna looked up and shrugged her shoulders. He could determine from her expression she did not understand. He raised his hand pointing to his mouth and then over emphasizing his actions formed his lips and let out a quiet whistle. Onna looked up with an astonished face smiling. He whistled several more whistles with each one a little more loudly until the last one was so loud a smiling Onna put her hands over her ears. It was more of a playful gesture than to protect her ears.

Harjo pointed to his mouth and said, "Whistle."

Onna repeated the word, "Whistle."

"Can you whistle?" Harjo asked.

Onna made several futile attempts and smiling as though it was a game said, "No can do"

"We need an alert technique, a danger signal. Perhaps you could just yell."

"Danger," Onna said as though she had a solution. She then put her hands together forming a "cup or bowl shape" that put her thumbs together. Taking a deep breath, she blew through the knuckles of her thumbs to produce a loud, strange whistling sound. She stopped and looked at Harjo laughing. She formed her hands and whistled again then, showing off; she altered the pitch of the whistle by opening and closing the palm of her hand. The pitch was very loud and should carry a long distance.

Now curious, Harjo got down on his knees in front of her and said. "Show me." Smiling, Onna opened her left hand and put her fingers together. Harjo reached up taking her hand and turned it so as to see. Onna reached out her hand touching his, then turned her hands to afford him a better view.

She continued to demonstrate her technique. She placed the combined fingers of her left hand at the palm base of her right hand then wrapped her right hand around then cupping her left hand so that her thumbs were adjacent. She then blew on the knuckles of her thumbs, which formed a small opening into her cupped hands. The loud whistle came out.

"Danger!" she said.

Harjo made several unsuccessful attempts at the hand whistle. They laughed together as though enjoying a game. Onna took his hand helping him form the correct hand configuration. He remained unsuccessful however, at producing the hand whistle. But it would make a perfect danger signal. It would carry far and more important, there would be no mistake in its meaning. Harjo wanted to make certain they had an understanding.

"If there is danger," he said making a serious face, "you use hand whistle. Understand?"

"Yes!" she replied. "Hand whistle for danger."

"Yes," Harjo agreed, "Good. I will come running for you. I will come fast. Understand?"

Onna looked at Harjo with an expression of relief. "You will come I, yes danger? You will help I, yes danger?'

"Yes, said Harjo with a sincere expression looking into her face. Onna saw the sincerity in his face and smiled.

"The hand whistle is only for danger," he said sternly. "Understand?"

"Yes," she replied. "Hand whistle-danger only-you come, run I. No uses-you come I. Use danger-only!" Onna said "only" as though she was giving herself an order.

"Good," said Harjo and they both seemed pleased with their plan.

Harjo got up then took his spear from the adjacent rock and held it out. "Understand spear?"

"Yes," she replied, "harpoon."

Harjo chucked to himself because the harpoon was the weapon the Canineqmiut men use to hunt sea mammals. But harpoon was close enough for now. Harjo took his spear and demonstrated how to hold it using a fighting stance. He held it with both hands separated about shoulders length with the lethal point aimed at approaching danger. Onna watched intensely.

"If danger comes," Harjo said in a serious, fatherly voice, "Stand with harpoon—face danger-do not run. Understand?"

"Yes," she replied with a serious manner.

"Danger comes," said Harjo still in his fatherly tone, "You talk me."

Onna looked up for a moment, deep in thought, and then she answered. "Danger hand whistle-stand hold harpoon-face danger-no run."

"Very good," said Harjo well pleased. He laid his spear across her lap.

Onna looked up. "You can have harpoon—you danger."

Harjo pointed to his darts. "I have little harpoons." Onna then recognized Harjo's darts and atlatl then realized he was well protected. She was familiar with all hunting weapons. She noticed Harjo's atlatl. Carved from ivory, she saw it was an extraordinary weapon.

He pointed to her clothes tied and draped on the braided rawhide line. "I washed your clothes. They should be dry."

"You wash clothes I?"

"Yes, I did." Onna was becoming overwhelmed. No one had done such things for her, at least, not in so many long seasons.

"Thank you," did not seem enough but it was what she said.

Harjo walked over to the stack of pelts and supplies, grabbed the woman's bag his mother had given him for the journey then returned to Onna getting down on his knees in front of her. Onna immediately recognized a well-sewn woman's bag.

"You can have good bag Harjo; same grandma can sew."

"Yes," he replied, "my mother made it for me to use during my journey."

Then Harjo recalled the poor condition of Onna's bag and his mother's words, expecting that he would give the bag to a pretty girl. He handed the bag out to Onna.

"I give this bag to you."

Onna paused. She was taken back. She looked into his face with a serious expression. "Harjo, mother you, give you journey."

"Yes," he answered, "and she told me to give it to a pretty girl. You are the prettiest girl I know. You have-you keep-for our journey to the land of the mammoth."

It was all too much for young emotional Onna. She hugged the bag to her breast and began to softly cry. Still wrapped in the bison rope and hugging the bag, she stood up. Instinctively, Harjo also stood. Onna stepped toward Harjo and put her head against his chest. With caution, Harjo put his arms around her and gently pulled her to him.

She gently cried as she spoke. "Harjo, thank you, thank you." She wanted to say more but that was all her limited vocabulary allowed.

Harjo held her for a while then he gently took Onna's shoulders and sat her back down on the end of the sled. Cautiously, he opened the bag, sorted through it, and brought out the small pouch of soap and handed it to her. She opened the pouch to immediately recognize the substances and smiled.

"I can wash?" she asked.

"Yes," he replied.

Onna put the pouch in her lap with the ladle and bag drawing in her breath and making an "oh" sound. Then she lightly clapped her hands together and turned to Harjo then exclaimed, "Thank you, Harjo!" She clapped her hands again.

Harjo was surprisingly taken back. He had never seen anyone clap their hands together to express joy or delight. Her unknown gesture brought a smile to his face. Chuckling, he answered, "You are welcome."

"Servant girl no can wash."

"Yes" he answered, "I thought so."

Onna held up the soap pouch and asked, "How you talk?"

Harjo thought for a moment. The Canineqmiut do not have a word for soap, only urine. So, he told her in Muscogee. "Soap, it is called soap." Onna repeated the word over to herself.

Harjo stood up. "Alright," he declared. "I will go hunt. You can eat, drink tea, you have warm water, wash, put on dry clothes and rest."

Onna reached out, taking his hand then kissed the back of it. She then looked up and smiled at him and whispered a gentle, "Thank you." The gesture was the same the Muscogee people use to show thanks and appreciation.

"You are welcome," said Harjo.

He donned his belt with his attached fore shaft quiver and knife, his dart quiver, and slipped his atlatl in to his belt. He grabbed the bird dart and a small game bag from his supply pile then turned to walk away but remembered something and turned back. "We should make sure that our danger whistles are good."

Harjo could tell she did not quite understand, so he repeated, make sure. "I'll go hunt. I'll make one loud whistle. You hear. You make one loud hand whistle. Make sure danger whistle good. Understand?"

"Yes," Onna replied. "One whistle you-one whistle I-make sure good."

With an approving nod, Harjo headed down slope. He turned and looked back at Onna. She still sat on the sled with his "harpoon" in her lap and she smelled the pouch of soap then she looked up, smiling at him. He returned the smile and went on.

"What a beautiful, but smelly girl," he thought to himself. "She comes far from the west. But just where is that and how did she pass over the great glaciers?"

Harjo decided he would hunt down the little stream toward the coast. If by some chance the Canineqmiut came from the village, they would need to pass him to get to Onna and the camp. Lions and bears very seldom range to the coast. In fact, the only possible dangerous animal would be the musk ox, but they would not approach the camp or the fire. Onna would be perfectly safe. In fact, she will never be safer than where she is now.

After he had gone a distance, he stopped. He let out one loud whistle then waited. Then he heard one of Onna's hand whistles. He waited a little longer. All was silent. "Good," he said to himself then continued on to find some ptarmigan.

Onna eagerly took advantage of this moment alone. It had been so long since she had any privacy. First, although naked but wrapped in the bison robe and barefoot, she walked away from the camp to leave dung and urine behind the large stones and tall grass, then covered the remains with snow. Next, soap and warm water.

It was wonderful, gloriously wonderful, to bathe and to wash her hair and even though the air was stingingly cold, the fire and the robe warmed her. While she was bathing, Onna felt, then examined, the stinging welt marks left on her bottom from her master's wicked switch. In one respect she felt lucky-at least he did not rape her. Usugan managed to stop him from forcing her.

"I must forget this," she said out loud to herself, "and enjoy the small comforts I have now been given." She dressed in her old worn clothes but at least they were reasonably clean and dry. She then filled up on the delicious mammoth stew and tea. Oh, it had been so long since she had tasted mammoth. It seems as though it were another life, so long ago. Again, she warned herself to stop thinking about it or she would start to cry.

Then, she snooped around Harjo's pile of furs and supplies. Not unstacking anything just "snooping around." She then went through her new woman's bag, a gift from Harjo, which held the soap and bowls and found a comb. She knew a woman packed this bag; a man would not pack bowls or a comb. Men use tied bundles of stout twigs to care for their hair for some reason and seldom use combs. At first, she thought "his wife" but remembered he was on his Rite-of-Passage, so he was not married. His mother or sister probably packed the bag for him as a gift for his journey. She likewise went through her old woman's bag taking a quick stock-her rabbit skin, rabbit skin fur, grass pads for menstruation, and sewing kit. She carefully packed those items into her new bag.

She gathered some wood and tended the fire and was then content to sit on the soft mammoth bed on the sled and comb her hair. She had not felt good for so long. She found herself singing and also enjoyed the antics of the busy snow buntings. Then, she reminded herself she must cut some roasting sticks for the small game Harjo would certainly bring back to camp. Also, she must take the mammoth bed from the sled and make a bed in a good spot on the ground. They would both need the bed tonight.

She was apprehensive about sleeping with Harjo. She was afraid of sex. Then she said to herself out loud. "He is a brave boy with deep honor. He is like my father and he would not hurt me." Now that she thought about it, it would be a relief to sleep with someone who would protect her.

Cheparney taught Harjo and the other boys as well, to practice every day with dart and spear. "Every day," he would say, "not every other day and the morning was best to be prepared for the day's events." He fondly recalled his advice. Often his father would remind him and his brothers to practice every day while they were practicing.

Harjo manufactured a fore shaft just for practice. It did not have a stone point but instead was hafted with a straight bone point without barbs or shoulders. Stone points would, of course, break during practice, but a bone point could be used over and over again.

Selecting a clump of grass as a target, Harjo took many practice throws from various distances. He also practiced with both hands. He could not throw a dart very well left-handed; he could, however, launch his spear equally well with either hand. He rarely missed the target with dart or spear. After a little practice, he looked for some small game.

Harjo was able to bring down five ptarmigan, which would make a tasty meal for two. He pulled the heads of each bird to bleed it a little, then carried them in his small game pouch. He did not want to get the blood of the birds on his parka, pants, or boots. A successful Mammoth Hunter carried no scent, even that of a bird. He was proud of one throw as the bird took wing fast in a straight-out flight. Harjo struck him in the air a good distance out. It was early afternoon, so he headed back to camp to see how Onna was doing.

As he approached the camp, Harjo saw Onna sitting on the bison robe combing her hair. He had hoped she would rest but noticed she had been busy around camp. She had moved the mammoth bed placing it in a likely spot on the ground then taken some short sticks placing them inside the bed to prop it open to air it out. She washed his caribou shirt and had it drying on the rawhide line. He also noticed cut roasting sticks and a fresh pile of firewood stacked by the fire.

When she saw Harjo, Onna got up and ran to him greeting him with his name-Harjo. He returned the greeting with her name-Onna.

She held out the comb and said, "I use comb, yes?"

"Yes, it is good you use. We will share."

He had already learned to recognize her expression just before she asked a question. "What is share?"

"Share is-you use, and I use, same."

"Yes, share," she smiled then stuck the comb in her hair. "I wash." She held her arms out then turned around so he could see her back and front were clean.

"Very good clean girl." Harjo reached into his bag and held up the ptarmigan.

Onna's face brightened up, then she clapped her hands together. "Oh Harjo, white bird-good eat. Canineqmiut boys catch white bird, I no have eat."

"Well then, I'll clean the birds and we will eat them," said Harjo as they walked toward the camp. He slipped the game bag over his shoulder.

Onna reached out and gently took the birds. "Onna clean, cook birds, you fire."

Harjo decided to wash while there was still lingering sunlight. He undressed and wrapped in the bison robe, went to a somewhat secluded spot by the stream. He then decided to take a "very quick" dip in the icy stream. Onna heard his splashing and yelps and watched as he ran back to the fire wrapped in the robe. This whole antic set Onna to laughing in a way she had not laughed for so long. Harjo put on his second pair of pants, boots, and his caribou shirt then tied the clothes he wore this day up on the line to dry.

Onna cleaned the ptarmigans and slowly roasted the succulent game on the fire coals. They feasted on the birds, left over mammoth stew and tea. Harjo thought they should stop drinking the Canineqmiut tea. He wanted to take the tea to his mother but was beginning to like the taste of it as well as her. He would pick and dry some Mammoth Hunter tea as it remained abundant in the Coastal Zone. He was reminded the Canineqmiut call the tea *ayuk*. Then he and Onna watched the sun sink into the distant horizon. There were no clouds to reflect the flush, but the sunset remained beautiful, nonetheless.

"Alright," announced Harjo. "Let's make a plan."

"Yes, yes," responded Onna, clapping her hands. "Make plan."

"Can you sew?" asked Harjo.

Onna looked at Harjo with an expression to say of course, silly. "All woman can sew, Harjo. I can sew good clothes. No clothes same grandma-good clothes."

"Yes, of course-good. Tomorrow you will sew a good pair of boots, *mukluk*, for you. Use any of the sea mammal pelts you need." He pointed to the stack of pelts.

"You have needle and sinew?"

"Yes," Onna replied, becoming excited.

"I have needles, sinew, awls, and other sewing tools," explained Harjo. "We share."

Onna was so excited she thought she might not be able to sleep. To be allowed to sew a new pair of boots that she could own and wear thrilled her. She clapped and repeatedly said "Thank you" over and over. But she also knew she must tell Harjo of her fear of sex. She must always be truthful with him.

"Harjo?" asked Onna. "I, you sleep, mammoth bed?"

"Yes, of course," he replied. "Why do you ask?"

"Harjo, I want sleep you, I afraid sex.

She wished she could explain in a more elegant manner, but she could not in this Yupik language. She started to say something else, but then just cupped her hands together under her chin in the same manner as before and lowered her head.

Harjo reached out, touching the side of her face and she looked up. "We just have sleep. No sex." Onna looked into his face and saw his sincerity. She reached up, taking his hand, then turned her head to the side and kissed his palm.

"Go sleep now?" she asked. Harjo smiled and nodded his head yes.

Harjo walked away from camp to urinate as Onna took off her clothes arranging them by the bed so they would air out and dry. Her clothes were not wet, so she did not need to tie them on the rawhide line. She then climbed into bed.

When Harjo returned and seeing Onna in bed, he thought to himself, "How do girls go so long without urinating?" Harjo made certain all was prepared. He looked around finding a least traveled spot on the edge of camp away from the fire and bed, then looking up into the night sky, he first located the Big Dipper and then the North Star. He drew a line in the snow with his foot that aligned with the star and topped the line with a point. Then he loaded wood on the fire and made sure his first set of clothes was drying on the line. He placed his weapons by the bed, took off his boots, pants, and parka placing them by the bed and got in.

Harjo and Onna lay side-by-side facing each other. Harjo closed his eyes and seemed to be going to sleep but Onna lay awake looking at Harjo. She could just make him out by the light of the camp fire and could feel wonderful heat coming from him. Onna's mother told her that body heat was the sign of a good husband. A good husband always had an overabundance of body heat to share with his wife especially on cold winter nights. Good body heat from the man means a long happy marriage.

"Harjo," whispered Onna.

"Yes," mumbled Harjo.

"You sleep, yes?"

Harjo could not help but smile. "I sleep, no."

"Harjo, bottom cold-switch hurts."

Harjo thought for a moment. He had forgotten about the welts on her backside but then recalled the skin was not broken so there would be no infection, but still lingering soreness.

"Do you want to move against me? Don't be afraid, I remember, no sex." "Yes-good-thank you Harjo," she whispered.

Onna rolled over and vigorously snuggled her cold and still painful bottom up against Harjo's hot stomach. She also welcomed that he put his warm, muscular arm across her shoulder and breasts then tenderly cupped her left breast in his powerful, calloused hand.

Harjo could smell her. As some strange exotic flower, she emitted the most pleasant and exciting female aroma he had ever experienced. In addition to her scent, she was marvelously soft and warm, and he could not help but achieve an erection.

Onna could also feel his erection but it did not alarm her. She knew he would keep his word and he was so wonderfully warm. She felt comfortable and safe. They slept as would two satisfied lovers. Onna had not slept this content in so many long seasons.

Chapter 11:

SEWING

Perhaps the morning sun or the chattering snow buntings woke Onna. She did not want to get up, but she had to wet and knew she could not wait much longer. Then she suddenly realized she was alone. She reached out felling for Harjo, but he was gone. Taking a deep breath, she sighed a sleepy moan. It was wonderful sleeping with him. She smiled to herself as she stretched. He was warm, strong, and he smelled so good. Not only did she feel warm and comfortable, but also safe. She felt relaxed and without fear. She had not slept safe, void of fear, since she slept with her parents-so far away-so long age. Then she realized she had to see what he was doing which motivated her to quickly sit up.

Now, fully awake, she saw he was practicing throwing his darts. She also noticed his harpoon was still next to the bed where he left it for her, and a fire was burning. She asked herself, "How could he get up, get dressed, build a fire, and go throw darts and not wake her up? Do I sleep that soundly?" She also noticed the bison rope was on the bed with her clothes. He must have placed it there.

She slipped out of bed, wrapped herself in the bison robe, and stepped off toward the rocks and tall grass. She flushed some snow buntings on the way. The busy little birds flew only a short distance then landed to chatter at her. She turned to see if Harjo was watching and saw he was busy throwing a dart, so without hesitation, she squatted. She then made her way to the small stream where a flat rock, adjacent the bank, created a perfect location to reach the water. The air was cold this morning and so was the rock. Braving the cold, however, she got down and plunged her hands into the icy stream and washed out her mouth and drank. "Oh! Oh!" she reported out loud as the water was nearly frozen. Nonetheless, she quickly washed her face, vulva, vagina opening, and behind which were all she could endure on this crisp morning.

She then returned to the bed, dressing as quickly as she could. She went to the fire hoping there was warm tea. "Oh, wonderful," she said to herself, "Harjo brewed some morning tea." She drank a ladle full, picked up Harjo's harpoon, and then ran toward him.

"Harjo," she called out as she ran to him, all in smiles. He stopped, turned and likewise smiled as she came up to him.

"Morning, Harjo," she said still in smiles.

"Yes, morning," he replied as he held out his hand to her and she responded with hers. He took her hand and kissed it. Her heart suddenly fluttered like the snow buntings.

"He kissed my hand," she thought. Now blushing and smiling, she held out his spear. "I can throw?" she asked.

"Most certainly," he answered.

"Show I yes?" she asked again holding out his spear. Harjo slid his atlatl into his belt and took the spear. Onna would ask about his throwing board later but now watched. She made a face as Harjo pulled the fore shaft from the spear and pushed it into his fore shaft quiver. Then he pulled the practice fore shaft from the dart and was attaching it to the spear.

"Why no can have sharp?" asked Onna still with a puzzled expression.

Harjo taught the term 'point' and explained the use of practice points so as to spare breaking the projectile point, wasting the hard work required to manufacture one. He also demonstrated the fighting stance then allowed her practice under his supervision using a newly acquired "fatherly voice" he reminded her.

"Allow the charging danger to run into the spear. Never forget, keep fighting. Anything can be a weapon, rocks, and sticks, even dirt. If you have no weapons, fight with your hands." Onna listen intensely.

Harjo then demonstrated how to make a fighting lunge by taking a small step and by driving with the force of her back leg not just her arms. She was strong, and with practice, he told her she would be able to drive the spear completely through an animal or an Enemy Warrior. Finally, he showed her how to throw a spear. Onna was serious but these instructions were also to a large extent fun for her. It had been long since she played or enjoyed anything fun. Harjo's companionship and learning from him was all the more wonderful. She then attempted her first throw at the target. It was a disastrous toss. The spear traveled only short distance then hit flat on the ground. Laughing, Onna ran to retrieve the spear.

Harjo chuckled to himself. She runs and throws like a girl. He recalled when he and his boyhood playmates laughed and made fun of the way girls ran and threw. Now he thought of it in a different light. He enjoyed watching her run and throw "like a girl."

Onna attempted several more unsuccessful throws and was disheartened by her futile efforts. Harjo encouraged her and explained not to worry about throwing. It only takes practice. The fighting stance and lunging were the most important. Onna had never learned anything about using a man's weapons and she thoroughly enjoyed it.

"Enough practice for today," declared Harjo. "We should eat, and we have work to do. You have boots to sew."

"Oh-yes-yes!" cried Onna out loud and laughing. She placed the spear on the inside of her forearm the way Harjo did and clapped her hands with delight.

As they walked back to camp, they heard a distant ptarmigan. "Uh oh," laughed Onna. "Maybe can have white bird tonight-eat."

"It's a male," declared Harjo.

Onna looked at Harjo with a puzzled face. "What is male?" she asked.

"Do you know male and female?"

Onna thought for a moment. "No understand."

Harjo pointed to himself and said "man" and then pointed to Onna and said "woman."

"Do you understand?"

"Yes," replied Onna still smiling but she wondered what he meant.

"Male is man animal and female is woman animal. Understand?" asked Harjo.

Onna rolled it over in her mind saying the words, male and female, then with a little smile, reported. "Yes, man and woman-human. Male and female-animal."

Onna looked at him again with an adorable puzzled look on her face. "How you know bird male?"

Harjo explained it was the beginning of early mating season and the males were calling to locate and attract a mate. Harjo made the different calls explaining the male and female sounds. Onna tried at producing the low whistles and chuckling sounds of the ptarmigan. Alas, her calls were not very ptarmigan like. She looked at Harjo smiling then declared, "Take practice!"

Harjo just laughed but went on to explain an adult pair will raise a brood of chicks of eight to twelve. As the chicks mature, the brood becomes a covey, the parent birds and young adult chicks. Eventually, the parents break away and will raise another brood the following season. The adult chicks remain together as a covey from one summer to the next but eventually break up seeking mates of their own and to raise their own brood.

They ate hurriedly. Onna was anxious to get started. They went over to the stack of sea mammal pelts. Harjo told Onna she could select the pelts she wanted to use. He became stern with her.

"Do not work fast. Go slow, do good work, sew good boots. We can stay here today, tomorrow, and next day. As long as needed. Understand?"

"Understand," she replied, "Work, sew slow, good, no fast."

Hunting was a man's life-long occupation and sewing was a woman's. Tailored clothing, sewn by women from the pelts of a vast variety of animals, allowed men to hunt in the unforgiving landscape of the Mammoth Steppe. Without tailored clothes, survival would be bleak. The small, seeming insignificant, bone needle in the hands of a skilled seamstress remained an apogee of importance as a tool of survival. The needle, which in turn produced tailored clothes, was the heuristic invention that made the difference between human life, human culture, human aspirations, and animal existence on the great cold steppe.

Men could likewise sew and carried basic stitching tools while on distant hunting trips. A cut or ripped boot left unmended on snow-covered ground rendered disastrous and deadly consequences. A man cared little for aesthetics or craftsmanship only survival. Accordingly, Harjo carried a sewing kit and additionally, his mother packed extra sewing tools in his women's "gift" bag.

Even a poor servant girl like Onna was allowed to keep a sewing kit and a woman's bag. A complete woman's sewing kit would contain needles, needle cases, spindles of sinew thread, awls, boot sole creasers and crimpers, and knives. Men crafted sewing tools for women from bone, or better still, from ivory. A man took pride in carving and decorating sewing tools for his woman, especially needle cases and awls. Carved by a man from ivory and finely decorated, an awl or a needle case was a woman's most treasured possession. Combining the sewing kit Onna brought with her on her escape from Up'nerkillermiut, with Harjo's emergency kit, and the excellent tools provide in the kit by Harjo's mother, Onna was well equipped to sew a pair of boots, even though none of the tools were decoratively carved or the type of sewing tools treasured by a woman. Although her *uluaq* knife served well for skinning and scraping hides, it was not the best tool for cutting hides.

Thus, so motivated, Harjo took one of his fore shafts and cut the shaft so as to create a knife handle instead of a fore shaft. He wrapped the handle with a strip of rawhide forming a good knife for Onna. He reworked the end so that it would still fit into a spear socket and thus fashioned a short but still effective spear point. When Harjo presented the knife to Onna, she was nearly driven to happy tears. No man had ever made such a beautiful knife for her and she did not know such spectacular red stone existed. Onna wanted to show her deep gratitude to Harjo but did not want him to think she was sexually teasing him. She wanted affection but the idea of engaging in sex still frightened her, but still she needed to be honest with him and herself. She paused for a moment and slowly but with purpose, moved against him then reached up and put her hands on the back of his hooded head.

"No same sex," she said, "Same thank you."

She stood up on her toes then gently pulled his head down and reaching up, kissed him full on the mouth. The kiss ended but she was still looking into his face.

"No one good I, much long, Harjo."

A simple, "You are welcome," was all Harjo said.

"I make *mukluk*," said Onna. "I work slow," she said as though giving herself an order. Harjo agreed.

Although to herself Onna thought, "His kiss was wonderful, and his breath was warm and pleasant. He is so strong and healthy. Am I falling in love with him?"

Onna selected her seal pelts. She took one of the large thick pelts of the bearded seal to use as the sole, the most important part. These types of seal the Canineqmiut call *mukluk*. In fact, Onna recalled they also use this term to mean boot. She also noticed one hide of the small spotted sea mammal and selected it for the tops of her boots. In Yupik the term is *issuriq*. Women appreciate that colorful spotted pelt. She gathered all the tools and laid everything out on the bison robe then began to work. She was excited and had to force herself to stay calm and to follow Harjo's instructions to work at a slow, steady pace and not hurry the job.

She laid the large pelt "fur down" and using a fire-blackened stick, traced out the pattern of both her feet to use as a guide for the sole. Keeping the pelt fur side down, she cut out the sole patterns. Her new knife of red chert was keenly sharp. Again, she thought, "What a wonderful gift." She would also sew a sheath for it. She knew Harjo would re-sharpen it for her when it became dull. To complete her sewing kit, she also cut a small round "thumb size" piece of pelt and cut a long slit in it to become a thimble. Eventually, she would cut the boot tops from the spotted sea mammal.

A sea mammal pelt is exceptionally thick and hard. Therefore, it requires the use of the awl to punch stitching holes. Once the stitching holes were made, Onna would bend the soles up around the borders and crimp about the heels and toes with the crimper tool. Then, carefully she sewed the parts together using the sinew thread, and of course, needles. She could take extra stitches, as necessary, allowing the thick sole was difficult to stitch without awl-punched holes. The boot tops, however, could be pierced by the needles alone. Finally, she planned to attach strips of rawhide to the side at the ankles as tie straps to wrap around the ankles and tie at the tops. Later, she planned to attach strips of hare pelt at the tops and perhaps on the ends of the tie straps as decoration.

Harjo likewise stayed busy. He followed the stream, locating a stand of tall straight willow trees just the right size to fashion Onna a spear. He cut one of the smaller trees, stripped the bark, and shaped the head. Harjo carried two extra spears or dart sockets. He attached one to Onna's spear. Then, he shortened one of his fore shafts, reshaped the end, and fit it into the socket. Finally, he sharpened and fire-hardened the butt end. Onna now had a good spear her own size. Also, she could fit her newly created knife into the socket as a fore shaft to form a short, but still lethal point. And for a finishing measure, he fashioned a wooden point she could use for practice throwing.

Harjo also took advantage of the hard wood stand to cut poles to construct a "pole-travail" should it be necessary to transport more load later in the journey. He notched the poles for fitting but left them unassembled. For now, four poles were easily attached to the sled and could be drying out for future use.

Late in the afternoon, Harjo went out hunting and returned with a hare. Onna wanted to keep the hide so he staked it out on the ground at the edge of camp. He also found a patch of mammoth hunter tea and picked some leaves to start drying.

After a meal of rabbit, they sat by the fire watching the sun set. Onna took Harjo's arm and then putting it around her, leaned against him.

"Oh Harjo, wonderful day."

Harjo agreed. Suddenly, a shadow caught their eye and they looked up to see a snow owl silently fly by overhead.

"Big white bird hunt night," stated Onna. They watched as the owl silently flew on. Harjo was beginning to anticipate Onna's questions. She was uniquely inquisitive.

"Can see day Harjo?" she asked.

"Yes, they often hunt in the day."

"Have call?"

'No, they are noiseless."

"Hunter quiet-kill animal."

"Yes," he answered. There was a short quiet pause.

"Why do you talk so much?" Harjo asked smiling.

"I girl Harjo," Onna replied laughing. "Woman, girl, talk all day. Woman, girl sew, weave, make eat, talk. Men hunt, no talk. I like talk you, Harjo. You like talk I?"

"Yes, I do," replied Harjo. "I enjoy talking with you. And I am fond of hearing you talk. Your voice is-well, pleasant to hear."

Onna reached her hand up and lovingly rubbed his chest, smiled, and snuggled up against him.

"Speaking of talking, I will need to teach you the Mammoth Hunter's language," Harjo said in a matter-of-fact tone as though he dreaded the thought.

Raising her head up, Onna looked in to Harjo's face. "I can talk Mammoth Hunter's language," she replied with a sly little vixen smile.

Harjo was just beginning to realize just how quick witted she was. "You need to learn the Muscogee Mammoth Hunter language."

"Can talk Yupik," suggested Onna as a language alternative.

"Yes, we can," Harjo replied slowly. "But in the Wind Band, only my mother, sister, and I speak Yupik. And my father speaks a little Yupik. But everyone else speaks the Muscogee Mammoth Hunter's language, which is the language you need to learn."

Onna took in a deep breath and expelled it as though exhausted. "Yes, yes, can. Teach I Mammoth Hunter talk."

"First learn I, my and me in Yupik," stated Harjo in his fatherly teacher voice.

Onna repeated, "I, my, me," as though it was one word, smiling.

Harjo looked at her with a stern expression as she smiled back. "I, my, and me are three words, not one," he stated.

"I-my-me, three word, no one," she spoke as though playing a game rather than learning a language.

"Now, if I were to say, I want to kiss you," stated Harjo.

Onna cocked her head with an adorable expression, smiling. "You want kiss I?"

Harjo could not help but to laugh out loud. He continued as seriously as he could, Onna being such a delightful learner, quickly caught on to the use and meaning of I, my, and me.

"Enough for today," said Harjo with less than an enthusiastic pitch.

"Enough today," repeated Onna, her voice patient but weary.

But then, she thought of something that brought a little zest to her tone.

"I teach you language my Tribe—they far away."

Her last statement caused Harjo to pause, thinking to himself. Where was her homeland and Tribe? He knew only it was far to the west, but he also realized the story of how she came to the Canineqmiut village must be a tragic tale laced with death and abduction. When she felt comfortable enough, she would tell her story, but Harjo realized it must be difficult to now relive the sorrow. Besides, Harjo was not ready to make a language learning trade, so he did not say anything more. He was tired and Onna as well.

"Bed," said Harjo.

"Yes, bed," answered Onna.

As they lay in bed, Onna was thinking to herself and inspired with some philosophical thought concerning sleeping with Harjo. It was like the two sides of her new knife blade. The strength and power of his arms excited her; it was almost like power she could use or at least direct. But on the other side of the blade, it was also frightening because that same power could easily crush her. She knew he would never hurt her. But she also believed it would be different if he had little or no strength in his arms. The emotional feeling was similar to a lion that was both thrilling and yet frightening. This, by paradox, made it all the more exciting. She sighed, snuggled up against "her warm strong" paradox then drifted off to sleep.

Late in the morning on the next day, Onna called out to Harjo. He had spent part of the morning dressing and tanning the rabbit skin for her. He now recognized when Onna called his name, in the way she just did, it meant to come here and see this. Harjo just finished adding a second harness to the sled rigging. He turned and walked back to the campfire where Onna set on the bison robe working on her boots. As he approached, she was holding up both boots with a big beautiful smile on her face.

"New boots, Harjo!"

He sat down on the robe and she handed him her completed task for his inspection. He examined her wares with a pull then a tug, here and there. Harjo was impressed. Onna sewed a sturdy pair, not fancy, but very usable. She was a far better seamstress that her young age indicated, and she had worked under less than perfect conditions.

"Very good job, Onna, very good. You sew well."

Onna clapped her hands loudly and laughed. "Not good same grandma, but good same girl," she said smiling. She then quickly began to pull off her old boots, grass socks, and pads as Harjo continued to examine the foot wear. Her laughter and joy sent a good feeling through Harjo.

Suddenly, in her bare feet, she crawled across the robe. Harjo looked up to see an unusual serious look on Onna's face as she crawled toward him. She edged close to his face and placed that part of her cheek, which is next to her mouth against his cheek and gently rubbed against him. Then, gently sliding over, she moved her lips to meet his and gave him a kiss.

As the kiss ended, she slowly moved her head back and whispered, "Thank you, Harjo, thank you, skins, tools, make boots."

Harjo was also moved to a moment of seriousness. He reached up and put his hand under her chin and placed his thumb on the front of her chin. He gently pushed down and following his lead, Onna opened her mouth and closed her eyes. Harjo then leaned to her and kissed her full on her open inviting mouth. She was warm, tender, sweet and incomparable.

As they separated, Onna was breathing heavily. She opened her eyes and looked into his face. "Harjo, I afraid, sex. She paused, swallowed, and briefly looked down.

Then, looking back into his face, she asked, "You understand?"

"Yes," he answered without hesitation, "I still understand."

"You can like me, Harjo?"

"Yes, I like you," he answered smiling. "You will be ready when you are ready."

Onna did not say anything but leaned into him giving him another playful rub on his cheek with her cheek.

"Go for walk with your new boots," suggested Harjo.

"Oh, yes," declared an excited Onna as she took the boots and quickly put on her grass socks, stuffed in the grass pads, and pulled on her new footwear. After lacing up the boots, she stood up in all smiles walking around. Harjo also stood up and Onna held out her hand and he took it. "Take me walk, Harjo."

"I'll take you hunting," he replied.

"Oh yes, go hunt," replied a jovial Onna.

Harjo pointed with his spear to her spear on the robe. She bent down, picked it up, and sternly reminded herself, "Always take harpoon-no forget."

The hunting pair combed the small stream. Onna carried her spear and the game bag while Harjo handled his bird dart. It was fun. Onna marveled at how Harjo could bring down a bird both on the run and in flight as she ran to retrieve a downed bird and the dart. They found an appropriate clump of grass to use as a target and Onna took some practice throws with her spear. She was improving. She admired Harjo's weapons, especially his atlatl.

"Harjo, you have good thrower. I can touch?"

"Most certainly," he replied and handed it to her. She examined it, realizing it was an extraordinary piece, manufactured by a craftsman of great skill.

"Talk me thrower?" she asked.

"Certainly," Harjo replied. He paused for a moment than began.

"My grandfather's name was Fus Chate or Red Bird. He was one of the most renowned carvers in the Muscogee Tribe. He carved the atlatl, which has been in my family many, many seasons. Fus Chate wanted his youngest grandson to carry the weapon then pass it on to his son. It is a family heirloom and belongs to all the men in the family. I have been given the honor to carry and use it."

Harjo explained and demonstrated to Onna that the atlatl was carved from bone and the nocking end was an exquisite carved figure of a bird. The "bird beak, nocking end" held the "nock" end of the dart. On Harjo's atlatl, the bird beak end was actually the carved beak of a whole bird. The bird's head was curved so that the bird beak nearly touched the bird's breast and so the dart was "nocked" against the bird's beak and lay along the breast. A grooved channel extended along the length from the bird beak, along the breast of the bird, then to the handle. The dart lay along the channel. Perfect finger grips were carved into the handle and the raised grips served the function of pegs. The atlatl could also be used as a club and was an effective weapon in hand-to-hand combat. Harjo paused for a moment as Onna continued to admire the atlatl.

"My grandfather once had a vision. He saw a beautiful bird, completely red in color with a crested top-notch. It had a yellow bill but also black color around the eyes and bill. No one has ever seen such a beautiful red bird on the Mammoth Steppe. In his vision, the Wind Band was migrating south, and this bird led the way. This is why his name was Fus Chate or Red Bird and why our family is named the Fus Chate family."

"It so beautiful, Harjo," said an admiring Onna with an expression of awe. "You teach me thrower?" asked a wide-eyed Onna as she handed the atlatl back.

Harjo looked up toward the sun to calculate the amount of daylight remaining in the day. "Alright," he replied, "but tomorrow. There is not enough daylight today." Onna put her hands together clapping and smiled.

Onna's boots passed the test. Her hard work brought just rewards. There was absolutely nothing fancy about them, but they were well made and would hold up under the rigors of the Mammoth Steppe for several seasons.

They returned to camp. Certainly, this was an exceptional camping spot but there was nothing to hold them here now. "Tomorrow we leave for the land of the mammoth," confirmed Harjo. Onna could not contain herself, nor did she try. She jumped up and down, clapping her hands.

ᖰᖱᖰᖱᖰᖱ

They eagerly completed their evening chores, drying out their socks and clothes, washing and cleaning the ptarmigan for the evening meal. Onna now had a second pair of boots she could use in emergencies, or better still, to wear around camp while her new pair dried out. As they sat by the fire roasting the birds, Harjo contemplated something important, he must talk with Onna about in preparation for their journey. He also considered their language barrier.

He realized this would be a complicated explanation and probably one of many to come. But he would demonstrate, explain, and they would work through the process. Onna listened intently and she often, although politely, asked questions. Even though she was limited in her grasp

170

of the Yupik language, Harjo was beginning to realize how quick witted and intelligent she really was. She grasped and understood the meaning of complex situations that she otherwise may not be able to explain in Yupik. He needed to teach her Muscogee but that would require several seasons. With her attention, he began.

"Onna, if something should happen to me, you continue on. Take the sled "At this point, a surprised Onna reached up to gently tap Harjo's lips to interrupt with an anxious expression on her face. "No something happen you Harjo. You, me, go same. You take me land of mammoth."

Harjo reached over and took her hand giving it a gentle squeeze. Onna was quiet but wore a worried expression. He continued. "Take the sled, mammoth bed, food and supplies, and continue onto the land of the mammoth and the Echota River Valley. Leave the seal pelts, travel with little weight."

He then picked up his atlatl next to him handing it to her. "Take this atlatl to my family. My mother and sister speak Yupik; my father knows some words as well. They all will welcome you into our family."

Onna looked at the atlatl, gently handling the magnificent weapon. She then looked at Harjo and slowly nodded her head yes. Harjo looked into her face and smiled.

Now Harjo retrieved two types of small game traps from the woman's bag, both were simple but effective. One, a snare trap, was just a length of narrow strong rawhide with an open knot tied at one end to create a noose about the size of a man's fist. The remaining length stretched through a long section of small hollow bone. The end was tied to a branch adjacent a small game trail, usually used by hare, so that the animal running along the trail would be caught by the neck. The bone kept the animal from chewing the rawhide apart. The trap could be set in the evening to snare the prey over night while the hunter slept, hopefully to awake in the morning to an easy meal.

The second was a "death fall" trap utilizing three small, straight sticks, each about a forearm's length. The sticks had been modified and notched so as to be fitted together forming a triangle shape. Then, a heavy weight, a large flat rock worked best, was set on end, leaning with the weight held up by the sticks. One stick, which extended under the raised rock, was baited. The small animal, usually a hare, was attracted to the bait. Then, by moving and jarring the baited stick, the whole triangular shaped sticks collapsed-the rock fell-killing the small animal. Ptarmigan were also taken if willow buds were picked and placed under the bait stick.

Harjo presented the two traps to Onna who laughed. "Yes, yes, understand, can do. Father teach me." Onna took the two traps demonstrating to Harjo how the traps worked. It was as though she was playing a game. Harjo watched in amusement. They would keep the traps in the woman's bag on the side of the sled. Onna may not be successful in hunting but she could certainly trap small game especially hare and ptarmigan. Harjo now asked Onna his final question.

"Do you know about lions?"

"Little," answered Onna. "Father teach. No run from lion! I hear other men talk, but I don't know. You teach me?"

"Of course, I will. That is why I asked you."

Onna first smiled at Harjo then became quiet looking at him listening intently. She wanted to listen and learn. She was a good student.

"Mammoth are the smartest of all animals. They are one-smart. But lions are next. They are two-smart. You already know, do not run from lion. You cannot out run a lion; if you run, he will catch you and kill you. Onna shook her head yes. "Understand."

"Very good," said Harjo. He paused for a moment to make his next point then continued. "You must recognize a male lion. You must know the male lion. He is large. He has longer fur on his neck. He has a loud roar." Harjo paused temporarily to gather his thoughts, then he continued. "He acts like male." Do you understand?"

"Yes, understand," she answered.

"The male lion is not afraid of anything," continued Harjo. "He will attack anything. If you meet a male lion and he has a kill-food, he will attack. If there are baby lions, he will attack. If he thinks his female is in danger, he will attack. If he thinks he can kill you easily, he will attack. But, if you have a spear or a harpoon and you stand, ready to fight, maybe he will not attack. Maybe he will let you back away."

"The female lion is different. She is not like the male. She will attack to protect her babies. Maybe she will attack, if the male is fighting, to help the male in his struggle. But usually, the female will not attack. She will go away herself if you let her or she will let you back away. I know that was a lot of words. Do you understand?"

"Yes!" Onna said seriously. "Teach me more."

"During the spring and summer when they have babies, the male and female are together. The female stays with the babies nursing them. They stay safe and hidden while the male hunts for her."

"Same man, woman," said Onna. Harjo had not thought of it like that before but "yes," he said, "same as a man and woman."

"The male will make a kill. Then, with a loud roar, he will call the female. She will come to eat then go back to the babies. When the babies are older, they will come with her to the kill. Occasionally, the male will drag the kill closer to the female and the babies. Every so often, I have seen the male pull a part of the kill off, the back leg, and carry it closer to the female if the kill is too large to drag. The male is smart. He knows other predators or other lions can follow him if he drags or carries the kill and maybe find his female and babies. So, he will not take the kill all the way to the female and the babies. He stops before he is too close, then calls for them."

"The male and female are together when they have babies and then they generally break up when the babies are old enough to take care of themselves. But some pairs remain together even after the babies are grown. I think the older ones stay together. It is the younger ones that separate." Onna remained quiet-listening intently. "Understand?"

"Yes! Yes!" Onna exclaimed smiling and clapping her hands together. "Tell me more."

"Remember, there can be two. Always watch your back. One may be in the front while one may be in the back. Recognize which one you see, male or female. Consider the season-summer or winter-then you will have a better chance of knowing what they will do. Always be prepared for an attack."

"This is important," Harjo said sternly, "This is what we do if we see a lion. Slowly take off your harness, allowing it drop to the ground. Take your spear, then go to the back of the sled. The sled is between you and the lion. You must watch the back. Call out and tell me if there is another lion at our back. You stand ready to fight with your spear. Watch the back, but glance-look to the front. Understand?"

Onna paused running some of the words in her mind then replied. "Yes, understand."

"The way you move is important. Not fast, not like throwing your spear, but a slow steady movement. Fast movement, especially the head, may create a flash of sunlight on your face. If it does, it will cause the lion to charge.

Do not move your head fast. Move your eyes, not your head. You can see a wide area without moving your head. We will practice tomorrow."

"Oh, yes," said a joyous Onna. She started to clap but then just clasped her hands together under her chin. She laughed and shook with excitement. What wonderful adventures awaited them tomorrow? And more importantly, she was free. Free from the cruelty of a Canineqmiut servant girl. Harjo had given her freedom.

As Harjo advised, they both made good use of the fire and the wood. During the four- or five-day's journey across the treeless Costal Zone, they may camp without a fire. They both washed. Harjo learned that Onna, similar to him and the Mammoth Hunters, was very hygienic. She washed often, combing her hair at least once a day often twice. Of course, she came from a tribe of Mammoth Hunters; nonetheless, he appreciated sleeping with a healthy smelling girl. Because of excitement, Onna thought she would find difficulty sleeping. But, once snuggled against her warm human hearth, her liberator, she soon drifted off.

Chapter 12:

RETURNING

The dawn of great adventure showed bright. Harjo was up kneeling by the fire drinking tea when he heard Onna's quiet, soothing voice. "It morning Harjo-you-I go." Harjo looked to see her setting up in the mammoth bed smiling. She always woke up cheerful, which rubbed off onto him. "Yes, it is a beautiful morning, Onna and yes, we go."

Naked she got up, wrapped the bison robe around her, then took easy steps to the fire and bent over to kiss Harjo. Then she stepped off toward the tall grass to urinate and wash, as was her morning custom. She returned, dressed, drank a healthy portion of tea and ate with Harjo. It did not take long to prepare this morning. They loaded and tied down the sled, and they were ready to depart.

"I will teach you to use the throwing board, atlatl, another day, alright?" Onna shook her head yes in agreement.

They practiced as Harjo described-dropping the sled harnesses-Onna moving with smooth, deliberate motion to the back of the sled. Harjo cautioned, "We will see muskox in the Coastal Zone the next four days. We should not see lion, bear, or bison until we cross over the Coastal Zone and reach the tall grass. We will probably not see mammoth until we reach the Echota Valley. We can always see bad men, and we must always be ready."

Onna shook her head yes with excitement. They stood side by side looking around the camp. Onna thought to herself she would remember this lovely little camping spot for the rest of her life, the place where Harjo had given her freedom and they began this incredible journey.

Harjo noticed Onna held a rawhide chord in her hand, but he did not say anything, although he had an idea what she intended to do with it. Then a question came to Harjo. The answer did not matter to him and he already could nearly guess the answer, but he was still curious.

"How old are you?" asked Harjo.

Onna looked at him with a slight surprise then answered with a smile. "Twelve summer."

"How old you?" she asked.

"Sixteen summers," he replied.

"How many day land of mammoth?" she asked.

"Sixteen," he answered.

"Same old you." She held up her chord. "I count," she said tying a knot in the chord.

They walked to the sled. Onna tied her count chord on the sled, and then they slid their harnesses over their heads. Harjo pointed a direction. "Southeast," he said. They leaned against the sled together and began.

Although the loaded sled was heavy, with Onna's help, it moved easily across the snow-covered tundra as Harjo continued to be surprised by Onna's strength. The morning was anything but quiet and boring, as Onna remained full of endless questions and Harjo stayed eager to explain new discoveries. She confirmed she was much more intelligent than he first imagined, and her lack of understanding was a lack of understanding the Yupik language, rather than of concepts. Although, common to all women and girls, she lacked survival skills. He also came to realize that her homeland, far to the west, was not that much different than his and that she was likewise a child of the Mammoth Steppe.

Harjo began teaching Onna the Muscogee language and although she eagerly learned any other area of wisdom, she was not enthusiastic to learn Muscogee. He explained that as she gained knowledge of the Muscogee tongue, she likewise gained a greater depth of Yupik, as it was the language of communication between them. He also realized his mother will delight in having another female around who spoke Yupik. His sister was maturing and will soon marry and leave with her husband to live in another band.

"Harjo?" she asked. "Someone say I will do. What word?"

He thought for a minute. "Do you mean-promise?"

"Yes!" she replied with the joy of discovery. "Prom-prom. Tell me again!"

He repeated the word slowly. "Promise." She repeated the word out loud then replicated it in a whisper to herself.

"Harjo, must I learn Muscogee language?"

"How else can you live in the valley of the Muscogee with the Muscogee Tribe?"

"I no want. It hard. I no understand Muscogee language."

"You are very smart, and you will learn the language easily."

"I learn Muscogee language; you can learn my language?" she asked in the most pleasant of voices she could conjure.

Harjo stopped, turning to her, as she did likewise. "If I learn your language will you be happy?" he asked.

"Oh yes!" she replied with a glowing face and a smile. "Yes! Yes! Yes!"

"Alright," he replied somewhat begrudgingly. "You learn the Muscogee language and teach me your language."

"Promise?" she asked with that beautiful, vixen smile.

"Yes-I promise"

Onna fitted her spear to the inside of her bent left arm to free her left hand and clapped her hands together. All smiling, she replied. "Harjo, you can make me happy." She again grasped her spear in her left hand and embraced him in a fashion they would repeat often, and she spoke her playful words. "Give me kiss." With a kiss, they were off again.

"What is your language?" he asked.

Onna stopped and Harjo followed. He could tell she struggled but spoke for the first occasion about her past.

"My people-Dyuktai-same our language. I live Valley-Oklan River-winter village name Palana." He reached out, taking her hand and kissed it. She smiled, then they headed on.

"You already know one Muscogee word," Harjo announced.

"I can speak two, you name Harjo and soap," she said with a smile.

Harjo was learning a little more each day how clever she really was. "Yes, my name and soap, but you also know another Muscogee word."

"What word?" she asked.

"Mammoth!" he replied.

"Mammoth?" she asked.

"Yes, mammoth." he answered.

"The Yupik term for mammoth is-*equgaarpak*. But the Canineqmiut seldom use the Yupik word, they use the Muscogee term-mammoth-and not the Yupik word. I don't know why. So now you know three Muscogee words, Harjo, soap and mammoth."

Onna thought about this as they moved on and then replied. "And you four Dyuktai words; Dyuktai, Oklan, Palana, and Onna," she said with a childish smile.

Harjo thought for a moment then responded equally with a less than enthusiastic tone. "I suppose so. And I suppose you will teach your language to your children."

Onna smiled, reaching out and grasped his hand. "Yes! Baby nurse, mother sing, talk baby, baby learn language. Baby learn more language at same-same you."

Harjo chuckled to himself as he recalled on numerous occasions how he, his mother, and sister talked Yupik in front of his father as he sat unaware of the conversation. Occasionally, they talked about him, although he usually intercepted those exchanges. So, it seems history may repeat itself.

Approximately midday, they stopped on top of a small hillock. "Rest and water?" asked Harjo.

"Oh yes," Onna replied. She was panting but she looked at Harjo with such a big, beautiful smile and her cheeks were flushed red. Her smile prompted Harjo to also smile. Harjo slipped off his harness and Onna followed. He took the water pouch and some jerky from the bag and they rested.

"I must teach you something," said Harjo in his fatherly voice.

Onna was always ready to learn something new. "Yes, ready."

"You must pay attention to what is going on all around you, in front, behind, and to the sides. Since we left camp this morning, pulling our sled, have you looked behind us?"

Onna glanced up toward the sky but without moving her head for an instant she then replied, "No look."

"You must learn to look behind you habitually. Lion, bear, and wolf can and will sneak up behind you in deadly silence. Mammoth too, they are usually noisy, but they can be quiet, and they can and will come up from behind and kill you."

"Yes, I know. Father teach. Mammoth same quiet, can walk-can kill. So, can bad men," replied Onna.

Harjo was suddenly taken back by her reply. "Yes," he answered, "And so can bad men." He marveled to himself at her insight.

"How you say bad men?" she asked.

He thought for a moment then answered, "Enemy Warrior".

She repeated the words to herself in a whisper. "How you say bad child?"

Again, Harjo thought for a moment then answered, "Naughty."

Once more she repeated the word to herself, then looked to Harjo seemingly ready to proceed.

Harjo replaced the water bag and they returned to the harnesses. He surveyed the circular horizon, as did Onna. However, Onna took a 'put on' serious face, placed her hands on her forehead as though shading her eyes, and used an exaggerated motion to survey the horizon. Then she looked at him with such a big beautiful grin.

"No see lion."

Harjo could not help but start laughing then he stopped to find his fatherly voice.

"This is serious Onna," he attempted to say with a straight face. "You must look for danger behind you."

Onna tightened her lips to keep from smiling and shook her head yes. And managed a "yes, understand" without too much laughter.

Harjo tried to be serious but still with subtle laughter, they pulled the sled on. He had a good idea of the next camping spot.

⁓◦⁓◦⁓◦⁓

Early in the afternoon, they came to a wide shallow ravine with a small drainage flowing through the rocky gully. It was only a pace wide, but the water was clear and cold. It supported a thick patch of willows and grass, providing a welcome change from the tundra of the Coastal Zone. Harjo camped here on his way to the coast thus he realized this may be the last camping site with any brush or small trees until they reached the grasslands.

Unexpectedly, a small herd of eight to ten muskox flushed from the brush, running away from Harjo and Onna. When she saw them, she called out excited, "Look Harjo, look!"

The shaggy beasts ran but a short distance then formed a circle standing shoulder-to-shoulder with their heads outward. The aggressive lone bull ran around on the outside of the circle, prepared to charge any intruder as last year's yearling calves stayed protected on the inside of the body circle.

"They usually are not dangerous," said Harjo. "If they do charge us, use the sled for protection. Onna understood, shaking her head yes.

The muskox were not large, standing chest high and about three paces long. The stocky animals were not abundant but ranged over the whole steppe from the coast to the interior. Short, stout horns covered the entire top of their heads, curving down and out to a point. Both males and females carried horns on a large thick head. Long hair similar to the mammoth flowed nearly to the ground from their robust shoulders and flanks. The rugged animals seemed to endure anywhere and did not migrate. Abruptly, the bull took flight again out in the lead and the cows followed, shaping into a spear point formation with the calves still in the center. Soon, they were gone.

"I see animals same as Zaliv Valley, Harjo," stated an exuberant Onna. "Oh Harjo, wonderful animals you call muskox!"

"No danger?" asked Onna.

"Danger if you hunt them. The bull is unafraid and will attack anything to protect his herd. There are few in the grass steppe but many more here on the Coastal Zone."

"You eat?" asked Onna.

"I remember only once. They are hard to hunt. Small numbers and they do not migrate, so it is difficult to predict where they will be."

"I eat, no remember," concluded Onna.

Although it was early, they camped on a flat area above the stream. Onna would not admit it, but Harjo could tell that she was tired. She worked hard the first day. Harjo went hunting while Onna rested. The small brushy oasis supported an abundant small game population enabling Harjo to kill several ptarmigan and two hare. They roasted them on the fire. After a short nap, a hot meal, some tea, and the evening tasks completed, the two sat together on the mammoth bed against the sled. Onna discovered she was not too tired for complex questions.

"Harjo?" asked Onna in her alluring childlike voice. "You have wife, yes, what you want her promise?"

Chuckling quietly, Harjo replied, "I have wife, no."

Onna looked at him with a curious frown on her face then stated, "No, you have wife, no!" She then repeated herself, "You have wife, yes, what you want her promise?"

Harjo now realized she was asking a question in her strange but often humorous way without using the word "if" but he also realized she was serious. "Promise?" he asked, seeking clarification.

"Yes," she said politely, "Tell me wife promise you. Harjo now realized she wanted him to lay out what he wants from a wife and what he expected her to promise him.

Putting together his thoughts, Harjo responded. "I want wife to work hard-take care of our babies-cook good food-sew good clothes."

"Yes," said Onna, "Good promise, good wife, good mother." She then held up her hand extending her little and adjacent finger to make the count two followed by saying "two" with a little smile on her face.

"Two," repeated Harjo, "Wife will not have sex with any other man, only me."

"Yes!" said Onna, "good wife have sex, one man, husband."

Content with those questions and answers, Onna sat quietly snuggling against Harjo. Soon, he discovered she had fallen asleep on his shoulder and it required some effort to move her from on top the mammoth bed to in it. Harjo chuckled to himself at the rough manner he could manhandle her, nearly picking her up, to move her around while she remained asleep. He finally managed to get her tucked in, then retired himself. But even in her sleep, affectionate Onna, with the instincts of a baby hare, snuggled up against him.

The following morning found no hesitation with Onna to get started. With the sled loaded and secured, she hastily-but with purpose and poise-moved to the front of the sled, slipping the harness over her head. She was more than willing to do her part in pulling the sled. Harjo followed likewise affixing himself in the harness. Onna turned, looked into his face, then with a beautiful broad smile exclaimed, "Let's go!"

Harjo could not help but return the smile then answered, "Yes, go!" And together they began the morning trek.

Onna brought such a new, different, wonderful view of the world to Harjo he often was not sure if it was really happening. Every new discovery was exciting to her and Harjo delighted in her childlike, joyful reactions to a new discovery. He would not have believed he would enjoy talking so much to a woman, especially considering their language barrier. Harjo told himself he would begin to use Muscogee words when Onna asked "what something is" and she asked "what is" constantly.

They had not gone far when Harjo stopped. As he did, Onna followed and looked at his face to see what direction had caught his attention, then she likewise looked that way. But now, Harjo was studying the area just ahead of them and the tracks in the new thin snow cover. Onna could see the tracks but had no idea what animal had made them. She assumed the worst.

"Lion?" asked Onna, with an excited voice.

"No," Harjo replied. Thinking for a moment, he answered, "Lynx".

Onna looked at him smiling. "That not Yupik word," she said, "that Muscogee word." Onna noticed that Harjo was also smiling. She thought for an instant then replied. "Alright, yes," she said, teach me Muscogee, language of Mammoth Hunters, I teach you my language.

Harjo was not happy with this whole exchange of language development, but he reluctantly agreed.

"How say Yupik?" she asked. Harjo stated the word in Yupik, "*niutuayaq*" and Onna repeated the word to herself.

"How say Muscogee?" she asked.

"Lynx," Harjo replied.

185

"What is lynx?" she asked. Harjo began to describe the admirable feline.

"It is cat," began Harjo. "Not lion, not big like lion, same size as a wolf. It has pointed ears, hair on ears, and very little tail."

Suddenly, Onna reached her two fingers up touching his lips to interrupt. "Yes! Yes!" she said. "I know, have in Dyuktai land same as muskox. Is called "leuk," but no hurt, it run away!"

"Yes," Harjo replied.

"Tell me more!"

"Alright," he continued. "Size of a wolf but it has big paws-feet. Not white like a lion, but white on the bottom, brown/white on the top with black spots. Some say it has beautiful fur. It has fur on the top of the ears and the side of the face. It kills mostly hare, other small animals, and occasionally birds.

Onna was excited about seeing the tracks of an animal that ranged westward into her distant territory; however, she looked at Harjo with a puzzled expression. "How you know not lion?" she asked, "look same."

They pulled the sled adjacent to the tracks. Harjo pointed to the tracks with his spear. "Lynx have big paws, but they are still not as big as a lion. A lion is much larger, so it takes a larger step. See the distance between the tracks. Too short, so it must be a lynx not a lion. When we see lion tracks, you will see the difference."

Onna looked up at him. "Man, hunter, know much animal-hunt and no hurt.

"Yes, that is true," he replied with a smile. Little boys begin to learn from their fathers. It is the same with the Canineqmiut boys and I am certain boys from your tribe as well."

"Father can teach girl same," said Onna. "Father teach me same you, see lion-no run! I afraid lion, Harjo, but no afraid have you."

Onna became silent looking at Harjo with an alluring expression and then turned standing on her tiptoes giving him a tender kiss. Then, Harjo took her in his arms and even with the constraints of the sled harness and his weapons, he managed to give her a long passionate kiss. His action took her by surprise, but she willingly responded, kissing him back. They looked at each other for a short moment, then following a little panting, they both instinctively leaned into their sled harness and continued on their journey.

They stopped midday for food, water and rest. Harjo wanted to insure Onna could find her own way, if need be, so he took advantage of the rest to ask his own question.

"Do you know what direction is north?"

Onna thought for just a moment then replied, "No understand north."

Harjo pondered his question. "Do you know what direction we have been going?"

Again, she had that pretty but serious look on her face as though she was forcing thought. "Direction?" she repeated clumsily more in a question that a statement.

He pointed north. "What way?"

She smiled that beautiful childlike smile then pointed east. "Sun come," she said. Then pointing west, she said, "Sun go down." Continuing, she pointed south and said, "Great Sea," then pointing southeast she said, "Canineqmiut village." Finally, pointing to the north, she looked at him grinning, "Big Ice."

Harjo was impressed. "Very good!" he said.

Most women of the Muscogee Wind Band had little knowledge of directions or locations and relied on men to

guide them. Onna, however, appeared to possess an understanding of geography and landscape.

"Can you find the North Star at night? The star that
points to the direction of the Big Ice."

"No," said Onna. "You teach me?"

"Most certainly, I will."

"Line you make on ground, night, go Big Ice Star?"

"Yes, and I will show you Big Ice Star tonight.

That evening found Harjo and Onna enduring a cold
camp. The early evening was clear, but it looked as though
it might become cloudy. They gazed at the stars as Harjo
pointed out the North Star to Onna, which she called the
Big Ice Star and then he drew his north line. He would
follow up with some direction tips tomorrow. Harjo became
serious, needing to insure himself that she understood.

"We must always travel southeast or east to reach the
Echota River. Do you understand?" A smiling Onna shook
her head yes.

"Now you tell me. What direction?"

"Always go to sun come up and lower. Go Echota River,"
replied Onna. Harjo smiled approvingly.

Anticipating snow, Harjo made a shelter with the
bison robe, the sled, and the travail poles as support. They
found comfort and warmth in each other, secured in the
warm mammoth bed. As the light vanished, Onna was not
quite ready for sleep. She looked at Harjo with a serious
but puzzled expression holding out her open palm then
asked. "How you say?" Now Harjo looked puzzled. Onna
pointed with her left finger drawing a circle around her right
open palm.

"Oh," said Harjo. "It is called palm."

She repeated the word then looked to him for correc-
tion and Harjo nodded. She then closed her hand to a fist
and asked, "How you say?"

Harjo reached out gently running his fingers over her fist. "Fist," he answered and again she whispered the word to herself. There was usually meaning and intent in her questions, but Harjo could not find one tonight. Onna remained inquisitive.

"Harjo, I speak you something, you no tell. What word?" she asked.

He thought for a moment then replied, "Secret."

Onna leaned over close to Harjo's ear then began to whisper to him as though someone else might hear her. Harjo laughed to himself. She was so wonderfully childlike.

"Harjo," she whispered, "I speak you secret, women know, no men."

His expression said, "Alright."

"Wetness inside man's mouth. Woman swallow, some eat. She want get sex with him. He want kiss her. He get tongue in her mouth, she suck same baby. She want sex, before kiss, she no want. Mother tell me. She speak, for women, no speak man. I speak you."

"Let me see if I understand," replied Harjo. "If I kiss a woman, any woman, she will want to have sex with me finding it hard to say no?"

"Yes!" Onna answered.

Then she suddenly stopped. Harjo looked into her face and could see she was in deep thought reconsidering possible repercussions of this divine secret. She looked at him with a serious expression. "Maybe no true," she said.

Harjo could not help but burst out in a loud laugh and Onna followed his path. She laid her head on his chest. They soon drifted into sleep.

Chapter 13:

LEARNING/LOVING

The two young adventurers lay awake at dawn under their lean-to shelter snuggling in the warm mammoth wool bed Harjo's mother made for him for this journey. The bed was sewn together from one long length of tanned winter mammoth pelt. The long course winter mammoth hair had been removed and the remaining wool, a hand width thick, had been combed, rubbed, and sheared into a soft warm layer. The two ends were folded together then one side sewn from the bottom "foot" fold to the top. The other side was stitched from the bottom end up to about knee high. When laid flat, the top layer could be folded back to expose the body or brought up over the head and shoulders for greater warmth. Harjo realized his mother made the bed large enough to accommodate a sleeping man and a woman wondering if there was any purpose in her sizing.

Finally, a reluctant Harjo gave Onna a quick kiss and climbed out of the mammoth bed. As he was taking his clothes from the drying line when he heard her soft voice.

"Harjo. Bring me clothes-please," She drew the word please out with her childish accent.

Harjo took Onna her clothes, then she proceeded to dress under the mammoth bed covers with plenty of warm smiles and a thank you. Their conversation focused on teaching Onna the Muscogee language and presumably teaching Harjo the Dyuktai language of Onna. Even though Harjo spoke three fluent languages it soon became apparent that Onna was the linguist. She was not inspired to learn Muscogee, nonetheless, she learned and recalled every Muscogee word Harjo taught her. On the other hand, Harjo struggled to remember the simplest of words in Onna's language.

After the sun rose, warming up the snow-covered landscape, Onna was eager to learn about the atlatl and its use. Even though she had watched men and boys of her tribe use the atlatl all her young life, she had not given any thought to why or how it functioned. She did not recall ever touching one. Harjo decided to offer her the "long story" even though the language barrier remained difficult. He discovered he had more patience than he ever realized possible, but Onna's patience was unending which kept him from being frustrated.

"The throwing board or atlatl," began Harjo, "propels the dart at a much greater speed, distance, and accuracy than a man could throw by hand alone. No two are alike as each hunter crafts his atlatl to fit his own hand and individual throwing style, but each function in the same manner being similar in basic design."

Harjo explained and demonstrated the complicated process to Onna. Excited and smiling, she held the atlatl and dart as he held her hands. She did not really understand most of Harjo's words, but she enjoyed listening and learning from him. She also enjoyed the attention he gave her. Still, through his demonstrations, she grasped his meaning.

Onna attempted several disastrous throws. She was having so much fun it did not matter to her how terrible her throws were, and she also realized she may never grasp the atlatl and dart technique.

"It takes a long while to learn," stressed Harjo. "First, learn to throw your spear." Onna agreed with Harjo.

They walked to the North Star snow line marked on the ground. Harjo pointed, "North to Big Ice." He now explained they could begin toward the southeast or east horizon using physical terrain locations, if any are present, on the horizon.

Onna had a good grasp of direction and navigation. She said her father had taught her similar tricks and how to use the sun for navigation. Harjo retained confidence she could reach the Echota River on her own. They started another day.

⁓⁓⁓⁓⁓⁓⁓

The farther inland they journeyed, the more breathtaking the horizon. The aroma of the air also began to smell different. Now the wind carried the fragrance of the tall steppe grasses and low shrubs, in particular the sage bush, as opposed to the salt air and the tundra landscape of the Great Sea coast. The promise of reaching the land of the mammoth offered by the new fragrances also enhanced Onna's zeal for conversation.

"Harjo, what is word, husband go, leave wife, no come back?" Onna asked as the two leaned against the harness pulling their sled up a gentle incline.

"No come back," repeated Harjo.

"No come back," said Onna.

"That would be-abandoned," Harjo replied, although he wondered why Onna used the words husband and wife as opposed to man or woman. Onna repeated the word to herself as she generally did; thus, it would now be implanted in her vocabulary.

"What you think good husband do?" asked Onna as it was now obvious where she was taking Harjo on this conversational journey.

"Do you want to tell me what you think is a good husband?" asked Harjo.

"Yes," she replied.

As they reached the top of the incline, they stopped to catch their breaths. "Alright, tell me."

Thinking to herself, Onna looked up with her eyes putting her words and thoughts in order. She was so adorable when she formed this expression, but Harjo also realized she was deeply serious. He also took on a serious attitude.

Now ready, she held up her little finger and said, "One: good husband, good hunter, bring food, skin-clothes, build house, me and children have."

Holding up her little and adjacent finger she stated, "Two: good husband no abandon me and children. No say gone, long hunt or trade. I say go, no come back. You know-abandoned."

Now holding up her little, adjacent, and middle fingers to make the sign of three she said, "Three: no have secrets. I tell husband, husband tell me. Husband want girl, sex, he tell me. We can buy her. Maybe I want her-same. Maybe I want husband have two wives.

Onna started to hold up four fingers but then she stopped. She stuck the sharpened end of her spear in the ground then reached out with both hands picking up Harjo's hand. She gently held it. She marveled at how large his hands were-how rough and calloused his palms.

She could feel the powerful strength in his hands and yet, equally she could feel a gentleness-a tenderness in the way he would touch the side of her face. She could envision him gently holding a newborn baby. She looked into his face.

"Husband no hit me face." She then closed the fingers of his hand to make a fist and said, "Husband no hit me fist. Husband no hit me switch. I bad, no good wife, husband can hit me same this." She turned around giving herself a slap on the buttocks. "Husband can give me spank same naughty girl, no wear parka or pants. Husband no let people see, no let children see, he give me spank. Husband me alone see, he give me spank."

Holding his hand and feeling the rough hardness of his palms and the strength, not only in his hands but his arms as well, Onna thought for a moment. "What a painful, severe spanking he could deliver." But she also believed it unlikely to ever come to that. She was confident if he were to slap her buttocks it would be more to embarrass her or to scare as a naughty child, rather than inflict real punishment.

Onna now held up all five fingers of her right hand. She began to choke with emotion as she spoke. "Five: if Enemy Warriors or lion come, good husband will fight, no let lion or warrior hurt me or children. Five things for good husband."

Still holding his hand, she looked deep and serious into his eyes. Harjo could see tears swelling in hers.

"Oh, Harjo," she said in a near whisper. "Enemy Warriors take me-you come for me-please come for me-please Harjo, come, bring me home!"

Without hesitation, Harjo also planted his spear into the ground and reached up as Onna let his hand go free then he put his hands on the sides of her face. He looked into her face-deep into her beautiful blue eyes. Onna had never heard Harjo speak with such seriousness. She would remember his words the rest of her life.

"If Enemy Warriors ever take you, I will come for you. No matter how far they take you, no matter how long it will take, I will come. If Enemy Warriors ever take you-you stay alive. Whatever it takes, you stay alive. If they take you to the end of the Mammoth Steppe or to the end of the world, I will come, and I will bring you home."

"Harjo," she whispered. Onna put her arms around him, then placed her head on his chest softly crying. Harjo held her tightly and caressed her beautiful summer-grass colored hair. He did not know how long he held her, and it did not matter.

They stopped for a mid-day break sharing water and mammoth jerky. Sitting on the bison robe, they were surprised to watch an artic fox make her way across the open tundra, seemingly unaware or unconcerned of their presence. A freshly killed hare was clamped in her jaws. The hare was nearly as large as the fox and yet the vixen was able to carry the white furred prey with seemingly little effort.

"Fox good hunter same you Harjo," pointed out a cheerful Onna.

"Oh, she is a much better hunter than I am," remarked Harjo.

"She no kill mammoth," responded Onna.

"Well, that's true," said Harjo with a smile.

"Harjo, why bear big, more big lion? Lion can hunt bison-bear can hunt bison-lion no big same bear. Why?"

Harjo chucked to himself at the manner Onna asked questions, but he could also see her serious expression. "I'm not sure," he answered. "My uncle killed a bear. He knows much about them. I'll tell you what he told and what I think." Smiling Onna shook her head yes.

"Bears live alone. There are few-not many-that range in a large open area. My uncle says they do not hunt. They steal the prey from lions and wolves. That is why they are so big, so they can steal food. They cannot run fast as a lion or wolf, but they can run a long distance."

"I see bears, family we move camp. See bears run long away-one see close." Onna got up pulling up her parka then bent down on her hands and feet looking back over her shoulder at Harjo. "Bear on four paw-tall same man."

Harjo thought to himself how sexually inviting she appeared in that position, but she remained childishly innocent.

Onna then reached her hand up tapping the top of her head, then she stood up and again tapped her head, smiling.

"Yes," Harjo replied. "As the bear stands on four paws its head is taller than a man. If we meet a bear, Onna, the same as a lion—understand?" Onna nodded yes.

Then, following a short pause, Onna stepped toward her "harpoon" which still lay on the ground. Harjo's spear was still stuck butt first, as always, in the ground. Onna picked up her harpoon then sunk it into the ground and with her hands on her hips she boasted.

"I ready go. You ready go, Harjo?" Laughing, Harjo got up and they returned to the sled, pulled the harnesses over their heads, and were off again.

Toward the end of the day, however, they stopped to rest. Harjo pointed out a clump of trees on the horizon that might provide a good camping location. After some water with bites of meat, Harjo walked some ten paces from the sled to view the horizon with a different perspective. Suddenly, from nowhere a lone raven circled low overhead. The large ebony bird reflected momentary flashes of rainbow colors off its black feathers as it called. Suddenly, it abruptly swooped down and landed on the sled. Onna stood by one end of the sled with the raven at the other.

"Look Harjo, look," called out an excited Onna.

Harjo turned to see the raven fluff up its feathers, then call to Onna. She held out her hand with a piece of meat. The raven called again and then walked across the sled to Onna taking the meat from her hand. It made a strange call with the small piece of meat in its bill, then took off into the air. As it lifted up, a black feather drifted down to Onna.

"You see, Harjo, you see. Big black bird give me feather. How you say, Harjo, how you say?" asked an excited and delighted Onna.

"It's called a raven," answered Harjo.

Onna picked up the feather running to Harjo saying "raven" over and over to herself. She stopped in front of Harjo holding up her feather.

"It's very pretty," said a smiling Harjo. "The raven left you a magical gift." Onna remained excited the remainder of the day. They quickened the pace and although late in the day, they came to a welcomed tree oasis with a small spring. They had finally crossed the Coastal Zone.

Rocks surrounded the little spring. It was only about two paces across, but the water was deep and clear, offering a delicious taste. It formed a short, narrow bushy channel that drained off to the east. A cottonwood tree patch supported several medium-sized trees and more importantly, an abundant supply of wood. It was not long before the travelers were drinking hot tea and warm mammoth stew before a large roaring fire.

Harjo was very proud of Onna. She was weary, near exhaustion, but had not complained once. He pulled a flat seashell from the pouch of shells he had traded at the Canineqmiut village, then drilled a hole in the center and took a hare tail he had kept and tied it and the raven feather all together. He then braided three strands of Onna's hair just behind her left ear then tied the raven feather ornament to it. The white hare's tail and the black raven feather both stood in stark attractive contrast to Onna's bright yellow hair. She was very thankful to Harjo for the gift and very proud of her magic raven feather. She would wear it now and into the future.

Onna fell asleep leaning against Harjo with her drinking bowl in hand. He took off her clothes, as he had some experience in that pleasurable exercise, and laid a naked little Onna to bed, then hung up her clothes to dry. They would sojourn here a day or so allowing Onna to recover her strength. A long, harder journey remained.

Onna slept late into the morning while Harjo carved on the sewing tools, as he did not want to leave camp with Onna sleeping. Although only on the fringe, they had entered lion and mammoth country. He would hunt later after she was awake.

Onna woke and was pleased to learn they would rest here for a day or two. She eagerly heated a pouch of warm water then bathed and sat combing her hair by the fire.

Harjo was unloading the sled because he wanted to rebalance and retie the load when suddenly he pulled the "fancy parka" out from the sled, which had been stacked among the seal pelts. He had completely forgotten about it. He approached Onna then handed it to her.

"It's for you," he said. Her eyes suddenly grew wide with excitement and the smile on her face was a glow like the early morning sun shining on a snow-covered meadow. She took the parka, holding it out in front of her repeating

"Oh Harjo!" over and over again. "Where you have beautiful parka?"

"I traded a Canineqmiut man for it," he answered. "I presume his wife or some other Canineqmiut woman made it."

"Is for me?" she asked, as tears began to swell in her beautiful eyes. "Please no tease me, Harjo," she said nearly crying as she held the parka in front of her wrapped in her arms.

Suddenly, Harjo felt something stir deep inside of him. Something he had never before experienced. He did not know what it was or how to define it. The only word he could relate it to was "seriousness" and that utterance seemed so incomplete. He did not consider how to react or what to say, it just came from him with the honesty of youth. He stepped up in front of Onna and faced her. He reached out his right hand gently touching the side of her face. He could feel tears swelling in his own eyes. A Muscogee man-warrior and hunter of mammoth-did not cry in public, especially in front of a woman. But Harjo did not care at that particular moment. He was moved by something he did not understand, but he knew he must speak his heart.

"I will never tease or joke you, Onna, in a way that will hurt you. Never! I never will."

Onna looked up into his face. Although she was nearly crying herself, she saw the wet eyes of sincerity in Harjo's face. "Oh, Harjo!" she said, as tears began to seep into her eyes. She embraced him, looking up into his face.

"No one nice me, long, Harjo. I servant girl. I no have nothing-I no have family. I belong you. You can keep me, you can send me go. You saved my life, without you I die. I want belong you. I love you, Harjo!"

Harjo did not say anything and Onna did not expect him to. She stood up on the tips of her toes to kiss him. She kissed him in such a manner as he had never been kissed before, not even by her. The kiss seemed to embody all things. It was warm and tender, but it also expressed joy-a deep gratitude of thanks. At the same instant, it was also arousing and sexual. He would remember this kiss and this fond memory for the rest of his life.

Onna stepped down and back, and then somehow still holding the parka in her arms, she gently jumped up and down, clapping her hands together in that delightful gesture Harjo had now grown so fond off.

"Harjo! Thank you! Thank you! Thank you!" she cried with such delightful excitement. "I can wear?" she asked.

Harjo could only smile, laughing to himself. She enchanted him. "Of course, you can wear it. It's yours."

Onna held the new parka out to Harjo as he instinctively took it. She then reached up around her neck pulling her old parka off over her head then stood before him bare from the waist up. She handed him her old parka and he returned the new one. He gazed at her. As he did, he lost himself in her new gesture of boldness or perhaps it was her trust. He had seen her naked before and slept nude with her, but it seemed different now that she was awake. He saw the slenderness of her waist and stomach and the loveliness of her small but firm breasts. Her nipples were the same color as her mouth. A beautiful strange color he had yet to conjure up a name in any language. It was a type of red. But not red like the chert tool stone or a red like the red ocher paint. It was similar in color to one of the small berry fruits. Again, the name of the berry plant now escaped him.

Then it came to him- "the dawn." Her lovely nipples and warm soft mouth were the color of the dawn flush. The color of a snow-covered hill or mountain as the sun first broke the horizon. He was still not certain of the color's name. Perhaps the color did not have a name, but he would call it flush.

Onna noticed he was staring at her and she smiled, holding the parka up in front of her as she turned her back toward him. Still smiling, she looked back over her shoulder at him. Harjo was now afforded a close view of her small, narrow but strong shoulders and back and the curve at the small of her back. He could also see the top of her buttocks with their shape faintly outlined by her pants. She continued to turn to now face him again with a more serious look on her face.

"You think I pretty, Harjo?" she asked.

His answer could have been coyer but wasn't. Without thinking, he simply blurted out in his typical, young, honest self.

"You are the prettiest girl I have ever seen," he answered.

Instead of putting on the new parka, Onna laid it on the bison pelt and then took off her pants. She was not wearing any boots, as usual, and now stood completely nude in front of Harjo. She held out her arms to him. He picked her up off the ground.

Onna's warrior, hunter and protector remained a paradox. Harjo was strong, lethal, and fearlessly cold in that he could snuff out a life, both human and animal, with no hesitation or remorse. And yet, he was warm, gentle, tenderly loving. Onna's apprehension concerning sex lingered. The past experience of her abduction still held her emotions trapped in anxiety. Although she had not been abused during her captivity, another woman who was captured with her had been beaten and raped. Consequently, those images, like paintings on a cave wall, were not easily worn off. Anxious yes, but she was not afraid, and she wanted to have intimate relations with Harjo. She knew he would not hurt her.

Harjo carried a beautiful, naked little Onna in his arms. At first, she laughed and kicked her legs but then pushed his parka hood back to reveal his head then placed her hands behind his neck gazing into his face. Harjo did not see a smile, but a serious look, a look of anticipated longing.

He glanced along her warm body, her small firm breasts and flush nipples, her flat stomach, rounded hips, and the light tan colored little patch of pubic hair and her female essence. He could not resist her.

With his parka hood pushed back, Onna stared into his face-deep into his bright, dark, nearly black eyes, so thin and narrow. She noticed his high prominent cheekbones and dark brown face, but she also noticed he did not have any scars on his face. Most men of her tribe carried some scars if not from injury at least from frostbite. She was glad her young warrior had no scars and marveled that even though his face was dark it still contrasted with his straight black hair.

Onna moved her face close to his. She wanted to kiss him, but first she wanted to smell his breath. She slowly licked her lips and breathed heavy hoping he would do the same. Then, when he did, she moved her nose to his mouth moaning as she drew his breath into her nostrils. Taken from her mother at such a young age, her training in sex, reproduction, and infant care remained incomplete. And her mother certainly did not tell her a man's breath could be so enticing. She again inhaled his breath as if to draw it deep into her. Then, she kissed him full on the mouth and could not help but whimper as she did.

Now that she had inhaled his breath, she wanted his wetness and his tongue. He obliged as though he sensed her longing and inserted his tongue into her warm wet mouth as she sucked on him. She did not try to control herself as she whimpered and moaned out loud. She wanted to suck all of him into her.

Their embraces ended as she looked into his face panting. He carried her to the mammoth bed then laid her down on it. As she lay breathing heavy, her first impulse was to spread her legs, arch her back raising her hips, but he was still dressed. He stood and pulled off his parka. Then, the ever vigil Harjo raised the palm of his hand to her, then stepped away from the bed to retrieve his spear, then he returned and laid the spear on the ground by the bed. He sat down on the bed taking off his boots.

Onna reached up to rub his muscular back. He brings his two hard spears to bed she thought, but one will be mine. He turned, but for a moment watching her beautiful breast rise and fall with heavy breathing.

"Hurry, Harjo," she panted in a whisper.

Standing, he untied the draw chords to his pants then pulled them off. Finally, a naked Harjo lay down beside Onna as they embraced and kissed with the eager passion of youth. Suddenly, as they stood at the entry to the mysterious spirit world, everything around them was lost. There was no tomorrow-no yesterday-only now and each other.

Harjo kissed Onna's neck. Now that he had taken in her sweet warm breath, he now understood why the Father Creator was called the "Master of Breath." Now he wanted her scent, her young female scent. He moved his face to her armpit, kissed her, drawing in her intoxicating scent in deep breaths sucking on the little patch of her under arm fur. She had very little hair on her body and it was all the same wondrous color as her hair locks-yellow as the winter grass. The soft little hair that grew on her ankles was nearly invisible and was only noticeable when the sun shined on her bare legs.

He kissed her again, long-hard. Onna sucked his tongue as though she could suck all the wetness from his mouth and all the male fluid from his tongue. He kissed her throat, then slowly dragged his tongue to her breast.

"Oh, yes, Harjo, yes," she whimpered again and again.

She wanted him to suck baby milk from her and more. He kissed, licked, flicking his tongue on one turgid nipple then the other. Onna caressed his head, his neck, and shoulders-any part of him she could reach.

Then, he slowly slid his hand down her stomach to her bladder. His large powerful hand on her stomach, her bladder, and her womb where she would carry his baby sent chills down her spine to her pelvis. Knowing where his hand was going prompted her to curl the toes, arch her back, and raise her hips. She whimpered and moaned out loud again.

"Yes, Harjo, yes" over and over.

Harjo carried her to the edge of the spirit world. Now he would carry her into that mystical realm as her passion and excitement lifted beyond control. His fingers lingered to twist the soft little patch of her pubic fur then slowly moved down to her wet swollen vulva. He sucked on her left nipple then took all of her breast into his mouth sucking her hard. Onna could feel the tension pull from her breast down through her stomach and into her vagina. Exactly how she felt this tension she did not know, nor did she care. His hand slid farther down as he gently massaged her vulva, and then his fingers tenderly caressed her clitoris. Onna strained, convulsed, and contracted as every muscle in her body tightened.

"Yes! Yes!" she cried out. "Water, Harjo, take girl water!"

And he did. His fingers rubbed her fluid out of her as he carried her over into the spirit world. It was, however, only a quick journey into the mystical, unknown world of the spirits. But he would take her deeper, much deeper.

Harjo rose up to kiss her again, noticing the flush color in her neck. Onna panted and moaned with passion-she wanted more. He kissed her again, then her breast-her nipples. He repositioned himself slowly kissing and licking his way across her stomach, her bladder, her pelvis, and her female scent. He lightly kissed her vulva, drawing in deep breaths of her warm, fragrant, female essence, more exhilarating than any aroma he had ever breathed and much more intoxicating than the female aroma of the two other women he had known. Even though Onna had not yet touched him, he bore a hard erection since their first kiss. But now, adding her wonderful aroma, forced his swollen manhood to throb.

Harjo rose to his knees. Onna spread her legs and he moved between them. He kissed and sucked on her inner thighs, teasing her, licking ever so close to her womanhood. Until finally, he kissed her sweet female secret, drinking in her innocence. Onna stroked his head as she rolled hers back and forth. He was taking her again to the spirit world, but even deeper. Harjo was glad for the lessons he had learned from Chufe and Ciriiq. He first kissed, then licked, and then sucked on her clitoris. Again, she arched her back, raising her hips as she contracted. Again, he took her female fluid drinking it out of her.

As her spasms ended and she slowly returned to the edge of the spirit world, she looked down to see Harjo on his knees, ready for final rite. She reached down touching him and gently grasped his manhood. How could he be this large and hard, she asked herself? Even though she had felt his erection against her while sleeping with him she had not considered is actual size. She had watched him urinate and shake his soft penis on numerous occasions. Like all females, particularly girls, she was hesitant to urinate in front of men, even Harjo. But all men, especially fearless Harjo, had no qualms of urinating in front of women. How did he grow to such size and hardness-harder than bone or mammoth ivory? She wanted penetration but feared it. She feared the pain but wanted it if there was no other way of penetration. But, ultimately, she trusted Harjo and knew he would not hurt her.

Harjo stayed on his knees then moved into position. She released her grip on his manhood reaching up to grasp his sides. She looked into his face. He, too, was in passion, breathing hard, but also in control. Unlike her, he kept his senses, at least in part and she was glad-glad that he was deliberate. His manhood found her little vagina opening and slowly pushed through. It hurt, only a little, a wonderful hurt, but still hurt.

"Please slow, Harjo, please slow," she whispered in her adoring childlike voice. He looked into her face, somehow managing to smile. She could tell he was in passion, still breathing hard, but he was also still in control.

"I will my love, I will not hurt you."

"You call me love, Harjo, you call me love."

Once more, she lifted her bottom raising her hips. She wanted all of him-she wanted him to surround her, engulf her.

Although she wanted all, she could only take less than one-half of him. As he slowly penetrated to that point, she cried out.

"Oh stop, Harjo, stop. Hurt Harjo, hurt!"

He stopped and slowly withdrew to the head of his organ, but he was far from finished. Onna thrust her hips up in rapid motion, moaning, crying.

"More same, Harjo, more same!"

He again pushed to that point of pain. He could feel it when reached. Thus, he pushed in and withdrew, again and again.

"Yes, Harjo, oh yes," she franticly repeated as he lifted her spirit up again to carry her to the mystic world. She raised her arms inviting him to embrace her.

"Hold me, Harjo, hold!"

He moved to first put his hands down on either side of her head then dropped to his elbows. Now he overpowered her and engulfed her. She put her arms around his powerful chest and back. She kissed his chest over and over then moved her face to his armpit to take in his breathtaking male odor.

He thrust his manhood in and out of her warm, wet womanhood sinking only to that depth of her young innocent pleasure. She continued to raise her bottom off the mammoth bed raising her hips and moving with him in the rhythm of pleasure-the rhythm of love-and the rhythm of life.

Nothing that Harjo had ever experienced before was as wondrous or exciting as Onna. Her exotic appearance, beautiful and healthy. Her manner, the way she acted and the way she talked. Her mystic aroma and the sweet taste of her kiss and body. The wonderful way she felt, warm, soft, wet, and tight. Her love and love making, all combined into an extraordinary Onna. He could not possibly meet or ever know another girl like her.

Harjo was not a talker but Onna talked enough for them both. He turned his head to the side so that he could kiss her as she kissed him back, lost in love and passion. All that he could say was, "I love you, Onna, I love you." But those few simple words meant everything to Onna. As he looked into her face, tears filled her eyes as she cried whispering back to him, "Harjo, Oh Harjo, I love you-I love you!"

They continued to move, locked in the rhythm of love, rocking with the pulse of passion. But now, he pushed faster and faster still taking her deeper and deeper into the light. Then he altered his thrust so that his rigid male organ stroked across her female organ which forced her to release her female fluid for the greatest and final moment. He too released his male fluid.

When Onna felt him release, she grasped his buttocks because she instinctively wanted to insure he stayed in her to discharge all his fluid. She knew she would not become pregnant, but by instinct, wanted him to fill her with a baby-fill her with his male fluid that somehow, through the Father Creator, would grow to a baby.

Again, Harjo lifted Onna up and again carried her off to the magical spirit world. But not the dim spirit world of dark shadows but one of brilliant lights and glowing mists-the bright amazing spirit world of enduring love and sensual pleasure.

As Onna returned from the spirit world, her faithful Harjo was still with her. He was so strong, she thought, so much strength in his arms he could stay on top of her during their complete journey and not lay his weight on her. So strong, he could shift his weight to one elbow leaving one hand free to caress the side of her face and kiss her. She loved it when he put his hand across her chin, pushed her chin down to make her open her mouth, then kiss her full on her open mouth. She loved it more now.

He moved off her but not away, only to his side then rolled her so that they faced each other on their sides. He put his arms over her shoulder holding her so that she looked into his eyes. Onna reached up and touched his lips. She had never known such happiness. She began to cry again.

"Sex-you-wonderful, Harjo. I afraid-I know you no hurt me. You call me love, Harjo, you say, you love me Harjo." Tears swelled in her eyes.

"I do love you, Onna."

"Harjo, I same baby, Harjo, I cry same baby!"

Harjo gently laughed as he had before and caressed her hair. "You are free, remember, you can cry when you want."

"Harjo, Harjo," cried Onna as she put her head to his chest then openly wept tears of joy.

Harjo held her, caressed her, and gently kissed her. They were each changed forever, but they did not appreciate it because they were so young. But that is the true beauty of youth, to trust, to love, to change unaware. To change and step from a bittersweet world that you can never return to and yet never realize it.

Chapter 14:

MAMMOTH AND LION

The landscape changed with noticeable subtleties. With their sled in-tow, Harjo and Onna journeyed from the flat, treeless, coastal tundra plain, blanketed by a continuous snow cover into the interior region of the Mammoth Steppe, a domain of an endless sea of thick grass, rolling hills, and wooded streams. The interior was also covered by a shallow mantle of dry snow, dotted with areas of exposed surfaces. Onna tied seven days in her chord.

According to Mammoth Hunter law, a girl belonged first to her father, then to her husband. Although Onna's circumstances remained extraordinary, there would be little doubt among any Mammoth Hunter Elder that Onna now belonged to Harjo. Additionally, even though neither had completed a Rite-of-Passage and thus not eligible for marriage, the vast majority of the same Elders would declare Onna and Harjo married by Spirit Law. That is, no law was absolute. Circumstance could intervene creating an unusual situation in which the action taken was more justifiable than obedience to the proper law.

The young lovers laughed and talked throughout most of the days often stopping to survey the circular horizon, especially the view to their backs, insuring nothing dangerous was behind them. Now more familiar and daring, Harjo was inclined to take a taste of Onna on those brief halting periods. Once their backs were cleared, he would reach out taking her hand gently pulling her toward him. Onna now eagerly came to him any moment he beckoned. With her spear in her left hand moved aside, she wrapped her right arm around the small of his back then pressed her breast against his stomach. Harjo likewise repeated her actions, only holding his spear in his right hand then enveloping his left arm around her neck. She moved her face up close to his, beaming like the morning sun. Then, with the playful voice she used on such occasions she said, "Give me kiss!" Each occasion, as Harjo reached down to kiss her warm beckoning lips, he could not help but grin, often laughing at the way she said-give me kiss-which of course was part of her purpose.

Late morning, they struggled climbing a steep hill as they headed for a small rock formation covered with brush when suddenly Harjo stopped listening with solemn intensity. Onna followed. She started to say something but a raised hand from Harjo silenced her. Following a short pause, he turned, speaking in a low voice, "a mammoth."

Onna's eyes grew wide as she opened her mouth with an, "Oh" taking in a deep breath.

"It is strange that a lone mammoth is out here this far from the Echota River during migration season." He pointed. "It is over in that direction." Onna looked with her excitement building. "We will go to the top of the hill to those rocks but keep a sharp watch. Understand?"

Onna whispered, "Yes, understand."

They continued to the top of the hill, stopping at the rock formation. They left the sled then climbed up the small outcrop to obtain a good view. Harjo pointed-below at a far safe distance-a bull mammoth used his tusk and feet to clear the shallow snow to get at the winter grass.

"Oh, Harjo!" sighed an excited Onna. She wanted to clap but just clasped her hands together.

"We must be cautious and careful," spoke Harjo in a low voice. "An old bull, separated from the herd and away from the valley far too early. He will be dangerous.

We can rest and watch. It will be safe here. I don't think he will come up the hill, but if he does, he can't climb these rocks."

Harjo paused momentarily then continued. "I know you are from a Tribe of Mammoth Hunters, but do you know about mammoth?"

"Men, my tribe hunt mammoth-know much. Women and girl sew, make clothes, keep baby, know little mammoth. Mammoth can kill!" She replied.

"Yes," he answered.

"You teach me?" she asked. "So, we can-let's go see mammoth-and no get kill. I can learn same much mammoth?"

"Yes!" he replied, "of course I will teach you about the mammoth and this is a perfect place to learn, rest, drink water, and eat some mammoth pemmican."

They retrieved their supplies from the sled, setting their pouches on the ground near the rocks, and then sat down making themselves comfortable. Onna took a long drink from the water pouch.

"Water good from spring, Harjo," she whispered. Harjo agreed. The old bull seemed content to stay eating the winter grass and searching for any new green shoots under the snow. As they watched, Harjo began.

"You must pay attention to the direction-way-the wind blows." He reached down pulling out a handful of grass blades then let them fall indicating the wind direction.

"The wind generally blows east to west and north to south on the great Mammoth Steppe and occasionally it will blow up or down the river valleys. Animals can smell men," said Harjo. "Mammoths can smell a long distance."

"Yes!" Onna replied. "I remember men talk, I girl. Father tell me, animals can smell people."

Harjo took this pause to look around especially behind them as he habitually did while Onna, following his lead, did likewise. Thoughts quickly raced through his mind. She was very intelligent, more intelligent than he had ever presumed. Harjo was a very young man and he had not considered the astuteness of a woman. His considerations of women had been more focused on their beauty and sexual possibilities. To his own surprise, he discovered he was attracted to Onna's intelligence as much as he was to her beauty.

His thoughts were broken by the distant call of the mammoth, prompting them to look at each other smiling. "The wind blows" continued Harjo, "It brings the mammoth scent or smell to us. If the wind blows now, from sun go down-to sun come up-the mammoth could smell us and know we are here. Do you understand?"

Onna looked at him, her mouth slightly opened in astonishment. She looked out toward the distant mammoth then back to where they were setting. "Yes!" She replied. "Mammoth smell from mammoth to us-wind blow from us to mammoth," she said.

"Good," said Harjo, "Very good."

"Mammoth no can see same far?" she asked as though she knew the answer but was asking for certainty.

"No," they can only see a few paces. We can sit in the open on rocks and the mammoth cannot see us."

"Mammoth can smell from us to horizon?" she asked.

Harjo smiled, "Yes, they can smell as far as we can see, from us to the horizon."

"We hear mammoth," she said, "mammoth call. Mammoth hear you, me?"

"He cannot hear us talking," said Harjo, "Maybe if we were to yell. But they can hear their own trumpet calls for a great distance, as far as they can smell."

Harjo now employed his fatherly voice. "Always pay attention to the direction where the wind blows. When you see an animal, any animal, know the wind direction then you will know if the animal can smell you. Understand?"

"Yes," replied a cheerful Onna. She reached down, pulling up a handful of grass then allowed it to drop being caught by the wind then pointed toward the mammoth.

"Big, old mammoth, no can smell us, no can see us, can hear us, maybe can-we call same yell."

Harjo grinned with pleasure-such a smart little learner. He then leaned his spear against the rocks, placing both hands to his face, took a deep breath, and let out a loud mammoth trumpeting call.

The loud call surprised Onna and she jumped, grasping her harpoon with both hands then whispered loudly, "Harjo!"

She was further surprised when the old bull raised his head to answer Harjo's call. Onna now dropped her harpoon, quietly clapping her hands and smiling.

"Harjo, you can talk mammoth?"

Chuckling Harjo replied, "Yes, mammoth have many calls."

"Harjo, you can teach me mammoth talk?"

"Most certainly," he answered.

A grinning Onna leaned over close to his face. "Give me kiss."

Harjo complied, then he stood up taking his serious fatherly tone.

"Show me the direction we should go."

Onna also stood up, surveyed the horizon circle and looked toward the sun, then she pointed. "Echota River!"

Harjo nodded his approval.

Onna pointed again. "Look Harjo, little water." She then moved her hand in a serpentine motion. "Little water have trees, go Echota River. We go, camp."

Harjo looked to see the small wooded stream in the distance. He was very impressed and was now certain Onna could find her way on her own if need be. Then, often predictable, often not, Onna surprised him.

Smiling she said, "Mammoth can smell you!" Then, as with a kiss, she reached up on her toes, placing her nose and mouth on the side of his neck, she smelled him.

"I can smell you same!" she laughed.

She returned flat-footed but still in front of him, dropping her hands to his arms. "You smell good," she said. Then she reached her hands up and pushed her hood back then raised her chin, turning her head to the side inviting him, then asked, "And me?"

Accepting the invitation, Harjo moved downward placing his nose and mouth on the side of her neck. He inhaled, taking in her aroma.

"You smell good!" he exclaimed, "Very good!"

Onna smiled and giggled, seemingly pleased with his response. Then, suddenly, she pointed as the lone bull decided to move on. "He look for mammoth-you make call!"

Harjo agreed. "The old bull is moving on to find the other mammoth he thinks he heard. Good, now we don't need to go around him."

Onna was only now learning there were many tricks to know how to survive on the Mammoth Steppe. As they reached their sled, she reached down to pick a handful of grass then dropped the yellow blades to check the wind. It was still blowing west. She then scanned a full circle around them, then pointed southeast toward the Echota River and the small wooded stream. They both reached for the sled harnesses slipping them over their heads. They looked at each other, smiled, then leaned into the harnesses and headed down the hill.

The mood on the Mammoth Steppe changes much like the mood of a woman. They had not gone far when Harjo quickly stopped. Up ahead of them in the snow, the tracks were clear. "Lion," said Harjo. Instinctively, they both did a horizon survey as the mood changed to matters more serious. They pulled the sled up to the large paw imprints in the snow. Harjo looked at the directions-the origin-and where the tracks led. Onna bent down placing her hand on one of the full-sized tracks, much larger than her hand.

"A large male," said Harjo. "We'll keep a close watch." Onna shook her head in agreement. Then they were off again heading toward the small stream.

The hilly terrain proved much more difficult to negotiate than expected thus when they reached the little wooded stream, it was later than Harjo anticipated. It was a good camping spot, so they stayed for the night. Harjo had killed several ptarmigan on today's march. As they ate, Onna again surprised Harjo. She was full of surprises.

"You chew food-give to babies same me?" Onna asked.

Harjo thought for an instant to be sure he understood her question before he replied. "Yes," he answered.

She took a bite of the suckling roast ptarmigan chewing it for a while. Then she reached over moving her mouth close to his as if to kiss him. She opened his mouth with her tongue and slid the bit of masticated bird into his mouth. Taking the bite, he chewed it a little more then swallowed.

Onna looked at him with a satisfied smile. "Now you, she said.

Harjo took a bite of the game bird and also thoroughly gnawed it. Repeating her action, he leaned over close as if to kiss her. She willingly opened her mouth to receive the chewed portion, and then swallowed it. Again, she looked at him with satisfaction-smiling. But her smile quickly turned to a more serious, even longing expression.

She slid over next to him slowly reaching up with both hands to each side of his face then moved her face close to his. Extending her right hand, she gently touched his chin. "Open," she said in a whisper. He slightly opened his mouth then she leaned in and kissed him long and gentle. The kiss ended but her mouth was still a breath away from his.

"Give me tongue," she whispered.

He wrapped his arms around her adjusting to kiss her. She opened her mouth as he slid in his tongue as she gently sucked him in for a long passionate kiss. He was not sure how long the kiss lasted but as they embraced cheek-to-cheek Harjo marveled at the wonderful aroma of her breath, slightly scented with the taste of the roast ptarmigan. He also realized he was developing an aching erection.

Then, Onna slowly, but purposefully, reached her hand to his groin. Harjo did not flinch or jump. He completely trusted her. With her hand on his groin, she felt his erection as she gazed into his face smiling and gently caressing him. Onna was now certain he would be a good father.

"Take me bed, Harjo," she panted. The mammoth bed laid only a few paces from the fire, but Harjo picked up Onna and carried her to bed. She loved to be carried to bed.

The next morning Harjo drew a map in the snow as Onna watched intently. He pointed north stating he should explain the succinct geography of the Echota Valley. "The Echota River comes from mountains to the north. The mountains always have ice. Not the "Big Ice" but the same direction. The river flows south toward the Great Sea, but before that it empties into the Big River."

"River Canineqmiut call Kuigpak?" she asked.

"Yes," he answered. "The Big River flows from sun up, east, to sun down, west, then southwest to flow into the Great Sea."

"Land toward sun down, I can know, I come there," she said. Has tall mountains with ice, land same this. What land toward sun up?"

"The old Lion Shaman told me," replied Harjo, "that the land toward the sun up is a great wall of ice."

Onna's face turned puzzled. "Big River?" she asked.

Harjo once again marveled at her thoughts. "You're right," he said. "Some say the Big River creates a valley through the wall of ice and beyond the wall of ice is a great land-a Mammoth Steppe."

"I want see Echota Valley, Harjo."

"Well then, we should head in that direction."

Onna agreed. Thus, they made their way to their sled but Onna suddenly stopped. "Look, Harjo, look!" whispered an anxious Onna with the excitement of a new discovery as she pointed toward the small wooded thicket. "Little bird with black," she patted the top of her head.

"It's a chickadee," replied a smiling Harjo. The small active little bird was about the size of a snow bunting with grey back and wings, a white breast, and the top of its head and throat conspicuously colored black.

"I see little bird, my land, Harjo. Tell me colors, Harjo, tell me colors, please!" An excited Onna grasped Harjo's arm.

Harjo named the energetic little bird's colors as it darted about limb-to-limb and limb to ground. Then it landed upside down on a branch pecking on the limb. A delighted Onna quietly clapped her hands together. "Look, Harjo, he…" She stopped not knowing how to say upside down but turned her head to the side as far as she could to express the action.

Harjo laughed out loud; she was completely adorable. He then went on to explain "upside down" but it was all so much of a new Muscogee language to take in. The little chickadee had more amusement.

It picked up a small bit of food, perhaps a seed, and flew to the trunk of a large cottonwood and stuck the tasty morsel into the bark to cache it. Onna looked at the bird and back to Harjo. "Look, Harjo, little bird hide food!"

"Yes," replied Harjo, "that is how they survive the winter by storing and hiding food." Onna put her hands together still delighted.

Harjo whistled a birdcall and the chickadee answered. "Harjo, you can talk same little bird."

"I can make that whistle, they usually answer. I want you to learn to whistle and to make the chickadee call."

Onna attempted to whistle then laughed. She could produce a quiet "whistle like sound" but little more. "You teach me make bird whistle, Harjo?"

"Of course, but you can learn yourself, just keep practicing."

"Practice," she replied, "same throw harpoon."

"Yes," Harjo answered.

"Yes, yes, Harjo, men, hunters my village make bird talk, whistle can talk, no scare animals." Again, Harjo replied with a simple yes.

Onna looked into Harjo's face. She reached up, brushing back his long black hair. He is so handsome she thought to herself. No scars or blemishes on his face.

"Thank you teach me Harjo. Thank you make me happy." She put her arms around him and with her head on his chest, hugged him.

Harjo gently stroked her hair. "You are most welcome, Onna."

There was a moment of silence then Onna whistled with loud puffs of breath with her head still against his chest. "Sound same little bird, Harjo?"

Harjo chucked out loud. "Just keep practicing and you will improve."

Such a beautiful spring morning thought Onna. So clear, so bright, so calm and peaceful. Green began to appear across the landscape as young moist grass shoots stretched out from their yellow dry parents or through patches of snow seeking the sunlight and warm air. The Father Creator was calling forth all his children and soon the whole Mammoth Steppe would be blanketed with ripe green grasses, lovely colored flowers, and playful baby animals and birds of all kinds.

Harjo, too, was content with the beautiful still morning then realized the usually talkative Onna was quiet, simply taking in the cool sunny morning as they pulled the sled. With their parka hoods pulled back exposing their heads and face, Harjo still marveled at the comparison between beautiful Onna and the early spring steppe landscape. Her eyes, blue as the clear, deep, distant sky and her hair the color of dry yellow grass blown by the wind. Her lips and now her cheeks, exposed to the cool morning air, were the color of flush-the snow-capped mountains at dawn-her face the color of the light distant horizon. When she smiled, light hearted and free as she frequently did, her smile was a perfect snow-ivory-colored smile.

As the snow covered waned and melted, resulting in exposed patches of dry grass, the sled pulled harder across the ground; however as long as they did not yet pull against the tall green grass of late summer, the journey remained enjoyable. The distant faint call of a raven broke the still morning silence. Harjo recognized the call, but it did not sink in. It was the raven's call upon seeing something dead. A deceased animal on the steppe usually means the presences of a deadly predator or scavenger. Perhaps he was enjoying the peacefulness too much. Suddenly, he stopped and Onna followed. She looked over at his face then followed the direction of his stare. The site took her breath as fear pierced through her as would icy cold water. Ahead, about 30 paces-a lion.

It lay crouched on his stomach facing them, a large male devouring a fresh kill. He had not yet seen them being predisposed as its large white fangs crushed the carcass with the blood of its fresh kill on its face and front paws. Onna slowly turned her head back to Harjo's face.

With a cold and emotionless expression, he moved his eyes to the side then gently, ever so slightly, moved his head to the same side. A signal to remind her-to prompt her into action the way Harjo had taught her and the way they had rehearsed for just this event. With smooth, deliberate, quiet movement, she reached up and pulled the harness over her head allowing it to drop to the ground. Gently, she stepped to the back of the sled, her spear in hand. She was to watch their backs and call out to Harjo if she saw another lion behind them. As Harjo had taught her Onna moved her eyes, instead of her head, as much as possible. She discovered she could see the lion, Harjo, and ground without moving her head at all.

She watched as Harjo had already dropped his harness and pulled two darts from his quiver and then with the same deliberate, smooth, movement was attaching fore shafts to the darts. The lion now saw them and stopped chewing on the carcass. It stared motionless at them. Onna continued to watch Harjo as he eased his atlatl from his belt, and then with the same even motion nocked one of the darts into the butt end point of the atlatl. All the while his spear was somehow leaned into his inside left forearm.

Now at the back of the sled, Onna grasped her spear ready in both hands. Although Harjo had told her to watch the back, taking glances to the front, she found herself doing the opposite as the deadly beast in front of the sled overwhelmed her. Then, the lion opened his jaws, showed its deadly white fangs, and made a loud, low hissing sound. Onna expected it to growl, but it did not, it hissed, and she could see pure terror in its bloodcurdling face. Then suddenly, in a deadly, silent, flash of white, it charged. Onna's heart cried out in fear, but she stood her ground, also in silence glancing behind them, at Harjo and at the lion.

Harjo held ready the atlatl nocked with a dart. Then, with the same emotionless face, he brought his arm forward with a rapid movement seen only in a flash releasing the lethal dart. Onna thought she could see the dart fly as though a streak of color.

Suddenly, in a flash through her mind sent from the spirit world, she pictured the lion leaping on Harjo, tearing at his limbs, biting through his neck and chest, a dream that flashed like lighting, white and blood red. She wanted to scream in terror but did not. It all seemed to happen so fast, only a few blinks of an eye. Then she saw the dart as it struck the lion in the chest about ten paces in front of Harjo. It sunk in deep.

The lion roared a piercing, horrible cry, nearly like a human scream. It hit the ground on his chest then rolled over on his side. The desperate beast struggled, squirmed, and fought against the dart as blood squirted out in all directions. Its rear paws clawed at the embedded dart.

Trembling, Onna still watched their backs but also took glances at the lion and toward Harjo who had already placed the second dart in his atlatl. He took about three short side steps with his spear in his left hand then stuck the butt end into the ground.

With his back paws, the lion dislodged the dart in his chest, sending it flying out as though thrown by a human hand. At that exact moment, Harjo released another dart. With a slightly side angle view, Onna saw the dart flash in flight but only an instant flash. Then it too struck the huge cat in its now blood-stained white chest.

Once again, the wounded animal released a high-pitched scream as it clawed and fought against the second dart with even greater violence and agony. On its side, it seemed to claw at the ground and the embedded dart at the same moment. At one point, it leaped into the air but then fell back to the ground in a desperate struggle. Then, unexpectedly, it stopped thrashing about and lay still. It panted for a few quick breaths gargling blood and air-then-it lay silent. For an instant, everything was silent and still. Then a sudden breeze blew, ruffling the white fur on the still, soundless, beast.

Harjo now had a third dart loaded with a fore shaft and nocked in his atlatl. He was prepared to make another throw but at the same instant appeared more relaxed. His eyes did not leave the lion as he pulled his spear from the ground with his left hand and continued to watch the motionless beast as though he expected it to leap into action.

"Harjo," Onna said in a low trembling voice nearly a whisper.

"Stay there," he replied without taking his eyes off the motionless animal. "Watch our backs."

Onna continued to hold her ground. She trembled as she watched toward the rear taking quick glances back at Harjo then at the lion. Harjo waited, watching the motionless animal, poised to cast another dart. Finally, after what seemed to Onna to be an eternity, Harjo slowly advanced step by step. He held his spear by the butt end stretched out to full length, point end toward the still terrifying creature. When he was close enough to the animal, he reached his spear out and touched the lion's eye with the spear point. It did not move. It was dead.

Harjo now relaxed and lowered his weapons. He walked back toward Onna but still surveyed the ground behind her. As he drew near, Onna leaned her spear against the sled throwing herself into Harjo's arms. He found it difficult to return her embrace as he held weapons in each hand, but he did his best.

"Oh, Harjo," she cried with her face muffled against his chest. "I much afraid. I much afraid he hurt us."

Harjo managed to lean his spear against the sled then held Onna with his left arm. "Well, he's dead and harmless now. Certainly, he was alone, a single male, or his mate would have attacked by now."

Harjo began to feel his own heart, now beating fast, as he could feel Onna's fast thumping heart. "It seems our plan worked."

"I try to watch back Harjo, I much afraid. I watch you-I watch lion. Lion's face, he charge. It scare me much!"

Her voice and gentle sobs were still muffled against his chest. Harjo thought she might crack one of his ribs as she hugged him so hard. Again, he was reminded just how strong she was. He returned her hug, kissing the top of her head. After a while, her calmness returned.

Harjo carefully pulled the fore shaft from the dart, replacing it and the dart into their respective quivers then slid the atlatl into his belt. He took his spear from the sled with his right hand and held out his other hand to Onna. "Let's go have a look at this fearsome cat."

Smiling now, Onna likewise took her spear from the sled and Harjo's hand then they slowly walked to the slain lion. They stood together hand in hand gazing down in quiet awe at the magnificent white creature. It lay on his side, the final dart imbedded into its bloody chest.

"Harjo," said Onna in a whisper, "he much scary-and much beautiful, same."

"Yes," he answered as he kneeled down beside the beast and but his hand on its side. "He still has his thick winter fur."

Onna also knelt down and reached out to touch the lion. But, just as she did, Harjo made a deep loud growling sound. Frightened, Onna quickly drew her hand back with a surprised "Oh!" Harjo burst out laughing.

Onna tightened her lips then with her fist gently hit Harjo on the shoulder. "Harjo! No scare me!" she said seemingly angry but also laughing. Harjo reached up and taking her hand brought it to the lion's side. They petted the beast together.

"Harjo," Onna said in a whisper smiling at him. "His fur so soft."

"Let's take his pelt," announced Harjo.

Onna looked at him with wide blue eyes. "Yes, yes!" she answered clapping her hands together laughing.

"Plan," declared Harjo.

"Yes, plan," replied Onna as she looked at him listening intently.

"You go and cut some meat from the lion's kill. I think it is a young bison. Take food for maybe two or three days. I'll skin the lion. Then we will go and find a good camping place. We'll eat fresh meat, scrap the lions pelt and leave this place of death and fear for the ravens before it attracts other predators."

"Yes, yes!" Onna replied laughing with excitement. She hurriedly reached into her woman's shoulder bag to pull out her red chert knife and sheath. She leaned over and gave Harjo a quick kiss, picked up her spear, then she got up and ran to the lion's kill.

As she reached the carcass, she noticed that Harjo was right, and the lion's prey was a young bison. Onna thought to herself. "How could he have noticed that? When I saw the lion, I did not pay any attention to its kill." She went down on her knees beside the bison, glancing back over to Harjo and watched him for a few moments.

He stuck the butt end of his spear into the ground then pulled his atlatl from his belt, laying it on the ground. He must have picked up the first dart the lion dislodged from his chest when she was running to the carcass as he now held it in his hands. He examined it closely from end to end and smoothed out the fletching on the end. He then slid his dart quiver off his back and replaced the first dart into the quiver. Then gently, but deliberately, pulled the second dart from the lion carcass. The fore shafts and points of both darts remained embedded in the lion. Onna knew he would cut them out before they left. He closely examined the second dart as he had the first and satisfied of its condition, slid it back into the quiver with its comrades. Then, pulling his knife from its sheath, he got down on his knees by the lion. He rubbed the great beast's blood-stained white chest. Then, to Onna's great surprise, Harjo stared off into the distance as though deep in thought-seemingly in a daydream or drifting into the spirit world. Onna mused to herself, "What was he thinking about? Perhaps he pays homage to the spirit of the lion." Then, just as suddenly, he returned from the spirit world with a jerk of his head and began cutting into the lion's underside.

Onna now got up. Following Harjo's lead, she stuck the butt end of her spear into the ground. She selected the tenderloin along the rear back of the bison and began to cut away its hide. She pondered to herself about Harjo.

"He is only four summers older than I am, and he is not yet a man. But he has just proven himself to be a brave, skilled hunter and warrior. He stood between me and charging white death without the slightest notion of fear. How any man could throw a dart and strike a charging lion, I cannot imagine. I know I am a girl; I am 12 summers in age and I behaved like a girl my age. I accept that fact. Harjo, too, is a boy, but he does not act like one. His behavior and manner are one of a veteran hunter and warrior, a leader, a headman of a band. He behaves in the way I remember my father behaving and I love that about him."

If there was ever any doubt about Harjo, Onna now put it beside her. This young Mammoth Hunter, slayer of lion, was for her. He would be her husband and mate-her hunter-her warrior-her protector. She was not sure exactly how, but she was certain it was her destiny. Only just days before he had saved her life, offered her hope, and a chance for freedom. They had shared sexual intimacy and made love. Making love with Harjo was wondrous beyond her imagination. It was magical. It was of the spirit world. And, he did say he loved her. She knew now her future was with Harjo. She wanted to belong to him.

Now, she thought, just how to convince him that she was his destiny and future. Little ideas began to light up in her intelligent little head. Maybe she should just tell him. She was not sure what to do. As she worked on the bison, ravens were calling and gathering overhead. She heard another call and looked up to see a great soaring bird. It was black with a white head and tail. Another scavenger she thought. All the scavengers would enjoy a great feast including her and Harjo.

Chapter 15:

PROMISES

The small, wooded, unnamed stream provided another pleasant campground. Harjo constructed a sturdy drying rack for the lion pelt while Onna set up camp, made a fire, then roasted the bison steaks over the open coals. The fresh meat provided a welcome change.

Onna realized the near-death experience with the lion brought everything around her to life. How much more wonderful was the fire, the smell of the smoke, and the roasting bison. At only 12 summers of age, her life experiences had been traumatic. She had been abducted and taken by force from her family and country. Most likely her family had been murdered. She had been traded into slavery and kept as a servant girl by strange people under a cruel master. She endured several near-death experiences, saved twice by Harjo. The Mammoth Steppe promised no one, young or old, any guarantees. She must take life now as if was offered.

Onna stopped eating and looked over to Harjo. Her tears melted her vision of him into a silver glow. Harjo felt something as well, perhaps in her silence, and he looked over to see a serious, tear-stained face Onna.

"You think I same baby-I cry same baby, Harjo?"

Harjo smiled. "You can cry when you want. You are free."

"Harjo," She got up on her knees and reached out her oily hands to him. Harjo sensed she was very serious, so he likewise faced her and reached out taking her hands.

"I love you Harjo. I know you love me. I no know how I know, I know. I want marry you, Harjo." She started to say more. She wanted so deeply to say something more elegant than what she just said. To convey so much more than her inadequate Yupik and now very limited Muscogee languages would allow. She stopped. She hoped Harjo knew she was deeply sincere. She held both of his hands hard, bowed her head, and wept.

In the history of the Muscogee Tribe, no woman has ever asked a man for marriage. But there is always the first occasion. Harjo knew Onna was right. He did love her and wanted to marry her even though neither could formally marry, although that would change. He would never find another girl like the one that sat before him now.

"I will be your husband," pledged Harjo, "and I will keep the five promises to you."

Onna looked up into his face. She could just make it out. She wanted to look deep into his eyes, but her tears blocked her vision. But, even without clear vision, she could feel the intense seriousness in his voice. Gripping his hands as tight as she could, she whispered her vow.

"I good wife Harjo, I love you always-always."

They held each other's hands. And, as they looked into each other's face, they became lost-lost in their reflections-lost within in each other-lost within love.

On one side, the promise of marriage seemed to lift a huge burden of life from their shoulders bringing a welcome relief. Conversely, on the other side, the promise of marriage seemed to add an equally heavy burden, but it was different. It was different because they chose to accept what weight marriage would hold.

Harjo finally broke the silence. "Alright, it is settled. After we reach the Wind Band camp and after I become a man, we will marry. You will join the Wind Band and my family."

Tears of joy continued to run down Onna's pretty face. She went to Harjo and embraced him, then put her head on his chest as he held her tight. She whispered, "Yes. I love you-I love you-I love you."

A light, late spring snow had fallen during the night promising an easy day of travel, as the sled would glide easily over the new fluff of white cover. The two young travelers should be motivated into an early start to take advantage of the snow but the warmth of the bed and each other pitted against the cold clear morning air was too much of a challenge for early rising.

Harjo was reasonably sure they were camping on the periphery of his homeland—the land of the Muscogee Tribe-land of the mammoth. He reckoned that with but a short walk, they should come into view of the wide valley of the Echota River. He had not told Onna they were this near the river, but she diligently kept her knot counting string thus, she likewise knew they were in the vicinity of the valley.

Sitting up, under the lean-to, Harjo leaned against the sled enjoying the sunrise and the flush of the new snow cover while Onna slept soundly, nestled against him. He smiled down at her face. She was so beautiful he thought, as beautiful as the sunrise even when she was drooling a little with her hair in her mouth. He reached down and gently brushed her hair out of her mouth. Suddenly, off in the distance, he heard a familiar sound. It was one of those few sounds that were so distinct it could never be confused with any other noise. Onna stirred a little-she was waking up and returning from a deep, night's long sleep. The distant sound rang out again and her eyes bolted open-she awoke—she, too, heard the distant, extraordinary resonance. She looked up at him with eyes wide with excitement and the thrill of discovery.

"What that?" she asked in whisper as though she might frighten the noisemaker away.

"It was the call of the mammoth," Harjo replied. "They welcome you to their valley-the valley of the Echota."

With the palm of her hand, she playfully slapped him on the chest. "No tease me," she said making a serious expression then repeating her question. "What that?"

As the call rang out again, Harjo smiled. "It's the call of the mammoth."

Onna now too heard the distant call and instantly recognized it. She quickly jumped up, grabbed his hand, and pulled him with a child's excitement, shouting in a whisper. "Come! We go! Hurry, Harjo, hurry! We go see them!"

It did not take long to strike camp that cold snowy morning and soon the pair moved together, pulling the sled through shallow new snow up a long gradual incline. Although Harjo could tell Onna was trying to keep control, each instant they heard a mammoth's trumpeting call, she nearly jumped up and down and turned to him laughing with joyful anticipation. Her excitement was catching. Soon they reached a small rocky outcrop situated on top of a low promontory where they stopped; before them now laid the Echota River Valley.

The wide, tall grass plain extended as far as they could see. Now covered with a shallow thin blanket of snow, the grass tops clearly pushed through the new flurry layer. In the distance, they could see the meandering Echota, lined with groves of trees. The brilliant sun reflected off various sections of the great frozen river. Here and there, tall clumps of forested spots dotted the tall grass terrain. Although the new blanket of thin snow covered the ground, emerging signs of spring filtered through. The trees were budding; small patches of green reflected in the light, especially at the base of large trees, and the green tips of low bushes peaked through the snow. The view was breathtaking.

As Onna first glimpsed the wonderful valley, she drew in her breath making an "Oh" sound as she lightly clapped her hands together. Then, she turned to Harjo with a broad beautiful smile and tears in her eyes.

"Harjo," she whispered, "It so beautiful!"

"Yes," he agreed, "It is very beautiful."

They both dropped their sled harnesses. Onna came to Harjo and put one arm around his waist as he followed by putting his arm around her neck and they embraced. Then suddenly, Onna pointed and with joyous excitement, nearly shouting in a whisper, exclaimed, "Look, Harjo, look! Mammoth!" Harjo turned to the direction she pointed out to see a small herd of the great, stately beasts, lumbering along below.

Onna tried once to stick the butt end of her spear into the ground, as a good hunter should, but when it would not stay, she let it fall to the snow. She turned to Harjo, embracing him with both arms and put her head to his chest. She then quietly wept. Harjo did sink his spear's butt end into the cold, snow-covered earth. Then, he embraced Onna with both arms. And, placing his hand on her head, he held her tight.

Part Three
Spring Migration

Micco Yarda again rose. "As soon as the mammoth begin to leave from around Coweta, the Wind Band will initiate Spring Migration."

Chapter 16:

ECHOTA RIVER VALLEY

The breathtaking Echota Valley shaped the physical world, the landscape, and the heart of the Muscogee Mammoth Hunter's domain. The wide low valley was carved and fashioned by the clear shallow Echota River long before human memory-long before the beginning of legend. The river formed and headed from the vast glaciated Apalche Mountain Range far to the north and west. Three glaciated mountains shaped the eastern portion of the range while the solid Koryak Glacier fashioned the western extent. The Koryak Glacier created a solid mountain of ice that reached to the Great Sea. Of the three glaciated mountains, the Cheaha Mountain was of particular awareness to the Muscogee Mammoth Hunters as it supplied tributaries and springs that fed the Echota River, which in turn flowed and meandered southward to empty into the Big River.

Adjacent and northwest of the Cheaha Mountains loomed the larger Tokonhe Mountains, which supplied water for two river systems. The first and larger was the

Kolavinarak River system that flowed southeast to the Great Sea. Named by the littoral Canineqmiut, their several winter villages were located near the coast but inland and situated on this river. On occasion, the Muscogee hunters visited the upper region of the Kolavinarak but otherwise rarely utilized the watercourse. Much of the mid-section of the river flowed near the Koryak Glacier supporting a cold and inhospitable environment. The second was the smaller Etowah River system which emptied into the Echota River just south of the Cheaha Mountains. Finally, to the northeast of the Cheaha Mountains were the more isolated Ochone Mountains. Whatever water drained from this range did not flow down into the Echota Valley and so it was presumed its runoff coursed northward to the Big Ice. The more isolated Ochone Mountains were situated on the other side of the Cheaha Mountain nearer the Big Ice. Consequently, this region remained cold and unwelcoming; accordingly, Muscogee hunters did not explore it.

A system of low foothills formed around the base of the Apalche Mountain Range and its four mountains. All the rivers, which drained from the range, supported narrow wooded valleys as each meandered through the foothills. The southeastern extent of the foothills system formed a set of isolated hills named the Ronoto Hills by the Muscogee. A smaller river, the Coosa, flowed from these isolated hills southeast to empty into the Echota. Bison left the open plains in early summer, moving to the foothills where they calved. They grazed and reared their young throughout the summer and fall in the foothills, then migrated to the upper regions of the Kolavinarak, Etowah, Coosa, and Echota Rivers to survive the winter.

The upland areas and headwater regions of these rivers formed a substantial component of the Muscogee homeland. The several bands of the Muscogee Mammoth Hunters spent the summer and fall seasons along the three rivers of the Etowah, Coosa, and in particular the Echota, but all the bands migrated through the Echota Valley.

Far to the southeast, a large river, similar to the Big River, flowed from the mountains of ice and glaciers that formed the eastern extent of the Mammoth Steppe. The Canineqmiut called this river Kusquqvak and the Muscogee utilized their term. But, as the Big River flowed due west to the Great Sea, the Kusquqvak River flowed south. The Muscogee did not know if the river emptied into the Great Sea or the massive Hetute wall of ice.

Farther still to the southeast, a great solid glacier mountain extended from the Great Sea north and east. The Muscogee Mammoth Hunters called the massive glacier Hetute. It was larger and more massive than anyone could comprehend and just how far it reached southwest, out into the ocean and to the north and east no one knew. Perhaps a strong, young Canineqmiut hunter, skilled in ocean travel paddling a sleek skin kayak could go around the glacier on the Great Sea to the southwest-or perhaps not. A skilled daring traveler could possibly travel far to the north and then east, making his way around the colossal glacier-or perhaps not. No known Muscogee Mammoth Hunters had ever traveled to the Hetute Glacier however, other glaciers had been explored and the glacier environment was well known. Life near the glacier was not possible.

Immense outwash plains, powerful katabatic winds, and major flooding during the summer warming characterized the glacier's inhabitable environment. The vegetation cover was dominated by grasses and sage, but as a result of bitter cold winters followed by short dry summers, mammoth and nearly all herbivores avoided the region. It was a formidable barrier and believed impassable except by flying creatures.

Migrating birds, especially the passerine birds that nested along the wooded rivers and drainages, left the Mammoth Steppe in the fall taking a southeastern course. They returned to nest in the spring. The birds must fly either over or around the massive ice. They could not live on an enormous glacier, so there must be a substantial landmass on the other side.

Similarly, to the northwest, the Koryak Glacier rose from the Great Sea and extended northeast. This huge ice mass, however, was known to be part of the extensive Apalche Mountain Range. Thus, the Great Sea Coast was once thought to extend from the Hetute Glacier in the southeast to the Koryak Glacier in the northwest. But, according to the information Harjo received at the Canineqmiut village and Onna's story and information of her abduction from her home village, it was now known the Koryak Glacier did not block the Great Sea. And that great wall of ice extended a much greater distance southwest than anyone in the Muscogee Tribe could have ever realized.

Spring's awakening across the Mammoth Steppe loomed equally a blessing and a curse-the promise and hope of summer but also the discouraging results of winter. And so, it was with the endless herds of wandering mammoth and the several Muscogee Bands that hunted and followed them. The wooded valley of the enormous Big River provided the mammoth and the other steppe animals' protection against the winter winds, sufficient water, and meager forage from the thick brush and tree bark. The dry grasses could be found under shallow snow in the adjacent protected meadows but the budding spring and the subsequent summer within the vast open plains of the Mammoth Steppe promised to provide an endless panorama of tall green grasses, forbs, and an abundant water supply in the numerous streams, shallow lakes and ponds. This unmatched bounty of nourishment, in turn, provided the means of survival to nursing infant mammoth.

Consequently, mammoth and other herbivores of the vast Mammoth Steppe premeditated the birth of their offspring to early spring as the snow cover melted and winter waned. The new growth of grasses and other vegetation would indirectly provide an endless supply of mother's milk. This bounty lasted all spring and summer and then into the fall, nearly one-half of a complete cycle. This extraordinary abundance gave the infants a season of plenty in which to grow strong and healthy, affording them the best chance to endure the most dangerous season of their lives-their first winter.

To achieve this birth period, the mammoths began to migrate northward from the protected shelter of Big River following the wide Echota River valley in late winter thus reaching the Echota's headwater region and the immense open steppe in early spring. It was a dangerous but necessary trek. Much of the ground still lay frozen and snow covered. If babies were born too late in the spring or later still into the summer, they would not have the full length of spring and summer necessary to grow and gain the strength needed to make the return migration to the Big River Valley. Conversely, if they were born too soon, there would not be sufficient supplies of green, ripe grasses available to their nursing mothers, thus ending the hope of future life. Spring offered the promise of summer but also the effects of a long, harsh winter.

Although each Muscogee band prepared for migration, the mammoth dictated when it actually began. Something in their instincts placed there by the Father Creator told the mammoth when to begin migration. Also, their long experience with weather patterns and seasonal changes likewise helped make that determination. The old bulls initiated migration behaviors by loud trumpet calls to each other. It was a clear, distinctive call as the bulls of each family group sounded out to each other across the herd at large. They recognized each other's calls. They also became restless and impatient, pacing about with aggressive ges-tures-they scrapped the snow with their tusks and pushed against trees.

Next, the old cows followed the bull's behavior and began calling to each other throughout the herd, and as the bulls, they too could recognize each other's calls. Soon, the younger ones caught the calling frenzy, copying their parents. There was little difficulty in distinguishing the dif-ferences in their calls. The old bulls, the young bulls, old cows, and young females, were all distinctively different. All the calves and youngsters, male and female, generally sounded alike.

The boisterous trumpeting continued about three days. Then, on the fourth or fifth day, the old bulls walked through the herd energetically, loud, and aggressive. They each rousted their harem, persuading them to move out. As each family group began to travel, the old patriarch initially led the way accompanied by the dominant cow. Once on their way, the old bulls fell to the rear to guard the families back, making sure each member stayed in formation and did not fall behind. The dominant cow then led the way to the calving grounds.

The Muscogee Tribal Council met on several occasions throughout the winter. Once after all the bands were set-tled at Coweta, another at mid-winter, and finally just prior to spring migration. Certainly, the miccos of each band attended and often the larger bands supported a second authority. Now and then, a band micco would request the presences of his band shaman. Other band miccos often requested Micco Yarda to ask the Lion Shaman to attend, as he was renowned throughout the Tribe for his wisdom and experience. Cheparney generally accompanied Micco Yarda to the meetings, which were most often held at Micco Yarda's mammoth lodge.

The Wind Band took a certain amount of pride that the tribal meetings were conducted at Micco Yarda's lodge. They took assurances that it was kept in good order because it served as a representation of the band. Similar to all mammoth lodges, the main floor was an excavated pit about waist deep. Four selected wooden structural posts were set into the floor out from the pit corners. If possible, a fork created by the limbs of the tree was left to form a fork at the top of each post. Two cross beam posts were laid across the post set into the forks, then two more beams lay across those beams to form a structural square. Selected mammoth tusks were then attached to the structural cross beams usually three to each side. The tips of the tusks were tied to the beams and the bases set on the ground but outside of the floor pit. The structure was then covered with fitted mammoth hides with the wool and trimmed hair on the inside for added warmth. A rock wall weighted down the edges of the mammoth hide cover.

Micco Yarda asked Cheparney if he would take word to all the band miccos that the Tribal Council will meet tomorrow, late morning. Music will make the announcement. Band Miccos usually sent energetic boys to deliver messages from one to another but to announce a Tribal Council meeting required a warrior of some renown. Cheparney agreed.

The Wind Band musicians played at the Council Meeting; the men played flute and percussions instruments. The women singers, however, did not perform. This was strictly a man's world and women were forbidden to attend or to even listen in on such meetings. As directed by Micco Yarda, they first played outside his lodge to call the meeting. It was loud, especially the drumbeats, but it was not really a song, more of a summons. As they noticed the leaders of the other bands approaching, the musicians moved inside and sat on Micco Yarda's platform bed so as to leave ample sitting room around the hearth. Now they played actual songs and the pleasant music created an agreeable atmosphere as the miccos and other Elders and leaders from the various bands slowly, and with a certain air of dignity, filed into the Micco Yarda's mammoth lodge.

They first came into the entry room of the lodge. Any weapons were generally left there and several used sticks to knock off any snow from boots or clothes. They then descended the entry tunnel to the cold trap. The entry tunnel to most mammoth lodges was just the slanted dirt floor. In Micco Yarda's lodge, however, wide steps were cut along the entryway, about hand high, and faced with small support logs. The steps facilitated entry plus added a touch of prestige. At the cold trap, they step up the entry steps and through the entryway as it was covered with a heavy mammoth hide and into the main room.

Many of the miccos and Elders carried backrests and or robes or furs to sit on and found a place on the ground around the hearth, while the second order of leadership usually stood behind the circle of Miccos and Elders. The stone hearth was set in the center of the room between the four structural posts with a skylight cut into the mammoth hide above the hearth to let out fire smoke and allow light to fill the interior. The skylight could be covered when the fire hearth was out. Several long posts were attached to the bottom of the structural post at shin and knee height and many of the visitors used the post as a backrest. Cheparney stood behind and near Micco Yarda. When Micco Yarda determined all were present, he asked the musicians to stop and a somber quiet fell across the crowd.

It was suggested and agreed that Micco Yarda preside over the council, as he usually did, and he accepted. He was actually rather comfortable sitting on his large bearskin against his backrest near the fire, but duty called, thus he rose to speak.

"We have but one pressing issue. Are there any sightings, signs, or word of knowledge of any raiding parties from any hunters, adventurers, traders or boys returning from their Rite-of-Passage?"

The leaders looked around to note if any had knowledge to offer. The old Micco of the Wolf Band did not rise but spoke. "A trader from the Wolf Band went to the Caribou Hunters this winter and has recently returned. He reported to me the Caribou Hunters have not suffered any encounters or attacks this winter or last fall or summer. For better or for worse, the Enemy Raiders do not appear to have been active for several seasons."

Head shaking and agreement followed. Micco Yarda set back down but continued. "Is there anything else to bring before this Council?

The respected micco of the Caribou Band slowly but with determination left his backrest and got up to speak. When he stood, Micco Yarda spoke out. "Micco Yahu has risen to speak. Let us all listen."

The longstanding micco first cleared his throat, coughed, and then spit into the hearth. "Late summer last, a young but mature man took his pregnant wife and two daughters out from our summer camp to pick berries. The girls were something of eight to ten summers of age. They were attacked by a war party of four or five Enemy Warriors. The foolish man was killed—the two girls abducted. They did not take the pregnant wife. She was lucky. They did not rape, beat, or harm her in any manner. The man knew better than to go out so far away from camp without other warriors, without guards, without protection. His wife talked him into the trip. I dispatched a group of warriors, but they were unable to find the raiding party. I suspected they quickly headed north, back into their own land."

Micco Yahu paused, allowing the council to talk among themselves. As he began to speak again, the council grew silent. "Those of us who dwell on the edge of the Echota Valley, such as the Caribou Hunters or the Muscogee Caribou Band, are more susceptible to Enemy Raiders attacks; therefore, it remains prudent for us to take more precautions. Tragedy will befall the man who listens to the childish desires of a woman instead of his own mind and wisdom. Women think with their hearts and stomachs, not their heads. The dead man's brother took the pregnant widow into his lodge and shelter. She may yet find contentment." Slowly the old man returned to his backrest.

The micco from the small Antelope Band did not stand up but instead raised his hand. Then he spoke. "You may have heard the tragic report. A father and son were killed this winter on a dangerous mammoth hunt. They leave a grandmother, a widow of some advanced seasons, and a pregnant young widow without hunters, warriors, or men to pull-sled. You all know we are a small band. Any men who could help these women pull-sled this migration would be appreciated."

Micco Yarda thought to himself. As the Wind and the Lion Band were the two largest bands, he or the Lion Band Micco should offer help, but he really did not want to give up any of his young unmarried warriors this migration. The Micco from the Wolf Band solved the problem.

"We have a youngster just returned from his Rite-of-Passage and publicly acknowledged. That boy's mother died last summer but the father remains unmarried, for too long in my opinion. I will ask those two to pull-sled for your widows and perhaps match-up widows and widowers on each side of our bands." There was general agreement with positive head nodding throughout the Council, then a long silence.

Micco Yarda again rose. "As soon as the mammoth begin to leave from around Coweta, the Wind Band will initiate Spring Migration. Is there any other word?" He looked around the Council. "Then let us go in peace with the joy of music." He turned holding his hand out toward the musicians who began to play.

The leaders rose, slowly and deliberately. As they began to file out of the mammoth lodge, they talked and saluted each other. Outside the weather was sunny, clear, and warm. Several of the old men grabbed the front of their parkas pulling forward so as to circulate some air, laughing and commenting on the warm weather. Restlessness filled the air. In the distance, mammoth bulls could be heard trumpeting migration calls.

Chapter 17:

LEAVING COWETA

A healthy hunter, traveling across snow-covered ground and pulling a sled could complete a journey along the full length of the Echota River Valley from the Cheaha Mountain to Big River in 22 days, give or take three days. A migrating band, however, required many more days to travel the full length of the Echota Valley. Children and the elderly must be taken into consideration during a band migration.

As the Muscogee bands left their winter village at the confluence of the Echota and Big Rivers heading north through the Valley, they did not migrate all the way to the Cheaha Mountain but stopped in the lush open grasslands on the periphery of the mammoth calving grounds well before the mountain. Each band required 20 to 24 days to complete the migration each spring going north and each fall returning south as they followed the migrating herds of mammoth.

Micco Yarda sat on his bearskin leaning against his backrest by the comforting burning hearth. He was planning and calculating the Spring Migration as he had done as far back as anyone could remember with the exception of the Lion Shaman.

"The Wind Band counted 62 people—no wait," he said out loud, "Yahola and Kak-ke's new baby would bring the total to 63. A baby does not necessarily count in numbers except that a young woman, who could have otherwise pulled a sled or helped push one, will now carry a baby. I must be getting old," he chuckled, "Harjo is gone so we are back to 62."

One or two people added or subtracted to the total number was not a concern, but he would miss Harjo. Young unmarried boys of Harjo's age were particularly good at the many assigned duties of the migration and eagerly volunteered. They especially enjoyed tasks that afforded the opportunity to travel out alone. They enjoyed being away from their families and the band over a night or so. In particular, the duties of rear or forward guard positions appealed to older boys and Harjo was exceptionally reliable and mature.

"Harjo had always been mature." The old Micco continued to talk to himself out loud. "Even as a small boy. Oh, he liked all the things that all boys liked, but his behavior more resembled an adult. The seasons go by so fast now. It seems only a few seasons ago Harjo was just a boy playing the fox chase game and now he travels on his Rite-of-Passage. Alright, the migration," he grumbled as he returned to his planning.

He counted 33 sleds, which should be enough allowing two or three, perhaps four empty sleds or with light loads to take on any additional pack such as an accident, injury or an unexpected birth. He did not think any of the women were due now, but he would ask at the band meeting. Micco Yarda preferred to begin the migration with two empty sleds. Two or three unmarried girls were generally cooperative at pulling empty sleds or the Ptarmigan Band of boys would often volunteer to pull an empty sled along with their own. He was counting on Cheparney's girl, Chucuse, to pull an empty sled. She is as beautiful as her mother and most likely to be married soon, perhaps by this summer. Consequently, he would be wise to utilize her during this upcoming Spring Migration because she will likely be married and living with another band by Fall Migration. Now he should consider the most important aspect, the Forward Guard.

Two hunters traveled out as the "Forward Guard" one or two days ahead of the sled pack to select a campsite one day's journey ahead. The distance was most important. If the distance was too far then the sled pack was stressed to reach it in one day's march. Conversely, if it were too short the Wind Band pack would require more days than necessary to reach the final destination, the edge of the mammoth calving grounds. Young hunters tended to go too far which was why he generally assigned a team of one veteran and one youngster. Cheparney and one of his boys often took the Forward Guard, but now Harjo was gone, and Yahola was married with a new baby. Also, should Harjo return during migration, he will likely bring his own sled load of sea mammal pelts and seashells? Micco Yarda laughed to himself. "The females are going to be after Harjo if he returns with a sled load of sea mammal pelts and seashells. I can appreciate youth and Harjo's unique circumstances. "I would not be surprised if that bunny Chufe has already got her pretty eagle claws into him."

If necessary, Micco Yarda could assign two level-headed youngsters as the Forward Guards at the beginning of the migration as the pack followed along the Backbone

Mountains the first several days. That trail was replete with good camping locations. But once they reached the northern end of the valley, however, the daily estimated distance would be more critical; then he would assign a veteran hunter to the task.

The Forward Guard pulled one sled loaded with one-half of the Chokofa "communal" Tent and several pre-cut dried poles. The Chokufa Tent provided summer lodging for the band at large during the long summer camps. It was made of two separate large mammoth hides with all hair and wool removed. With pre-cut holes, it was easily re-titched during the summer as the single Chokufa Tent and separated during the winter and during migration travel. Going ahead of the sled pack, the Forward Guard went out the appropriate distance and selected a likely camping location. Occasionally, a previously used campsite fell within the appropriate distance. They set up the Chokufa hide using the poles they carried and what was available at the location. But more importantly, they were required to locate a raised location safe from mammoth attack. Usually a lean-to configuration was best served. Then they gathered firewood and if possible, they hunted. In the optimum situation, the Wind Band pack would arrive late in the afternoon, before dark, to a shelter cleared of snow, a comfortable fire, warm water or tea brewing, and roasting fresh meat. The sleds were set up around the shelter forming low walls and protection. The people could unpack their bedding, eat, relax, and be in bed for a good night's rest, ready to leave in the morning. All 62 people together under one hide often presented interesting situations, packed in as two young lovers. The children loved it; to them it was a fun game. To the adults, it was tolerable and even enjoyable for a night or two and then slowly edged into stressfulness.

Some families, who counted several young unmarried hunters, might pack their own small shelter. Cheparney's family often did, but now without their two unmarried hunters, they would probably change tactics.

The Forward Guard also provided a measure of protection against attacks by Enemy Warriors. Hopefully, the guards would spot an ambush, but with any sign of Enemy Warriors, they would quickly return to warn the band. There always remained the threat the Forward Guard itself might be attacked however; Enemy Warriors were foremost interested in capturing women. Secondarily, they wanted food and hides. Consequently, a single, lightly loaded sled of two men may not be worth the risk of attack. Katchu, Chufe's father, in addition to his troublesome daughter, also counted three strong boys in his mammoth lodge, one he named Ayo. Micco Yarda would first assign Katchu and one of his boys to the Forward Guard. That would leave Katchu's wife and two boys to attend to his family sled, leaving Chufe to pull an empty one.

The Forward Guard also kept the fires burning and guarded the camp overnight. After two or three nights, several warriors would come to Yarda volunteering to stand night guard. They became too restless trying to sleep in the Chokufa Tent around all the gossiping women and playful children.

Next to consider, the Lead Sled. A single "Lead Sled" attended by two warriors positioned itself roughly 200 paces in front of the sled pack. Their primary purpose was to spot an ambush or any other dangerous threat and to warn the band. If there was an all-out assault from ambush on the whole pack, the attackers would need to consider the Lead Sled and the opposition it would bring. This condition would give the Wind Band an advantage, however slight, they would not otherwise have. "Every spring migration," grumbled Yarda out loud, "it's suggested a warrior and his wife take the Lead Sled because usually a man/wife team pulled the family sled, which would leave one warrior free for another duty." Micco Yarda shook his head frowning. He opposed the idea of a woman assigned to the Lead Sled. If there was an attack, the woman would be stranded from the protection of the pack and would also provide a tempting hit and run target. Also, if the main pack was assailed, the two warriors on the Lead Sled would provide a cross-throw of darts but lessened in power if there was only one warrior.

Since his youth, Cheparney emerged as the most capable warrior of the band. Ever alert, he would spot an ambush before anyone else. That's why Yarda often assigned Cheparney to the Lead Sled and he often assisted him helping to pull or push Cheparney's sled. Cheparney's boys could handle his other family sleds. But Cheparney was aging, as was Yarda, and Ayuko could not pull a sled by herself anymore even an empty one, at least not very far.

"Well," Yarda mused out loud, "I'll begin the migration with Cheparney and myself in the lead for a day or so then see where to go from there. Surely, we two old men can still pull one sled, spot an ambush, and whistle the alert."

Micco Yarda eyes widened as though he had just reminded himself. He tightened his lower lip then curled his tongue-just so-and gently blew out to create a whistling sound. It took a few attempts before he produced an actual whistle rather than silent blown air. "Out of practice," he grumbled to himself. All Muscogee men and boys over ten summers of age, including some women, knew how to whistle loudly, and used the whistles to communicate, especially as an alert call. The various whistles were commonly understood throughout the band and the whole Tribe for that matter. Yarda noted to himself to practice the alert whistle before migration.

The main body of the sled pack was formed into four rough rows. Yarda preferred a row of seven sleds on the left side of the pack. In the event of an attack, the sleds would provide the only cover in open ground. If there was an attack, the sled pack formed two protective circles, a smaller one inside and a larger one outside similar to the defensive circles formed by the musk oxen. If the order was given "defensive circle" the left two rows of seven sleds pulled left forming the smaller circle. The center row, followed by the right-side row, followed behind to form the larger circle around the smaller. Women, children, and elderly men took refuge in the smaller circle. Armed warriors formed a circle on the inside with the outer circle of sleds as protection and thus engaged the attackers.

"We will rehearse a defensive circle," Micco Yarda said, "as soon as the sled pack reaches its first open ground with room to maneuver. Let's see Flanker Guards."

A single warrior was positioned on each flank of the sled pack as the "Flanker Guard." Their duty was to sound the alert in an attack, giving the pack the opportunity to form a defensive circle. A young, swift-of-foot warrior was always assigned this duty. Hopefully, the young Flanker Guard could spot an ambush, sound the alert, and be able to run to the safety of the pack. It was presumed, however, in an all-out attack by a large force, the Flanker Guard would likely be lost. Hopefully, he would take an Enemy Warrior or two with him to the other side. Micco Yarda believed he would assign Ayo to one flanker position. He could recognize the other boy he had in mind but could not remember his name. He found it difficult these days to remember any of the youngster's names, both boys and girls.

The Trailing Sled provided nearly the same function as the Lead Sled only at the rear of the pack and with less focus on protection. During the last several migrations, Honeche's family volunteered for the Trailing Sled duty. Honeche and his wife had four older, unmarried kids, two boys and two girls and an elderly grandmother. As Micco Yarda recalled, they all pulled a sled except of course the grandma.

"Finally," said Yarda with a sigh, "the Rear Guard." A single warrior pulls an empty or near empty sled trailing far behind the pack. The obvious purpose was of course to guard against a rear attack. Yarda preferred two young warriors assigned to the Rear Guard position but often one carried out the duty as there always seemed to be a shortage of warriors. The Rear Guard also insured that no stragglers were left behind which was why he pulled an empty sled allowing him to load and pull anyone that may otherwise be stranded.

The Rear Guard accomplished another important duty. The greater part of the mammoth herd migrated north on the eastern side of the Echota River, then crossed the river to reach the calving grounds. A smaller segment of the herd migrated on the western side of the Echota, moving ahead of the Wind Band. It was most certainly unsafe to move in front of the herd, consequently, the band waited until this smaller segment left, then followed behind the herd. Mammoth could, however, cross the shallow Echota virtually anywhere along its course and they can be unpredictable. Thus, the Rear Guard also kept a close watch to the rear for mammoth to ensure the band was not surprised by a migrating group, large or small, moving up behind them. Such an encounter would most certainly have fatal results.

Although far from ideal, this configuration formed the "desired formation" of migration but there were always changes. There never seemed to be enough warriors to fill all the positions and women complained, if allowed to, that they were overburdened pulling sleds as their husbands or sons were assigned guard duties. On occasion, older people felt they were causing a burden as a young warrior may be assigned to pull them that would otherwise take a guard position.

The Muscogee Mammoth Hunters survived the Mammoth Steppe because they learned long ago to adapt, adjust, and improvise. Changes were constantly made to the migration formation depending on the circumstances. Often the Forward Guard could not be sent out a day in advance but only just ahead of the pack with a full sled to set up camp, leaving no opportunity to hunt, and thus they could not provide fresh meat for the band. Occasionally, only a single hunter went ahead to provide fresh meat and thus the Wind Band pack was burdened with camp set up after they arrived.

But Micco Yarda knew the Wind Band wanted leadership, order, and planning on migration. He would make assignments with the full complement of guards for the first day or so. All would know their duty and responsibility on the first day of migration. Once underway, he would make changes and rotations as needed.

He called a meeting of all adult men and they met in front of his mammoth lodge. The band would leave tomorrow morning, late. He called out guard assignments. There were no questions or dissent and the Muscogee Mammoth Hunters of the Wind Band returned each to their families to make final preparations.

The early morning excitement brewed throughout the Wind Band winter village as every mammoth lodge household was up and active. Each family and family group were busy packing and securing their sled loads. Items were carried out from each mammoth lodge but occasionally an item added too much weight to the load and was returned to the lodge. A sled's load remained critical. If the sled bore too much weight then items may be abandoned along the trail or given away to another family.

In addition to the excitement of migration, the warmth and sunlight of early spring raised optimism, leaving behind a waning winter and lifting the hope and promise for the impending joys of summer. The mammoth herd began leaving several days ago and the Forward Guard left yesterday. The Wind Band was generally the first band to leave Coweta and the continuing trumpet calls throughout the mammoth herd heightened the excitement. The remaining bands would all strike out within the next two or three days.

Micco Yarda and Cheparney leaned against the Lead Sled as Yarda shaded his face with his hand looking skyward toward the sun. "Are you ready to go brother?" Yarda asked.

"No!" Cheparney growled but also smiled. "I would rather be headed off on a trading expedition or better still to explore the upper regions of the Big River."

Micco Yarda laughed. "You've completed more trading journeys to the Caribou Hunters than any hunter in the band, perhaps the whole Tribe. I would think you would be tired of those journeys by now."

"One never knows where the Caribou Hunters are going to camp, so it is always an adventure to find them," Cheparney exclaimed.

"Well, I am sure Harjo will be taking plenty of trading trips to caribou country bringing back more hides than Ayuko can sew. He speaks their language and I would not be surprised if he returned with a young caribou girl on his first trading trip."

Both men chuckled followed by a silent pause broken by Micco Yarda. "I expected Harjo to return to Coweta before Spring Migration. Are you worried for him?"

"No," replied Cheparney. "I look for Harjo to meet us south of Wetumka."

Micco Yarda shook his head to mean he understood. "Well, let's get started. We are not growing any younger," he laughed. With some reluctance, Cheparney shook his head in agreement then moved to the front of the sled to harness up. He looked back and waived to his family group who stood waiting by four sleds although daughter Chucuse pulled an empty sled for band use. They returned a spirited wave especially Ayuko who smiled, waiving enthusiastically retaining a youthful excitement during migrations.

Micco Yarda turned to the awaiting Wind Band and held his atlatl up over his head then called out. "Wind Band-move out!" There was an outburst from the Wind Band as everyone shouted something, many cried out "Yahola!" Cheparney leaned against the sled harness as Micco Yarda stuck his atlatl into his belt and then with both hands, pushed against the sled. Spring Migration was underway.

The several migrations in pursuit of the mammoth herds were necessary for the survival of each band but likewise strained the people's strength, endurance, and patience. To the children, camp movement was a great adventure, a daylong game of endless surprise, fun, and camaraderie with their playmates, especially for the boys. In particular, there was a gang of five boys who called themselves the "Ptarmigan Band."

They pulled their own sled, self-constructed with contributing help from family adults, especially uncles and older brothers. They loaded the sled down with their own supplies including pelts for a tent and a wooden support frame. Along the way, they hunted and killed small game taking turns at pulling the sled, hunting, and riding. Rabbits and birds were the expected quarry especially the ptarmigan. Those abundant birds were not only delicious food but were nearly always unpredictable which made the thrill of hunting them all the more exciting, that is, to a boy of 10 to 12 summers.

The sled caravan including the Ptarmigan Band's sled flushed ptarmigan as singles, pairs, or coveys continuously throughout the day's migration. Frequently, the birds might run on the ground ahead of the boy's sled and then take flight one after another. Other occasion, a covey would break open in a single flush as 10 to 15 birds took to the air in one sudden burst. One could not predict if the startled birds would run or fly some distance ahead or fly up just under boot-covered feet.

Their weapons were not toys only smaller child versions and the young hunters were deadly accurate with their atlatl throwing boards and bird darts. Instead of a stone point, a bird dart was tipped with three curved pointed bone prongs opening outward and cut to create rows of small, back-slanting barbs. Certainly, there were misses, but each boy could bring down a bird on the wing or a hare on the run.

At the end of the day's march, the boys would set up their shelter, build their own fire, and cook the day's quarry. On other days, one or all of the boys might forego the Ptarmigan Band tent, choosing to eat and retire with their own families. For them and the other children of the band, each day of Spring Migration seemed to be an adventure.

Chapter 18:

ACROSS THE VALLEY

The stunning Echota River Valley, akin to so many geological and landscape features across the vast Mammoth Steppe, offered a projectile point contrast with two sharp cutting edges. On one edge, the valley offered open tall-grass plains and meadows filled with mammoth and herds of other herbivores, beautiful camping locations, an abundance of wood, and plenty of clean drinking water. On the other cutting edge, however, the threat of mammoth and lion attack remained constant. Harjo must now take extreme caution in selecting an overnight camping site. Ideally, an elevated area surrounded by large rocks was preferred; conversely, open flat locations were to be avoided in all circumstances. If mammoth came across a human encampment situated in flat open ground, they would charge through, trample the camp and its human occupants. Harjo recalled the first days of his journey and the early morning mammoth encounter at his camp. Higher elevations, steep terrain, large rocks, and even a large felled tree would prevent the deadly beast from a fatal charging attack. Lions would also approach a campsite, posture in quiet lethal stealth to ascertain if an easy kill could be realized. A large fire, alert hunters, and visible dangerous weapons would generally send an opportunistic lion away to search elsewhere for easier victims.

Given his young age, Harjo had already migrated up and down the Echota River Valley many seasons learning by heart a plethora of comfortable and safe camping locations. As the bulk of Echota River mammoth herd migrated on the east side of the river, most Muscogee bands migrated on the west side. Those bands that spent the summer and spring near the Ronoto Hills located eastward of the Echota crossed the river once they reached the narrower and shallower sections of the stream in the north. One or two bands actually crossed the river at the beginning of the migration near the confluence with the Big River while the river remained frozen. It was risky because the freezing thickness of the river was unpredictable from season to season. During the course of one winter, it may be so cold the river may freeze solidly enough that a mammoth could cross, although they seldom would. Conversely, another winter might prove dangerous for the ice to hold up a child. One could generally determine by the severity of the winter, but each band's Micco made those decisions.

An overexcited Onna and an equally jubilant Harjo pulled their sled down a gradual grade into the Echota Valley. Harjo would lead them all the way to the wooded edge of the river then northward to eventually find the Wind Band. They may meet other bands on the way as the Wind Band was usually the first to begin Spring Migration and likely to be several days out in front of the other bands.

As the several bands of the Muscogee Tribe continued northward, each spread out and followed minor drainages east or west to their preferred calving areas of the mammoth herd. The Wind Band branched off to the northwest. Two bands would follow the Coosa River, a tributary of the Echota, to the northeast to the Ronoto Hills and the headwater region of the Coosa River. Two other minor tributaries fed into the Coosa from the Ronoto Hills.

Onna's grasp of both the Muscogee and Yupik languages improved daily. She remained exhaustedly inquisitive although her questions now focused on the more social-cultural aspects of the Muscogee Mammoth Hunters and the Wind Band rather than survival skills, as she would join the Wind Band through marriage and adoption. By luck, they came across a low brushy rock "up crop" that supported several trees and although void of water, it provided a very safe place to camp. They sat quietly together watching the fire. After so many days of travel across the Coastal Zone and the western region of the steppe, to finally camp in the Echota Valley provided a sense of comfort.

But curious Onna would not remain quiet for too long as she noticed a flash and fluttering movement. "Look, Harjo," she whispered with a hint of excitement, "little birds with red on top—red here." She tapped her breast with the palm of her hand. Harjo looked to see the busy little flock chattering around the rocks and brush.

"Yes, I see."

"What name, Harjo?"

"Finches, red finches," he answered. He watched the small brown and white striped birds about two fingers in size with a bright red spot on the top of their heads and a lighter, flush color, breast. He saw the birds often during the spring and summer paying them little attention but now marveled at their flush colored breast for it was nearly the same color as Onna's lips and her nipples.

"The color of the bird's breast," said Harjo, as he tapped his chest, "is the same color as your lips." He leaned over giving her a kiss.

Onna kissed him back then announced, "I no see color my lips, Harjo. Same bird?" she asked as she licked her lips then squinted to look down her nose as though she might see her own lips.

"Yes," answered a cheerful Harjo smiling at her antics, "same as the bird."

Onna was pondering a question for Harjo. Within reason, she understood Harjo's Rite-of-Passage and what was required for its completion. Rite-of-Passage seemed to be a difficult phrase for her to pronounce so she used the term "Man-Journey" in its place or its female counterpart.

"Harjo?" asked Onna. "Girls you band have Woman-Journey?"

Harjo thought for a moment then understood. "Yes, girls have a woman's Rite-of-Passage."

"You tell me?" asked an enthusiastic Onna.

"Certainly," he replied as he gathered his thoughts together. He then realized it would be more complex than Onna was going to appreciate.

"For a woman of the Wind Band, her Rite-of-Passage begins at her first menstruation. Her family prepares a special hut for her located at the edge of the camp or village. Also, each band maintains a small permanent mammoth lodge just for this purpose to house any girl should her menstruation occur during the winter. There she remains isolated for a period of some seven to 14 days. Her mother and other female family members bring her food, other necessities, and the comforts of life." This was the component

Harjo was sure that Onna would object too. But she did not say anything, at least thus far, so he continued.

"During her stay, she is expected to produce an article of value. Nearly always the girl makes an article of clothing by sewing although some girls may weave something from mammoth wool. Also, during her stay, female Elders of the band will come by to visit offering her words of encouragement or wisdom on achieving a successful adult female life."

Onna reached up, then gently tapped his lips with her fingers and he stopped. "I no like, Harjo, it hard."

"Do you want me finish?"

A frowning Onna offered a sad "Yes."

Harjo cleared his throat and continued. "When her stay has passed, she visits a council of village Elders which usually consists of the village Micco, the shaman, and other female Elders of some renown. They examine her created article and ask her various questions. If all goes well and the council is satisfied that she is mature enough to accept the responsibilities of marriage and family life, they declare her Rite-of-Passage complete."

"This part you will like." Harjo looked to see a still unhappy frown on Onna's face but still attentive. "At a public gathering, the village Micco declares her an adult female and that she is eligible for marriage. She is also presented with a carved ivory or bone female figurine to be worn as a necklace. The figurine often depicts enlarged female breasts and or buttocks. Many believed the large breast and buttocks will attract the Father Creator who then sends many babies and plenty of mother's milk to the woman. A plain female bust without enlargements is equally popular for the same reasons. All are a sign of fertility and to symbolize her acceptance into the band and the tribe at large as an adult female. Girls proudly wear these figurines during the next few seasons of theirs lives. Eventually, as they mature, marry, have children, and come to own other types of necklaces, these Rite-of-Passage necklaces are worn less frequently. But still, women keep these first simple figurines for their entire lives often using the carved pieces to attach to their menstruation counting chords."

"Dyuktai girls have same Woman-Journey," offered a still unenthusiastic Onna. "Girls have woman carving have big breast and bottoms." Onna reached up and grasped both her breasts then reached around grabbing her buttocks to emphasis her words. Harjo chuckled at her gestures.

Still wearing a sadden frown on her face, Onna laid her head on Harjo's chest. "I no want sleep hut alone, Harjo, I sleep you."

Harjo smiled and stroked her hair.

"No send me hut, Harjo, please"

Harjo still smiled but he could tell by her voice she was scared and serious. "I will not send you to a hut. You will sleep with me," said a smiling but serious Harjo.

"You promise?" asked a little whinny Onna voice.

"Yes, I promise," answered Harjo as he continued to stroke her hair. "Are you smiling?" he asked.

"Yes," she answered with a hint of laughter, then she snuggled up against him. "Harjo?" asked Onna.

"Yes," he replied.

"What hut?"

Harjo laughed out loud, but also explained to Onna the meaning of a hut.

Two caribou herds roamed within the realm of the Muscogee Mammoth Hunters north of the Big River and south of the Cheaha Mountain simply called the Large and the Small Herds. The Large Herd's extensive calving range lay southeast of the Ronoto Hills. Each winter that herd migrated south to the Big River, far west of the Echota River. The Caribou Hunters followed the Large Herd that provided for all of their needs.

The Small Herd calved on the western fringes of the Echota Valley migrating south for the winter to the Big River, just west of the Backbone Mountains and the Coweta winter village. Caribou migrate subsequent to the mammoth. Most animals learned long ago to not migrate in front of the huge mammoth. Besides, the caribou have a shorter migration distance and their endurance enables them to cover long distances without rest.

The only predictable phenomenon of the Mammoth Steppe remained its unpredictability. One day a hunter may observe a mammoth crashing through the forest in such a loud clamor that it scares all other animals in the area away. The next day he may turn around to discover the same mammoth has come up behind him in a soundless march, threatening his life. Life on the Mammoth Steppe teaches you to take nothing for granted and take advantage of all your opportunities.

Early morning found Harjo and Onna as they continued on but the usually talkative Onna remained quiet-listening to the sound of spring in the Echota Valley. Suddenly, a strange whistling sound caused them both to stop, searching the immediate landscape for the noisemaker. Then, a smiling Onna pointed with her spear. "Look Harjo, look," speaking in her loud whisper voice. A mere 20 paces to the east, a large ground squirrel type animal perched on a rock pile sitting up on his back legs whistling and barking at them.

Excited, Onna reached her small left hand up and caressed the right breast of her parka. It was outlined by the circular shape of the dark stripe of fur from the marmot and still supporting a broad beautiful smile, she turned to Harjo.

"Same animal, Harjo, same my parka!"

Harjo likewise smiled as he looked to Onna pointing at the animal as it persisted to whistle alerts, and as Onna continued to caress her parka.

"What name, Harjo, what name?"

"Marmot," answered Harjo.

"Why we no see, Harjo?"

"They hibernate all winter and much of the spring and fall."

"What mean, hi-ber-nate?"

"They sleep during the winter and cold weather in burrows deep underground. They live in large family groups with one strong male and several females."

Onna turned toward Harjo and stuck the butt end of her spear into the ground. She looked to him with an adoring expression. "Marmot fur make pretty parka. I no have good clothes-you give me. Thank you, Harjo."

Harjo also planted his spear, then reached out taking Onna by her arms and pulled her to him. She eagerly came to him and stood up on her toes, her mouth close to his, beginning to breathe hard. She completely belonged to him now. He could take her any moment he wanted-she would not refuse him. He could take her now simply by pulling her pants down, turning her around, and bending her over. He smelled her breath. It was always so sweet. He kissed her long, but gentle.

"I will always love and provide for you Onna-always."

Onna remained touched by Harjo's kindness and generosity. She stretched her arms around him, placing her head against his chest and softly wept. Harjo folded his arms around her and held her. Onna could feel his warmth and his strength. She could also feel his courage and commitment to her.

Harjo held and comforted her until he could feel she had finished crying. He then took her hand and his spear, and she followed. With the smiling look only young lovers wear, they continued on.

Late morning, the Echota Valley terrain provided its own traveling hardships. Harjo and Onna enjoyed a well-deserved rest on a small knoll adjacent a wide game trail. Mammoth and other migrating animals left their sign on the trail including caribou from the Small Herd. Harjo decided to take a long rest, so he pulled the bison robe off the sled, then he and Onna sat back to back supporting each other and drinking water. Onna was quiet for some reason. Harjo presumed she was tired.

Suddenly, Onna tapped Harjo on the leg. "Why is she tapping me?" thought Harjo, Onna is never too tired to talk. As he turned, she raised her hand and pointed. Harjo looked to see a small group of 10 to 12 caribou following the trail not more than 20 paces from them. He had removed his dart quiver and atlatl, laying the weapons on the sled, which was a short distance away, but his spear was at hand.

Harjo slowly rose up, hurled the spear, and it struck a young cow in the chest that was unfortunately the nearest target. The red chert point sank deep and the wounded animal bleated a ghastly call as it bolted into a blind run taking the small group with her. A now excited Onna jumped up.

"Look, Harjo, you harpoon her!"

"Yes," replied Harjo, "It's a mortal wound."

An energized Onna grabbed Harjo by the arm with both hands as he moved to the sled and she followed. He picked up his dart quiver and pulled a dart, then slipped the quiver over his head. He armed the dart with a foreshaft and pick up his atlatl. They both kept a keen watch all around them, the horizon, and especially the trail in case a predator followed the caribou.

Onna was somehow able to keep both her attached to Harjo's arm as he pulled on his dart quiver and armed a dart. How she managed to do these seeming impossible little maneuvers Harjo did not know.

She then pointed, "Look, Harjo, look, she fall!"

"Alright," he replied, "Let us go find her."

Onna clapped her hands, laughing with a jump or two. "Harjo it long I have ..." She stopped short in her sentence then turned to look a Harjo with a childish frown and wrinkled eyebrows. "How you say, Harjo?"

Smiling, Harjo answered, "Caribou!"

She repeated the word as she reached for her spear leaning against the sled and once in the harness, they pulled toward the fallen caribou.

"I can learn throw harpoon same you, Harjo?" asked Onna as they approached the caribou.

"Of course, you can Onna, it only takes practice." Onna had practiced with Harjo "nearly" every morning and she was now inspired to practice "every" morning. Onna did not want to go hunting with men every day, but to be able to cast her "harpoon" and strike a caribou would be a magical accomplishment.

They stopped a few paces from the carcass and dropped their harnesses. "I can find dead, Harjo?" asked a serious Onna.

"All right," he answered, "watch and be careful,"

A solemn Onna nodded her head yes and took her harpoon by the butt end, then approached the caribou with stealth and caution. Once in position, she touched its eye with the red chert point prepared to thrust if necessary.

269

There was no movement. She stepped back and turned to Harjo smiling. "Dead, Harjo."

"Very good," said Harjo with since of pride. He was proud of her. "Given another season or two," he said to himself, "he would teach her to kill a caribou. Boys her age could kill a caribou and she carried more than enough strength."

A single hunter on his hands and knees, with limited vision and hearing, concentrating on dressing an animal that could attract scavengers and predators alike was taking a risk and asking for a deadly ambush. With fresh blood in the air and a fresh kill on the ground, an approaching male lion would most likely attack. Harjo would stand as armed guard while Onna dressed the caribou. She took off her fancy parka laying it on the sled and picked up her old one. Harjo would have discarded it by now but Onna kept it just for such occasions as this. She would have completed the dressing task bare breasted before risking blood and guts on her new parka.

It did not take Onna long to dress the caribou while Harjo guarded for predators and scavengers, although he would step in and help with moving and lifting the animal. "Winter hide Harjo, no good, no can sew, we no keep." Harjo shook his head in agreement.

He pulled out the poles he cut many days ago and fashioned a pole-travail complete with harness. The dressed caribou carcass loaded well on the pole-travail. They carried an ample water supply and they used plenty to wash off the blood and other dressing remains. Onna pulled the pole-travail while Harjo took the sled. A kill site was exciting but equally tense due to the threat of predators and scavengers but as they moved away to a safe distance, the tension eased. They stopped for water and Onna decided she would trade her parkas again and wear her new one. She pulled off her old parka which was spared a blood bath by Onna's careful caribou dressing. Harjo could not help but notice a beautiful naked Onna.

She noticed Harjo watching her. She smiled and put her hands behind her neck arching her back, then in a teasing yet seductive voice asked. "You watch me, Harjo?"

Caught staring, Harjo was not afraid to admit it. "Yes, he smiled, "you are very beautiful."

Onna appreciated that answer. Keeping a seductive smiling manner, she stepped up against him then turned around and looked back over her shoulder. "You want sex me Harjo? Be careful, lion catch us." She bent over just slightly and rubbed her bottom against him still beaming as she looked over her shoulder.

"You are an adorable little tease, aren't you?" he said as he drew his hand back and gave her a hard spank on the bottom. Onna reacted to the spank with a childlike squeal and bunny jump. "I'll sex you tonight, little bunny, but now we need to keep moving and find a campsite." Harjo scanned the horizon and the sky.

It did not take long and still early in the day, they came to a wide, shallow little wooded brook, which eroded and formed a curved steep bank and an excellent safe camping location. The high terrace bank lay in full sun, which had melted the snow leaving a welcome mat of short, thick green grass. Soon a large fire burned roasting fresh caribou meat. Enough sunlight remained to dry meat strips as well. Harjo dug a pit, lined it with rocks, and burned a fire in the cavity. Then he wrapped the hindquarters in grass and buried it in the pit. The meat would slowly roast overnight and in the morning, they would enjoy a tender roast.

Using ample warm water, Onna took a complete bath with soap and with the afternoon sun and green grass, it was nearly like summer. She also washed her old "animal dressing" parka in the stream, calling out to Harjo to tell him how cold the water was. Little wonder Onna marveled as Harjo bathed in the stream and she laughed at him yelling out "oh Harjo, it too cold-cold-cold!" With all the evening chores complete, the meat cured and packed away, they set by the fire enjoying a fresh meal.

"Harjo?" asked Onna, "Mammoth Hunter men and women greet same?"

Harjo pondered her question momentarily then reasonably sure he knew what she asked, answered. "No, they greet differently. Muscogee men greet each other by clasping hands or wrist. They use one hand more formally and two hands for those well acquainted, similar to the Canineqmiut men. Family members and good friends may also embrace but men never kiss. A father may kiss his sons at any age but usually only when they are boys. As they mature to adults, they will embrace but seldom kiss."

Onna shook her head yes with an understanding expression. "Same, women?" she asked.

"No," he replied, "Women are just the opposite. They kiss each other, friends, and family on many occasions throughout the day. However, women will not kiss a man outside of her family, perhaps a lifelong male friend as the rare exception or perhaps a young boy who has given her a gift. But she does kiss men within her family and most certainly her sons, daily."

"Women greet each other with a prescribed kiss. An older dominant woman will kiss a younger submissive one in the same manner as a man or her husband would kiss her. A man dominates a woman and penetrates her in sex and likewise penetrates her mouth with his tongue in a kiss."

Smiling, Onna interrupted, "I like you give me man kiss, Harjo, pen-e-trate, tongue. I like you, do-min-ate."

Chuckling, Harjo continued. "In the same manner, a dominant woman of higher status will address and kiss a younger, submissive woman of lower status. In particular, the mother of the household will kiss her daughters and the young wives of her sons in this manner."

"Mother you, Harjo, give me man kiss with greet?"

Harjo thought for a moment. "I don't think so. You know she is Canineqmiut, so she will probably rub noses. She may kiss you, but not as a man."

Onna smiled then playfully she made a deep sigh, rubbed her stomach, and fell over on Harjo so that her head lay in his lap. "I no can eat more, Harjo," she said with a groan and frown.

"You're stuffed," answered Harjo, laughing as he reached over rubbing her stomach, "You feel pregnant."

Onna rolled off Harjo on to the ground holding up her arms and still using a groaning voice, "I no can walk Harjo, carry me bed."

Of course, she could walk but Harjo got up to comply and picked up a laughing Onna who kicked her legs as he carried her to bed. The simple pleasures of life and loving company are the memories most cherished. Another day ends on the Mammoth Steppe, full and complete with the promise of tomorrow.

The next early morning was cool and sunny and found Harjo awake with Onna snuggled up tight against him soundly sleeping, as would a milk stuffed baby hare. Harjo wore a mischievous smile across his face brought on by the idea of a prankster trick. He snuck out of bed, ensuring Onna was still covered and found the bison robe and laid it on the ground several paces from their mammoth bed. He returned to the bed to pick up naked Onna and carried her to the bison robe then laid her on it still sound asleep. He returned to the mammoth bed and got back in. It did not take long for a shivering Onna to wake and realize where she was and what had happened.

She called out, "Harjo! You, naughty boy! Harjo, you naughty! She jumped up and ran back to bed. Harjo laughed out loud and threw back the top mammoth bed cover and stretched out his arms to welcome her back into the bed. As she climbed in, he pulled the cover and his arms over her, but she still made a fist and now laughing, pounded on his chest.

"You big naughty boy, Harjo, you naughty!" She pointed her finger at his face. She wanted to be stern but could not help but laugh.

"You get switch, Harjo, you get switch!"

She also wanted to give him a stern lecture, but she first wanted to snuggle against him to rewarm her cold, naked body. This story was told and retold to children and grandchildren on many occasions. Harjo embraced Onna as he held her tight and they laughed together in the way only two playful children of the Mammoth Steppe can.

Chapter 19:

REUNION AND ATTACK

The two brothers struggled with the sled. Micco Yarda pulled against the harness as his cold breath, illuminated by the bright sun, formed around his hood as if it were campfire smoke. Cheparney was likewise huffing deep breaths from within his chest as he pushed the loaded sled. Micco Yarda stopped and then turned around toward Cheparney.

"Whistle for the pack to take a breather," he gasped as he let the sled harness fall to the snow-covered ground, then walked around to the side of the sled.

Cheparney turned to the following pack of sleds and whistled the signal to stop, waving his hands over his head and then he joined his brother leaning against the side of the sled. He untied the water pouch-took a long drink-then handed the pouch to Yarda who followed with a drink.

Some 30 paces toward the river stood an ancient "mammoth tree." In the distant past, a bull mammoth had vented his frustrations on a young cottonwood tree, pushing it over and breaking off several limbs. The tree survived, however and continued to grow but in a deformed condition. The tree was now very old and most certainly outlived its mammoth attacker, his calves, and their offspring.

Yarda pointed to the ancient tree. "Do you remember that mammoth tree when we were boys, Cheparney?"

Cheparney glanced toward the tree then nodded his head yes.

"The band pulled sleds just past the tree and we often took rest stops here as we are now. You and I and the other children played in the tree as the band rested."

Again, Cheparney shook his head yes as he recalled similar events.

"But now," explained Yarda, "the trees, bushes, and saplings have grown, expanding from the river some 30 or 40 paces."

"I know," concurred Cheparney, "the forested drainages are expanding and taking over the grasslands. I've noticed theses subtle changes over many seasons."

"I can tell you more," continued Yarda. "The Lion Shaman told me when he was a boy, the band pulled sleds during migration on the other side of this same mammoth tree near the banks of the Echota. Something else, last summer, as we camped near the mammoth calving grounds, the old Lion Shaman had his helpers take him out on travail because he wanted to see the herd. I went along."

"Yes, I recall," replied Cheparney, "most people thought the behavior strange, except that it was the Lion Shaman, who already is strange."

"Well, we made our way up to the top of a low rock outcrop for a good view of the herd. The shaman told me when he was a boy there were twice the number of mammoth in the herd than now. He said he had been watching all of his life. Each spring, a few more mammoth migrate up the Big River, north and east. He presumes there is another river valley upstream, a tributary of the Big River, and that the mammoth are moving into that valley. He also presumes there are other calving grounds. He told me these two events are related. The Mammoth Steppe is changing as the forest areas expand into the grasslands supporting fewer mammoth. Thus, they move eastward, a few each spring migration. It is not so noticeable from season to season, spring to spring, but over a long lifespan, it becomes very apparent. Eventually, most of the animals, the grass eaters and their predators, will leave the Echota Valley."

"Perhaps," pondered Cheparney, "we should encourage our young warriors throughout the whole Tribe to journey eastward up the Big River on their Rite-of-Passage journeys and begin to explore the lands to the east."

"I think that would be wise," added Yarda. "Next winter I may bring this up as a topic of discussion at the Tribal Council."

Cheparney shook his head in agreement as he took another long drink of water.

"I miss my boys, Cheparney, killed in a mammoth hunt." Cheparney looked at his elder brother but did not respond and instead took a deep breath. Micco Yarda's remorse was short lived as he returned to lighter matters.

"I wish you had more boys, Cheparney," laughed Micco Yarda. "In fact, I have always hoped you would purchase a second or even a third wife. You could certainly support them. I am looking forward to the days of being pulled by your boys in a warm, soft sled when I am too old to walk."

Cheparney laughed out loud. "Ayuko is all the woman I can endure. Besides, I am too busy looking for wives for your young nephews."

"Exactly what I mean," smiled Yarda. "While you are busy assisting your sons with their wives, you could easily pick up one or two young girls for yourself. I understand pretty Chufe might be bought at a low price."

Both men laughed out loud as they resumed their respected positions on the sled. Cheparney whistled to the sled pack to move out and Spring Migration continued.

Early in the day, with ample remaining sunlight, the Wind Band reached a good camping location often used during Spring Migration. The Forward Guard had the camp setup with a large fire burning although they had not been successful in killing any fresh meat.

Ayuko was glad. She was tired and looked forward to a long night's rest. The whole family had gone off with Cheparney, including Kak-ke with her baby and Chucuse to see something they all concluded was interesting and important. The girls usually stayed with her, but she remained alone with their sleds as she proceeded to build a fire. She gathered some wood and was looking around to see the nearest family with a fire going to use a fire stick, when she heard a shrill whistle that she recognized immediately. She sucked in her breath and whispered her son's name, "Harjo."

She turned to see the distant figure of Harjo, his sled, and a small female figure beside him. She now called his name out in a joyful yell then ran toward him. Harjo planted his spear and dropped his sled harness and Onna followed. He took Onna's hand then walked toward his advancing mother. As they grew near, Ayuko threw herself at her son, hugging him with all her strength. Releasing Onna's hand, Harjo returned her embrace.

"Harjo! Oh, Harjo! I am so glad you're back. I've missed you so much," she said, seemingly laughing and crying at the same moment in such a way only a woman can do. She rubbed Harjo's nose with hers then showered his face with kisses.

She held him for a long moment, then took his hands and stepped back to look him over. "Are you alright?" she asked still smiling and crying. She added the motherly side of her to her voice. "Now don't tell your mother a story. Are you alright?"

"I am alright mother—I am fine."

Ayuko still held her son's hands as she looked over to Onna. She took in her breath in surprise and looked back to Harjo. "I see you will have some tales to tell. Who is she, Harjo?" Harjo dropped his mother's hands and put his arm around Onna.

"Mother this is Onna."

Onna held out both her hands and Ayuko took them and then gazed into Onna's face in astonishment. Having asked Harjo how to say various words, Onna had rehearsed and constructed her own greeting in Muscogee as she now proudly spoke up.

"Glad to meet you. I hope you are well. I am Onna. I belong to Harjo. He is my hunter, my warrior, and my protector."

Ayuko was taken back. "Thank you very much, Onna," replied a smiling Ayuko still in astonishment. "I am glad to meet you." She noticed that Onna wore the woman's bag she had made for Harjo to take on his Rite-of-Passage Journey and that he had indeed given it to a pretty girl. She then gently pulled Onna toward her and leaned into her face to rub noses with her. Onna immediately recognized the

Canineqmiut welcome and replied in kind. Ayuko then kissed Onna's cheek and again, Onna returned the greeting.

They released hands and Onna wrapped both her arms around Harjo's left arm. Ayuko turned to Harjo. "I am not sure I believe what I see, Harjo. What a beautiful, strange girl and the color of her hair and her eyes. Where does she come from?"

There was not the opportunity to answer for now as the whole Wind Band circled around them greeting Harjo and welcomed his return. All the band, young and old, marveled at this stunning extraordinary girl. Soon Cheparney and the rest of Harjo's family returned, as they had not gone very far. Onna saw the reaction when Cheparney called out Harjo's name and Harjo returned the call. Onna reluctantly released Harjo's arm so that he could properly greet his family, but she smiled at the joy and smiles on their faces especially when father and son embraced. She was overwhelmed by the greetings and the astonishment for her and she was also moved by the warmth and affection she received from Harjo's family.

When she took Cheparney's hands, normally she would have been fearful and reluctant as he was such a tall, strong, seemingly fierce warrior. But instead she felt an inner strength in him, spirit strength, something that told her only the enemies of the Wind Band need to fear him- that he would never harm her. She felt the same inner spirit strength with Harjo.

Onna also marveled at how Harjo, Ayuko, and sister, Chucuse, switched back and forth between the Yupik and Muscogee languages seemingly with little effort and apparently for no particular reason. Except for brother Yahola's wife Kak-ke, the whole family could add in words and phrases in Yupik to the conversation, especially Cheparney.

The Wind Band built a single large fire then the whole band gathered around it to eat and to hear Harjo's stories and to ask questions to and about Onna. She was overwhelmed and shy but not afraid. Onna clung to Harjo most of the evening and very seldom let him go. Watching them together and their sincere affection for each other brought smiles to many faces especially to older women.

The Forward Guard had not been successful in hunting but the adventurous boys, eager to explore, discovered a large patch of potatoes in early bloom. The small white flowers and the grass-like leaves identified the plant. They carefully dug the root tubers making sure that roots remained in the ground to insure future growth. The tubers, about the size of a baby's fist, were relished especially when roasted around the edge of a fire. All were grateful for the boy's find and their efforts, and along with mammoth jerky and hot tea, the meal was most enjoyable and as memorable as the First Kill Feast during the summer.

All marveled at the story of how Onna came to be at the Canineqmiut village, her escape, and her journey with Harjo from the coast of the Great Sea. It was likewise an ironic story because Cheparney and Ayuko had made a similar journey from the Great Sea many seasons ago. Everyone, perhaps with one exception in the person of Chufe, was pleased that Harjo and Onna apparently would marry. By Mammoth Hunter wisdom, they were already mated by "spirit law" if not yet by legal action. Micco Yarda declared the band would stay to rest at least one day. They had pulled hard the last several days and this camp was a good location. Perhaps some fresh game could be felled.

Although the large Chokofa communal tent was erected and many families slept under its shelter, other families, including the Fus Chate, setup their own family tents usually in the form of a lean-to. Ayuko later learned the big attraction that Cheparney had taken the whole family off to see, leaving her alone to greet Harjo and Onna, was the clean dry bones of a young mammoth, consequently the tusks were just the right size to form the opening of a lean-to tent. The men carried the tusks and other long bones back to camp. With the ends of the tusks lashed together and propped up by several poles, they formed a lean-to frame supporting an arch opening. Once covered by their furless bison skin covering, the lean-to provided a comfortable, private shelter. The Fus Chate woman made the beds inside the shelter although Ayuko did not allow Chucuse to sleep with her brother and had not for many seasons although she was welcomed to bed with her and Cheparney as she often did on the cold nights of Spring Migration. Harjo and Onna set up their little shelter next to the family lean-to. As Onna became more familiar with the family, they too would sleep inside the family shelter.

The day of rest was welcomed. The whole band shared in Harjo and Onna's arrival in one way or another, but spring migration will not wait, and they must take advantage of the snow that still blanketed the ground. It would not last long. The air warmed, the winds relaxed, and the mammoth maintained a steady pace toward their calving grounds. Harjo and Onna found themselves in the middle of the caravan sled pack situated on the outside of the left flank. They laughed and talked as they pulled their sled with the same youthful optimistic outlook, they nourished on their journey from the Canineqmiut village and the Great Sea. Without the weight and load of the seal pelts now distributed throughout the family members, Onna could pull their sturdy sled by herself. During the majority of the day's journey, they pulled together but occasionally each pulled alone to give the other a restful moment. Harjo periodically left Onna with the sled to go up to the front of the pack to check with Cheparney and Micco Yarda on the caravan's progress.

Onna attracted the children, especially the girls, with some type of unseen magic. Throughout the day's march, children gravitated to Onna's sled, asking to ride and talk with her. Some would come over, walk beside her, hold her hand, and ask her questions. They did not realize she was still learning Muscogee but nonetheless delighted in her unusual voice and pleasant laughter. Onna learned a children's song from Ayuko and would periodically sing the song as children would run to her sled to join in. Although she didn't really know what the Muscogee words meant, the children enjoyed the song and everyone in the band remarked on her beautiful singing voice.

A youngster named Ayo was assigned sentry duty on the left flank of the caravan, however, Harjo did not trust the lad. He was only two or three summers younger than Harjo, but the boy did not take matters seriously and often paid little attention. Harjo thought him immature and guarding the caravan flank proposed a serious task.

"He's too far out," said Harjo.

"What?" Onna replied.

Pointing to the distant figure, Harjo repeated, "The Flanker Guard Ayo is too far out."

Onna looked and replied "oh" with a smile not really understanding the preferred distance of a Flanker Guard.

Harjo took off his harness. "I am going up front. Maybe I'll ask Micco Yarda and dad if I can relieve Ayo for a while."

"Yes," Onna replied, then smiling and holding out her chin, she said, "Give me kiss." Smiling, Harjo kissed her, then slid his spear into the bindings of the sled and pulled a dart from his quiver attaching a fore shaft. He thought he would carry a dart for a while and then he started off in a slow jog toward the front of the caravan.

A young girl of five or six summers approached and asked Onna if she could ride with her. Onna didn't completely understand what she said but she knew what she meant. She picked the girl up, gave her a kiss, and set her on the sled. She then saw a beautiful sight off to the left. A small patch of yellow flowers peaked through the snow surrounded by bunches of green grass. Unable to resist, Onna pulled the sled over to the flowers to pick them. Smiling she smelled. What a wonderful scent she thought. She handed the bouquet to the girl. "These are for you," she said smiling. The girl took the flowers and said thank you. Smiling she made an "mm" sound as she smelled the fragrant bouquet. As she reached for the sled harness, Onna looked up and out across the landscape of the left flank of the caravan expecting to view the lone distant figure of Ayo on guard. Instead, she saw three warrior figures running at top speed toward the caravan. Fear swept through her like a cold chilling wind-Enemy Warriors.

She did not panic. Without hesitation, Onna put her hands together blowing the strange alert call she had shown Harjo as loud as she could. She then quickly picked up the child and set her on the ground and yelled out "attack" as loud as she could. She then called out "run" to the child and at that same instant, drew her spear from the sled turning to face the three silent attackers. She would stand and give the child a chance to run from danger. Although the girl did not recognize the words, she understood Onna's commanding voice and ran toward her parent's sled.

When Harjo heard Onna's hand-whistled alert, he instantly pulled his atlatl from his belt and at the same moment, he whistled to alert the whole caravan of the attack. He turned and came running at full speed back toward Onna and their sled with a dart in his left hand and his atlatl in the other. He saw the three attackers bearing down on Onna.

He paused, only for a moment, notched the dart, and cast the lethal weapon with all his strength. He pulled another dart from his quiver and quickly attached a pointed foreshaft to the second dart. He continued to run in full stride as fast as he possibly could.

Onna stood fast, holding her spear as Harjo had taught her. Fear struck Onna as would ice cold water. She was as afraid as when she was abducted but she remained determined to stand and fight and protect the child and her new family. She repeated over and over to herself, "No run from lion, no run from lion." She saw the flash of Harjo's dart as it struck the warrior on the right. The warrior went down, falling head first onto the snow-covered grass.

Harjo also saw that the throw was true and the warrior fall. He slowed his pace and cast his second dart. Then, he ran as hard as he could toward Onna.

Suddenly, Onna saw the flash of Harjo's second dart and it too struck its mark bringing down the running warrior on the left. But the warrior in the center continued on. He was so close now, Onna could see his face as it expressed strain as though he was yelling but he remained silent. Her heart was beating faster than she thought possible.

Again, she saw something flash to her right as Harjo ran in front of her to meet the assailant. The attacker held a thrusting spear in his right hand. He stopped and turned to meet Harjo only a few paces in front of Onna. The attacker thrust his spear at Harjo's stomach and Onna's heart cried out in terror. But Harjo turned his body to the left and the point of the spear plunged by him. Somehow, he reached out and grasped the spear. He pulled it forward with the onward motion of the thrust, managing to pull the spear from the attacker's hand. At the same instant, he swung his atlatl in his right hand at the attacker's head. But the agile attacker ducked, and Harjo's atlatl club flew over his head. Harjo brought the atlatl club back in a backhand swing and at the same moment, Onna watched as Harjo somehow twirled the attacker's spear in his left hand so that he now held it point first. As the attacker again ducked Harjo's backhand swing, Harjo thrust the attacking warrior's own spear into the right side of the assailant's chest.

The spear sunk deep into the attacker's chest, but he was not finished. He also grasped a spear foreshaft and point in his left hand, holding it like a knife. Again, Onna's heart cried out as she saw the smaller but still lethal weapon. Her impulse was to charge in to help Harjo in his struggle, but she knew it would be better to stand her ground. She told herself, however, if Harjo went down, she would then charge in and try to thrust her spear into the warrior.

As Harjo's atlatl club flew past over the attacker's head in his back-swing motion, the attacker raised his left and brought the point down. It slashed across the right side of Harjo's face. Onna saw the blood as it poured down Harjo's face, spilling onto his parka. Her young heart cried out in agony but there was still nothing she could do-she could not charge in now as she might cause more harm than help.

Harjo now brought his atlatl around in a circular motion and down on the attacker's forearm, knocking the pointed fore shaft from his hand. As the attacker was now falling backwards from the thrust of the spear into his chest, Harjo again brought the atlatl around in a small circular motion and struck the attacker on the head and then drove him to the ground with the spear. Blood spit out from the wound on the assailant's forehead. He then grasped his own spear with both hands, hitting the ground on his back. He opened his mouth to cry out in pain, but blood gushed out and with a gurgling sound, the ill-fated attacker laid lifeless on the ground. It all seemed to happen so fast and was all over in the twinkling of an eye.

Suddenly, another Muscogee warrior appeared on the left. It was Harjo's brother, Chilocco. Onna pushed aside her girlish fear and focused on action. With hurried instinct, she drove the sharp butt end of her harpoon into the ground then turned to the sled and quickly untied her woman's bag and withdrew her large hare buckskin.

Harjo put the palm of his left hand on his wound as it gushed out blood but held up his right hand as he grasped his atlatl club. "I'm alright!" he called out to Onna, "stay there!"

Blood ran down Harjo's face as it would a fawn caribou hung upside down with a deep throat cut. Onna paid no attention to Harjo's order and ran to him with the buckskin folded up and pressed it against his face. "Stop blood-Harjo-stop blood," she cried out but not in tears but as a warrior chieftain might shout an order to his band.

Now Cheparney ran up to the scene from the Lead Sled. "Prepare for attack-prepare for attack," he called out. "This could just be the first assault!" He grasped Harjo's shoulder and looked at his face and the wound and saw that he was in good hands.

"Take care of Harjo, Onna" he called out in perfect Yupik. "Harjo, do what she says!"

A much slower runner than his younger brother, Micco Yarda ran into the midst of the sleds. He held his atlatl in the air over his head and made a wide circular motion. Pointing to the other side he yelled, "Warriors, watch the other direction! These three may be a decoy!"

Immediately, the whole band burst into action. Well-rehearsed, the Wind Band pulled and pushed the sleds into double concentric circles with a smaller circle in the center and a larger one on the outside. Women, children, and the elderly dashed to the smaller circle. A large heavy mammoth hide prepacked on top of a particular sled was brought out to cover the top of the inner circle and secured to the sleds. This hide would help protect the occupants from incoming darts. Armed warriors spread out along the outer circle of sleds ready to repel any possible attack.

"Check them and make sure they are dead," called out Cheparney, "and be careful, remember wounded animals!"

Honeche was now on the scene with spear in hand and he approached the warrior Harjo had killed with the attacker's own spear. He reached his spear out and touched the attacker's eye with the point. There was no movement. Meanwhile, Chilocco and Cheparney cautiously approached the other two attackers who lay motionless on the ground and repeated the eye touch check.

Onna held Harjo and pressed the buckskin material against his wound as hard as she could, and it began to impede the flow of blood. As she walked him toward the circle of sleds, she called out in Yupik "Shaman-shaman!" Ayuko repeated the call in Muscogee but the Lion Shaman was already in preparation and stood with his medicine bag over his shoulder along with his two apprentices in the inner sled circle. They had not completely covered the inner circle of sleds with the mammoth hide and the shaman's older apprentice was busy making a fire. With luck, much of the ground in this area was free of snow.

Suddenly, Micco Yarda called out. "Cheparney, take three warriors and check on the Flanker Guard. Be careful, there may be an ambush!"

Cheparney stepped back and looked over to the circle of sleds and called out the name of a young warrior, "Ero!" He immediately vaulted over the sleds and jogged up to the group. Cheparney looked at each warrior, Honeche,

Chilocco, and Ero. "Ready?" he asked." They each nodded they were.

"Yarda," called out Cheparney. "If we walk into an ambush, we will attempt to retreat in a fast run back to the sleds with Ayo. We will count on our warriors to provide cover. Throw over us and take out as many as you can."

As the four warriors headed off toward the flank, Micco Yarda responded, "I understand."

The Lion Shaman motioned for Onna to escort Harjo toward him. Meanwhile, another warrior had gone out and pulled Harjo and Onna's sled into the circles.

"I don't think the wound is all that bad," growled Harjo, "and no need for all this fuss."

"Cut bad, Harjo. You no talk-you obey!" snarled Onna with a firm voice of authority.

"I need the girl and Ayuko. The rest of you stand back," ordered the crusty Shaman in a voice so stern that no one would dare disobey.

"Onna, sit down on the ground." To the surprise of all, the Lion Shaman spoke in Yupik.

"Hold Harjo," he barked, as he reached up and took the buckskin bandage Onna pressed to his face and ordered Harjo to hold it. Onna obeyed and sat down and the Shaman draped another buckskin hide over her lap.

"Harjo, lie down and put you head in her lap," snarled the shaman. "He will stay still if the girl holds him." Onna removed Harjo's hand and once again held her pressure bandage on the wound.

The older Shaman's apprentice managed to start a diminutive fire and was holding a tool in the small flame. The younger apprentice stood by with a water pouch in one hand and buckskin material in the other. "Wet the buckskin!" ordered the Shaman"

The young apprentice followed instructions and handed the soaked buckskin material to him. Slowly but deliberately, the old man got down on his knees by Harjo. Ayuko did the same but on the other side of Harjo adjacent his knees. The blood flow was stopped. The Shaman reached up and removed the bandage then washed the wound with the wet material. With both of his hands-on Harjo's face, he stared into the wound as though it was a living creature and he possessed the power to read its thoughts.

The wound appeared clean and open, but only for an instant. Then the blood again flowed, running down Harjo's face, over his chin, and down his neck. Onna could no longer remain stoic as tears filled her eyes and began to run down her checks as Harjo's blood ran down his. She took Harjo's hand and cupped it in both of hers.

"You my love, Harjo, my brave warrior. Lion Shaman have great power, Harjo, he make better." Harjo looked up at Onna and smiled. He also smiled at his mother.

The sight of her son's blood brought cold chills through her heart. Still, she patted his leg to reassure him. Unemotional, Harjo remained composed.

"It's ready!" called out the apprentice at the fire."

"Bring it!" shouted the Shaman."

The apprentice rose and carried a tool to the Shaman as though he handled some precious or sacred object. The artifact resembled a large sewing needle but was made from ground stone, not flaked. How the Shaman managed to shape stone to this size was a mystery. Perhaps it was a lucky find as a gift from the Father Creator or he cracked off a small section of river cobble and ground it down to this needle or bird bone size. The large end was shafted into a handle of antler. It resembled a pressure flaking tool used to remove small flakes and to finish a flake tool such as spear points. The tip of the strange small tool now glowed red hot.

The apprentice handed the tool to the Shaman who blew on it as though it were a hot coal. He looked at Harjo. "You are a brave young man. Remain still." Harjo nodded he understood.

The Shaman gently turned Harjo's head so that he looked at Onna, removed the pressure bandage, then quickly brought the tip of the red-hot tool to the wound and cauterized it. The wet skin sizzled, as all burning meat will, while smoke drifted up along with the odor of burnt flesh. Onna kissed the back of Harjo's hand then held it to her face and wiped the tears from her eyes and fought them back. Harjo again looked up to her and smiled, and she smiled back.

The Shaman did not just randomly smolder the wound nor burn it entirely but instead isolated the severed blood vessels and sealed them. Again, he cleansed the cut. Meanwhile, the older apprentice had left the fire and had gone through the Shaman's medicine bag and was preparing needle and thread. Unaware of the crowd around him, the apprentice threaded the needle with a hair-sized length of sinew which can be pulled to any size a seamstress can manage even a hair size or smaller. Some women use hair as thread, especially the long strong guard hairs of the mammoth for certain delicate sewing tasks. He handed the threaded needle to the Shaman as Ayuko watched in amazement.

The needle was miniature. Perhaps it was manufactured from a bird bone or a sliver of ivory, carved and ground down to such an incredible tiny diameter. How the Shaman was able to drill such a small hole in the head of the needle she could not fathom. If someone had told her, especially a gossiping woman, she would not believe it possible, but she watched as the Shaman stitched up Harjo's wound with just such a remarkably small needle.

She was equally astonished at the sewing skills of the old man and how could his vision remain so keen at his age? He did not stitch the wound as a garment but rather pulled and tied "cross stitches" along the length of the cut, which extended just beside Harjo's eye, down his check, and stopped near his mouth.

Ayuko thought to herself. "It could be worse. The point could have struck his eye or his mouth." She caressed Harjo's leg near his knee. "How terribly painful and yet her brave son did not flinch or even grimace," she thought. Quite the contrary, for he occasionally looked at Onna and smiled.

Meanwhile, Cheparney, Honeche, Yahola, and Ero headed toward the flank. "Why would just three warriors attack?" asked a young Ero.

"I don't know," answered Cheparney, "It doesn't make any sense to attack here with just three warriors. This is a poor location for an ambush. Perhaps we will learn more when we find Ayo."

"Now listen!" said Cheparney to his men. "We may be walking into an ambush, but we will not leave one of our warriors behind. Be ready for an attack. Spread out and form a spear point-shape. I'll go ahead. Stay alert!"

As the small war party made its way toward the general direction where the Flanker Guard Ayo was last seen and what was apparently the hiding location of the attacking warriors, the ever-emotional Onna fought back her tears. Although she remained focused, she could not hide her anxiety, so distraught was her face as she continued to hold Harjo's hand. Harjo remained still and in good humor. It often seemed as though he was calming Onna and Ayuko more than they him. But finally, the stressful task was complete.

The Shaman's apprentice and even the young helper were well trained preparing ahead at each stage of the treatment. The apprentice now handed the Shaman several wet leaves. Ayuko recognized the distinctive leaves but she could not recall the plant's name. Canineqmiut Shamans likewise used the plant to treat wounds and village men occasionally took the plant into the steam baths to use as an antiseptic. She presumed the plant was a coastal adaptation and had not noticed it growing in the Echota Valley. Of course, she had not looked for it, but would now.

Onna concentrated on Harjo but Ayuko carefully focused attention on the activities of the Shaman and his apprentices. She had observed the Shaman treating wounds in the past, but she had not ever watched this close. The Shaman laid the wet leaves on the wound along with a moss material. Then, he took a small cut section of buckskin to use as a bandage which had been taken from a soft fur animal such as a ground squirrel and applied a wet sticky substance to the edges of the bandage. Ayuko knew the substance was made from the juice of a plant put did not know the procedure. Somehow, the ingredient and the Shaman's treatment of the material, allowed it to remain sticky for an extended period, in fact for several days. Consequently, the sticky material would secure the bandage over the wound but then allow the bandage to be easily removed and washed off from the skin.

With the dressing complete, the Shaman gave his instructions to Onna and Ayuko in perfect Yupik. "Insure the bandage stays in place and the wound remains clean. I will see him every day for the next several days. He should not walk but ride a sled and otherwise stay off his feet and in bed for three days. To tear open the stitches, invites danger. In seven days, I will remove the stitches and in 10 days, he should be healed."

The Shaman looked at the two women and waited silently as if to respond to any questions, but his instructions were very clear. Always expressive but honest, Onna reached out her hand to the Shaman and holding back tears spoke.

"Thank you, Lion Shaman, thank you."

To Ayuko and Harjo's surprise and anyone else who was watching, the Lion Shaman reached out and took Onna's hand and smiled. No one had ever seen the Lion Shaman touch anyone other than a patient, much less smile. He then called out and the older assistant helped him to his feet. They gathered up his medicine kit and tools and he returned to his own sled.

The four Muscogee warriors found a semi-conscience Ayo. The Enemy Warriors managed to sneak up and club him. Cheparney checked his ears and found no blood so most likely there was no concussion or real damage. The Lion Shaman would later provide a complete examination. His embarrassment would last longer than his headache. The two young warriors, Yahola and Ero, assisted Ayo back to the sled caravan while Cheparney and Honeche provided rear cover.

"Recover all the weapons and tools worth taking from the three dead warriors," called out Micco Yarda. Cheparney and Honeche complied and returned to the caravan.

"Yarda, the three appeared to be adults but were very young, certainly inexperienced," concluded Cheparney. "The best explanation is the three hapless youngsters snuck away from a larger raiding party and foolishly decided they could attack the caravan on their own and somehow claim some misguided honors."

Micco Yarda agreed. "Well, in any case, the appearance of three young Enemy Warriors almost certainly means a larger raiding party is likely in the area."

"Should you send messengers, Yarda, to the other bands?" asked Cheparney.

Micco Yarda considered the action then answered. "No, it is not worth risking one or two warriors going alone. Besides, each band must stay vigilant while migrating. Let's drag the three bodies up close to the trail. Any passing Muscogee band will certainly recognize the Enemy Warriors and surmise they are fatalities of an unsuccessful attack, left to warn the migrating bands."

When the sled and two warriors in the Rear Guard came within sight and saw the sleds encircled, they came in on the run and joined the circles. Micco Yarda called a quick council of the veteran warriors. Should they stay here or press on to the next camp location? All agreed to press on at least to a better defendable position if not the next camp location. Young Ayo's family could pull him in their sleds. Micco Yarda assigned a veteran warrior to the Flanker Guard positions. The protective mammoth skin cover for the center sled circle was removed and repacked as everyone was busy checking their sleds in anticipation of moving out.

"I can certainly walk," remarked Harjo, "It is not that bad of a wound."

Standing by his side, Onna put her hands on his now blood-stained parka. "Please, Harjo, please ride sled. No break my heart." Tears begin to form in her beautiful blue eyes. Onna was able to influence Harjo's decisions with honest tears and by asking rather than by demanding.

Harjo resigned to his fate and Onna helped him to the empty sled. Then, Micco Yarda called out to Onna and Chucuse. "Can you two girls pull a sled loaded with Harjo by yourself?"

Chucuse translated to Yupik for Onna. Smiling, Onna called out in a loud voice "yes" in Muscogee, which brought smiles and laughter to everyone's face. Micco Yarda was good at relieving band tension.

"Alright!" he yelled waving his atlatl in a circular motion above his head. "Flankers and Rear Guard out-Cheparney and I will take the lead! Onward to the next camp location! Everyone stay alert!"

Onna and sister Chucuse pulled young Harjo to the next camp and during the next several days. The Ptarmigan Band of boys volunteered, and together the five boys and two girls pulled the three sleds, one loaded with Harjo. Harjo turned his temporary handicap experience into a fun game and for the next several days of travel, the small group laughed, played, sang songs, and seemed to thoroughly enjoy the migration.

During the next few days, Harjo's initial wound remained ugly, red and swollen but it slowly healed. The Lion Shaman proved to be an extraordinary physician. Perhaps he possessed magical power or was afforded mysterious assistance from the spirit world or from the Father Creator. As the shaman predicted, in a few days the swelling and redness abated. He removed the stitches in seven days and the wound seemed to heal over. In 10 days, the wound itself was gone leaving the scar that marked Harjo the rest of his days.

Thus, the Wind Band of the Muscogee Mammoth Hunters continued on their Spring Migration camping at the several pre-selected camps without further engagement. If a large raiding party of Enemy Warriors was on the prowl, they did not materialize. But all would remember this day's events and this story was often recounted around glowing night campfires. The people of the Wind Band would remember the heroism and amazing warrior skills of Harjo. And they would fondly recall the courage of Onna, the extraordinary young girl who came to them from such a distant, faraway land.

Chapter 20:

SUMMER STRATEGY

Cheparney approached his older brother with an offer of a late spring strategy. "I'll take Harjo and a boy, maybe one of Honeche's boys, and pull a sled to Wetumka moving in advance of the mammoth herd. We'll set up a forward camp and undertake to ambush a mammoth at the Spirit Tree. We should be able to move ahead of at least part of the herd past the First Echota Mammoth Crossing. If we are lucky and able to down a mammoth, we will send word back with the boy to come on to Wetumka. Harjo and I will stay to guard the kill and complete what dressing we can."

"I like that strategy," agreed Micco Yarda. "If there happens to be an early summer followed by an early southward advance of the herd, we may be able to make another kill at Wetumka avoiding a summer camp movement."

Cheparney shook his head in agreement. "I thought the possibility of two kills at Wetumka could work into the plan," he added.

"Settled," exclaimed Yarda. "Will you leave tomorrow?"

"No, we'll head out now and travel this afternoon. Many mammoth will cross the Echota in one afternoon and I want to be ahead of them."

"Alright!" agreed Micco Yarda. "I'll keep the band here for two days and if we do not hear from you, we will move toward Wetumka on the third. Tomorrow will count the first day. Perhaps we can reach Wetumka in one long day's sled pull. I'll presume Harjo's wound is now completely healed."

"Completely," replied Cheparney. "I predict many women, especially Caribou Hunter women, will be attracted to that scar."

Micco Yarda chuckled. "Ah, one more item. You realize Ayuko will need to sit on that yellow haired girl. I know she belongs to Harjo, but you may need to say something to insure she stays with the band."

"You're right, Yarda. I will," replied a solemn Cheparney.

Cheparney made his way to the Chokofa Tent and presented his hunting plan to Honeche who agreed but also volunteered to join the hunt.

"I think it is better if you stayed with the band," said Cheparney and then explained. "Once Harjo and I depart there will be a shortage of manpower to pull sleds. Micco Yarda preferers that the stronger men stay to insure all the sleds arrived at Wetumka."

Honeche again concurred but added, "I have two sons, Cheparney, which one would you prefer?"

"The younger boy, some 12 or 13 summers. I have noticed him practicing atlatl and dart on several early mornings and he seems to be quiet, mature, and a leader of the Ptarmigan Band.

"His name is O'pa and he will be ready and honored," concluded Honeche.

Sensing this day's halt in the migration may be more than an overnight stay, Ayuko directed her boys to erect a more permanent shelter. They constructed an admirable lean-to in a sunny location between two small trees and in a new growth of green grass. Once he arrived at his own families' new shelter, Cheparney introduced the impending hunting plan.

"Father," said Yahola, "Chilocco and I would like to join the hunt."

"I realize that, boys, but we need the band men to stay and pull sleds to Wetumka. However, I want you to go out hunting and provide fresh meat if at all possible. You know that caribou and antelope are migrating. I think you should journey westward onto the grasslands away from the wooded river. Always remain ever vigilant, as lions will likewise hunt those moving herds." This was not the boy's first choice, but they also knew not to differ with their father and besides they were reasonably satisfied with their hunting task.

Cheparney, Harjo, and O'pa completed loading the empty sled that Chucuse had been pulling, then Cheparney and Harjo went to say their farewells to the family. Ayuko and Cheparney embraced, smiled, and kissed, so often had they said farewell. Ayuko smiled up to his face as she pushed his black hair back over his ear. She noticed his hair was streaking with grey.

But a poor anxious Onna was not so easily consoled. She was extremely fearful that Harjo would be hurt or killed and was convinced, somehow, her presence would prevent misfortune. This would also be the first occasion she would sleep without Harjo and the loss of his warmth and comfort added to her stress. She implored Harjo to allow her to accompany him, but to no avail.

"I can go, Harjo," pleaded a desperate Onna. "I have harpoon, you teach me harpoon, I quiet, I watch, I can pull sled!"

"No, Onna," said Harjo in the sternest voice he could summon.

"Please, Harjo, I can go," pleaded Onna wearing such a worried expression.

Finally, Cheparney stepped in and up to Onna, gently putting his hands on the side of her face. "You will stay, Onna. I will watch Harjo's back and he will watch mine and all will be well." He spoke in Yupik. Harjo did not realize his father could speak Yupik so elegantly. Apparently, he knew the language better than all in the family presumed. He did not raise his voice, nor did he speak in anger or even sternly, but his tone was final. Onna knew the discussion had ended. She nodded her head yes then looked to the ground, fighting back tears.

Cheparney smiled, drawing her to him. He kissed her forehead, then patted the side of her face. Onna wrapped her arms around his waist and hugged him. She then went to Harjo and took his hand. The three headed toward the sled and an awaiting O'pa.

Even though Harjo told Onna on several occasions she was free and could cry when she wanted, she hoped to avoid any tears. Her high-strung emotions, however, often overruled her plans. They stopped near the sled and embraced. With her head against his chest, she held him as tight as she could.

"Harjo, you pay attention, all," she scolded him as she sniffed her nose.

"I will," he promised as he held her tight and petted her head.

"You come back me, Harjo!"

"I will," he repeated. He reached down and took her chin with his thumb and forefinger, lifted her head and kissed her.

He then turned and joined his father and O'pa who had waited patiently by the sled. O'pa did not understand the Yupik that Harjo, Onna, and Cheparney spoke but certainly did the situation. He stood harnessed to the sled and Cheparney stood alongside. Harjo walked up behind the sled and grasped the back with one hand as his other hand held his spear, and he gave it a push, and the three hunters headed off. Onna stood for a while with her hands clasped under her chin as silent tears now rolled down her face. Harjo turned, looked back and waved. Onna smiled, returning his wave. Then, without a sound, they were gone.

Onna returned to the family shelter. Yahola and Chilocco had already left the camp on an exploration trip to survey the area. They would certainly take advantage of any game opportunity that presented itself, but they would leave early in the morning before dawn to hunt in earnest.

Yahola's wife, Kak-ke, sat comfortably in Cheparney and Ayuko's bed nursing her baby, who seemed content, dressed in a caribou skin and woven grass diapers, enjoying her meal. She kissed the baby's head. "Such a poor hungry little baby," she smiled. "Ayuko, why does she make so much noise when she nurses?" she asked.

Ayuko laughed, "I don't know child, some babies do." She and Chucuse sat by the fire. Ayuko was making tea and Chucuse was sewing a baby parka. Ayuko remarked watching Chucuse sew. "I am so glad my boys are growing older and buying wives. I love my boys, but I have grown ever so weary of sewing clothes for them. I will gladly let their wives take up that burden!"

Onna entered the shelter and approached Ayuko crying. She stood with her hands folded on her breasts and tried not to cry, but she could not help herself. "I no can go hunt. I no brave, Ayuko, I naughty girl. I no brave same Harjo. I afraid he get hurt."

Ayuko's motherly instincts quickly took over and she went to Onna and hugged her. It is such a bitter-sweet moment for a new young wife when her hunter first leaves on a dangerous hunt. "Don't worry so much, Onna, don't worry."

"I no brave same Harjo I cry same baby I afraid he get hurt I naughty." cried a distressed and frighten Onna.

As Ayuko held Onna, she could feel her trembling as she petted and comforted her. "You are one of my girls now Onna. I will be your mother. Understand?"

Onna shook her head and managed a quiet, "Yes."

"Believe me, if you are naughty, you will hear it first from me. You are not a naughty girl," replied Ayuko in her motherly voice. "We try not to let the men see us crying when they leave on dangerous hunts. They have enough to concentrate on and worry about rather than worry over women's tears. But child, you must certainly understand there will be danger. Harjo has told us that you were born into a band of mammoth hunters, so you must know, Onna, there will always be danger-always. I know you are afraid but don't be."

Ayuko lifted up Onna's head and wiped the tears from her face then held the side of her face. "Cheparney is one of the greatest hunters and warriors throughout the whole Muscogee Tribe and Harjo learned from him. So, don't be afraid for our Harjo. The mammoth is not yet born that can harm him. And you have seen what will happen to a lion foolish enough to attack him. He will bring that pelt home for you to sleep on."

A sniffling Onna now managed a partial smile and was somewhat reassured. Ayuko reached down and brought up a ladle of warm tea and held it up to Onna, giving her a drink as she would have a small child.

"The men usually leave for hunts early in the morning and we women stay in bed together late into the morning, drinking tea, comforting each other, easing our tension, and sleeping late on the first day the men leave. Even though it is now late in the afternoon, let's join Kak-ke and the baby back in bed."

Ayuko turned and called to Chucuse. "Do you want to join us in bed for tea, Chucuse?"

"No, mother," she replied, "I want to finish this parka for the baby."

"Onna, if you do not know how to nurse a baby," offered a motherly Ayuko, "now would be a good opportunity to watch and learn from Kak-ke." Onna shook her head yes.

Ayuko escorted Onna to her bed and helped her take off her parka and other clothing. She pulled back the mammoth blanket and gave Onna several loving pats on the bottom.

"Slip down into bed and join Kak-ke and we'll take an afternoon nap. Then you and I have several women's issues to discuss. You were taken so very young from your mother, surely your training was not complete." Onna did not speak but shook her head yes.

"Do you understand the law of marriage for the Muscogee Mammoth Hunters?" Onna looked up, thinking with that pleasant childish expression she wore when she searched her memory then looked back to Ayuko and shook her head no. Ayuko smiled at Onna.

"Would you care to know?" she asked. Again, Onna shook her head yes.

"We will have that discussion later," said Ayuko as she undressed. She then got down on her knees and slipped into bed. The three women with one infant gently snuggled each other. Ayuko held Onna in the same way Harjo did. Onna was comforted, and soon the three women fell asleep.

Yahola and Chilocco hoped to encounter the most curious looking animal across the whole Mammoth Steppe, the antelope. Its large inflatable and moveable nose give its head a bulging appearance as the top of the snout curves outward from the eyes nearly parallel with the ground. These small animals are less than two paces long and just over knee high at their shoulders. They wear a white coat in the winter turning brown in the summer. The male supports a pair of long single horns, slightly curved.

The small curious animals are fleet afoot, plentiful, and migrate in large herds. Surprisingly, the males migrate in one herd and the females in another. As the females reach their fawning grounds, most will give birth to twin fawns simultaneously in large numbers. This was the circumstance Yahola and Chilocco hoped to find. A group of birthing females would be an easy meal.

A small flock of gray jays called out from the treetops as the two brothers left the wooded Echota River onto the open grasslands. They both then stopped, surveying the area as the large birds, similar to ravens and magpies, often called out an alarm upon sighting predator animals. They glanced up, admiring the birds.

"Micco Yarda and father have both said those gray birds cache more food, meat and bugs, than anyone could count," declared Yahola.

Chilocco agreed, "Enough food to last all winter." But Chilocco had more important subjects he wanted to discuss with Yahola.

As they walked, Chilocco talked about "wife buying" with his older brother. "I wasn't hurried to purchase a wife,

Yahola, but now that both you and Harjo have wives, I suppose I should give it more serious consideration. What do you think about Chufe?"

"Well," replied Yahola, "no one would argue that she is exceptionally attractive and certainly one of the most lovable little bunnies a hunter would want to bundle up with on a cold winter night. But wife?" he shook his head with a frown, "I don't know. My advice, enjoy all the sex you desire with her, but I would not purchase her before talking it over with father."

Chilocco pondered his advice. "I like her, and I do enjoy sex with her, but you're right," he answered, "Maybe I'll ask father about her."

Yahola laughed, "Harjo promised Chufe he would bring her back a handful of shells from the coast and of course, he did not know he would return with Onna. He wanted to keep his promise but not upset Onna."

"I did not hear," responded Chilocco with a surprised expression. "What did he do?"

"Well, he took Onna with him and handed Chufe a bag of shells. And, I think he introduced them," answered Yahola.

They both laughed. "Well, that brother of ours is a smart one," replied Chilocco.

"I have an idea for you," offered Yahola. "Remember two winters ago when I went with father to the Caribou Band across the Echota to announce to their Micco the Tribal Council meeting?"

"Yes, I recall, because mother was quite worried about you and father crossing the Echota, fearing you two might fall through the ice."

"Well, it was very cold that winter and you know how shallow the river is. Anyway, father told me to bring along a treated hare pelt. I didn't ask why. I traded a bird dart with one of the Ptarmigan Boys for one. As we sat around the hearth in the Caribou Band Micco's mammoth lodge, his daughter brought in a pouch of tea then left. I decided to follow her out and attempted to talk with her. She was close to her Rite-of-Passage but not yet mature. She was not beautiful but very pleasant and friendly. Then I remembered the pelt. I told her she could have the hare pelt if she would give me a long kiss. She giggled, blushed, thought about it, then agreed. I pulled her to me, pushed her hood back, and kissed her straight on the mouth-a long wet kiss and she kissed me back. I gave her the pelt and she smiled, rubbing it on her face. Then, suddenly, and taking me by surprise, she grabbed me, pulled me to her, and kissed me again. I managed to put my arms around her. Then she ran to one of the other lodges. She must be mature by now and I would say she will have her Rite-of-Passage this summer. She was very pleasant to kiss. I would have waited for her to mature but I found Kak-ke."

"I am leery of the Caribou Band," responded Chilocco. They live on the other side of the river in winter separated from the other bands and they hunt caribou more than mammoth. Father says, they are more similar to the Caribou Hunters than Mammoth Hunters."

"Well, maybe so," said Yahola, "but the girl seemed sweet and pleasant in my opinion. You asked my advice-I would certainly keep her in mind."

Yahola and Chilocco did seek out and find a small herd of birthing females and dispatched two and their fawns with ease. They gutted the animals and returned early in the afternoon with the carcasses. The women took over and quickly processed the kill. The thick white fur of the adult females would provide very usable pelts.

The Fus Chate women and Yahola and Chilocco roasted all the meat and shared portions with others in the band whose hunters had gone out but had returned unsuccessful.

The fresh meat was welcomed as they ate and talked around the family fire. Chucuse raised several questions about marriage law and Ayuko used the opportunity to explain marriage law to both girls, Chucuse and Onna. Yahola, Kak-ke, and their baby retired to the shelter and Chilocco left to find other company, perhaps to stroll by the family shelter of Chufe leaving the three females by the fire. Besides most of the language would now be in Yupik.

"To the Muscogee Mammoth Hunter," began Ayuko, "marriage is a simple fact and defines the role, relationship, and status of men and women. A man reigns as head of his household even if it includes only him and his wife. As you see around the Wind Band, that condition is very rare. More commonly, just like ours, the households are more extended, comprised of a man and his wife, grown sons and their wives, grandchildren, and others. A woman belongs to a man-first to her father-then to her husband and his household."

"Yes, yes," interrupted Onna, "I belong Harjo!"

Ayuko smiled, "Yes, Onna, and even though you are not married by legal law you and Harjo are married by spirit law."

Onna shook her head in agreement and liked the idea of being married by spirit law.

"To be eligible for marriage, both boys and girls must reach sexual maturity and complete a Rite of Passage hence children, as you know, are not married. Elderly people whose spouses die and journey to the other side generally remained unmarried. Otherwise, every member of the Tribe is married."

"Will Chilocco buy a wife, mother?" asked sister Chucuse.

"Most certainly, child, but often it takes a young warrior several seasons after completing his Rite-of-Passage to find a girl he wants and to accumulate the wealth necessary to pay bride price."

"But brothers and sisters may not marry?" asked an inquisitive Chucuse."

"Most certainly not," responded Ayuko, "incest is strictly taboo. And although kinship is determined only by the father, the mother's ancestry is also considered concerning an impending marriage to insure close biological relations and interbreeding does not occur. Brother and sister marriages are strictly forbidden and generally cousins, as well, depending on other circumstance. Age, however, is not a factor. A successful hunter of mature age, especially one from a prominent family, may purchase a youthful girl usually as a second wife. But generally, spouses are near the same age."

"I hope father does not sell me to an older man," anguished Chucuse. "I want to marry a young handsome man." Ayuko did not respond but continued.

"If not elderly, being a widow or widower due to the death of a spouse is a temporary situation. Following an acceptable mourning period, a new marriage is arranged. If a woman's husband dies, she becomes the property of her dead husband's father and occasionally she is given to one of her husband's brothers as a wife, often as a second wife. If a widow's father-in-law is also deceased, then the oldest uncle as next in line takes charge of the widow. For a man, it is much easier. Following a mourning period, he simply goes out and purchases another woman as wife."

"Why doesn't a man buy Chufe as a wife?" asked a still inquisitive Chucuse, "I think she is very pretty."

"I am certain some man will buy Chufe from her father Katchu before the summer is out," added Ayuko.

Chucuse looked over to Onna frowning. "Her father gives her hard switchings. Oh, her poor bare legs!" and she reached down and rubbed the back of her thighs.

"Well, every now and then," added a stern Ayuko, "Chufe is disobedient. You two girls should keep that in mind." Chucuse and Onna looked at each other. They each bit their lips but said nothing.

"As a young man completes his Rite-of-Passage and becomes an adult male member of the Tribe, he may purchase any unmarried adult woman, within the confines of incest, from her father or the man who owns her. The process is simple."

"Same Harjo," exclaimed a smiling Onna, "but he no buy-any girl-he get me!"

Chucuse and Onna took each other's hands and laughed. Ayuko took a deep breath, shook her head, and thought to herself. "These two girls, was I this silly when I was their age?" Attempting to remain serious, she then continued.

"A man approaches a single woman's father or the man who owns the woman and offers him a "bride price" for his daughter or the woman in question. A whole dressed mammoth pelt would be considered an extraordinary price for a bride; conversely a hare pelt would be an insult. Food in the form of cured meat is always a welcomed price, in particular pemmican. I expect a man with a mammoth lodge full of noisy young girls might accept less in bride price than a man with a solitary girl. If the father agrees, the marriage is set." Ayuko studied her charges making sure they each understood, especially Onna, then continued.

"A public announcement of the marriage follows, usually at a public gathering and typically by the band Micco. The ideal gathering would be during the First Kill ceremony, but a Micco can command a band gathering at his prerogative."

Onna clapped her hands with excitement, "Yes, yes, First Kill. I marry Harjo!"

Chucuse reached over and again took Onna's hands. "You are so lucky Onna, to be in love with the man you'll marry, and I'm so happy for and Harjo, Onna. Your marriage will be wonderfully different." Ayuko did not reply but continue on with her discussion.

"Often the husband's family will sponsor a feast to include the immediate families and on rare occasions, a lavish affair to include the entire band at large, depending on the wealth and status of the husband's family. Finally, the new wife will gather her personal belongings and move into the mammoth lodge of her husband and become a legal member of his family and his band. She is no longer considered a member of her father's family. In the course of the seasons, as the young wife becomes pregnant and gives birth she is attended by her husband's mother or perhaps his aunts. Her parents have nothing to do with the birth and the child is not related to her parents but only to her husband's parents. Now this you have seen with Kak-ke. She belongs to our family now. I am now her mother and helped her with the birth of her baby as did Micco Yarda's wife. Soon, Chucuse you will become a member of another family. This law is hard for me."

Ayuko stopped and caught her breath. Both girls sensed a stressful pause and reached out taking Ayuko's hands. She smiled and squeezed their hands then continued. "I was a Canineqmiut. Cheparney brought me from the Canineqmiut village of Up'nerkillermiut and I became part of his family. In some ways, Onna, it seems strange to me because you will do the same as I did, so that experience bonds us together." Onna still held Ayuko's hand, smiled and nodded her head yes.

"I did not return to my former village nor have I ever seen my Canineqmiut family again. Kinship relations of the Muscogee Tribe are often difficult for me to grasp considering the Canineqmiut recognize kinship through both parents, both fathers and mothers. Always remember girls. A Muscogee woman's future and the insurance of her old age rest in her sons not her daughters."

Ayuko paused for a moment to allow that information to sink into their young minds and making sure Onna understood the Yupik words. Confident her message was learned, she carried on with her teaching.

"Now, girls, you must truly understand that men dominate this world. And what a Muscogee man, hunter and warrior, desires from family life, more than all else is harmony-peace and harmony."

"Chucuse, one day very soon, you will be married and leave our family to join another. But your father still loves you and he wants you to be happy. To your father, your marriage will be about harmony not about bride price. And the boy you will marry, his father is also concerned about harmony. Any father will avoid bringing a young wife into his shelter who will cause discord and stress. Consequently, fathers are well advised by wives and daughters as well as to who would and who would not be an appropriate husband for their daughters. Make no mistake, we women have no legal status but only a foolish father would proceed contrary to advice destined to lay an unharmonious path of discord and discontent."

"Mother?" asked Chucuse, and then she waited for her mother's response.

"Yes, child?"

"Did you talk with Yahola before he bought Kak-ke?"

Ayuko smiled, "I made some suggestions, but I did have some serious talks with your father. He will listen to me and seriously consider my advice more readily than most other Muscogee men will concerning advice from their wives. But remember, all Muscogee men desire that the wives of their sons will bring harmony with them rather than stress as they move into their lodges."

"Mother, will father ever purchase a young girl as a second wife?" Ayuko laughed and reached out to stroke Chucuse's hair. "Oh child, well, I don't think so. I am sure he would talk it over with me before he did. Now this you should also remember, girls. In many examples, it is the wife who wants her husband to purchase a girl as a second wife especially if she has several boys. Before those boys are old enough to buy a wife, the mother will do all the sewing. It is long tedious work making all their clothes. And also, the weaving for grass and mammoth wool socks including menstruation pads. After they are married, the wife will sew for her son, but before, it will be the mother even though a grandmother may also help. So, a wife with two or three boys and or girls who are too young to sew, will be over-burdened with work and she will want some help. A young second wife could solve that problem and help her with her work."

"Harjo promise," spoke up Onna, "he want sex other girl he tell me. He can buy other girl for wife. But I hope he no want."

"Harjo will always keep his promises, Onna, but I don't think he will ever want another girl. I think he will always want you."

Onna clasped her hands together and held them to her breast with a big broad smile. "What a beautiful smile she has," thought Ayuko to herself and then noticed the raven feather in her hair. She was thus reminded of another marriage custom.

"Onna, I thought of something else you should know-a marriage custom. The left side of a woman's head signifies that she is married and the right side that she is not. Young unmarried girls, like Chucuse, might weave a small braid in their hair on the right side of their heads and attach a white feather to the braid. The white feather creates an attractive contrast against her black hair. The white tail feathers of eagles are very popular with women as decorations and ornaments. This announces to the whole band that she is unmarried. A married woman, however, follows the same decoration format only she uses the left side of her head which announces to all she is married. Hence, she warns adventurous young men to keep their distance. During cold weather when hoods are worn, women decorate the appropriate side of their parka hoods with feathers and or seashells to announce their marriage status."

A smiling and excited Onna reached to touch her raven feather, rabbit tail, and seashell ornament. "Harjo make for me. He twist hair, he tie this side."

Ayuko reached out and touched Onna's raven feather ornament. "Harjo is a sly trickster. He was telling you then, Onna, that you were to be his wife." Onna touched the raven feather again. Now knowing Harjo's intentions when he made the adornment and with the story of the raven, the ornament now held an even deeper memory for Onna.

"Let me see," mused Ayuko, "Oh, yes. Caribou Hunter men and the seal hunters, the Canineqmiut, offer their wives and daughters in sex to friends and guests as hospitality. To them, it would be an insult for a guest to refuse. I don't know about the evil Enemy Raiders, but I expect all their women are slaves. Onna, Harjo is an adventurer and trader. He is like his father and will be away on long trips specially to trade. But what he brings back to our family is much appreciated and brings wealth to us. Do you understand?"

"Yes, he sex Caribou Hunter and Canineqmiut women. He can go trade."

"He will not break his promises, nor will he lie to you, Onna, but you must understand."

"He can take me trade, I can pull sled," offered a smiling Onna.

"You have certainly proven you can pull sled and I am certain he will take you on occasion, but not always," replied an understanding Ayuko.

"One final warning, girls, one you must always remember. Men may have sex with other women, but a Mammoth Hunter wife may not. A Muscogee wife caught in adultery will bring sorrow and disgrace on herself and to both the families of her husband and of her father. A wife's adultery may also end in death. Look to poor Chufe. She was caught in adultery but fared better than she might have. She was not killed nor switched in public. She is so beautiful; yet see the sorrow she brings on herself. Do not follow her path."

There was a long silence as the two girls looked at each absorbing this wisdom. Finally, Ayuko stretch and yawned. "It is getting dark, girls; let us get ready for bed. Onna and Chucuse agreed.

"I can sleep you same Harjo?" Onna asked Ayuko.

"Certainly, child," replied Ayuko, "If you want." Smiling, Onna nodded her head yes. "We will all three sleep together." They made their way toward the family shelter.

Chapter 21:

FIRST KILL

The three Mammoth Hunters made their way north following the wooded edge of the winding Echota River. They made camp just before dark and gathered wood for a protection fire following that with a cold meal of jerky and water, they slept. The next morning, they were on the move before dawn. Late in the afternoon, they crossed the Wekiwa Stream and camped at the Wetumka summer camp. There, they set up a more substantial camp and sat around the fire considering tomorrow's hunt.

"Father," said a serious Harjo, "I want to make the kill."

Cheparney remained silent for a moment then responded. "I thought you would ask, Harjo, but I am reluctant. You are a new husband with a new, young wife, although technically you are not married yet nor an adult male."

A solemn Harjo replied. "I know if something happened to me, Father, you would take good care of Onna. And you know I would take care of Mother. We both have two young brave brothers and sons who would also see to the needs of our wives."

For such a young man, Harjo was always so practical thought Cheparney. "Alright Harjo," replied a still hesitant Cheparney, "perhaps better now than later. You will be able to supply the mammoth meat for your own Rite-of-Passage feast and for the First Kill Ceremony. We can ask the old Lion Shaman, but I don't think that feat has ever been accomplished before. Well, it will be difficult to sleep but we all need the rest. The dawn always arrives too early."

The majority of the mammoth herd migrates north along the eastern side of the Echota, then the great shaggy beasts cross the river to arrive at their calving grounds westward of the great river. A smaller portion of the herd migrates on the western side of the Echota, moving ahead of the Wind Band. Mammoth could actually cross the shallow Echota River nearly anywhere along its winding route but preferred several selected crossings that supported solid rock or gravel beds. The heaviest used crossing was located just north of the Wekiwa Stream as it emptied into the Echota near the Wetumka summer camp. This crossing was often referred to as the First Mammoth Crossing. Once the mammoth crossed here, they spread out through the meadow extending between the Wekiwa Stream and the Echota River. The Spirit Tree was located on the Wekiwa upstream from the Echota.

In the dim light of the early morning, the three hunters stopped at a low rock formation overlooking the Wekiwa Stream. The Mammoth Steppe remained still and quiet as they made final preparations. Harjo stood upright holding several clumps of tall grass stained with mammoth urine in one hand and his spear in the other while Cheparney crushed sagebrush leaves in his hands and rubbed the aromatic foliage on Harjo's back. Meanwhile O'pa, down his knees, did the same with the sage leaves to Harjo's pants.

"Alright," said Cheparney as he stopped. He patted Harjo's back then put his arm around his shoulders and hugged him. "Pick up some fresh mammoth dung on your way, follow the edge of the trees, and stay out of the meadow."

"I will," replied Harjo with a smile.

"Everything will go well, Harjo," said O'pa still on his knees and looking up to Harjo's face. "I know the Father Creator watches you."

"Thank you, O'pa," Harjo replied, and he reached down and patted the boy on his hooded head and then turned, heading off toward the Spirit Tree.

Cheparney and O'pa made themselves comfortable and watched as Harjo made his way along the stream's edge.

"Thank you for asking me to come with you, Cheparney," said a humbled O'pa. "It is an honor."

"You're welcome," replied a solemn Cheparney as he continued to watch Harjo's trek.

"Can I ask you a foolish question?" asked a serious young voice.

Cheparney turned his head to the boy. "There are no foolish questions, O'pa, only foolish answers. Ask your question."

"Well, when you've waited to kill a mammoth and you are alone, are you afraid?"

Cheparney looked again at the boy and smiled. "I will tell you something I taught my boys when they were about your age and my father taught me. Fear is nothing to be ashamed of O'pa. Fear is a gift from the Father Creator. Fear helps us to survive."

"I don't understand," responded O'pa.

317

Cheparney paused momentarily then continued. "The Father Creator gave all animals and humans a spirit of fear. It gives us extra strength and helps us to survive. We must learn to channel that fear. When an antelope sees a lion, his spirit of fear is summoned, and he runs. Fear gives him added strength and he runs faster to avoid the lion. But an antelope can out run a lion. When we humans see a lion, we have the same fear spirit and are likewise given added strength. But if we run, we waste the added strength and we are doomed. But if we stand and fight, we may survive the lion's attack. We learn to channel our fear by skill and talent—skill with a spear and skill with an atlatl and dart. We learn to channel the added strength with a throw of the spear and the point sinks deeper into the lion. We move faster and perhaps we can hit the lion with two darts rather than one."

"Practice with your weapons and learn all your skills. When you have mastered those skills and you have faith in yourself, then you will rechannel that fear. When you have practiced and your weapons are true and you can hit the target from 20 paces each and every throw, you have mastered that skill. Then it matters not if the target is a clump of grass, a hare, a lion's chest or an Enemy Warrior. You will strike the target."

The boy smiled with added confidence. "Thank you, Cheparney."

"Remember, practice every day or twice a day and every so often all day."

O'pa quietly shook his head yes, then pointed. "Cheparney, Harjo is at the tree."

Cheparney looked and could just make out the still dark figure of Harjo at the Spirit Tree, preparing. "Now we wait," said Cheparney, "often this is the most difficult part."

While still dark, mammoth rise from their beds and eat what nearby grass they can and only occasionally trumpet call. But they remain noisy with low snorts and blowing sounds and clearing the shallow snow with their tusks. Slowly, but with true certainty, light fell upon the Mammoth Steppe and the Echota Valley. As the dawn awakes, the calls of mammoth soon roll across the valley both near and distant. Generally, each family group heads for water. Once the sun is up full, ravens and magpies call out all across the valley, adding their voices to the trumpeting mammoth.

Near the rock formation that concealed Cheparney and O'pa was a secondary ford, crossing the Wekiwa Stream, utilized by a variety of migrating animals. As they watched, a small herd of caribou crossed the wide shallow stream. O'pa pointed and whispered. "Cheparney, we could kill a caribou. Should we?"

"No," Cheparney replied, "we will wait for a mammoth to investigate the Spirit Tree and for Harjo to respond."

Then, to their surprise and excitement, a large family of mammoth crossed the stream. They stopped, drank, showered, and trumpeted loudly in the stream and provided an excellent opportunity for close observation. O'pa moved close and whispered into Cheparney's ear. "They are so loud." Cheparney smiled and shook his head in agreement.

Eventually, the patriarchal bull made a loud trumpeting call which was picked up and confirmed by the dominant cow and she began to move on out of the stream and onward as the family filed in behind her. The bull came up behind a dawdling youngster and pushed his tusks against her rear end to move her inline and the boisterous family group moved on.

Not long after their departure, two bulls appeared at the crossing and likewise stopped to drink. They were unusually quiet and then moved on seemingly to follow the family group.

"There is a lifesaving lesson," pointed Cheparney. "Notice the bulls are young but very mature. Often, one or two young bulls will follow a family group intending to challenge the old bull to a duel of death or with ambitions of sneaking in to breed with some of the females. Eventually, the old bull's daughters grow to maturity and may be reluctant to mate with their father and might seek out a mature bull. It is important to remember that once a family group has passed, one or two bulls may follow. Do not think it is safe to walk out behind the family. The trailing bulls will run you down." O'pa shook his head, grateful for the knowledge.

Cheparney glanced down to the Echota River crossing to see a large group of mammoth crossing the river. He pointed, "This could be it, a large group of young bulls."

"How can you tell they are young bulls from this distance?" inquired the inquisitive youngster.

"By the manner of their walk and their gait, same as a human. You can recognize a girl from a distance, can't you, by the way she walks?" The boy smiled and shook his head yes.

The group of mammoth spread out across the meadow after they crossed the river, but some ventured near the Spirit Tree. Then two broke off approaching the tree. Cheparney gripped his fist, quietly held his breath, and watched in unemotional anxiety.

This was all the more dangerous, two bulls at the tree. Harjo may not know there are two. If he steps out to take the one in front, the one in the back may attack him. He would have little chance to survive.

Both bulls rubbed on the Spirit Tree then one moved to the side of the other. The second bull stopped rubbing and they moved on together side by side. Cheparney and O'pa watched in silent apprehension. Harjo stepped from the tree, spear in hand and delivered the thrust to the near bull; the other remained on the other side of his companion thus he could not harm Harjo.

The wounded bull raised its head, struggled, and thrashed about in anguish. Both bulls stampeded in panic as did other nearby mammoth. The call of the injured bull reached Cheparney and he could determine by the sound that Harjo had thrust a mortal wound.

The injured bull came charging straight toward Cheparney and O'pa. "Alright, notch your dart. If he runs in front of us, rise and throw. Remember, I'll aim for the shoulder and you the hip. Do you feel the spirit fear? I feel it as well, but we will control and channel our fear into strength and accuracy. We know we have the skill to hit our marks and we will stay focused on the targets."

O'pa was overwhelmed with excitement but did just that. But there was no need. The bull dropped to the ground before it reached Cheparney and O'pa. Harjo had delivered a lethal strike.

Considering the danger of traveling alone, Cheparney now thought about sending Harjo back to the Wind Band or going himself to deliver the message of Harjo's mammoth kill instead of O'pa. But, O'pa remained tremendously excited on the prospect of taking on that small challenge and adventure. The boy certainly knew the way and had conducted himself in a mature manner. Besides it may not be any safer to stay and guard the mammoth, thus engulfed with excitement, O'pa headed back to the Wind Band encampment.

As O'pa returned to the camp, he went first to Micco Yarda who usually could be found in and around the Chokofa Tent. "Micco Yarda, Micco Yarda," he called out. "Harjo has killed a mammoth at Wetumka. Cheparney says to bring the band to Wetumka and the kill site. He and Harjo will stay and guard it!"

As the excited O'pa turned to run and join his own family, Micco Yarda called him back and patted the boy on his back. "Good son, good effort. Now whistle an alert for me."

The boy looked at Micco Yard with a curious expression. "An alert, Micco?" he asked."

"Well, no, not an alert, but a loud whistle for attention." The boy did as requested, then he turned and ran to his own family.

Micco Yarda then called out in a loud voice. "Harjo has killed a mammoth! Break camp and move to Wetumka!" Whistles and calls of joy rang out throughout the camp, then suddenly and deliberately the band moved into action.

A still apprehensive and frightened young Onna heard the order, but she only translated a few words. In the confusion of languages, she understood three words; "mammoth-kill-Harjo" and added to that the boy's shrill whistle which she understood only as danger. The sudden announcement sent her emotions off like a gust of wind. She grabbed her "harpoon" and her woman's bag and without word to anyone headed off in a run northward.

Luckily, Ayuko noticed the escaping girl. "Onna," she called out, "What are you doing?"

Onna stopped only briefly and turned to answer Ayuko. "I find Harjo," she called out now in tears. "Harjo hurt, Harjo hurt! I find Harjo!"

"You stop right there," called out Ayuko in the loudest and angriest voice she could manage. She ran to Onna, turned her around and put her hands on her shoulders then shook her hard. "What do you think you are doing? Where are you going? Do you want me to pull your parka up and switch your legs?"

"Harjo hurt-I find Harjo-Harjo hurt-I afraid!" cried out Onna in desperation as she pulled away to continue her flight.

Ayuko maintained her grip on Onna's parka and shook the emotional Onna again. "Listen to me, Harjo is not hurt." Onna stopped and looked at Ayuko, her face still strained with stress.

Ayuko quickly called out to O'pa whose family shelter was just next to theirs and he was but a few paces away. "O'pa, come here and tell Onna that Harjo is alright. The boy ran up and looked at Ayuko and then Onna.

"Harjo is alright, Onna. He killed a young bull. It was so exciting!" He reached out and patted Onna's shoulder then returned to his family.

Onna was relieved to hear Harjo was safe but remained emotional as she dropped her spear and stood crying. Ayuko pulled Onna to her and embraced her. Onna returned her embrace but continued to weep. "It's alright now," said a comforting Ayuko as she caressed Onna's hair. As Onna began to calm down, she took her again by the shoulders. "Oh, Onna, think what you are doing, child, think. To run off from camp alone and you don't know where you are or where you are going. Oh, child, that is so very, very dangerous."

"I no brave, same Harjo, same you, I afraid he hurt," sobbed a still anxious Onna.

"I understand," said Ayuko now using her soothing mother's voice. Onna was now calm but still sniffed and went to Ayuko and put her head on Ayuko's shoulder.

"Now, are you going to be calm?" Ayuko smiled as Onna shook her head yes still against her shoulder.

"No more running off?" Again, Onna nodded.

Again, Ayuko took Onna by the shoulders. "You need to learn the Muscogee language, don't you?"

Onna whispered a little "yes" as she continued to sniff loudly. "You tell Harjo I naughty-I get switch," asked a humbled Onna.

Ayuko quietly laughed to herself but maintained her motherly attitude. She was also not sure how Onna used the word "get" to have so many different meanings in both Yupik and Muscogee. "No, not for this naughty but your next naughty, yes."

Ayuko gently put her fingers under her chin then lifted her head smiling into her face. "Now, we'll pack and move to Wetumka. It is such a beautiful camp, you'll see. And we'll find Cheparney and Harjo, and his first mammoth kill."

A now smiling and enthusiastic Onna clapped her hands together. "Oh yes, oh yes!"

Ayuko also smiled but marveled at Onna's strange clapping.

Onna turned to run back toward their sleds but stopped, reached down, and picked up her spear. "Good hunter no leave harpoon," she boasted with a smile, then ran toward their sleds. Ayuko took a deep breath and sighed but smiled and likewise walked toward the family sleds.

Veteran warrior Honeche took the Lead Sled with Micco Yarda while his son, O'pa, was again honored as a Flanker Guard and the Wind Band trekked on in migration formation. Onna easily won the hearts of the Wind Band with her smiles and warm pleasant attitude and manner. Her strength and endurance likewise earned praise. With Chucuse's help, Onna pulled her and Harjo's sled the whole length of the day and continued to work hard helping with camp setup. Cheparney and Harjo did what they could do to process the mammoth, managing to remove the intestines to help keep the meat from tainting. But just when needed, the Wind Band arrived and a core of 20 or more adults descended on the slain mammoth. With a few days of very hard, sullied work, the meat was cured and stored, and the Wetumka summer camp was set up. The Wind Band prepared to enjoy a long pleasant summer season. It would be especially memorable to those who completed their Right-of-Passage and accepted the duties of marriage.

Part Four

SUMMER SEASON

Micco Yarda now put a hand on Harjo's shoulder and the other on Onna's. He called out in a loud voice. "Harjo takes Onna in marriage as his wife. Onna now belongs to him and belongs to the Fus Chate family. All of you come and congratulate them."

Chapter 22:

WETUMKA

A series of interconnected rock outcrops formed the beautiful summer camp of Wetumka that included a rock shelter, large springs, and deep spring pools at each end of the uplift. It appeared as an isolated elevated and low grassy ridge surrounded by rock formations of various sizes. The most impressive formation lay at the southern end of the ridge, reaching the height of three or four men and supported a large deep rock shelter. Tents or lean-to structures could be erected in the shelter for added protection in case of intense storms, but seldom were. More importantly, the shelter served as a focal point for the annual summer celebration of "First Kill" and the revered location for rock paintings and music.

The southern end also supported several large springs which formed a number of pools and a wide shallow stream which meandered southward to empty into the Echota River. Along with the springs, this stream, the Wekiwa, captured run-off water and served as a tributary artery to the Echota River. Instead of flowing directly to the Echota, it paralleled the great river creating its own micro-valley. The stream was heavily wooded and several large rock outcrops formed along its winding route. Mammoth followed this small valley on the north/south migration along the Echota Valley at large. The sacred "Spirit Tree" where Harjo single handedly killed his first mammoth was situated along this stream near its confluence with the Echota. Cheparney, Grandfather Fus Chate, and other brave Wind Band hunters had also used the tree as well.

Another beautiful spring, which supported a waterfall, was located at the northern end of the low ridge. The spring initially pooled on the high top of the outcrop then cascaded down creating a wonderful waterfall hence the name Wetumka "sounding water." The spring formed a large pool at the falls and then flowed out in a stream eastward to empty into the Echota. The falls and the pool offered an incredible site for drinking water and bathing. Mammoth Hunter children spent many summer days playing in and around the pool. Adults regularly bathed at the pool and women spent as many opportunities as they dared to bathe, comb their hair, and talk. The pool also provided a meeting place for unmarried youth to become acquainted. Girls who were just becoming eligible for marriage during the summer found an excuse to visit the pool at least once a day.

Both spring pools and flowing streams were riparian and supported a wooded zone of cottonwoods, willow, and alder, especially the Wekiwa Stream, where many large cottonwoods thrived along its banks including the giant Spirit Tree. Additionally, a wooded zone extended along the western edge of the rocky uplift connecting the two riparian streams creating an exotic, almost dreamlike zone of large rocks and trees extending along the back of the camp. This zone formed a favorite playground for children and a secret haunt for lovers seeking privacy.

Wetumka provided the Wind Band a safe and secure haven. Lookouts could be posted, usually adolescent boys, on top the rock shelter formation with a spectacular view of the surrounding landscape where they could easily detect approaching game and or Enemy Warriors from a great distance. Wetumka had never been attacked. The size of the Wind Band and its number of capable warriors generally encouraged an enemy war band to seek a smaller less formable group of victims. Also, the Echota River formed the heartland of the Muscogee and once an attack ended, the enemy raiders must escape and return to their homeland without engagement from a Muscogee war band which may pursue them. Consequently, Enemy Warriors concentrated their evil work on smaller, less formable bands and other groups situated on the fringes of the Echota Valley.

These elements all combined to make Wetumka the favored summer camp location for the Wind Band. The most important element of any summer camp, however, was a mammoth kill. Wherever summer kills occurred along the Echota River or throughout the whole valley, the Wind Band moved and set up a camp at the kill site. They stayed at least long enough to dress and process the meat and hide. Then, depending on the kill site location, the Band settled in at the kill site or packed up and relocated to another area and hence an enhanced living site.

Moving a summer camp, however with the added load of the processed meat of a mammoth loomed as a difficult task. Pulling loaded sleds across snow-covered ground remained difficult enough. Pulling travails, along with sleds, across the open summer grasslands was a formidable task. Consequently, all bands of the Muscogee Mammoth Hunters most often camped at or near a kill site especially a summer kill. Nonetheless, the Wind Band, if at all possible, would spend summers at Wetumka.

The elevated oblong ridge of Wetumka surrounded by rock formations created a nearly impassable barrier for mammoth in particular but other herbivores as well. Few campsites provided such a safe location against roaming mammoth that otherwise my stumble or even stampede through a camp with deadly consequences. Covered with thick grasses and dotted with tall trees, the low ridge provided an excellent location to erect summer tents. In addition, three important constructions at Wetumka provided the Wind Band with central areas and focal points of social interaction, the Chokofa Tent, the Chunkey Yard, and the Square Hearth.

In construction, the Chokofa Communal Tent was comparable to a mammoth winter lodge, but without the floor pit. The tent centered on a super structure of four up-right posts connected at the top by four lateral or horizontal posts. Four trees had been selected with a suitable trunk size and a fork notch which formed from where a main limb branched off from the trunk. The trees were felled and trimmed to manufacture four posts with a forked top. The base of each post was treated with mammoth oil then set in the ground as four corner posts reaching just higher than a man could reach. Then, four lateral posts were laid using the forks to secure two of the posts with the others laid on top to create a four "post and lintel" super structure of the tent. Then, the ends of six mammoth tusks were attached to the two parallel posts, three on each side with one at each corner and one in each center. The base end of the tusks was not buried in the ground; however, another length of post was attached to base of the three tusks on both the left and right ends. Now the mammoth hides, which were sewn together and cut to fit, were stretched across the curved super structure. A skylight window about two paces square was cut into the top of the covering and thus centered on the four structural posts and hearth. The window could be covered with translucent mammoth intestines if necessary. Then mammoth bones, especially long leg bones, and rocks waited down the ends of the hides on the ground at the base of the mammoth tusks.

The Chokofa Tent served the Wind Band as a communal shelter although, over the course of a long summer, many families moved into their own family tent shelters and lean-tos leaving the Chokofa Tent as a gathering shelter rather than a sleeping shelter.

On occasion, groups of men, in particular, hunting or exploring parties, would spend a night or two in the Chokofa Tent to insure an uninterrupted early morning start. Occasionally, the Ptarmigan band of boys would sneak away from their family shelters for a frockling night in the great communal tent.

A Mammoth Hunter's family summer shelter was used primarily for sleeping otherwise most activities occurred outside throughout the camp. Inclement weather may encourage the people to move into their shelters in particular, the Chokofa Tent but generally a family shelter remained empty during the day except when privacy was needed.

Following tradition, Micco Yarda and his wife, Us'se, were the only permanent residents of the Chokofa Tent. He had a platform bed constructed of small sturdy limbs using two of the four corner posts. The front side of the bed was also made into a solid wall and thus used as a backrest. Micco Yarda often conducted band business on the floor in front of this bed. Us'se strung up hide curtains around the bed to provide for a measure of privacy for sleeping.

In front of the Chokofa Tent, the large communal hearth called the Square Hearth, served as a band gathering location especially at night. Several large natural rocks at the hearth and four large logs served as seats as did the ground, bison robes, and back rest.

Two large natural rocks formed two corners and the seating logs were laid out to create a square about the hearth, hence the name "Square Hearth." A large circle of rocks inside the square enclosed the fire. Everyone helped to keep the fire going. Boys were especially useful at supplying wood. To them it became an enjoyable game to venture out and return with a load of wood. A small group might leave and take their darts and atlatls for practice and small game hunting and often they would take a travail and return with it loaded with firewood pretending to return with a big game animal. Many families cooked and ate at the hearth just at dusk and storytelling was a popular social event especially for the children.

Toward the southern end of Wetumka and in front of the rock shelter, the Chunkey Yard provided a convenient location as a dart and spear practice field but more importantly it was used for the Fox Chase game. The four corners of the yard were staked and marked with white feathers. Other stakes marked off other boundaries around the yard. Several low hillocks and seating logs lay along the southern edge and seated spectators during the Fox Chase games although many sat on the ground or on robes and the elders most certainly used their back rests. The top of the highest hillock on a robe with a backrest was a favored location generally reserved for Elders.

It normally required three days for the Wind Band to process a fallen mammoth depending on the location of its final resting and if the hide was kept whole or cut in to sections. Whole hides were desirable as dwelling covers for either the semi-subterranean winter mammoth lodges or the summer lean-to tents but were also more difficult to process. The hide belonged to the hunter(s) who risked their lives providing for their people.

After the first mammoth kill of the summer had been processed and the meat equally distributed to each family, all bands of the Muscogee Tribe celebrated the annual summer ceremony of First Kill. Each band may have its own special proceedings, practice, or order of events associated with First Kill, but each ceremony included a feast of the fresh mammoth meat, the First Fire Ceremony, a Communal Tea, wall painting ceremonies, and public recognition of Rites-of-Passage, marriage, or other achievements. Music accompanied the events throughout the ceremonies.

A beautiful, late, warm afternoon laid still, and quiet, and distant mammoth trumpeting calls rang out but seemed to blend with the afternoon stillness rather than clash. Harjo, Onna, and Ayuko made their way across the Wetumka camp to the Chokofa Tent at Micco Yarda's request to speak the tale of Harjo's Rite-of-Passage journey and to formally meet and question Onna. Harjo carried a pouch in one hand and held Onna's hand in the other. Micco Yarda often conducted band matters at the Central Hearth located in front of the Chokofa Tent but this afternoon, he sat on the ground on his bearskin and other bison robes were spread out in front of his platform bed with the Lion Shaman seated next to him. Green shoots of spring grass were bursting through the thick mat of yellow winter grass which covered the ground throughout the whole Wetumka camp and under the Chokofa Tent.

As he always did for Rites-of-Passage conferences, the Lion Shaman dressed in formal attire punctuated by his lion skin headdress and cover. He presented a strong, fearsome presence. The Shaman frightened Onna and she hoped he would not ask her any questions but realized he likely would.

"Don't worry so much, Onna," said Ayuko as she tried to comfort the anxious girl as they neared the communal tent. "Remember, you are probably the only human the Lion Shaman has ever touched, not including patients, and most certainly the only one he has ever smiled at."

Still, as they entered the tent, she released Harjo's hand in order to cling to him. These formal meetings, even though intended to bring positive results, were often anxious but Micco Yard had long experience with easing tensions.

"Welcome, welcome, come in and sit down," exclaimed a jubilant Yarda as the three made themselves comfortable on the robes. Once the three were seated, he continued.

"Harjo, my thanks and congratulations on your mammoth kill. The Wind Band is fortunate to have a hunter so young with such skill and courage."

"You're welcome," replied a modest Harjo.

"Well now, Harjo," continued Micco Yarda, "Tell us about your journey and your vision. It was obviously quite an adventure."

Following custom, Harjo related the tale. He was not a good storyteller but a confident speaker and accurately presented details and facts of his journey including his vision. He concluded, "You saw my sled packed with sea mammal skins. I have shared the pelts with my family. I followed the Lion Shaman's advice and received my vision although I am still uncertain of the meaning." He then handed Micco Yarda the bag, "Shells from the Great Sea."

Micco Yarda opened the bag and reached in and brought out a handful of seashells. "Congratulations, Harjo, well done. You bring honor to your family."

Out of turn, Ayuko spoke up. "Oh, I can hardly wait to sew some shells onto my parka!" No one replied, and she noticed a stern look from Micco Yarda. She cleared her throat and returned to silence.

"Perhaps the Lion Shaman can address any insight into your vision, Harjo," suggested Micco Yarda.

The Shaman turned then looked at Harjo. "You are 16 summers?" he asked.

Nervous little Onna feared for Harjo, so she nervously looked over to him, but she saw no sign of fear in his face. He held the same expression as he did during their encounter with the lion on their journey from the Great Sea. Also, she could not feel any tension within him as she clung to his arm. "I am," answered Harjo in a fearless yet respectful tone.

"Your vision is a complex matter. I will ponder the details and render my interpretation to you on another day."

"Thank you," replied Harjo.

"Alright, my son," broke in a jubilant Micco Yarda. "At tomorrow's Morning Tea and First Fire Ceremony, I will publicly announce that you have successfully completed your Rite-of-Passage and have stepped from the realm of childhood into the world of an adult man of the Wind Band." There was a quiet but joyful calm and all smiled.

"Onna," stated Micco Yarda, forcing her to look up with an anxious face. He looked into her face with a pleasant expression. "We have never seen anyone like you Onna. Your appearance is strange but still you are very beautiful."

Onna did not understand all his words but enough to blush and smile. Her smile could warm anyone's heart, even the seemingly cold heart of the stern Lion Shaman.

"We would like to hear your story," suggested a calm Micco Yarda.

As presupposed, Harjo related Onna's tale as all listened in silent wonderment. After he completed it, there was a pause. Then, the Lion Shaman leaned over and looked into her face. She cringed and squeezed Harjo's arm. Harjo reached his arm over her shoulder which calmed her. The Shaman spoke and even though he had conversed in perfect Yupik the day he tended Harjo's wound; he delivered his questions in Muscogee.

"What did you hear from the Elders of your village concerning these matters? How far does the Mammoth Steppe extend to the west of your former lands? What is to the east, south, and north of your former homeland?"

Harjo related the questions to Onna, and they discussed the answer. Ayuko also added to the discussion although her comments were more because she was a woman and could not remain silent for too long. Micco Yarda listened in some wonderment to the Yupik language. He thought to himself and realized that although he had heard this strange language spoken by his close kinsmen, including his brother, all these many seasons, he still understood very few words in Yupik.

Finally, Harjo related Onna's answers. "I heard from my grandfather and other Elders that the Mammoth Steppe extends far to the west and ends at a great ocean. The Great Sea lies to the east of my former homeland. To the south, are great mountains and glaciers. No one knows what lies beyond. The Big Ice is far to the north. Some said the great ocean to the west and the Great Sea to the east are the same, others said no. No one really knows." The Shaman leaned back, seemingly content with the answer.

Micco Yarda broke a short pause with a question. "Ayuko, you wish to address us?"

An enthusiastic Ayuko spoke up. "Yes, Onna has reached the age of female maturity. She sewed the boots she now wears and wore on her journey with Harjo from the Great Sea. She has been adopted into the Fus Chate family

338

and we desire her to be recognized as an adult female of the Wind Band and the Muscogee Tribe."

Micco Yarda looked over to the Lion Shaman who stared off past everyone without emotion. "It is done," he said. "I will make the announcement tomorrow." Onna recognized enough Muscogee to realize the answer of yes and released Harjo's arm, clapped her hands and squirmed with excitement.

"Anything else?" asked Micco Yarda in such a way to reveal he knew there was.

"Yes," stated Harjo. He put his arm around Onna and pulled her to him. "I will take Onna in marriage as my wife."

There was a wonderful silence, gently broken by Onna who put her head on Harjo's chest and then gently whispered, "Oh, Harjo."

"I will be glad to make these announcements at tomorrow's ceremonies," related a joyful Micco Yarda. He rose as did all except for the old Lion Shaman and the trio left the Chokofa Tent with a gently weeping Onna still clinging to Harjo.

Chapter 23:

CELEBRATIONS/MARRIAGE

The ensemble of Muscogee Mammoth Hunter music consisted of a flute player, singing voices, and percussion. The most celebrated musician was the flute player named Yuhi'ke. As leader of the Wind Band musicians, he was respected not only as a musician but also as a craftsman for the manufacture of his flutes. He played both melodies and accompanied the singers. Normally, two women supplied the voices for the songs. They blended with the flute player depending on the song. On some occasions, they sang the melody and the words accompanied by the flute player and on other occasions, the reverse and the female voices accompanied the flute player who took the lead if the song did not have words. There was no set order, but it was related to how they rehearsed, working out the songs, although tradition established a precedent. The Wind Band audience expected certain songs to be performed in a certain way and also expected to be surprised in the presentation of others.

Three percussion instruments completed the ensemble with the drums being the most noted. Similar to the flutist, the craftsmanship employed in the manufacture of a drum was complex and held in high regard. The drummer's name was young To-wa-tol-ku, a recent addition. His father played the drums for as long as anyone could remember. To-wa-tol-ku took his place. He was equally as skilled as his father having learned from the master since boyhood. A flat, thin length of wood formed the base of the drum about wrist to forearm size. Split, smoothed, and cut to size, the piece was then bent into a circle with warm water and steam or by utilizing green wood. Once the circular rim-base was fixed, it was covered with an animal skin and stretched taut and tied. Additionally, a drum covered with treated mammoth intestines was highly prized for its sound and the extra effort required in processing the intestines.

Two remaining percussion instruments completed the group. A rasp was simply made by cutting notches along a caribou long bone, a slither of mammoth ivory, or a length of hard wood. A smaller stick or bone was pulled along the length creating a strange rasp sound. Finally, two small pieces of bone or wood were taped together to create a high-pitched sound. Although these instruments, the rasp and the taper, were simple to construct and play, satisfying musical sounds were not created by accident. The musicians manufactured these implements with the same care as the others and worked hard to locate material that produced the desired sounds.

Many rehearsals over several seasons were required before the musicians could perform songs that pleased the ear. The three percussion instruments, the drum, rasp, and taper required more rehearsal than many realized so that the drumming and striking sounds flowed with a pleasing beat, fitting together into a soothing blend. The two girl singers were often replaced, as the girls were married and then moved to the bands of their husbands. Chufe had been a welcome voice but was purchased by a young warrior from another band. Now returned, perhaps she would sing with the musicians again. Once flute player Yuhi'ke heard Onna sing, he became anxious to have her voice join in but would wait until she mastered the Muscogee language.

The ground was now thawed with winter snow nearly melted. Only shallow pockets lingered in north facing shaded areas, adjacent rock formations, or large trees along the streams. Small groups of women began gathering forays, venturing out from the summer camp with armed warriors as escorts to search for and harvest bear root. With projectile point-shaped leaves and striking purple flowers, this bushy herbal plant can reach knee high. The taproots are edible with a delicious, unusual flavor. The harvester, however, must remain cautious because some related or "look alike" plants can cause an upset stomach.

Bears also relish the plant, which is why the Mammoth Hunters call it bear root. Along with berries, this plant is the only vegetable the carnivorous bears consume which was another reason why armed warriors accompanied the women. Hunters out on early spring and summer hunts or other excursions likewise harvested the plant and carried back as much as possible to their families. All the Muscogee bands relished this vegetable addition to their meat heavy diet.

"I can guard same warrior," boasted a confident Onna. "I can throw harpoon, Harjo teach me. No need warriors, Chucuse, I can go find bear root."

Onna was so anxious to go and dig bear root she tried to convince Ayuko that she and Chucuse could go alone without warrior escorts stating that she could provide all the required protection. Ayuko, however, was not about to allow the two daring girls to leave camp without escorts even in the relative safe region of Wetumka. Onna and Chucuse quickly learned, however, that if men in their family were not available to provide warrior escort duty plenty of other warriors in the band, young and old alike, eagerly volunteered to escort the attractive women of the Fus Chate family, especially the unmarried Chucuse.

The days warmed and lengthened as the sun moved steadily northward before it dipped past the horizon often with colorful and spectacular sunset results. But to the Mammoth Hunters, the return of the robins remained the clearest and most noticeable sign that summer was approaching Wetumka. The grey back, red-breasted birds were most abundant along Big River but nested all along the wooded streams and were particularly fond of the Wekiwa Stream, the Echota River and the open meadow between them. Ground disturbances came from the migrating mammoth herd as they congregated at the Echota River crossing then through the meadow. The adjacent woodlands facilitated the robin's search for insect food. Displaying little fear of the Mammoth Hunters, the robins nested in the trees and thickets all around the Wetumka camp. Apparently, the local human disturbance likewise assisted in their continuous quest for insect food for themselves and their offspring.

The bulk of the mammoth herd had now migrated on northward to their calving and spring feeding grounds, which was much too far to hear their trumpeting calls. Only the occasional call of a late straggler broke the otherwise peaceful Echota Valley. But the male robins sang a beautiful song every morning notifying all, especially other male robins, they lay claim to a nesting area and the female within it. The robins were fearless in their search for insects throughout the campgrounds, providing games for small children who tried to catch them.

The joyous song of the robins provided a bittersweet melody to Onna. Bitter because it reminded her of her distant homeland and lost family, but sweet because she was also so thankful to be living in the Echota River Valley with Harjo and soon through marriage to formally belong to him and his family. This particular First Kill ceremony would remain in the hearts and memory of both Harjo and Onna all of their lives but was also recalled as an important occasion by everyone who took part. It began in the morning with the drinking of communal tea and lighting the "First Fire."

Micco Yarda, ready to conduct the ceremonies, gave the word for the musicians to begin to play, summoning the people to gather at the village's Hearth Square. The Wind Band was fortunate to have such talented musicians who were often asked to play at the tribal council meetings held during the winter at Coweta. They began to play what was commonly called the "Gathering Song" and although the voices blended in an appealing harmony, the song did not have words. The people assembled at the Hearth Square, each brought a bowl or ladle to enjoy a taste of a special tea brewed each season by Micco Yarda's wife, Us'se.

Called simply yellow tea, the rare delicacy was highly favored for its unique delicious taste. The tea was made from a knee-high bush, which supported bright yellow flowers with large petals, hence the name, and projectile point-shaped leaves. The plant preferred a rocky terrain on the edge of wooded areas. The rare plant was easily recognized but infrequently encountered. Us'se collected the leaves of the plant throughout the warm weather seasons in order to brew enough tea for the whole band. She brewed the tea at her own hearth and quietly stood by her boiling pouches with a ladle in hand, ready to draw out tea for all who wanted. The people thanked her and appreciated her contributions to the ceremonies.

The observance began with a quiet, peaceful moment. The people gathered around the Hearth Square drinking tea, talking, and listening to the music, as they waited for the arrival of the Lion Shaman to perform the First Fire ceremony.

Eventually, the old Shaman arrived with his two helpers, an apprentice of about 20 summers and a boy possibly one-half that age. The boy walked in front of the Shaman and the older apprentice off to his right but behind. The only solemn portion of the First Kill ceremony was lighting the first fire perhaps because the Lion Shaman performed the task but more so because it invoked, however slightly, the spirit world.

Dressed in full ceremony apparel, the Lion Shaman approached the Square Hearth. He wore his lion cape over his bare chest but also carried his staff of spruce mounted with an elegant ivory carving of a lion's head. His long pants and boots were a single unit. He wore an unusual and impressive necklace. It was constructed mostly of shell and bone. The central necklace ornament, however, was a wide stone projectile point with a finger sized hole through its middle. No one was really certain exactly how to drill a hole through a stone point but could see the point was knapped by a master craftsman. His shoulders were bare and revealed the scars of lion claw marks on each shoulder. His presence commanded reverence and attention.

The two young apprentices of the old Shaman cleaned and restacked the hearthstone to prepare the Square Hearth some days earlier. They swept out the old ash and debris exposing the bare fire hardened baked ground. They also stacked a pile of dry wood in the center for a fire. Much more than a random wood stack, selected wood, kindling, and tender were consciously placed to create a pre-set camp-fire about waist high. A large stack of random wood lay nearby to be added to the ceremonial fire as needed.

They rebuilt the large circle of stones around the ceremonial woodpile. The sitting logs and the large stones formed a square about the hearth-hence the name Square Hearth. They also selected four larger logs about waist high and about the size of a young woman's thigh, which also lay near the ceremonial woodpile.

As the Shaman approached, the gathering stepped aside, clearing a path for him and his helpers. He did not speak or greet anyone on this solemn occasion although he seldom did on normal days anyway, except for perhaps Micco Yarda or Cheparney. His face usually displayed little or no emotion and more so on this day as he appeared to be in a trance. He stared straight ahead—he did not seem to even blink. His left hand grasped the shoulder of the boy who guided him. The Lion Shaman truly was not completely of this world. He was, in ways few could understand, linked to the spirit world.

The trio stopped near the ceremonial woodpile. The boy carried a small blanket sewn from hare pelts and he spread it out on the ground near the pile. Then, they both assisted the old man down to his knees on the edge of the hare blanket. Micco Yarda raised his hand and glanced toward the musicians who halted play. Silence fell across the camp. A deathly silence, so still that even the robins and other birds ceased to sing as though they also listened with hushed reverence.

The older apprentice, also on his knees and with his fire starter kit in hand, began to draw the bow. At the same moment, the old Lion Shaman began to sing a song, a weird, eerie, almost frightening sound but also strangely hypnotic. It was as though the song filled all with anxiety and yet all wanted to hear it. No one understood the words, but it did not seem to matter as the unnatural resonance fixated all.

Finally, the apprentice blew on the fire stick and the small now smoking fire hole. The Shaman held a large wad of tender in his hand. He stopped singing, touching the wad to the fire stick hole, then the wad instantly ignited. A few 'oohs' and 'ahs' came from the lips of those standing by. Holding the flaming tender in his hand, he then put it into the ceremonial wood stack which burst into a large flame causing the people standing close to the fire to jump back, startled but joyful. Instantly, a healthy fire burned in the Square Hearth. No one knew how the Shaman created this feat, but it brought the gathering to excitement and calls of joy. The first fire was now ignited.

All the families gathered together, including the Fus Chate family, now laughing, applauding, and embracing each other. Onna released her seemingly ever-clinging grasp on Harjo's arm to clap her hands and jump with excitement. Never afraid to show her feelings, a smiling Onna stood on her toes to give Harjo a quick but tender kiss. Igniting the First Fire signified the end of winter and a completed Spring Migration. The first mammoth kill would provide enough food for at least two full moon phases over 60 days. It was the beginning of summer and a new beginning for all.

The two apprentices helped the old man up and escorted him to one of the large rocks, respread his blanket, then assisted him to sit back down with the rock as a backrest. The boy sat down next to him, but the older one returned to the fire. Then, taking the four large logs, he placed the ends of the logs into the fire so that the distal ends pointed to the four directions, north, south, east, and west. Throughout the course of the ceremonies, the two helpers would tend the fire and keep it burning until the four logs were consumed.

Later and over the next few days, all the families would light their first campfires from this First Fire.

Micco Yarda made his way to the front seating log. The end section of the log was split and therefore flat. He stood up on this section obviously ready to make announcements. He took a final drink of tea from his cup, which was actually an old ladle with a broken handle. Many laughed to themselves that a man in his position, a band micco, used something his wife once discarded or gave to a little girl as a toy as his favorite drinking vessel. He motioned all to draw near and spoke.

"The First Kill ceremony, above all else, is a season of new beginnings, a season of birth, of maturity, and of marriage. It is a season to renew old pledges and the dawn of the promise for the future." He stopped, cleared his throat and continued. "I know we all enjoy this delicious tea provided by my wife. Take the opportunity today to thank her for her efforts." He paused as the crowd nodded their heads with approval.

"We all have the good fortune to come this early in the season to Wetumka and to celebrate the First Kill at his beautiful camp. If we are able to make another kill, perhaps we can tarry here for four full moons. If the seasons remain in our favor, the possibility remains that the band could remain at Wetumka during the warm seasons leaving from here on the Fall Migration back to Coweta. The possibility of only two migrations to complete the whole seasonal cycle seems to be in our grasp." That announcement brought loud cheers of approval from the gathering. Another short pause and he continued.

"The first kill was made by Harjo. It is his first mammoth and he shares it with us. We are all grateful to him." Another joyous outburst from the gathering sounded out and many shouted out-Yahola!

Onna understood these words and turned to smile up to Harjo. She stood on her toes to gently kiss him in the ear, whispering. "Thank you, Harjo." Anyone standing near Harjo reached out to touch and thank him.

"Harjo and Onna come up here," called out Micco Yarda and motioned for them to approach. Onna again wrapped both her arms around Harjo's arm and clung to him as an infant might cling to her mother's breast as they moved up and in front of Micco Yarda.

"Harjo has returned and successfully completed his Rite-of-Passage journey. He has traveled from boyhood to manhood and is now an adult man of the Wind Band of the Muscogee Tribe of Mammoth Hunters." Again, the voices of joy filled the air.

"Harjo, I am bound by family heritage to inform the band that the splendid atlatl you carry-the same that bears the likeness of the strange red bird seen in our grandfather's vision-will be your token of manhood."

Ayuko, standing next to Cheparney, reached out and took his hand as tears filled in her eyes. Such a bittersweet moment as a mother's youngest son becomes a man.

"Harjo's journey," continued Yarda, "was quite the adventure. I am sure we will all hear about it tonight around the Square Hearth and as you know, he did not return alone."

"Onna," said Micco Yarda. Hearing her name, she turned to look up at Micco Yarda smiling then turned back to the crowd still smiling but she would not release Harjo's arm. Her adorable expression brought smiles to all the Wind Band.

"Onna, my father, Harjo's grandfather, was not a Shaman but nonetheless he was a man of vision—a man with strong spirit power. He was also a master carver.

Interpreting one of his own visions, he carved this female figure of a beautiful girl."

Micco Yarda held up a carved figurine necklace. Carved from ivory, the necklace was shaped as two connected figures. The first was a bust of a beautiful female form. The bust was linked by interconnected rings to the second piece which was the head of a raven. They appeared to be two separate, connected figures but they were not. They were one solid piece of ivory. Only a master carver of extraordinary skill could carve two or more pieces that interlocked by circular rings from a solid piece of ivory. Some believed this rare skill required assistance from the spirit world, perhaps the Father Creator himself.

"The face of this girl in the carving," continued Micco Yarda, "is one none of us had ever seen. We have never seen the likeness of any people captured in this carving. We did not know such people existed. I believe this face is an image of you, Onna. And through Fus Chate, the spirit world, perhaps the Father Creator himself was sending us a sign that you were coming to us. Accept this necklace as a token of your maturity for you have now crossed over from the realm of a girl to the realm of a woman. Onna, you are now an adult woman of the Wind Band of the Muscogee Tribe of Mammoth Hunters. We welcome you."

Micco Yarda reached over and lowered the necklace over Onna's head. As Onna took the figurines in her hands and saw the images, tears began to swell in her young eyes. Once more, the sound of approval came from the gathering.

Micco Yarda now put a hand on Harjo's shoulder and the other on Onna's. He called out in a loud voice. "Harjo takes Onna in marriage as his wife. Onna now belongs to him and belongs to the Fus Chate family. All of you come and congratulate them."

The totality of the ceremony overwhelmed young, emotional Onna and she could not help but cry. All of these life changes at one moment; completing her Rite-of-Passage and becoming an adult woman, being accepted into the Wind Band and into the Fus Chate family and now being married to Harjo overwhelmed her youthful heart. Additionally, by her reckoning, her marriage would be strong because Harjo had not purchased her from her father. She had chosen him and he her. They had spoken marriage vows and promises. It was a day, a moment in her life, she would never forget.

Suddenly, Onna became somewhat embarrassed by her tears. As she blushed, she wanted somehow to hide. But the Wind Band people recognized and appreciated her honesty, her sincerity, and were happy with her. Harjo sensed something. He put his arm around her shoulder, so she put her head against his chest, which helped relieve her uneasiness.

The Wind Band filed by offering congratulations to both, taking their hands. Many kissed Onna's hand, especially the children, to further demonstrate her acceptance. Cheparney and Ayuko, who also remained in tears, were first to kiss and hugged them both, then the whole Fus Chate family came with embraces and kisses.

Chapter 24:

Painting/Games

Save one, all skills were the product of many seasons of practice, learning, and tutorage under the watchful patience of a skilled Elder, usually one's parents. A girl began learning the art of sewing from her mother at a very early age and a boy the skill of hunting from his father. All continued to learn, improving those skills throughout their entire life. All of these skills were learned and acquired with the exception of one, the art of painting.

The skill and ability to paint a good painting was a gift from the Father Creator. No one was taught or learned the art of painting but a chosen few were endowed by the Father Creator with this special gift. Usually a man, a hunter and warrior, received the gift but not absolutely because the Father Creator may choose to bestow his endowment on a woman or even a child. Certainly, a woman or in particular, a child, may be reluctant to come forth in open public and paint a picture on the rock shelter wall during an important observance of the First Kill Ceremony, but as Micco Yarda would say, "If anyone is so inspired, come forth." Be assured, anyone can physically paint a picture but only a few are blessed with that unique gift to do it well.

Painting a picture on the rock shelter wall at Wetumka or any other location was an expression of appreciation to the Father Creator for his gifts that sustained life. Most commonly a painting depicted an animal that contributed to the survival of the Muscogee Mammoth Hunters but not absolutely. Every now and then human forms, for example, of hunters or warriors were painted especially relating to an encounter and subsequent battle with Enemy "raiding" Warriors.

Harjo was not a good painter, nor had he ever painted a picture during the First Kill Ceremony or ever been so inspired. His contribution was to provide the paint. He knew several locations where good quality red and yellow ocher clay could be excavated. He shared several locations with anyone in the Wind Band, but he also kept one particular location to himself. The Wind Band, especially those who painted, appreciated that he journeyed out to return with liberal amounts of the material and likewise produced good quality paint that he generously shared with all.

Late in the morning, the sun shone bright into the rock shelter and revealed otherwise dark corners and crevices providing adequate light to facilitate wall paintings. At the appointed moment, Micco Yarda directed the musicians toward the shelter and they took their place along the sidewall. Traditionally, they performed throughout the painting, providing a stimulating background.

The whole band gathered on the floor of the shelter sitting comfortably on bison robes, blankets, and mats, many with supporting back rests. Watching the artist paint was both an enjoyable and spiritual experience and meant to be shared. Young and old set on the ground next to each other touching and embracing. Many quietly sang the songs along with the music. Only the youngest of children remained uninspired by the ceremony as it was always a moving and satisfying experience.

All were gathered at the rock shelter including the reclusive Lion Shaman who sat with his helpers near the side, more or less out of the way. Harjo and Onna sat on their bison robe, wrapped in arms embrace and likewise surrounded by their Fus Chate family. Katchu was one of the gifted artists in the band and was painting a picture of a horse. Onna appreciated that he painted a horse. She was very fond of the horses. They seemed more abundant in her homeland than in the Echota Valley and the painting reminded her of that distant land. Suddenly, Onna became disturbed and almost frantic. She took Harjo's arm and seemed to cry out in a whisper.

"Harjo! Harjo, I see picture on wall!"

Harjo put his arm around her. "Yes, there are many beautiful pictures on the wall."

"No, Harjo," she said in such a frantic whispered intensity. "I see picture, I see picture, but no picture!"

Distressed, Onna spoke with such serious intensity but Harjo did not understand her meaning. "I don't understand, Onna."

Onna thought for a moment then she held out her left hand and tapped it with her right-hand fingers. "No picture, Harjo. I see picture." Then she pointed to the rock shelter wall.

"You see a picture on the wall, but there is no picture there?" asked Harjo.

"Yes, Harjo, yes! I can paint, Harjo. I can paint."

"You can paint a picture, Onna?"

"Yes, Harjo, but I afraid!"

"You want to paint a picture on the wall, Onna?"

"Yes, Harjo, want"

"But you are afraid to?"

"Yes, Harjo, I afraid."

Many Muscogee men may have shrugged off the idea of such a young girl participating in such a solemn, serious ceremony. But Harjo took Onna's hand and together they rose. He picked up his tray of paints and led Onna out from the crowd to the rock shelter wall. He stopped a few paces from the wall. "Where?" he asked quietly.

Onna looked at him and smiled humbly and pointed. He led her to that spot, then guided her up to the wall. He set his paints down on the floor and put his hands on her shoulders. "Paint your picture, Onna."

Onna looked at him and put her hands on his chest. "I can paint picture, Harjo?

"Yes, Onna. Paint your picture."

"No one mad me?"

"No, Onna, no one will be mad. Anyone can paint a picture on the wall."

"Thank you, Harjo," she whispered.

Loud murmurs and voices of disbelief came from the gathering. Not objections, more of surprise. Onna turned and touched the wall.

Generally, an artist preferred a flat surface avoiding any rough texture or cracks, but Onna put her hand on a course, jagged surface. She touched and rubbed her hand across the rough texture of bulges, ridges, and cracks. Still murmurs and disbelieving voices emitted from the gathering, but no one spoke out. Micco Yarda himself had often said, "The Father Creator touches all hearts. If a woman or even a child is so inspired to paint, come forth."

Onna reached down and picked up the container of black paint, dipped her finger in, and began to draw an outline on the wall. She utilized and manipulated the rough bulging surfaces as parts of the drawing. At first what she painted seemed odd, but as she applied more paint it soon became clear and all could see she painted the outline of a mammoth. A large, round, bulging, rough textured area on the wall was transformed into the mammoth's shoulder and a nearby smaller bulging area became its head. Onna's eager fingers changed a long, curved, ridge into one of the animal's tusk. On the rear of the animal, a wall crack was manipulated into the area between the mammoth's hip and stomach. Now all could see a clear black outline of a bull mammoth, magically brought out from the wall by Onna.

Onna stopped and looked around as all eyes of the gathering were on her. Whispers still filled the rock shelter and filled her with apprehension. Harjo was not going to let her stop now. He put both hands on her shoulders and whispered into her ear. "Do not worry about those watching. They will be pleased. Keep going and paint your picture. Work slow, work good. Remember, you can sew good boots and you can paint a good picture. I will stay here by your side holding your paints."

What had been fear and timidity, Harjo transformed into confidence. Onna was inspired and now wanted eagerly to continue. She took the red paint container and still using her fingers, began to paint in the image while Harjo held the two yellow and black containers. She would stop, look and study, dip her fingers into the pigments, and paint.

Perhaps inspired by Onna's painting, Yuhi'ke led the musicians in a favored song about a young hunter from a poor family without a father or brothers. His band looked down on him. He sets out alone one day to singled-handedly kill a mammoth, sharing it with his family and his whole band. In legend, he became renowned in his band and was the first hunter of the Muscogee Tribe to accomplish such a feat. All were inspired as they watched Onna paint.

Now and then, Harjo whispered words of encouragement into her ear and tickled her ear with his breath, which brought a smile to her face. Even though she smiled she remained focused. She seriously studied the wall, the textures, and the paint. Finally, she finished with the black and smoothed out the contour lines.

Onna stopped. She was finished. She looked at Harjo and smiled. "New painting Harjo-mammoth." Harjo gave her a final kiss and whispered into her ear.

"It's wonderful, Onna; it's the prettiest painting I have ever seen." Onna set down the paints and took Harjo's hand and they stepped back from the wall.

At the conclusion of the painting ceremony, those who had painted went out first and stood outside the shelter. The Wind Band filed by and congratulated each artist on their accomplishment. As Harjo predicted, all were well pleased with Onna's painting. The textured surfaces and cracks gave her painting a dimension not before seen. It was quite remarkable. There was something magical in her painting and something magical in her. Harjo stood with Onna and all of the Wind Band came by and took her hands. Some, especially the children, kissed the back of her hand to show appreciation and respect. Even the old Lion Shaman came by and although he did not touch Onna, he stopped in front of her and spoke. "You are indeed touched by the spirit world. You will fare well." He then went on with his helpers.

The sun reached its high apex to announce the beginning of the games as the Wind Band assembled on the side of the Chunkey Yard on the low hillocks and the log seats to enjoy the first of two games, the dart throwing contest. The Elders, both men and women, were afforded the best seats on top the low hillocks and were assisted by grandchildren up the hills to robe seats and backrests. Similar to a covey of ptarmigan, the little girls gathered on the ground in front of the log seats each with a toy doll. They enjoyed each other's company as much as the games. Interspersed with burst of laughter then solemn quiet, they exchanged dolls, giggles, whispers, and secrets.

Older boys, with assistance from some of the older men, manufactured a dart target from old caribou skins and parkas by sewing and stretching the material into an animal shape then stuffing it with grass. Once attached to poles, including other slight modifications, the target resembled an animal. It was then set into place in the Chunkey Yard.

The younger boys assembled first in front of the seated crowd with their darts and atlatls. Then, one after another, they each took a throw at the target. Applause and cheers rose from the crowd when the target was hit, conversely oohs and ahs when the target was missed. After each round, the target was moved back until it was out of reach for all the boys. The boy to score a hit from the longest distance was awarded a prize.

Micco Yard kept a collection of artifacts to serve as prizes. As a renowned knapper, he owned a large collection of well-crafted, fluted points which were a treasured prize to a youngster. Later, a victorious boy hafted the point to a knife handle or spear, proudly showing it off when given the opportunity.

Chilocco and Yahola sat together deep in discussion, probably concerning a fall bison hunt, so Kak-ke took a seat with Harjo and Onna. Next to Cheparney, Ayuko indulged her grandchild. Holding the baby gave young Kak-ke a rest. Her baby was quiet, strong, and healthy and Ayuko was sure it would live. Drawn to her brother, Chucuse sat down in front of Harjo, braced against his knees, then leaned her head back on the top of his knee to talk to him or Onna. Onna's Muscogee language summarily improved and everyone throughout the band was impressed with the rapidity she learned to speak. Harjo already knew how clever she was and her uncanny ability as a linguist in both Yupik and Muscogee, not to mention her native tongue.

"I can throw harpoon," announced a proud smiling Onna to Kak-ke. "No atlatl, hand. Harjo teach me. He take me hunt caribou soon."

"Yes, I know, said Kak-ke "You were so brave and ready to fight the Enemy Warriors when they attacked. Everyone was so proud."

Holding fast to Harjo, Onna hugged his arm and smiled at Kak-ke. "Harjo teach me, stand, fight with harpoon. No run from lion."

Kak-ke could not resist adorable Onna and reached over gently, drawing Onna to her then tenderly kissed her. Onna blushed; the open affection of the Wind Band women with each other often surprised Onna. Kak-ke gently stroked her hair. "I am so glad you came to us Onna and will stay with our family."

Suddenly, there was an outburst from the crowd as the last remaining boy hit the distant target. Micco Yarda came forth, and then with the approval of the gathering, presented the proud boy with a fine point. The target was moved back as older and more experienced boys took the field and the contest continued. Eventually, the target was set at such a distance only the best of the veteran warriors could strike the mark. Each warrior took a turn or not, as they choose or were persuaded by the crowd.

Several veteran warriors attempted a futile cast but were nonetheless applauded by the crowd for their efforts. Even Honeche, who was one of the most skilled throughout the whole tribe, attempted an unsuccessful throw. The band called out for Cheparney to make a throw, but he declined, smiled, and waived them off. He put his arm around Ayuko and fussed with his grandson.

The crowd called out for Harjo who was reluctant especially since his age group had passed by. But with light-hearted jostling and kidding, especially from brothers Yahola and Chilocco, he rose to step onto the field. Using another's atlatl and dart would present even more of a challenge as like most men he didn't bring his weapons to the games as there were plenty on hand.

Harjo briefly examined the set of weapons he was handed. Then, armed with the atlatl and dart, he positioned himself on the field. There was a slight moment of silence as he made the throw. The dart flexed and arched through the air. There seemed to be plenty of distance as the dart descended striking the target in the chest. The force knocked it off the poles.

A loud cheer erupted. Many shouted out "Yahola" to show genuine congratulations. Onna reacted as only Onna could. She stood up and jumped up and down clapping her hands loudly. Clapping was unknown to the Mammoth Hunters, but all were amused and delighted at her frolics. Onna was easily winning the Wind Band heart. She was honest and sincere.

There was something magical about her. More than her beauty and her smile, there was something that could not be seen. Something in the warmth of her presence that seemed to touch the most hardened of hearts, even the heart of the Lion Shaman. As Harjo returned to the log seat, excited Onna hugged and kissed him. The other women around him likewise took the opportunity to embrace him.

The second game, favored among the boys throughout the whole Muscogee Tribe, was called the fox chase. The boys played the game by themselves without supervision throughout the summer but often during the First Kill Ceremonies, an older man served as an overseer and announced the games. Micco Yarda was always a welcomed announcer. The gathering showed its approval as he came out in front of the crowd.

Onna realized something new was about to begin. She squirmed with excitement. Ayuko called over.

"Chucuse, explain the game to Onna. You may need to speak Yupik."

"Alright, mother," answered Chucuse as she turned around placing her arms up on Harjo's knees.

"This is called the fox chase game, Onna" and she explained the rules and how it was played with occasional help from Harjo. Watching the boys play the game, it did not seem difficult to put in plain words, but it was a lengthy discussion to include Onna's questions.

"This is a chase and tag game, Onna," explained Chucuse. "First, they make boundaries on the Chunkey Yard by four stakes, one at each corner making a big square in the yard. All the boys are supposed to stay in the boundaries. Then two more stakes are pounded in at each end in front of the other stakes on the edge of the Chunkey Yard and this makes a line across the end of the yard. Can you see where all the stakes are?" Onna shook her head yes. "Anyway, the ends of the yard are called dens. They are safe areas for the players."

"Now you can see, Onna, each boy wears a tail of some kind and of course, they like foxtails the best. They don't wear parkas or boots. Those boys spend the whole summer barefoot and the soles of their feet are hard and tough just like mammoth rawhide."

"Anyway, one boy is chosen as the 'Catcher.' They have a special way of choosing the Catcher which is a hand game, a matching game. They use one hand and they make a rock, a point, and an animal skin. Harjo can show you how they do it later, alright?"

Onna agreed and watched as boys paired up and matched each other using one hand and thus one would win. Then, the losers matched each other until finally only two boys remained—the last loser became the Catcher. It took only the blink of an eye to decide. Onna thought it would likely require adults the entire afternoon to make such a decision, but the boys completed the task in a few moments.

"Well," continued Chucuse, "the Catcher is the least liked player in the game but, over the summer, all the boys play it. Once a boy was a game's Catcher, he is excused from that for other games that day until all boys play the Catcher."

Onna now watched as the game began. Every boy, wearing a foxtail, rallied at a den on one end of the Chunkey Field. The Catcher positioned himself as close as possible to the den, but he could not cross the imaginary line established by the stakes on the side of the yard. The Catcher now counted out in a loud voice 1-2-3-run! All the boys took off trying to run to the safety of the den at the other end of the Chunkey Yard and once they made it there, they were safe. The Catcher tried to yank the tails out of as many boys as he could.

"Scuffling is not allowed between the Catcher and a fox," a laughing Harjo told Onna. "The foxes can evade, turn, twist, and out run the Catcher but no wrestling or contact except for hands on the foxtail."

"The boys who lose their tails are far from being eliminated from the game," continued Harjo. "They now change sides and become the Catcher's Helpers—and they have just begun to play. The Catcher's Helpers cannot pull a fox tail, but they try to hold and detain a fox until the Catcher arrives to pull his tail. Now wrestling and scuffling plays a fun and important role."

Harjo explained to Onna that sportsman and games-manship were admirable qualities, consequently hitting and or kicking were strictly forbidden and only wrestling, and scuffling was allowed. Boys who broke this rule were eliminated from play for the entire day. Also, older and larger boys were warned against hurting younger and smaller boys. A boy who would hit another or harm one younger or smaller boy was looked down on by the Wind Band at large as a matter of honor. Such boys may be considered as having less than warrior skills. The infraction seldom occurred except by accident. On the other hand, a good scuffling and wrestling match by boys of near equal size and age was appreciated.

Excited, Onna watched as the Catcher and his helpers would advance to the line on the end of the Chunkey Yard. When all were ready, the Catcher would call out the order for the boys within the den to run. They took off like a covey of ptarmigan in many different directions, trying to reach the safety of the den at the other end of the yard without losing their tail. The Catcher's Helpers attempted to catch and hold on or hold down a boy until the Catcher arrived to yank his tail and turn him over to their side.

As Onna watched the game progress, she saw the boys were good sports and many fun incidents occurred throughout the game. For instance, when a little boy became a Catcher's Helper, older boys may only pretend to run fast and allow the little one to catch and hold them or they may wrestle with a little Catcher's Helper allowing him to win and hold the older boy down until the catcher arrived. Another crowd pleaser occurred when a larger fox would have a little Catcher's Helper sit on his foot and wrap his arms and legs around the larger boy's leg, the fox would then try to reach the fox den with the heavy little load riding on his foot.

As the foxes ran more, more lost their tails becoming Catcher Helpers. It thus became more difficult to reach the safe den at the other end. Eventually, only one or two boys remained—the fastest and most elusive runners. This was the climax of the game. If these remaining one or two boys were able to run the field reaching the safety at the fox den on the other end, a great cheer would explode from those watching the game on the side. If a boy was able to run the yard without being caught, he was awarded a prize. Eventually, he would be caught, ending one game and beginning another.

As the Fus Chate family sat watching the fox chase game, the crowd shuffled around and Ayuko was now seated next to Onna and Harjo.

"I have a story to tell you Onna about Harjo," announced Ayuko. An unemotional Harjo groaned under his breath but an energetic Onna clapped her hands, laughing out loud, "Yes, yes."

"When Harjo was a little boy," recalled Ayuko, "and he played the fox chase game, he was often the last boy with a tail even when he played with his older brothers who were stronger and faster but Harjo, was well, he was elusive. He was just so agile and evasive, and he was a trickster."

"I remember once," continued Ayuko, "he was the last boy waiting to run. The Catcher called out run and Harjo started to go, then suddenly stopped and looked up in the sky. He hushed the boys as though he heard something up in the sky and he looked and pointed up. Many adults on the side also looked up. When the boys on the field looked up, sly little Harjo took off and ran past most of the boys before they realized he had tricked them, so he easily reached the fox den on the other side. Everyone on the side watching cheered for such a sly trick, many were themselves fooled.

Harjo was awarded a prize, and everyone said those were wonderful games."

Cheparney and Chucuse sitting near Ayuko listening to her story also laughed. Onna laughed and smiled at Harjo. Even the stoic Harjo managed a slight grin. Onna put her arms around Harjo's arm-her sly trickster.

Chapter 25:

FOUR SUMMERS WAIT

Prepared to leave on a scouting trip with his father and brothers, Harjo returned to the family shelter to say farewell to Onna. The family converted their lean-to shelter with the mammoth tusks "arch opening" into a larger conical shaped tent lodge which afforded more privacy. Constructed of wooden poles and their bison skin cover, it resembled a Caribou Hunter summer tent in appearance and construction. Onna emerged from the shelter all in smiles as she carried Kak-ke's baby.

"Look, Harjo, poor baby no have name."

A smiling Harjo approached, gently touching the baby's head. "They will give it a name if it lives until next summer."

"You and men family hunt, Harjo?" she asked.

"We are going to scout the bison," he replied.

"Bison scare me Harjo, you can have careful."

"I will," he said as he cupped her face, pulled her to him, and gave her a long passionate kiss.

Onna met his passion with her own and beckoned for more embrace.

As the kiss ended, Onna was breathing heavily. "Baby make me want you sex me Harjo-give me baby."

"Yes," Harjo agreed; the baby does the same to me.

The baby squirmed and squealed then tried to suck on Onna's breast through her parka. "Oh, no, baby hungry," smiled Onna.

Harjo gave Onna another quick kiss then turned to go and Onna went back into the tent shelter.

Kak-ke took the squirming baby from Onna and began nursing. Meanwhile, Chucuse stood naked before Ayuko as she examined her daughter. "Mother, when I will start menstruation?" asked the inquisitive girl.

"Soon, child, I would guess before fall migration."

"Mother, does Kak-ke and your menstruation happen together?"

"Why yes child, we do."

"Will Onna's happen with you and Kak-ke?"

"Yes!"

"Will mine?"

"Yes, Chucuse, it happens to all women who live together."

"Why, mother?" asked Chucuse.

Ayuko just laughed but saw that Onna and Kak-ke also looked to her with an inquisitive expression. "Well, girls, women have asked that question for many generations. My old grandmother told me that long ago, in the far distant past, it was safer for women of a group or band to have their babies at the same season, close together. Perhaps when there was more food in much the same manner as the females in a herd of animals, such as the mammoth."

Onna and Kak-ke covered their mouths and snickered. "All band, they can have sex same day," joked Onna as all three giggled and laughed.

Smiling, Ayuko took a deep breath and continued her examination. She got down on her knees and inspected Chucuse vulva. Then tenderly, after wetting her fingers, she examined her vagina opening.

"Mother," squealed a squirming Chucuse.

Ayuko hushed her. The girl's vulva appeared as in previous examinations and continued its preadolescent size, color, and backward position and certainly there were no signs of pubic hair development. Ayuko put her hands on Chucuse's hips as she massaged and gripped them in examination then turned her around to examine her buttocks and anus. Satisfied, she gave her girl a loving spank of the bottom. "Alright Chucuse, you can dress."

Ayuko got up and washed her hands with the water pouch. The anus was always examined last so that no other areas of the body were touched with the hand that touched the anus. Then the hands were thoroughly washed.

"I hope I don't start my menstruation and then have my Rite-of-Passage during the winter. I don't want to stay in that cold little mammoth hut at Coweta," moaned Chucuse.

Ayuko sighed, "Oh, Chucuse, once there is a fire and lamps burning along with blankets and mammoth beds, that small mammoth lodge is quite comfortable and warm."

Frowning, Chucuse still protested. "I still don't want to."

Ayuko smiled, kissed her index finger, then reached out and gently tapped Chucuse's lips with her finger. "Don't fret. Besides, if another girl begins her Rite-of-Passage, the same as you, then you will share the little lodge with her and have some company. Otherwise you will be in a summer shelter by yourself."

Chucuse took a deep breath and mumbled something to herself then moaned, "Well maybe it would not be that bad, but I still hope I have my journey during the summer."

Ayuko went to Onna taking her hands. "You're next Onna, so you will need to undress."

Onna was aware this examination was forthcoming, but she remained hesitant. Ayuko gently touched Onna's face. "Don't worry child, this is women's business and only us women are here." With firm motherly patience, she helped Onna undress.

Ayuko gave Onna a thorough and complete examination including her anus which embarrassed the shy little Onna. Ayuko was primarily concerned with her vulva and more importantly her pelvic area. On her knees, she gently and motherly scrutinized Onna's hips then tenderly pressed in following her pelvic opening. Then, having turned her around and with her fingers between her buttocks, felt the base of her spinal cord. She then massaged Onna's firm little bottom and marveled at the wonderful shade of her light-colored skin.

Ayuko rose and told Onna she could dress. "You are very beautiful, Onna and I am glad to say you are very healthy and have very good hygiene, but you are much too young to have a baby."

Onna picked up her parka and held it in front of her. "No understand?"

"Your hips and pelvis are much too narrow. You are simply not ready to have a baby." Onna still did not understand but with an additional effort in both languages Ayuko conveyed her decision.

"You cannot have a baby. You will wait three summers, maybe four."

A now anxious Onna held up her hand and counted beginning with her little finger. "One-two-three-summers, have baby. I want have Harjo baby."

"I know you do, child, but it is much too dangerous."

The emotional Onna began to move to tears and again held up her three fingers. "Three summers long. I want Harjo, baby."

A stern Ayuko took Onna's shoulders. "Yes, three summers, maybe four. I know it seems long, but there is much danger.

"Danger," replied Onna. She understood that word.

"Yes, danger, big danger. I will not risk your life and I certainly will not watch you die. You are so young-you will have many summers to have many babies." To make her point, Ayuko moved her hand to Onna's vulva, which forced a little "oh" from her.

"You may still have sex with Harjo, as much as you want. You can be sore or 'have little hurt' nearly every day if you want."

"I like Harjo give me little hurt," replied a now smiling Onna.

All the females in the lodge laughed, even young Chucuse who was not quite sure what 'little hurt' meant.

Ayuko removed her hand from between Onna's legs and again took her shoulders giving her a slight but firm shake. "Sex, yes-baby no! If you become pregnant, you must lose the baby."

Onna was still naked holding her parka, then she put her hand on her stomach and formed such a sad face. "I not want lose baby, Ayuko, no want."

"I know, child, that would break all our hearts, but I will not risk your life for a baby. Understand?"

Onna nodded her head yes, beginning to see the wisdom in Ayuko's decision. She now cupped Onna's face in the same manner as Harjo. "These can be such wonderful seasons, Onna, before you have babies. You can go on trips, journeys, and adventures with Harjo."

"Harjo promise he take me hunt caribou," announced Onna with a smile.

"And he will, child, but think, if you were pregnant or had a baby, he would not take you. Enjoy these seasons of your youth," implored Ayuko, "enjoy sex, but you will not become pregnant! Do you understand?"

Onna slowly nodded her head yes. "You speak true, Ayuko. No baby three summers, four maybe."

"Good girl," praised Ayuko, and she pulled Onna to her, giving her a warm embrace.

Admiring Onna's parka, Ayuko reached out and rubbed it. "What a beautiful parka, Onna, we have all admired it but have not had the opportunity to ask you about it. Did you sew it?"

"No, Harjo trade Canineqmiut, he give me, more better I can sew. A proud Onna bent over and picked up her boots. "I sew boots," she declared with a smile.

Ayuko took Onna's boots, "Yes, your Rite-of Passage boots. "Girls, we will all need to examine Onna's boots and parka before we begin on the beautiful sealskins Onna and Harjo brought from Imarpik. If there are enough skins, we will all have seal skin boots to wear in winter. If there is not enough material, at least our men will wear seal mukluks."

The pace of life often moves fast on the Mammoth Steppe and Ayuko, Chucuse, and Kak-ke, who laid her now fed and contented baby down for a nap, had forgotten all about Harjo's sled load of seal skins and Onna's fancy parka. But now they all converged on naked little Onna, the center of attention, to examine her parka and boots made of the strange skins.

"I am always nervous," declared Ayuko, "When the men hunt or go on trading journeys during the winter. Seal skin boots will help insure warmth and protection from frost bite."

All the females handled, examined, and commented on Onna's beautiful parka and when they finished, she quickly, but with motherly assistance from Ayuko, slipped it back on. Then their attention turned to Onna's boots as they likewise prattled over the exotic material, as only women can.

Onna was curious about something and as they examined the pelts, she asked. "Ayuko, how Harjo can talk Caribou Hunter language?" I ask, he say have friend when little boy, he Caribou Hunter. He no can tell me."

"It's a very sad story," answered Ayuko. "Harjo does not like to talk about it. Are you sure you want to know?" Onna pondered the question and then nodded her head yes.

"Alright," said Ayuko and began her tale. "When Harjo and his brothers were too small to accompany Cheparney on trading ventures to the Caribou Hunters, Cheparney would go with his hunting and trading partner, Honeche. His children are about the same in age as ours."

"The pair would plan to leave early in the fall usually at the first snow. They would pull a sled laden with mammoth pelts and other materials to the land of the Caribou Hunters, then locate a band eager to trade. With luck, they would find the Caribou Hunters as they had just completed their fall migration and caribou hunts when they have fall hides on hand and willing to trade. Then, Cheparney and Honeche would rejoin the Wind Band on its fall migration to the Coweta Winter Village."

"One fall, Cheparney and Honeche returned to the migrating Wind Band from a trading journey with a sled load of caribou pelts and a small Caribou Hunter boy about eight summers in age. The poor child had been abandoned by his band."

"When I asked Cheparney, he stated, 'I don't know the reason he was left behind. Perhaps his parents were killed or too poor to care for him.' "Cheparney explained that mentally and physically handicapped children were left behind to die. The Caribou Hunters are admirable men in many respects, but they also follow many strange customs. They commonly abandoned children and often killed girl babies for reasons he did not understand."

"Well," continued Ayuko, "the abandoned boy turned out to be physically well and mentally alert. We understood his name to be Honea. He understood what his fate would have been, left alone during the winter, and was grateful to Cheparney for rescuing him and he fully appreciated being a member of our family. I adopted him as I had Cheparney's two older boys. I tried to overwhelm him with love and affection."

"Onna, Honea became a model child and the occasion never arose to punish him or to switch his legs. He and Harjo became the best of friends and constant companions. They slept together, played together, and ate together all day, every day. Oh, they had other friends and along with Yahola and Chilocco, were proud members of the Ptarmigan Band, but they seem to always be together."

"No one spoke his language, however, and communication remained awkward at first. But from one summer to the next, he and Harjo shared each other's language and by the second summer's end, Honea spoke Muscogee and Harjo the Caribou Hunter tongue with fluency. Everyone in the band was amazed at how quickly they shared each other's language. They often spoke the Caribou Hunter tongue, laughing as they talked about everyone while eating around the family hearth and no one knew what they were saying.

Cheparney understood Caribou Hunter words and phrases because of his trading experiences but certainly he could not converse. He would let it pass or not pay any attention to the two silly boy's antics, but I caught on. Are you boys talking about us, I would scold? They would laugh, pleading innocent. Cheparney would then remind me that I, Harjo, and Chucuse conversed in Yupik frequently. Different languages had long been spoken around the Fus Chate family hearth especially at meals."

"But Onna, the ending is terribly sad. Tragedy befell Honea during he and Harjo's eleventh summer. They left our summer camp venturing out only a short distance then decided to race back. Each took a different path. Harjo returned first and looked for his friend, but he was not in camp. Suddenly, distant screams and cries were heard. Harjo, along with a few other warriors, raced to the distress call to reach a gruesome, heartbreaking scene. Honea had been attacked and killed by a lion. One of the warriors quickly carried his mangled bloody body to the Lion Shaman but to no avail. He was dead." Tears formed in Ayuko's eyes. She paused, sniffed, and continued.

"All the family mourned, especially Harjo and I, but Harjo was heartbroken. We buried little Honea according to our custom. The men dug a grave and lined it with mammoth long bones. We washed his broken small body and blood-soaked clothes in a stream as well as we could, then laid him in the grave. We placed his meager belongings, weapons and toys in the grave. Harjo painted a caribou hide in red ocher paint that depicted the journeys, hunting trips, and games that Honea liked the best, adventures he and Harjo shared. He covered his friend's body with the painted hide. The gesture touched everyone's heart. Then, silently, we covered the grave with dirt and piled a rock cairn on it for remembrance. The cairn is at another summer camp and one day I will show it to you if you want. I still miss my Caribou Hunter son. I think I always will."

"Cheparney took grieving Harjo aside to offer what words of wisdom he could. I asked him and although he would not tell me everything he said to Harjo, this is what he told me that he said. 'I can offer you no words of comfort my son, I can only offer you words of truth. I know you seek revenge upon the lion, but it would be a shallow reward. You will never know if you killed the attacking lion or not. Harjo, the lion is not evil. Father Creator gives the choice of good and evil only to men, not to animals. A lion will never commit an act of evil against us or an act of good. A lion will simply act as a lion. I guarantee you the day will come, and you'll be given the opportunity to take revenge on a lion and it will likely be necessary to save your own life.' Cheparney told me he put his arm around the tear-stained face of Harjo, and they walked back to camp. Harjo would never paint another painting nor ever have a friend like Honea. That is until you, Onna."

Tears streamed down Onna's face. "Poor little Harjo. I so sorry, he lost friend." Sensitive Onna continued to cry, unable to stop as she went to Ayuko for comfort. Ayuko, also in tears, put her arms around her now grieving charge. She held her, kissed her, and rocked her in her arms as she would a child.

Cheparney and Chilocco left Wetumka on band business. At Micco Yarda's request, they journeyed to the Lion Band's Summer Camp with three tasks to complete. First, to deliver word of the attack by Enemy Warriors on the Wind Band during spring migration and second, to attend the Lion Band's First Kill Ceremonies. The third was inform them of Onna. All bands of the Muscogee appreciated guests and visitors from other bands especially during the important ceremonial summer season.

During the evening, while gathered around the Lion Band's communal Square Hearth, Cheparney asked Chilocco to tell the story of the attack as a close first-hand witness. Lion Band warriors were impressed that a young warrior named Harjo, who just happened to be Chilocco's younger brother, single handedly, killed the three attacking warriors. One assailant had been slain in hand-to-hand combat using the attacker's own spear as the lethal weapon.

During the telling of the tale, both Cheparney and Chilocco answered question from the crowd and in so doing, added sidelines, which included other important information concerning the same young warrior named Harjo namely that he had also single handedly killed a mammoth for his own Rite-of-Passage feast and a charging lion on his return trip from the Great Sea with a sled load of sea mammal pelts. Finally, Cheparney also told them of Onna.

He described the exotic girl's appearance, fair skin, yellow hair, and blue eyes. But more importantly, her and her band of people lived on the other side of the Koryak Glacier. This was something unusual and important, especially for the Elders to consider. He announced the Wind Band would remain all summer at Wetumka and perhaps through the fall. He explained the girl was Harjo's wife, but they were welcome to come and meet her this summer. Or they could wait until the Tribal meetings this winter where Micco Yarda would introduce her to the other Band Miccos.

Cheparney had ulterior motives as well. A girl from a family he knew would be publicly announced as eligible for marriage during the Lion Band First Kill Ceremony and he wanted Chilocco to see her, perhaps meet her, and talk with her father. Now that Chilocco had asked him about Chufe as a possible wife, Cheparney thought it prudent to edge

Chilocco into a more harmonious direction. Following his father's suggestion, Chilocco carried with him a bag of seashells from the treasure Harjo brought back from the coast. On their journey to the Lion Band summer camp and sitting around the evening fire, Cheparney had a fatherly talk with his son and offered his advice.

"Once you see the girl, Chilocco, perhaps talk with her, and see that you are sure you want her then barter a bride price with her father. Especially if other suitors are present, ready to propose an offer-some actions cannot wait. If you successfully purchase the girl, you could leave the bag of shells as a promise to return with the agreed upon bride price. If you are not certain you want to marry her, then leave the shells as a gift for her and her mother. Such actions will impress the father and the family. Later, if so inspired, you can return with bride price with full knowledge that attractive healthy girls do not remain unmarried long subsequent to their Rite-of-Passage completion."

At the Wind Band camp, the busy Fus Chate family engaged in chores around the family campsite. The women were laying out the seal pelts Harjo and Onna brought from the Great Sea coast. They clattered loudly about the prospects of sewing boots from the precious hides. Chucuse and Kak-ke were eager to gain from Ayuko's and Onna's experience with seal pelts.

Meanwhile, Harjo and Yahola had just returned from the Ronoto Hills area with a collection of red chert bifaces. Harjo sat on the rocks at the edge of camp knapping on new biface material that had just cooled off from heat treatment. Most men knapped at the edge of camps to keep sharp flake debris more concentrated, otherwise it might spread throughout the camp at large and into barefoot children.

Onna also enjoyed watching Harjo knap and when possible, she would help, especially when he struck the fluted
flake from a near complete point. "Harjo?" asked the always
curious Onna, "Dyuktai men make flake on side of point
same you, why?"

As he held a biface in hand Harjo explained. "The fluted
flake is the final large flake removed from each side of the
base of a large point, especially if I am knapping a spear but
also dart points."

Onna anxiously shook her head yes as she understood
that portion as she urged Harjo to get to the important
explanation.

Harjo continued, "The flute scar thines the point but
more importantly it creates a 'slot' to securely haft and
attach the point to the foreshaft."

The delicate procedure required caution as many points
were broken at this final stage particularly by inexperienced
knappers. Consequently, when Harjo was ready, he called
to Onna to come and help, and she eagerly ran to him. He
used his heavy caribou antler mallet and his pressure flaking
tool for the fluting job. The pressure flaking tool was the
small sharp end of a caribou antler tine set into a handle of
wood. Harjo also used the tool as a finishing flaking tool.
Onna would lie down on her stomach holding the target
point tightly between her thumb and forefinger at arm's
length. She held the point vertically with the tip set on a
thick piece of mammoth hide which in turn rested on a
flat section of wood. Harjo placed the tip of the pressure
flaking tool on the end of the base of the point and struck
the flake. The trick was to hold the point still. Onna's trust
in Harjo was complete and she would not flinch. She buried
her face in her other arm to guard against being struck in
the face by the fluting flake as it flew off the point. She held
the point perfectly still and would call out "ready." Harjo

would strike the flake then repeat the process on the other side of the point.

Onna held the finished treasure in the palm of her hand, smiling. Spirit power lingered in such a well-crafted point. Harjo was a master craftsman, rare for a man of his young age. All the adult men in the Fus Chate family were master knappers. Micco Yarda was renowned throughout the whole Tribe as elite. Not only for themselves but the Fus Chate men kept their women well supplied in beautiful, superiorly crafted stone tools. Other band women were envious, not begrudgingly, but envious nonetheless.

"I can have?" asked Onna.

"Certainly, if you wish," responded Harjo.

Holding the red chert point in the palm of her hand as she would a baby bird, Onna leaned over and thanked Harjo with a kiss. She gave him three kisses, calling out "thank you" with each kiss. Onna remained emotionally inundated. She still found it hard to believe she belonged to such a brave, loving warrior and a member of such a wealthy, generous family.

The three Fus Chate females sitting at the family hearth and anyone else watching could not help but chuckle at Onna's antics as she assisted Harjo in knapping the point. Ayuko shook her head laughing. Harjo was so stoic and "adult like" while Onna so adorably "childlike" the two were nearly opposites. Perhaps that is why they were so attracted to each other. Ayuko had never seen a man and woman or husband and wife enjoy being together as much as Harjo and Onna. Ayuko loved Cheparney and she knew he would lay down his life for her in an instant without hesitation. She was blessed by the Father Creator to belong to Cheparney, but she did not necessarily enjoy his company beyond being wife. She much more enjoyed conversation with her girls or her mother figure, Us'se. How it was that Harjo and Onna enjoyed each other's company remained inexplicable.

Two Caribou Hunters pulled a travail laden with caribou skins and cautiously approached the Wetumka Summer Camp. They knew enough of the Muscogee language to announce their peaceful intentions and were then warmly greeted by Wind Band warriors. They had traded with the Wind Band on prior occasions thus they were recognized and known.

Yahola approached the family camp. "Harjo, they ask for you to come and interpret for the Caribou Hunters in trade."

"Alright, I am on my way. I thought that was what all the commotion was."

"I want go-I want go-I want see trade," called out an excited Onna.

"No, Onna, you stay here," voiced a stern Harjo as he rose. "This is a man's work and gathering. Women are not allowed."

"Please, please, Harjo, I can go. I quiet."

"No, Onna," said a stern final Harjo as he walked off toward the Chokofa Tent.

Ayuko added her motherly advice. "Now you stay away from those men, Onna or you'll be in trouble."

Onna was forewarned on several occasions-women are not allowed to attend the gatherings or meetings of men such as trading or in particular council meetings. If caught, women were punished for eavesdropping on such meetings. Micco Yarda's wife Us'se once had her bare legs switched for secretly listening in on a Micco's council meeting.

A frowning Onna shook her head, yes. Ayuko returned to the pelts and Onna walked off toward the area where women urinate and leave dung. The mischievous Onna shook her head "yes" but to her that meant she understood, not that she was going to obey.

Instead of going to urinate, the impish Onna turned off and ran to the edge of camp to the large trees and rocks. Then, she hurried along the camp periphery, around and behind the Chokofa Tent. The men were gathering at the front of the tent. Onna stopped and momentarily considered her actions. If caught, she could be switched. If the wife of a Micco was punished, how would a naughty girl escape that fate? But she convinced herself Harjo would somehow rescue her, and her curiosity was such a motivating force.

Harjo arrived at the front of the tent and provided a temporary distraction. Onna took advantage of the distraction, slipping into Micco Yarda's bed, obscured from vision by the animal hide curtains. She was then able to just part the curtains, look out, and watch the proceedings unnoticed.

Mammoth Hunters brought in sections of mammoth pelts and the men sat on the ground in front of the bed talking back and forth. Other men stood by and behind the bartering men sitting on the ground. Onna presumed there would be intensity; even anger at a trading session but to her surprise there was not. The men were calm, relaxed, and actually seemed to enjoy themselves. A pouch of cold tea was brought in and the Caribou Hunters seemed to appreciate the popular herbal drink. They also shared fresh roasted cold mammoth which was likewise respected. Onna could distinguish the two Caribou Hunters not only because they were strangers but also because they wore caribou fawn clothes. Oh, she would love to have clothes made from caribou fawns.

Harjo talked to the Caribou Hunters and Onna listened intensely to the strange language. She was impressed with her young husband. He was the center of the trading episode, talking first in the Caribou Hunter language then in Muscogee. He seemed to be in charge.

Then, for reasons unknown, Harjo looked over to the bed curtains and saw her peeking through. Onna froze. There was such a small opening between the curtains, he could not possibly recognize who might be behind the curtains, but she could tell by his expression he knew it was her. She continued to watch.

Then the session ended. Onna was surprised how short the gathering was as she anticipated it would be rather lengthy. As the men stood and bid farewell, all in high spirits, Onna snuck out the back way as she had entered. Again, she ran to the edge of the camp and to the women's urination and dung area, then she strolled back into camp as though she had just returned from urination. She met Harjo. She could see the anger in his face. She swallowed hard.

He took her hand and led her off toward the back edge of camp. He stopped momentarily, breaking off a small tree branch and stripped it of twigs and leaves. He held the switch in his right hand and swung it through the air so that it produced a painful switching sound. He took her hand again and led her beyond the camp behind the large rocks and trees. He stopped and released her hand as she stood with her hands folded in front of her and her head bowed but she looked up.

"Women are switched for hiding and eavesdropping on men gatherings, especially girls like you. Micco Yarda's wife was punished for such an offense!" Harjo's voice was angry and harsh, and he cut the air again with the switch, producing the same painful sound.

Onna's face turned distraught. She cried and tears ran down her checks. "You promise you no switch me, Harjo."

"I am not going to switch," he said as he threw the branch to the ground. "But I said I would use the palm of my hand," and he held his palm out.

Onna pulled her frock up to her waist exposing herself then turned around and bent over continuing her crying. "Please no mad me, Harjo. Please no mad me!"

She was crying such hard, anxious, honest tears. She asked Harjo not to be angry, but she did not ask not to be punished. She remained bent over, crying, and awaiting her spanking.

Her sincerity touched his heart and quelled his anger. He walked in front of her then took her shoulders and pulled her up and into his arms and she laid her head against his chest. She was crying very hard. He had not experienced her crying with such intensity.

"I sorry Harjo—I sorry. I want see trade—I no can stop. Please no mad me, Harjo, no mad me!"

He caressed her hair and kissed her. "I'm not mad, Onna, I'm not mad. It's alright now." He comforted her and slowly her crying eased.

"You mad me, Harjo?"

"No, I am not mad at you. I was angry but not now."

"Promise you no mad me."

"I promise, I am not mad at you," he whispered as he continued to caress and kiss her hair as her crying ceased.

"I get spank, Harjo?"

"No, I am not going to spank you."

Nearly calm, her head remained against his chest. "Harjo, you say you can see me watch?"

"No, I won't tell anyone I saw you."

Onna now looked up at him in a tearful smile. "We can have secret?"

"Yes," he smiled still stroking her hair, "we'll have a little secret."

Onna was now smiling. "I like have secret you Harjo."

Now, all in smiles, Onna stood up on her toes and kissed him and he returned her kiss. Harjo took her hand and led her back to camp.

∽∿∿∿∿∿∿∿∿∿

That evening, the Fus Chate family sat around their family fire eating, laughing, and enjoying each other's company. Onna was fond of feeding Harjo. She would take a small bit of meat in her fingers and put it in his mouth then lean over and kiss him.

"You same baby bird, Harjo," she would say as she laughed.

Suddenly, Onna noticed no one was speaking Yupik and she did not understand most of the conversation. Finally, a frustrated Onna spoke up in Yupik. "Talk Muscogee Mammoth talk. I no understand."

There was a hush pause around the fire as though everyone knew something but Onna. "We are speaking only Muscogee, Onna" stated a motherly Ayuko, to help you learn the language."

Displeased, Onna formed a frowning but still lovely face. "I no like," she whined, "it hard." Everyone around the fire chuckled. She was such an adorable pouter, but she easily learned the Muscogee language in a few seasons as Harjo predicted she would.

∽∿∿∿∿∿∿∿∿∿

The task of collecting firewood generally fell to older children. Girls frowned and moaned when assigned the chore, but boys usually accepted it without complaint and ventured out in groups of two or three devising some amusement to lessen the small drudgery such as to pretend they brought back slaughtered game to each camp. Onna proved to be the exception and even though she was now a married woman, she still enjoyed little jaunts to the woods to gather firewood and viewed the chore as though but a small journey. The task generally fell to Chucuse who did not mind that Onna often volunteered.

Early one morning, with nearly all still asleep, Onna quietly walked into the woods to gather firewood for a morning fire and perhaps brew a pouch of tea, when she heard a strange sound. She could not identify the sound as she crept toward it but kept herself behind large trees as much as possible. She stopped at a large tree and peaked around it to discover the noisemakers-Chilocco and Chufe engaged in sex, muttering the peculiar low groans and moans.

Chufe was naked on her elbows and knees and had used her frock as a ground mat. Chilocco was behind her, also on his knees, with his parka pulled off and his pants down. He held her hips as his groin humped against her bottom with great vigor. Onna covered her mouth with both hands to keep from laughing. She did not want to invade their privacy, but she also wanted to watch. The lustful lovers paid little attention to anything around them and she was safely hiding behind the large tree.

Chufe's father left yesterday with his hunting band to pursue bison. Chufe apparently took these opportunities seeking out sexual exploits with Wind Band warriors even though she knew the consequences if discovered by her father.

Chucuse told Onna she once saw Chufe receive a switching and told her the full story. "Last summer, Chufe's husband brought her back to her father and gave her back to him because she was unfaithful. Now poor Chufe was divorced. This happened at another summer camp, not Wetumka. Several days later, I saw Chufe's father lead her by the hand away from camp on a trail through a small thicket out of view from the camp. There was a tree that somehow got pushed over and it grew funny and the trunk curved about up to the waist from the ground. He stopped at that tree with a switch in his hand. I could not help myself, so I followed to watch hiding behind a tree; I was so close to them. I was afraid but I wanted to stay and watch. Her father took out a long piece of buckskin and put it over her mouth. She began to cry but the buckskin muffled her sound, but I could see tears in her eyes. He tied the buckskin behind her head then turned her around and took her shoulders giving her a big shake. His voice was angry. He told her she had been warned what he would do if he caught her having sex. He said no man would marry her if she continued to have sex with every man or boy who came along. He then turned her around and pushed her up to the limb. He pulled her frock up to her waist and bent her forward over the limb. Then he switched the back of her legs with the switch. He did not make her bleed but left ugly red marks on the backs of her bare thighs. She put her hands on the ground and picked her feet up and franticly kicked her legs. Then, he switched her bare bottom. It was terrible, Onna. I cried and rubbed my own bottom and legs watching her. When he stopped and pulled her off the limb, I ran back to camp. She was crying when he brought her back to camp and he made her go into their shelter. I hope I never have a switching."

Onna wanted to watch longer but she considered the embarrassment if she were caught. She took one last glance around the tree. Chufe rose to her hands and Chilocco reached out, grasping her shoulders then grabbed her hair. He then leaned up toward her head to bite the back of her neck. Onna loved it when Harjo did that to her. Harjo nearly always took her woman's fluid when he bit her neck.

Harjo told her a male lion bites the neck of his mate to dominate her, forcing her to hold still as he penetrates her.

Onna used the tree to conceal her departure and quickly slipped away back toward camp. She then walked around the backside of Wetumka to the other side, gathered a load of firewood, and returned to the camp. As she walked toward the family hearth and shelter, she pondered.

"What if Chilocco bought Chufe from her father as wife and Chufe moved in with the Fus Chate family? That could produce a stressful situation. Although, Ayuko is a stern mother and matron, and it would not take her but a few days to put the mischievous Chufe on a straight path." Onna did not like Chufe and would not care to live with her. She did not appreciate how she looked at Harjo, as though she hoped Harjo would have sex with her. Onna would never say anything—she would not tell. But it would not break her heart to hear that Chufe got another hard switching from her father for having sex with Chilocco. Onna threw the load of wood to the ground by the hearth as hard as she could, venting a little anger as she thought about Chufe. This symbolical gesture, throwing Chufe to the ground, eased her irritation. Then, with a smirky little smile on her face, she sat down to start a fire.

Chapter 26:

THE BISON HUNT

Onna remembered that Cheparney, Harjo, and brothers Yahola and Chilocco would leave on a bison hunt and a wife-buying expedition for Chilocco, today. She wanted to go but knew it was beyond question, so she did not even ask. Bison hunts gave Onna pause but the thought of a new girl coming into the family brought excitement to her. The men's plan was simple. Kill one bison and process the meat, fat, and hide at their bison camp. It promised to be hard, unsophisticated work, generally performed by women, but there was no other way to avoid spoilage. Then, transport the processed meat, oil, and bison robe to the Lion Band summer camp along with two remaining sea mammal pelts that Harjo brought from the coast. All destined to be the bride price for Chilocco's wife. As she dropped the armload of wood by the hearth, Onna felt a shadow behind her. She quickly turned and jumped back, startled by a tall dark figure that snarled a low menacing growl. She then saw the figure was Harjo with a wolf cape over his head as he held his hands out as though they were lethal claws and growled at her again. "Harjo, no scare, me," she cried out, then began to laugh, jumping to him. "Harjo, you clothes same wolf man!" They both laughed as she grabbed his claw hands.

Harjo wore a long cape made from wolf skin. The near complete head of the black wolf including its ears were set on top of Harjo's head and the front legs extended down his arms and attached at his wrists. The back legs of the skin fixed to Harjo's legs and the wolf's long black tail hung down at his rump. Crawling on his hands and knees, Harjo would look very much like a wolf, which was exactly the strategy employed to hunt bison.

Onna listened closely a few nights ago as Cheparney explained the hunting tactic in detail. He rarely told stories around the Square Hearth but on this rare occasion, he described the bison hunt as the children, especially the Ptarmigan Band of boys and Onna, listened intensely. Chucuse and Harjo helped Onna in translation. Taking a common fatherly tact, his story was both instructional and entertainment.

"The wolves that follow a bison herd form a strange partnership with the bison," he began as all around the communal fire hushed up to hear. Excited, Onna gripped Harjo's hand listening intensely. "The wolves kill the bison and occasionally the bison will kill a wolf, yet they live side by side. The wolves only kill the weaker bison; the ones that are sick, injured, or old or a calf that is separated from its mother. The unfortunate ones are marked for death and would surely die in spite of the wolves. An adult healthy bison has nothing to fear of the wolves and does not show the slightest alarm. Even a cow with a calf has no dread as long as her calf is nearby."

"The wolf pack will isolate the marked bison doomed to a slow death and chase it down. Wolves can better bring down their quarry if the prey is running. But that sharp blade of death has another side because I've seen a young adult bull entice a pack of wolves to chase him as though he were hurt or sick. Then, he will turn on the pack to kill or injure as many as he can. It's a deadly outcome because a hurt wolf or any injured predator, lion, fox or lynx will not live long."

"Consequently, the bison and the wolf spend the day side-by-side paying little attention to each other. I have witnessed a female wolf with older pups sleeping, playing, and even nursing on a small hill surrounded by grazing bison that paid her only modest notice. I once watched a pair of wolves trot alongside the edge of a very large herd until they vanished from sight, only a few paces from the bison, who continued to graze with no regard for the wolves' presences."

Cheparney now changed his voice to a slow whisper. "This is why a hunter who wears a wolf's skin can crawl on his hands and knees approaching a bison herd so close he could reach out and touch one." As Cheparney spoke these words, he slowly reached out his hand touching and then petting the head of a little girl sitting in front of him. She opened her mouth and put her hands together, then shook and laughed at the scary proposition of touching a bison. All the listeners sitting around the great hearth laughed.

"Then, when the hunters are close, they rise up and cast their darts to strike the bison. But they must show caution. Once exposed as men and not wolves, the bison usually run away from the hunters, but not always. On some occasions, the bison herd may run in a circle appearing to retreat then suddenly return to overrun the hunters. Or, more dangerous still, a wounded bison will run to its death but before it falls, it may turn and charge the hunters. Any bison bull, wounded or not, may decide to charge."

"Occasionally, the whole herd may stampede for no apparent cause. Fire may startle a bison herd or perhaps a lightning ground strike with loud thunder. I have witnessed the whole herd take off on a run, apparently for no other reason except to move from one grazing location to another. A bison herd can be dangerously unpredictable, you never know for sure what they might do. But we all enjoy the bison meat, and some say the bison pemmican offers a better flavor than mammoth. Many of us Mammoth Hunters enjoy sitting on bison robes around the fire listening to summer stories on a warm summer night."

As Cheparney concluded his tale, Onna released Harjo's arm and clapped loudly and smiled. She delighted in hearing a story from Cheparney. Others looked and smiled at Onna's clapping, still not sure what to make of her unusual gesture. Harjo noticed some of the children looking at Onna, then copied her clapping.

"Tomorrow early," concluded Cheparney, "Harjo, Yahola, Chilocco, and I will leave to hunt bison."

Onna, Ayuko, and Kak-ke, with her babe in arms, stood and waved as their four hunters headed off. Ayuko and Kak-ke headed back to camp to begin their day but Onna stayed until the hunters were out of sight. She wanted to go, sincerely wanted to go. She feared for Harjo hunting bison perhaps more than the mammoth, but she had not made the effort to ask. Besides, she was confident Harjo would take her on an adventure when they returned. Also, a group of hunters returned to camp a few days ago with word they came across a large patch of potatoes and would return to dig more. Perhaps Ayuko and the hunters would allow her to go and she could dig some of the succulent tubers for her family if the location was not too far away. She would ask as nice as she could manage. Then, she too returned to camp where there was always work.

A plethora of varieties of grass blanketed the open plains of the Mammoth Steppe providing nourishment to the vast herds of herbivores that in turn provided meat to many carnivores including human hunters. After a long migration, the mammoth herds reached their calving grounds to give birth in early spring. They feasted on young tender green grasses which in turn provide high protein milk from the females to their nursing calves. The various species of herbivores preferred various species of grasses. Mammoth Hunters recognize certain species of grasses linked to the animals they hunt but did not specifically name others. As boys grew and learned, hunting with their fathers, they become experts on the animals they exploited including their diet and the environment they lived in.

Unlike the mammoth and caribou, the bison do not migrate south to the Big River to wait out the cold winter. Instead, the great shaggy beasts remain in the foothills and the upper regions of the Echota and Etowah Rivers. Mammoth thrive on the tall blue grass that dominates the grasslands across the open steppe and their calving grounds spreading west of the Echota Valley and south of the Etowah River. But the bison prefer the shorter, knee high "bison grass" which blankets the foothill region including the Ronoto Hills.

Herds of bison share the open calving grounds and the tender young blue grass shoots during the spring but then migrate to the foothills in early summer to calf. There, the thick lush bison grass provides them with plentiful forage and nutritious milk for their young throughout the summer into the fall. Then the herds move into the upper Etowah and Echota River systems to endure the winter then renew the cycle again in spring. Horses follow nearly the same seasonal patterns and similar to the bison, thrive on the lush bison grass.

Depending on the terrain, the Mammoth Hunters anticipated they would traverse, they may or may not pull travail with them as they departed for a hunt. If they journeyed across an open flat landscape over many days, they most likely would load their supplies on travail and drag it with them. Conversely, if the impending hunt took them through a hilly or rugged landscape, they would usually carry backpacks then later construct travail to carry the load of the quarry on return. As they typically hunted bison in the rugged foothills of the Apalche Mountains or in the Ronoto Hills, Cheparney and his three sons generally employed the later strategy.

A shallow gully meandered a considerable distance across the foothills collecting water and creating various water holes and pools along its course. The standing water stimulated the growth of grass. Both attracted bison. Most of the puddles were not deep but occasionally a deeper pool formed in a low rocky area. One such permanent deep pool supported a thick grove of trees and solid green grass.

The four Mammoth Hunters set up camp in this thin peninsula-shaped grove. This singular camp had been used by three generations of Fus Chates as Cheparney's father, Fus Chate, brought him to this camp when he was a boy and he brought his sons since they were old enough to make such a hunting trip. In turn, the three Fus Chates brothers would most certainly bring their sons to this same bison camp.

All and all, the rocky, thick island grove was a pleasant camp and along with the deep clear pool, provided everything the hunters would need including a relatively safe location. These foothill areas were the domains of the bison and few mammoth trod this region. Although bison grazed all along the gully, they avoided this wooded promontory, consequently Cheparney and his sons could sleep comfortably at night around a large fire.

"We'll cut grass and pile it up a distance out from the grove," suggested Cheparney, "that will attract a few bison. The closer to camp we make the kill, the better." The four hunters walked out from the grove onto the open steppe to a likely location.

As his boys cut the grass, Cheparney was taken back in memory and fondly recalled one summer day in the past. He escorted his three young sons out from their summer camp to learn about grasses, bison, and to pass on other words of wisdom. None of the three boys had completed his Rite-of-Passage and he smiled to himself and drifted back in memory.

"This type of grass," lectured Cheparney, "dominates the Mammoth Steppe and is the favorite food of the mammoth." He grasped a handful of the head-high grass and pulled it out of the ground by its roots. His three young charges, Harjo, Chilocco, and Yahola attempted in vain to pull the grass out by the roots, so they dropped to their knees pulling their knives and began to cut the grass.

Smiling at their enthusiasm, he continued. "It is called blue grass. Notice that the tips of the grass leaf blade have a bluish color as it grows from the joint of the stem. Then, as it grows to head high, the end of the grass blade retains that bluish color. Women weave this grass to make socks and mats which is why we are taking a stack back for your mother."

As the energetic boys cut and piled the grass, Cheparney watched the circle horizon. "The Caribou Hunters use a special knife to cut grass, perhaps because they use so much of it. Their women cut tall piles for flooring and bedding in their winter lodges. To make those knives, the men cut slots into a length of antler and insert small sharp flakes of chert. It is as very useful knife and they also use it to dress caribou. They use a similar method to make spear points."

"Can we go with you, father, when you next go to trade with the Caribou Hunters?" asked an enthusiastic Yahola.

"Perhaps, Yahola, I think you are old enough and I am considering taking you and Chilocco as well. You may yet be too young, Harjo."

A frowning little Harjo looked up. "I speak the Caribou Hunter language."

"Yes, you do son and remarkably well. But I think you may still be too young. Don't fret; your season to join me will come. Listen boys, all things have their season. Be patient. Only a patient hunter can kill a mammoth at the Spirit Tree."

All three boys accepted his wisdom and continued to cut grass including a disappointed Harjo who realized his father was probably right.

"There is beach grass that grows along the coast of the Great Sea," continued Cheparney. "It is favored by Canineqmiut women for weaving baskets. What it is called?"

The boys looked at each other, pronouncing several words in Yupik in asking voices. A fluent little Harjo spoke right up. "It is called *taperrnaq*," he boasted with a broad smile.

Cheparney likewise smiled at Harjo's young grinning face and thinking to himself—he looks so much like his beautiful mother. "I always try to bring back a stack of that beach grass for your mother on those rare occasions I travel to the coast."

"Father, how big is the Great Sea?" asked Yahola.

"No one knows, son. But I can tell you a man can stand on the highest mountain next to the sea and look out to see it still extends past the horizon."

"I would like to see the Great Sea someday," spoke up an adventurous Harjo. "I would too," said Yahola. "And me," added Chilocco.

"I hope each of you do. It is a wonder to behold. Well, do we have enough grass?"

Three boys all shook their heads in agreement. "Alright, let's tie the grass into one big stack and move onto a bison herd."

As they cut and stacked a pile of grass, Yahola asked a question and brought Cheparney back to the present.

"Father, who will crawl out and make the attack tomorrow?"

"Well, the bison will belong to Chilocco, so certainly him. Then one of us, it doesn't matter."

"I'll match you, Father, as the boys do during a fox chase game to determine who goes."

Cheparney laughed as he held out his hand and he and Yahola went through the gesture.

"I win, you're out of practice, Father," laughed Yahola. Then he stepped over to Harjo and matched him. The boys laughed again as Harjo merged the victor.

Yahola turned to Chilocco and Cheparney, "Harjo always wins at this game, doesn't he, Chilocco?"

Chilocco smiled and shook his head, "nearly every match!"

∽⌒∾⌒∾⌒∾

The next morning, the four hunters rose before dawn. Without a campfire, they consumed a cold breakfast with water and tea. Harjo and Chilocco wore the wolf capes as the four crawled to the edge of a low promontory and gazed out over the hilly terrain. They waited, prone on their stomachs. The rising sun smiled on them as the bison herd edged closer and the animals slowly grazed toward the gully but more importantly, a pair of young bulls took their bait and moved to their grass pile to take advantage of the easy forage. Harjo and Chilocco crawled out.

Initially, the two young bulls paid little attention as a pair of wolves was a common daily sight. Harjo and Chilocco crawled closer on their hands and knees with darts and atlatls in their hands. Harjo had wrapped two strips of buckskin around each knee as a cushion before the long crawl. His father and brothers paid it little attention. Chilocco had briefly noticed Onna cutting and sewing the knee pads back at summer camp but had given it little thought. It seems his little brother had thought up another brilliant idea as the hard ground dug into his knees. He would certainly consider kneepads on the next bison hunt.

As the two wolf figures drew near, the bull bison grew agitated and snorted, shaking their heads but still remained more interested in the grass than approaching wolves. Now, they were so close that one bull pawed the ground, kicking dirt and grass back over his shoulders and eventually he stomped with a threatening lunge. Impressive, but Harjo and Chilocco still interpreted his actions as display threats or a challenge and they did not think he would charge.

Cheparney and Yahola watched from the low promontory, still on their stomachs in the tall grass. "They seem close enough to me, father," whispered Yahola into Cheparney's ear.

"The hunters must make that decision, Yahola," also whispered Cheparney. "Their experience and the bison's behavior will direct their attack."

Finally, Chilocco stopped and slid his dart over, then notched it into his atlatl and held his second dart in hand.

Harjo did likewise. As the closest bull put his head down for a mouthful of grass, Chilocco raised and Harjo followed. Chilocco cast his dart with great speed and superb accuracy, striking the bull in the shoulder just behind its shoulder blade-the dart sank deep, past the foreshaft.

Harjo also made a good throw and as intended, struck the animal in the hip near the joint. Each notched another dart but did not cast as there was no need. Chilocco's dart was a near perfect hit. With one dart in his heart and his rear leg crippled, the bull would not run far.

The mortally wounded bull did manage to run a short distance and then fell into the dust and grass of the Mammoth Steppe as his partner continued on to join the distant herd that seemed unaware or concerned about the loss of one member. Harjo embraced his brother, both laughing.

"Excellent throw, Chilocco!" called out the usually stoic Harjo.

Chilocco laughed and pointed at Harjo's kneepads. "I am going to ask Onna to make a pair of those for me! My knees are bloody!" He reached down and massaged them.

"She will," laughed Harjo, "She will!"

Cheparney and Yahola also celebrated. Cheparney put his arm around his oldest son as they walked out to join and congratulate the two successful hunters.

"Well, boys," exclaimed a jubilant Cheparney, "Now the work begins, and we will regret that we did not bring any women with us!"

The whole bison required processing at the kill site; the meat cut into strips then dried and or smoked, the fat rendered into oil, and the hide scraped and tanned to produce a bison robe. Mammoth Hunters relish bison robes. Because Cheparney, his boys, and other Mammoth Hunters as well had used this campsite over the past many seasons to kill and process bison, drying racks and poles were left in place which would expedite the processing. Luckily, the kill was made in the morning leaving the entire long summer day to accomplish the work.

That evening, they enjoyed fresh roast bison and each other's company. They asked Harjo to relate the story of his lion kill. They were all awed and proud of the young Harjo. And Cheparney, a veteran warrior and hunter of noted accomplishment, was not easily impressed but he was of Harjo's lion kill.

"Father told me," continued Harjo, "my opportunity to take revenge on a lion concerning a long overdue debt would come; he was right." They each knew Harjo meant the death of his young Caribou Hunter friend, Honea, so many long seasons ago. As part of the conversation, Cheparney described their next destination while Harjo and Yahola were interested in their brother's impending wife.

"You remember at Yarda's request, Chilocco and I traveled to the Lion Band to attend their First Kill ceremony. The band set up shelters and their Chokofa Tent at their favored summer camp along a wooded tributary of the Etowah River," explained Cheparney. "The stream meanders by a beautiful open meadow adjacent to a series of low, flat, rocky hills. The stream is easily crossed but forms a deep pool at the camp site and provides a perfect location to swim and bathe."

"Ah, yes," interrupted Yahola, "but how did you work it out, Chilocco, that you saw the girl naked? That's what Harjo and I are dying to know."

Cheparney and Chilocco laughed. "You should relate this story, Chilocco," said Cheparney.

"Well," began Chilocco. "Father and I sat at the family hearth with the girl's father. Her name is Hokose and her father is the Lion Band's Second Chief. I overheard Hokose ask her mother if she could go for a swim. Her mother answered in common mother language and said something like, 'alright child, but don't stay long because there is plenty of work before the celebrations' or something like that."

"So, I excused myself," continued Chilocco, "and father and the Second Chief continued to talk and didn't seem to care if I stayed or not."

"Yes, yes, yes," interrupted an impatient Yahola, "skip all that and just go to the naked part!" The others laughed out loud.

"Alright," said Chilocco. "I planned it out, but it was also just luck. I simply waited and then walked up to the stream by a big rock where the girls swim and she was standing there naked. Her back was to me, but I was certain it was her. She had a beautiful figure and gorgeous buttocks. I just stood there only a pace or two from her. Other girls swimming in the stream yelled out to her, so she turned around. She stood there, completely naked, surprised with her mouth open. Then, she covered her breasts, turned around, and dove into the stream."

"Then what?" asked Yahola.

"Then, I waited a short distance down the path. When she walked by, I stepped out and walked with her back to camp. Other girls were with her, but they ran on ahead. I talked with her. She was shy, polite, and friendly and I realized she was for me. We returned to camp where she went to her mother and I went back into the shelter where father and Hokose's father still sat talking. I sat down and began to discuss a bride price."

"And she had not completed her Rite-of-Passage?" asked Yahola.

"Not completely because there had not been the public announcement," answered Chilocco.

"Bold move, Chilocco, bold move, I am proud of you," exclaimed Yahola.

Again, they all laughed. "It takes a bold move to bring home the prize," offered Cheparney. "Well, it is bed for me; plenty of unpleasant work remains tomorrow."

Chapter 27:

TRAGEDY

Cheparney and his three sons processed the bison hide the next day and with the four men working together, the drudgery lessened. In the afternoon, they smoked the hide, gave it a final washing, and then stretched it on a rack to dry overnight. A little more softening in the morning would render the hide ready for use and trade.

Early the next morning, they packed and prepared to travel. The meat was more than the hunters could transport with three travails. Consequently, they left a portion behind in a skin pouch suspended from a high tree limb. The tree had been cut and modified for just this purpose by other hunters in the past. Scavengers could not reach it from the ground. A lion might climb the tree but would be afraid to go out on a limb for fear it would break. Of course, if the limb broke, the lion would claim the prize, but he possessed the mind of a lion and not the intelligence of a mammoth, so suspended, the meat could hang for several days.

They used a length of *babiche* to secure the pouch. Babiche are strong caribou skin lines used to secure or tie.

The lines are made from a single skin of caribou cut in a circular manner to a great length. The lines were also braided to form an even stronger rope. The term was an Athabascan term borrowed from the Caribou Hunters and incorporated in the Muscogee language.

"Boys," called out Cheparney, "I am going to make one final check of the processing site and see if there are any tools worth taking. I think I dropped my ivory handled knife there."

The brothers concurred and Cheparney headed out from the camp to the processing area now marked by ravens, magpies, and a few jays. Eagles circled overhead deciding if the remains were worth their effort to land. The bison herd had moved away as the smell of blood unsettled them. A still, calm morning with the distant calls of the scavenger birds at the kill site and circling overhead were the only sounds floating on the winds across the open rolling hills.

Then, a distant disturbance reached them as a faint rumbling sound prompting Harjo, Yahola, and Chilocco to look at each other with puzzled expressions. "Distant thunder?" asked Yahola. Harjo and Chilocco shrugged their shoulders. The three brothers stood listening with pondering expressions, unable to identify the distant, muffled resonance.

Suddenly, with only that slight warning, the distant sound rolled on them as it were clashing thunder or a glacier cracking with huge ice sections falling to the ground as might occur in late summer. The clamor overwhelmed them. "Stampede!" called out Harjo as loud as he could. The entire massive bison herd was on them appearing as an enormous bison robe, rippling and stretching to the horizon.

"The trees!" again Harjo called out as he jumped into the nearest tree quickly climbing up. Yahola and Chilocco followed and the three brothers found safety in lofty perches.

But the huge herd stampeded around the grove of trees and their campsite which was one of the reasons Fus Chate had selected it so many seasons ago. The blanket of stampeding bison charged around the camp but reunited farther down in the gully. The ground shook and the pounding hooves blocked out all sound as dust and grass filled the air swirling around them.

Then abruptly as it had charged upon them, the massive bison herd ran over the nearby hill and out of site until the three brothers could only hear the distant rumbling as when it had first come upon them. The sound was now etched forever in their memory. What dust and grass blades that did not settle around the grove a gentle breeze took away as a strange, almost eerie calm, fell upon the camp. The three brothers slowly climbed out from the trees. They could have stayed safely on the ground because other than the thin blanket of dust, the camp remained untouched by trampling hooves. They looked at each other and the dread of death cast its fearsome shadow upon their faces-their father-Cheparney.

As though terror stricken, they ran toward the bison processing area, each brother's heart ached for fear of what they might find. As they reached it, out of breath, a gruesome, heartbreaking site greeted them. Cheparney's body lay on the ground trampled and mangled. They could identify the body because of the clothes; otherwise they would not have been able to recognize him. Yahola and Chilocco grasped hands and fell to their knees weeping. They had always been and remained partners, understandably so. Harjo stood alone as tears flowed down his face.

The three brothers did not remember how long they mourned by the mangled body of their father. But it was the youngest, Harjo, who led the way. Bones of the slain bison lay scattered around the area now trampled. It is surprising how it only requires perhaps two or three days for the sun and scavengers to clean and dry out bones from a recent kill. A hunter can stumble upon scattered bones and surmise the kill occurred perhaps last season and it may have occurred only days prior. Harjo found a shoulder blade from the bison and began to dig a grave. Soon, Yahola and Chilocco took some implements in hand and joined Harjo.

When the grave seemed deep enough, Harjo stopped digging and again his brothers followed as they stepped up to their father's body. Yahola reached down and took Cheparney's atlatl. It was intact and finely carved from antler by Cheparney's hand. "I will keep this," he said in a solemn statement.

The others said nothing but looked to Chilocco. "I want nothing," he said.

Harjo held up Cheparney's carved ivory handle knife with a broken blade. The same knife Cheparney had gone out to recover from the kill site.

"I will keep this," he repeated Chilocco words.

Harjo then reached down and grasped Cheparney's parka. In so doing, Yahola and Chilocco took his pants legs and together they moved the body to the grave. His darts still fixed into his quiver and his foreshaft quiver remained attached to his body. They quickly looked around for any other tools or weapons that might also go into the grave but found none. There were no mammoth bones to line the grave and so they quietly covered the body.

"Such a shallow grave for such a great warrior and hunter," spoke Chilocco.

"True," answered Harjo, "but if we remember him, he will be content in the spirit world." The three brothers returned to camp.

"What do we do?" asked Yahola.

Harjo looked at his brothers. "We go on," he replied in a final tone. "That is what father would want. We head for the Lion Band summer camp and Chilocco will buy his wife. Then we decide our course of action from there. We will not have the added benefit of a single warrior as point guard, but we may still use a single 'lead travail' as a point travail and the other two travails will follow behind about 200-300 paces. Any attacking war band must divide its force to attack both our positions or leave us with a flanker to counter attack them. Either way, it is a small but still an advantage we would otherwise not have. Chilocco, you know the best path from here to the Lion Band summer camp thus you should take the point guard. Yahola and I will trail."

Harjo held out his hand and Yahola and Chilocco reached out and grasped it. Then, without further conversation, they each grasped a loaded travail and as planned, Chilocco headed out first with Harjo and Yahola following at the appropriate distance.

The three Mammoth Hunter brothers struggled with the heavy-laden travails across the rolling hills of the Cheaha Mountains. Having visited the Lion Band summer camp earlier during the summer, however, Chilocco led them on a direct path and the trio reached the Lion Band encampment without incident.

Chilocco's impending wife, Hokose, was the daughter of the Second Chief. The Fus Chate brothers met with him in his shelter and presented him with the agreed upon bride price. He accepted the price and Hokose now belonged to Chilocco. They would be bound and married by spirit law until Micco Yarda made the public announcement at the Wind Band summer camp. The meeting was bittersweet as the Second Chief was deeply saddened to here of Cheparney's tragic death.

"I knew your father when we were boys," he recalled. "One spring, the Lion and the Wind Bands migrated together. Your father and I were Ptarmigan Boys, and we pulled the same sled. Cheparney was the best of us boys with a bird dart and could bring down a bird in flight. He impressed us all. He was a long-trusted friend. I will miss him and remember his name."

They stayed but one night in the Chokofa Tent and likewise talked with the Lion Band Micco. He, too, was saddened to hear of the heartbreaking loss, having also known Cheparney most of his life as a brave warrior and hunter. The Lion Band leaders held concerns for Hokose's safety on the return trip and proposed two Lion Band warriors accompany them. The Fus Chate brothers gladly accepted. The Lion Band Micco and the Second Chief also had other reasons as well.

This journey provided an opportunity for warriors seeking a wife to visit the Wind Band and take a look at and perhaps talk with Chucuse as she neared maturity. The budding girl of the Fus Chate family would inspire numerous warriors, young and old, from across the Muscogee Tribe to bid for her hand. One of the warriors chosen to go was the son of the Lion Band Micco. Also, the Lion Band leaders thought it prudent to send condolence on behalf of the Lion Band to Micco Yarda for the tragic death of Cheparney. Harjo, Yahola, and Chilocco decided they would return to the bison camp and retrieve the cached bison meat then return to Wetumka. The Lion Band leaders concurred. It would be a shameful waste to leave the cache hanging to spoil.

The next morning, they packed their supplies and Hokose loaded her meager belongings onto a travail.

Hokose bid a bittersweet farewell to her family that rejoiced in her marriage but was saddened in losing a daughter. Her father reminded both her and Chilocco they were bound by spirit law until their marriage was finalized by public acknowledgement at the Wind Band. Initially, the two young warriors from the Lion Band took the point position, as they were well aware of the location of the bison hunting camp. The three Fus Chate brothers pulled the travail. Hokose walked along side of Chilocco. Harjo and Yahola now saw why Cheparney had moved Chilocco toward buying Hokose. She was not only attractive but also quiet and pleasant in her moods and manner. She would bond agreeably with the females of their family.

Even though now tarnished with tragic memories, the bison camp remained an excellent and safe camping location. Fresh tracks and claw marks on the trees provided signs that both lions and wolves investigated the meat cache but were unsuccessful in claiming it. Consequently, they built three large fires, standing guard shifts throughout the night. The next morning, they loaded the cache of meat and made the long journey to arrive at Wetumka without incident.

"Chilocco, perhaps you should break the news to Micco Yarda, and Yahola and I will tell mother, Onna, and Kakke," suggested Harjo. The brothers solemnly agreed. The Mammoth Hunters were a hardy people-hardship and death an everyday reality. Nonetheless, Cheparney's tragic loss rendered the whole band to a despondent state. Everyone mourned. Ayuko and Onna were grief stricken, and their sorrow would not be easily overcome.

Micco Yarda sat down in disbelief. He presumed all his life that he would journey to the other side before Cheparney and that his brother would thus take over the duties as Micco. He was now unsure of the future. Us'se likewise collapsed with the terrible news. She was a mother to Ayuko and more of a grandmother to Ayuko and Cheparney's children than an aunt. To Hokose's credit, she immediately stepped in to comfort the aging Us'se and soon endeared herself to the whole family.

A band micco is not allowed the luxury of mourning as his responsibilities loomed in the present. He welcomed Hokose into the band and told Chilocco the public announcement of his marriage must wait a day or so although all would certainly realize that Hokose belonged to him. Micco Yarda then ordered a band gathering.

The musicians performed a sad traditional song, which also summoned the band to gather for the solemn occasion. Yahola and Chilocco asked Harjo to address the band relating the story of Cheparney's death and he did. Despairing Onna clung continuously to Harjo or Ayuko.

"I ask all of you," requested a somber Micco Yarda, "to remember Cheparney's name and stories of his deeds. Tell your children about him and how he served the Wind Band and the Muscogee Tribe with unfailing courage and unlimited generosity."

The Wind Band built a rock cairn as a monument to Cheparney on the edge of Wetumka. Everyone carried at least one rock, even the smallest child. All of the Wind Band mourned, his family grieved and wept. Emotional young Onna was heartbroken more than anyone could imagine. As she carried her rock, she wept uncontrollably and placing it on the stack, fell to her knees with her head against the monument overwhelmed with grief and emotional weeping. Harjo reached down, helping her to her feet.

"I lose two fathers now Harjo!" she cried as she reached out and grasped his parka. "I miss him, Harjo, I miss him. My heart broke, Harjo."

The weight of her sorrow was so much that Onna collapsed but Harjo picked her up and carried her away. She buried her face into his chest and cried without control. Those standing close as Harjo passed with Onna in his arms reached out and gently touched her. Harjo carried her all the way to the Spirit Tree. The trip required most of the morning and several stops.

But at the tree where Cheparney and his fathers before him had killed many mammoth, perhaps the power of the tree and the spirit of the mammoth would help heal Onna's broken heart. Perhaps, thought Harjo, he could help heal her grief.

"Do you remember?" asked Harjo, "you asked why I can speak the Caribou Hunter language." Onna nodded her head yes as it was buried against his chest. "And you know I had a Caribou Hunter friend as a boy who was killed by a lion." Again, Onna shook her head yes. "I will tell you what Cheparney told me back then when I was dreadfully broken hearted. Perhaps his words will help to heal our two hearts."

Onna listened as Harjo spoke their father's words. "All of us Harjo, all of us, suffer loss. I know you grieve now. We all do, but I know you are heartbroken. But I can guarantee you, the sorrow will pass. One day you will look back and remember your friend Honea with happiness and joy and recall the wonderful boyhood adventures and games you shared. Believe me, son, this sorrow will pass. Grasp each day of life you are given Harjo and take all the fullness it has to offer."

Onna's crying began to ease. She got up and took Harjo's hand and reached out with the other, touching the Spirit Tree. She raised her head back and looked up at the top of the giant cottonwood then looked at Harjo's face. Tears were still running down her face, but she was not weeping.

"Take me back Wetumka, Harjo." Harjo gripped her hand and together they made their way back to the summer camp.

Part Five

LAND OF THE CARIBOU

The huge bull wooly rhino challenged with a deep threatening wulf. He pounded his feet and scrapped the ground in a backward stiff-legged motion with his head and horn held high. "Move to the rear," ordered Harjo in a whisper as he notched an armed dart into his atlatl. "No," answered a scared but determined Onna under her breath, clutching her spear. "I stand with you."

Chapter 28:

DEPARTURE

Although at first reluctant, impatient young Onna waited a full four summers before she became pregnant. On one side she was too immature to safely have babies but on the other side, she was eager and desperately wanted to bear Harjo's children. Fortunately, she did not have a choice. Ayuko was a stern matron and mother and through her guidance, Onna saw the wisdom in the decision to wait. Eventually, Onna matured and her narrow little girl hips and pelvis developed into the wide, fuller hips of a woman.

Throughout their child-bearing age, Mammoth Hunter women will bear eight to ten babies. More than one-half will die during the first several seasons of infancy. Following this common life practice, Onna bore eight babies. Four died, a heart-breaking experience for the young emotional Onna, but four lived, three older boys, Chate, Echo, and Fus and the youngest a girl, Loni.

During Loni's third summer, Ayuko convinced Harjo to take Onna on a long trip alone, just the two of them.

Ayuko thought Onna would jump at the chance to go but she was devoted to her children and did not want to leave them. She was more difficult to convince than Ayuko would have believed and remained reluctant to go.

"I don't care how many babies you have had Onna, you are still one of my girls and you will obey," lectured a stern Ayuko.

"What about the boys?" asked Onna, "often they are rowdy and loud."

"The boys will be fine. Their aunts and I will watch them. They're good boys but if they become too raucous, I'll ask Yahola or Chilocco to step in. Micco Yarda and Us'se would enjoy having the boys stay in the Chokofa Tent for a few days. The boys will think it is fun."

"But Loni will need to nurse."

"Oh, Onna," groaned an impatient Ayuko, "this is Loni's third summer and she does not need to nurse every day. If she fusses, there are several nursing women in the band who will gladly fill Loni with milk. In fact, it might be a good opportunity to wean her. If you become full, you can milk yourself off or let Harjo suck off the pressure. He'll enjoy it."

"Do you remember, Onna?" continued a stern, now impatient, but equally convincing Ayuko. "Before you were pregnant, Harjo took you caribou hunting. Remember how excited you were?"

"Oh, yes," recalled Onna. "What a wonderful memory."

"I practiced throwing my harpoon nearly every morning with Harjo when he was in camp and I asked him to wake me when he rose. He taught me all the fine techniques and I developed, grew, and advanced in skill worthy of any boy my age or older. I remembered waiting in the hunting blind with Harjo in the late summer as the small caribou herd began its southern migration back to the Big River. A small group approached and I nearly shook with anticipation. Harjo whispered into my ear. 'You have the skill to hit the target. A clump of grass or a caribou shoulder, it does not matter. It is just a target. Stay focused on your target-one small spot on the shoulder. When the target is in the best range-rise and throw.' Harjo's confidence in me," continued Onna, "and his composed voice calmed me down giving me confidence. The same when I first painted a picture of a mammoth on the Rock Shelter wall. As the small herd approached into range, I rose, casting my harpoon. My aim was true and deadly, and my harpoon struck the mark. My excitement rose as to the top of a glacier."

Onna looked and smiled at Ayuko. "Together, Harjo and I dressed the caribou, tanned the hide, and processed the meat. That evening we camped at a beautiful location-feasted on fresh caribou-and made love throughout the night."

Ayuko went to Onna, gently taking her shoulders. "Oh Onna, you worked so hard on your backpack, excited as you made it, and you have never used it. Do I need to ask Harjo to make you go?" Onna did not say anything but shook her head no.

"Now find that backpack, fill it up with supplies, and go with Harjo on a trip. Go collect some paint. Remember how you were so enthusiastic when Harjo would take you on trips to collect paint?"

"Oh, yes, Ayuko, it sounds so wonderful."

Ayuko smiled and pulled Onna to her, then tenderly put her hands on her face. Ayuko gave her a long kiss. She then stroked her hair and the side of her head. "Alright, it is settled. Now go find your backpack and prepare."

Onna's backpack was a smaller version of the one she sewed for Harjo. Some women used rawhide because it is stiff and does not require a frame, but it is difficult to stitch

417

and punch holes through. Additionally, if it becomes wet, it softens, then it is just a pouch. Most women will ask their husbands to construct a light frame; caribou ribs are often used, and then cover it with hide. Some women will use the transparent, light and waterproof mammoth intestines as the hide itself or as an added cover. Onna carried her whole caribou buckskin robe rolled up and tied on top of her pack. She also sewed a sheath on the side of the backpack to house her knife; a beautiful red chert blade hafted in an antler bone handle. Harjo carved the end of the handle so it would fit into the socket of her spear and thus served as a second foreshaft. She attached the sheath under her left elbow so that she could draw the knife as she wore the backpack.

Harjo carried his caribou bed likewise rolled up and tied to the top of the pack. The caribou bed was light of weight and warm enough during the summer. Oddly enough, it was just wide enough to sleep two, provided one occupant was small, maybe about Onna's size. He then mounted his dart quiver on the side. He also carried a large piece of mammoth intestine to use during the infrequent rainstorms. Thus supplied, Harjo could spend many days on long-distance travel across the Mammoth Steppe as he often did.

Onna longed to return to the ocher paint collection area. It was a beautiful clear sandy little stream by a grassy knoll. Harjo brought her there the summer they were first married. It became their secret camp and hide-a-way, remaining dear to Onna's heart. She also wanted to see the great caribou herds at their fawning grounds, witness the Caribou Hunters hunting fawns, meet the Caribou Hunters, and trade with them for fawn hides in one of their camps. She adored fawn hides as summer clothing.

Harjo, too, was hesitant. Such a trip would be long and hard, not to mention dangerous. Ayuko put as much pressure on her son as she dared and in addition, all the family members encouraged Harjo to take Onna. Then Harjo realized he was becoming old and too cautious. He likewise recalled the many trips he and Onna took together before she became pregnant. Wonderful trips of two adventurous youths. And yes, occasionally dangerous. But it was the longing desire in Onna's beautiful blue eyes that influenced his decision. He agreed.

With their backpacks loaded and all preparations made, they were ready to depart. Onna gave all her children many more kisses than they would ever want. They went by Cheparney's monument and Onna laid another rock on it, then they were gone. They followed the Wetumka Creek to the Echota River, then the Echota down river for a short distance, then crossed the river at the Second Mammoth Crossing.

They laughed as Onna carried Harjo's boots and he carried her barefoot across the river. Onna had not been this excited and full of adventure for many seasons. To return to the ocher paint collection area, to see the vast caribou herd now with fawns, and to visit a Caribou Hunter hunting camp was nearly more than she could tolerate. She glowed with excitement as they followed an old and remembered route. They talked, laughed, and Onna practiced her chickadee calls. She would also practice throwing her "harpoon." It had been so long, but she still kept her practice throwing foreshafts.

In the distance, they noticed a lone rock outcrop adjacent a small hill and made their way toward one of their favorite and most unusual campsites. Many hunters from the Wind Band and other Muscogee bands utilized this camp, which appeared as a large, isolated rock and also a rock shelter. The mystery of how this huge, solitary, wedge-shaped rock came to be situated on the open flat steppe could not be solved.

The bottom of the pointed wedge area of the rock had broken off to create a small rock shelter. It was deep but only about chest high. Long before living memory, other portions of the rock cracked, broke, and fell over the sides of the wedge, creating walls on each side with the point of the rock forming the opening of the shelter. Over many seasons, hunters had also stacked up rocks on the side and built a hearth at the entrance. During inclement weather, especially snow, the little cave with a fire burning in the front provided a warm comfortable shelter. Hunters usually cached dry wood in the shelter.

Throughout uncountable seasons, the winds had blown soil against the back of the rock and formed a steep mound covered with grass and brush. One large lone tree grew on top the rock mound. Certainly, the wind can carry seeds a great distance but to see a single tree on the mound was most unusual. Harjo believed some Mammoth Hunter planted the tree there many generations ago.

The sides of the rock were perpendicular thus shaping a straight up and down cliff face and the grass mound formed a steep angle, consequently the rock mound formation was difficult to climb. Even a lion would find some challenge in scaling to the top so the camp provided not only a safe sleeping bed but also a good lookout and vista.

Onna did not enjoy camping in the shelter because of the dirt floor so they climbed to the top as they had on many other occasions. Some other hunter, probably from the Wind Band, recently dragged a large limb up to the top which provided seats and backrest as well as firewood. They sat by the hearth quietly watching the view. The sun moved high across the summer sky and daylight lasted so long that Onna was not sure when to go to bed. Also, she did not pay

420

that much attention to the length of the day and besides, she just went to bed when Harjo did.

Throughout the day's hike and this afternoon at camp, Onna had been pondering a serious consideration and now believed she had it thoroughly worked it out in her thoughts. She had long brooded over and pondered the question of a young, second wife for Harjo and their household and had finally derived a conclusion.

She now had four children. The work required in sewing alone to keep four children and a husband in clothing meant dawn to dark work every day. This work demand would last for many long seasons until the boys were grown and married and brought a young wife into their household. Even her girl, Loni, would be of little assistance. By the season a girl becomes old enough to be an actual help with sewing, she is purchased by another man and leaves to join his family.

Onna had several long talks with Ayuko on the subject of a second wife and Ayuko held strong opinions on the subject. Ayuko raised Harjo and his siblings as Cheparney's only wife. She admitted she was afforded substantial help from Micco Yarda's childless wife, Us'se. Micco Yarda and Us'se had lost their two sons during a tragic mammoth hunt. Us'se adopted Ayuko, as mother and mentor, and she remained grateful to her. Ayuko would argue, however, she never had a childhood as she stepped from child to mother of four and labored endlessly from day to day-season to season.

Consequently, Ayuko encouraged all her girls who had more than two children to persuade their husbands to buy a second wife. In particular, a very young girl who must wait several seasons before giving birth herself and thus devoting all her energy to working for the first wife and her children and not her own child. Ayuko also divulged to

Onna that while she knew that Cheparney had loved her, she did not hold the unique persuasion over him as Onna did over Harjo.

The idea of a young woman coming into their shelters or mammoth lodge-sharing her bed-more importantly sharing Harjo-loomed as a serious consideration. When she was first married to Harjo, the thought of sharing him with another woman was completely absent from her way of life. Now, eight births and four children later, she formed another opinion on that subject. During the last five summers, since Fus was born, she did not believe there was one day she did not work. And as Loni grew older, Onna would have four children and a husband to care for and the workload would expand. She had reached the conclusion that she wanted a young second wife to help with the labor and that she would pose the possibility to Harjo during the first days of this wondrous journey.

"Harjo?" asked Onna as pleasantly as she could manage.

Harjo looked over to her. He didn't say anything but raised his eyebrows as in the manner of the Caribou Hunters of saying, "Yes, what is it?"

Over the many seasons, Onna had learned little of the Caribou Hunter language, although she did recognize many of their facial expressions often used by Harjo.

"Harjo, I want to ask you a question but don't answer too hastily, alright, promise."

Harjo chuckled. "How short a moment is too hastily?"

"Harjo, you know what I mean."

"Alright," he smiled, "I promise I won't answer too hastily."

Onna cleared her throat. "Harjo, will you buy a second wife?"

"Do you mean will I ever buy one in the future or do you mean will I buy one tomorrow?" he asked with a sly smile.

"Will you buy one in the future?"

"I don't know. I have not considered it."

They sat by the hearth. Now that summer nights were warm, they had not built a fire and here lions would pose little threat. Onna was sewing and mending a rip in her pant legs from a small tough sage bush and Harjo was inspecting his darts. Smiling, she went to him and first kissed his scar, his ear, and then his lips. "I know Love, so I am asking you to consider it."

"Do you want a second wife living in our household?"

"Oh, yes, Harjo, yes!"

"Alright, I'll consider it." Harjo returned to his darts.

As she sat next to him, Onna responded. "Harjo, I know just the type of girl you want!"

Harjo laughed out loud, sensing the path she was taking him on. "Oh, you do, do you?"

"Yes," she answered with a wide smile. "You will want one very young and very pretty. It will be many seasons before I allow her to become pregnant because of her age. She will be obedient, quiet, and very submissive. She will never make you angry or very seldom, if ever, give you cause to switch or spank her. In fact, I am thinking you will not even be aware she is in the mammoth lodge except when we sleep with her. You will take pleasure in her sexuality; we both will."

Again, Harjo laughed out loud. "Have you found such a rare beauty?" "Not yet, but I have some girls in mind. May I begin, Harjo, please, just looking?"

Harjo pondered her question. "Alright," he answered. "You may look among the females available for marriage. But," he raised his index finger as if to say one. Onna was quiet and listened intensely.

"No promise. I may say no. And, you may look but you will not talk about a second wife. Understand?"

"Yes, Harjo, I promise. I will only look. Thank you, Harjo," and she clapped her hands loudly and squirmed with excitement. Then, with a seductive smile, she slowly moved closer to him. She took a deep breath through her nose and soothingly rubbed the side of her mouth against the side of his mouth in the same manner a female lion will do to her mate as she feels her days of heat and fertility nearing.

The next morning, they broke camp continuing on across the Echota Valley for the next several days. Eventually they would journey out of the valley onto the great open plains of the Mammoth Steppe to a landscape more favored by horses and antelopes. Harjo led Onna to the small end of a low peninsula-shaped ridge top to show her a sight he knew she longed to see, a herd of horses. They watched and rested quietly. Onna put her hand on Harjo's arm then whispered into his ear.

"I so enjoy watching the horses, Harjo. Thank you for bringing me with you. It's been so long since you've taken me on a trip."

Harjo smiled, "You're welcome Onna." He chuckled as Onna gently kissed and tickled his ear.

They lay on their stomachs watching a herd of some 20 horses. It appeared as a common herd consisting of a stallion, his mares, and their colts. The excited stallion pawed the ground and shook his head in courtship display as he circled a reluctant filly in attempts to seduce her. Occasionally, she seemed willing as he mounted her then she would change her mind, running off from under him kicking her back legs at him.

"She can't make up her mind," chortled Harjo.

"All young females don't know what they want, Harjo," whispered Onna, "They require a mature, patient male to seduce them."

The hesitant filly pranced in a circle then urinated. The stallion pawed the ground then strutted over and likewise urinated in her exact spot. Onna giggled. "I think you should urinate in the same place that I do, Harjo, to make sure you mark me."

Harjo quietly laughed. "The horses elicit the animal instinct in you."

"Indeed," she whispered as she leaned over smelling his neck, then gently bit his ear lobe.

"I think he has finally won her over," announced Harjo.

Onna watched the would-be lovers touched muzzles then the stallion rubbed his nose against the reluctant filly's neck and effectively mounted the bashful little female. Drawing on his long experience and calm patience, the stallion successfully inserted his huge erection into the now willing filly. He secured her with his front legs and hooves locked on her chest and humped her to completion.

Onna still whispered into Harjo's ear and reached her hand down, attempting to grasp his buttock but settled for the small of his back. "He is well endowed just like my stallion." Harjo smiled at her naughtiness.

Once the mating was completed, the whole herd joined the filly and the stallion in post-courtship antics. They seemed to approve, especially the old mares. Then, in playful excitement, several of the colts darted off running in a wide circle around the herd. They did not go far but still the frantic mares called out in unrest and went after their rambunctious offspring.

"Look Harjo, the colts run faster than the mares." Harjo nodded in agreement.

"Naughty colts, they worry their mothers," said Onna in a stern voice. "They won't stay close by. They each merit a hard nip on the rump."

Harjo looked at Onna. "They want to get away on their own and explore. I know someone similar." Suddenly, they whole herd bolted.

Onna reacted and pointed, "Look, Harjo, wolves!"

Two wolves, one black, the other grey, charged down on the escaping herd. "They are good hunters, Harjo; I did not see them stalking the herd. Did you?"

"No, I didn't," replied Harjo.

"Oh, Harjo," exclaimed a mournful Onna. "I hope they escape and outrun the wolves."

"They probably will," added Harjo, "unless there are more waiting in ambush down the horse's trail. Even so, the stallion can fight off one or two even if the wolves catch one of the horses."

Onna rubbed the small of his back and stretched farther to pat his rump with the palm of her hand. "Remember the horse meat and hide you and your brothers brought back to camp one fall?" chuckled Onna. "Remember?"

A grinning Harjo shook his head yes.

"The meat tasted odd, so lean," laughed Onna. "And the hide was thin and weak, I think we cut it up and used it for diapers."

Harjo recalled the episode. "It was more of a reaction to reflex than hunting. The herd came running by, nearly over us. We heard the distant hoof beats and ran to a small rock pile just as they were on us. The pile was large enough to send them around us on each side. We responded with the opportunity, casting our darts, and one of us brought down a young mare."

"I am so glad you don't hunt the horses, Harjo. I just feel sad if you kill one, especially a colt. They are so playful, just like playful naughty boys."

"Yes, they are very clever and difficult to hunt, which makes them dangerous. They are too unpredictable."

With that, Harjo rose to his feet and Onna followed. They returned to their backpacks a few paces away. They lifted their packs to their backs and continued on.

Chapter 29:

OCHER CAMP

The narrow perennial stream was born high in the Ronoto Hills. It slowly meandered its way through the upper regions of the Echota Valley to empty into the Coosa River, a major tributary of the Echota. A child could jump the shallow rivulet anywhere along its course except at natural pools where it may reach two or three paces wide and perhaps knee deep. This whole region at large, where Harjo and others collected ocher, was underlaid by sandstone and thus formed locations consisting of unique sandy soils and sandstone outcrops.

Ocher deposits, both red and yellow, could be found at various locations throughout this sandy, hilly region. One popular location often visited by Mammoth Hunter warriors was a low cliff face of sandstone impregnated by a narrow vain of ocher deposits. Generally, fist size chunks of the mineral material were knocked off the wall face then ground into a powder. The material was then washed to separate the soft fine powder pigment from the coarse sand. The powder pigment was then mixed with mammoth oil to create paint. Other bonding materials were also used.

Glue made from rabbit skin fleshing provided a strong paint although somewhat cumbersome to prepare. The skin fleshing was boiled in water until the water evaporated leaving the glue material. Boys often used egg yolks as a convenient method to prepare paint. They seem to be fascinated with bird egg collections; no one knows why. But adults often cautioned boys against collecting the robin eggs around summer camps, especially Wetumka. Mammoth Hunters enjoy the robin's songs and wished them to remain undisturbed.

Nearby their Ocher Camp, Harjo discovered a unique collection area known only to him and Onna. Water seeped from a small sandstone outcrop in a brilliant red color. It formed a wet patch in the ground then trickled down slope to dissipate a few paces from the seep. This ground was covered with a thin layer of perfect wet powder, a radiant red. Occasionally, Harjo and Onna found solid chunks of the pure powder pigment, some reaching fist size. Nearby, Onna discovered a similar situation forming a yellow color, only the water seep had long ago ceased leaving a dry surface deposit of near pure chunks of pigment. Over many summer seasons, Harjo and Onna had modified one unique location they dubbed Ocher Camp.

At their Ocher Camp, a large, flat, sandstone rock laid adjacent the stream near a small natural pool. Harjo modified the pool. He dug it out to widen and deepen it and built an overflow dam to impound more water. The pool formed an exceptional sandy and sandstone bottom bathing pool warmed by the summer sun. Other areas of the stream, as it flowed through the sandy soil, provided wonderful drinking water. Beautiful flowers and thick green grass thrived around the sandy rock-lined pool, but small willow bushes and other various brush flourished above and below the pool.

Mammoth Hunters recognized two distinctive low shrub willows because they eat the leaves which are among the earliest foliage to emerge in spring. Throughout the warm seasons, the young, tender, whole leaves or the soft leaf tips are collected and eaten raw. Some families store the leaves in pouches of mammoth oil, and some combine them with berries into pemmican. The tea-leave willow is perhaps the favorite. The low bush grows throughout the warm seasons, sprouting new leaves all spring and summer long. No one knows why it is called tealeaf, as there is no relationship to the various plants used to brew tea and the leaves are generally oval shaped with pointed tips. The sprouting leaves of the ptarmigan willow bush are likewise consumed but perhaps with more caution. Mature leaves and the bark of the shrub produce a numbing effect in the mouth and throat. Some say this will cure sores in the mouth. More relevant, the mature leaves are bitter in taste. This thick low shrub provides excellent cover for the ptarmigan, hence the name. Both plants are generally found growing together and the tasty noisy birds are usually found in the same area.

Near the pool, a low steep hillock stood out in the otherwise flat surroundings.

It appeared distinctively circular, some eight to ten paces across and was outlined with large sandstone boulders. With the boulders as barriers and too steep for mammoth or other herbivores to negotiate it, the hillock provided a safe and comfortable campsite. Harjo could imagine the hand of man involved in its formation as much as a unique work of the Father Creator.

A thick short grass blanketed the hill. The Muscogee did not have a name for the grass as few animals ate it because of its low height, especially the mammoth that required a tall grass such as the blue grass to wrap their trunks around. This short grass was not rare, growing in small patches across the steppe. Harjo was not sure why it flourished on this small hill. Perhaps because of the drainage or the sandy soils but for whatever the reason, the thick grass provided a relaxing bed.

Harjo cleared the few small trees and brush that grew on the hill, leaving four trees forming a perfect square shape. He tied limbs to each tree parallel to the ground to create a good support for a shelter. Each trip to the Ocher Camp he laid willow branches across the limbs forming a shelter top. With a rock hearth constructed next to the shelter, the comfortable camp was complete.

One late summer, on a trip to the Ocher Camp, Onna found several clumps of the delicious yellow tea bush and collected a small pouch of seeds intending to sow the seeds all along the pool and the stream. The conditions proved favorable and the plant flourished, providing not only tea but also the beautiful yellow flowers. In fact, Onna picked flowers or seeds on every trip to the Ocher Camp and replanted them at the encampment. As a result, the colorful flowers bloomed in abundance around the campsite and their perfume filled the air with a delightful aroma. There is something about the brilliant colors of flowers and their sweet aroma that seems to render women into a romantic mood. No one knows why.

The Ocher Paint Stream attracted ptarmigan in abundance. The shallow narrow watercourse, sandy soil, low willow thickets, and thick grasses all combined to draw the noisy birds. But it was the Ptarmigan Bistort that lured the birds in great quantity, keeping them there through all seasons. The plant grew to about the length of a man's hand. The delicate white flowers packed together at the top of the stalk while the "spear point" shaped leaves crowded the bottom. The flower bulbils that did not open into flowers clustered just below the blooms and provided the preferred food of the ptarmigan and likewise tasty treats for Mammoth Hunters as well. Caribou, ground squirrels, and lemmings also relished the bulbils. Lemmings stored them in their burrows as a winter food cache. During late summer and fall, before the first snow, Mammoth Hunter children raided the lemming's food caches for handfuls of tasty treats, which included the Ptarmigan Bistort bulbils, along with other grass seeds and roots. The caribou gathered at their fawning grounds to the south, but the ground squirrels and lemmings thrived in the environment of the Ocher Paint Stream.

Harjo and Onna followed the clear, small stream, stopping at an area of dense, waist high willow thickets some distance from their Ocher Camp. The brush had been trampled by an animal herd creating wide paths with wads of fur and wool clinging to the broken branches. The large round tracks immediately identified the herd as rhinos.

Onna was witness to rhinos on many occasions in her early youth for they were common in her childhood homeland as were mammoth and horses. They reached six or seven paces in length and at their shoulders, were taller than a man. Their thick wooly fur reminded her of mammoth wool and was nearly the same color. But the most impressive aspect was their horns. The end of their snout supported a long horn, longer than a man's arm. A shorter one was set between their eyes. Their heads were huge and reminded Onna of a horse.

Harjo squatted down next to a pile of dung and tracks. "The sign is old," he said, "but we will keep a close watch."

"Can we rest here, Harjo?"

"Alright," he said rising to his feet. They followed a path through the brush, stopping at the stream's edge where they dropped their packs in a trampled area. Onna collected a handful of the rhino wool from the branches.

"Their wool is similar to mammoth," she said as she squeezed the material in her hand.

"The rhinos ramble all through the brush scrapping their winter wool off. They also relish the new growth of grass emerging under the brush cover," said Harjo.

"I hope they don't go to our Ocher Camp, Harjo, trampling our brush. I am sure they would destroy our little pool."

Harjo chuckled, "Well, I think they will stay clear of our Ocher Camp, perhaps human smell makes them cautious."

Due to the rhino dung, they did not drink the water as they sat by the stream but Onna did wash her hands and neck. Harjo had taught her about rhino behavior, but she wanted to be reacquainted with the dangerous beasts. "Tell me again about the rhinos, Harjo." He agreed.

"The adult bulls live a solitary life," he explained. "With dung and urine, they mark out a hefty territory and defend it with their lives against other bulls. Females live in small groups of 10-14 centered on a mature female and her off-spring. Occasionally, sub-adult males will also follow a female herd. Females do not mark or defend ground. Similar to mammoth, their eyesight is poor but their sense of smell acute. As the adult females come into heat, a dominant bull will join the herd for several days for breeding. During this period, the bulls are very aggressive and very dangerous. They rub their large horn on the ground just before they charge."

Once refreshed, they continued to follow the stream and it brought them to their Ocher Camp. They stuck the butt end of their spears into the sandy soil and stood in silence at the sight of their favored hide-a-way. This camp was dear to Onna. Harjo brought her here the first summer of their marriage. They returned on several occasions each summer before Onna became pregnant. It was their private, secret place where two young lovers, mere children, had laughed, loved, and played. It would be a magic place to return to as aged grandparents. They could watch their grandchildren play and slip back in memory to the wonderful summers of their youth. The ever-emotional Onna wiped the tears from her face with her hands, then embraced Harjo with her head against his chest. She didn't say anything nor did Harjo, he only held her. Although Harjo returned frequently, Onna had not been to the Ocher Camp since pregnant with her first baby, Chate, who was now nine summers in age.

It did not take long to set up the camp. They cut fresh willow branches to secure to the top of the shelter while they snacked on the young willow leaf shoots. And they gathered dry wood and started a fire. As they worked on the camp, a pair of ground squirrels just downstream of the pool chattered, barking their disapproval at the pair of busy Mammoth Hunters. A small hillock covered with sandstone and grass was obviously their den nest as they would disappear under the rocks, then reemerge to chatter their condemnation. Ground squirrels dig deep borrows for hibernation during the winter, tunneling under any pile of sandstone rock or hillock.

Unfortunately, the vocal little squirrels concentrated too much on Harjo and Onna, who posed no threat to them, rather than on the real threats to their lives silently soaring above. As one unaware squirrel stood on the open top of the hillock in continuous chatter, a large red-tailed hawk swooped down from the sky and snatched up the nosey rodent. The raptor's sharp lethal talons sunk deep into its prey's shoulders and neck while with only a slight struggle, it remained aloft and carried its unlucky victim away.

"Look, Harjo, look!" shouted out Onna. Harjo looked up to see the hawk make its way parallel to the ground with its struggling quarry and then it rose into the sky.

"Poor little squirrel," whined Onna. "He wasn't paying attention." Harjo shook his head-the Mammoth Steppe remains unforgiving.

With the camp prepared, Harjo went off to hunt ptarmigan for this evening's fare, but he would not journey far. Onna took a long bath in the shallow, sandy bottom pool. She bathed daily in the clear cool pools at Wetumka but here the sun warmed the shallow water. Even though the air and wind were chilly on her wet skin, the warm water pool remained inviting. Often at Wetumka, she sat on the edge of the pool with just her feet submersed before she gained enough inspiration to dip into the cool, often chilled water. But more importantly, the privacy of just her and Harjo was welcomed. She combed her hair for such a lengthy period, laughing that she could allow herself so much leisure. She carried her large buckskin pelt and harpoon to the sandstone rock and lay naked in the sun, sleepy, and content.

Harjo returned with several ptarmigan and whistled the chickadee song as he approached. Instead of the traditional answer, Onna called out, "I'm here by the pool Harjo!" She didn't open her eyes as she lay on her stomach but felt his shadow pass.

Harjo glanced down at the lovely naked Onna as she laid on the rock, eyes closed. "What a beautiful little victim," he thought, "but at least her spear lies nearby." Apparently, some of his teachings had rubbed off over many long summers.

"You're going to sunburn," he warned in his fatherly tone.

"I am relying on you to come and roll me over before I cook on this one side." Her eyes remained closed, but she smiled a childish grin.

Harjo considered splashing her. Instead, he kneeled down on one knee and gave her a hard swat on the bottom.

"Ouch, Harjo. Don't spank me!"

"You've become as bossy as an old bull mammoth," chuckled Harjo.

"I'm not bossy," laughed Onna, still with her eyes closed. "I'm decisive."

Harjo laughed out loud. "Well, beautiful 'decisive,' roll over before you burn."

Smiling and keeping her eyes closed, Onna rolled over on her back as Harjo rose and went on downstream to dress the birds. He left them to hang in the branches of a bush just above the water in the shade which would keep the birds cool. He returned to Onna and sat down beside her, laying his hand, purposely wet and cold, on her stomach then rubbed her.

"No-Harjo-no," whined Onna, "don't splash me and don't spank either!"

"I have a tea pouch full of cold water," warned Harjo, "and I am waiting for just the right moment to dump it on you!"

"No-Harjo-don't," cried a still whining Onna but she also laughed and opened her mouth. "Don't splash me but give me a drink!"

Harjo continued to massage her stomach. "You'll need to sit up for a drink."

Onna now opened her eyes then looked up at him in a curious fashion. "Harjo," she then paused and took a breath. "Do you think I'm still pretty?"

Harjo looked to her face to see that same childlike expression she wore when she asked honest questions. It was a silly female question, but nonetheless asked honestly.

"You're prettier now than when you were a girl," he answered calmly.

"I've had eight babies, Harjo, and you can see my stomach is scared from the greatness of pregnancy and it is not flat as it once was."

"You're shaped like a woman now," remarked Harjo. "When I first took your clothes off, I noticed you were pretty, but you had a little boy's butt. In fact, you looked like a little boy."

"I didn't have a little boy butt and I didn't look like a boy!" argued Onna. "I just had narrow hips."

Harjo laughed as he lowered his hand to gently touch her small patch of soft pubic fur. Onna smiled and moaned a tender sigh as she stretched her arms over her head. Her pubic hair and the little tuft of hair under her arms glistened in the sunlight like moist winter grass, as it is first uncovered from snow, both the same color as her hair. Again, Harjo thought, as he had over so many seasons, that there really was no color name for the shade of Onna's hair. It wasn't exactly yellow, as yellow ocher paint nor was it a tan color as the underbelly of a caribou doe. Nearly, the color of winter grass, but there was no name for that color.

"Harjo," sighed Onna as he continued to caress her pubic hair as she smiled and squirmed. "Do you want my women's fluid?"

"Later," he responded as he reached his hand into his game pouch and withdrew a handful of Ptarmigan Bistort bulbils.

Upon seeing the tasty treats, Onna quickly sat up and clapped her hands, taking Harjo's hand bringing it to her mouth, then lapping up a bite of the bulbils. She chewed, laughed, and reached up and pushed his hair back over his ears.

Very early dawn, twilight, the stars glowed bright and clear as the near full moon set toward the northward horizon. A full moon would rise tomorrow. So quiet, the morning birds were not yet ready to welcome the sun with morning song. Harjo could just make out sleeping Onna's face and listened to her soft but heavy breathing. She drew air through her nose with a closed mouth. Harjo leaned over and caressed her face, tenderly kissed her, and gently tapped his fingers on her lips, a trick he learned from her. She lightly squirmed and softly sighed. Harjo smiled to himself. Often, he could entice Onna to talk in her sleep using this method; he gently tapped her lips again.

"Oh, Harjo, no-no drop Onna in snow. I no naughty," she whispered and whined in an adorable child voice. Chuckling, he again gently tapped her lips with his fingers. She now opened her eyes and sighed. She smiled at him, then he leaned over to softly kiss her.

"Harjo," she said in an excited whisper, "I dreamed I was a naughty little girl and you were carrying me, intending on dropping me in a deep snow drift!" She reached her fist up from under the caribou bedcover and gently hit him on the shoulder. "That is not nice, Harjo!"

"Well, were you being naughty in your dream?" he asked in a mild voice.

Onna chuckled as she reached up to gently stroke the side of his mouth with her finger. "Maybe," she answered in a childlike accent.

Again, he leaned over, giving her a stronger kiss on her warm moist lips. She stretched and sighed.

"Are you going to sex me, Harjo?"

"Yes, but later," he said quietly. "Look at the moon."

Onna looked around and when she saw the bright setting moon, she sucked in her breath and whispered out loud.

"Oh, Harjo, what is it? What is happening?"

What she saw was both wondrous and frightening. The top portion of the nearly full moon showed bright, glowing as a hot ember. The remaining section of the glowing disk, although visible, was blotted out in a nimbus haze and a brilliant incandescent glow formed around the thin circular edges.

"It's called an eclipse," said Harjo, "a moon eclipse. The moon is covered as in a shadow."

"Oh, yes, yes, I've heard Harjo, but I have never seen one." Suddenly, Onna felt a little uneasy, perhaps a little fearful, as she made a little whiney sound and snuggled up next to Harjo. Sensing her uneasiness, he put his arm around her, and they lay watching the wondrous site.

"How does it happen, Harjo?"

"I don't know. No one knows how it occurs, but I do know the earth, the sun, and the moon are not flat but are great spheres. Our father, Cheparney, taught me that long ago."

"Yes, Harjo, and you taught me, but how do you think it happens?"

Harjo paused for a moment then answered. "The moon, earth, and the sun were created by the Father Creator," he explained. "Somehow, each exists individually but also they move together in a great plan of the Father Creator. The sun must somehow create a shadow on the moon. It must be the same way the sun creates shadows on the earth from the smallest pebble to the tall great mountains; all things cast shadows from the sun."

Onna thought to herself. That seemed a plausible explanation. She wondered how someone could figure that out.

She smiled to herself, her brilliant hunter. "Is the eclipse a good or a bad omen, Harjo?"

Harjo thought for a moment. "Some say it is good, some say it is bad, some say both."

Onna looked at the moon again, then leaned over and rubbed noses with him. "I want to know what you believe, my love."

"I do not think it is either. It is simply a rare phenomenon that is seldom witnessed. Most people are asleep when it occurs. The Father Creator provides much wonderment. Each season, the yellow grass turns green, the green grass grows tall and the flowers bloom, the snow and ice melts, and babies are born. All of these are also wonderments, but these marvels happen each season, so we accept them as normal occurrences without explanation. The eclipse, the moon's shadow, is just very rare and tells nothing of our future."

Onna rubbed and patted his chest, then again rubbed noses with him and kissed him. Harjo could explain an "occurrence" that might otherwise be fearful and turned them into wonderment. The eclipse now appeared as an amazing sight, nothing to fear at all. This was one of many reasons why Onna loved Harjo.

"Take me to urinate, Harjo."

"Alright," responded Harjo, as they both rose naked from their caribou bed. Harjo picked up his spear and the caribou buckskin robe, shaking it off. Onna glanced up at the moon and saw that about one-half remained in shadow and the remaining portion shown bright. The sun had not yet crested over the distant hill, but the sky radiated in a beautiful bluish hue. Onna wished there was blue paint. She glanced at Harjo as he surveyed the circle horizon.

Onna took his hand and led him to edge of their soft grass hillock and squatted to urinate. Harjo stood behind her and covered her backside with the robe. She looked back over her shoulder to see that he still silently watched the landscape all around them. She smiled to herself. No creature would ever sneak upon her while she was with Harjo-her brave vigilant warrior was always watching-always.

As she finished, she rose, and he wrapped the robe around her as she then stepped behind him. Harjo now urinated in her exact wet spot. She chuckled to herself, placing her head against his back. Was she now to be his filly? Harjo finished and they walked back to their bed. Onna took down the water pouch and rinsed out her mouth then drank. She also took a handful of water and washed her vulva with her hand. She handed the pouch to Harjo and he also washed out his mouth and drank.

"I'll start the fire," said Harjo.

Onna smiled a yes, then returned to bed. She glanced up at the mysterious and still somewhat disconcerting yet stimulating moon. She watched a naked Harjo rekindle a morning fire and in so doing, began to kindle a fire in her heart and her groin. She felt moistness springing between her legs.

She folded the top cover of the caribou bed down and lay on her stomach slowly rubbing her pubic area against the bed. Then she gently reached back and began to massage her buttocks and also reached her fingers to stimulate her milk-full breast. As Harjo approached the bed, she looked up at his face over her shoulder as a slight whimpering sound escaped her lips. Harjo got down on his knees, then with one hand on her waist, he began to rub her buttocks with the other. Onna had always marveled at the size and power of his hands and how the palms were mammoth hide hard and calloused. His strong hands on her waist and buttocks moved her to breathe heavy as she began to moan.

Then he raised his hand and brought it down on her right cheek-she felt the impact and the sting. A high pitched "oooh" escaped from her lips. Was he going to spank her into submission as an impatient rough warrior would a young reluctant girl until she cried, squirmed, and with red burning buttocks implore him to stop as she surrendered to his dominance? No-his hand was open, and the fingers spread not closed together to deliver a hard slap. Instead, he gripped and massaged her cheeks. She could still hear and feel each smack, but he did not deliver a spank to punish-he squeezed and rubbed her cheeks.

Feeling the strength and power in his hands, Onna reached her own hand to her pubic area as her fingers found and stimulated her small female organ, now rigid and hard. His rough hands continued their labors on her soft behind until her woman fluid flowed out from her organ and little "ooohs' escaped her lips in moans of ecstasy. She loved being dominated by him.

He could easily hold her down and punish her with the palm of his masculine hard hand as she remained helpless in his grip. But instead he stimulated her-forcing her to give him her female fluid. It was this contradiction, this wide contrast that stimulated her bonding her to him and had since she was 12 summers of age.

His hands stopped, then roughly massaged and squeezed her bottom. He grabbed her hips. Was he going to pull her to her knees and take her like the forceful male lion does his smaller female, holding her by her neck with his great jaws or better still as a stallion does a mare? The vision of the stallion mounting his reluctant filly they had watched just days before now flashed through her thoughts. No-he rolled her over on her back then came down to her and kissed her warm, moist lips. His tongue then penetrated her mouth-deep into her mouth and she sucked on him as hard as she dared.

Next, he spread her legs and moved between them as she reached out grasping his rigid male spear. Warm and hard, she could feel his member as it throbbed and pulsated as did his heartbeat. She released him and reached around to grasp his muscular buttocks. Then, she raised her chin and arched her back. His hardness searched the warm moistness of her womanhood until it found her secret opening and slowly penetrated her.

Cautiously, Harjo did not push his rigid member to full penetration. He stopped short at a depth that long experience had taught him was a maximum penetration her warm soft fissure would comfortably accommodate on his initial incursion. Onna moaned in delightful ecstasy, squeezing his buttock's firm flesh as hard as she could. Harjo came down to his elbows and against her, then moved over and above her. The strength and power of his masculine chest brushed against the tip of her nose, overwhelming her. She kissed his chest, his nipples, then under his arms, inhaling his potent male scent. The smell of his intoxicating male aroma and the huge hard wetness of his penetration forced her to again give up her female fluid and she convulsed as her hard, little female organ released her juices against his massive male organ. He would take her surreptitious woman's liquid again and again.

Harjo now moved in and out, slowly at first, so that his thick hard spear impaled her as it smoothly slid across her female organ and then, as in a dream or foggy vision, his powerful essence picked her up to carry her deep, ever so deep, into the mysterious spirit world. Her hands and fingers continued to squeeze, even claw his rump, the small of his back, and up higher on his back. With her open mouth against his chest, Onna groaned an "oooh" from deep inside her, matching the rhythm of each of his thrusts, lifting her bottom off the caribou bed so that her pelvis met each penetration. As she exploded in orgasm, she made a gurgling sound from deep inside her stomach.

He now lowered himself close to her and cupped her face in his dominant hands and slowly, but with certainty, pushed the complete length of his maleness into her. He filled her completely and as he rubbed his pelvis against her, she felt her woman's fluid building to spew once more and again she shook with orgasm.

Harjo bent his head down to kiss Onna's lips, which were dry until she licked them, and then she breathed heavy into his mouth. She wanted to suck him, his male essence, into her and to smell his life's breath, strong, hot, and powerful. He withdrew his organ then slowly penetrated her again-then again-and again. She rocked with him in the rhythm of life as he increased his pace, faster and faster until he pounded her as a stallion does one of his mares, then he exploded his male fluid deep inside her. He had remained quiet until now as he groaned a sound deep from inside his chest. His orgasm drove Onna to another and she convulsed with him as her whole body flexed.

Then they both relaxed and panted as though they had run a great distance. Harjo maintained his strength and did not flatten out atop Onna. He would not squash her, but he did roll over on to his side and brought her with him, then they lay side by side.

They slowly returned from the foggy, mysterious, yet enchanting spirit world. Onna moved up to look into Harjo's face.

"I love you, Harjo, so very much. Do you still love me after all these many seasons?"

Harjo looked into her eyes and smiled. "I will always love you-Onna-always-from now until forever." Always emotional, tears formed in Onna's eyes as she likewise smiled then began to cover his face with many kisses until they both laughed and sighed.

Such a beautiful morning, warm and still as the wonderful scent from the flowers filled the air. Onna wanted to stay. She could only guess how long would pass before she would see the Ocher Camp again. But she also wanted to leave to experience the great caribou herds and to find a Caribou Hunter camp. They started a large fire, taking one last trip to the pool. Harjo took a dip, but the morning water was much too cold for Onna who washed off on the pool's edge on the big rock then ran back to the fire to dry and then dress-Harjo followed.

They collected several skin pouches of ocher paint, red and yellow. The yellow chunks Onna found were a deep solid hue, the best examples she had ever seen. They enjoyed a large breakfast of tea, ptarmigan, Ptarmigan Bistort bulbils, and willow leaves. They extinguished the fire, loaded their backpacks, and in a bittersweet mood, silently moved on.

The wooded groves that Harjo and Onna encountered as they trekked across the open steppe grassland offered favorable camp sites but also provide slight obstacles to maneuver around. As they followed the edge of one small grove, the chattering magpies in the tops of the trees caught their attention. They glanced up at the long-tailed birds smiling at each other and presumed the birds alert calls were directed at them.

Suddenly, they came to an abrupt stop-ahead a large bear feasted on a caribou carcass. They failed to see the bear due to the thick density of the grove of trees and overlooked the magpie's alert calls. They had walked so close they could now hear the bear's powerful jaws crushing caribou bones.

Onna slowly raised her spear and grasped it at the lower end, then assumed a defensive stance. She glanced up at Harjo who had drawn a dart and proceed to arm it with a foreshaft. He gestured with his eyes, then a very slight movement of his head. Together, with cautious determination, they began to slowly back up.

They had not taken many steps when the bear looked up seeing the two human figures. It growled a loud roar raising its head. It jumped, seemingly both startled and aggressive. Then it took two or three aggressive steps walking over the caribou carcass toward the intruders.

Onna and Harjo continued to slowly back away-Harjo held his atlatl armed with a dart poised to throw. Onna knew that if the bear charged, Harjo would cast the dart then step in front of her to take the bear head on with his spear thus giving her an opportunity to escape. Harjo made her promise she would follow this course of action in these life-threatening situations, but she had deceived him. She would not leave him. She would remain-attacking the bear the way he had taught her-as best she could.

The fearsome beast continued to growl, displaying aggressive and threatening behaviors. It jumped forward stiff legged, then scrapped the ground in an instinctive effort to mask the scent of its dead prize. Then, it snapped its enormous jaws together creating a loud smacking sound with its deadly teeth.

The pair continued to slowly back up. As Onna watched the frightening bear, she could feel her heart pounding. Although she could not see his face very well, she again glanced up at Harjo who likewise watched the bear with his usual, unemotional facial expression.

Onna's heart did more than pound. It seemed to jump as the bear rose up on its back legs with a loud roar. Its size alone beleaguered her, looming as tall as a mammoth. The great fearsome bears, however, have few equals. They take prey away from lions and wolf packs with little effort. Pairs come together for short periods to breed and sows raise their cubs but otherwise they maintain a solitary existence. Consequently, they hold little fear from any creature including humans.

As Harjo and Onna withdrew to a safe distance, the great bear returned to his meal convinced the intruders were of no threat and his carcass prize remained safe. Harjo took Onna's hand, leading her a good distance off, out of harm's way. Then, he stopped and pulled her to him embracing her as best he could-both wearing backpacks.

The ever-emotional Onna put her head against Harjo's chest breathing hard. "Harjo, I was so afraid. I thought it was going to charge!"

"So did I," he replied rubbing Onna just under her armpits. "Micco Yarda once explained to me that bears seldom charge when you encounter them with a prey carcass, unlike a male lion that always will. 'But you can never be sure about bears,' he added.'"

Onna stepped back, still holding onto Harjo but looked up into his face. "When it stood up on its back legs-Harjo-I thought I might urinate!" She then looked at him with a blank expression. "Maybe I did!"

With a childish expression, Onna raised her parka, reaching her hand under to check to see if she was wet. Harjo laughed. "I don't smell anything, Love."

Satisfied she was dry; she took another deep breath. "I don't want to repeat this encounter Harjo, but it was exciting. It makes me feel alive! Is it the same for you?"

"Yes," he replied as he pulled her close to him, face to face. "Such deadly encounters remind us how short and precious our lives are. It is folly to waste a single day."

Onna sighed. Her brave warrior and hunter turned philosopher. She was pleased. As she was already up on her toes, she leaned forward and kissed him. "I am excited to keep going, Harjo. Take me closer to the caribou herds."

Remaining close to his mouth, she wanted him to speak-this close-so as she could smell his breath. "Alright," he calmly replied.

The aroma of his breath caused her to smile and to tingle inside. Excited, she took his hand. "I am more anxious now than ever to see what is ahead! Hurry, Harjo let's go!" Hand in hand, they continued on toward the caribou fawning grounds.

Chapter 30:

CARIBOU HUNTERS

F all stood as the preferred season to take caribou skins for clothing and many old men said the only season. During the winter, the dense brown underwall and long guard hairs are too thick to sew into comfortable attire. Some Mammoth Hunters appreciate the thick winter pelts as bedding albeit it sheds conspicuously. During the spring, the caribou molts thus the shedding pelage likewise makes for poor clothing. Throughout the summer, the animals may be infested with parasitic larvae of the warble fly that burrow through the skin of the unfortunate victims leaving holes in their pelts. Because of the flies Mammoth Hunters prefer to avoid the caribou altogether during the summer. There was an old saying often quoted by Elder hunters, "do not hunt caribou until the first frost of fall lays on the grass."

Summer fawns were the exception as they were not infested with the larvae and the soft fur of the fawn was preferred for summer clothing or in particularly as an under garment during cold winter periods. Fawn meat also proved a unique flavor, although fawns were small as were their pelts and so too, the amount of meat they provided.

The land of the caribou, north and northeast of the Echota River Valley, reminded Onna of the flat, nearly tree-less landscape she crossed with Harjo on their epic passage from the Great Sea so many seasons ago. Subsequent that grand journey, she had not been this far from the Echota River. Prior to having babies, Harjo took her on many trips along the Echota, to their Ocher Camp, and once to the red chert quarries that supplied the tool stone for their beau-tiful red chert tools, but never this far. She had longed to see the great caribou herds, but they were such a far distance from their summer camps that Harjo would not take her. She had seen the small herds that roamed the area southeast of the Echota but not the great herds of the north or the Caribou Hunters who followed them. On many occasions, Harjo described to Onna the life patterns of both the car-ibou and caribou hunting bands.

"Caribou follow a dynamic life," he explained. "Their migration paths, fawning, feeding, and wintering grounds change altering from season to season, and thus they are not consistently predictable. Consequently, the lives of the Caribou Hunters are equally erratic."

"The Caribou Hunter's principal hunt occurs during fall migration as the herds move south to the Big River feeding grounds and when the caribou hides are in pre-ferred condition to render as clothing and their meat lined with winter fat. The members of each band assemble under the direction of a chief who organizes a drive. The animals are ambushed and herded into a corral and thus dispatched by the hundreds. The meat and hides are divided equally among the families with respect given the chiefs and other drive leaders. The fall hunt remains the only season when a band unites. During the other seasons, the bands disperse into extended family groups of two to four families."

"That seems terribly strange, Harjo," stated a curious Onna. "Our band and all the bands of the Muscogee Tribe stay together throughout all seasons. Surely, the Caribou Hunters must stay in touch with each other?"

"They do," answered Harjo. "Family groups remain in contact operating within a loose band range and territory. It is not a strict land division but usually all the families within one area at large belong to one band. A band chieftain may call a band together under exceptional circumstance but otherwise the fall communal drive and hunt remains the only occasion a band at large unites."

"They continue to hunt individual animals during the remaining seasons especially during the summer as they concentrate on taking fawns. Same as you, they want the fawn skins for summer clothing and the tender meat as a delicacy. Small family camps can be found throughout the caribou fawning and summer feeding grounds."

"I surely hope we find a family group, Harjo!" exclaimed an excited Onna as she clapped her hands. "It will be so exciting to visit one of their camps. Afterwards, I am anxious to make clothing and to sew the fawn's skins!"

Harjo laughed and reassured her, "We will," then he continued. "During the winter, they camp near the herd's wintering grounds along the upper Big River. And as we have experienced on many occasions, winter caribou provides fresh meat, notwithstanding very lean and thick hides for cold winter bedding and floor mats. I have often been told winter hides are too thick to sew and for manufacturing clothing."

"They are, Harjo, you know it is not worth the effort."

"Harjo," asked the always-curious Onna, "do Caribou Hunters speak one language?"

"Yes," he answered. "They call their language Athabascan."

Onna repeated the strange word to herself. She had heard the word before but now committed it to memory. Harjo sensed she was not through with her questions and waited for her next one.

"Harjo, what language do the Enemy Warriors speak?"

"A Caribou Hunter chieftain once told me the Raiding Warriors also spoke Athabascan, but it was not the same nor was it intelligible with their language. You know the Enemy Warriors have taken many Caribou and Mammoth Hunter women captive. Some say they speak a mongrel or mixed language."

"What do you think?" asked Onna.

"Their tribe and bands are probably similar to our family and band. I believe they have a foundation language, an Athabascan language, similar to the Caribou Hunters that they all understand in the same way that we have the Muscogee language. Individuals, however, will speak other languages, Caribou Hunter Athabascan and Muscogee." Onna shook her head yes, as this seemed sound reasoning.

Harjo also reminded Onna that the Caribou Hunters have many admirable traits in some respects but not so in other aspects. "On one side, the men are brave, skilled hunters and warriors showing little fear of danger. In trading, they are generous and fair and once they give their word, they rarely break it. But on the other side, they show little respect to women who are often beaten; equally, they display even less regard for children. Men offer their wives to other men as a form of hospitality. Children are often abandoned, especially girls, to die alone of hunger or at the claws and fangs of wolves and lions. A baby, even a newborn, may be left naked in the winter with its mouth stuffed with snow to slowly succumb to cold."

Onna sighed a heavy sigh. "I just can't imagine abandoning a child, Harjo, especially infants and to stuff their mouths with snow-such cruelty. Please, Harjo, if we find any children left behind, we must bring them with us. It would break my heart to leave a child." Harjo looked to see the sincerity in Onna's face. He didn't answer but nodded his head in agreement.

The first view of the vast caribou herds seen from the edge of their fawning grounds stretching to the horizon delighted Onna more that she had ever imagined. With the butt end of her spear stuck into the ground, she wrapped both arms around Harjo and rubbed her chin against his chest. Then, she stood on her toes, kissed his neck, and gazed out over the innumerable herd in shear wonderment.

"I don't believe it, Harjo. I've never dreamed there were so many. They extend beyond the horizon."

"They do," replied Harjo who had witnessed the vast caribou herds on many occasions, yet likewise remained in awe. "They number more than anyone could ever count, more than the stars."

Harjo led Onna to a small rocky uplift. There the grass had escaped trampling and hungry caribou over many seasons to grow head-high. It provided a perfect vista and hiding location. To the east, a low gully extended northward to a small wooded grove. Smoke streamed upward from the grove. Harjo pointed, "A Caribou Hunter camp."

Onna boiled with excitement like an overheated tea pouch. She wanted to clap her hands but managed to restrain herself and gripped her spear instead, grinning a beautiful smile. She did jump up and down, although with caution. Onna's enthusiasm was always contagious. Harjo smiled and put his arm around her. He welcomed that she remained so young at heart, and he delighted in her honest, yet childlike antics. She brought a welcome element of joy into their lives.

They removed their backpacks and constructed a small blind so that they could sit and refresh themselves unseen by the herd and watch. The wind was in their favor. Slowly the herd grazed, moving closer.

Onna could see that the caribou formed small herds of 10-12 does with their fawns and one or two bucks. She had seen caribou all her life and had sewn many sets of clothing from their pelts and buckskin including the clothes she and Harjo now wore. Still, watching the enormous herd inspired her to describe the animals to herself as though she were first seeing them as a child.

They were all a brownish color with lighter, nearly white necks, underbellies, and rumps. The bucks were easy to recognize, much larger than the does, supporting large magnificent curved antlers. The antlers dropped off during winter and begin to grow again in early spring. Now nearly grown, the antlers were covered with velvet. The bucks would scrape off the velvet and sharpen their antlers in preparation of the rutting season and combat over mating rights in early fall. Onna remained astonished that the backs of the bucks were such a dark brown color providing a striking contrast of light and dark hues. Many of the does also supported antlers although much smaller than the bucks, often mere spikes. Their backs were a lighter brown color than the bucks. The little fawns appeared as an even lighter brownish-grey color. As with all youngsters, the playful fawns ran and jumped around when not nursing.

Harjo had told Onna that the caribou sense of smell was very keen as are so many animals of the steppe, but caribou do not have intelligent vision. "I believe they see about as good as we do," he said, "but they do not have smart vision.

They are easily fooled. Hunters can employ unsophisticated disguises and approach with the wind, well within killing range of the herd. You and I would see them and easily recognize them as hunters, but the caribou do not."

Suddenly, Onna gently tapped Harjo's hand, pointing, she whispered, "Harjo." Two strange figures emerged. They must have been concealed in the gully and now approached the herd downwind. They were hunters. Each one wore a strange hooded cape seemingly with caribou antlers attached. They bent from the waist and mimicked the caribou gait using their arms as front legs.

"They wear caribou heads and antlers, Harjo," whispered Onna.

"Yes," answered Harjo. They use the skin from the head, shoulders, and back of a caribou. The antlers are actually carved from wood and occasionally painted-much lighter than heavy antler. They hunt the fawns."

The two hunters moved slowly and methodically toward the herd that continued to graze on the green grasses, milling around completely unalarmed at approaching death in disguise. Excited, Onna squeezed Harjo's arm, she knew they were well within dart range. Onna was just as thrilled as when she had killed a caribou with Harjo so many seasons ago.

Simultaneously, both hunters rose and launched their darts. One struck a doe while another hit a fawn. The herd bolted in panic, but each hunter managed to cast another dart with one bringing down another doe. The wounded fawn lay still on the spot but the two does reacted violently to the impact of the darts. The first jumped and squirmed near where she was struck but the second ran a short distance before falling to the ground to die in kicking convulsions.

A surprised Onna reacted. "Harjo, the fawns stay with their dead mothers."

"Yes," replied Harjo. "Once attacked, during some hunts, the fawns might run with the herd, especially the older ones, but more often they stay with their dead mothers to be easily killed. Consequently, the hunters will attempt to hit one doe with a fawn and one separate fawn. They know if the fawn stays with its wounded mother, they can easily cut its throat and not damage the hide with a dart point. If the fawn runs with the herd, however, they will still have a dart-hit fawn and a doe's meat and hide to use if necessary."

Onna watched and listened intently. She had long wanted to witness the Caribou Hunters and a fawn hunt and she remained excited with this new adventure. Each hunter approached a live fawn and dispatched it with a single knife swipe.

"One hunter is skilled with atlatl, Harjo; he hit the doe on the run." Harjo agreed.

The two hunters tied the three fawns onto a pole. Then, leaving the two slain does, they carried their quarry off toward the distant camp. "We will wait until they are close to their camp then we will follow and approach," said Harjo in a near whisper.

Onna agreed then suddenly smiled and pointed. "Look, Harjo, horses!" Harjo turned to see a distant herd as they came to an abrupt stop. Mares allowed their colts to nurse as they nibbled on grasses while others milled around pawing the ground and shaking their heads. The anxious stallion nervously trotted around the perimeter of his harem. Onna and Harjo watched for a while. Then suddenly, the herd bolted into a gallop to continue on across the steppe, seemingly with no particular destination.

"Alright," said Harjo as he rose, "we'll follow the hunters to their camp." Glowing with excitement, Onna followed and they slipped on their backpacks and then headed toward the gully. They noticed two wolves trotting toward the slain does.

"Wolves watch the hunters during the summer throughout the fawning grounds," explained Harjo, "having learned they may leave a slain doe in their pursuit of fawns." Harjo and Onna trailed the hunters along the gulley then into the wooded grove. As they neared the camp, Harjo stopped. In front of them some 20 paces-a Caribou Hunter.

Onna was certain the wind was blowing before they saw the Caribou Hunter but now the air seemed still and quiet so that the Caribou Hunter could hear Harjo's voice. Over the past many seasons, Onna became certain the wind would nearly always pick up or lay still in favor of Harjo. As was planned, Onna quietly slipped behind him.

"We are Mammoth Hunters!" called out Harjo in the Caribou Hunter tongue. "I am Harjo of the Wind Band, and we come to trade!" Onna now wished she knew more of the language.

"I have heard of you," replied the Caribou Hunter. "So, it is true you speak our language."

"I do," answered Harjo.

"I am Dina of the Deg Hit'an Band," he announced as he advanced.

Harjo likewise walked toward Dina and Onna followed. As the men approached, they exchanged spear hands to reach out their right hands, free of weapons in a display of friendship, and grasped each other's wrists.

"What do you seek?" asked Dina.

"Fawn pelts," answered Harjo.

"What do you bring in exchange?"

"Red chert," was Harjo's answer.

"Red chert," replied Dina with an air of amazement. "I am sure we can agree on a trade."

Dina glanced past Harjo to Onna. Harjo could see the surprise in his face when Dina saw the fair skinned, yellow haired Onna. Although common with Caribou Hunter emotions, his reaction remained very subtle. Harjo thought Dina would be more amazed when he was close enough to see Onna's blue eyes.

As the men talked, Onna peeked around Harjo and looked the Caribou Hunter over. She saw a striking figure, as tall as Harjo and well adorned in handsome fawnskin clothing. She first noticed his pants and boots were a single unit. A dark nearly black strip of fur lined the outside of each leg. Onna presumed an aged caribou buck provided the dark strip. Black wolf fur lined the area about knee high as though to fringe the top of the boots if separated from the pants.

His frock was equally well made. The edge reached his hips in length and was cut in a wedge shape, pointing just at his groin rather than cut straight across, seemingly to draw attention to his groin, perhaps a hint of ego. The entire edge was fringed with adjacent thin strips of buckskin. Each strip was individually attached. This alone displayed an arduous sewing task. The neck, the long sleeve, and the outside length of the arms were lined with a strip of the same dark fur. He also wore a seashell necklace. The wealth in his clothing including the necklace told Onna he was a man of some rank within his band.

Suddenly, Harjo spoke to her. "Alright Onna, his name is Dina and we'll follow him to his camp. Remember our plan." She shook her head yes.

Onna remained both apprehensive and excited as she followed Harjo who in turn followed the Caribou Hunter named Dina single file along a fallow caribou trail to his camp. They were not in danger, but she was apprehensive because she did not want to be the cause of the trading session to go awry. The adventure of being in a Caribou Hunter camp on a trading mission excited her. Harjo's instructions repeated in her memory.

"As we enter a camp and approach a hearth, take off your backpack. The Caribou Hunter will invite me to sit down and I will. But you remain standing behind me some two or three paces. Then, after I tell you, sit down. Keep these things in mind about Caribou Hunter women. They do not sit with men at the hearth and seldom speak unless spoken too. They are treated with little respect and you may be witness to slaps, perhaps a beating. Sit calmly, say nothing, and remain quietly pleasant." Onna promised she would follow his instructions.

They came to a wooded grove surrounding a small clearing. Three conical shaped lodges constructed of long poles and caribou skins lined the edge of the clearing while a smoking, large stone hearth occupied the center. Several smaller hearths smoked near the lodges. The signs of caribou processing were clearly evident including the unmistakable odor that filled the air. Several caribou fawn hides were stretched on wooden frames even as others lay staked out on the ground. Strips of meat hung from drying racks, with one particularly large rack built over a smoking fire.

Presumably, three families occupied the camp, one for each lodge. One man and several women and children were gathered to one side of the camp. Obscured by the foliage but apparently skinning a fawn, the man appeared to be one of the hunters they witnessed killing the caribou. Next to them, several fawns hung by their back legs from pole racks waiting processing. One woman was busy scraping a hide staked to the ground. Next to her, another nursed an infant.

A second man, still wearing an antlered hooded cape, was engaged in whipping a girl in front of one of the lodges. His left buckskin boot-foot was braced on top of a large log with the girl draped over his knee her buckskin frock pulled up over her waist. The man brought a rawhide strap down hard across the girl's buttocks as she cried and kicked her legs.

Dina called out, "Leave that girl alone!" The man stopped whipping her but answered back, "She's a lazy little bitch!"

"They all are," growled Dina, "but we have Mammoth Hunter guest." The man looked over to Harjo and Onna, then pushed the girl off his knee. She got up, pushed her buckskin frock down and grabbing her buttocks, ran into the lodge. The whipping Caribou Hunter walked over, as did the other man.

"My wolf pack and our bitches," laughed Dina who began a somewhat lengthy introduction between the other two hunters and Harjo. As the three men conversed, Onna remained behind Harjo but exposed enough so that she could watch. She noticed Dina's spear point.

It was a type common to Caribou Hunters. Harjo had often described the points and once brought one back from a trading journey. The point was made of bone or antler the length of a man's hand and the size of his middle finger. The top portion was shaved to a flat "spear point" shape. The sides or the foreshaft of the point was grooved with parallel slots on each side. Then, small "flake blades" of chert were inserted within the grooves. Onna noticed the chert was grey in color. The point produces a bloodletting wound. Harjo also informed Onna they use a similar tool or the points themselves to cut grass. Suddenly, Dina's loud voice surprised her.

"Back to work," ordered Dina and the two men returned to processing fawns.

Dina motioned for Harjo to sit. Harjo took off his backpack, retrieved the bag of chert bifaces from the pack, and then sat down with his spear next to him. The hearth was surrounded with caribou skin rugs. As instructed, Onna stood behind Harjo.

"I would like my wife to sit," said Harjo.

Still standing by the hearth, Dina looked at Harjo, up to Onna, then back to Harjo who could detect that Dina was still surprised about Onna but remained seemingly unemotional. He smiled a pleasant smile, then gestured with his hand, "by all means."

Harjo turned around to Onna. "Come sit, Onna! The other two hunters are Dina's brothers. He leads this small family band which includes his brothers, their wives, their children, and some other young ones, somehow related."

Onna picked up her backpack and came to sit next to Harjo with her pack placed behind her. As she sat down, she laid her spear next to her. She remained calm but inside she jumped with excitement. She was in a Caribou Hunter camp and so many questions came to mind, but of course, only Harjo spoke the caribou language and she knew she must follow his instructions. She wished again she knew more Caribou Hunter words.

Dina pulled his atlatl from a buckskin belt he wore around his waist and took off a dart quiver he wore on his back similar to Harjo's. He then sat down on a caribou rug. Onna noticed his atlatl.

It had finger loops of buckskin or rawhide rather than a handle, as did Harjo's. Also, she did not see a foreshaft quiver. Harjo told her Caribou Hunters often use small darts, which are not compounded and made without foreshafts. The points are hafted directly to the smaller shaft. Such darts cannot be reused but are easier to carry.

Dina sat across from them and called out over his shoulder, "Bring us some fresh fawn meat on roasting skewers and some cooked meat!" One of the other men repeated the order and the poor whipped girl quickly emerged from the lodge then hurriedly began to comply with the order.

Again, Dina briefly but intently studied Onna. Harjo could sense Dina's curiosity but the Caribou Hunter remained cautious. "Your bitch seems to be obedient and well-trained Harjo. How often do you whip her?" asked Dina.

Harjo smiled and answered. "More when she was younger but seldom now." Dina nodded his head in agreement accepting the answer.

"Caribou Hunters have dragged travail loaded with hides to trade with the Wind Band when we are summer camped at Wetumka," stated Harjo.

"Do you mean the large camp with a rock shelter between two small streams just west of your Echota River?" asked Dina.

"Yes," Harjo replied, "that same camp. Summer last, Caribou Hunters named Giye and Curliq of the Deg Hit'an Band came on a trading journey."

"I know them as I know all men of the Deg Hit'an Band, but I have not heard late of any Caribou Hunters planning to journey to that camp to trade," stated Dina. "But I have heard from those who have traded there that the Wind Band are fair, generous traders and hosts. They share all but not their women. I have also heard that their interpreter, called Harjo, is a fair trader. It is said he even barters to the benefit of the Caribou Hunters."

"The traders that make the journey deserve at least a slight edge," remarked Harjo.

Again, Dina appeared to agree with Harjo's answer, then moved his head, slightly glancing at Onna as though he might achieve a different perspective of her. Next, he looked backed to Harjo with a curious smile as he spoke.

"Around blazing winter fires, fur traders who have returned from a trading journey with the Wind Band Mammoth Hunters tell stories of a strange woman among them with fair light skin and hair the color of winter grass. They say she comes from far away on the other side of the great western glaciers. They say that she is Harjo's bitch."

Harjo formed the Caribou Hunter's facial expression as to say what he was hearing was true. "What you have heard around winter fires was accurate."

"They also say that Harjo can kill a mammoth without the help of any other hunters. Is this true?" asked Dina wearing a facial expression that told of his sincerity.

"It is," replied Harjo.

"Extremely remarkable," answered Dina still wearing a face of sincerity. "You must tell me how that dangerous task might be accomplished."

"I will," replied Harjo.

As Dina shook his head, seemingly satisfied with the discussion thus far, the whipped girl cautiously approached with food in bowls and raw meat on skewers then stood quietly by. As the two men continued to converse, Onna looked up to see the timid girl was only 10 or 12 summers. She appeared attractive and otherwise healthy but ill groomed as Harjo had foretold of Caribou Hunter appearance. Her knee length frock and knee-high boots were both well sewn and tailored, made from buckskin but lacked any adornments or fringing. She was dirty-her hair had never felt the pull of a comb. She smiled a little smile at Onna who smiled back. Dina waved his hand and she began to distribute the food to each, then ran back toward the lodges.

They each set the skewers up so as to cook on the coals and ate the cooked meat from the bowls. Onna leaned over and whispered into Harjo's ear. "The meat is very good,

Harjo, will you thank him?" As instructed, Onna had thus far remained silent. She was on her best behavior.

"The meat is very good," praised Harjo, "She asked me to thank you."

Dina looked at Onna. "I am very impressed with your bitch, Harjo; would you consider selling her?"

Harjo smiled, "No, she has been with me many seasons."

"I understand you have much invested in her, but I can make it well worth your efforts." Again, Harjo shook his head no.

"Another consideration," said Dina as he rose and called out a name. Harjo watched as again the whipped girl approached the hearth. "Hurry," he yelled, and the girl now ran.

As the girl cautiously came near, Dina took her by the shoulders and turned her toward Harjo. "This little bitch has just attained marriage age. I think she is a virgin. I'll trade you one afternoon delight for another, and I'll throw in a pile of fawn pelts as extra incentive." As he talked, he reached down and pulled her frock up to expose her. "You can take her into a lodge or to the edge of camp and I'll do the same with your bitch."

Uncovered, Harjo and Onna could see the girl was slender built and saw her small patch of black pubic fur. Then, Dina turned her around. "Her butt is already whipped red in preparation if you want to take her in that manner. Is it a trade?"

"No," said Harjo, now sternly. "My wife is dear to me and I will not trade, exchange, or sell her."

"Not even for a pile of fawn pelts?" ask Dina.

"No," repeated Harjo, using a final tone of voice and with no hint of a smile.

Dina let the girl go and waved her off. "Well, I am sure I don't understand you Mammoth Hunters," he exclaimed as he sat back down.

"Tell me, Harjo, it is true your wife comes from the other side of the great glacier to the west?" asked Dina.

"Yes, the glacier we Mammoth Hunters call Koryak.

"Is it then also true, Harjo, you bought her from the strange coastal people who hunt mammals in the ocean?

"Yes, it is," answered Harjo.

"Then, you have seen the Great Ocean?" asked Dina with a hint of excitement.

"That I have," replied Harjo, "and of course, so has she."

"I am amazed and somewhat envious," exclaimed Dina. "I did not know or consider there was anything on the other side of the glacier and presumed it was the end of the world. And now I learn another tribe of strange people live there. I have never met anyone who has seen the Great Ocean and now I meet two and one a woman. I do not want to offend you, Harjo, but I would appreciate moving close to her face and looking into her eyes. I will not touch her."

Harjo paused then turned to Onna. "Dina wants to move close to your face and look into your eyes. He says he will not touch you. Once they give their word, they will not break it."

Onna thought for a moment then responded. "Alright," but she turned around to her backpack and pulled out her knife and held it in her lap.

Harjo nodded his head yes and Dina slowly move around the hearth close to Onna who turned to the side to accommodate him. He glanced at Onna's knife and smiled then slowly moved close to her face.

He first looked up to her hair. "Inexplicable," he whispered, "Her hair is the color of winter grass. I don't know a name for the color." He moved even closer.

Onna could smell him. His breath and odor were strong, not necessarily foul or bad but strong and pungent. She swallowed hard.

"Clear blue eyes," he continued, "the color of the sky, remarkable, simply, remarkable and her lips are beautiful, irresistible. The same as her hair, I don't believe there is as name for the color of her lips."

Dina moved back to his caribou hide. "Luck is surely with you, Harjo, to own such a beautiful, exotic woman. Quiet and obedient and she shows courage as well."

"As I have spoken," said Harjo, "she is dear to me."

Dina shook his head yes in response. "Now to trade. How many prepared fawn skins do you desire?"

"Enough to make her and me a long frock."

"Is that all? Easily done," exclaimed Dina.

He called out again over his shoulder for the whipped girl to bring a pile of prepared hides. While they waited, they ate more cooked meat, tended and turned the skewers of cooking meat while Harjo explained to Onna what had thus far transpired.

The girl approached with two arms loaded with fawn hides and laid them on the ground then stood.

"She may select what she wants," stated Dina.

Harjo translated the words to Onna who, smiling, clasped her knife handle in both hands. Harjo could tell she was resisting an urge to clap. Then, Onna rose and returned her knife to her backpack sheath. She moved her pack off the caribou hide she was sitting on and dragged the hide over to the pile of hides. She motioned for the girl to sit down and she sat as well and began to examine the hides.

Harjo handed the pouch of red chert bifaces to Dina who opened the pouch and took out a biface and examined it. "High quality," he mused, "a very high-grade quality and a beautiful red color. Our tool stone sources are grey."

"Strike one of the bifaces," instructed Harjo.

Dina looked around and found what appeared to be a boiling stone on the ground. Then, holding the biface in the palm of his hand, he struck the edge, dislodging a large flake. "I like the sound," he reported. He examined the biface and the flake and held the flake up to the sun. "This may be the finest material I've ever seen. Where is the source?"

"The Ronoto Hill," responded Harjo pointing northward.

"Will you tell me the location?" asked Dina.

"I will," replied Harjo, "but even with detailed directions, I do not think you could find it, but I will take you there someday."

"You would take me there," pondered Dina. "It is a great source of wealth and you share it with a Caribou Hunter?"

"I would," explained Harjo. "The Father Creator left such resources for all men to use. The wealth lies in bifaces, points, tools, and a man's skill to craft such tools, not in the natural stone. There is an old Mammoth Hunter tale that says-the hide of a mammoth has no value as long as the mammoth wears it."

Dina laughed, "Sound wisdom, Harjo, sound wisdom."

"Keep all the bifaces in exchange for enough skins to sew two frocks," offered Harjo.

"That is more than generous, and you are the one that journeyed," responded Dina.

"I am content," said Harjo.

"Then we have a trade," replied Dina. "And I will take your offer to show me the location of the source of the red chert one of these days, Harjo, and listen while you explain how a hunter might single handedly kill a mammoth."

"Agreed," said Harjo. "You'll find our summer camps due west on western tributaries of the Echota River. If we are not camped at Wetumka, then you will find the Wind

Band to the north." Dina held up one of the bifaces and shook his head in agreement.

Harjo spoke to Onna to inform her a deal had been struck as she and the girl continued to look over the pelts. Then, the shy girl spoke.

"Shut up, bitch, before you feel another whipping!" growled Dina.

Onna spoke up, "Harjo, what did she say?"

"She asked if she could touch you," responded Harjo.

"She may touch me, Harjo; ask Dina if it is alright."

Harjo translated and spoke to Dina, as the girl looked over to him. "Alright, alright," grumbled Dina. He continued to inspect the bifaces then knocked off more flakes.

The shy girl smiled at Onna and began to raise her hand then quickly withdrew it with a frightened expression. "It's alright," said Onna in her calm, soothing voice. Onna slowly reached out and took the girls hand bringing it to her face. The girl smiled again and caressed Onna's face. She reached for Onna's hair and again pulled back. Once more, Onna took her hand and placed it on her hair.

"It's alright, you may touch my hair. Onna sighed, "Poor abused child, you have such a beautiful smile. I wish I could take you home; you're little more than a servant. It is shameful the way you're treated."

Onna now noticed the girl was looking at her breasts. "I know I must seem so strange to you," said Onna in a calm, gentle voice, "but I am the same as any other woman." Again, Onna took the girl's hand and laid it on her breast. The girl sucked in her breath with amazement and gently caressed Onna's breast.

Onna looked over to Harjo. "Harjo, will you tell her I've nursed four babies?"

"Certainly," replied Harjo and he translated.

The girl glowed with amazement. Onna gently took her hand and moved it to her other breast. After the girl gently felt Onna's breast, she withdrew her hands. Onna selected several hides, rose and returned to the hearth. The girl ran back toward the group still preparing hides.

Dina spoke up, "Be sure she has the hides she wants, Harjo. There is another stack of prepared hides near the lodges and she is welcome to search through those as well.

Harjo translated. "These are the hides I want. I am satisfied," said Onna as she began to role the hides up and stow them in her backpack.

Harjo rose. "I believe we'll be off."

Dina likewise rose. "Stay the night," offered Dina.

"No, thank you," answered Harjo. "I want to cover more ground toward the Echota River today. He slipped on his backpack.

Dina walked around the hearth, extending his hand. Harjo took his wrist and Dina followed the same gesture.

"Come visit me, Dina, at Wetumka!"

"I may do just that," Dina replied with a smile. "Take the skewers of meat to eat on your way."

Harjo retrieved the skewers of meat as Onna picked up her spear. She smiled at Harjo and handed him her spear. He took both spears in his left hand and offered Onna the skewers of meat. She accepted the offering and took his hand. They held hands and Onna took a bite of meat as she smiled at Harjo as they began to walk away.

Dina had never seen a man and a woman hold hands in that manner as though they enjoyed it. "Mammoth Hunters are strange creatures," he said to himself.

"She picked up that spear with an air of experience," he called out, "as though she can handle it."

"She can!" called back Harjo over his shoulder.

"What is her name," asked Dina"

"Onna, her name is Onna!"

"Farewell, Harjo and Onna!" shouted Dina.

"Farewell, Dina!" replied Harjo in a loud voice.

"Farewell, Caribou Hunter," called out Onna over her shoulder in the Caribou Hunter language. She smiled at Harjo with that witty little smile of hers and took another bite of the fawn meat.

"Clever little linguist," thought Harjo. He did not recall teaching her those Caribou Hunter words.

Chapter 31:

ORPHANS

White smoke bellowed from a large campfire apparently aided by green limbs and leaves. Presumed as a distress call, Harjo and Onna were sidetracked from their return to Wetumka to investigate the smoke. They approached cautiously, stopped, and slipped off their backpacks. Harjo untied his dart quiver from his backpack and carried it in hand. Then they slowly crawled to the edge of a low ridge that overlooked a small stream and a campsite. They looked down on a gruesome scene.

The encampment had been attacked. Bodies of the fallen victims lay around the camp, stripped of their clothing. Several hide tent shelters were ransacked with the coverings ripped away, leaving only the bare poles with small tattered pieces of attached hides. They could see two figures by the fire.

One was a small child; a boy who sat on the ground by the fire and the other was a woman who appeared to be pregnant. The woman tended the fire then waddled to a pile of wood stacked near the fire and carried back a branch in one hand, throwing it on the flame; all the while she held her other hand over her lower swollen belly.

Onna reached over and touched Harjo's forearm. "Oh, Harjo," she whispered in a low distressed voice. The villagers have been attacked and murdered. But the Enemy Warriors left the pregnant woman and the boy?"

"They are Caribou Hunter victims," answered Harjo. "The pregnant woman and the small boy, if taken, could not keep up on the long march back. Accordingly, the Enemy Raiders left them to take hostage on another day, should they survive."

"Can we help them, Harjo? Please, can we help?"

Harjo did not answer but surveyed the scene and the area without emotion. Onna knew he was formulating a plan, but she also knew he would not put her at risk.

"This could be a trap," replied Harjo, "and we will not walk into it." There was another long quiet pause, then Harjo announced his plan.

"You will stay here. Keep quiet and hidden out of sight. Have some water and jerky. I'll circle the camp on the ridges and high ground and make sure there is no hiding band of Enemy Warriors waiting to ambush anyone who approaches the camp. I'll return here from that direction." He pointed off to the northwest. "You should be able to see me at several points as I circle the camp. Once I return satisfied that no ambush awaits us, we'll go down."

Harjo held up his index finger, so she knew there was more. "If I encounter raiders, I will call out a danger whistle. Once you hear the whistle, you will leave everything but your water and your weapon and you will run back to Wetumka."

Onna sucked in her breath and her face filled with distress. "No, Harjo, don't make me leave you. I cannot leave you if you are in a fight. I could come with you to check for Enemy Warriors."

"No," he replied in a quiet but final voice. "That is the plan. We will follow that plan or we will both sneak away and leave them."

"Please, Harjo, we cannot leave the little boy or the pregnant woman. They will most likely die if we do."

"They will die if we leave them, but I will not jeopardize your life or your capture for their lives."

There was another short but intense silence as Onna tightened her lips in thought and looked skyward. On other occasions, this was one of her charming expressions but now the matter she pondered was deadly serious.

"Alright Harjo, I will wait here. If you sound an alert whistle, I will take the small water pouch, my harpoon, and run back to Wetumka."

Harjo reached out and took Onna's chin with his thumb and forefinger then turned her head to look into her face. "I want to hear a promise."

Onna's face again turned to a distraught expression but she answered. "Yes, I promise."

Harjo smiled and leaned over and kissed her. "Move to a better hiding spot." He began to crawl backwards, and she reached out touching his arm and whispered his name, "Harjo."

He smiled again. "Follow the plan. We will help these two and all will be well." He crawled backward below the ridgeline and slipped his dart quiver over his head. After a quick inventory of his weapons and with spear in hand, he moved off out of sight.

Along with both of their backpacks, Onna moved to a better hiding location to endure a long anxious wait. She remained concealed in the tall grass and rocks on the ridge top, but the woman and child remained in view. The nearby stream provided water and they drank from a water pouch. Once, she watched the boy walk to the stream to fill the pouch. The woman was large with child and Onna thought she was near due. She could hardly move. How could they ever walk back to Wetumka?

She noticed a small gray and black chickadee flittering about with a small bit of food in its beak. It then flew to a nearby small tree with a tiny hole in the trunk. It landed on the side of the trunk as wide beaked baby bird heads emerged from the hole. The parent fed one of the babies then flew away to find more food. Onna was reminded to practice her chickadee call.

On three occasions, she caught a glimpse of Harjo as he made his way around the camp and crossed the small stream at each end of the little valley. He exposed himself to her line of sight to lessen her worry. Finally, he returned.

She heard the whistling song of the chickadee and with relief, answered Harjo with the same bird song. Harjo approached crawling up from behind to lie next to her. She reached over and laid her hand on his and rubbed the side of her head against his shoulder. He petted her hair and kissed her head.

"It does not appear to be an ambush. I think the attackers are long gone. Let's go down."

Harjo retied his dart quiver to his backpack, and they each slipped their packs on to descend the ridge approaching the camp. The smell of death and rotting flesh permeated the air. Onna's face frowned at the repugnant odor. She thought she might vomit but she looked up to Harjo who remained unaffected wearing his usual unemotional expression. She thus fought off the urge to throw up.

The two figures were alerted as they approached but Harjo called out in Caribou Hunter language. "Do not fear! We will not harm you! We are Mammoth Hunters! I am Harjo of the Wind Band!"

To Onna's surprise, the little boy, perhaps this his third summer, came running to her, arms out-stretched. He was crying and repeating one word over and over in such a mournful child voice. Onna got down on her knees as the boy threw himself to her in a tearful embrace.

Harjo reached down and petted Onna's head. "He calls you mother."

The emotional Onna burst out openly in tears and embraced the crying boy. "We will help you, baby, we will help. My poor little child, we will help you."

Harjo stepped up to the pregnant woman who got down on her knees and held up her hands. In tears, she cried out in a desperate pleading voice. "Please help us, Harjo, please help us. I have heard my people talk about you; I know you will help us."

Harjo reached out and took her hands. She was very young, a mere child. Mammoth Hunters remained appalled at the young age Caribou Hunter girls are allowed to become pregnant; little more than babies themselves.

Harjo planted his spear, brought the girl to her feet, then reached down and scooped her up. She was similar to Onna in size and slender in build but huge with child. Onna wiped the tears from her eyes and prepared herself for the task at hand. She knew Harjo had a plan. He turned toward her. Onna could also see the pregnant woman was but a child. The girl clung to Harjo with her head against his chest weeping.

"Can you carry my spear?" Onna nodded her head yes. "Bring the boy," he ordered, "and we'll move away from this stench and death trap."

Onna grasped both her and Harjo's spears in one hand then picked up the boy with the other and followed Harjo. The girl must weigh as much as a frisky mare she thought, but Harjo carried her with little effort. Onna still marveled at his strength even after all these many seasons together.

As they followed the wooded creek downstream, Harjo talked with girl as they moved along. They did not go far. He led them away from the stream to a little grove of several small trees that grew close together in a narrow open area but was nearly surrounded by thick cover. It would provide temporary concealment. Harjo set the girl down and took off his backpack and Onna followed. He pulled out their mammoth jerky and they both came to him as famished wolves. He untied his dart quiver and the caribou bed, then spread the bed by the group of trees.

"They were attacked three days ago. All the men in their family band were killed and the women and children taken hostage. Her husband and the boy's father were killed, his mother taken captive. She is not related to the boy. Most certainly, the Enemy Warriors have gone but we won't take any chances. As you can see, they are hungry. Stay here, stay hidden, and quiet. Feed and comfort them as best you can. Her name is Sanh and she is due any day now. The boy's is Nigeday. I'll return shortly."

Onna shook her head yes and Harjo pulled his dart quiver over his head and left heading back toward the grue-some camp. She noticed he left his spear. He did not forget it but left it on purpose. All these seasons with Harjo had taught her that there was purpose in everything he did.

Harjo was not gone long. He returned packing several of the Caribou Hunters lodge poles, remnant lodge skin covers, and lengths of rawhide rope. He left his spear behind in order to carry the poles. As he approached their secluded spot, he was greeted with a touching scene. Onna set on the ground with her buckskin frock untied and her right breast exposed. The little boy was under her arm nursing as she gently caressed his head. The girl was curled up under her other arm not nursing but perhaps should be. Onna likewise stroked her hair. Although told to be quiet, Onna was gently whispering and singing a song caressing and comforting them both.

Harjo smiled at the touching scene and Onna smiled at him. "They both smell horrid, Harjo, but they are so adorable. I think we have two new children. Or, if you want, a second young wife, this one is very pretty, and she comes ready pregnant."

Harjo laid down his burden smiling. Onna would adopt all the orphans across the whole Mammoth Steppe if he allowed her. He grasped one of the poles and began to cut notches and then broke off a shorter length of pole.

Onna now saw his plan. "Travail?" she asked.

Harjo answered, "Yes."

"I can help, Harjo."

"No," Harjo replied. "Keep doing what you're doing. Keep the orphans fed, quiet, and comforted." Onna nodded in agreement.

Does the girl's name, Sanh, have a Muscogee translation?" she asked.

"Yes, Sanh means summer."

"Oh, that is wonderful. That is what I am going to call her-Summer. And the boy's name?"

Harjo thought for a moment. "Nigeday means hawk."

"There are too many hawks in the Wind Band. We'll keep his name, Nigeday."

Harjo quickly spoke. "We will do our best to save them, Onna, but be sure you understand. I will not sacrifice you for them." His voice was stern and final.

"I understand," she answered and looked at his face so he would know she was serious.

Onna suddenly cried out "Oh," then she reached up and caressed the boy's head. "He sucks so hard," she said smiling up at Harjo.

It did not take Harjo long to manufacture a sturdy travail which included sides, a foot brace, and a front brace which elevated the front end off the ground. He helped "Summer" onto the buckskin bottom of the travail then secured their backpacks and spears onto the sides. Harjo lifted the front braces of the travail and Onna carried Nigeday and they were off across the Mammoth Steppe in a desperate race for life. If the girl delivered before they reached Wetumka, she and the baby would most likely perish. A long difficult journey lay ahead.

Harjo struggled with the weight of the travail. Sweat poured down his face, his breathing was hard. Onna continued to feed Nigeday with masticated mammoth jerky which provided a lighthearted moment. "Harjo, watch," she said as she had a baby size mouthful well chewed. The little boy put his hands on the side of her face and took the food from her mouth as though a big long tender kiss. Then, when he had sucked all the food from her mouth, he smiled, chewed, and bobbled up and down in a happy motion. "Harjo, he is so delightful."

Harjo laughed. "That is truly a hungry kiss."

Once full of meat and Onna's milk, the boy slept. Harjo stopped momentarily so Onna could lay him in the travail with the girl. "I can help pull the travail, Harjo."

"No, just carry yourself." His voice remained stern and completely final.

"I should carry my harpoon and watch our back."

"Yes," Harjo replied just as stern.

"I want to do something to help, Harjo."

"You are helping. Taking care of the orphans is important to their survival. We are not yet out of danger."

"I know," said a quiet Onna. "When we return to Wetumka, the first thing I am going to do is give them both a hot bath with soap. And comb that poor girls' hair," lectured a motherly Onna.

Harjo quietly agreed then lifted the travail and they continued on. With her spear in hand, Onna kept a close watch behind them.

They came upon a safe, comfortable camping location just at dark and stopped for the night, but the weary travelers did not enjoy the camp to its fullest. Harjo built a fire, but they did not brew any tea nor enjoy the flame. The fire was more of a precaution to keep lions at bay. They ate and drank water, and then Harjo instructed Onna to take the two orphans and crawl into the caribou bed. They were all three soon asleep. Harjo guarded the camp. The night was surprisingly warm and gloriously bright. Harjo did not need to take a directional bearing from the North Star, but he easily located it in the brilliant starlit sky. Onna and the two orphans slept soundly. They were exhausted from today's travel. It is well they slept; tomorrow would be more difficult than today.

The beautiful steppe morning beckoned all sleepers to arise as the desperate travelers were up and on the move with little ceremony. Harjo guided them away from the stream and out across the open treeless steppe. He set a grueling pace. He believed if the girl went into labor before they arrived at Wetumka, her chances for survival would be slim. Onna agreed.

Late in the morning, they came upon a family of mammoth and from a safe distance, waited for the herd to pass by. The patriarchal bull was very large, and the herd followed his leisurely pace, grazing along the way. Summer was delighted and got up from the travail to watch. Mammoth are not abundant in caribou land. As they stood watching, Onna held the boy and noticed that Summer put her arm around Harjo. She smiled to herself. She did not say anything nor was she jealous. Under these circumstances, she anticipated the orphaned girl to fall in love with him. She did not blame her.

The herd moved too slowly for an impatient Harjo. He put his hands to the side of his face and made a loud mammoth call. The mammoth responded, especially the bull and at his urging, the herd stopped feeding and pressed on at a quicker pace. Onna was witness to Harjo's clever calls to mammoth on various occasions, enticing them to do his bidding. His trickster calls were always enjoyable. But Summer was overjoyed and laughed out loud. Laughter and joy would benefit the young mother to-be, who had suffered terrible loss and endured such trauma. The mammoth soon passed and when they reached a safe distance, the travelers pressed on.

Summer days are long on the Mammoth Steppe as the sunsets move to the north than west, but now the days were not long enough, and darkness fell too soon. They camped at a poor location with no cover from possible mammoth attack. There was little choice, but most of the mammoth herds now tarried far to the north at their calving grounds. They did build a fire, burning dried mammoth dung and brewed some tea, which helped calm the orphans. Little Nigeday was especially delighted, perhaps his first taste as Caribou Hunters seldom brew tea. Harjo again guarded the camp and again at dawn, with little ritual, they traveled on across the steppe. Wetumka was still too far away.

By midday, sweat dripped from Harjo's face as he silently strained under the travail's burden but at least now they crossed a more level terrain, which Onna presumed, would be to their advantage. Not necessarily so. Harjo suddenly stopped. He recognized the distant thundering sound of heavy footsteps pounding the thick green grass and the loud blowing snorts. Onna also heard the distant clatter but she was not sure of the origin of the clamor.

Harjo quickly looked around but within the immediate area laid only flat tall grass, no rocks, trees or brush, gullies or hills. There was nowhere to escape. Onna looked to Harjo's face as he tightened his lips and frowned in a rare show of emotion. Onna turned to the front and took in a deep breath at the sight of the noise makers-a herd of rhinos which had stopped a mere 30 paces to the front.

Onna had never been this close. She was taken back by their size. She instantly recalled the perils of mating season and the aggressive bulls that joined the female herds. She recalled Harjo's words-the bulls rub their horns on the ground just before they charge.

Such was the dangerous situation at hand because a huge snorting bull charged to the front of the herd. The bull challenged with a deep threatening wulf. He pounded his feet and scrapped the ground in a backward stiff-legged motion with his head and horn held high.

"Move to the rear," ordered Harjo in a whisper as he notched an armed dart into his atlatl.

"No," answered a scared but determined Onna under her breath, clutching her spear. "I stand with you."

"If the bull kills us both in a single charge, the orphans have no chance. One of us may live if we separate. Now, move to the back of the travail and help the girl to her feet.

If he charges, he will first attack me, giving you and the orphans the opportunity to flee to safety-move!"

Onna now obeyed as ordered. Summer was already on her feet and stood holding the boy's hand. The noise from the herd blocked out all other sound-the loud blows, wulfs, and snorts. The bull now scrapped his horn on the ground. A charge was inevitable. Life is often all too short on the Mammoth Steppe.

Then, Harjo put his hand to the side of his face and called out a loud mammoth trumpeting sound. Onna recognized the call as one of a charging bull. Suddenly, to their surprise, the whole rhino herd lifted their horns and snouts, then froze completely still. Only the strident sounds of their wet sniffing and snorting pierced the otherwise calm air. Facing almost certain death, it was as though an eternity had passed, but it could only have been several blinks of the eye. Then, Harjo repeated his loud mammoth call. Unexpectedly, a large female grunted, turned, and ran away from the travail and the four wanderers. The whole herd followed her, leaving the bull alone. Solo he stood, still and frozen with his head and lethal horn held high. Then, just as suddenly, he grunted a loud snorting sound and turned to follow the fleeing herd.

The four figures now stood alone on the vast Mammoth Steppe. The pounding steps of the fleeing rhinos slowly dissipated until there was silence. The stillness was then interrupted by the relieving wind as it blew across the tall grass.

"Oh, Harjo!" cried Onna in a desperate heavy sigh. "I was terribly afraid." She leaned her spear against the travail and came to him wrapping both her arms around him, laughing and crying simultaneously. Onna told herself she belonged to the cleverest hunter across the whole Mammoth Steppe. Summer also came to Harjo in tears of joy and relief, then following Onna, she clutched at Harjo with her arms and laid her head against his chest.

Harjo put his arms over both females as best he could, holding his atlatl and dart. He looked to Onna's smiling face and kissed her. Little Nigeday stood beside them, looking up but not sure what to do. Then, Summer moved from Harjo and reached out and gently took Onna's hands in her two hands and kissed them. She then held Onna's hands to her face and wept. Onna looked to Harjo with a wondering expression.

"She thanks you," said Harjo. "Caribou women kiss in the same manner as Mammoth women do," offered Harjo.

Onna leaned over and gently kissed Summer, who eagerly opened her mouth to accept Onna's kiss and to show her submissiveness. Onna moved to help Summer back onto the travail but Summer spoke.

"She asks if she can walk," reported Harjo. He answered her. "I told her only a short distance, then we must move with haste."

Onna put her arm around Summer who did likewise, and the two women walked together. Little Nigeday spoke up in a loud voice and was pointing. "He wants to pursue the rhinos," reported Harjo. Everyone laughed as they moved on.

Late in the afternoon, Harjo struggled pulling the laden travail at such a crushing pace. He was nearly exhausted but still pushed on. He drank plenty of water but did not eat the meager rations, saving it for Onna, Summer, and the boy. Only on one rare occasion did he allow Onna to help him pull the travail, but she carried the boy as much as she could. Harjo made a simple sling from rawhide strips and Onna carried Nigeday on her back. He enjoyed it. The ever-emotional Onna remained astonished by Harjo's endurance, but she fought back any possible tears, staying focused on the difficult task at hand.

Harjo stopped and they all drank water. Onna assisted Summer up to stand for a while as she drank. Onna was grateful, even with the food shortage, that they had carried ample water.

She reached up and wiped the perspiration from Harjo's brow and looked into his exhausted face. In her memory, she could see the face of that young boy as she first saw him, and he first smiled at her. He was so handsome. Then, so many seasons ago, he saved her life and gave her freedom. More than freedom, he gave her hope. She brushed back his long black hair. Did she see some grey in his hair? He was still handsome, but older. She touched the scar on his face. Again, she smiled because the scar wound was inflicted as he again saved her life. He gave her that same wonderful smile, the same as when they first met, although now he wore a weary smile. He lifted the travail and they pushed on.

Finally, Onna began to recognize the terrain and then with great relief, they reached the Echota River. As might be expected, she reacted with an emotional outburst as she clapped her hands and laughed out loud as they approached the beautiful river at the Second Mammoth Crossing. Onna could have found her way back following the streams and trails but she remained mystified and wondered to herself how Harjo could guide them from the Caribou Hunter camp across the Mammoth Steppe in nearly a straight route to this location on the river so far away-mystified but thankful.

The three figures stood on the river's edge as both Onna and Summer wrapped their arms around Harjo. Nigeday laughed and splashed at play in the shallow clear water. Harjo should be exhausted. Many men would have collapsed long before now from the speed and distance he had pulled the travail with little food or sleep.

But, with a sudden outburst of laughter, Harjo swept Onna off her feet and carried her across the river. She laughed, kicking her legs and with her arms around his neck, she laid her head against his chest. She could hear his great heart beating.

"Harjo, are we really here?"

"Yes," he said smiling, "we are at the Echota River and the Second Mammoth Crossing."

"Thank you, Harjo, for saving them, our two orphans. And you saved us all from the rhinos." She smiled into his face, kissed him, and stroked his long black hair.

"Don't thank me yet, we are still not at Wetumka," he said as he set her down on the opposite side of the river, then turned and waded back across. He then scooped up Summer who likewise kicked her legs and with a few wobbles, he carried the laughing heavy girl across. Instinctively, Summer put her arms around Onna as a daughter would as soon as Harjo set her down.

Harjo returned for the third trip to carry the travail across and for the fourth to collect Nigeday, who all along paid no attention to the river crossing but played on the water's edge.

Harjo surveyed the area and the meadow. It was always prudent to follow the edge of the Wekiwa or the Wetumka streams to avoid an encounter with mammoth in the open meadow. Few mammoth were this far south during the summer. Thus, Harjo led his small band, wife Onna and two orphans, across the open meadow and arrived safely at Wetumka, the summer camp of the Wind Band.

Chapter 32:

BIRTH AND SECOND WIFE

Onna opened her eyes, taking a long leisurely stretch as she yawned then lay silently listening to the peaceful early morning sounds. She heard the robins singing from the trees along the creeks and thought she could just detect the faint sound of the waterfall. With another long stretch, she breathed a deep sigh. She had been on a wonderful trip with Harjo despite the desperate retreat from caribou land. She would long recall this adventure. But still, it was good to be back at Wetumka sleeping in her mammoth bed. She slowly sat up, then looked over to Harjo who lie next to her, sound asleep. On the other side of Harjo lay the pregnant Caribou Hunter girl she called Summer. This was one of the rare mornings she woke before Harjo. It only occurred when Harjo returned from a long trading or hunting trip, completely exhausted. She knew what a light sleeper he was and did not want to wake him. Still, she could not help herself as she reached over to gently caress his face, then leaned down and softly kissed him. He did not stir, deep asleep in the spirit world, but he did move his lips. During their desperate flight to reach Wetumka, he pulled a hastily constructed travail loaded with Summer and often the little boy for three days without food or sleep. She pushed his hair back over his ears. Did he know how grateful she was?

Summer also stirred as she slowly woke. The heavy pregnant girl could not easily rise but managed to roll over, come up to her knees, then sat on the side of her hip. Onna laughed to herself having endured eight pregnancies. Summer smiled at Onna then whispered something in Caribou Hunter language. Onna looked at the girl's face, "What a beautiful smile," she thought. Given the circumstances of their frantic flight, Onna had not actually taken a close look at the girl. Summer was very attractive and Onna thought she resembled the poor abused girl at the caribou fawn hunting camp. Harjo explained that all the groups within that area would most likely belong to the same band, so perhaps the two girls were related.

Again, Summer whispered in her language, looking at her as though asking a question. Then, she reached down, gently touching Harjo on his lips. Onna had an idea what she was saying and asking, so she nodded her head yes. Summer struggled but managed to lean down to softly kiss Harjo. She then reached out and gently took his hand. Onna did not want Summer to wake Harjo but she was also reluctant to stop her, trusting she, too, would not arouse him. She gently brought Harjo's relaxed hand to her face then softly kissed the back. Harjo told her the gesture meant thank you. The gesture held the same meaning for the people of her childhood, the Dyuktai, and the Mammoth Hunters as well. She then held his hand to her face as silent tears flowed from her eyes, down her cheeks, and onto Harjo's hand.

Summer's tears and gesture touched Onna's heart. "Yes," she whispered. "We are both so grateful to him. He is so easy to love, isn't he? I should know." Onna knew Summer could not understand her but continued in a soft low voice. "Do you know he will give all he has for us, his heart, his body, his spirit, and his life?" Summer did not understand but listened to Onna. Then, Summer gently laid Harjo's hand back down on the bed. Exhausted, Harjo did not stir.

Onna rose and quietly came around the bed to help Summer up. "Come along and meet the Wind Band and the rest of my family," she whispered. Little Nigeday was equally exhausted and most likely would sleep most of the morning. "I am so desperate to bathe you-wash your clothes and your hair. Poor child, you are so unkempt! Didn't you have a mother?"

The labor of birthing fell strictly within the domain and supervision of women. When a woman gave birth, all the males who resided within the shelter vacated, except for very young boys who remained under close care of their mothers or other women of the family. An older, experienced woman performed the duties as midwife, generally the mother of the expecting woman's husband. Although, there was usually two or three elderly women within each band who were revered in their knowledge of birthing babies who could be called upon to assist with very serious labor if necessary. Lastly, the Lion Shaman could be summoned in a dire situation. He could cut open the mother in a final act of desperation to save lives, although baby nor mother seldom lived.

The most dangerous, life-threatening event a Mammoth Hunter woman would face throughout her existence was giving birth to a baby. Within the security of her family, her husband, and within the protected confines of each village or camp surrounded by armed hunters and warriors, a woman remained generally safe. Wild animals or even

Enemy Warriors rarely approached a large band encampment close enough to be a threat. Even under the dire circumstance of an Enemy Warrior attack, abduction remained the threat to women and girls but not death.

A young pregnant girl fell under the supervision and care of her husband's mother or the family matron. Even though she may have learned about birthing and had been witness to women of her family giving birth in her father's shelters, it would be the women of her husband's family who insured the girl was well versed in prenatal care and pregnancy. A family matron continued to bestow wisdom on the various stages of pregnancy, the nature of the birthing process, the various breathing exercises utilized during labor, and infant care. The opportunity to prepare young Summer for this life-threatening event would not be realized, nor could it be helped.

Full of mammoth pemmican and still groggy, Harjo made his way to the pool to bathe. He greeted Katchu on his way who congratulated him on rescuing the Caribou Hunter girl. Word must have spread through the band and rightfully so. Such an attack was cause to worry even though it occurred a safe distance from Wetumka and to another tribe.

Harjo was uncertain how long he had slept as he bathed, dressed, and relaxed by the pool. The sound of the waterfall remained soothing. He thought he might fall asleep again as he sat by the pool when he suddenly heard a distant cry of alarm. He looked up to see his sister, Chucuse as she called out his name running toward him.

"Harjo—Harjo, come to the Chokofa Tent-hurry! The caribou girl is having her baby-they want you!" called out a frantic Chucuse.

As Chucuse ran up to Harjo, she took his hand pulling him to his feet. "Hurry-Harjo-hurry!" Distraught and anxious, Chucuse held tight to Harjo's hand, turned and ran as he followed. As they neared the communal tent, Harjo heard the voice of Summer crying and calling out his name. Entering the tent, he saw naked Summer laying on a bed with Us'se and Onna by her side. A worried Ayuko met Harjo, taking his arm. "You must calm her down, Harjo or we are going to lose her!"

Harjo stepped up to Summer then bent down beside her. Upon seeing him, the crying frantic girl held up her hands. "Harjo-Harjo," she cried out! Harjo took her hands and she grasped them with all her strength.

"I am here," he said calmly with confidence. "I will stay with you. Now you must calm down!"

"Harjo-Harjo-help me, Harjo!" cried out a poor frantic Summer in agonizing labor.

Harjo released her hands and to all's surprise, he slapped her hard across her bare shoulder. Summer froze but for an instant, wide eyed.

Harjo took her shoulders in a strong grip and looked sternly into her face. "Now you breathe with me!" Harjo began a breathing exercise. His voice was so commanding, and he spoke with such authority, Summer began to breathe with him.

Harjo did not really know any of the women's breathing exercises used during labor but of course he was aware of them. He recalled Yahola's wife Kak-ke practicing her breathing with Ayuko prior to giving birth but he had hardly paid any attention. With Summer, he just made one up.

But, fortunately, it was successful. Harjo's presence calmed the girl and he persuaded her to breathe, to focus, and the contraction passed. Summer lay calm, she even smiled. Harjo comforted her, kissed her and stayed with her throughout her whole labor. Ayuko and Onna gave Harjo quick lessons on the proper breathing exercises and sequences, which he completed with Summer during each contraction. Ultimately, the baby was born.

Onna was extremely proud of her husband. Harjo surprised all the women by performing so well. So, it seems a man can be a good birthing partner, but of course, he was the only one who could speak Summer's language.

Harjo, as with most men of the Muscogee Tribe, had watched various animals deliver babies but had not been witness to a human baby's birth, even his own children. He admitted it was quite magical.

In the end, Summer fared well. The beautiful shy girl was strong and in three days, had recovered and was up and around. But the baby did not and died in a few days. Both Harjo and Onna surmised the tragedy of the last several days before birth, the mother's lack of food, and perhaps the apparent need of overall prenatal care contributed to the baby's death. Death of a newborn, however, remains common on the Mammoth Steppe.

Harjo buried the unfortunate infant with little ceremony. He carried the small body out from camp alone in one arm and an antler pick in the other. After digging a deep grave, he covered the little body without marker, prayer, or observance.

The other women of the Fus Chate family comforted the young grieving mother, especially Onna. Even though she did not know her language, she cared for her as a loving mother. She made sure Summer ate, held her while she wept, and took her to bed with her and Harjo. "It is not good for a very young mother who has just lost a baby to sleep alone and grieving," insisted Onna.

Summer immediately adopted little Nigeday. He was a clever little boy and fit right into the Fus Chate family charming all, young and old. Adopted by both Onna and Summer, he was overwhelmed with love and affection but also endured the discipline of two mothers. Nigeday and Loni became playmates and as though twins, were together day and night. Cunning Onna, long range little planner, told herself in secret that technically Nigeday and Loni were not brother and sister and thus could marry. In that way, she would not lose Loni to another family and most likely to another band as well.

Even though Nigeday and Loni would not nurse that much longer, Onna and Summer shared milk-feeding duties. Usually, the two little playmates wanted to nurse simultaneously and came running to their two mothers as a pair of baby birds. Often, they would race each trying to reach a nursing mother first.

Harjo explained to Summer that he would take her back to Caribou land, to her band or she could remain with his family as second wife. The choice remained with her. This in itself marveled Summer-that she was allowed to choose, and the decision not forced on her-such was the way of the Caribou Hunters. She considered her circumstance and the two choices.

Everyone in her family was gone. Her husband and father killed, her mother and sister taken captive. Besides, she had received more love, affection, tenderness, and attention in the past several days than in most of her young life with the Caribou Hunters. She had never gone this long without feeling the burning sting of the woman's strap across her bare backside. The generosity of the Mammoth Hunters and the Fus Chate family was a bounteousness she had not experienced.

Moreover, the Caribou Hunter family she would be left with would not be hers. Perhaps the same band but distant relatives at best. She could expect to be treated with little more respect than a servant girl enduring sexual abuse from all the men to include frequent whippings. Summer looked at Harjo and to Onna who stood next to him.

"I want to remain with you and Onna and be your second wife," stated Summer in her soft, childish, but determined voice.

"Make certain you understand," explained Harjo taking on his stern fatherly attitude. "You will be submissive, obedient, and you will respect Onna. Your status will be little more than an older daughter. You will not be a servant girl, but you will work hard every day."

Summer considered the conditions then meekly asked questions. "Will you give me to other men for sex?"

Harjo smiled to himself. He had forgotten she was a Caribou Hunter. "No, I will be the only man you will have sex with," replied Harjo.

"Will I have sex with Onna?" asked a soft voiced Summer.

"You will be obedient and submissive to Onna and you will sleep with Onna and I. When the men are gone hunting or trading, all the women of the family generally sleep together and work out their own sexual affairs with each other."

"Understand," concluded Harjo, "if you are lazy, disrespectful, or disobedient, you will be severely punished."

Summer looked into Harjo's face. She did not speak but smiled and he returned her smile. She knew deep in her heart he would not hurt her. He might, given good cause, take her over his knee to discipline her as if a child or frighten her as he might a little girl, but not to severely punish. She also knew she would endeavor with all her spirit never to give him or Onna cause to punish her. "I want to stay with you as second wife," she answered, and her choice was final.

Harjo described their conversation to Onna and Summer's answer. Ever emotional, Onna reacted as usual with laughter, clapping, and excitement. This was what she had hoped for, and Summer's decision could not be better. She and Harjo had talked over this matter at length. Onna asked desperately if Summer could stay with them as Harjo's second wife. He agreed.

Harjo then reached out and grasped Summer's shoulders. He pulled her to him, and she stepped with his tug. Then he lifted her up so that she was on her toes.

"He is powerful," she thought to herself. "His physical strength and strong character were both frightening but also exciting." He then pulled her to him and kissed her. It was a wondrous feeling. She had kissed him once before but only when he was asleep. Tears began to fill her eyes. She had never experienced such an affectionate people and such gentleness from a man. A man who had saved her and Nigeday from a certain slow death at her devastated camp, carried her on a travail across the whole Mammoth Stepp without food or rest, became her birthing partner and once again saved her from dying on the birthing bed. How could she say no as wife to such an extraordinary man, even as second wife?

After he set her down, Summer reached out, taking his hand, kissed it, then got down on her knees holding his hand to her face. Smiling, Harjo gently helped her to her feet.

Summer then stepped in front of Onna and repeated the same gesture. Tenderhearted Onna reached down, laying her hands on the side of Summer's face then looked over to Harjo. He could see tears swelling in her deep blue eyes.

"Thank you for taking her into our family, Harjo. She will be a good second wife; I feel it deep in my heart."

"I believe you are right," replied the ever-stoic Harjo.

Onna lifted Summer up to her feet and could not resist the impulse to embrace. Then, in her childish, soft voice, Summer spoke to Onna, who looked to Harjo for translation.

"She asks if you will teach her the Mammoth Hunter language," answered Harjo.

Onna smiled and petted Summer's hair. "Yes," she answered in one of the few words she knew in the Caribou Hunter tongue.

The Fus Chate family grew in numbers as the brothers married and their wives bore children-too many to pack into one summer shelter. Yahola and Chilocco with their households slept together in one shelter and Harjo's household in another adjacent shelter. Ayuko generally stayed in Harjo's shelter but often resided with Micco Yarda and Us'se who had been mother as well as matron to Ayuko when she first married Cheparney and bore her first child.

A girl from the Fus Chate family, upon reaching marriage maturity, was highly sought after by men both young and old throughout the Muscogee Tribe and striking Chucuse, more so. The reputation and renowned beauty of her mother preceded young Chucuse. Also, she spoke the Yupik language as did Harjo thus similarly could claim kinship with the Canineqmiut all of which could only prove beneficial to any trading venture with the Sea Mammal Hunters.

Men from all the other bands attended Chucuse's "public announcement" as being eligible for marriage and discussed a bride price with Micco Yarda. Renowned veteran warriors of noted wealth and status inquired as to the price for the hand of Chucuse. Micco Yarda, however, remained careful in his selection. He would not sell Chucuse as a second wife. It was his intention for Chucuse to belong to a young man of distinction from a noted family as first wife. She would, with age and maturity, be the matron of her own household.

The oldest son of the Micco of the Lion Band eventually bought her. The young warrior impressed Micco Yarda with the story of his single-handed kill of a mammoth and a trading venture to Caribou land. He had heard of Harjo's successful trading venture to the Great Sea, contemplating such a venture himself. Chucuse would be well provided for especially as the young warrior remained "heir apparent" as Micco of the Lion Band. Other members of the Fus Chate also whispered into Micco Yarda's ear that this tall handsome warrior was more than suitable.

A long beautiful late summer day came to an end as the gorgeous sunset filled the sky with a blush of color inspiring the male robins to lift their voices and bid the sun farewell. Off in the distance, the wolves howled to summon the entire pack to an evening kill. Meanwhile, the Fus Chate family enjoyed a late meal at the family hearth by their shelters. Other Wind Band families gathered in front of the Chokofa Tent and the Square Hearth as they did every evening. Although Micco Yarda and Us'se usually ate at the Square Hearth, this evening they dined with the family and Micco Yarda spoke with Harjo, Yahola, and Chilocco about the need for a mammoth kill, soon. Onna had grown wiser at concealing her anxieties. The Wind Band was fortunate as many brave and skilled warriors and hunters filled its ranks, but her Harjo always seemed to be in the forefront of any dangerous venture. To her, it seemed he was always one of the first to risk his life.

As the children began to fall asleep around the fire, the households retired to their own shelters. Ayuko carried a sleeping Fus to spend the night with Micco Yarda and Us'se.

The last of the daylight filtered through the top poles of their lodge to allow vision. Onna went to Chate and Echo who lay sound asleep in bed, exhausted from playing the Fox Chase game all day. She laughed to herself as she drew a buckskin blanket over their dirty bare feet and smelly little bodies. "When boys prepare for bed," she whispered, "they really don't do anything, they just go to bed as they are." She wanted to kiss them but settled for just petting their heads. She would send them to the bathing pool tomorrow.

Harjo lay naked on his back in their bed under fur blankets with his hands behind his head. Summer sat on his left side nursing both Nigeday and Loni. Onna came to their bed, then removed her buckskin frock and boots, hanging them up on the lodge poles with the other clothing. She then relieved Summer the burden of one nursing child as she took Loni and carried her to the other side of Harjo and sat down on the bed. Loni fussed only long enough to find another nipple, then again nursed in comfort drifting off to a deep sleep.

When both toddlers were asleep, Summer and Onna laid them on each side having wrapped them in buckskin diapers stuffed with grass or grass pads, then they snuggled to each side of Harjo braced on their elbows. Onna reached down and tenderly touched the side of his chin and turned his head toward her then lowered to him, giving him a long passionate kiss. Instinctively, he penetrated her open mouth with his moist rigid tongue. When she finished, Summer followed the same gesture and as she kissed Harjo, Onna reached out, combing Summer's hair back over her ear. When Summer finished kissing Harjo, she smiled at him as she caressed his chin with gentle fingertips, then she looked over to Onna, continuing to smile. All the while Onna kept her hand on the back of Summer's neck then gently, but with determination, pulled Summer to her, giving her an equally passionate kiss.

Content and smiling, Onna and Summer snuggled up under Harjo's armpits. They each slid a hand down his chest and with locked fingers gently grasped his now erect manhood and testicles. Harjo raised his hands over his head in a stretching motion then wrapped each arm around Onna and Summer. Soon the three drifted off to a deep sleep walking the mysterious domain of the spirit world. Each one was content with this day's outcome and eager to experience what the Mammoth Steppe offered tomorrow.

Part Six

PAST AND FUTURE

Onna looked up into her abductor's sneering face and stared as deep as she could into his eyes. Then, in a low, mystical whisper she replied. "You are wrong-dead wrong. One man will come for me, the man who loves me. He is a strong, fierce warrior-he is brother to the wind."

Chapter 33:

WINTER JOURNEY

S imilar to their summer shelter, one single winter mammoth lodge was no longer of adequate size for the growing Fus Chate family. Even though Cheparney's family lodge was larger than most lodges, as the three brothers became men, took wives, and had children of their own, the family constructed a second mammoth lodge. Yahola and Chilocco moved into the new lodge while Harjo remained with his family in Cheparney's old mammoth dwelling. Although she had spent so many winter seasons in the Cheparney's family lodge, widowed Ayuko was content to move around. Generally, she stayed with either Harjo or Yahola and Chilocco but would also spend many days with Micco Yarda and Us'se. Eventually a third lodge would be required as life continued on and the family prospered-grandchildren grew to adult men who took wives, who in turn had their own children.

Onna tightly held her hands to her breasts against her full-length parka and unsuccessfully tried to hide her anxiety.

On every occasion the hunters in her family ventured out from their villages, her worry and emotions surfaced.

"It was so clear and cold last night I saw a wondrous display of the mystic lights-oh, such a deep green color." She paused and sniffed her nose becoming teary eyed. "The lights offer a good omen for your trading journey." Three of her hunters stood in front of her in winter dress with their parkas and pants turned fur side in-ready to depart.

Onna stepped in front of Nigeday, her adopted Caribou Hunter son who had turned 11 last summer and now was nearly as tall as she. Smiling, she pushed his hood back with both hands then brushed his hair. "Now, be a good boy, Nigeday," she ordered, "and pay close attention to everything around you."

"I will," he answered glowing with his charming smile.

She kissed him on both cheeks as he closed his eyes tight. He had already endured kisses and embraces from sister Loni, who was his same age, and his second mother Summer. He was completely adorable. Females in his family took every opportunity to shower kisses on him as did women throughout the whole Wind Band. "Don't you dare stay with those Caribou Hunters, Nigeday, you return home, understand!" she warned.

"I will," he repeated still smiling.

Onna now stepped in front of son Echo, who at 16 summers, had completed his Rite-of-Passage journey last summer and joined the world of the other adult males of the Wind Band. She likewise brushed his hair back and kissed him as he returned her kiss. She spoke Dyuktai. "I am so proud you are a man now and eligible for marriage Echo, but don't bring back a Caribou Hunter girl. Now promise your mother."

"I promise I won't, mother," he answered smiling because he had not considered marriage with a Caribou

Hunter girl although this trip would provide the perfect opportunity to investigate that proposition.

"Be so very careful, Echo." She whispered becoming more emotional, "and stay alert to all things around you."

"I will," he answered still smiling.

Onna now stepped to Harjo. She looked up into his face then gently reached up caressing her fingertips along the length of the scar on his face then nervously adjusted his parka. "You will sleep with a Caribou Hunter woman?"

"I don't know, probably," he answered. "You know their custom of hospitality and that it would offend them to do otherwise if offered. But you also know how strange and unpredictable they are."

Onna looked over to the two boys. "I presume you will all sleep with Caribou Hunter females." Her two young and inexperienced sons stood quiet not exactly sure of her meaning or how to answer.

"Probably so," responded Harjo.

Onna again looked to Harjo's face as she fussed with his parka. "I hope she smells, has bad breath, and becomes pregnant," she smirked.

"So do I," responded Harjo with a partial smile.

"I'll need to give each of you a hot winter bath when you return," said Onna trying to laugh but beginning to cry. "And while I have you naked, I should give each of you a good switching!"

Harjo reached out and pulled Onna to him and kissed her full on the mouth, then wrapped his arms around her and held her. "Come back to me, Harjo and bring our boys with you" she whispered with her head against his chest.

"I will," he replied with a gentle smile.

The three departing hunters had already bid farewell to the rest of the family in the mammoth lodge. Chate stood by his new wife, Hokte, who was pregnant and sister

Loni stood with Summer who held a baby-her two toddlers remained asleep in bed. At 14 summers of age, Fus was mildly disappointed as he had hoped to accompany his father on the winter trading journey, but he also realized Nigeday deserved his first opportunity. Besides, he would accompany Chate on several winter caribou hunts that promised to be equally exciting.

"Outside boys before we start to sweat inside these parkas." Harjo pulled the front of his parka repeatedly to create a draft against his chest. Fus stepped up to Echo and Nigeday for a final farewell using their silly hand gestures.

"Harjo!" called out Onna. "Remember, Harjo, please, if you come across any abandoned children, don't leave them, bring them back."

Harjo shook his head yes, "I will." And with that, the three hunters collected their weapons and departed through the mammoth lodge tunnel.

The remaining family members gathered around Onna. Summer moved next to her, still holding her baby and put her head on Onna's shoulders and Loni followed, standing next to Summer with her arm around her waist. Fus moved to Onna's other side as she put her arm around his waist. She noticed he was now taller than she was. Chate came to Onna and gently kissed her. "All will be well, mother," he said in Dyuktai. Onna wiped the tears from her eyes, found a partial smile, and shook her head in agreement.

Two sleds awaited in their mammoth lodge entry room. Harjo secured his spear in the tie downs of one sled loaded with mammoth pelts and took its harness while Echo grabbed the harness of the other sled packed with supplies. Nigeday would push one or the other sled as needed.

"Now, don't just ride on the sled runner, Nigeday," joked Echo, "be sure you push the sled!"

"Hey," called out Nigeday, "That is a good idea, I didn't think of that. I could just ride on the runner and you could pull me all the way to caribou land!" Both boys laughed out loud, excited to finally be underway.

Willow and alder grew in abundance forming vast thickets in the low flood plains east of the confluence of the Echota and Big Rivers at the Mammoth Hunter's winter village of Coweta. West of the convergence, however, in the Backbone Mountains, the higher elevations and rocky terrain suppressed the spread of the tickets. Not only were the willow/alder thickets difficult, if not impossible barriers to cross, but they were equally dangerous. Mammoth herds wintered along the thickets, and deadly encounters would be unavoidable.

The Great Caribou Herd likewise wintered along Big River but east of the willow/alder thickets. Consequently, an indirect route to the Caribou Hunter land following the edge of the immense thickets was the wisest and most prudent path even though it was the longest.

The three Mammoth Hunters pulled sleds in a single file. Harjo went first with the heavier sled loaded with mammoth pelts while Nigeday usually pushed this first sled. Echo followed behind with the second sled of supplies. Harjo stopped every so often to catch their breath and survey the circular horizon. When he did, Echo pulled up alongside.

"Father tell us again. Where will the Caribou Hunters be camped?" asked Echo.

Harjo looked over at his son's bright flushed face and smiled. "I have a good idea, but you never know for certain. Their winter camps are near the caribou winter-feeding grounds but those change from winter to winter. But boys, that is part of the adventure of trading with the Caribou Hunters-locating their camps."

"What is the name of the Caribou Hunter or a certain group of hunters we hope to find?" continued the curious Echo.

"We will explore the region utilized by the Deg Hit'an Band. I have traded with many of them over the seasons. But we will seek a certain chieftain named Nigighun. I know him by reputation only, but I hope we are able to establish a long-term trading relationship with him."

"I was from the Deg Hit'an Band," stated Nigeday. "Will they recognize me, Father?"

"No, you were just a baby then. But you both remember our discussions of how we will keep Nigeday's birth to ourselves?" reminded Harjo in a fatherly tone.

Nigeday and Echo shook their heads yes. Then, with a jubilant reaction, broad smiles and their breath blowing cold frozen air, the trio leaned into the sleds and continued their adventure.

Harjo planned the winter trading journey well in advance. It began late in the fall when he successfully killed an autumn mammoth. That hide provided the pelts for this trading venture and the meat would provide food for the whole band nearly all winter. The Wind Band completed fall migration and set up winter camp at Coweta.

Each fall, the various bands of Caribou Hunters organized their large fall drives and hunts as the caribou herds struggled with fall migration. Once the numerous hides were cured and the meat preserved, several bands would also complete their fall migrations to erect winter camps along the upper Big River and its other tributaries.

Early winter provided the optimum season to negotiate trade with the Caribou Hunters who were now wealthy with tall stacks of caribou pelts and deep caches full of meat.

Later into the winter, as the stockpiled resources dwindled, they would be less reluctant to trade. Once the Echota River froze and the ice could be safely crossed, the early winter season became ripe for the journey.

The trio stopped for a rest. Suddenly, Harjo pointed off to the distance. "A pack of wolves are having a meal-it appears to be a caribou." The boys looked on as a pack of five to seven wolves devoured the caribou unaware they were being watched.

"I wonder if the wolves killed the caribou or found it dead?" asked Nigeday.

"There is no way to know," answered Echo.

"Many caribou," added Harjo, "the weak and young, die during the winter as do other animals. It was likely killed by the cold. Winter is a hard season for the caribou but an easy one for the wolves."

The two boys called out a wolf howl which caused the wolves to stir and return the howls. They looked at each other smiling, then gave the other a silly hand gesture. Harjo smiled, shaking his head, then pulled his sled on, but he would admit that he could not distinguish the boy's howls from the wolves.

The three figures pulled their sleds across a narrow stream nearly frozen solid then up its steep embankment. The stream, along with an adjacent ancient deep channel, formed a steep hillock. No mammoth could easily ascend the steep banks thus it created an ideal camping location. Harjo used this campsite on several occasions over many past seasons, first stopping here as a boy when he and his bothers journeyed with Cheparney.

On top the natural mound, four medium-size trees grew in the shape of a square. Four horizontal poles were attached to the trees, forming a square that could support a cover of buckskin to create a shelter top or sides if necessary. A large log lay across the back of the shelter.

Bull mammoth often vent their frustrations on trees by pushing them over or breaking them off then smashing the limbs. The log was the result of one such bull's frustrations, which lay broken and virtually de-limbed near the campsite. Harjo and his brothers, including young Chate, dragged the log up the hillock to serve as a backside windbreak. Trees that suffered attacks by irritated bull mammoths also provided convenient firewood, as did this tree.

The three Mammoth Hunters pulled the two sleds, one to each side of the trees, to help form the sides of the shelter. A large piece of sewn buckskin covered the top and portions of the shelter sides.

After clearing the ground of snow in and around the shelter, and with the addition of a roaring fire burning in the hearth situated at the open shelter's end, the Mammoth Hunters were now afforded a comfortable camp. The trio would sleep together in a mammoth bed actually sewn to accommodate two but little Nigeday could easily squeeze between Harjo and Echo. They sat around the large fire enjoying pemmican, hot tea, and each other's company. Overhead, the Northern Lights provided a spectacular display.

"No matter how often I see the Mystic Lights," declared Harjo in a quiet voice, "each moment is always inspiring." Harjo raised his hand, "Listen, you will be able to hear the lights."

The two boys also stared up into the otherwise dark sky illuminated by the fascinating and mysterious green spectral of lights. "The lights make the sound of a fire crackling," remarked Nigeday in a whisper.

"Do you know what causes the Mystic Lights, Father?" inquired Echo.

"No, son, I don't."

"Does the Lion Shaman?"

Harjo smiled. "I don't think anyone knows the cause of the Mystic Lights," he explained, "but I will tell you what I know." He paused briefly then continued. "Usually the lights are a greenish color as now but occasionally the lights reflect a reddish-bluish hue. Usually the lights are visible in winter, especially when it is very cold, but I have also witnessed the lights in summer."

"In summer?" questioned Nigeday.

"Yes, during the summer. Many believe the lights are caused by the cold. I am not so sure. I think their visibility is related to the dark. I think the lights may be present during the summer or all the seasons, but we do not see them because the sky is so light. Also, the lights may be visible during the summer when it is dark but then most people are asleep and for that reason, they do not see them."

Both boys looked at each other and shook their heads in agreement but the display still caused an eerie feeling in their young hearts. "Do the lights predict good or bad luck?" asked Echo.

Harjo smiled again. "Neither. Your mother tends to think such phenomena, especially the Mystic Lights, reflect a good or bad omen. I do not believe so. The lights are a gift from the Father Creator-beautiful-fascinating to behold. I believe the sun somehow creates the lights. Remember, although it is dark here where we are, but somewhere far to the east or to the west, the sun shines on the Mammoth Steppe."

The boys seemed content with their father's answers but remained as curious as their mother. "How will we find this Caribou Hunter chieftain called Nigighun, Father?" asked Echo.

"We will make our way to a certain small stream. I believe he will be camped there. Caribou Hunters will certainly set up winter villages on that stream so if he is not there, others will be. They will likely know the location of Nigighun's winter camp and will tell us. Then we will decide if it is worth our effort to find him or trade with the other Caribou Hunter families along that drainage."

Again, the two boys looked at each other in agreement and were also pleased they were included in the decision making and thus not only considered sons but also partners with their father on this trading venture.

"I am glad I got to come with you, Father, on this adventure," said a thankful Nigeday, his handsome face and smile all aglow.

Harjo grinned. "I enjoyed my first journey to the Caribou Hunter territory as a boy with your grandfather Cheparney," related Harjo. "He taught me the best route from Coweta was to follow the Echota River north along the fall/spring migration trails. Then, cross the Echota heading east along the edge of the willow/alder thickets and the open steppe. The thickets narrowed ascending Big River and thus the path gradually turns southeast eventually intersecting the river. Winter camps of the Caribou Hunters can be found in that area along the several southward flowing small tributaries of the Big River."

Echo and Nigeday quietly listened.

"Once the Caribou Hunters have completed their fall caribou drives and hunts, they establish their winter settlements with sled loads of treated caribou skins and caches full of meat and pemmican. This is the season to trade with them before the woman began to utilize the hides as clothing and lodge covers and before they consume all of their food supply."

"But your grandfather also taught me," continued Harjo, "that the other side of winter travel provides its own unique hazards and limitations, cold being the most obvious winter challenge but limited sunlight being the other. Nearly all winter days are clear and bright but short lived thus travel distance is likewise short. Waiting in camp for the sunlight is often the most difficult challenge. If the moon is full, then night travel is possible but more of a desperate decision than a wise one."

"Father?" asked an inquisitive Echo, his thoughts now turned to a more romantic subject. "I know I am now a man, but I have not thought very much about marriage, so maybe I should. But mother warned me not to bring home a Caribou Hunter girl. I've certainly not considered a Caribou girl, but could I marry one?"

Harjo could not help smile while Nigeday spoke right up. "I'll help you learn Caribou Hunter language, Echo, it's not that hard!"

"Thanks, Nigeday," said Echo, "maybe I should learn more of the language."

"Your mother was just emotional, Echo; she worries so much about us all. If you like, I can tell you what I know about Caribou Hunter marriage."

"Yes, Father, do," replied Echo.

"Yeah," spoke up Nigeday, "Maybe I'll marry a Caribou Hunter girl too!"

Harjo chuckled then started his story. "Marriage among Caribou Hunters is very strange to us. It institutes a unique twist, which in turn forms unusual family memberships. The young man seeking a wife leaves his family and moves into the household of his bride-to-be. There he resides hunting for the family of his intended throughout a full cycle usually summer to summer. All that he kills belongs to them. This long stay constitutes his bride price. Once the cycle is completed, the price is paid, and the wife belongs to him. The young hunters, however, will often remain with his wife's family. He fathers children and may abide with his wife's family indefinitely, then ultimately start a household of his own."

Echo and Nigeday looked at each other frowning as they considered this strange marriage custom. Harjo allowed a moment for that first thought to sink in. "Consequently," he continued, "a common Caribou Hunter household includes the hunter, his wife or wives, their younger children, the parents of the wife, and the grown daughters including their husbands and children. But boys, also consider that Caribou Hunters are endless travelers and wanderers because they follow the caribou herds. Socially they organize into loose family groups. A single-family unit, in particular a young hunter, his wife and children, may move in and out of several bands or extended family groups from season to season. A Caribou Hunter family is not necessarily a stable unit."

"So, if I wanted to marry a Caribou Hunter girl, I would be expected to live with her family and hunt for them?" asked Echo.

"Yes," answered Harjo, "but of course, there are unusual circumstance such as those that brought Summer and Nigeday into our household."

"What would happen," continued Echo, "if I just approached a Caribou Hunter father and offered a certain price for his daughter, would he accept?"

"I am not sure, Echo, probably not. It is more than just price; it is part of their customs and those sink deep into a people and are often difficult paths to stray from. And to make matters more complicated, if a Caribou Hunter husband dies, a brother takes over the husband's responsibilities and the widow, at least for a while, becomes his wife. I am not sure of all the possibilities, but I have been told this whole situation can become complex."

Echo and Nigeday again looked at each other frowning. "Too much trouble, and just for a wife," concluded Nigeday. The three Mammoth Hunters agreed.

"Father, will you tell us about the Caribou Hunter settlements?" asked an excited Echo. "I know you have before but will you again?"

"Alright," responded Harjo, also realizing the dark period remained long, often boring, especially for youngsters.

"I've seen plenty of Caribou Hunter settlements," boasted a childish grinning Nigeday.

Echo reached over and pushed him on the head. "You're so silly, Nigeday; you were just a baby then."

"I know, but I still saw them," laughed Nigeday.

Harjo chuckled and shook his head. "Caribou Hunters reside in mobile tents throughout all seasons including winter. Their basic shelter consists of a conical shaped tent constructed of wooden poles and caribou skins. The shelters range from a simple single unit housing with only one or two adults to a complex unit constructed of several large and small single units interconnected by various forms of entry rooms and tunnels."

"The poles that form a basic lodge are some four to six paces long. First, snow is cleared from the area. Then, the ends of the poles are set on the ground in a circle with the opposite ends joined and tied at the top with babiche thus forming a conical shape. The poles are then covered with caribou skins cut and sewn together in a form that best fits the conical shape."

"I do remember the lodges had the caribou fur left on," recalled Nigeday.

"Yes," answered Harjo. "Summer lodges are often covered with buckskin, but the pelage is left on the hides that cover winter lodges consisting of an inner and outer layer."

"The outer cover is laid over the poles fur side out, reaching from the ground to the top of the poles. A circle of rocks holds the cover to the ground. The bottom edge is also banked with snow and often piled to waist high or higher. The inside cover is stretched and tied to the poles inside the lodge with the fur side facing the inside of the lodge. It does not necessarily reach the top of the lodge but is at least head high. Finally, a circle of rocks in the center of the lodge serves as a hearth and fire while the top opening allows smoke to escape. Similar to a parka, the double layer adds insulation so that the lodges remain quite warm."

"Willow branches, occasionally woven into loose mats, surround the hearth over laid with piles of grass then are covered with caribou skin provide seating around the hearth. More willow branches, overlaid with thick piles of grass, are laid around the edge of the lodge as beds, which are then covered with thick winter caribou pelts. Finally, weapons, tools, and other utensils are hung from the poles. Many Caribou Hunters, especially elderly men, use back rests similar to Mammoth Hunters elders."

"I remember," said Echo, "you once brought home those strange knives and spear points the Caribou Hunters use and they cut grass with those knives." Harjo smiled in remembrance.

"But they don't use those spear points manufactured with little flakes of chert for darts, do they Father?" asked Echo.

"No, they don't Echo. For their darts, they use small points attached directly to the dart shaft without a foreshaft. Perhaps those types of darts are more efficient for smaller game such as caribou and antelope, but less so when facing a mammoth."

"Tell us more about their settlements, Father, and maybe the type we will stay in," asked a now eager Nigeday.

"Alright," answered Harjo. "A more prosperous or rich Caribou Hunter will own three perhaps four winter lodges all interconnected by an entryway tent. A typical two-sided tent is about head high but usually only covered with a single layer of hide. The entry way is also used as storage for firewood and sleds."

"One of the more unusual features of a settlement is the cache pit. It is a simple rock lined square pit of various sizes as required. The bottoms and tops are also lined with rocks, especially large flat types as large as they might find and carry. Food, of course, is stored in the pit then it is covered with a small conical lodge. Not as elaborate as a winter lodge, more similar to a summer shelter."

"You both know," continued Harjo, "lions are the menace of food caches. Even those sturdy rock-lined Caribou Hunter caches will eventually be dug up by lions if left unguarded. You also know that lions are excellent climbers and they can take caches tied in trees and fixed on babiche lines. The same as our settlements, lions are leery of the Caribou Hunter lodges and will not enter one. But, of course, they will occasionally stalk near a settlement hoping to catch a lone child or a woman who has wandered away too far."

"Father?" asked a humble Echo. "We have often heard mother tell the story of how you killed a lion when you were just my age. You never talk about it."

"No," replied a modest Harjo. "Your mother is a good storyteller."

"I don't think I could kill a lion. I would be afraid," spoke up an honest young Nigeday.

Harjo admired his son's honesty. "Your mother killed a caribou when she was your age. Can you kill a caribou?"

Nigeday shook his head to say yes.

"Then you can kill a lion. Remember, both of you. Fear will give you strength and help you sink your dart into a lion's chest." There was a short pause as the boys considered this wisdom. "Well, are you boys ready for bed? I am. We will take the first daylight tomorrow to practice with our weapons, making sure we have our winter throwing arms."

Both boys quietly realized that fortune had certainly smiled on them to be the children of such remarkable parents. The three adventurers made ready for a cold winter's night but a warm deep sleep. Tomorrow promised to be another hard, chilly journey with more to follow.

Chapter 34:

CARIBOU HUNTER TRADING

The sun showed bright through a clear blue sky reflecting off the blanket of shallow dry snow as the three Mammoth Hunters pulled their two sleds along a small riparian stream through an open meadow when a small caribou herd brought them to a stop. The hefty antlers of the larger bucks had shed by now but the slighter does still retained their small antlers into the spring.

"With no antlers, it's hard to tell the bucks from the does," noted Nigeday. The others agreed.

"Look! Look!" pointed Echo. "They chew the antlers that are still on the other heads. I thought they only chewed the antlers after they fall off."

Echo and Nigeday looked at each other with surprise, then looked to their father. "Oh, yes," said Harjo, "it's very strange to witness. We find the gnawed antlers on the ground, so we presume they were gnawed after shedding. They usually are, but occasionally the antlers are chewed still attached. I've noticed it is usually the does chewing on the antlers of other young does, perhaps their own fawns."

The herd took to their hoofs and scampered across the drainage. The boys were delighted at this new experience and so the three Mammoth Hunters trudged on.

Even though the trees and underbrush were barren of foliage throughout this small wooded drainage, visibility remained difficult as the sunlight, bright snow, tree trunks, underbrush, and dark shadows all mingled and mixed into visual deceptions. Suddenly, Harjo stopped, and his two young companions followed. Ahead of them, off in a distance of less than 30 paces, a human figure stood but remained ignorant of their presence. The standing figure presented his back to them.

"It's a Caribou Hunter," related Harjo quietly.

"How can you tell, Father?" asked Echo in a whisper.

"He wears a hat with ear muffs rather than a hood, a subtle but distinctive difference."

"Oh yeah," replied Echo, now recalling a lesson delivered by his father just before they departed.

Standing next to him and smiling, Nigeday pointed to his head with his mitten hand, moving his hand back and forth, then in a circle. Echo reached up to tap Nigeday on his hooded head, likewise with a mitten hand and smiling.

"Seriousness is now required," related Harjo in a stern yet whispered voice, although he could not help but chuckle to himself over their silly boyish antics.

The figure turned and now saw the trio. Harjo called out, "I see you are a Caribou Hunter!"

The figure remained still but answered. "That is correct, Mammoth Hunter. How is it you speak our language?"

"I am Harjo of the Wind Band of Muscogee Mammoth Hunters. I seek Nigighun of the Deg Hit'an Band. We have come to trade!"

"You have found him, Harjo," related Nigighun with great enthusiasm. "Your reputation precedes you, Harjo," he exclaimed as he approached Harjo and his sons, "and I welcome trade."

Nigighun walked straight up to Harjo with a broad grin extending his hand. "By the looks of your sled, Harjo, mammoth are still plentiful in the Echota Valley."

Harjo reached out, taking Nigighun hand with a firm shake. "Not as abundant as when I was a boy but still plentiful and mean," he replied. "And how was the caribou migration this season?" asked an enthusiastic Harjo.

"The best in my memory," responded an equally enthusiastic Nigighun. "We killed and dressed more caribou this fall than in any I can recall."

"Splendid," said Harjo. "These are two of my sons, Echo, the oldest and Nigeday."

Echo extended his hand and greeted Nigighun in the Caribou Hunter language followed by Nigeday who spoke several words as he shook Nigighun hands.

Nigighun looked at Harjo. "They speak Caribou Hunter well, Harjo. I am impressed. Come, my lodges are near."

The three Mammoth Hunters pulled their sleds and followed Nigighun. "It's been cold this winter, Harjo, and I think it will be colder."

"I believe you're right," replied Harjo.

"If you desire any winter pelts, this would be the season to take them. The caribou fur has never been this thick, at least in my memory, and I've noticed an abundance of white fur in the caribou this winter. I have only fall pelts to trade."

"Fall pelts are what we seek but if the opportunity presents itself, we may take a winter caribou or two."

They followed Nigighun along the wide trail and stopped on the edge of a small clearing. Across the other side of the clearing, the three Mammoth Hunters could see a Caribou Hunter winter settlement. Suddenly, Nigighun pointed to fresh tracks in the snow and all looked. Harjo looked at the Caribou Hunter. "Lion," exclaimed Harjo with a scowl, "the size of tracks show me it's a male."

Nigighun agreed. "Two or three stalk our camps each winter. This one is the first. We will need to deal with him straight away." With serious expressions, Echo and Nigeday surveyed the circular horizon.

"Perhaps the addition of three hunters at your camp may encourage the lion to move on," offered Harjo. Nigighun agreed and the group moved across the meadow to the lodges.

They arrived at the complex of three tall conical-shaped tent lodges all interconnected with a low triangular-shaped tent. Several other caribou lodges were visible in the distance, also situated on the edge of the meadow. Harjo was very familiar with a common Caribou Hunter winter settlement, but his two sons looked around observing and learning the landscape with excited faces.

The complexity of Nigighun's residence pointed to his wealth and standing. The three conical-shaped lodges were erected in a row. The first lodge was large and appeared to be the main living quarters. The second center lodge was smaller than the other two and Harjo recognized it as a cache lodge. The third appeared to be a smaller living and sleeping quarters. A low "head high" entry tent interconnected the three lodges. With Nigihun in the lead, the three traders pulled their sleds past a large hearth outside the entry tent as they stored their supply sled in the entryway then pushed the sled loaded with mammoth pelts into the main lodge against the left sidewall.

Inside, the lodge was large, spacious, and warm. Bright sunlight shown down through the top and live coals burned in the hearth in the center of the lodge. Two women sat by the hearth sewing, both adults but one older and one younger. They both looked up with open mouths and faces filled with surprise at the sight of the three strangers.

Nigighun looked around. "Where is Yixgitsiy?" he asked sternly.

"She has gone out for firewood," replied the older woman, now even more perplexed by the question.

"Anyone else outside?" he asked still in a rough voice.

"No," again the older woman made an anxious reply. "She is the only one."

"A lion is near the settlement. Make sure everyone stays inside. I'll go bring her back," said Nigighun as he headed back toward the entry.

"I'll follow along," said Harjo as he likewise stepped for the entry. Echo and Nigeday followed. "Stay alert and ready," exclaimed Harjo as he addressed his two sons over his shoulder.

Outside, Nigighun pulled a dart from his quiver and loaded it in his atlatl. As he did, he called out the name, "Yixgitsiy!" The three Mammoth Hunters also loaded darts. Nigighun called again and in the distance, they heard a slight "yes" reply. He jogged off toward the answer and Harjo and his two sons followed with weapons in hand.

Yixgitsiy was not very far away and the four hunters soon ran up to her. The three Mammoth Hunters could now recognize Yixgitsiy as a small girl, younger than Nigeday. She stood with an arm load of firewood. "What is it, Father?" she asked.

"Fresh lion tracks are close to the lodges," replied Nigighun.

The girl's eyes grew wide and she opened her mouth with an "oh" sound. All four hunters continued to visually scan the area. "We'll head back to the lodges," ordered Nigighun. The girl shook her head yes and as they walked back to the settlement, Harjo watched their backs.

Once back inside the lodges, all was well. Nigighun told the females to take precautions. He ordered them not to go outside alone and only for firewood and nature calls. He instructed them to build a large fire in the outside hearth. He then went to the lodge complex next to his to spread the word of caution throughout the camp and to light outside fires. Upon his return, he sent Yixgitsiy to his adjacent lodge to inform the two other female occupants, who were also his grown daughters.

Soon, the anxious atmosphere calmed and Nigighun told his three Mammoth Hunter guests to make themselves comfortable. "I'll send a group of hunters out tomorrow to track the lion and perhaps persuade him to move on," stated Nigighun. Harjo nodded in agreement. With little reserve, Nigighun took off his parka and pants and pulled on a pair of buckskin pants, then sat down by the hearth. Harjo and his two sons followed Nigighun's lead and removed what clothing modesty allowed and found seating by the warm fire, making themselves comfortable. As pre-instructed, young Nigeday brought in a wooden bowl full of mammoth jerky from the sled and neatly placed the frozen meat around on the hearth stones to heat.

"I believe we should enjoy a taste of mammoth," offered Harjo.

"Excellent," replied Nigighun, "It has been many seasons since I've tasted mammoth."

Nigighun stood as a man of wealth and a leader within his band. He organized the caribou drives and as a chieftain, renowned hunter and warrior, claimed a large share of the caribou wealth from the communal hunts and drives. He owned two wives, one older and one younger. The older was his first wife of many seasons and the younger came into his possession due to the recent death of his younger brother. The anxious women stood behind them, along with two girls, one about 10 summers in age and the other 12 to 14 summers.

Nigighun frowned as he waved his hand motioning them away. "Move away and leave us alone and let us eat and talk in peace!"

"Please, Nigighun," implored the older woman, "let us sit by the fire to talk and listen. We've seen so few Mammoth Hunters and never one who speaks our language. This may be our only opportunity to talk to a Mammoth Hunter."

The younger woman, seeming more cunning, also spoke. "I hear that Mammoth Hunters eat and talk with their women, Nigighun. Maybe he would feel more at home if we joined you and perhaps lessen any potential bartering tension."

As this proposal seemed reasonable, Nigighun looked at Harjo. "Would you care if they sat?"

"No, certainly not," replied Harjo. "And she may be right. Once their curiosity is cured, we will be able to negotiate in peace without interruption."

"Alright, sit down," grumbled Nigighun. As the excited women squeezed their way into the circle, one on each side of Harjo, he noticed the girl of about 10 summers quickly left through the entry. She soon returned with two other young women, apparently Nigighun's married daughters with babes in arms and toddlers in tow and they also found seating around the fire. The two youngest girls served fresh, nearly frozen caribou meat on skewers, then squeezed in next to Echo and Nigeday.

"Soon the whole lodge will smell like female," snarled Nigighun.

Harjo laughed, "Perhaps my sons will appreciate the aroma."

Nigighun looked first at Harjo, then his two boys, then he put his head back laughing and shook his head in agreement.

The younger of Nigighun's wives looked into Harjo's face and smiled. "He is very handsome," she thought to herself. "He has a scar on his face. It must be from a knife cut, yet it does not distract from his appearance, in fact, it adds character to his attractiveness."

"My name is Na'aa," she said in a soft yet bold voice. "Are your boots made from mammoth?"

"Yes," Harjo replied.

"May I touch them?" Na'aa asked.

Caribou Hunter women remain very cautious about touching a man or any of his positions. They learn to ask first. The sting of the women's strap teaches hard lessons.

Harjo did not answer but he reached down and untied one of his boots, pulled it off, and handed it to her.

"Thank you," she replied with a smile as she began to examine the boot in detail.

"Did your wife sew these boots?"

"Yes," Harjo answered.

Na'aa looked up to Harjo. "She is a very talented seamstress."

She then looked across to Echo who sat quietly eating. "Is that boy her son?"

Harjo nodded his head yes.

"I see she is also very beautiful."

"She is indeed," replied Harjo.

"I would like to touch them," spoke up the older wife.

"By all means," said Harjo. "Pass the boot around so that all the women may examine it."

"That is my first old wife," stated Nigighun, "her name is Vi'ot.

The older and delighted Vi'ot took the boot and began her examination.

Echo took another bite of meat. The silent girl sitting next to him gently reached over and tapped his shoulder then pointed at the bowl of mammoth jerky. Echo looked over to Harjo. "Father?" he said as in a question.

Harjo smiled. "I believe she wants to taste the mammoth and probably examine that bowl as well."

"Oh, yes," said Echo as though he should have known. With a cheerful expression, he picked up pieces of meat, placed them in the bowl, and handed it to her. She accepted the bowl from Echo with a smile then tasted the meat.

"Harjo?" asked Na'aa, pronouncing his name with only minor difficulty. "Can you kill you a mammoth by yourself?"

Harjo looked at Na'aa, somewhat taken back. She was bold and outspoken for a Caribou Hunter woman. "Yes," was Harjo's modest reply.

"I've also heard you killed a lion when you were just a boy. Is that true?"

"Yes, it is," replied Harjo as he now noticed that Na'aa studied his face.

"Stories are told around campfires that you journeyed all the way to the Great Sea and returned with a beautiful young woman from a faraway land—from the other side of the great western glacier. Are they true?"

"That story is, and you just commented on the apparent beauty of my son's mother."

"Yes, I did. And do you also have a young Caribou Hunter woman as wife?" inquired Na'aa.

"Again, your question is true, Na'aa," answered Harjo. "You seem to possess considerable knowledge about me, and we have never met."

"Oh, but we have heard numerous stories about Mammoth Hunter men," exclaimed Na'aa. "In particular, many stories about a Mammoth Hunter warrior named Harjo. He often comes to trade with Caribou Hunters and he speaks our language."

The older wife, Vi'ot, passed the boot onto a younger woman seated next to her. They fussed and whispered over the boot but also listened intensely to the questions Na'aa posed to Harjo and equally important his answers. Mammoth Hunter men are a source of strange fascination to Caribou Hunter women.

Accordingly, Na'aa found herself becoming excited over Harjo and his simple, direct answers heighten her attraction. She could not help herself. Being seated next to a Mammoth Hunter who could single-handedly slay a mammoth, the largest most dangerous beast on the Mammoth Steepe, lifted her emotions and desire. She felt herself becoming aroused and moist between her legs but maintained calmness in her voice and continued to find questions.

"You and your sons appear relaxed, sitting and talking with women. So, it must be true that Mammoth Hunters eat with their women. As Harjo took a bite of caribou meat on a small skewer, he looked at Na'aa answering yes with a Caribou Hunter facial expression.

"But I have also heard that Mammoth Hunters beat their women's bare legs with a switch if they are disobedient. Is that true?"

"Some Mammoth Hunter men do," replied Harjo.

Na'aa became bolder and unable to help herself; she reached out to touch Harjo's hand. "Have you ever switched the bare legs of your wives?"

Harjo lowered his eyebrows in a near squint as he looked into Na'aa face. His expression was a Caribou Hunter facial gesture to mean annoyance. "No," replied Harjo, "I have not."

Na'aa smiled, seeming very content with Harjo's answers.

Harjo's boot completed the circle gathered around the fire and Na'aa again took it in hand. She smelled the inside then looked at Harjo. "I have heard that Mammoth Hunters smell offensive," she said with a coy smile.

"I've heard the same of Caribou Hunter women," said Harjo.

Na'aa smelled inside Harjo's boot again while she looked at him. "The odor is quite foreign but far from offensive, in fact, I would call it compelling." She then passed the boots on for another trip around the hearth.

Harjo then took off a mammoth wool sock. "Would you care to touch woven mammoth wool?" he asked.

Na'aa sucked in her breath. "Oh, yes, thank you," was her delightful response.

He handed her the sock and she eagerly examined it. Caribou Hunter women do not weave wool or grass, relying nearly completely on caribou and other animal skins. Socks or interior boot linings were made from hare or other soft furs such as marmot, ground squirrel or fox. Na'aa examined, pulled, and smelled the sock seemingly fascinated with the material and the craftsmanship.

"I had no idea the wool was so soft and such a beautiful pale-yellow color," she spoke, smiling at Harjo.

The other women compelled her to pass the sock on. More questions followed. The women were also fascinated with the Mammoth Hunter's parkas, supporting attached hoods. They all openly enjoyed examining the parkas.

Meanwhile, Nigighun had his own questions he wanted to pose to Harjo. "I saw something last spring, Harjo, that I have not witnessed before," he exclaimed. Harjo looked at Nigighun and raised his eyebrows in the Caribou Hunter manner of facial expressions as if to ask-what?

Nigighun continued, "A small herd of mammoth migrating northeast."

"Northeast?" questioned Harjo.

Nigighun shook his head yes. "All my life, the very few mammoths I have seen in caribou land always migrated northwest. And that adds another oddity, Harjo. When I was a boy, I would see mammoth only on rare occasions-very rare. Now I see mammoth in our land more frequently, in fact, they have become almost common. Not in any great numbers, more individuals or small groups, but certainly more common."

"What do you make of it?" asked Harjo.

Nigighun formed a facial expression as if to say I am pondering the question and will speak after I have formulated an answer. "I believe," he responded, "the mammoth are relocating eastward. Perhaps they follow the Big River and," added Nigighun, "so are the caribou. Some caribou have always migrated northeast in the spring, thus they must have fawning grounds to the north and or east. But those numbers are growing, many more migrate northeast than when I was a boy."

"And I will tell you something else. Perhaps you have noticed the same in the Echota Valley. Certain areas, especially the meadows that were once filled with tall grass, are now overgrown with trees. One of my favorite summer camping grounds is on the edge of a small meadow between two small streams-we have camped there since I was a boy. Now it is overgrown with trees, including those cottonwoods."

Harjo agreed. "Nigighun, you and I have both lived long enough to understand the Mammoth Steppe continually changes his face. The Father Creator expands and shrinks through the generations. Elders have told me when they were young the Wind Band once followed the edge of the Echota River on migration. Now, with the growth of trees, we pull our sleds farther and farther away from the river as we follow the forested edge. Some Elders will say the number of mammoth at the calving grounds is far less than when they were young. For better or for worse, Nigighun, the Mammoth Steppe is changing. Wherever the mammoth herds go, we the Muscogee will follow, and your people will likewise follow the caribou."

Nigighun nodded his head in serious agreement, then smiled. "Is there any more of your mammoth meat? I would never in my wildest dreams attempt to kill one of those shaggy beasts, but I could become accustomed to the flavor of their meat. Now, let's talk about trade."

The actual trading transaction did not take very long. Each man was honest, trusting the other and desired to continue trading long into the future. More importantly, neither was greedy and Harjo's long reputation of generosity preceded him.

With Nigighun and Harjo's approval, Nigeday got up to examine a pile of caribou skins stacked near the edge of the lodge. Once given permission, the excited females hurried to the sled and after untying the load, examined the mammoth pelts with a prattling clamor.

"You women, quiet down before I whip you all!" growled the loud voice of Nigighun. "Caribou women can have an orgasm over mammoth pelts," he laughed.

Grinning, Harjo and Echo looked over to the sled surrounded by the women who now voiced their excitement in loud whispers. "Mammoth Hunter women react similarly to caribou pelts and more so to a lion hide," offered Harjo. Nigighun raised his head back, laughing out loud.

"Father?" spoke a low quiet voice. The three men seated around the fire turned toward Nigeday standing by the stack of caribou pelts. He spoke in the Caribou Hunter's Athabascan tongue. "A good stack of pelts and there are two that are nearly white. I hope mother will use those to sew a new parka for me."

"I am sure she will," replied Harjo as a smiling Nigeday returned to the fire.

Another outburst came from the caribou women still going through the mammoth pelts. Nigighun reacted in anger. "Vi'ot, you keep those women quiet. If there is another outburst, I will whip here in front of our guests!" Vi'ot raised her hand and hushed the other women and quietly but sternly silenced them.

"Nigeday speaks Athabascan well, Harjo," observed Nigighun as Harjo's youngest son sat down.

Harjo thought it best not to confirm or deny that Nigeday had been a Caribou Hunter boy and from Nigighun's band, the Deg Hit'an. If questioned, he would relate the story but otherwise the three Mammoth Hunters would keep this subtle knowledge to themselves.

"I do own a Caribou Hunter as second wife, Nigighun, and she nursed Nigeday as a baby. There are many languages spoken around our family hearth. My first wife's language is the strangest of all and every one of my children speaks it, including Nigeday."

Harjo spoke the truth and still maintained Nigeday's boyhood identity secret. Nigighun nodded his head, content with the answer. Meanwhile, the women returned to the fire silent but excited. "It is a wonderful stack of pelts, Nigighun," reported Vi'ot.

"A trade then?" asked Nigighun, as he reached out his hand.

"It is a trade," responded Harjo as he also reached out and took Nigighun's wrist.

Everyone sitting around the hearth expressed delight in smiles and headshakes. Echo and Nigeday each clapped their hands twice in unison and then lightly touched their fists together. Their hand clapping was influenced by their mother and the other, a silly antic, was a Ptarmigan Boy gesture.

Nigighun chuckled at the two boys' antics. "You are lucky to have boys, Harjo. You can teach them to hunt and share in their growing up."

Harjo looked at the two smiling boys and likewise smiled. Then, Echo and Nigeday got up and with the two girls unloaded the mammoth pelts from the sled then stacked and reloaded the sled with caribou pelts.

"It seems I only produce females," declared Nigighun "and two of my unmarried girls there." He pointed to Sanh and Yixgitsiy who were handling pelts. "Sanh is my first wife's daughter and she is ready for marriage, somewhere around 14 summers old, I think. The younger one is Yixgitsiy, my second wife's daughter. As you can see, she is not mature but soon will be."

With all the pelts loaded, tied, and stacked, the four youngsters returned to the fire. Young Yixgitsiy spoke up as she sat down, "I am 10 summers!"

Nigighun gave her a stern look. She lowered her head and bit her lip hard as she realized such outbursts could earn her a taste of the women's strap.

Nigighun continued, "Among the Caribou Hunters, with the death of a woman's husband, she becomes the wife of her deceased husband's brother. Na'aa's dead husband was my younger brother. A young Caribou Hunter, who wishes a wife, comes and lives with the brides' family for one full cycle, usually beginning in the summer. That is the bride price. Often, he remains with the young wife's family ultimately to establish his own lodge and family. The husbands of my two daughters and their children reside in the second lodge. Those two boys are good hunters and they are friends, nearly brothers. They are away on a winter hunt as I anticipate a long cold winter."

Nigighun paused momentarily, but there was purpose in his silence. "What if one of your sons married a Caribou Hunter girl, Harjo?" he suddenly inquired.

"It would be difficult to give up any of my boys," stated Harjo.

"Oh, yes, understandable," replied Nigighun, "but we both know, nothing remains fixed on the Mammoth Steppe. You follow the mammoth herds and us the caribou. Often, we will set up a camp for one season never to return, while you return to the same winter village over many winters. A caribou family moves from one band to the next, from season to season, while your family will stay within one band a whole life span. Once the young Caribou Hunter has paid his bride price, he may stay with the girl's family, return to his own, or elect to join a completely different band. Caribou Hunters are notoriously mobile. A young hunter may take his wife to a different band each season."

"Consider, Harjo," illuminated Nigighun, rubbing his hands together, "if one of your sons married one of my daughters, we would establish a trading bond that may last many generations. Young Nigeday there speaks Athabascan better than I do. Nigighun held out his hand to Nigeday. "How would you like to marry one of my daughters, Nigeday?"

Nigeday was taken by surprise as his eyes grew wide and his mouth open but he answered with a boyish reflex, "Which one?"

Everyone around the hearth laughed and Nigighun rolled his head back and laughed out loud. "You see, Harjo, he fits in already!"

"I will give the matter serious consideration," replied Harjo.

"Good," answered Nigighun, satisfied with the answer.

Although profitable, the day had been long and hard, and it was now late in the night; morning would come all too soon. "Harjo, I am glad to offer you and your sons the comfort and hospitality of my women, please accept," offered Nigighun with a tone of clear sincerity.

Harjo anticipated this Caribou Hunter custom and he did not want to cause any hurt feelings or more importantly, anger. If a guest turns down such an offer from a Caribou Hunter, it would mar the image and the sensitivity of the female being offered, stating she was not good enough and thus anger the host by presenting himself as an elitist. "We eagerly accept," he replied.

"Excellent-good," voiced the jubilant Nigighun. "Na'aa, see to it that Sanh and Echo-Yixgitsiy and Nigeday are bedded down, then you sleep with Harjo. You and the younger women will bring in some more firewood. Remember the lion. Let's all get some sleep."

With the command given, all the household females rose, stirring into action. With caution, some stepped outside to bring in wood and urinate while others made up beds. Harjo asked Nigeday and Echo to escort the women outside and they gladly accepted. Once their outside duties were complete, Echo and Nigeday pushed the sled loaded with caribou pelts out into the entry to make more room in the main lodge, then brought their mammoth bed and other supplies in from the supply sled. Following a brief stop outside, Nigighun and Vi'ot peacefully retired to their bed.

After motivating her two young charges, Na'aa approached Harjo. "Harjo, may I take your mammoth bed and set it up?" she asked.

"Certainly," he replied.

"I've made a new bed of fresh grass and piled it high," boasted Na'aa. "I have never slept in a mammoth bed." She stepped in front of Harjo so close her breast rubbed against his chest. "I am looking forward to sleeping in one and sleeping with you." She looked into his face and slowly moved against him, then she lifted up on her toes and leaned into him to kiss his neck near his ear. Then, with a seductive smile she went to set up his mammoth bed.

Sanh and Yixgitsiy brought in several loads of firewood and soon built a bright fire that burned warm, illuminating the whole interior of the lodge. The shape of the opening formed by the diagonal poles, tied and fixed at the top of the lodge, created a draft pulling out the smoke. Articles, tools, and weapons hung from the poles including the rawhide woman's strap. The sinister instrument measured the length and width of a man's forearm and hand and hung readily available to sting the buttocks and legs of the female occupants of the lodge who displeased Nigighun.

The two girls insured that the layers of small branches and piles of grass were overlaid with caribou skins, which provided seating around the hearth, remained a safe distance from the fire. They also made their way toward the edge of the lodge where the same idea was employed to provide beds. Large piles of grass supplied bedding along with thick winter caribou hides. They arranged and fussed with the bedding.

Afterwards, and to his surprise, Sanh took Echo's hand and began to lead him toward the entry. He stopped. "Uh, Father, where is she taking me?"

Harjo posed the question and the shy girl calmly answered. Harjo translated, "to the adjacent lodge where her two sisters sleep. Their husbands are gone, and the sisters sleep together leaving an empty bed." The girl said something else.

"She said it is very warm there. It will be fine, Echo-take your weapons."

Echo released her hand and picked up his atlatl and darts. He smiled at his father, then stretched out his hand to the grinning Sanh who took it and then led him through the entry.

Meanwhile, two snickering youngsters, Nigeday and Yixgitsiy, undressed and climbed into bed seemingly piled high with caribou skins and furs. They disappeared under the pile of furs.

Sitting on the mammoth bed, Na'aa pulled off her boots then stood and pulled her parka over her head laying her clothes at the foot of the bed. "To have a child as old as her daughter Yixgitsiy," thought Harjo to himself, "Na'aa remained young and quite striking. Onna and his mother often displayed contempt at the young age Caribou Hunter girls bore children. Na'aa could not have been more than a child herself when she bore Yixgitsiy."

Naked Na'aa pulled the top cover back then lowered herself down on her hands and knees on the mammoth bed and slowly rubbed her hands over the thick wool. "I've always wanted to sleep in a mammoth bed," she whispered as though anticipating a luxurious experience. "It is delightfully soft." She put her nose to the wool, taking a deep breath.

Her displayed buttocks and the dark area between her thighs offered a seductive pose. She rose back to her knees and held out her hand. "Come," she whispered to Harjo.

Harjo went to the bed and undressed. Na'aa took Harjo's hand as she slid down under the cover while Harjo followed her. They lay face to face. Her smell filled Harjo's nostrils. Her woman scent was strong, but not unpleasant. Caribou Hunters only bath every five to seven days even during the summer compared with Mammoth Hunters who habitually bath every day including winter.

Meanwhile, Nigighun and Vi'ot were soon asleep as strong breathing sounds came from their bed. But giggling and hushing sounds were heard from the bed of the two naked youngsters. Harjo and Na'aa looked at each other smiling.

"I think they are too young to have sex," softly laughed Na'aa.

Harjo looked over toward their bed then back to Na'aa. "Do you think they will try?"

"No," pondered Na'aa, "I don't think so. They will just play with each other, but they will enjoy each other's warmth."

Na'aa gazed at Harjo's scar then into his eyes. "May I kiss you?" she asked in a whisper.

"Yes," he replied.

Na'aa leaned to Harjo and kissed him, gently at first, and progressively with more passion. She began to whimper as they embraced. As with her body odor, her breath was strong but not distasteful.

"All my life I've heard that Mammoth Hunter men were well endowed. Caribou women gossip and laugh about it frequently. May I touch your manhood?"

Harjo did not reply which Na'aa took to mean yes. She slowly reached both hands out and touched his chest. Then, absent any objections, she slowly slid her hands down to his groin and ever so gently massaged him. She cupped his testicles as if to determine their weight. Next, she moved one hand to grasp his erect manhood. "It is true," she sighed, "you're heavy, large, and very hard."

Whimpering, Na'aa rolled over on her side and pulled her knees up. She then squirmed and wiggled her bottom against him then slightly lifted her leg. Still tenderly holding his manhood with one hand and whimpering louder, she guided him into her.

She was wet and swollen. He penetrated her full length, leisurely but certainly, he entered her in one slow fluid motion sheathing his erect foreshaft into her warm wet female opening. She released her grip on his manhood, reaching back to grasp his thigh pulling him into her. Instinctively, Harjo grasp her hips as she whimpered, jerked, and convulsed into orgasm easily surrendering her woman's fluid to him. She journeyed, although not deeply, in and out of the spirit world.

Then, she twisted her head and shoulders back toward him and reached her hand back over her head to take hold of the back of his neck. Harjo could feel the strength of her arms as she gently, but still with a steady force, pull his head to her. "Kiss—kiss me," she urged in a desperate whisper. He reached over with his hand on the side of her face and kissed her passionately.

She then reached up and pulled his hand to her breast then slightly rolled with a slow rhythm and whispered little "ooohs" pushed her buttocks against him. She released his hand thus Harjo held both her hips and in the same smooth pace, wet and warm, soft and hard, moved in and out of her.

Her whimpered ooohs began to rise in pitch. Again, she took his hand and brought it to her mouth and sucked on his fingers then pushed his hand down to her groin and her vulva. His moistened fingers sought out her clitoris and once found, she again convulsed, jerked, and flowed wet and fluid into the wondrous, mysterious, realm of the spirit world. Harjo also released his male fluid and although he did not journey to the spirit world, nonetheless, it felt good.

As Na'aa returned from the spirit world, she reached down and brought Harjo's hand up to her mouth and kissed it. "Thank you, Harjo," she whispered and sighed.

He kissed her neck and replied, "You're welcome." She sighed again and wiggled her buttocks against him. Then, holding tightly to his hand, they drifted off to sleep.

Chapter 35:

RETURN TO COWETA

Breaking dawn, as the rest of the caribou lodge occupants slept, Harjo brought in wood from the cold entry room and rekindled the fire. He looked around and found some heating stones and placed them on the hearthstones to heat water for tea. Taking his spear, he then ventured outside for a moment, then returned, leaving his spear at the entryway. Afterwards, with a water pouch in hand, he made his way into the small cold and unheated conical tent with just enough light sneaking through the top allowing him to wash. He now sat by the fire and enjoyed the hot tea.

To his surprise, naked little Yixgitsiy crawled out of bed grabbing her boots and parka then hurried to the hearth. She sat down by the fire, unembarrassed by her nudity and proceeded to pull on her boots, smiling at Harjo. Then, her facial expression turned serious.

"We must be quiet, Harjo," she said in a low whisper. "If I wake up my new father, he will be angry, and he will whip my behind with the women's strap. Oh, it stings so bad-see." She then turned around to show him her buttocks and pointed to old strap mark bruises now faded to a more yellowish, almost ocher color, dotted with dark red spots.

"We'll be quiet," whispered Harjo, "and not wake him."

Again smiling, she turned around and sat with her legs spread. Her exposed open vulva was absent pubic hair and her flat breastless chest left little doubt of her immaturity. She obviously remained several seasons from menstruation. But it was equally obvious she would grow into a striking young woman similar in appearance to her mother. Harjo took this more private opportunity to ask questions.

"Do you like my son, Nigeday?"

"Oh, yes," she responded with a giggle. He's fun to sleep with and to play with too."

"How old are you?"

She pressed her lips together pondering the question as though she must provide an exact answerer. "Ten summers, last, and two more seasons." She fussed with her boots. "I have never seen any Mammoth Hunters before and now I have seen three and slept with one. I want to tell my friends when I see them. They will be jealous."

Yixgitsiy then paused and her expression changed again to a solemn look. She crawled across the floor still nude and boldly put her hands on Harjo's leg. She stared into his face. "Can I touch your scar?" she asked in a childish yet serious voice.

Harjo thought for a moment. "You may," he answered.

Slowly but without hesitation, she reached up and put her little fingers on his face smiling. She grew bolder. "Can I kiss your scar?"

Harjo was momentarily taken back then agreed. "You may."

Leisurely but deliberately, Yixgitsiy moved close to Harjo's face and kissed his scar. In doing so, she made a kissing sound. She then shifted slightly back but was still near his face. Then, without asking, she moved to his face and kissed his lips. She moved back with a big smile on her face, apparently very proud of herself.

"Harjo, will you make me a promise?" she asked maintaining a serious childish tone.

"I might, but I don't know what it is," he answered.

"When you come back to trade, can I sleep with you?"

Harjo pondered her question, and then replied. "I thought you liked to sleep with Nigeday?"

"I do," she replied, "but you can kill a mammoth."

"One day," answered Harjo, "Nigeday will be able to kill a mammoth."

Yixgitsiy pondered that proposition. "Would he kill a mammoth for me?"

"I think he might," replied Harjo.

"Well, I still want to sleep with you. Will you promise?"

Harjo thought for a moment then replied. "I promise when I return to trade, I will want you to sleep with me."

Smiling, Yixgitsiy seemed very content with that answer and set back down and returned to her boots. "I hope I get to sleep with you and give you many kisses."

There was another stirring and Na'aa came to the fire. She had her frock on and sat down to pull on her boots. "Harjo, are you seducing my daughter?"

Harjo looked up at Na'aa then over to Yixgitsiy. "No, but I believe she is attempting to seduce me."

Na'aa quietly laughed, "Well, I am not surprised."

Yixgitsiy looked up to both the adults. "What is seduce?"

Na'aa chuckled again. "Come, let's go out for a moment."

"Oh, yes," said Yixgitsiy now rushed. She quickly finished with her boots and pulled her parka over her head and the two headed out through the entrance.

"Remember the lion," stated Harjo, "so don't go far." Na'aa acknowledged with a head nod.

As Na'aa and Yixgitsiy left the lodge, Echo entered. "Good morning, Father," he whispered. Harjo returned his greeting. He sat down and found the ladle with hot tea. "Father, should I wash?"

"Not necessarily, Echo, do what will make you feel comfortable. But be aware that lions are attracted to the female scent, especially the males. One may follow us all the way back to Coweta."

Echo began to laugh then glanced around the lodge to determine if his laughter had disturbed anyone sleeping. "May I wash in the food cache lodge?" he asked quietly.

"Yes," answered Harjo. He handed Echo the water pouch who again looked around then got up and went outside.

Harjo stood up by the now blazing fire and rubbed his hand over it. He looked over to see if he could any signs of life from Nigeday but only saw the large pile of caribou and fur blankets. He smiled to himself. As if a little ground squirrel, Nigeday hibernated under the furs. Suddenly, Nigeday crawled out from under the blankets, sat on the bed, and pulled his boots on. Still naked, he crept to the fire but dragged a caribou blanket with him then wrapped it around himself.

"Good morning, Father," he said with a long yawn, still drowsy.

"Good morning, son," whispered Harjo has he hugged Nigeday and rubbed his head.

"Outside," said Nigeday still with a yawn as he again wrapped the caribou blanket around him and crept to the entryway.

"Go all the way outside, Nigeday, not in the entryway," stated Harjo in his quiet fatherly voice. "But not too far and take a weapon with you-remember the lion."

"Alright," answered Nigeday as he reached out and grasped Harjo's spear then turned to look at his father asking permission with a Caribou Hunter facial expression. Harjo approved with a nod. Then Nigeday smiled and made his way through the entry.

Later in the morning, Nigighun and Vi'ot rose out of their caribou bed from a long night's sleep. Nigighun and Harjo bid farewell. Nigighun told Harjo he would camp on this drainage next winter. "If you decided to return to trade next winter Harjo, look for me here."

Harjo agreed to make every effort, understanding that nothing on the Mammoth Steppe was certain. Nigihun concurred and reminded Harjo that his daughters were ready and prepared for marriage. Harjo again told Nigighun he would seriously consider the proposal. Nigighun went out to visit the nearby lodges to round up a small group of hunters to track the lion, a task not to be taken lightly. They hoped to persuade the deadly predator to move on from the encampment. But, when you pursue a lion, especially a male, there always remains the possibility he will attack.

Meanwhile, Echo and Nigeday were making final preparations to depart. Harjo was not sure where the rest of the household women and girls were, but he sat at the fire with Na'aa who remained full of questions-always a calculating female.

"Harjo, I have heard that Mammoth Hunter boys make their own decisions. Is this true?" questioned Na'aa.

Harjo looked up realizing she was planning, not seeking knowledge. "Not completely," he replied.

"They are influenced by their fathers?" she continued.

"Most certainly," he confirmed.

"Then you could persuade one of your boys to journey to the Caribou Hunters seeking a wife?"

"I could."

"And convince him to come to Nigighun who has unmarried daughters?"

"Tell me what it is you are after, Na'aa."

"Alright," she now seemed enthused. "Echo appears to be of age now and so is Sanh, and Nigeday looks as though he will be of age in three or four summers as will Yixgitsiy."

"You remain correct," answered Harjo.

"I am just pointing out possibilities, Harjo, and you do know I am Nigighun's wife by law. My bride price was paid seasons ago by my dead husband. By Mammoth Hunter law, could you purchase me from Nigighun as wife?"

Harjo nodded his head yes.

"Then it would be legal for you to purchase me by both our tribal laws. You could buy me from Nigighun in the future or," she paused and smiled at Harjo, "you could buy me now."

"You would want to be third wife in a Mammoth Hunter's lodge?"

"I would be third wife in your lodge," answered Na'aa with a serious expression.

"And your daughter?" asked Harjo.

"I would certainly miss her, but she will soon start her own life, with her own husband and family," she answered. "But also, Harjo, you could buy her as well. I think Nigighun would be relieved to have us both gone and when she matures, she will make an excellent wife for any of your sons."

Boldly, Na'aa moved closer to Harjo capturing his hand. "May I kiss you?"

"Alright," he replied.

Na'aa slowly leaned into him and kissed his lips. "I only tell you this to remind you of your options." She spoke, slightly panting, with her lips gently pressed to his.

"I will consider all my options," answered the ever stoic Harjo.

Smiling, Na'aa kissed him again. Then, seemingly satisfied, she stood up.

Echo called in from outside. "There is not much daylight left, Father!"

"Alright Echo, we're leaving," Harjo said as he headed toward the entry.

"Harjo," asked Na'aa in a low almost childlike voice.

Harjo stopped and turned. He was reminded of the same manner that Onna called his name when she was about to ask a question, which in reality compelled him to do something.

"Will you promise you will return to trade?" Her facial expression added please.

Harjo thought for a moment. "Yes, I can promise that," he said with a smile then exited through the entry.

Na'aa likewise smiled and began planning to herself. She knew he would keep this promise and return.

⚬⌒⌒⚬⌒⌒⚬⌒⌒⚬

The three Mammoth Hunters began the long hard trek back to the Echota River and Coweta with the sleds now loaded with prized caribou pelts. They stopped for their first breather side by side as Nigeday looked up at his father with a puzzled expression.

Harjo knew the vast array of facial expressions that Caribou Hunters used woven into the wool of their language. Nigeday was no exception although he was brought up from a young age as a Mammoth Hunter. Following Summer's loss of her first baby, however, she attached herself to Nigeday and remained both his surrogate mother and older sister. Onna and Summer raised Loni and Nigeday together sharing both nursing and motherly duties.

Consequently, Nigeday's languages contained all the subtleties of Caribou Hunter facial expressions. Nigeday and Summer often amused themselves and the family with their facial expressions especially during long winter meals around the family hearth.

Nigeday's expression changed as though he had somehow answered his own mysterious question. "Father, I like sleeping with naked girls," boasted the honest Nigeday, which prompted both Harjo and Echo to laugh out loud. Nigeday formed his "Why is that funny?" facial expression as he looked to his brother and father.

"Beware, Son," replied a joking Harjo as he laughed, "I've heard that sleeping with naked girls is habit forming."

Now Nigeday formed his "I don't understand" facial expression and looked to Echo for an answer asking, "What is habit?"

Echo copied Nigeday with an "I don't understand" gesture thus Nigeday turned back to Harjo.

"What is habit, Father?"

Harjo reached out laughing, putting his arms around both boys' shoulders and hugged them. He thought to himself, "Are all boys this age silly or just mine? We'll pull sled for now but when we take our next breather, I'll explain habit." Echo and Nigeday looked at each other, shaking their heads in agreement. Harjo and Echo leaned into their harnesses while Nigeday pushed one of the sleds. Thus, the three Mammoth Hunters continued homeward bound across the cold, snow covered Mammoth Steppe.

Chapter 36:

Summer Kill

Onna finished pulling off her boots then laid them with her woman's bag on the large tree branch next to Harjo. She looked toward the processing party as they drew closer with two trailing figures. Shading her face and smiling, Onna pointed, "It will take old Micco Yarda the remainder of the day to arrive."

Harjo glanced toward the advancing group. Many lugged wooden poles and pulled travails while several of the men carried axes and nearly every woman held a long handled scraping tool. Chuckling, Harjo responded, "Well, Yarda enjoys supervising the processing-he always has."

"Harjo, I just remembered, now don't get mad," implored Onna as she stepped up to Harjo putting her hand on his shoulder.

Harjo looked up, "What did you do?"

Onna took a deep breath. "I know Nigeday is to guard the camp during the processing and help set it up, but I told him he could come down to see the mammoth-he was so excited Harjo and he is so proud of you-he desperately wanted to see the mammoth-I just couldn't tell him he had to stay in camp-so don't be mad, alright?"

Harjo chuckled, asking himself, "How could she weave that many different words and thoughts together and somehow still make some sense? It's alright, Onna; I didn't mean he could not come down and see the mammoth."

A cheerful Onna clapped her hands, "I was certain you would not be angry, Harjo." Then she paused glancing skyward, pondering an important question with the same endearing expression she has had since she was a mere child.

"Of course, you know, Harjo, Nigeday and Loni are not siblings and as you know they have no kinship heritage."

Harjo knew where she was going but asked anyway. "What are you striving for?"

"Well, legally then, by Mammoth Hunter law they could marry."

"Perhaps Nigeday will not want to marry Loni," proposed Harjo with a 'you should know this' expression.

"I know, but he'll do what you ask, Harjo."

Now Harjo took a deep breath. "You're missing the target. Let us wait and allow them to grow to maturity, complete their Rite-of-Passages, and then discuss marriage."

Onna sighed a deep breath. "Oh, alright-I suppose you're right and we should wait."

Onna turned toward the fallen great beast. "Harjo, I am anxious to process the mammoth and I also dread starting," fussed Onna with a heavy sigh.

Harjo did not reply but turned toward the advancing group. As the assembly of Wind Band processors approached, the small figure of Nigeday sprinted out in front, running up to Harjo who now stood up. Nigeday threw his arms around Harjo who laid his hands on his son's shoulders and hooded head.

"I tried to pretend I was not afraid, Father, but I was. I was afraid you would be hurt by the mammoth!" Nigeday clutched his father.

"It's alright to be afraid, son."

Standing next to Harjo, Onna reached out and pushed Nigeday's hood back to brush his hair with her hand. Nigeday looked up, "Thank you, Father, for killing the mammoth for us."

Harjo looked down at his young smiling face and took hold of his shoulder. "You are very welcome, Nigeday. Now go examine the mammoth and take a close look at the entry wound."

"Alright," responded an excited Nigeday who glanced both at Harjo and Onna, then ran to the great beast. Onna put her arms around Harjo's arm. She felt silent misty tears forming in her brilliant blue eyes.

⁓✺⁓✺⁓✺⁓

Dressing an animal requires nearly the same process whether processing a small hare or a gigantic mammoth. The scourge of the hapless hare are the fox and small Mammoth Hunters boys who can dress and butcher a hare within a few moments depending on if he wishes to keep the hide for tanning or not. If not, a hare can be skinned simply by pulling the hide off by hand. Conversely, if the boy desires to tan the hide, it is carefully cut from throat to groin then cautiously removed. The process still only requires a few moments, but the same concept applies to a mammoth.

It is much easier to tan smaller cut sections of a mammoth hide that might then be utilized for making boots or for bedding. Uncut whole hides, however, were preferred as winter lodge covers and it remained a challenging task to tan a complete mammoth hide. Nonetheless, whether the hide was kept whole or not, it still required an intensive effort from every member of a Mammoth Hunter band who has reached ten summers of age or older to dress, butcher, and process the meat and hide of a full-grown bull mammoth.

Boys 10-12 summers of age were generally assigned guard duties standing watch over the camp and the processing area while girls of the same age, with guidance from grandmothers, took care of young children while their mothers worked. One or two young nursing mothers would join the childcare group and feed the entire number of nursing babies in the band.

The Wind Band had processed many mammoth, untold numbers, over countless long seasons in both warm and cold weather. Everyone generally took up a task they preferred or that they just seemed to always do and embark on the tasks without direction. Still, it was beneficial to have Micco Yarda on hand to direct the whole process, settle disputes, and answer questions.

Aided by Fus, old Micco Yarda finally arrived at the kill site as the Wind Band had already began the daunting task, but spirits were high as the work proceeded amidst laughter and jokes. Generally, the men carried out the heavy lifting, disjointing, and skinning the great beast while the women cut up the meat and scrapped the hide. Younger ones were generally assigned general labor, primarily transporting meat, firewood, and constructing drying racks. A general sequence was followed.

First, the men disjointed the legs of the mammoth at the knees and the leg hides removed. Then, the women took over the leg segments stripping and drying the meat. Leg meat is tough and primarily utilized in pemmican where it is pulverized or perhaps it might be boiled in water as a stew.

Then, the mammoth head was removed which eliminated massive weight. Little of the head was used accept that the brains were needed in the tanning process.

Next, a cut was made along the whole length of the underside from the neck, along the chest and abdomen, to the groin. The hide was now carefully cut and peeled back toward the back exposing the meat and fat. Selected sturdy tree limbs were laid on the ground in a row by the under-belly with the butt ends pointing outward with additional limbs laid in a crisscross pattern to form a pallet base which was then overlaid with old pelts and grass mats. The belly was now carefully opened up to expose the internal organs. Now the whole viscera sack containing all the vital organs was cleaned out onto the limb pallet. Micco Yarda directed a group of young men who took hold of the butt end of the pallet limbs. Then, under his command and in unison, they dragged the pallet clear of the carcass.

Some of the internal organs were consumed on the spot such as the heart especially by the men, more so the younger men. Drummer To-wa-tol-ku, one of Honeche's sons, was particularly fond of the heart and often organized a group of young men who sliced up and consumed the dark bloody organ. This local feasting was repugnant to many of the women, in particular younger women, who made faces in disgust at the gruesome eating. But more importantly, sections of the large intestines would be utilized as a durable translucent material as window covers on mammoth lodges that kept out the cold but allowed in the light. The liver was also taken and saved.

The hide was carefully peeled back all the distance over the back of the carcass to as close to the ground as possible. Now the precious meat and fat was taken. Most of the meat was cut into strips then dried or smoked. Drying and smoking racks littered the processing area. Every tree limb that could support a strip of meat did so. But the tenderloin and choice roasts were roasted in pit ovens or on an open fire. The fat was rendered into oil by heating it in skin boiling pouches with boiling stones.

Fleshing was initiated on this exposed portion of the hide even though it remained attached to the carcass. The edges were staked to the ground and women began to scrape the flesh and fat from the "flesh side" of the hide—the fur side lay against the ground. Many varieties of fleshing tools were utilized but the most common was a spear sized wooden handle about a forearm in length with a perpendicular top about a hand's length in size. A thin stone biface of red chert was attached to the top. The goal was to scrape all the meat and fat from the flesh side of the hide thus any tool that facilitated this goal was used. Several women used hand-held bifaces.

Once all the meat and fat were taken from this side of the mammoth, the carcass was rolled over. Strong babiche ropes were attached to the legs and the stakes removed from the portion of the hide that secured it to the ground. All present took hold of the ropes and directed by Micco Yarda, they pulled in unison rolling the carcass over. Most of the workers were sullied with oil and blood but Onna was completely dirty—covered from head to foot. Harjo stood behind her as they pulled. This joyous event was celebrated with laughter and cheers.

Onna turned prankster and pretended she was going to jump into Harjo's arms. He caught her by the shoulders, keeping her at arm's length. "Hug me, Harjo, hug!" she cried out. She then carefully leaned over and up to kiss him without touching him with any part of her oily, bloody body, except her lips. Harjo helped her maintain balance by holding onto her shoulders. Their childish antics brought the crowd to laughter. Onna maintained the heart of a child and even the stoic Harjo, with his serious expressions, likewise remained young at heart.

Once the great carcass was rolled over, the Wind Band processors let out a loud call of joy and cheered as the other one-half side of the meat was exposed to easier reach. The whole hide was now removed. Yahola led a group of some ten men to move the now detached hide. They cut slits in the hide's edges to use as hand holds-some attached lengths of rope through the slits. Then, with a unique sense of unison and cooperation, they dragged the hide to a prepared location near the Wekiwa Stream. There, a group of six isolated trees formed a circular configuration several paces larger in circumference than the mammoth hide. Tree branches and brush was cleared from in and around the whole area. The men pulled the hide to within the circle of trees. The hide was then attached to the trees with ropes, pulled through the cut edge slits of the hide and pulled taut, fur side down. Edges of the hide between the trees were staked down where necessary, so that the whole hide was stretched tight.

Meanwhile, the women took breathers to refresh themselves while enjoying fresh roasted mammoth meat, water, and tea. Most of them walked to the stream to bathe in the cool clear water even though they realized they would be soiled again with blood and oil when they returned to processing the meat and the large raw mammoth hide. Several women brought soap to share with the others as they washed their hands, arms, and faces. Ravens and their scavenger cousins, the magpies, packed the trees throughout the area filling the air with their strident calls. Other birds were likewise drawn to the kill site in search of an easy meal. Even though each mammoth kill attracted a plethora of scavengers, the Wind Band people still marveled at the bird's abundance and their occasional antics including acts of daring to steal a bit of food. Onna's pet raven joined her at the creek for a drink, bringing smiles to the faces of the women as Onna cupped her hands full of water and the raven drank from her hands. After quenching his thirst, the large black bird briefly landed on Onna's shoulder then returned to the carcass for more feasting.

Chate's pregnant wife, Hokte, remained at the Wetumka camp along with Loni, Ayuko, and two other young women with nursing infants. This female group joined forces and together they all cared for the band's younger children including Summer's three young ones. Summer remained anxious about leaving her young children but as long as the female group included Loni and Ayuko, she was less apprehensive.

Summer sat next to Onna on the stream bank as the women rested. Onna wet her hands then gently washed blood and oil from Summer's face. Summer usually wore a pleasant expression but now appeared forlorn. "Why such a sad face, Summer?" inquired Onna.

"Something for long, but I no want say," replied Summer.

Onna again wet her hands in the stream and once more washed Summer's face. "It's not good to keep something that troubles you to yourself, Love. You may tell me."

Summer's facial expression said she agreed. She tightened her lips, looking to the ground, then took a calm deep breath in the manner of the Caribou Hunter's facial displays to mean she was preparing to speak of something important. "Onna, I much afraid when Harjo and boys hunt. Mammoth hide and meat much work but I happy we have much food and good lodges. I much afraid they have harm and ..." She struggled with Muscogee then continued. "Soon Nigeday hunt-he same my baby boy."

Understanding, Onna reached up to gently push back Summer's hair, then with her hands on the side of her face, pulled the fretful young woman close and kissed her. "Sweet child, I will tell you something that Ayuko once told me long ago when I was just a young girl and I also worried for Harjo's safety. 'Don't worry for Harjo,' she said. 'He is one of the greatest hunters throughout the whole Muscogee Tribe. The mammoth is not yet born that can harm him.' And I think the boys including Nigeday are the same." Somewhat relieved, Summer smiled a partial smile, and the two women embraced.

Suddenly, old Micco Yard called out toward the group of women. "Onna, the men have the hide stretched out. Lead the women and start to work on the hide. Most of the morning is already gone!"

Onna was not necessarily a women leader although, according to custom, she did own the mammoth slain by Harjo. As Ayuko aged, Onna was seemingly developing into the matron of the prominent Fus Chate family, consequently many band women now followed her lead. And even though Kak-ke and Hokose were older, they likewise often followed Onna's advise. Onna waved her hand to Micco Yarda to acknowledge his order as he turned away, limping, to check on some other work area.

Onna then looked around at the group of women. "I suppose we should head for the hide," she laughed, "before the old micco threatens to take a switch to us." Some women smiled while others laughed as they slowly rose to make their way to the stretched hide. In direct contrast to Muscogee men, Muscogee women were open and honestly affectionate toward each other, displaying unabated public fondness. Various women held hands or walked arm and arm with each other. They seemed to be especially tender during any group gathering. Onna and Summer held hands while Kak-ke and Hokose walked with their arms around each other's shoulders and waist.

The women circled the hide, armed with a variety of fleshing tools prepared for the task at hand. A few of the younger women carefully walked out to the center of the hide to reach that area. They had partly fleshed portions of the hide when it was attached to the mammoth carcass but now, they could reach all of it and complete a more thorough job. Keeping up high spirits amidst laughter and gossip, the women scrapped the meat and fat from the raw, bloody, wet side of the hide. With knives and cutting tools, they also thinned the hide around the neck, tail end, and along the spinal section where the hide was much thicker.

Meanwhile, work continued throughout the processing site. Various men, along with the remaining women, continued to strip the meat from the carcass and then carried it to a variety of racks. Thin strips of meat hung from drying and smoking racks constructed throughout and all around the vicinity of the processing area. Chilocco supervised a pair of youngsters and constructed an oven pit; soon large portions of delicious tenderloin roasted in the pit.

Yahola, with assistance from his son, Chepane and nephew Chate, removed the mammoth's eye cutting away the membrane and flesh from the eye socket. Now they could reach into the skull, extracting the mammoth's brains. Mixed with the liver, oil, and fat in a large pouch, the brains produced a tanning solution, which would treat the rawhide converting it to a cured usable pelt.

Micco Yarda wandered around the processing site offering words of encouragement and wisdom, usually in the form of jokes or stories as the women completed fleshing the hide. Now a group of men attached several long sturdy poles to the circle of trees holding the hide about waist high forming a sturdy rack. The hide was now stretched between the poles. With assistance from the women, they raised the hide off the ground, keeping the flesh side up to about waist high, attaching it to the poles. Then, they pulled it as taunt as possible and then secured the hide within the tree rack. Now it was ready for tanning.

The women rubbed the tanning brain solution into the hide. Then, utilizing flat bone or wooden scrapping tools, scrapped the concoction off but in the same gesture forced the gruesome mixture into the hide. This was hard, exhausting labor. As during the fleshing, several younger women crawled out to the center of the hide applying the tanning solution to that hard to reach area. Once the tanning solution had penetrated the hide and was likewise scrapped off, the hide was washed. Hot or warm water was preferred. To that end, the women carried several pouches of water that had been left in the sun all day just for that purpose. After washing, another coat of the brain tanning solution was applied but this layer would be left overnight.

As evening approached, night preparations began. The valuable hide and the yet unprocessed meat required overnight protection. The bulk of the meat had been dried or smoked, stored in skin pouches or wrapped in grass mats and transported to Wetumka. Numerous trips were made throughout the day with travails loaded with cured meat or full pouches latched to poles carried by two men. Meat that remained to be smoke cured during the night was affixed to racks situated near the hide. Fires were lit surrounding the curing hide and meat. The sentries would likewise protect the carcass, but their efforts would center on the hide and smoking meat.

Micco Yarda assigned Chate to supervise the guarding squad. The boys enjoyed the task and the threat of danger heightened the sensation. Certainly wolves, maybe lions, perhaps the elusive large bear would steal into the processing site to scavenge what remains they could. The boys must remain armed and ever vigilant.

As night fell, the tired processing crew made their way back to Wetumka. Many paused to wash in the Wekiwa Stream, while others gathered at the Wetumka pool. The Wind Band members who had remained at the summer camp had not been idle. The Chokofa Tent had been erected, fires roasted fresh meat, and warm tea brewed along with hot water. The Wind Band enjoyed a fresh meal around the Central Fire but soon all found a bed in the Chokofa Tent. The evening was early but so too would be the dawn.

Although he had guarded the camp all day and helped set it up, Nigeday was anxious to join his brothers at the processing site. With hugs from Onna to include last moment instructions to stay ever alert and a smile from Harjo, he slipped his dart quiver over his head, then hurriedly made his way to the processing site, atlatl and dart in hand.

Early dawn came as the Wind Band took pleasure in a hearty breakfast of fresh mammoth roast slow baked overnight in a pit oven along with potatoes, and fresh young willow leaves all washed down with warm tea. Each member remained grateful to Harjo including the youngest of children for risking his life and limb and for sharing his kill with them. But each member also took satisfaction with a measure of pride that they also contributed to the processing of the mammoth and thus contributed to the well-being and survival of the band. As they gathered around the Central Fire, the atmosphere remained calm-spirits were high. Such unique moments bonded the band and held them together.

Eventually, old Micco Yarda called out, "Follow me Wind Band and let's finish this mammoth today!" He gradually got up and headed toward the processing site. Slowly, but certainly, all followed and soon passed him by, but loyal Loni walked with the old man lending him the strength of her shoulders.

Little remained of the meat processing thus it was soon completed. Each family was secured with its share of dried and smoked meat including many pouches of mammoth oil. Women of the families would thus combine the meat and oil to produce pemmican, often adding various other ingredients, especially berries and secret family herbs. Sections of the large intestine were likewise processed to be used as a translucent material for lodge windows or skylight covers. The work today, however, would focus on the hide.

Once again, the women circled the hide. With renewed vigor, they scraped the tanning solution into and off the flesh side. Younger women and girls such as Loni crawled to the center of the suspended hide, working the central areas. They also jumped up and down throwing themselves into the air stretching the hide by using the elasticity of hide as it was pulled taunt above the ground. The girl's childish antics brought smiles and laughter to the whole group. Once the tanning mixture was scraped off, a third and final application was applied utilizing all the remaining tanning solution. Finally, the hide was thoroughly washed. The men now joined the women and together, having first cut the ropes that secured the hide to the rack and leaving the ropes attached, they dragged the hide to a specially prepared rack.

Yesterday, Harjo with help from his sons, cut a long sturdy pole and attached the ends to the forks of two adjacent trees about the same height from the ground. The hide was now draped over the horizontal pole flesh side down. Approximately one-half of the group grasped one side of the hide while the remainder took the other side. Then, under Micco Yarda's cadences, they pulled the hide along and over the pole. One side pulled while the other provided just enough resistance so that the flesh side of the hide rubbed hard and taunt against the pole. This action stretched and softened the hide to a usable condition. Now, just one final step remained.

The edges of the hide were staked to the ground to form a tent shape. Then, a slow smoking fire was made under the tent. The purpose was to "smoke" the hide. Care was taken to insure the hide was not burned but smoked. This final process cured the hide. Once complete, the untreated rawhide edges were trimmed. Sewn together with other treated mammoth hides, this hide was destined to serve as a mammoth lodge cover.

Chapter 37:

ONNA'S STORY

During the first several evenings of the First Kill ceremonial season, nearly all of the Wind Band gathered at the Square Hearth to eat, visit, tell stories, and listen to the music. Informal and unrehearsed, those gatherings formed the social bonds within the band more than any other assembly. The formal ceremonies such as the Morning Drink, the First Fire, Public Announcements, Wall Paintings, and the Mammoth Feast were all important, emotionally, and spiritually moving. But the informal gatherings, achieved without any prescriptions, bonded the band together in unexplained ways.

Story telling was one of the most enjoyable events especially for the children. Good storytellers were held in high esteem among the Muscogee Mammoth Hunters and good stories could be told and heard over and over again. Onna was a popular storyteller and she could usually be enticed, especially by the children, to tell a story or two.

Her personal story concerning her abduction from her far way homeland was a special favorite to all. There seems to be something about a faraway land with strange and unusual names, exotic but yet familiar, that entices and fans the flames of imagination. Such stories, somehow, become fascinating.

Harjo warmly recalled the first occasion Onna related the story of her abduction to him. It was on one quiet evening on their journey from the coast as they set by the fire and Harjo held her in his arms. Young, emotional Onna cried through most of the telling as she struggled with the Yupik and Muscogee languages. She was not emotional as she told the story nowadays even though she often held tears in her eyes but continued the narrative unbroken and smiling.

Also, that same epic journey when Harjo brought Onna from the coast of the Great Sea to the Echota River Valley was another popular narrative. Children enjoyed the frightening portion of the story of how she and Harjo survived the attack by the lion on that journey. Children, for some reason, take pleasure in being scared; no one knows why.

Aside from her stories, Harjo believed the Mammoth Hunters were in part fascinated by Onna's manner of speech and the sound of her voice. It required only four or five seasons for Onna to become completely fluent in Muscogee. She had a gift with language. Also, as directed by Ayuko, the family stopped speaking Yupik for nearly a season, forcing her to learn Muscogee. She retained, however, a unique and pleasing accent. Her manner of speech captivated Harjo from the first words he heard her say. Her voice still fascinated him. It was soothing, non-threatening, and warmly pleasant to listen to.

Often when she told the story of the lion attack, she would bring out the lion pelt and the listeners would touch and feel the pelt and pass it around as she related the story. Children and women were especially enthralled with the pelt. Harjo could not believe it lasted these many seasons especially under the conditions it was taken, but Onna took extraordinary care of it.

The setting sun painted a breathtaking scene on the evening sky and a few thin clouds captured the brilliant flush color. On many such evenings, the male robins and their close cousins, the varied thrush, sang songs in the same manner as they did to each and every summer morning. The wolves were also performing as their melodious howls echoed from the distant Echota River. They were gathering, as were other scavengers, at the mammoth kill site where plenty of free morsels could still be found.

The boys seated around the Square Hearth copied the wolves' howls. The future hunters were delighted and celebrated if they were able to fool the wolves and entice them to answer their calls. The gathered people were amused and smiled to themselves at the boy's antics. Many of their wolf howls were realistic and only an expert hunter could distinguish between them, but now and then, they howled with some ridiculous sound and laughed at their own silliness. Obviously, there were some secret meanings to their boyish pretend wolf calls.

Most of the Fus Chate family was also at the Square Hearth as was nearly Harjo's entire lodge. Chate and his pregnant young wife, Hokte, had slipped off together, and Loni had escorted Ayuko to the hearth and helped her to sit. Now publicly acknowledged into manhood, Echo, remained the center of attention as he might for several days. Fus and Nigeday sat with the wolf howling boys and were full and complete participants in their childish, albeit, entertaining frolics. Onna sat on one of the seat logs with Summer next to her and Harjo sat across from them.

Harjo noticed Onna was wearing her Rite-of-Passage necklace. The bust of a female in the likeness of Onna and the head of a raven interconnected by interlocked circular links all magnificently carved from a single piece of ivory by grandfather Fus Chate. She also wore her raven feather-hare tail and seashell ornament he had made for her on their journey from the Great Sea. How she managed to hang on to these small items without losing them over so many seasons, he did not know.

Yahola and Kak-ke and Chilocco and Hokose, with their children and grandchildren, took up nearly one complete log seat. The apprentices of the Young Lion Shaman were tending the First Fire and soon had it flaming again and the Four Logs, representing each direction, continued to burn.

Several began to ask Onna to tell the story of her homeland and abduction. It had been last summer since she last told the tale. Summer handed Onna her baby while she and Loni went to retrieve Summer's two little boys who were always on the run and took every opportunity to attempt an escape from the clutches of their mother. No one knows where adventurous boys of two to four summers believe they are escaping to. The third, a toddler girl, was content to stay put at Onna's feet. Ayuko asked Onna to tell the story. Onna would not refuse her mother, so she agreed. Everyone gathered around, especially the children who collected at Onna's feet. Then, with smiles and shifting around, she began.

"My people were the Dyuktai and so named the language they speak. Similar to the Muscogee, the Dyuktai are mammoth hunters. The Dyuktai lived in a great beautiful plain called Zaliv. It is located far to the west on the other side of the Koryak Glacier and the Kamchatka Mountains. The Zaliv Plain is surrounded on three sides by tall glacier mountains. The Koryak lies to the east and the Kamchatka on the south. Also, to the north and the west are breathtaking mountains. The mountain's name is difficult to say in Muscogee, but it is Kolymskoye. Finally, to the south lies the Great Sea. The Dyuktai call the Great Sea Okhotsk." Onna laughed, "That is another Dyuktai word that is difficult to say." She addressed the children seated in front of her. "Can you say the word Okhotsk?" The children pronounced the word together "Ok-ho-t-sk" which brought a smile to the faces of the adults.

"To me as a child, the Zaliv Plain was the center of the world. Now, I know it was not as large as I presumed. Dyuktai hunters traveled out in all directions reaching the mountains and the Great Sea and returned with wondrous stories of adventure. A great river flowed from the mountains to the north, southward to the Great Sea. The Dyuktai called the river the Oklan and it divided the Zaliv Plain. Other rivers flowed from the mountains east and west to the Oklan River. My Dyuktai family and band lived on the Tymlat River which coursed westward down from the Kamchatka Mountains into the Oklan River."

"The edges of the river were wooded with large trees and thick forests and the plain was covered with tall grass and many animals, mostly mammoth. The Echota River reminds me so much of the Tymlat River I lived on as a child. Just the same as here, the mammoth spent the winters in the wooded edges of the rivers then migrated out to the open plains in the spring and summer and the Dyuktai followed them."

"I heard my Dyuktai father and other Dyuktai warriors talking and they said the Kamchatka Mountains were a great peninsula that stretched far to the south surrounded on three sides by the Great Sea. The Koryak Glacier rested on the northern end of the peninsula. They also talked about a strange people with dark skin and black hair who lived on the other side of the Kamchatka Mountains. From a large village on the coast, they hunted strange sea animals in watercraft made from the skin of the sea animals. They seemed to be a terrifying people."

"But the men said the dark-skinned men could not bring their watercraft around the Kamchatka Peninsula because it reached too far to the south. The Great Sea would freeze before they reached the end of the peninsula. And even though rivers flowed from the Kamchatka Mountains, no one could cross over the glacier-but they were wrong."

"My Dyuktai grandfather told all of us children stories. He once told us that his grandfather told him the Dyuktai came from the west across the Kolymskoye Mountains from the valley of the Aldan River. He told us the Zaliv Plain, surrounded on three sides by glaciers and glacier mountains, was but a small patch of the Mammoth Steppe. To the north was a region of solid ice, larger than anyone could know or understand. He called it the Big Father Ice and all the mountains and glacier around us were his wives. Some seasons, the wives were skinny young girls and other seasons they were fat and heavy with babies. Some seasons, the wives were disobedient, so Big Father Ice spanked them until they cried big tears that flowed down the mountains. The ice and glaciers expanded and waned-grew larger-or shrank smaller-throughout the many generations."

"Our winter village was located where the Tymlat River emptied into the Oklan River. The Dyuktai called the village, Palana, and I remember it was so beautiful even in winter. We lived in large underground earth lodges. Usually in early spring, my Dyuktai band followed the mammoth out onto the open plains. But one winter, after a late winter mammoth kill, the band chief decided to stay at Palana into the summer and then migrate and catch up to the herds in late summer. Everyone believed that spending at least a portion of the summer at Palana would be a wonderful experience, but we were wrong."

"One early summer morning, a large band of warriors attacked our village. They were evil strange warriors with dark skin and back hair. My Dyuktai family was up and dressed, enjoying a morning fire when they were attacked. My father told my mother and myself to hide, then he grabbed his weapons and ran out of our earth lodge. My mother put me in our bed and covered me with our mammoth blanket. She told me to hide there and keep quiet. She then took my baby sister and left. Outside, I could hear the sounds of fighting and screaming. I see now my mother thought if she separated her children, she would give each of us a better chance to survive."

"I tried to stay hidden-I was terribly frightened. Two warriors came into our lodge and found me. They tied my hands and feet and carried me out of our lodge. Then, one of them threw me over his shoulder and carried me off."

"I cried and yelled. I could hear the screams and shouts from our village, but I could not see very well thrown over the man's shoulder. As he carried me away, the heartbreaking sound of the attack on our village faded. I could tell there were several warriors walking in a line and other female captives because I could hear them. I squirmed and cried. The warrior hit me hard on my bottom with his hand. I wore a parka and pants so it did not hurt, but he could certainly deliver a painful strike if he wanted."

"He surprised me when he spoke, 'Keep still and quiet,' he ordered with a growl, or I will beat you and tie a gag to your mouth!' I kept still, trying to be quiet, but I still whimpered."

"Just a child, I did not realize it then, but he spoke the Dyuktai language. Certainly, there must have been a long relationship with at least some people of the Dyuktai Tribe and the raiding warriors. But this was the first occasion I had ever seen any people with dark skin and black hair."

"We stopped and he set me down on the ground. I could now see that another girl about my age and an older young woman had also suffered my fate. We sat together. The young woman was several, perhaps five or six summers, older than I, and I knew she was married and had a baby. Five warriors held us captive. The leader appeared to be Dyuktai, with light-colored skin and brown hair, and he spoke the Dyuktai language, but the other four were dark skinned with black hair-such strange, fearsome warriors."

"They untied our hands and feet then began to attach a length of rawhide around our necks. Suddenly, the young woman took off in a desperate run. All the warriors looked at each other and began to laugh. She did not go far; one of them pursued her, caught her, and pulled her back."

"The leader growled an order, 'Hold her!' He looked at me and the other girl captive with a cruel expression. 'Now you learn the fate of naughty little girls who try to escape,' he snarled as he spoke."

"One warrior stood behind her, holding her arms as another lifted up her parka, untied the drawstrings on her pants and pulled them down. Then, they laid her face down on the ground with her parka pulled up over her waist. One warrior held her ankles and another grasped her wrists."

"The leader got down on his knees beside her. He raised his hand high above his head and brought his palm down hard on her bare buttocks. He raised his hand again and repeated the hard slaps over and over. As his hand rained down, she squirmed, fighting against her hold to no avail. The poor young woman cried and cried, finally begging him to stop."

"Her buttocks burned red when he finally stopped. 'Are you going to be a good little girl?' he growled in anger as he panted out of breath from slapping."

"Yes-yes-yes!' she replied through dreadful tears."

"'Are you going to try to run away again?' he asked still in anger."

"'No-no-please!' cried out the poor desperate girl"

"Meanwhile the other girl and I hugged each other crying out of fear and sympathy for the punished young woman. Finished, the leader got up and came to the other girl and I as two other warriors stood by us. We cringed in shock and fear."

"He looked at both of us with a face void of compassion. 'The same thing will happen to you,' he threatened, 'if you are bad little girls and try to run away! Do you understand?' I shook my head yes as I cried, and the other girl put the palms of her hands to her mouth also shaking her head yes."

"Meanwhile, the poor spanked young woman stood crying, rubbing her backside. The two warriors who had held her down stood by laughing and sneering, obviously making fun of her in their language. Then, one of them took her arms from behind and held her as the other grabbed her hair on each side of her head then roughly kissed her. He then reached one hand down and began to massage her womanhood as she continued to cry and whimper."

"The leader looked over, yelling out something in their language, so they released her. He then ordered the woman to pull her pants back up and then growled out another order in their strange language. The whimpering young woman came to me and the other girl, so we took her to us. We embraced her, comforting her as best we could together on the ground. The other warriors proceeded to tie the buckskin ropes around our necks."

"I had not noticed before, but each warrior carried a backpack, side-pouch, water pouches, blankets, bedrolls, and an array of weapons. They sat together taking stock of their supplies, apparently planning their next course of action. The leader did most of the talking then growled out orders. They broke, came to us, and taking hold of our arms pulled us to our feet. A long, hopeless journey began."

"They led us single file. The leader went first followed by a warrior leading each of us captive by the buckskin rope attached to our necks. The remaining warrior fell behind, presumably to guard our rear. The poor punished young woman whimpered most of the day. I was so afraid."

"That evening we stopped, and they fed us with pemmican and plenty of water to wash it down. They took us together and the leader told us to urinate. It was embarrassing as the other warriors watched and sneered. After we were finished, they tied our ankles together. The tie was loose so as not to cut circulation, but the knot was tight. We could not untie the knots and they had searched us to ensure that we did not have any cutting tools. They put us down on a caribou blanket by a large tree and covered us with another. We three captives huddled together for comfort and warmth. The night was cold in the mountains, the sky clear and the stars bright. We slept well considering the circumstances. I did not want to admit it but deep down I knew. There would be no escape."

"The next morning, after a meal of pemmican and water, they again allowed us to relieve ourselves under the same embarrassing manner. Then again, we were on a single file march. The wooded valley they led us through was beautiful, crossed by many small cold, clear streams. Under other circumstances, it would have been a wondrous adventure, crossing those formidable mountains."

"The long difficult trek continued each day, but they stopped frequently, allowing us to rest and drink water. At first, we were embarrassed as the warriors laughed and sneered as we urinated and left dung, but soon that novelty wore thin and they paid us little attention."

"On the third or fourth evening, they built a large fire now assured that we were not being pursued. Two of the warriors came and took the young woman and forced her to have sex with them. They pulled her clothes off as they roughly kissed and fondled her then made her get down on her hands and knees. One man got down on his knees in front of her and held her by her hair and continued to kiss and molest her with his hands while the other was also on his knees behind her with his pants down, rubbing her still bruised backside. To no avail, she cried and begged them not to hurt her."

"I was terribly afraid and painfully sorry for her. I covered my ears and closed my eyes huddling with the other girl. After they brought the young woman back to us, we held her close offering her comfort as best we could. My heart was broken for her."

"The next evening, the warriors engaged in a big argument. I hoped they would fight and kill each other. Apparently, the leader was not going to allow the others to have sex with us or abuse us. He became our protector. I am not sure if he was concerned with our welfare or if he calculated we would bring a higher price if we were spared beatings and rape. Either way, it was to our benefit."

"One evening was the same as another. We rested, they fed us, and we slept together, although they no longer tied our ankles. It seems as though we had cleared the pass through the mountains, but I was not certain. It felt as though the nights became warmer and our trek seemed to generally slope down. I cannot recall how many days and

571

evenings passed and often when I think back, it seems as though it were a whole life."

Onna stopped to catch her breath. She smiled looking around at the many eager faces anxious to hear her continue the saga. Summer's baby who had been content to sit quietly in front of her now fussed, beckoning Onna to pick her up. Onna could tell by the manner of her whining she was not hungry and did not want to nurse but only to be held. Onna brought her to her shoulder as she put her thumb into her mouth, now content. Onna continued.

"Then, one warm afternoon, we came into view of the Great Sea. The sight was breathtaking and even though my circumstance and those of my fellow captives remained dire, I'll never forget the overpowering emotion of the sea."

"They brought us to a very large coastal village, larger than any I could have imagined. I heard them say the name of the village was Ostrov. I also understood them to say there was another coastal village of equal size located farther south called Ushki. I could not count the number of the many earth lodges aligned side by side and the structure posts scattered throughout the village. Also, skin lodges of many different shapes and sizes dotted the coastline. In addition, many types and sizes of sea crafts manufactured from animal skins appeared to be all over the village. I have never seen so many people gathered in one place. The men all seemed to be engaged in sea mammal hunting and the women in processing the hides. Except for the one warrior leader and us three captives, all the people had black hair and dark skin. The size and complexity of the village including the various activities simply overwhelmed me."

"The corner of a large earth lodge provided living accommodations for the five raiding warriors and their three young female captives. Our captors came and went with regularity, always leaving at least one to guard us. Soon we were elevated to the center of attention. Throughout the day and much of the evening, warriors came by to look at us and presumably, discuss our worth. I recognized several strange languages."

"They took us out on several occasions during the day and allowed us to attend to personal needs and exercise. Those excursions also provided the occasion for the men in the village to look us over in the bright daylight."

"Late one sunny morning, they took us out to where a large crowd of men were gathered. I remember the wind blew in from the Great Sea carrying such an unusual aroma-a strange scent neither pleasing nor offensive but lasting in memory. My captors lifted me up onto a small, waist-high platform constructed of earth and rocks. They took my parka off and pulled my pants down and I stood naked before the large crowd of staring interested men. Then, the men shouted out strange words while the leader of my captors answered-selling me to the man who offered the most in skins or other valuables."

"The Canineqmiut man named Tangkak offered the highest price. They allowed me to dress while the leader of my captors spoke to me. 'You belong to this man now and you will go with him. He seems to be a gentle man and I do not think he will hurt you.' Then he turned and walked away."

"That was the last occasion I heard the Dyuktai language spoken until my children were old enough to talk. I do not know what became of the other female captives from my village. I presume they suffered the same fate. Tangkak took me immediately to the shore where he lifted me into a large open skin craft the Yupik call an umiak. Several men were in the boat, and we launched out into the open expanse of the Great Sea. We followed the shore line northward."

"Similar to the long journey over the glaciated mountains, traveling in an open boat on the Great Sea would have been a great adventure under other circumstances. That first day was sunny and bright but the many days that followed found the coastline of the sea cloudy and cold. Chilled wind blew from the sea but Tangkak gave me a warm blanket of sea mammal skin. During the day, Tangkak and the other men paddled the craft and at night, we went ashore and camped."

"The warrior leader was correct, Tangkak was a gentle man. He did not hurt, humiliate, or abuse me. He did not force me to take my clothes off. We slept together but for warmth and perhaps for my protection from the other men. I remember his offensive smell, but he did me no harm. The other men paid me little attention. They paddled the boat, talking among themselves. I sat by Tangkak as he paddled. Early on, he began to teach me Yupik words."

"After many days of travel, we reached the Koryak Glacier and I must tell you it was a thrilling sight. I was too young and naïve to realize how treacherous the glacier could be. The men took the craft out into the open sea away from the shoreline in the event a large chunk of the glacier might fall off and wreck the craft. The enormous glacier loomed dangerously beautiful. It was white and clear, the same as the ice on the Echota River but also a beautiful strange blue color. It cracked as it thawed in loud crashes that I believe could be heard all the distance to the horizon."

"We did not go ashore but stayed in the openness of the Great Sea. The men took turns sleeping, paddling, and moved the craft onward throughout the night. I also took turns at paddling which helped ward off the cold and wet of the open sea and boredom of just sitting in the craft. Once, a huge chuck of the glacier did fall off. It crashed into the sea far behind us. I tell you it was a spectacular sight, showing me how dangerous it would have been to be near the glacier. Eventually, large movements of water rocked our craft. I actually thought it was fun, at least it added some excitement."

"I also saw many strange sea animals; some would swim up close to the craft. A few were larger than a mammoth, perhaps as large as a mammoth lodge. They could have easily overturned the craft, but they seemed to be just curious, not dangerous. Yes, I must admit, watching those large sea animals still lingers as a thrilling experience."

"Finally, the shoreline curved away from the glacier which extended on inland and we could safely come ashore. All of us laughed as we were able to stand on the ground, build a fire, drink hot tea, and sleep lying down. We continued to follow the shoreline pulling in and camping at night."

"The sun again appeared early in the afternoon with mild winds and a calm Great Sea as the men paddled the craft into a large bay and to the Canineqmiut village. Most of the Canineqmiut had already moved up river to summer camps but many of Tangkak's family and friends remained at the coastal village. A happy reunion with his wife awaited him but also with his brother."

"Tangkak greeted his family and friends. It was so odd to see them rub noses in greeting but they also kissed, and he embraced his wife who was named Usugan. His brother was called Ilalke. I came to know these two well but not so much the others. He introduced me and explained my presence. For the moment, I was a novelty. They had never seen anyone like me-yellow hair, blue eyes, and light-colored skin. They were all curious and examined me. We all spent the night in a large dirt lodge including the men who had brought us in the umiak. I slept with Tangkak and his wife, Usugan."

We spent the next day treating the skins of all the sea craft with oil from the sea mammals, including the umiak that had brought us across the Great Sea. Tangkak's family owned several skin crafts. The long narrow sea craft used by a single man to hunt seal on the sea was called a kayak. They also owned an umiak."

"The following morning, we all left. The men who had brought us returned to the Great Sea in their craft and headed southward, presumably back to their Ostrov Village. Tangkak's group loaded their umiak and kayaks and we headed up the river they call Kolavinarak to their summer camps."

Onna paused again and looked around at the children's faces. "Can anyone say that long Yupik word-Ko-la-vin-a-rak?" The children repeated the word out loud together. This always brought a smile and light laughter from the listening crowd.

"I stayed with Tangkak and Usugan at their family summer camp. Then, in the fall we moved again and finally in the winter, once again. In winter, many of the dispersed Canineqmiut families and bands came together in a large winter village. We lived in large underground earth lodges. All the men stayed together in large earth lodges and women and children live together in smaller ones. Most of the day and night, I spent with Usugan and slept with her at night."

"Even though I was a servant girl, I was not treated badly. Tangkak did not beat me or sexually abuse me and Usugan also treated me with kindness. Oh, I terribly missed my own family and people, but I had resolved that I would never see them again. And for all I knew, they may have been killed during the attack."

"Early in the winter, however, my situation took a turn for the worse-Tangkak died. Accordingly, to Canineqmiut custom, his brother Ilalke became husband to Usugan and my master. Ilalke was a cruel man and treated Usugan and I with little respect or dignity. On several occasions, he hit me. He wanted to force sex on me but somehow Usugan was able to stop him. I am grateful to her. She protected me. What little I did receive in food and kindness came from her. Luckily, all the men stay together and the small earth lodge that Usugan and I lived in belonged to her. Consequently, Ilalke was obliged to visit her lodge to attempt to abuse me."

"Then, early in the spring, the whole village loaded all their belongings onto sleds including the many sea craft and moved to the coast of the Great Sea to the large spring village they call Up'nerkillermiut. The living situation remained the same-all the men stayed in large underground earth lodges and the women and children in the smaller "women's houses" with Usugan and I living in her small but warm house. The men hunted the seals and the women worked very hard processing the meat and seal hides. I worked very hard. I thought some days I might just drop to the ground unconscious. But at least there was plenty of food and I slept comfortably with Usugan in her warm little earth house. But I knew I could not go on. Ilalke continued to force his sexual attentions on me. Once he pulled my pants down and whipped my backside with a switch. Usugan stopped him, but I knew she would not always be able too."

"Then, one day everything changed. As if by a miracle, I was given hope with a chance for a new and better life. A young Mammoth Hunter came to the village to trade. He impressed all the villagers. They all said he was generous and brave. Once inside one of the large sod houses where the men lived, he stopped Ilalke from beating and hurting me. Usugan told me I should take my chances with this Mammoth Hunter. She gave me a new pair of well-made grass socks. So, when the young Mammoth Hunter left to return to his land, I sneaked out of the lodge and ran away from the village to follow him. I nearly died but he found me. He saved my life."

Onna stopped, then looked around at the children's faces. "Do you know who he was?" All the children looked, pointing at Harjo and they all said his name at the same moment "Harjo." Onna smiled at the way children are able to spontaneously synchronize their words, seemingly without practice or forethought.

She also looked over to Harjo, smiling. Harjo returned her smile with only a slight blush as he had now grown to expect being singled out by Onna having heard this story on more than a few occasions over the many seasons.

"Yes," said Onna still smiling and looking at her husband. "Harjo gave me hope-he gave me my freedom and he brought me across the Mammoth Steppe from the coast of the Great Sea to the Echota Valley." She now glanced around at all of the children at her feet. "But that journey is another story for another evening-The End." The children laughed and clapped; the gesture learned from Onna while all the listeners applauded her story.

Onna turned her eyes back to Harjo. Seeing her face, Harjo could not help but smile as her eyes moistened with joy. She spoke to him in her language knowing only he and their children, who were likely not listening, would understand her words. "I love you, Harjo. Thank you for giving me freedom and life. I will belong to you always."

Harjo likewise responded in Dyuktai. "I love you, Onna, from now until forever."

Chapter 38:

EXPLORATION

T he Fus Chate family appeared as a migrating small band as they readied for their summer journey to Coweta to construct a family mammoth lodge. Several sturdy travails, loaded and secured with complete mammoth hides including other supplies, awaited in a line. Chate's young wife, Hokte, drew near to birthing her first, consequently Onna would remain at Wetumka as a midwife as would Ayuko, Summer, and her children. Originally, Loni was to remain with the band but she offered such a desperate appeal to go, that Harjo finally agreed.

"After all, Father," she pleaded, "Mother made a more dangerous and longer journey when she was my age and she grew up to be wise and beautiful."

Onna, children and grandchildren under 12 summers of age, the elderly and pregnant women would remain, while the rest of the family under Yahola's leadership would make the journey. A trip of such a lengthy distance, with the added load of the mammoth pelts, was guaranteed to be long and difficult. Additionally, once at Coweta, the strenuous labor required to construct the mammoth lodge would test all. Nonetheless, the voyage still promised to be an adventure, especially for the women, who were rarely afforded the opportunity to experience such an expedition aside from camp movements and migrations. Moreover, the occasion to visit the winter village site and the Big River during the summer when not blanketed in snow and the water frozen solid, remained a thrilling proposition to all.

Constructing a winter mammoth lodge was no easy task requiring several seasons of toil and preparation. Certainly, a whole band, even a small one, could productively complete the task but only a large prosperous family could hope to successfully accomplish such a complex undertaking. The most challenging aspect was that most of the labor had to be completed during the summer or at least during the warmer seasons. Consequently, just access to the winter village of Coweta and the long journey was in itself a challenge. Several seasons were necessary to cut the required number of structural posts, sidewall poles, and to locate, then transport mammoth tusks of the appropriate size and curvature. Just processing a single mammoth hide might be beyond the capability of one family much less the several hides required to cover the lodge superstructure. Finally, excavating the pit presented a large investment in labor and likewise had to be accomplished in warmer seasons, as the frozen winter ground could not be penetrated.

A considerable amount of knowledge and experiences was likewise required. For instance, if the pit was excavated too large, the hides would not cover the super structure. Conversely, if too small, the lodge would be smaller than it otherwise could be. The same held true concerning the pit's depth.

During the preceding winter seasons, some progress could be made. Occasionally, appropriate tusks were located from the expansive bone bed, but the snow-covered frozen ground usually impeded a successful hunt for tusks. Winter trees for construction material likewise remain hard and frozen and many axe blades were broken on winter wood.

Meanwhile, as the family journeyed to Coweta, Harjo planned to travel upstream of the majestic Big River to explore that region. His mission was to ascertain if that region supported a large mammoth herd, a fruitful new river valley, and perhaps a new homeland. This topic had been discussed at length within the Fus Chate family including Micco Yarda but also discussed with other Wind Band leaders. It was now accepted that Harjo would make the journey. Onna was not happy that Harjo would travel alone. He had considered a traveling partner but finally decided to make the journey solo.

Last summer, Harjo led a party of his sons and one nephew, Yahola's boy named Chepane, to Coweta to dig the pit, collect mammoth tusk, and cut construction timbers for the new mammoth lodge. For all five of the young men, the two older married men and the three boys, that summer is still recalled as an exciting adventure, especially for the two younger boys, Fus and Nigeday. The summer sights and sounds along the banks of the Big and Echota Rivers kept Fus and Nigeday inspired. Even though they lived on the upper Echota River during the summer, the mouth of the river where it emptied into the Big River was much different. Perhaps, more than any other aspect, the number and variety of birds caught their attention.

"Look, Fus, look!" called out Nigeday pointing to a flicker as it scaled the trunk of the tree. They had both seen the woodpeckers on the upper Echota, but they were rare and now sightings were daily occurrences. "It climbs the side of the trees!"

"Oh, yes," replied Fus. "Just think how tough their bill must be to peck that hard and fast on the trees. And they are so loud!"

"Can you make their call, Fus?" asked Nigeday. "I have tried but I can't."

"No, not very well," answered Fus. "Father can make their call; I don't know how he does it. Also, Father says other birds, like the chickadees, nest in the holes the flickers make. They peck to make holes for a nest and to find bugs to eat."

Suddenly, the brown woodpecker took flight, sounding its distinctive call. "Look at the flashes of yellow color, Fus. That must be why they call it a flicker because of the flickers of yellow."

"I think you're right, Nigeday. Their flying reminds me of a flashing dart in flight." Both boys agreed as they watched the bird fly away.

It was difficult, hard work digging a waist-high pit for the new semi-subterranean lodge. The work crew of six cut and collected support timbers from the Big River but also carried mammoth long bones and tusks to the winter village from a nearby bone cemetery. One man can lift a mammoth tusk, but it takes two men to carry the heavy ivory piece any distance. Nonetheless, along with the hard work, it was enjoyable being away from parents, family, and young wives for an extended period of the summer season. Summer at Coweta provided another rare opportunity for young Mammoth Hunters.

Although living spruce trees were easily found during the winter, to locate any driftwood was nearly impossible during the frozen season. But now, along the banks of the flowing deep water, each was able to collect that highly prized raw material.

Harjo's spear was constructed of strong spruce driftwood. All the young men of his family examined it with awe, and perhaps a little envy. They did not covet the spear itself but the skill of the craftsman in its manufacturing and the rare material. Harjo related the story to his sons and nephew. Although heard on several previous occasions, they listened intently.

"I was lucky enough to find several lengths of perfect driftwood spruce here on the banks of the Big River. One summer season, long ago, I was chosen along with my father, brothers, and other men and boys to journey to the winter village with the instructions to construct a new entryway to Micco Yarda's mammoth lodge. I was just about Nigeday's age but I did not manufacture a boy's spear. Over several seasons, I carefully crafted a man's spear. I intended to use the spear when I became an adult and took it with me on my Rite-of-Passage. Good driftwood spruce can last a whole life."

Harjo's young work crew also considered themselves lucky for the opportunity to collect spruce driftwood. The idea of manufacturing a longer man's size spear to use as an adult appealed to Nigeday. He would do just that.

Throughout the course of their expedition, Harjo also discussed his plans to explore the upper areas of the Big River next summer. One of Harjo's strategies was to cross the Big River here at Coweta and the confluence with the Echota River then go upstream on the southern side off the great wide river. To his recollection, no Muscogee warrior had ever crossed the river-that alone appealed to Harjo's since of adventure.

Harjo and Chate stood together on the banks of the Big River as Harjo considered his plan to cross the mysterious river next summer and then follow it upstream. A large log also piled with other wood debris slowly drifted by. The wide river flowed slow and lazy.

The trumpeting calls of a large flock of cranes overhead caused Harjo and Chate to look up. The large birds flew in projectile point formations with a single bird at the point leading the way. Their wingspan spread longer than a man's height with their long narrow necks and legs of equal length. Adult birds supported a grey-colored plumage with a bold red crown while juveniles were a dull brown color. They came each spring in great numbers and nested in the open steppe in the upper regions of the Echota Valley following the Echota and Big River on migrations. On the ground, they resembled dancing human figures during the strange hopping and jumping antics of their courtship display. Once their young were reared, they migrated again in great flocks still following the Echota and Big Rivers south and southeast then over the massive Hetute Glacier.

Young Chate pointed to the flock of birds. "Father, perhaps because they are so vocal, large, and obvious, the cranes, more than any other bird, show the evidence that the Hetute Glacier is not the end of the Mammoth Steppe. A land mass, able enough to support the cranes and other birds through the winter, must lie on the other side of the glacier."

Harjo turned to Chate. "Wise thinking, Son. I have for many seasons held the same opinion.

"Something else, Father," said Chate as he turned to Harjo with a stern expression.

"There are only two sides of a river, Father, so what difference would it make which side you followed?" asked Chate in a disagreeable tone.

Harjo looked at his son, noting his serious expression. "Aside from the adventure of it," he answered, "it makes little difference."

"It seems to me to be an unnecessary risk to cross the wide Big River on a raft," declared Chate. "Besides, once on the other side you don't know how extensive the willow thickets are. You may be left with no choice except to struggle through the thickets to reach the edge or follow the muddy banks of the river itself."

Harjo laughed, putting his arm around his oldest son. "Have you become more cautious in your maturity?"

Chate now smiled. "Maybe so, Father, but I know you want to explore the upper river region and not the thickets of the lower river just on the other side."

"You make sound judgments, Chate. It does seem wiser to follow the thickets on this side of the river then reach to the river's edge as the thickets allow."

Chate felt good. He admired that his father would listen to anyone's advice regardless of age or status in the band. He was proud that his father was a true leader.

As the boys searched the bone bed, Chepane called out. "Uncle Harjo, I think I found several good tusks here!"

"Good," answered Harjo as they all converged on Chepane. Harjo inspected the long-curved ivory, concluding these several mammoth tusks were indeed very suitable as lodge supports. The hunters handed their weapons to young Nigeday to carry while a pair lifted up each tusk and transported them back to Coweta. They piled them near the pit.

Harjo's young crew likewise spent several days cutting timber support posts. In particular, the eight up-right posts with forked ends-four to be set in the pit to support the main structure and four to form the main support for the entry room. But they also cut many long poles that would line the sidewalls of the pit as retaining walls. They treated all the wood with mammoth oil. When Harjo concluded that they had manufactured an adequate supply of structural material, they made their way back to the summer camp at Wetumka.

The parting farewell was lengthy and sorrowful. Emotional Onna was in tears from the beginning as she hugged and kissed little Nigeday although he was now nearly as large as her. She grew more emotional as she embraced each of her children then all her family members. Then, the other young women of the family began to cry and soon all the females were in tears to some degree.

As Onna held her head against Harjo's chest, she could hear his bold heart beating. "You come back to me, Harjo," she said gently in a tearful whisper.

"I will," he replied in his usual stoic manner.

Yahola waved his hand over his head, picked up a sturdy heavy-laden travail, and called in a loud voice. "Move out!"

The Fus Chate family with a line of loaded travails began their long journey southward to Coweta. At the same moment, Harjo headed eastward toward the Echota River at the Mammoth Crossing.

Onna, Summer, and Ayuko each held one of Summers babies and with pregnant young Hokte, held each other as tears flowed down all their faces. Through these next long summer nights, they would all most likely sleep together providing each with comfort and melancholy relief, although it remained common for Ayuko to spend nights, off and on, with Micco Yarda and Us'se. Before he was out of sight, Harjo turned and waved, and the women returned his wave. Then, he walked out of view.

Onna stayed as the other women headed back to their shelters. On how many occasions had she stood and watched Harjo walk out of sight knowing she may never see him again or ever learn what became of him. How many? Since she was a mere child, younger than Summer or Hokte. She still could not become accustomed to it. She fought back the tears, wiped them from her face, adjusted the baby in her arms, and followed the other women to the shelters.

Following the same trails he had tracked since he was a boy traveling with his father, Harjo skirted the edge of the vast willow/alder thickets that flourished along the flood plain of the Big River-the winter habitat of both mammoth and caribou who dwell within the Echota River Valley.

The willow/alder thickets, although immeasurable in distance, did not form a solid forested blanket but expanded and shrank as part of a mosaic of open grasslands, drainages, some forested-some not, and rolling hills. Occasionally, the thickets narrowed or disappeared completely, bringing Harjo to the banks of the Big River. Additionally, mammoth tromped out wide paths through the thicket that could be easily followed. There was a risk, however, following a mammoth trail as it may not cut through leading to the riverbank. A mammoth herd, especially during the winter, may wander throughout the thicket with no particular destination.

Having trekked now for many long days, Harjo followed a small brushy stream as it meandered through the open edges of the thickets flowing southward-presumably to empty into the Big River or a larger tributary. The clear watercourse was not wooded but supported an occasional patch of trees including a small grove of large cottonwoods. The trees had grown adjacent to each other forming a closed, protective barrier. Ptarmigan willow, tealeaf willow, and Ptarmigan Bistort flourished along the lucid stream, as did the small noisy game birds. Harjo had taken the opportunity to kill several ptarmigan with his bird dart and even though it was early in the afternoon with plenty of sunlight remaining, he considered camping in the inviting grove of large cottonwoods. Flickers were also attracted to the large cottonwoods. Harjo listened to the distinctive hard, loud pecking and their unique calls. With a smile, he mimicked their calls.

Suddenly, Harjo stopped standing as though frozen-mammoth lay just ahead. Three young bulls quietly feasted on willow buds and a new growth of green blue grass that had pushed its way through the yellow dried grass of last season. The youthful trio must have lingered at the wintering grounds while the rest of the herd migrated north to the calving and breeding grounds. Too immature to participate in the breeding rituals, young bulls occasionally did not migrate with the herd but went their own way. Next summer as they matured, it would be a different story but for now, they were dangerously close.

Caught in the open, Harjo lingered in a precarious situation-if discovered the bulls would most likely trample him to his death. But the wind blew in his favor-the mammoth did not catch his scent and remained ignorant of his presence. Drawing a dart shaft from his quiver, he armed it with a stone-tipped foreshaft then prudently made his way toward the grove of large cottonwoods. He could defend himself there and scale a tree if need be.

Suddenly, off in the distance, he saw a single mammoth. Nearly always an individual mammoth meant a mature bull. As he watched, he confirmed the lone mammoth to be a bull by his movements and gait. He put his hands to his mouth and called out a loud trumpeting mammoth call.

The three young bulls instantly responded. Now the single bull likewise trumpeted. As the wind continued to blow in Harjo's favor, the three juvenile bulls now picked up the scent of the single bull and began to move toward the older mammoth. Harjo had actually copied the call of a female in heat and even though the young trio of bulls was not yet of breeding age, they would still respond to a female call.

Once the three had moved away, Harjo continued across the opening. "Too bad," he grumbled to himself, "the grove of large trees would have been a welcomed camp site." Only mildly disappointed, Harjo continued on to find another camping site, perhaps a rock outcrop with a grove of large trees. He would take more caution in camp selection with mammoth in the area.

As the days passed, Harjo came to an open stream valley lush with tall blue grass and sprinkled with fragrant sage. The narrow clear stream was also open, supporting an occasional wooded grove. Harjo followed this stream southward until it emptied into the Big River.

The majestic Big River itself was changing. At the Coweta winter village and the confluence of the Big and Echota Rivers, the Big River extended wide from bank to bank as large logs and wood debris slowly drifted by on a long lazy journey to the coast of the Great Sea. But here, inland, the river narrowed, flowing much faster. The wooded areas were also changing. Downriver at Coweta, the woodlands appeared as narrow strips that trimmed and followed the two great rivers and nearly all drainages. Upriver, however the wooded strips widened into forest with spruce trees being much more abundant. Harjo also noted the abundance and variety of small passerine birds- some he did not recognize.

Harjo again headed north along the eastern edge of a vast willow/alder thicket. As he made his way, mammoth signs soon became copious and unmistakable. Harjo soon realized he was following the edge of the extensive wintering grounds of an enormous mammoth herd-larger than the herd that roamed the Echota River Valley.

As the days continued, Harjo came to a low wide river valley much like his beloved Echota Valley. Analogous to the Echota, the river flowed southward-clear and cool-most certainly born of mountains and glaciers to the north. As he followed the river downstream, Harjo encountered several rocky regions of the stream including a well-used mammoth crossing. The tracks at the crossing told Harjo an extraordinary number of mammoth crossed here, east to west, then trailed the river northward on their Spring Migration toward their calving grounds which must lay northward, west of the river. This migration pattern loomed nearly identical to the mammoth migration behavior within the Echota Valley.

As he continued to trail the unnamed river southward, Harjo came to a region formed by rock-laden mountains, low but steep, the likes of which he had not before seen. A wide, seemingly deep pit formation on the side of one of the mountain formations remained inexplicable. It required one lengthy day to follow the winding river alongside the base of the mountain formations. Along the way, several small wooded streams cascaded down the mountains to empty into the river. At the southern end of the steep formation, a larger wooded spring-like stream meandered through a narrow steep valley to likewise feed into the unnamed river. It flowed from the east as it quickly dissipated into several small drainages ascending the sides of the valley, especially on the northern slope.

A steep, long, high and open terrace formed along the edge of this tributary river just as it emptied into the unnamed river. This meadow-like terrace was surrounded by wooded groves of cottonwood, willow, alder, birch, and an unusual abundance of spruce. The terraces would be an excellent location for winter mammoth lodges. Mammoth could not climb the steep banks of the terraces. Wood and water were readily accessible and abundant.

Harjo could also determine by the formation and shape of the terrace that it was created by a large unknown water body back in the ancient past. The small spring-like river could not have created such a terrace. Harjo was reminded of the steep terraces he had seen along the coast, which had been created by the Great Sea. Could this terrace, similarly, have been formed by wave action of the Great Sea? This would mean that the Great Sea, long, long ago in the ancient past, long before memory, had extended from its current coastline to these mountain formations; it was difficult to imagine.

Harjo climbed the steep mountain slopes on the northern side of the small valley and reaching a high promontory, was offered a majestic view of the whole landscape. The Big River flowed from the northeast not the east. It formed a great bend following the base of the southern end of the mountain formations, curving southward then to the northwest to finally extend in a general westward direction toward the Echota River and the Great Sea.

The unnamed shallow river meandered southward from the northeast to empty into the Big River near the lower end of the great bend of the Big River. Directly below him, the small, spring-like stream flowed nearly due west and emptied into the unnamed river. Harjo took in a deep breath. The unnamed shallow river presented a breathtaking view, perhaps even more beautiful than his beloved Echota Valley.

From his vantage point, Harjo could now observe the expanse of the willow/alder thickets stretching from the confluence of the unnamed stream and Big River north and west as far as he could see. Harjo remained confident such broad wintering grounds supported a mammoth herd larger than the herd that followed the Echota Valley. Harjo could see another stretch of thickets along both sides of the Big River as it turned northward from its great southern bend. He had noted some caribou signs to the west but perhaps this large stretch of thickets provided winter forage for caribou.

Harjo ascended the mountain, crossing the small spring-like stream, heading south to explore the southern edge of the formation. Again, he found several areas of flat steep terraces, which appeared to him to have been formed by waves of an ocean, and yet the Great Sea lay such a great distance away to the southwest.

Harjo believed he was the first man to lay eyes on this region. "Oh, it's possible," he thought, "a young, adventurous Caribou Hunter may have as he did and followed the edge of the vast thickets which parallel the Big River thus coming to the banks of the unnamed river and likewise explored the area. But that was not the nature of the Caribou Hunters. Yes, they were without question nomadic and self-sufficient. They followed the elusive caribou herds. But they were neither adventurous nor inquisitive. They would not be inclined to explore a new area unless driven to do so by changing caribou migrations."

"Consequently," concluded Harjo, "I am the first man to view this beautiful unnamed river and the valley it formed and this great bend of the Big River."

As he made his way along the southern edge of the formation, suddenly, he spotted something on the ground-it appeared to be a small stone of bluish color. He reached down, picking up the stone and to his surprise, discovered it was not a stone, it was soft. He examined the material, smelled it, and then pinched the object between his thumb and forefinger. Again, to his surprise, the soft material was pigment-paint. It appeared nearly identical to the red or yellow ocher paint but was a beautiful, wondrous, blue color. Darker than the sky, it was nearly the same color as Onna's eyes-the material was inexplicable.

Anxiously, he looked around, discovering several more pieces which he collected, enough to fit into a small pouch. Grounded into powder then mixed with oil or glue, this blue material would become a beautiful blue paint. Onna will be thrilled beyond her imagination.

Harjo looked up, noticing a strange small vein extending along the side of the cliff. Every so often, he saw a small area of the blue material. He presumed the material was formed in the same manner as the ocher did only blue rather than yellow or red. He continued along the base of the cliffs turning northward, returning to the spring-like river where he would camp in a wooded grove with the protection of the high terraces.

The next morning, Harjo headed back to the Echota Valley, following the same route that brought him to this new unnamed valley. More exploration was required but he was convinced this new river valley could become a prosperous new home. The whole Muscogee Tribe could construct mammoth lodges along the protective terraces. Certainly, unanswered questions remained, such as the exact location of the mammoth calving and breeding grounds. If the calving grounds are located at the northern end of the unnamed valley, as he believed, how far to the north? Another consideration, was there a nearby mammoth bone bed to secure lodge construction material? He shrugged his shoulders. It was not a desperate consideration because other materials could replace the mammoth tusks such as spruce wood. Harjo smiled, he felt calm, relaxed,

and believed the possibilities of establishing a new homeland were good.

Chapter 39:

ONNA'S ABDUCTION

As Harjo neared the Echota River, he grew more anxious to see Onna again. Certainly, he missed his children, and his whole family including Summer. But, his beloved Onna loomed in the forefront of his memories. Many days and nights had passed since he left on his exploration journey and now the tall, head-high blue grass signaled late summer. He was also curious to learn how the work had gone with the construction of the new mammoth lodge.

Drawn to distant campfire smoke, he investigated. It must be Wind Band warriors, but the ever-cautious Harjo approached the fire with vigilance. He paused some distance from the camp and could see three figures around the fire. He whistled a signal.

To his surprise, he heard an answered whistle of alert-danger-a whistle of distress came from the camp. Harjo now knew the three were at least Muscogee men. He answered the distress signal then hurriedly ran toward the site.

As he came upon the camp, he recognized three Wind Band warriors, all had been wounded. Honeche's oldest boy, O'pa called out Harjo's name as Harjo ran up to him. He had taken a dart in the leg. Harjo saw that he had somehow been able to remove the deadly point and the foreshaft. Most likely the point had missed the bone and passed all the way through his leg. O'pa's son, Wakuche, lay on his back on a hastily constructed travail. He had been severely wounded in the chest-the point embedded-the foreshaft protruded. He was an adult but still very young having just completed his Rite-of-Passage only two or three summers ago. Katchu's son, Ayo, sat on the ground situated on the other side of Wakuche. He had taken a dart in the shoulder, but his wound did not appear severe, more of a glancing strike, consequently he was lucky and did not have a dart point embedded in him.

Harjo surmised they were attempting a desperate struggle to transport Wakuche back to the Wetumka camp but could not keep his wound from bleeding, so they decided to build a fire and cauterize his injury. Perhaps they intended to stop the lethal flow of blood on their own wounds as well. Harjo could see O'pa's leg had bled badly although Ayo's wound much less.

Breathing hard and fighting back the pain, O'pa cut open Wakuche's parka and holding a bloody piece of clothing, he pressed it to his son's chest and against the pro-truding foreshaft. He looked at Harjo with a grimacing face and related the tragic story.

"Onna was with us, Harjo. We came to pick berries. It seemed safe enough and she is hard to say no to. She was off by herself but only a short distance away. Five Enemy Warriors ambushed us. We were all three hit with darts as you can see. I feel stupid and foolish; I did not see them at all. I managed to throw a dart striking one warrior. I don't know how bad he was hit."

O'pa swallowed hard, grasping his blood-soaked leg then continued. "Onna fought with her spear—one warrior in front of her and one behind. She was brave, Harjo, but they overpowered her then bound her up. One warrior threw her over his shoulder-then they were gone. I tried to throw a second dart, but I collapsed."

"Hand me a fire stick! It should be ready now!" O'pa called out to Ayo but he did not respond.

Harjo quickly went to the campfire, picking up a small burning stick. He blew out the flame, then blew on the smoldering coal to insure it glowed red-hot. Then, he quickly took the glowing stick to O'pa who also blew hot breath on the red-hot ember. He pulled away the bloody clothing that he held pressed against Wakuche's chest, exposing his skin, the deep wound, and the foreshaft. As the blood began to seep, O'pa cauterized the wound. It sizzled and smoked as the smell of burning flesh drifted to their nostrils. Wakuche lay still as he was too unconscious to stir or react to the burning pain. It was obvious to Harjo, that little hope of his survival remained.

Harjo put his hand on O'pa's shoulder. "Now we each have our own desperate struggle, O'pa. You will fight to save your beloved son and I go after Onna!"

O'pa shook his head in understanding, then pointed. "They took her northward toward the Ronoto Hills. In that same direction, you will find where we were attacked."

Again, Harjo grasped O'pa's shoulder. He then reached over, gripping Ayo's leg. "Keep courage, Ayo. Help O'pa take Wakuche back to Wetumka." Ayo looked up at Harjo, his face grimaced in pain, but he nodded yes.

Harjo turned again to O'pa. "Tell my family not to pursue me. I will not return without Onna and I will follow her captors to the end of the Mammoth Steppe, if need be."

O'pa looked at Harjo fighting back the pain but nodded. Harjo rose departing in a run toward the direction pointed out by O'pa. It did not take him long to locate the ambush site-littered with darts, blood, berry pouches, Onna's backpack, and her spear.

Harjo cached her belongings along with his own backpack. He would travel as light as possible. He cut a length of strap from the large piece of buckskin stashed in Onna's backpack and attached it to his rolled up sleeping bag. He would carry his sleeping bag over one shoulder and his dart quiver over the other. He used Onna's small shoulder bag to carry her small water pouch, pemmican, mammoth jerky, and a few other items. This attire would be somewhat cumbersome for running. He first thought of leaving the sleeping bag with his backpack to give him more running speed then he had second thoughts. The nights are turning colder on the Mammoth Steppe. He considered this will be a long-distance pursuit. Thus, a good night's sleep may prove more important than any slight edge in running speed over the long distance and many lengthy days to come. He could see a trail left by his quarry in the tall blue grass heading northward.

As he began in a slow run, a heavy gust of wind blew along the trail, laying down the tall grass as if to show the way. As he ran, music crept into his head. He heard the song the Wind Band musicians played the very morning Onna painted her first picture of a mammoth on the rock shelter wall. The painting was still there continuing to be admired by all. The music, especially the beat of the drum, gave him a running rhythm. In his mind, he could see Onna's smiling face as he held his spear in one hand and the sleeping bag strap in the other-his boots hit the Mammoth Steppe in a determined cadence.

When he was a boy, Harjo could run without stopping a full long summer's day-from dawn until dusk. But now, at his age he would employ a simple but effective run/walk method—running as long as he could, then slowing to a walk until he regained his breath—then run again. He intended to keep this pace the length of the day stopping only to drink, eat, and sleep. The moon would not be bright enough to travel at night and even if it was, he would not take the risk of losing the trail during a moonlight night. No, he would sleep at night, as they will. Eventually, he will catch up to them.

Harjo ran up to the top of a small low promontory. Breathing hard, he took his sleeping bag and dart quiver off, then set down to catch his breath. He took Onna's small shoulder bag, pulling out a slice of jerky along with water. The open flat grasslands loomed expansively before him, especially to the north and west. Suddenly, he saw a large bear running along in a steady gait, likewise heading northward toward the Ronoto Hills. Bison, as well as caribou, congregated with their spring born young along the low hills of the Ronoto. Consequently, lion and wolves were likewise attracted to the hills to take advantage of the abundant calves and fawns as easy prey. The scavenging bears were also drawn to the region with more opportunities to commandeer prey from the apex predators. He was reminded of the dangers of running across the open steppe, inviting both lion and wolves, perhaps bears as well, to give chase and attack.

Harjo could also see a single trail meandering through the tall blue grass, subtle but clearly marked. His quarry headed north. Perhaps they followed the North Star. Onna would leave footprints whenever possible or any other method she could get away with to mark the trail. He rest assured she would leave clever markers for him to find.

Harjo made a fire his first night, deciding he would do so for the next few nights.

The fire glowed warm and comforting. Afterwards, he would sleep without a fire. He was now assured that bringing his sleeping bag was a wise decision. He first considered counting the days on a chord to know the exact number. This knowledge might be an advantage during his and Onna's return trip. He then decided no. It did not matter how many days it took to catch them; besides he would keep a rough number in his head regardless. He marked the North Star direction on the ground.

Harjo slowed to a walk. He panted hard. The subtle trail continued north through the tall grass, but the ground was hard. If his quarry had intermingled with a caribou herd or veered off, it would be difficult to notice. Suddenly, he stopped, on the ground a raven feather. No-it was more-a feather, a hare tail, and a seashell. It was Onna's hair ornament made by his own hand so many seasons ago on their epic journey from the Great Sea. He reached down and picked it up. Harjo realized back then just how clever Onna was and she was just as clever now. She marked the path unnoticed by her captors. Now there was no doubt he was on their trail. Harjo stowed the ornament in Onna's bag. He would give it to her again during an appropriate moment. Yet again, the wind blew from his back, across the grass, bending the stalk heads due north. The spirit brother also sends help, showing the way. Harjo took a deep breath then continued on in a slow but steady run.

Several days ago, Harjo stopped for water, filling Onna's water pouch at a small stream. Footprints marked the banks all along the stream including one very small noticeable print-Onna's. They too had stopped to fill their water skins. But now, the days had lapsed without any clear signs. Several trails extended northward including the trail he now followed-the most likely choice. Harjo began to worry they had changed course and he had somehow overlooked the change-then he stopped, breathing hard as a feature on the ground brought a smile to his face-a campfire. Onna's captors had not built a fire the first few days of their escape considering that Wind Band warriors may pursue. Now confident they were not being followed; they had built a fire.

He set down and refreshed himself. Signs lay all around the camp. Then, he noticed adjacent to the circle of hearth rocks, one clear small footprint. It was extremely unlikely anyone would step at that angle next to the campfire as though straddling it. No, it was clever little Onna, leaving yet another telltale sign.

The next day, up ahead in a small wooded grove, ravens from the tops of the trees told of death. Anxiously, heart pounding, Harjo approached the lone figure spread out on the ground. Relieved, he recognized the body of a dead Enemy Warrior. Certainly, the warrior wounded by O'pa who somehow had managed to survive this long.

"The Enemy Warriors don't bother to bury their own dead," scoffed Harjo out loud. Obviously, he found another of their camps. Harjo held his hand over the coals. "Still warm," he said with a smile. Then, he looked up to see a small bush with a small broken branch. He smiled again and whispered out loud, "Onna marks the way—soon—very soon,"

Onna sat on a rock. The Enemy Warrior leader stood next to her, adjusting his belt and atlatl. Onna looked up to his face. "How is it you speak Muscogee?" she asked in a calm, quiet voice.

The warrior leader looked around at the other warriors and raised his head back, laughing out loud. The others laughed as well. "Some of our bitch mothers were Muscogee, taken very young from one of your bands. Others came from the Caribou Band. Many of us speak your mongrel language but I will wager none of you speak ours."

The leader reached down and grabbed Onna's throat, pushing her head back. "You're brave and sassy aren't you and you're a beautiful little bitch," he scowled. "I am anxious to penetrate that tight little anus of yours. Never had it that way, have you?" The other warriors moved to also stand next to her. "Well, your sweet little butt is safe for now!" He released her throat with a hard push.

Another warrior spoke up. "I want to take her now. That old Shaman won't know or care!"

The enemy leader looked at the warrior with dismay. "That's where you're wrong, idiot, on both counts," growled the leader. "I know that old man and he will pay more for a virgin. Besides you will rip her apart with your passion and slap bruises on her butt. You'll lower her price!"

He turned to Onna. "No, pretty fox, your tight little anus is safe for the present. We'll just continue to strip you naked and enjoy watching you urinate and drop dung." All the warriors laughed out loud as they prepared to move out.

Harjo camped on a low rock rise. He would have a good view of the stars tonight and a long clear view of the landscape tomorrow. He located the North Star at full dark. As he gazed up into the sky, his heart jumped. On the horizon, nearly aligned with the North Star, he could see a campfire. It blazed high and hot, completely in the open. His heart began to sing. Suddenly, the wind blew through his hair and as in a vision, he could see Onna sitting by the fire. She seemed calm and unhurt. Then she quickly looked up toward him and gently smiled. Harjo smiled, too and whispered out loud, "Very soon my love, very soon."

The Enemy Warriors with their single captive moved along at a slow walking pace and generally maintained a single file order. The raiding leader went first, followed by his "second" who held the narrow strap attached to Onna's neck as she followed in third. Following behind Onna, the third warrior insured that she had no escape. The remaining raider kept a two to three pace interval with the trailing warrior. Thus, assigned the duty to guard their rear, he periodically turned, watching behind them. The leader stopped and turned around. The others followed his lead and likewise stopped.

"Rest!" he growled.

Onna went down to her hands and knees then sat on the ground. The four warriors formed a rough semicircle around her opened toward the direction they had come. "Give her some water," barked the leader. The raider next to her lifted his water skin from his shoulder, handing it to her. Onna unfastened the stopper and drank. Then, as inconspicuously as she could, she turned her head, glancing behind them, back toward the direction they had just traveled. The wily leader noticed her glance.

"She looks to see if her kinsmen follow," he said in a laughing tone. The others also looked toward their back direction and in so doing, chuckled and smiled at each other. The leader looked down at Onna, then reaching down, he grasped the line attached to her neck, giving it a quick yank.

"Why watch?" he snarled in a mocking voice. "Why do you keep such false hope? We are many, many day's journey ahead and near our own land. No one will come for you."

Onna looked up at him into his sneering face and stared as deep as she could into his eyes. Then, in a low, mystical whisper she replied. "You are wrong-dead wrong. One man will come for me, the man who loves me. He is a strong, fierce warrior-he is brother to the wind. He flies across the tops of the grass like a spirit of vengeance. You will not hear him-you will not see him. But for an instant, you will take one last breath as you feel the point of his spear when it touches your heart. Your life and evil deeds will flash before you and you will know it is him-brother of the wind-who has taken your life and snatched your last breath."

As she spoke the word 'snatched,' she reached up a small but defiant hand forming it into a clinched fist. As she stopped speaking, a sudden gust of wind blew through, lifting up her hair and just as suddenly it disappeared.

The Enemy Warriors all stood in silence, perhaps somewhat mesmerized by the mystical, quiet passion of her voice and her strange accent. Then, the leader let out a one-syllable chuckle. "Move out!" he said. "Less we make it too easy for this 'spirit warrior' to overtake us."

∽◠◡◯◠◡◯◠◡◯◠◡◯∽

The five figures proceeded in a single file through a narrow valley with a steep ridge on the eastern flank. They followed a long, straight well-used caribou trail past a small rock formation surrounded by tall head-high grass. Their marching configuration remained the same. The warrior leader went first as they tracked the caribou game trail, followed by the second warrior who held a rawhide rope attached to Onna's neck who trailed in third.

The third and fourth warriors fell behind in file order-presumably the fourth and last warrior guarded their backs. Now deep into their own country, however, and far from the Echota River Valley, the war party grew less cautious, remaining confident no warrior would pursue them this far. No woman was worth the effort especially one of advanced years as Onna, even though she was still very attractive but well beyond childbearing years. The raiding leader had a plan to trade Onna to an old, powerful, wealthy Shaman who was not interested in babies only in sex and status. Her uniqueness should bring a good price and more if she was not raped or beaten.

Several ravens flew overhead. And, even though the wind was still and calm, the ravens soared in great looping arcs. The large birds called out to acknowledge the presence of the human group, prompting each Enemy Warrior to glance up at the mysterious black scavengers.

Suddenly, as though he was a still deadly shadow, Harjo silently stepped out from his concealed position with his spear raised high, set for a deadly lunge just as the last warrior passed the rock and tall grass formation. His spear point hit the unaware victim in the center of his back with the same force that effectively penetrated the thick hide of many mammoth. The fine red chert point, true and sharp, emerged on the front side of the hapless warrior's chest a hands-breath past his parka coated with blood and with the tissue from his heart, clinging to its edges.

Unexpectedly, the spirit brother intervened. A loud gust of wind blew through the tops of the grass. The mortally wounded warrior may have made a gasping sound as he fell first to his knees, then forward on his chest, dead as he hit the ground. But the wind masked any noise he would have otherwise made as his spirit departed for the other side, without notice. But, the ever-sensitive Onna felt something; she was not sure, something in the spirit of the wind.

Before the warrior hit the ground, Harjo pulled out his spear shaft, leaving the foreshaft imbedded into his victim and rearmed his spear with another deadly foreshaft. The next warrior in line had advanced several paces completely unaware of any mortal danger.

With his arm back, Harjo hurled the spear with a lethal accuracy born from a life of training and it struck the warrior between his shoulder blades. Similar to the first victim, the thin, fine point protruded through his chest and was coated with blood and tissue.

The demise of this warrior, however, brought attention. He called out a gargled yell as he fell forward on his hands and knees looking up with a face wracked in pain. Onna turned around toward the noise of the cry, as did the other two warriors to see Harjo standing in the open, holding a lethal dart and knocking it into his atlatl.

"Harjo," whispered Onna. Her heart cried out in both joy and terror. She immediately realized she was in the direct line-of-dart-flight and so she instantaneously fell to the ground. The warrior immediately in front of Onna dropped the rawhide rope that attached to her neck. He first stood still in shock and disbelief but then managed to turn with his spear drawn back prepared for a throw. The wisdom of ages flashed through Onna's memory, taught to a young girl by a daring young warrior that "anything can be a weapon." The inventive Onna seized a hand-sized rock from the ground and brought it down with all her strength on the warrior's foot. He cried out in pain as he launched his spear. Onna watched in quiet terror as the spear flashed in flight toward Harjo. Her quick thinking, however, interrupted the warrior's aim and his throw. Although her heart nearly stopped, she saw Harjo, seeming with little effort, avoid the otherwise deadly projectile. The cowardly warrior now turned. He ran toward the tall grass, howling in pain and limping.

The remaining warrior, the leader, although evil, was an accomplished warrior. He too had knocked a dart into his atlatl, moving into throwing position. Having watched her own warrior on so many occasions launch a dart, Onna could tell by the way the warrior leader moved, he possessed skills and he released the dart with that warrior's skill and accuracy.

As Onna watched the dart flex and flash in a deadly ribbon of color, her heart cried out in more pain than can be imagined. But somehow, Harjo turned from the waist up at just the correct moment, as the life-taking dart cut across the chest of his parka and sped past her beloved warrior. In that same instant, more agile and swift than even Onna could realize, Harjo's arm was raised as she caught only the flash of Harjo's dart as it flexed toward the warrior leader. Onna turned to see the eyes of the warrior leader grow wide for just a moment. For only a moment, the blink of an eye, fear pierced his heart, as did Harjo's dart. The warrior leader called out a blood-curdling scream as he grasped the dart planted in his chest with one hand, the other still clutching his atlatl as he fell on to his back.

Onna now cried out, "Harjo!"

Harjo simply held up the palm of his left hand and called out. "Stay there!" His right hand was armed with dart and atlatl. He took aim at the cowardly fleeing man and with a few running steps, launched the dart at the distant figure. The fleeing man cried out in pain as the projectile struck him and he fell forward in the tall grass.

Harjo now stood over the body of his first victim and pick up his quarry's spear, quickly touching the point to the fallen enemy's eye to insure his death. Next, he quickly ran forward to his second kill, repeating the same gesture. Then, he ran to Onna with the spears of both his victims.

"It's not over, Onna, there is still danger!" He handed her one of the spears but managed to reach out and touch the side of her face. Onna reached up taking the spear but also grasped his hand. "Stay alert, stay ready," he said in a calm but urgent demeanor.

He ran toward the warrior leader with a victim's spear in hand and checked for life. The fighting had taken place along a beaten trail but now Harjo ran into the dangerous tall grass toward the final casualty. Onna could now see the threat of a wounded warrior concealed in tall grass.

She called out "Be careful, Harjo, be careful!" Harjo stopped a few paces from the final casualty who had apparently lived but not for long. Harjo launched the spear and fulfilled the coward's journey to the other side.

After insuring the demise of his final victim, Harjo now ran back to Onna, falling down on his knees, holding her as she held him. Onna cried anxious tears holding Harjo as tight as she could, calling his name over and over. Tears also formed in Harjo's eyes as he held Onna-embraced her and rocked with her. He looked into her face as tears of joy and passion ran down her cheeks and he kissed her face over and over to insure himself she was real.

Onna cried in such a frantic voice, "I knew you would come for me, Harjo, I knew you would come. You promised me so long ago when we were just children-I remembered-and I knew you would come!"

How long they embraced they do not know or remember. Eventually, Harjo took Onna by the shoulders, looking into her face. "We are not safe yet, Onna. There is still danger, we are deep in their territory."

Onna smiled. Reaching up, she wiped the tears from his face. "I am not afraid my love, my warrior. I know you have a plan."

Simple plans are often the most successful and Harjo's return plan was straightforward and uncomplicated. He would not make the same mistake his slain enemies had made, presuming no one followed him and Onna. He quickly went through the belongings of his victims taking food, knives, and their dart foreshafts. It required only a few moments for Harjo to reshape the ends of their foreshafts to fit into the sockets of his darts and his own spruce spear which he pulled from his second victim's back. Meanwhile, Onna took one of enemy spears with a short foreshaft and cut the butt end of the shaft to fit her size. Then, Harjo took Onna's hand leading her away and allowing all the scavengers access to a human feast.

Although it was more difficult traveling, Harjo led Onna over the ridge into the adjacent valley. Any pursuing Enemy Warriors would most likely presume they headed due south along the caribou trail, the most obvious route. Once in the adjacent valley, he would zigzag eastward and westward avoiding a direct due south heading. It would be nearly impossible for any would-be pursuers to follow them. He would stop and retrieve both of their backpacks, Onna's spear, and perhaps only then, head straightway for Wetumka. They avoided a campfire for the first several nights but Onna was more than content to sleep in Harjo's warm comforting arms. The first few nights, she gently cried tears of joy and relief.

A barefoot Harjo carried a laughing, kicking Onna across the Echota River as she carried Harjo's boots and their two spears.

"You're going to make me drop you if you don't stop kicking!" scolded Harjo.

"I can't help it Harjo-hurry-hurry!"

Once on the other side, Harjo put Onna down. He then quickly went to the ground and pulled his boots on, tying them in place. Onna reached out and took his hand, pulling him to his feet, smiling and laughing without control.

"Hurry—Harjo—hurry, let's run!"

In the lead, Onna held Harjo's hand as they ran across the open meadow toward Wetumka. "I have been running nearly all summer!" called out Harjo.

Onna turned around laughing, "Then the short distance across the meadow should be easy for you. Oh, Harjo, whistle a call!"

Harjo pulled Onna to stop, then whistled loud calls. Suddenly, whistles, calls, and yells echoed throughout the whole village, now alerted. Smiling, Onna jumped into Harjo's arms kissing him. As he set her down, she again took his hand, pulling him into a run. Suddenly, a raven flew out from the village in a direct line toward the running pair. The large black bird circled them screeching out calls. Smiling and running, Onna answered the bird.

Soon the whole village was alive with laughter and shouts. Harjo and Onna's children ran out of the Wetumka camp to greet them, as did other members of the Fus Chate family. In the tall grass meadow at Wetumka, Onna embraced and kissed each of her children and all the members of her family as joyful tears streamed down her face.

Chapter 40:

MICCO HARJO

Micco Yarda's death was a great loss but it was not tragic. Women and children cried at his burial, as they should, but his passing did not inspire the same emotions, as would the sudden casualty of a young hunter tragically killed by a mammoth or a young mother dying in childbirth. Micco Yarda was an old man who had served the Wind Band longer than all, but a few could remember. He died peacefully in his sleep. At his burial, the Wind Band said farewell to the remarkable old man as he journeyed to the other side. An eerie quiet fell upon the summer camp but it was fitting he died at Wetumka. They erected a stone monument over his grave adjacent to the one built for Cheparney.

The next morning, however, sparked activity as the men gathered and talked-a new Micco must be chosen. Harjo and Onna sat on their bison robe at the family hearth adjacent to the two tent shelters. Harjo built a fire, though the air was warm, and was having morning tea as Onna sat weaving a mammoth wool sock. Harjo laid out all his darts and inspected them, looking down the shafts and straightening the ones seemingly flawed. Onna smiled and thought to herself.

"His darts are in perfect condition; he is just looking for something to do."

Onna looked up and saw the men gathering at the Chokofa Tent, then glanced over to Harjo. He understood her expression and whistled a loud, specific whistle. Within a few moments, Nigeday and Loni came running up to the hearth.

"Go up to the Chokofa Tent and escort your grandmother and Us'se down to our shelter," spoke Harjo with more than a hint of an order to his two energetic children. "If either of them refuses, tell them I will come up and carry them down."

Loni opened her mouth then covered it with her hands. The two smiling youngsters look at each other then turned to go. "Children," added Onna, "be respectful!"

"We will," they answered in the same voice, then turned and ran to the tent.

Soon, four figures emerged from the large tent. Ayuko and Loni walked ahead arm-in-arm while Nigeday helped secure an aging Us'se and slowly brought her down.

As Ayuko and Loni approached, "I hope you have hot tea?" asked Ayuko. Now, both of you, get up and kiss your mother." She spoke Yupik so Harjo and Onna knew she was serious and rose to greet her. Ayuko rubbed noses and kissed them both, then the aging matron set down on the robe and took a ladle of tea.

Summer emerged from the family tent and went to Onna putting her arm around her. "Children sleep," she announced. Summer was not sure but knew something was brewing and joined Ayuko on the robe. Standing side by side, Harjo instinctively slid his arm around Onna's waist.

As Nigeday approached with Us'se, he called out. "Father, Chate, Echo, and Fus are at the Chokofa Tent! The men ask for you to come!" The stirring brought all the Fus Chate women and children who were not asleep out from the family's two shelters.

Harjo turned to Onna with a stern face and a serious tone. "You know what will happened if you sneak up to the Chokofa Tent to eavesdrop?"

Smiling, Onna stood on her toes and whispered into Harjo's ear. "Will you spank me? Remember your promise, Harjo, not to punish me in front of anyone especially the children."

"I will do both," replied a stern Harjo.

His voice said he was very serious. "I won't eavesdrop, Love, I promise. Besides I know what is going to happen. They will elect you Micco."

The ever-stoic Harjo sighed a deep breath and formed a serious frown. "I have never sought after, nor do I want to be Micco."

Onna reached up and fussed with his buckskin parka. "I know, my Love." She tilted her head as she looked into his face. "My quiet, brave warrior, but you will accept."

She brushed his parka with her hand. "I've neglected you. So many young children and young wives-you need a new parka. When I've finished weaving your new socks, I'm going to start a new parka for you."

Harjo took Onna's shoulders. At the same monument, she grasped his parka then again stood on her toes and kissed him. He then collected his spear and began to walk toward the Chokofa Shelter.

"May I come too, Father?" asked Nigeday.

"No, you're too young and so is Fus and I'll be sending him down to join you. But, put away my darts and atlatl!" called out Harjo in parting.

Normally, the boy would have been disappointed in not being allowed to join the other men at the meeting. But the opportunity to handle his father's weapons negated the disappointment and brought a broad smile to his face as he eagerly jumped to the task.

The men of the band were all gathered at the Chokofa Tent. Fus waited outside of the tent hoping somehow he would go unnoticed and be allowed to stay and join the men. As Harjo approached, he put his arm around Fus. "Be patient, son. Your dawn of maturity will come. Enjoy your childhood while you can but for now go on down to our shelter and join Nigeday." He patted Fus on the back who walked away disappointed but was glad his father always offered words of understanding and not just an order.

Harjo did not intend to "make an entrance" but did so, nonetheless. The men spoke his name as he entered the Chokofa Tent. Harjo looked around at the faces seeing his sons, brothers, and nephews. Honeche stood at the front of the tent and seemed to be taking charge of the meeting. He pointed to Harjo and spoke right out. "Harjo, the men want you to lead us. They ask you to be Micco." Approval was raised throughout the crowd.

"I've never desired to be Micco. You, Honeche, you're the man for this responsibility." As Harjo spoke, the crowd responded with some disapproval, but more voices rose in question.

"No, Harjo," replied Honeche's loud voice. "You are the warrior for the task. I will accept only if you refuse and the men ask me!"

Yahola spoke out. "Harjo, Micco Yarda once told me he hoped you would take his place. He knew you did not welcome the task, but he also believed you would not refuse it." Again, the air filled with approving voices.

Suddenly, to the surprise of all, the Old Lion Shaman, who had been sitting on the floor in front of Micco Yarda's bed unnoticed, rose up with the aid of his helpers. The atmosphere now seemed strange, nearly mystical, that he and his helpers had been setting there all along-unnoticed by all the men in the tent. It provoked a feeling that he had appeared by magic.

Once the ancient Shaman stood, a great hush fell upon the group of men. He reached out pointing his claw-like finger at Harjo. "It is your destiny to lead this band Harjo. Take up the task!"

The old man did not sit back down but began to walk out of the tent. Instantly, his helpers joined his side and took his arms to secure him. The group parted to create a wide path as the old Shaman walked with his helpers through the crowd and out of the shelter in near silence.

No Wind Band warrior spoke but all eyes turned to Harjo who looked around at the faces of the men, family, and friends he had known all his life. "Alright," he said, taking a deep breath. "I'll take up the task."

A jubilant uproar filled the Chokofa Tent as the Wind Band warriors called out Harjo's name and began to step up to him, taking his hands. His brothers, sons, and nephews embraced him, but Harjo called out over the voices.

"I will gladly relinquish the post at any moment to you, Honeche, or you, Yahola, or you, Chilocco!"

The Fus Chate women remained gathered at their family hearth and busied themselves with ongoing tasks such as weaving mammoth wool socks, sewing, or tending children. Loni now joined the women sitting with Summer and her three children. Onna shook her head smiling as she marveled as Loni conversed with Summer in the Caribou

Hunter language. Of all the languages spoken in the family, Loni seemed to be less fluent in her native Muscogee. Throughout the whole Wetumka camp, the women sat at their family hearths awaiting the outcome of the meeting. The camp boys including Fus and Nigeday, however, had gathered at the waterfall and pool, taking advantage of the rare opportunity when the pool was absent of women and girls.

Nursing her infant, Summer inquired of Onna concerning the meeting. "Men call Harjo name."

Onna reached over to stroke the nursing infant's head and smiled at Summer. She could tell by Summer's voice that she did not quite understand all the proceedings.

"Men call Harjo name," continued Summer, "He honored?"

Onna nodded her head yes.

"Micco same chief, yes?" asked Summer.

Onna again dipped her head and answered, "Yes."

"Harjo now chief, yes?"

Once more Onna answered with a yes.

"Women," she thought for a moment searching for word "respect."

Patient Onna allowed Summer to form her words and continue.

"Women respect wife of chief, yes?"

"Yes, most women do, Summer."

"And me-second wife?"

Onna reached her hand up from the baby's head and gently stroked Summer's hair. "I think most women will offer you a measure of respect as well, Summer. But with respect, we will both have added responsibilities."

Summer thought for a moment then smiled in agreement. She again reminded herself how lucky she was. All women of the Fus Chate family were offered a high measure of respect from both women and men throughout the whole Muscogee Tribe. With her husband as Micco, she welcomed additional respect and responsibility. She felt good as she shifted and adjusted her nursing baby.

Chapter 41:

BEGINNINGS

B irth and death, joy and sorrow, fear and calm, anger and forgiveness, love and passion-life continues on. While her abductors held Onna captive, Hokte bore Chate's first child-Onna and Harjo's first grandchild. Great grandmother Ayuko served as mid-wife so that young Hokte remained in good care and experienced hands. The baby appeared healthy as hopes were high the infant would survive.

Brave young Wakuche died of his wound. The young Lion Shaman pronounced him dead as he first examined the wounded young man. Desperate O'pa called out for the Old Lion Shaman to likewise examine his son, but the old man refused.

One of Honeche's boys, the musician drummer, To-wa-tol-ku, purchased naughty Chufe from her father, Katchu, as his wife, several summers past. Her only child, a boy, grew up strong and when his season came, he ventured out on his Rite-of-Passage journey. Poor worried Chufe fretted and cried nearly every day, seeking comfort from anyone, including Onna, until he returned safely. Micco Harjo proudly delivered the young man's public announcement. Small, but hard working, the Honeche family sent hunters out to secure a bison. They returned with a large store of roasted meat providing a feast for the whole band in honor of their lad's achievement and journey into manhood. Micco Harjo declared several days of celebration, similar to the First Kill Ceremonies but a smaller affair. The Wind Band also celebrated or remembered the completion of a new mammoth lodge by the Fus Chate family; the passing of an old micco and the selection of a new one; and Onna's safe return from abduction. That momentous summer would long be held in memory for better or for worse.

Music filled the air of Wetumka during the days of celebration. With proud musician parents, father To-wa-tol-ku playing the drum and the beautiful singing voice of mother Chufe, the Wind Band had never been treated to a finer sound. The music moved everyone's heart.

The Wind Band also held cave painting ceremonies. On this occasion, Onna painted a picture of a blue horse on the rock shelter wall employing the same techniques she utilized when she painted the mammoth so many seasons ago. All marveled not only at the wonder of the blue paint but also Onna's skill. Then, at the conclusion of the cave painting ceremony, the whole Wind Band was witness to a strange happening provided by the Old Lion Shaman.

It remained difficult for anyone within the Wind Band or throughout the whole Muscogee Tribe to believe the old "Lion Shaman" was still alive. He was older than old—some say older than dirt or stone. So advanced in age, he appeared more dead than alive. He gave up his practice long ago to the apprentice he had trained for 20 summers. The apprentice, now called the young "Lion Shaman" was a good doctor and rendered selfless service to his people. It was rumored the old "Lion Shaman" gave his power, his magic, and his lion spirit to the apprentice. Some believed the old Shaman also gave his lion parka to the young Shaman, but others contended that a parka, especially made from lion pelt, could not last that long. Nevertheless, the young Lion Shaman wore a lion parka that appeared to be the old man's renowned parka. Perhaps it did possess magical properties. The old man dressed in more normal attire and generally only wore a bison robe. The young Lion Shaman, with the aid of his family and other young apprentices, took care of the ancient Lion Shaman.

Nearly every day, even in winter, they took the old man to the edge of the village or camp with his back rest and ground furs and after building a large fire, left him there alone sitting on the ground with his back to the camp. They periodically returned to tend the fire and see to it the old man had food and water. Anyone could approach him, even asking for his opinion or for the wisdom of a long life, but few did. Most people were afraid except for the occasional veteran warrior.

As the cave painting ceremony proceeded, suddenly, as he had on other occasions, the Old Lion Shaman seemingly appeared from nowhere dressed in full regalia including his lion skin parka. The flame of the fire unexpectedly flared up in a loud thundering sound as it did when he started the First Fire. The old man, holding his staff in one hand, raised both hands over his head. The music stopped as all stood in reverence and some in fear. Onna stepped next to Harjo, wrapping her arms around his arm, making sure if he moved anywhere, she would follow. The mysterious Shaman now lowered his arms to address the whole Wind Band gathered in the rock shelter surrounded by the mystical paintings.

"I will soon go to the other side," spoke the old Shaman. "I have wanted to go for many seasons now, but I was required to wait for Harjo."

Being somewhat annoyed and called out in public, fearless Harjo interrupted the powerful old Shaman. "Wait for me," he abruptly replied! "How and why?"

The old man raised his hand to cut off Harjo's question and as if to say-listen and not talk-it will be revealed. Harjo shook his head yes and in a facial expression acknowledged he understood.

The old man continued. "I waited for Harjo to become a warrior and hunter of distinction, a leader, or perhaps our micco. I waited because he is destined to lead, not only the Wind Band, but also all the bands of the Muscogee. I waited because his vision is the same as mine and predicts what is to come. I waited and have not, through all these many seasons, revealed to you Harjo the meaning of your vision-I do so now. Our vision and what is to come is not of our doing. It is the work of the Father Creator "Master of Breath" Esaugeta Emissee. He sends us a glimpse of the future, but we have the will to act on it or not." The old Shaman paused for a moment then continued.

"The world is a great sphere larger than we can imagine or understand. Harjo knows this. His father, Cheparney, taught him this on the high ground at the winter village. What Harjo does not know is that I taught his father this wisdom when he was young on the same ground. I saw in Cheparney the same destiny as I see in Harjo. I understand now. Cheparney's destiny was Harjo and Harjo's destiny is the fate of the Muscogee people."

"The world is a great sphere of land and water-more water than land. That is why the Great Sea to the south meets the Great Frozen Ocean to the north. That is why the great Mammoth Steppe to the west meets the great Mammoth Steppe to the east. I believe a man can journey from this place going west crossing the entire world and return here to this location from the east, although it would require several life spans."

"The land and the water struggle against each other for domination. Occasionally the land grows out of the water-or the converse-the water covers the land. The land we live on, the Mammoth Steppe is doomed. You all see the changes coming yourself. The immense mountains of ice, the Great Sea, and the Frozen Ocean will melt and cover this region of the steppe. The mammoth and all the game will migrate either east or west and we must follow."

"People similar to us and people resembling Harjo's wife, Onna, live far to the west. That is why she was sent to us. So we would know. But to the east and then the southeast, there is a great Mammoth Steppe untouched and unseen by humans. Still farther to the east and the southeast lays another great ocean. The land near this great ocean in the southeast corner of the world is destined to be ruled by the Muscogee people."

"It will take many generations before the Muscogee people arrive at this land, but that long distant journey begins with us and Harjo as our leader. Many will say follow the mammoth northwest then west. But we must follow the mammoth east-northeast-then southeast. Our destiny lies to the east. We, the Muscogee people will be the first humans into that land."

The Old Shaman gazed across the cave room at the crowd, which fell so silent that all could hear the crackling of the fire. Some will say the children, even the infants were quiet-they too mesmerized by the mystic Shaman. Others will say the people just did not hear the children and the infants because they made as much noise as they always do. Then, without warning, the Lion Shaman turned and began to walk away. Instantly, the Young Lion Shaman went up to the old man and along with the young apprentice, escorted him out of the rock shelter. As Onna clung to Harjo's arm, she noticed Summer, next to her, was clinging to her arm. An uneasy stirring was felt through all. Harjo spoke out.

"We all appreciate the wisdom of the Lion Shaman. He has served the Wind Band since before any of us were born. We still have the remainder of the summer here at Wetumka to enjoy. Perhaps we should regard the prospects of a fall kill and most certainly we have fall migration to consider. You all know I have explored the upper areas of the Big River. That region appears to hold promise as a homeland but requires additional exploration and continued discussion."

Harjo paused then turned to the musicians. "So, musicians, let us have another song and perhaps we could all gather at the Chunkey Yard to watch the boys in a game of Fox Chase."

The boys in the gathering including Fus and Nigeday called out in approval while the musicians began to play the songs they often did as the gathering departed the rock shelter.

Honeche called out to Harjo. "May I speak to you, Harjo?"

Onna released Harjo's arm, patting his shoulder then stood on her toes offering a quick kiss the side of his mouth. "Go and talk, Love, we'll meet you at the yard."

"All right," replied Harjo. He then walked over to Honeche.

Summer was so upset she began to cry. Then Onna realized she might not understand what was happening. "Ayuko and Loni, will you two take Summer's children to the yard so I can talk with her?" Taking charge of the three youngsters, they escorted them to the yard.

Onna put her arm around distressed, tearful Summer brushing her hair back with her other hand. "What is it my Love, what do you not understand?"

"Wind Band go new land?" Summer asked in a low whimper.

Onna gently nodded her head. "Most likely we will go."

"I can stay you-Harjo, same now, yes?"

Onna stopped, placing her hands on the sides of Summer's face gently drawing her close. "Oh, yes, yes, my young Love. You and your children will always stay with Harjo and I. You will always stay in the Fus Chate family."

Relieved, Summer wrapped her arms around Onna to embrace her. Then she beamed as she sniffed her nose, bringing a smile to Onna's face. Then Summer's face showed the serious expression in the manner of the Caribou Hunters that she desperately wanted to ask questions.

"Yes, Summer, ask questions."

Summer swallowed hard then looked at Onna with her serious expression. "Harjo lead Wind Band west, over Koryak Glacier, to your land, yes?"

Onna paused for a moment-the words 'your land' moved her thoughts. Suddenly, she caught a glimpse of 'her land' as though in a vision. She saw her river valley childhood home, her village, and the faces of her parents taking a brief step into the spirit world. Those thoughts and vision brought a warm calmness and a smile to her face.

Then, she answered Summer. "No, he will lead us east."

"East?" asked Summer, "to big glacier mountain?"

"No," replied Onna, as she could not resist but to reach up, brushing back the hair on the side of Summer's beautiful face.

"Harjo will lead us to a land that lies between the glacier mountains. In the valleys of the Big River and a beautiful, wide valley formed by a shallow river that as yet has no name."

Appendix I

ANIMALS, PLANTS, AND BIRDS

Alder: *Alnus spp*
Antelope (Saiga): *Saiga tartarica*
Artic fox: *Alopex lagopus*
Beach grass: *Elymus arenarius*
Bear: *Arctodus simus*
Bear root: *Hedysarum alpinum*
Bearded seal: *Erignathus barbatus*
Birch: *Betula spp*
Bistort: *Polygonum viviparum*
Bison (Steppe): *Bison priscus*
Bison (Wheatgrass) grass: *Agropyron cistatum*
Blue (joint) grass: *Calamagrostis canadensis*
Canineqmiut tea: *Rhodiola integrifolia*
Caribou: *Rangifer arcticus*
Cottonwood tree: *Populus balsamifera*
Crane (Sandhill): *Grus canadensis*
Dwarf birch: *Betula nana*
Eagle (Bald): *Haliaeetus leucocephallus*
Gray jay: *Perisoreus canadensis*
Ground squirrel: *Citellus parryi*
Horned owl: *Bubo virginianus*
Horse: *Equus lambie*

Lemmings: *Dicrostonyx spp*
Lichens: *Sphagnum spp*
Lion: *Panthera leo spelaea*
Lynx: *Lynx*
Magpie: *Pica*
Mammoth: *Mammuthus primigenius*
Mammoth hunter tea: *Ledum palustre*
Marsh locks: *Potentilla palustre L*
Marmot: *Marmota caligata*
Moss: *Sphagnum spp*
Musk ox: *Bootherium nivicolens*
Potato: *Claytonia tuberose*
Ptarmigan willow: *Salix alaxensis*
Ptarmigan bistort: *Polygonum vivparum*
Raven: *Corvus corax*
Red-tailed hawk: *Buteo jamaicensis*
Red finches: *Acanthis hornemanni*
Rhino: *Coelodonta antiquitatis*
Robin: *Turdus migratorius*
Sage: *Artemisia alaskana and Artemisia arctica*
Sedges: *Carex spp*
Snow bunting: *Plectrophexan nivalis*
Snow owl: *Nyctea scandiaca*
Spotted seal: *Phoca vitulina*
Spruce: *Picea spp*
Tea-leave willow: *Salix panifolia*
Varied thrush: *Ixoreus naevius*
Warble fly: *Hypoderma tarandi*
White cottonwood tree: *Populus tremuloides*
Willow: *Salix spp*
Wolf: *Canis lupus*
Yellow tea: *Potentilla fruticosa L.*

Appendix II

PREHISTORIC MATERIAL CULTURAL

A s an archeologist, I study how people lived in the past through the cultural material they left behind, specifically, the Native American people of North America. Archeologists use two broad terms "artifacts and features" when discussing cultural material that may be recorded at a site. A feature is an item that cannot be easily transported or taken from a site, perhaps not at all. Features would include a fire pit, a house pit, rock art such as a painting on a rock shelter or cave wall, a rock shelter or cave, or a large rock slab grinding area. Conversely, an artifact is an item that can be effortlessly removed from a site. This would include baskets, pottery, tools made from stone, bone, and ivory, and small grinding stones. The list of potential artifacts seems to be endless.

In the world of archeology, organic material decays while stone endures. This is why stone "lithic" tools and lithic technology remain important to archeology. I have recorded many sites where the lithic tools are all that remain of what may have been a substantial campsite.

The reader may benefit from a more detailed discussion of cultural material, especially ancient weapons systems that utilized stone rather than the latter metal technologies of copper, bronze, iron, and modern steel. I focus on the artifacts of Alaska and hence Beringia and began with the material proper of that area-stone.

Tool Stone

Not just any stone could be successfully utilized as "tool stone" because only certain types of stone contain the molecular structure so that they fracture to create a sharp edge. It is called conical fracturing. The most important types are chert, obsidian, and basalt. Obsidian or volcanic glass and basalt are the result of volcanoes and are rare in Alaska and would have been rare on Beringia. The more common tool stone in Alaska is chert, a sedimentary quartz material scientifically called cryptocrystalline silicate. Even then, it is not abundant in Alaska. Also, I was taught in school that there was not a clear distinction between chert and flint, but more of a name difference. The material is called chert in the western United States and referred to as flint in the eastern United States and in Europe. The art and science of creating stone tools is called "flint knapping." I'm not sure why that is; it could just as easily be called "chert knapping." There are many people who are skilled in the art of flint knapping, in particular, archeologists, and they will tell you it requires many, many years to acquire sufficient skill to make good stone tools.

Skilled knappers will also tell you that stone tools were utilized very differently than metal tools. Stone tools were, however, very sharp, especially those made from obsidian. In fact, an obsidian edge is sharper than a steel edge, but stone breaks, so consequently the manner in which it is used is much different. A prehistoric stone tool using man would have carried his knapping kit with him.

I have recorded several hundred archeological sites in Alaska, including sites on the Bering Sea coast so in that sense, on Beringia. Many tools of the prehistoric and historic Eskimos were made of bone and or ivory (walrus tusk). Chert material was rare. I have recorded sites, however, where slate material had been ground to make projectile points and knives. It was not abundant, but still, along with chert, it was used as a tool stone material.

Also, we archeologists refer to stone points as "projectile" points, a point that was projected. An "arrowhead" is a type of projectile. In North American archeology, the arrowhead is actually a late arrival appearing in the record at approximately 600 A.D., some 1,500 to 2,000 years ago. The majority of the arrowheads people find in the recently plowed farmer's field are actually dart points. That is, Native American cultures used the dart in North American for some 10,000 years before they began to use the bow and arrow. Arrowheads are small, finger sized. An arrowhead the size of the first two finger digits (two inches long and one-half inch wide) would be large indeed. I have recorded many arrowhead projectiles that were no larger than the sharpened end of a pencil.

The weapons systems utilized by big game hunters throughout North America and into Beringia were the spear and the dart and atlatl systems. The spear was primarily a thrusting weapon, but it could be hand thrown a short distance with lethal accuracy. The primary projectile system was the dart propelled by the throwing board or atlatl.

Spear

Harjo's spear, or any hunter's spear, reflected the common craftsmanship displayed by Native American men and manufactured in three complex components: the shaft, foreshaft, and the joint socket. The stone point was attached, or hafted, to the foreshaft.

The shaft was constructed from a length of waterlogged and subsequently dried spruce collected from the Big River during a summer sojourn. It reached head-high and was approximately a handgrip in diameter. It had been whittled and smoothed down, so it was nearly the same diameter along its length, being slightly larger at the head. The tail end was sharpened to a point and fire hardened so the spear could be struck into the ground leaving the hunter's hands free but readily available at his side. The sharpened tail end could also be utilized as a weapon in the event of hand-to-hand combat. Spruce remained the preferred material used for shafts, although willow and some species of alder were likewise crafted into fine shafts. It required a major effort to create a shaft perfectly symmetrical and straight even though it was the least complex of the three components.

The foreshaft was the most complex of the three pieces as it held and secured the most important element of the spear, the stone point. Similar to the spear shaft, water drifted wood was preferred, but otherwise, cured hard willow was utilized. Occasionally, animal bone replaced willow and often proved to be a long lasting and durable foreshaft, but it was also more difficult to manufacture.

A foreshaft could be various lengths but generally measured the length of a man's forearm and approximately the diameter of a man's index finger. The craftsmanship extended to shafts was spent on the foreshaft to insure a straight and symmetrical component. A curved or bent foreshaft could potentially lead to disastrous consequences. The head end of the foreshaft held the thin, sharp spear point, knapped from fine chert. It was most important that the foreshaft's head end was "notched" and not split to accept and haft the point.

Once the base and bottom sides of the point were ground so as not to cut the bindings, the point was mounted in place and secured with sinew. If possible, the sinew bindings were coated with a protective substance. Only on rare occasions did a hunter find himself on the Big River during any season except winter. If such an opportunity did present itself, the hunter might coat the sinew bindings of all his stone points with the sap of the rare spruce tree. Sinew bindings were also coated with rabbit skin glue.

The socket joint remained as the final, smaller but equally important component of the thrusting spear as it attached the foreshaft to the main shaft. Carved from ivory or bone, the finger-size, round-hallowed piece fit snuggly over the tapered head of the shaft. The top one-half end of the inside diameter of the socket was slightly larger than the bottom. The bottom one-half was then tightly secured to the shaft head and wrapped with sinew. Now, the bottom or distal end of the foreshaft was carefully tapered to fit snuggly into the socket joint and thus the entire spear was complete.

Once a hard spear thrust penetrated an animal, the spear shaft was pulled back leaving the foreshaft and stone point deeply imbedded into the prey. Another prepared foreshaft could be quickly reattached into the socket and the spear was once again ready for use.

Most likely a hunter would have carried extra foreshafts in a quiver or pouch. Harjo used a quiver commonly adapted by most Muscogee men. It was sewn from a hard pelt with a thick circle of mammoth hide fitted into the bottom. The foreshafts were set in, point first, and rested on top the mammoth hide circle. Then the quiver was packed with mammoth wool to help protect the points from breakage or from cutting Harjo's leg. The quiver was attached to a belt around his waist and secured on his left side.

Atlatl

The atlatl or the throwing board was the tool used by ancient hunters to propel darts. Hand held, the atlatl allowed the dart to be thrown a greater distance and with much more power than a spear or dart could be cast by hand. The term atlatl is from the Nahuatl language of the Aztecs who still used the atlatl when the Spanish arrived in Central Mexico in the 1500s. Eskimo hunters utilized both the atlatl and dart (harpoon) for hunting and the bow and arrow for war. The bow and arrow would not have been effective for hunting sea mammals from a kayak.

The atlatl came in many shapes and sizes but functioned in the same manner. Imagine a round piece of wood some two or three finger-widths in diameter and roughly the length of a man's forearm. Then, split the wood section length wise in half. The flat surface of one-half is then like a board. A groove, about the size of the diameter of the dart, was cut along the length of the board surface. A "stop piece" with a "finger size point was attached to one end of the atlatl; it was usually made from bone or antler. The hunter held the other end of the atlatl usually with the aid of loops or finger notches. The dart lay along the groove in the flat surface of the board with the blunt end of the dart fitted against the stop piece and the point. Holding the other end, the hunter kept the dart steady with his thumb and pointing finger. Then, using the same manner of throwing a spear, he cast the dart, keeping a grip on the atlatl. The flex of the dart in flight gives it power and distance.

Dart

The dart was a small spear and constructed in the same manner as a spear, only it was fletched as an arrow. In the story, Harjo's foreshafts can arm both his spear and darts. He carries three darts in his quiver without the foreshafts attached. When needed, he pulls a dart from his quiver, attaches the foreshaft with the deadly point, mounts the dart in his atlatl, and throws.

Fire starting kit and method

As modern people carry keys, wallets, cell phones, and lighters at one time, prehistoric people carried fire-starting kits. A kit would consist of a bow piece, a drill stick, a fire stick, and a mouthpiece. Fire was started by friction. A fire kit such as this could also be used as a drill.

In making a fire, Harjo or any other Mammoth Hunter most likely would have followed the following steps. He first picked up the "bow piece" which was a length of finger-sized bone and although called a bow, it was only slightly curved. Holes were drilled at each end and a length of strong narrow rawhide was tied at each end through the holes. He then took the "drill stick" which was a long finger-size length of wood, similar to a foreshaft, roughly a forearm in length. He hitched the length of the bow rawhide around the drill shaft, pulled it taught and held in his hand.

Next, he positioned the "fire stick" down on the ground. It was a simple flat piece of soft wood with a series of holes drilled or notched into it, but not all the way through. Then, he set one end of the drill shaft into a fire stick hole and held the bow still and pulled it taught.

The curved flat mouthpiece was usually carved from bone with a tooth grip on one side and a drilled socket hole on the other. With the tooth grip side into his mouth and then on his hands and knees, Harjo put the socket side of the mouthpiece on top of the other end of the drill stick.

The fire was started using a drill operation that Harjo maneuvered by a back and forth motion. The rawhide length spiraled up and down the drill shaft and rapidly rotated it. The correct pressure was applied from the mouth piece, which also left both of Harjo's hands free, one to operate the bow and the other to hold the fire stick. If the fire stick was long, he could also hold it in place with his knee.

Once the drill was rotating in a fire stick hole, wood dust was worn off from the hole and grew extremely hot as to burn like a small coal. At first, the fire stick smoked and smoked until Harjo could see a tiny ember. Then, he placed the tender on top of the fire stick, took out the mouth-piece and blew to ignite the tender. He placed the burning tender under the small stack of prepared sticks and tender in the hearth. And then there was fire. The same method was utilized to drill holes. The procedure could be completed without the mouthpiece, although using it left both hands free.

I once watched a documentary film in a university anthropology class. It showed an old Australian aborigine man start a fire with his fire kit: a drill stick, a fire stick, and grass-like tender. He sat on the ground and rotated his drill stick in his hands after he spit on them. He held the fire stick with his foot. Once it began to smoke, he placed the tender on the fire stick and blew. It took him about 30 seconds or less to have a fire burning in the adjacent hearth.

Boiling Pouch

People have asked me how ancient people boiled water without ceramic or metal pots. The answer is easy-animal skin boiling pouches and heated rocks. The unsophisticated method has been used around the world for many thousands of years. I have not tried it myself but have watched it accomplished on documentary films. I have heated rocks and put them in a metal pan of water. It boils in a matter of seconds.

Constructed of thick mammoth rawhide, Harjo's boiling pouch had a head-size opening and measured about two hands-lengths tall. It was secured to four bone slats longer than the pouch and thus held upright. He placed a flat rock in the bottom of the pouch and nearly filled it with water. When the boiling stones were hot, red hot, he would drop the stones into the pouch and in a brief period, the water would boil. Such pouches were easy to carry and required little space. A traveling hunter pulling a sled often carried two or three. Harjo carried three-one for tea-one for stew-and one for plain water.

A Yupik "Eskimo" House

When I worked in Alaska, I recorded several hundred Eskimo houses from the Bering Sea coast of Nelson Island to the Kuskokwim River. These houses varied in size and complexity but followed a basic construction pattern. Such features are called semi-subterranean because the houses were built both above and below ground. They were used by Native peoples throughout Alaska.

First, a square house pit and entryway were excavated. Four meters square was a common house pit size. The entryway, about a meter wide, was dug deeper than the house pit floor because cold air sinks and hot air rises. Thus, the cold air would sink and stay in the entryway and not easily come into the house, creating a cold trap. Next, four vertical corner posts were placed, set in from the house pit corners, and four smaller upright posts were set in the entry tunnel. Horizontal logs connected the main corner post and upright entryway post. Horizontal roofing and sloping wall logs and "split log boards" enclosed the house. The sloping walls could extend beyond the pit to form a high bench within the house. Grass, tree limbs and branches, and grass mats were also used to cover the sloping walls. A square smoke and light hole was left in the center of the roof and usually covered with translucent seal gut. Sod blocks were then laid on the roof and sloping walls enclosing the whole structure. The sod could be two to three feet thick, especially on winter houses. A square or rectangular firepit was excavated in the center of the floor, and often it was rock lined. Logs and split log boards could line the dirt pit walls and floor. Grass could also be used as a floor cover.

Pole-Travail

The triangular shaped pole-travail consisted of two long side poles and three, occasionally four, cross pieces that supported the poles. The load was placed on the central cross section, then lifted at the narrow end and dragged along the ground by the wider ends. A shoulder harness could also be used to carry the pole-travail. Later, dogs would be utilized by the plains Indians of North America as beasts of burden to pull the pole-travails as they followed the bison herds and much later, the horse.

BIBLIOGRAPHY

Ager, Thomas A. and Lynn Price Ager - 1980 Ethnobotany of the Eskimo of Nelson Island, Alaska. Artic Anthropology 17(1):27-48.

Alaska Geographic Society - 1979 The Yukon-Kuskokwim Delta. Alaska Geographic 6(1).

Bandi, Hans-Georg - 1969 Eskimo Prehistory. Translated by Ann E. Keep. University of Alaska Press, College.

Barnette, Benjamin H. - 2009 Qaluyaaq: An Archeology Survey and Oral Histories Collection of Nelson Island, Alaska. Unpublished Ph.D. dissertation, University of Nebraska, Lincoln.

Barnouw, Victor - 1971 An Introduction to Anthropology: Physical Anthropology and Archeology. Dorsey Press, Homewood, Illinois.

Bettinger, Robert L. - 1991 Hunter-Gatherers: Archaeological and Evolutionary Theory. Plenum Press, New York and London.

Billard, Jules B. (Editor) - 1974 The World of the American Indian. National Geographic Society, Washington D.C.

Binford, Lewis R. - 1980 Willow Smoke and Dogs' Tails: Hunter-Gatherer Settlement Systems and Archaeological Site Information. American Antiquity 45(1): 4-20. 1978Nunamuit Ethnoarchaeology. Academic Press, New York.

Burch, Ernest S. - 1981 The Traditional Eskimo Hunters of Pont Hope, Alaska: 1800-1875. Borrow, Alaska, North Slope Borough.

Crabtree, Don E. - 1971Experiments in Flintworking. Idaho State University Museum, Pocatello. 1972An Introduction to Flintworking. Occasional Papers of the Idaho State University Museum, #28, Pocatello.

Dall, William H. - 1870 Alaska and Its Resources. Lee and Shepard, Boston.

Debo, Angie - 1941The Road to Disappearance: A History of the Creek Indians. University of Oklahoma Press, Norman.

Fagan, Brian M. - 1977 People of the Earth: An Introduction to World Prehistory. Little, Brown and Company, Boston and Toronto.

Fienup-Riordan, Ann - 1983 The Nelson Island Eskimo: Social Structure and Ritual Distribution. Alaska Pacific University Press, Anchorage.

Fitzhugh, William N. and Susan A. Kaplan (Editors) - 1982 Inua: Spirit World of the Bering Sea Eskimo. Smithsonian Institution Press, Washington, D.C.

Frison, George C. - 1978Prehistoric Hunters of the High Plains. Academic Press, New York.

Giddings, James L. - 1964 The Archeology of Cape Denbigh. Brown University Press, Providence.

Graf, Kelly E., Caroline V. Ketron, and Michael R. Waters (Editors) - 2014Paleo-American Odyssey. Texas A&M University Press, College Station.

Grantham, Bill - 2002Creation Myths and Legends of the Creek Indians. University of Florida Press, Tallahassee.

Hartman, Charles W. and Philip R. Johnson - 1984 Environmental Atlas of Alaska. University of Alaska Press, Fairbanks.

Hopkins, David M., John V. Matthews, Jr., Charles E. Schweger, and Steven B. Young (Editors) - 1982Paleoecology of Beringia. Academic Press, New York.

Jennings, Jesse D. - 1974Prehistory of North America. McGraw Hill, New York.

Kelly, Robert L. - 1995 The Foraging Spectrum: Diversity in Hunter-Gather Lifeways. Smithsonian Institution Press, Washington and London.

Kowta, Makoto - 1963 Old Togiak in Prehistory. Ph.D. dissertation, University of California, - Los Angeles. - de Laguna, Frederica - 1947 The Prehistory of North America as Seen from the Yukon. Memories of - the Society for American Archaeology, No. 3. Menasha.

Lee, Richard B., and Irven DeVore, (Editors) - 1968Man the Hunter. Aldine Publishing Company, Chicago.

Loughridge, R.M. (Rev.) and David M. Hodge (Elder) - 1964 (Reprinted by Permission) - English and Muskokee Dictionary. Creek Council House Museum, Okmulgee, Oklahoma.

Meltzer, David J. - 2009 First Peoples in a New World: Colonizing Ice Age America. University of California, Berkley and Los Angeles, California.

Mueller-Wille and D. Bruce Dickson - 1991 An Examination of Some Models of Late Pleistocene Society in - Southwestern Europe. In Perspectives on the Past: Theoretical Biases in Mediterranean Hunter-Gather Research. Geoffrey A. Clark ed. - Philadelphia: University of Pennsylvania Press. pp 25-55.

Murdock, George P. - 1967 Ethnographic Atlas: A Summary. Ethnology 6: 109-236.

Nelson, Edward William - 1899Eskimo About Bering Strait. Bureau of American Ethnology, Annual - Report #18, Part 1, Washington, D. C.

Olson, Dean F. - 1969 Alaska Reindeer Herdsmen: A Study of Native Management in Transition. - Institute of Social, Economic, and Government Research, Report No. 18, - University of Alaska. College, Alaska.

Oswalt, Wendell H. - 1962 Historic Populations in Western Alaska and Migration Theory. Anthropological Papers of the University of Alaska. 11(1):1-14. 1967 Alaskan Eskimo. Chandler Publishing Company, New York. 1990 Bashful No

Longer: An Alaskan Eskimo Ethnohistory, 1778-1988. - University of Oklahoma Press, Norman.

Pewe, Troy L. - 1975 Quaternary Geology of Alaska. Geological Survey Professional Paper - 835. U.S. Government Printing Office, Washington, D. C.

Ray, Dorothy Jean. - 1984 The Bering Strait Eskimo. In Handbook of North American Indians, Vol. - 5 (Artic). Edited by William C. Sturtevant, pp. 285-293. Smithsonian Institution, - Washington D.C.

Selkregg, Lidia L. (Editor) - 1973 Alaska Regional Profiles, Vol.6 (Yukon Region). Joint Federal-State Land - Use Planning Commission. University of Alaska (Arctic Environment - Information and Data Center). Anchorage. pp. 187- 195.

Soffer, Olga and N.D. Praslov (Editors) - 1993From Kostenki to Clovis: Upper Paleolithic-Paleo-Indian Adaptations. Plenum Press, New York and London.

Soffer, Olga and C. Gamble (Editors) - 1990The World at 18,000 BP. Volume 1: High Latitudes. Unwin Hyman, London.

Spencer, Robert F. and Jesse D. Jennings - 1970The Native Americans: Ethnology and Background of the North American Indians. Harper and Row, New York.

Taylor, Colin F. (Editor) - 1999The Native Americans: The Indigenous People of North America. Salamander Books, London.

Willis, Roxanne - 2006 A New Game in the North: Alaska Native Reindeer Herding. Western - Historical Quarterly 37. pp 277-301. -

AUTHOR BIOGRAPHY:

Photograph by Evan Smith, Grass Valley, California.

Benjamin H. Barnette has been a working "field arche-ologist" for over 35 years. He holds a Ph.D. from the University of Nebraska-Lincoln. His experiences include six years of work in Alaska on the Bering Sea coast in Southwest Alaska, so in that sense, on Beringia itself. Many of the descriptions of the Native people and locations in the novel were derived from his personal Alaskan experiences.

A Vietnam veteran, Dr. Barnette spent four years in the Air Force serving in Guam and Thailand in 1968 and 1969.

He later enlisted in the Army and the Air National Guard, serving a total of 20 years. He retired in 2007.

As a proud member of the Muscogee (Creek) Nation of Oklahoma, Dr. Barnette utilized his knowledge of the Muscogee (Creek) people and language as inspiration for the Muscogee Mammoth Hunters. He currently resides in Kailua-Kona on the Big Island of Hawaii.